I held the garment up, and the cloth rustled softly, shimmering in the candlelight. A real silk petticoat. I couldn't believe it. My hands trembled as I opened the other boxes. There were silk stockings as frail as cobwebs, two beige lace garters, a pair of pale orange kidskin slippers with elegant high heels.

The silk stockings felt heavenly on my legs, clinging to and caressing every inch of my skin, and it was strange wearing garters. I had never worn them before. The petticoat was just a little snug at the waist, and the bodice was cut daringly low, barely concealing my nipples. The skirt was very, very full, swelling out in luxuriant folds that swirled and rustled as I moved.

I had started my new life, and already I had shoes and a beautiful dress and a petticoat and my very own parasol, and I had a handsome and charming new friend who might become more than a friend. . . .

THEY CALL
HER DANA

Jennifer Wilde

BALLANTINE BOOKS · NEW YORK

For my Wish Brothers,
Richard Michael Morris and
Merle Wang, who make my world
a better, brighter place
because they are in it.

Copyright © 1989 by Tom Huff

All rights reserved under International and Pan-American Copyright Conventions. Published in the United States of America by Ballantine Books, a division of Random House, Inc., New York, and simultaneously in Canada by Random House of Canada Limited, Toronto.

Library of Congress Catalog Card Number: 89-90945

ISBN 0-345-34757-9

Manufactured in the United States of America

First Edition: September 1989

Book One

The Waif

Chapter One

I HAD THE DREAM AGAIN during the night, and it was the same as always, vague and puzzling and pleasantly disturbing. He was standing in the mist and his eyes looked searchingly into mine and there was water nearby, a great river, and then he took my hands in his and squeezed them and pulled me to him. He smiled then, and then the mist swallowed us both up and I felt that peculiar feeling, warm and kind of itchy, and sweet, like warm, sweet honey flowing in my veins. I moaned and turned in bed and the old springs creaked loudly and I woke up, still feeling that delicious feeling, groggy, thinking I must be going barmy, dreaming that same dream over and over again.

I sat up, rubbing my eyes, and the springs creaked once more. The corn husks that filled the mattress rustled noisily. It was still dark, although black was lightening to gray and I could see the outlines of the old dressing table and a murky silver blur that was the mirror. Almost dawn. Time to get up. Naked under the single worn sheet, I lingered in bed, thinking about the dream. Mama Lou could probably explain it to me. Folks in the swamp called her a witch and were scared of her, but they still went to see her whenever they needed potions or ointments or herbs. Mama Lou had the sight, and she knew things beyond the ken of ordinary folk. Why should I keep dreaming of the same man? He was tall and good-looking, I knew that, and he was wearing fine clothes, but I could never recall his features. Strange though it might seem, I knew that I would recognize him immediately were I to see him in real life.

Stuff and nonsense, I thought, climbing out of bed. He was just a figment of my imagination, and what chance would I ever have to meet a man like that here in the swamps? The rough oafs who lived hereabout certainly didn't wear elegant breeches and fine white silk shirts, and not a one of them had ever made me feel so . . . so taut, like I was stretched on a rack, aching pleasantly, suspended, waiting for something wonderful that was bound to happen as soon as the ache exploded inside.

Shadows were fading, outlines growing clearer, and a faint pink and gold mist was blending with the gray. No need to light the candle. I dipped the rag into the ewer of water I kept on the rickety old dressing table and washed myself. The water was wonderfully cool. My breasts seemed to swell, nipples like tight buds as I rubbed the damp rag over them. Why did I keep dreaming about him, and why couldn't I remember what he looked like? It was unsettling . . . and kind of spooky. Was I really going barmy? Wudn't likely, I told myself. I had just turned seventeen three months ago, and that was much too young to be losing your mind.

Forget it, Dana, I scolded. Get dressed. Get on with your chores. You ain't got time to get all fanciful, thinking about some mysterious man who keeps poppin' up in your dreams. Your problem is you ain't *had* no man yet and your cherry is gettin' too ripe. You need a tonic. Maybe Mama Lou will give you one when you go to fetch Ma's medicine.

I pulled on my ragged old white petticoat. The hem of the full skirt was torn and uneven and ended at midcalf, and the bodice was much too tight across my bosom, although I'd let it out twice already. Fancy owning a new petticoat that wudn't three years old. Fancy owning a new dress, I added, reaching for the tattered pink cotton frock that was the only one I owned. It was much too short, too, and the neckline that had been demure at fourteen was almost indecent now, barely containing my breasts. If I were to sneeze too hard, they'd likely pop right out. I adjusted the short sleeves that fell off the shoulder and smoothed the cloth around my waist. It was a snug fit, all right, but the dress wouldn't stand another lettin' out. I was going to have to get another one before long, else I'd have to clothe myself with leaves, like Eve.

The first thin rays of sunlight were slanting through the window now, all wavery and weak, and I could see myself in the murky mirror hanging over the dressing table. I examined myself critically, feeling the same disappointment I always felt when I was vain enough to study my reflection.

"Men are going to look at you, Dana," Ma had told me. "Men are going to want you, so beware, child."

Ma was wise, of course, and I loved her dearly, but she didn't have to warn me about men. They'd been looking at me since I turned thirteen, and I had long since learned to deal with them. You had to be sharp and you had to be quick and you had to be prepared to fight if need be. Men looked at me, all right, but I really couldn't understand why. I wasn't at all fetching. My hair was neither blond nor brown but, instead, a curious combination of the two, the color of dark honey, tumbling to my shoulders in thick, unruly waves. My eyes were hazel, flecked with gold, and my cheekbones were funny-looking, high and prominent. My lips were too full and too pink, and my complexion was a deep creamy tan.

I was too tall, with long legs and a narrow waist with far too many embarrassing curves above and below. Why would any man want to look at someone as plain and gawky as me? Beat all, it did. I guess men didn't really care what a girl looked like. They just wanted to get into her pants. They were a horny bunch, the lot of 'em. A girl had to watch out for herself all the time if she wanted to keep her virtue intact, not that many girls did here in the swamps.

Running my fingers through my hair to work out the tangles, I unlocked my door and started down the creaky old backstairs. My attic room was off to itself, originally intended for a maid's room. Clem O'Malley had never been able to afford a Negro maid, but he didn't really need one. He had me. I'd earned my keep ever since I was old enough to remember. Stepping into the kitchen, I shoved waves from my temple and got the fire started in the old pot-bellied black iron stove that gave me so much trouble. I poked at the coals, prodding them, and when they finally caught and began to glow, I sighed and shut the door and set a kettle of water on to boil.

I moved down the narrow, dingy hall and stepped outside, pausing on the sagging front porch. It was already warm and sultry, with wavering rays of sunlight streaming through the cypress trees and making pale golden patterns on the dirt. No grass grew here. Our farm, if it could be dignified with such a name, was completely surrounded by swamp. I could hear the pigs snorting unpleasantly in their sty, and the chickens clucked impatiently. How I longed to flee. How I longed just to take off and discover that world I knew existed beyond the swamps. One day, I promised myself. One day I would know something besides these swamps, this squalor.

I crossed the yard to the old barn. It was small, almost tumbling down, and I smelled damp hay and manure as I pushed open the door. Mollie stood in her stall, chomping with contentment on hay. She lifted her head and mooed when she saw me. She was a placid, stupid creature with huge bovine eyes and a mottled gray-tan coat, utterly indifferent as I picked up the tin bucket and pulled the three-legged wooden stool into place. I gripped the udders firmly and squeezed and tugged, and streams of milk spewed into the bucket. It was almost full when I had finished. Later I would separate the cream and churn it into butter. Mollie was still chomping hay as I left the barn and carried the milk inside to the larder.

Milking done, it was time to feed the chickens. They fretted noisily as I passed the coop on my way to the dilapidated old shed. A rat darted across the dirt floor as I reached for the chipped porcelain pan. It didn't bother me in the least. You soon got used to rats, and this one hadn't even been that large. I filled the pan with feed and stepped back outside. The Spanish moss hung limp and lifeless on the cypress trees, not a breeze stirring, and I could feel the perspiration on my body. Hardly daylight, and it was muggy as could be and I didn't have a single thing to look forward to.

Seventeen years old, I thought, and trapped. Out of bed when the sky was still dark. Start the fire, milk the cow, feed the chickens and cook breakfast for Clem O'Malley and his two sons, take a tray to Ma, clean the kitchen, sweep the floor and do my other chores and check on Ma and then start preparing lunch. Work and worry all day long, ignoring my stepfather's brooding silences and surly manners and avoiding my stepbrothers as much as possible, fighting them off if necessary. Seventeen years old, and I was little better off than a Negro slave. At least my cherry was still intact, and that was quite an accomplishment for these parts. If a lass wasn't married and a mother at seventeen, chances were she'd long since been despoiled, often by some man in her own family.

One day, perhaps, I'd give myself to a man, but he wouldn't be one of the oafs from these parts. He would be tall and clean and speak in a soft, cultured voice. He would wear fine clothes and look at me with love and see something besides a piece of tail. He would see Dana O'Malley, someone special, someone with a heart full of love and a head full of dreams. He would help me make those dreams come true. He wouldn't laugh at me because I wanted to better myself. He wouldn't scoff because I could read and write and speak French as well as English.

Those accomplishments weren't worth spit here in the swamps, I realized that, but out there in the world beyond, there must be lots of girls who were able to write their own names and read a page of the almanac without stumbling over too many of the words. How patiently Ma had taught me when I was a child, and how Clem had resented it. No need for me to learn to read and write, it would just give me airs. No need to be able to jabber in a foreign language either. Ma had been born French. I had spoken both languages from infancy on.

The chickens squacked noisily as I opened the gate and stepped inside the coop, and I was immediately surrounded by savage creatures with wildly flapping wings who clucked and pecked and did acrobatics in the air as I scattered handfuls of feed over the ground. Nasty, ill-tempered, greedy beasts, they were. I had been fiercely pecked many a time as I gathered eggs, but I still refused to wring their necks when it came time to take some to market. Jake did that, and with considerable relish, I might add. Jake was a bad one, a bully, genuinely vicious, and Randy wasn't far behind. Randy was twenty-one, Jake twenty-three, both hellions of the first stamp. If I was known in the swamps as the little wildcat, it was because since early childhood I had had to learn to defend myself against that pair.

Actually, Jake and Randy didn't bother me nearly as much as Clem. Clem had never laid a hand on me, treated me with surly disdain, yet somehow I felt he was a far greater menace than either of his sons. I had seen that brooding speculation in his eyes when he thought he wasn't being observed. I was safe as long as Ma was in the house, but if anything happened to her . . . I hurled yet another handful of feed into the air. The chickens flapped with frenzy, fighting each other for the grain.

Ma had had another bad turn last night. I had spent over an hour with her, holding her hand, bathing her brow with a damp cloth, trying to coax her into drinking a few sips of milk. I tried not to think of the racking cough, the blood-streaked handkerchief she had tried to conceal. It was . . . it was just the fever,

I told myself, and it would soon pass. Ma would be all right. I tried to believe that. I had to believe that. Without Ma I couldn't possibly endure this life. It was just the fever, and Ma would soon be on the mend. Ma wasn't yet forty, but she was already an old woman, so thin, so drawn, her honey-colored hair limp and streaked with gray. Life with Clem O'Malley had done that to her. Why, oh why, had she ever married him?

He had been an overseer at one of the larger plantations, I knew, a strapping Irishman with two unruly young sons whose mother had died giving birth to the younger. Ma was barely twenty, just recently widowed, and I had been born four months after she married Clem O'Malley. He wasn't my father, although he had given me his name. He had lost his job at the plantation when I was still an infant in arms, and we had all come here to the swamps shortly thereafter, poor white trash as far as the rest of the world was concerned, scratching out an existence raising pigs and chickens on this poor excuse for a farm.

Ma never talked about her life before Clem, quickly changed the subject whenever I tried to ask her about it. I had never known anything but these swamps, this run-down farm, the filth, the squalor, but Ma had known a much finer world, I sensed that. Long ago, when I was still a very little girl, I remember her speaking of fine carriages and gleaming silk gowns and perfumed gardens, promising me I would know that world, too, one day, but that was before her lovely hazel eyes were filled with permanent defeat, before her spirit was completely broken by the man she married and the bleakness of life here in the swamps. Who had she been before she married Clem O'Malley? Who was her first husband, my real father? These were questions that had plagued me for years, questions Ma staunchly refused to answer.

"It's better you never know," she had told me. "It would do no good. Know only that you—you're someone very special, my darling."

You could say that was just Ma talking, of course, but I *was* different. So was Ma. I had always known that. Ma didn't belong here, never had. She was too gentle, too refined, with none of that tough, gritty fiber that marked the other women of the swamps. Most of them were slatterns. Ma was kind and soft-spoken, dreamy, and her health had never been good. She had worked like a slave on the farm, trying to do her duty by Clem

O'Malley, but it seemed to me he had always despised her, as though . . . as though he knew something about her that gave him the upper hand. Ma never complained, but over the years she had gradually retreated into that dreamy world of hers, smiling gently as she did her chores, building a fragile wall around her that kept harsh reality at bay. How I wished I knew what went on in her mind when she smiled that gentle smile of hers and gazed into the past, remembering.

I didn't belong here, either, but I was made of sterner stuff than Ma. I dreamed, sure. Without my daydreams to keep me going, I would never be able to face the grim reality of my life, but I didn't retreat into that dreamworld. I accepted the reality and vowed to change it. I might just have one ragged dress, might not have time or opportunity to bathe properly or keep my hair clean, but I wasn't trash. I'd never gone to school—there wasn't a school in the swamps, wasn't a church, either, only a motley ragbag of shanties we called "town," three miles from our farm—but I *could* read if the words weren't too big, and I could copy the words on paper and write my name in big block letters. That was more than most folk hereabouts could do. They might poke fun at me, think me odd, but I wasn't ever going to let them pull me down. Someday, somehow, I was going to make a better life for myself.

I tossed the last handful of grain into the air and left the coop, fastening the gate behind me. It seemed even warmer than before. My dress was soaking wet under the arms, and my whole body was bathed with a sheen of perspiration. My face was undoubtedly streaked with dirt, and my hair was filthy. I returned the pan to the shed and started back to the house, thinking about the dream, the mist, the man, recalling that pleasant, tingling ache I had felt when I woke up. What did it all mean? Why did I keep dreaming the same dream? I was eager to ask Mama Lou about it.

Back in the kitchen, I discovered that the kettle wasn't steaming. Damnation, I thought, opening the door of the stove. The fire had gone out. I had to start it again, jabbing vigorously with the iron poker. I could hear loud clumping noises down the hall. My stepbrothers were awake, banging about as they always did first thing in the morning, ignoring the fact that Ma was so ill and needed her sleep. Sod the bastards, I thought angrily. They had no consideration whatsoever, never had a thought for anyone or anything but their own greedy appetites.

Jake came tromping in fifteen minutes later, brushing locks of dark blond hair from his brow. He was a tall, hefty brute with a square jaw, sullen blue eyes and a nose that had been broken more than once. Jake was a ruffian, the terror of the swamps. Liked nothing better than a good rowdy fight, a grin on his thick lips as he smashed a jaw or broke an arm. He was wearing old boots and snug gray breeches and an old blue silk shirt with full sleeves gathered at the wrists. It bagged over the waistband of his breeches where he had tucked it in loosely. Perverse as it seemed, a lot of girls found him exciting, and Jake never suffered for lack of tail.

"Mornin'," he growled, giving me a surly look.

"You and Randy might try to be a little quieter when you get up," I said coldly. "You know Ma's ill."

"Don't ride me," he snarled.

"You don't care, do you? It doesn't matter to you that—"

"Shut up, slut."

"Go sod yourself," I retorted.

"You're gettin' awfully lippy, girl. You don't watch it, one-a these days I'm liable to bust your mouth for you."

"Try it. You don't scare me none. I'll kick your balls so hard you won't *never* be able to have another whore."

Jake scowled, remembering the tryst behind the pigsty, remembering what I had done to him that time. Like most bullies, Jake picked only on the weak and defenseless, and he knew I was neither. He glared at me with blue eyes full of hatred, full of lust, too. I was the only girl around these parts Jake hadn't had his way with, either by force or with consent, and the fact that I was his stepsister didn't mean a thing. He wanted me, all right, but he knew full well I'd make good my threat.

"You think you're somethin', don't-ja?" he said.

"Maybe I do."

"Think you're better'n anyone else 'cause you can read some and write your name down and speak frog-talk. That don't mean nothin', wench. You're a swamp girl, just like th' rest of 'em, good for nothin' but spreadin' your legs for a man an' cookin' his food for him. One day I'm gonna—"

"You're gonna what?" Randy asked, strolling into the kitchen.

"I'm gonna show this lippy little wench what's what."

Randy chuckled. "That I'd like to see. I remember th' last time you tried to show her somethin'. Better keep it in your breeches, brother. You ain't no match for Dana."

"You think so?"

"I know so," Randy drawled.

He grinned and gave me a fond, playful look that didn't fool me for a minute. Randy came on all friendly and easygoing, but he was every bit as bad as Jake, only wily. Tall and lanky, he had a lean face with sharp, foxlike features and his father's auburn hair. His blue eyes were teasing, and a grin usually played on his wide lips, but Randy was, if anything, even meaner than his brother, cool and determined when in a fight or after a girl's favors. He was brighter than Jake, a sly, conniving scoundrel whose amiable mien was dangerously deceptive. Randy wore scuffed brown boots and tight, faded brown breeches and a silk shirt like Jake's, only tan.

"Hey, Dana," he said amiably, "when you gonna bake us another one of them peach pies?"

"I ain't got time to bake no pies," I retorted. "Besides, there ain't any more peaches."

"Me an' Jake are goin' to town this mornin', takin' the old sow and three piglets to market. I could pick up some peaches. I sure would like ya to make me one of them pies."

"Sod off," I said.

"Aw, come on, Dana. Don't be ugly this mornin'. I'm feeling real good. Just seein' my purty li'l sister makes me feel grand."

"Yeah, we can see it budgin' in your breeches," Jake told him. "Save it for Annie Cooper, 'less you wanna find yourself feedin' th' alligators. Li'l sister ain't havin' none."

"She'll come round," Randy assured him. "None of 'em can resist me for long."

Ignoring them both, I took the hoecakes off the stove and started frying the eggs. Jake and Randy sat down at the battered old wooden table and poured themselves strong black coffee from the heavy blue pot I set down. Randy began to butter the hoecakes.

"Your father come in last night?" I asked him.

Randy shook his head. "Reckon he'll be back sometime this mornin'. Reckon he was too occupied to make it back last night."

"He can whistle for his breakfast," I snapped. "After I finish this, I ain't about to start cookin' again."

" 'Magine he won't be thinkin' about food," Jake said. " 'Magine he'll-uv had his fill."

I knew what they were talking about. I knew where Clem O'Malley had spent last night, same place he'd spent any number of nights since Ma took ill. Jessie was a mulatto, a free woman of color who had her own shanty in the swamps. She must have been at least thirty, and she painted her face and wore an old red silk gown and had dangling gold hoops in her ears. Many of the men hereabouts went to see her when they had the money, and she did a brisk business, often taking produce or chickens or a piglet if the man didn't have cash. My stepbrothers had visited her, too, I knew, and she had shrieked to high heaven when they refused to pay. Jake had slapped her across the face and called her an old nigger whore, and Randy broke one of her chairs and kicked a hole in her screen door. They were a charming pair, all right, no question about it.

I slammed the plate of fried eggs down on the table and they began to eat greedily, talking about their plans for the day. I poured myself a cup of coffee and sipped it as I made Ma's porridge and toast. I never ate anything myself early in the morning, contented with one or two cups of coffee. Jake and Randy made fast work of their food and stomped out. I could hear the piglets squealing a few minutes later as I prepared Ma's tray: a bowl of porridge with cream, a pat of butter melting in its center, two slices of buttered toast on a blue saucer, a small pot of crab apple jelly and a glass of milk. I wished I had some flowers to put on the tray, but I hadn't had time to go into the swamp and pick any of the wild orchids.

Ma sat up as I entered her room. The curtains were parted and a warm ray of sunlight fell across her bed. How frail she looked, how drawn, but her color was bright, two pink spots glowing on her cheeks, her hazel eyes alight with a feverish sparkle. She smiled warmly, but I could see that it took a big effort. How beautiful she must have been as a young woman, I thought. Vestiges of that beauty still remained, despite the battering of privation and hardship. Her graying honey-colored hair was damp with perspiration, pulled back from her face and worn in a loose plait.

I returned her smile. When I was with Ma I felt all tender and gentle inside. I didn't have to keep my defenses up and pretend to be tough. I could be myself, be Dana, knowing those fragile feelings inside wouldn't be taken as a sign of weakness, wouldn't be ridiculed. How nice it would be if we could always be ourselves, I thought, without any need of putting up a front to protect us from the world.

"Good morning, my darling," Ma said in French. We usually spoke to each other in that language.

"Mornin', Ma. I've brought your breakfast."

"Just—just set it on the table beside the bed, darling. I—I'll eat it a little later on."

"But the porridge will get cold," I protested, "and I brought some of the crab apple jelly I made last year. I've been savin' it, hidin' it from Clem and the boys so you could have it."

"That was lovely of you, but—"

"Please try and eat some, Ma. You gotta keep up your strength. You didn't eat hardly nothin' yesterday, and—and it worries me."

Ma smiled again, a resigned smile, then nodded, and I placed the tray carefully across her knees. She looked at the food as though it were some kind of obstacle she must surmount. I sat down beside the bed and watched anxiously as she took a few bites of porridge and nibbled on a piece of toast. She took a sip of milk and indicated I should take the tray away. I removed it reluctantly from her knees and set it on the bedside table.

"I—I'll try to eat more later," she whispered. "I promise."

"At least drink the milk, Ma."

"I will, my darling. Later."

"I heard you coughing during the night," I said. "Was—did you cough up any—"

I couldn't bring myself to say the word "blood." Ma shook her head, smiling yet again as though I were being frightfully silly.

"It was just—just a little cough, didn't—didn't amount to anything. I don't want you worrying, my darling. I'm going to be all right."

"Course you are," I assured her. "I'm going to see Mama Lou this morning and get some more of that medicine. It—it'll help, I know it will. Mama Lou said it'd make you feel easy, and it did, didn't it? You'll be feeling as fit as can be in no time."

Ma nodded, pretending to believe the lie, just as I did. I took her hand and held it, loving her so, feeling so helpless, so lost. Ma looked at me with those curiously glowing eyes, and I could see the sadness in them, the fear. I knew the fear was not for herself, but for me.

"My poor baby," she said in a weak voice. "What is going to become of you?"

"I'm not a baby, Ma. I'm seventeen years old, and I'm tough. I know how to take care of myself, always have."

"You're so beautiful," she whispered. "Even in that ragged pink dress, even with dirt on your face. You have—you have something rags and dirt can't disguise. I—when I was young, I—"

"You're still young," I told her. "You're only thirty-eight. That isn't old. You're still beautiful, too," I added, smoothing a wisp of damp honey-blond hair from her brow.

"You look so—so like . . ."

She paused, and her lovely hazel eyes took on that faraway look. I could see her remembering, see the present melting away before her, a wistful expression on her face as the past shimmered in memory.

"I had it, too," she continued, slipping into that dreamworld, not really speaking to me at all. "I had that something special—like you—allure, I suppose you would call it. So many beaux flocking around like—like bees around a pot of honey, all of them handsome, wealthy, from the very best families, and I could have had any of them. . . ."

Her voice grew fainter, her eyes wistful.

"I could have had any of them," she continued after a moment, "but I had eyes only for him, and he—he was like a god. If only he hadn't . . ."

She paused again, looking at me through the mists of time.

"And he never knew about you," she whispered. "My little girl."

"Who, Ma? Who is 'he'?"

Ma ignored the question. "My little girl should be wearing fine kidskin shoes and a flowered muslin frock, attending an academy for young ladies, preparing to take her place in society. There should be teas and garden parties—the garden was so lovely, the azaleas and magnolia and, oh, the wisteria, spilling over the old gray stone walls like pale purple lace. . . ."

She fell silent, remembering, and I held her hand tightly, left out, wanting so desperately to hear more about that world she had known so long ago, before I was born. Why wouldn't she share it with me? Was there some . . . some terrible secret she felt must be kept from me? Questions were of no avail. Ma always evaded them. I knew she had come from a place called New Orleans—she had let that slip once—but I had no idea where it might be. Far away from here, I knew, far beyond the swamps. It was a place with perfumed gardens where ladies wore silk gowns and fine carriages bowled down the cobbled streets. It wasn't likely I'd ever see such a place. Might as well be the moon.

Ma sighed and looked at me, seeing me now, the past vanished. I squeezed her hand tightly.

"Was I—"

"You were driftin', Ula."

"Sometimes—sometimes it seems like . . ." She hesitated, frowning. "Like I'm no longer here," she whispered. "My poor baby. What—what will you do when I'm—when I'm no longer here?"

"That—that ain't gonna be for a long, long time," I said firmly, but my voice trembled nevertheless.

"I saw a redbird this morning," she told me.

"A cardinal? But, Ma, there ain't no—"

"I woke up and looked out the window and it was perched on a branch, looking at me—waiting for me, it seemed. It was bright, bright scarlet, the color of—of blood."

"You must of imagined it, Ma."

"It was very beautiful. I—I wasn't afraid."

"Ma—"

"I wonder what it means?"

Ma frowned again, her delicate brows pressing together, and I felt a terrible fear inside. I gnawed my lower lip, still gripping her hand. Several moments passed and then Ma pulled her hand free and placed it above her bosom and then began to cough, pulling out the handkerchief she kept tucked under her pillow. It was large and white and streaked with reddish-brown stains that hadn't been there last night. I quickly fetched another one from the bureau drawer, and she took it and continued to cough wretchedly. When the spell finally subsided, the fresh handkerchief had bright scarlet stains on it. Ma looked up and saw the expression on my face and shoved the handkerchief under her pillow. I poured a glass of water for her and she took it with a trembling hand and sipped and finally handed it back to me.

"I'm all right now," she said.

"Ma, is there anything I can—"

"No—no, my darling. I think—I think I'll just rest for a while."

"Will you be—"

"I'll be fine, darling."

"I'm going to Mama Lou's right away. I'll bring the medicine back. It'll make you feel better."

She managed a tiny nod. I looked into her eyes.

"I—I love you, Ma."

"And I love you, my darling."

"You're going to get well," I said hoarsely. "I—I intend to see to it. I—" My voice broke.

Ma attempted another smile, the corners of her lips fluttering weakly, and she lifted a paper-thin hand to stroke my cheek. I leaned down and kissed her brow, and then I left the room, closing the door quietly. I went to the larder and fetched the basket of brown eggs and the block of hard cheese wrapped in oilcloth that I had set aside earlier. I fought back the emotions that threatened to overwhelm me, and I fought back the tears as well. I left the house, moving resolutely past the barn, the shed, the filthy pigsty with the snorting beasts roiling in the mud. I moved past the cypress trees, strands of frail gray Spanish moss brushing my arms and face. I wasn't going to cry. I wasn't. I knew if I allowed myself to cry I'd never, never be able to stop.

Chapter Two

THE SWAMP WAS A DANGEROUS PLACE, but it held no fears for me. I was familiar with all its dangers, knew how to avoid them, for I had roamed freely through these parts since I was a small child. There were snakes, yes, but the cottonmouths lived in the water, and the other ones didn't bother you if you didn't bother them. The alligators were lazy, sluggish creatures who nestled in the mud along the water's edge like scaly brown-green logs, and they never snapped unless you disturbed them. There was quicksand that could suck you right up and swallow you whole, but anyone who knew anything about the swamp was able to spot those gummy gray-brown bogs immediately. The swamp was a damp, misty place, pale gray and green and tan, with thin yellow rays of sunlight filtering through the thick canopy of limbs above.

There were wildflowers, too, clusters of fragile pink and mauve blossoms growing in the shade and, here and there, long vines studded with bell-shaped crimson blooms. Loveliest of all were the wild orchids, hard to find but exquisite. Most were milky white with delicate mauve and red specks, but once, deep in the swamp, I had found one speckled with gold and bronze, the petals a pale yellow-white. There was beauty in the swamp as well as danger, if you knew where to look for it, but most folk were spooked and stayed away. I was at home here amidst the gnarled old cypress trees with their exposed roots and twisted limbs draped with ghostly gray moss, amidst the mud and profusion of damp green plants.

The ground was spongy beneath my bare feet, and the swamp was alive with the hum of insects and the cawing of birds. Sounds were strangely distorted here, giving off weird echoes that some-

17

times reminded you of tormented cries. Some said the swamp was haunted, full of evil spirits who called to each other, but I knew that was nonsense. I had roamed here all my life without ever seeing a ghost, though sometimes after a rain the mists grew thick and waved in the wind, taking on strange shapes that might remind you of spooks. I knew I didn't have to worry about supernatural beings. Those who had two legs with a dong dangling between 'em caused me worry enough.

I skirted a small brown stream with cattails growing tall on either side and turned and hopped over a muddy rivulet. The swamp was laced with these rivulets and streams, filled with ponds and lakes. A person really needed a small boat or a canoe to get around properly, as there was far more water than solid ground, but I moved with a sure foot, for I knew every inch of ground in these parts. Far from being uneasy, I felt safe and secure in the swamp. It was as though the damp, living gray-green walls protected me from the world outside. Here I could be free and drop those defenses I had to keep firmly in place at home. Randy and Jake never penetrated into the swamp if they could avoid it, nor did Clem. No one could find me here. No one could harm me.

I forged ahead, moving confidently, completely at ease.

Ma was going to be all right, I told myself over and over again, and after a while I almost believed it. Some things are so terrible to think about, you have to hide from them, have to trick yourself into believing they aren't so, and that's what I'd been doing with Ma's illness. Mama Lou would give me another bottle of the medicine and Ma would take it and the terrible coughing would cease and the feverish glow would leave her eyes and she would soon be strong again. I couldn't face the truth. I wouldn't. Ma was going to be all right. All she needed was some rest and some more medicine. How silly of me to get so upset just . . . just because she had coughed up a little blood and talked about seeing a redbird.

Cardinals were rare indeed in these parts, so rare superstitious folk believed you only saw one when you were about to die. Nonsense, of course, just like the ghosts who were supposed to prowl the swamp. Ma hadn't seen no redbird outside her window this morning. She had imagined it. I'd been up and about since daylight, and I certainly hadn't seen one. Ma must of just thought she was awake, must of dreamed it. I wasn't going to waste any more time dwelling on anything so foolish.

An alligator yawned nearby, making a curious hoarse sound that was followed by a splash as the creature slipped into the water. I moved on, shoving strands of moss aside, ducking under thick ropes of vine. It was very warm here, the air damp and muggy, and perspiration stained my pink dress, formed a sheen on my face and arms. I stepped over narrow fingers of water, like veins in the ground that swelled into rivulets and streams and eventually flowed into lakes. Water everywhere, stagnant pools and sluggish streams, the pungent muddy smell mingling with the smells of root and bark and damp greenery to form an earthy perfume that was strangely pleasant once you grew used to it.

It took me almost half an hour to reach Mama Lou's, for she lived deep in the swamp, as far away from other people as possible. Her shanty stood beside a small, flat brown lake, sticky white and yellow water lilies covering much of its oily surface. Though old and weathered, the shanty was in surprisingly good condition, not falling down like most hereabouts. The moss-green roof didn't sag at all, and a small verandah wound around the front and one side, providing shade on sunny days. Wild-flowers grew in profusion in the yard leading down to the lake, and in back there was a large herb garden, walled with stone to keep out the swamp creatures. It was a cheerful-looking place, not at all gloomy or forbidding.

Mama Lou had lived here for as long as anyone could remember, making her potions and medicines, shunning other people, her only companions a series of large, furry cats. She must be almost a hundred years old, folk said, and it was rumored her old master had given her her freedom after she put a curse on him and almost caused his ruination. She had come from Africa in chains, the story went, a wild and savage young princess who had been a medicine woman in her native tribe and steeped in the dark magic of that continent. Folk around here were convinced she was a witch and left her strictly alone, venturing to her shanty only when they needed herbs or medicine.

As I stepped into the clearing in front of the lake, a cloud passed over the sun, shadowing everything with gray. Superstitious folk would have taken this as an omen and shivered with apprehension, but I wasn't superstitious and I wasn't afraid of

Mama Lou. Once, years and years ago when I was a very little girl and not yet familiar with the swamp, I had lost my way and was very frightened and Mama Lou had come and taken me by the hand and led me back home, never saying a word. She had "seen" me lost, I knew, and had come to my rescue. After that, I had often slipped off to visit her, fascinated by the wizened old Negro woman who had the sight and was so wise.

I could smell the herbs growing in the walled garden and the overwhelming scent of the poppies that grew in wild profusion behind the house. Folk marveled that Mama Lou was able to make so many exotic things grow in the swamp, said it was black magic. She used the herbs in making her medicines, used the poppies, too, and the bark of several trees. I approached the verandah, carrying the cheese and eggs, and the screen door opened. Mama Lou stepped out onto the verandah. She was not at all surprised to see me. She was holding a small brown glass bottle full of thick liquid.

"I has the medicine," she said.

She knew. She had been expecting me.

"I've brought you some eggs and cheese, Mama Lou. I saved the best eggs, and I made the cheese myself."

Mama Lou nodded grimly and examined me with piercing black-brown eyes that always seemed to see so much more. She was small and stooped and gnarled, with a bony, nut-brown face that was a network of overlapping creases and wrinkles. Her lips were barely visible, her chin a hard, jutting knob. She wore a shapeless flowered blue smock, much faded, and a pair of cracked brown leather slippers that were too large for her feet.

"You doan have to bring me gifts, chile," she said in her raspy voice.

"I wanted you to have the eggs and cheese," I told her. "I— I would have brought some sugar, too, but there was just a little left in the canister."

"All these years little Dana comes to see Mama Lou. She isn't afraid of me like the others."

"You're my friend," I said simply.

Mama Lou nodded again, still examining me. Something seemed to be bothering her. One of her cats, an enormous, furry marmalade, came around the corner of the verandah and curled itself against her legs, looking up at me with visible hostility.

Ebenezer wasn't black, like the last one had been, but he was just as intimidating. Folk said Mama Lou's cats were her "familiars" and could transform themselves into different creatures. All witches had cats who acted on their orders.

"You knew I was coming," I said.

"Mama Lou knew."

"Ma had a bad turn, and—"

"I has the medicine you came for."

"Ma—Ma's going to be all right, isn't she?"

She ignored the question, those black-brown eyes aglow as she continued to study me. Several long moments passed, and I felt vaguely uneasy, gripping the handle of the basket, tiny streams of perspiration dripping down my back. Mama Lou grimaced and, reaching out, lightly touched my cheek. Her fingertips were as soft as velvet and seemed to vibrate with power.

"You is growing up," she rasped softly. "You is no longer a chile. This is good. This will help."

"What do you mean?"

"You is strong," she told me. "Inside you have the hidden strength, the will to overcome. This will see you through."

Mama Lou nodded as though in agreement with herself, her head bobbing up and down, and then she shooed the cat away from her legs and gave me the bottle of medicine. I slipped it into the pocket of my skirt.

"The last bottle helped a lot," I said nervously. "She was able to get some sleep. I—I feel sure she'll get better."

Mama Lou's eyes were sad. She didn't say anything, and I was afraid to ask her any more questions. Some things you didn't want to know. You wanted to keep them a secret as long as possible.

"Come on in, chile," Mama Lou said gently. "They's honey cakes. You always did love Mama Lou's honey cakes."

She opened the screen door. Her old leather slippers flopped noisily as she shuffled slowly inside the shanty. I followed, setting the basket down on the littered worktable. It was cool and dim inside. Drying herbs hung from the beams overhead, and a tall shelf along one wall was filled to overflowing with boxes and canisters. There were two battered old bamboo chairs, a small leather-bound chest between them. Mama Lou lighted a candle in a battered pewter holder and set it down on the chest, settling herself into one of the bamboo chairs. In the flickering candlelight I saw the strange masks hanging on the wall opposite the shelf. They were wonderfully carved and extremely ugly, one of them encircled with long dry grass like a lion's mane. The three savage faces seemed to grimace as the light wavered. They had been here ever since I could remember, and I wondered how Mama Lou had obtained them.

"You fetch the honey cakes, chile. Mama Lou doesn't get around as good as she did. These old bones are a-gettin' weary."

"I really don't want any honey cakes, Mama Lou."

"No," she said, "you wants to talk. Sit yourself down."

I sat down in the bamboo chair opposite hers, the candle flame leaping between us like a tiny yellow-orange demon trying to escape its captivity on the tip of the candle. Ebenezer jumped through the open window and perched on the sill for a moment, then jumped onto the old rag rug and marched over to sit at Mama Lou's feet. His yellow-green eyes glared at me, daring me to attempt any harm to his mistress. Through the window I could see that the cloud was still covering the sun, everything gray, dim, even though it was only midmorning. I looked at Mama Lou, and in the light of the candle her withered old face had a strange beauty, like one of the masks.

"Tell me, chile," she rasped.

"I—I've been having this dream, Mama Lou. I've been having it for some time now, and it—it's always the same."

She bobbed her head, waiting for me to continue, and I told her about the dream: the mist, the man I sensed was tall and handsome but couldn't see clearly, the great river nearby. I didn't tell her about the feelings I had when I woke up, for some reason embarrassed to speak of them. Mama Lou listened carefully, leaning forward in her chair, and when I had finished, she bobbed her head again, nodding.

"You has the sight," she said.

"The sight?"

"Everyone has it, chile, in one degree or another, only most folk, they's never even aware of it. It come and it goes, like a flash of lightning in the mind, and they just puzzled for a moment and forgets it."

"This dream—"

"It comes in dreams, too, chile, only most folk, they forgets they dreams as soon as they opens they eyes. Sometimes the sight come only once, faintly, like a shred of mist, and other times it come back again and again, like your dream.''

"Then—I—"

"You will meet this man."

"How will I know? I can never see his face."

"When the time come, chile, you will know."

"He will take my hands, pull me to him?"

"Beside the river, and you will feel like you feel in the dream."

"Is—is he a good man, Mama Lou?"

Mama Lou frowned and beckoned me to her. I got up and knelt in front of her, and Mama Lou placed her hands on my temples, peering intently into my eyes. Ebenezer made unpleasant noises, not at all pleased. Mama Lou shoved him away with her foot. The candle flame danced wildly, throwing shadows on the walls, and the bizarre masks seemed to change expression. Mama Lou stared into my skull for several long moments, her thin lips working at the corners, her eyes strangely flat. She might have been in some kind of trance. I trembled slightly as her velvet-soft fingertips pressed against my temples, gently kneading the flesh.

"What—what do you see?" I whispered.

Mama Lou didn't seem to hear me. Several more moments passed, and then she sighed and sat back, her hands dropping into her lap. She looked exhausted, her eyes closed, her fuzzy gray head resting against the back of the chair as she breathed deeply. It was some time before she opened her eyes, even more before she had the strength to speak.

"I sees many things, chile. They come in patches, and some of 'em don't rightly make sense."

"The man? Did you see him?"

"They's four men. One, he is good. One, he is bad and good. Good, but he does bad. One—" She hesitated "what he wants is unnatural, it is wrong and you must—" Mama Lou cut herself short, frowning deeply.

"I must what, Mama Lou?"

"You must not do this thing. It is wrong, against nature."

I stared at her, frowning. Mama Lou was frowning, too, and there was a puzzled look in her dark eyes.

"I—I don't understand," I said. "What is it I must not do?"

Mama Lou shook her head, the frown deepening. "It ain't

clear, chile. I gets a very strong impression, a feelin', but—it's patchy. All I knows is you must beware of this man.''

"Is—is he the one by the river?''

"Th' one by the river, he is one of the four, but—which one you must beware of—'' Mama Lou shook her head, scowling now, disappointed with herself. "Sometimes it's like that—you get the feelin', but you cain't see it clearly.''

"Four men,'' I said thoughtfully. "Will—will I love them?''

"Two of them you will love, with body and soul, and the other two . . .'' She hesitated, concentrating, trying hard to peer into that hazy realm. "The other two, you will not love them, but—''

She cut herself short, worried.

"But I must beware of one,'' I said.

Mama Lou nodded, her fuzzy head bobbing.

"They's more,'' she said.

She settled back in the chair and closed her eyes again, leaving me behind as she looked into the haze of future. I kneeled in front of her, very still, waiting. The candle flame danced, leaping, washing over the walls in bizarre patterns. Ebenezer crouched in a corner, purring angrily and glaring at me with hateful eyes. Several moments passed again, and then the old Negro woman sighed and shook her head, opening her eyes. When she spoke, her words were hesitant. She was plainly confused.

"It—it don't rightly make sense,'' she said, "but that's the way it is sometimes. I sees you an'—an' you is behind a half circle of lights an' you is wearin' a lovely gown, it seems like silk, yes, gold and white striped silk, an' you is wearin' sparklers, too, at your throat a necklace of sparklers—jewels, they is, maybe diamonds. The lights are flickerin' an' people—people, lots of 'em, they is watchin' you and makin' a big commotion, lots of noise, but—but you ain't frightened at all. You is smilin'.''

Mama Lou fell silent and opened her eyes, bemused by the vision.

"You're right,'' I said. "It don't make sense. Don't make no sense at all.''

"It will,'' Mama Lou said quietly. "When the time comes, when it happens, it will make perfect sense. You'll be where you belong, chile, an' you'll be—'' She hesitated, frowning, intent as she peered into the future. "You will be someone—someone they all know."

"Those people making the racket?"

She nodded. "You will be someone of note."

Someone of note? Beats me what she's talking about, I said to myself. It was thrilling to think of me in a silk gown, wearing sparklers, but what could the circle of lights mean? And all those people watching me and making a big commotion? My knees were beginning to hurt from kneeling there in front of the chair, but I still wanted to know about Ma. Mama Lou had been evasive when I asked her about Ma before. I asked her again now, and the old Negro looked at me with black-brown eyes that were full of concern. The corners of her mouth worked, and she hesitated again before speaking. Her voice was crisp.

"You takes her the medicine, chile. Mama Lou's medicine is the best. It'll ease her."

"But—"

Mama Lou shook her head impatiently and stood up, reaching down for my hand. I stood up, too, a wave of dirty honey-blond hair spilling across my cheek. I brushed it back, frustrated, apprehensive. She knew something, I was sure of it, but she didn't intend to tell me. Why? Was it . . . was it something bad?

"Mama Lou—" My voice trembled.

"Don't ask Mama Lou no more questions. Sometimes it ain't—it ain't a blessin' to have the sight. I has things to do, herbs to gather, petals to dry. I cain't spend no more time jawin' with you."

"Thank—thank you, Mama Lou. Next time I'll try to bring some sugar, too."

Mama Lou didn't reply. She avoided my eyes. I had the strange feeling that I would never see her again, that the old woman knew it full well. She led me out onto the porch, Ebenezer following behind us with a series of ugly hisses. The sky was darker than before, clouds covering the sun completely. Everything was flat pewter-gray and dull green and muddy brown. A frog leaped into the lake. The water lilies trembled, grew still. Mama Lou took my hand again and gripped it tightly, her own bony yet curiously smooth. Those black-brown eyes peered at me intently, but I sensed that they were seeing much more than a dirty-faced girl in a ragged pink dress. She didn't say anything for a long while, and when she finally spoke, her voice was tired, raspy.

"You's strong, chile, like I said. You's gonna see it through."

"Am—am I going to need strength?"

"They—they's gonna be hard times, little Dana, and you's going to suffer, but—you will know great joy as well. One day you will know great joy, a great love. The dream will come true."

There were many more questions I longed to ask her, but I knew it would be futile. Mama Lou had said all that she intended to say. She looked at me now with sad, dark eyes, and I felt sad, too, a tremulous sadness that seemed to well up inside me. It was all I could do to keep the tears from brimming over my lashes. This ancient Negro woman with her fuzzy gray head and withered black cheeks was the only friend I had ever had, and I knew somehow that I would never see her again. Mama Lou seemed to follow my thoughts. She nodded, as though to confirm the truth in them. She let go of my hand and moved back. Ebenezer curled his fat body around her ankles, hissing at me.

"Good-bye, Mama Lou," I said quietly.

"Take care, chile."

Reluctantly I left her, questions unanswered, new questions taking shape in my mind. I crossed the clearing beside the lake, and reaching the edge of the trees with their festoons of ghostly gray moss, I turned and looked back at the shanty. Mama Lou was still standing on the porch, absolutely immobile, looking like some petrified pagan statue with the furry marmalade cat curled about her ankles. The sky was still gray, the lake flat and motionless, but a few thin yellow rays of sunlight were penetrating the gloom. I lifted my hand in farewell, but the old woman made no acknowledgment of my gesture. I plunged into the swamp, filled with a multitude of conflicting emotions.

Moving through the dense, damp tunnels of gray and green, insects humming all around, birds shrieking in the distance, I thought about all that Mama Lou had told me. I wasn't a superstitious ninny like most folk here in the swamps—I didn't, for instance, put a bit of faith in the belief that seeing a redbird meant someone would die—but I knew Mama Lou really did have the sight, and I knew everything she said would come true, try though I might to convince myself it was nonsense. Four men . . . four I would love, one I must beware of. I guess I'm supposed to meet 'em while I'm cleaning out the pigsty or churning the butter, I thought. Me in a silk gown and diamonds, people watching me and making a commotion. That was even harder to believe, it was a real puzzler, but in my heart I knew that someday I *would* be standing behind a half circle of lights in that gown, those jewels, for whatever reason. I would be where I belonged, Mama Lou had said. Whatever could that mean?

I skirted a bad patch of quicksand and parted strands of trailing moss, reaching into my pocket to touch the bottle of medicine. Mama Lou's medicine was the best. Ma was going to get better. There were going to be hard times, just like Mama Lou said, but that didn't mean . . . It meant I would have to be very strong until Ma got over her sickness. I stepped over veins of sluggishly flowing green water, moved through clumps of cattails, smelling strong swamp odors. An alligator hissed and slithered into a nearby pond, sinking into the water like a brownish-green log. The anguish over Ma was like something live inside me, threatening to take over completely, and I knew I must keep it at bay. I couldn't give in to it. I had to be calm and cheerful for her. I couldn't ever let her know how worried I was.

The sun was high and hot when I finally reached the farm. Heat waves shimmered visibly in the air, and I could feel the perspiration dripping slowly down my back. The chickens were silent. The pigs were roiling quietly in the mud in their sty. Not a breeze stirred. The Spanish moss hung limp and gray from the boughs of the trees surrounding the farm. I paused in the yard, lifting my hands up to shove limp, heavy honey-blond waves from my cheeks. My breasts swelled, almost spilling out of the tattered dusty pink bodice. I smoothed my hair back, longing for a bath, longing to remove my filthy dress and shabby white petticoat and submerge myself in the crystal-clear water of the secret spring where I always bathed. It was deep in the swamp, and the soft green fern growing around the banks made a wonderful, creamy lather when dampened and crushed. Perhaps I could get away to bathe later on this afternoon, I thought.

It was as I adjusted the bodice of my dress that I felt the eyes boring into me. The sensation was so strong, so unsettling, that it was almost like physical touch. I turned, disturbed, and there he stood, near the corner of the barn. I had no idea how long he might have been there, watching me as I daydreamed about a bath, but I knew he had seen me tucking my full breasts deeper into the bodice. A blush tinted my cheeks. I felt embarrassment and anger and something else as well, the same instinctive apprehension I felt every time my stepfather stared at me with those sullen eyes so dark a blue they seemed almost black.

"Mornin', Dana," he said.

His voice was harsh and husky, so guttural it often sounded like a growl. I had never heard Clem O'Malley speak kindly, and I had never seen him smile. Not as tall as either of his sons, only a few inches taller than me, he had a strong, powerful body with thick chest, broad shoulders, muscular arms. His features were flat and coarse, the cheekbones broad, the nose large, the jawline hard, unyielding. His mouth was large and pink, the full lower lip curling with undeniable sensuality, and his thick auburn hair was brushed severely to one side. Clem O'Malley brought to mind a healthy, brutish animal acharge with strong red blood and tremendous energy.

The mystery to me was that so many women seemed to find my stepfather appealing. More than one woman here in the swamps had gone utterly daft over him. They seemed to revel in the rough, abusive treatment he gave them. He had quite a reputation as a tomcat and spent an inordinate amount of time in the pursuit of tail. He and Ma hadn't slept together for years, didn't even share a bedroom, and she had long since grown immune to his brazen infidelities. I wondered how Ma could ever have married such a man. What had driven her to . . . to accept such a brute after the graceful, gracious life I knew she had had earlier?

Clem O'Malley sauntered slowly toward me in that heavy-limbed, stealthy walk that reminded me of a panther. He wore tall black boots and tight gray breeches and a very thin white cotton shirt that bagged loosely at the waistband. The full sleeves billowed as he moved. The boots, I noticed, had been freshly polished, and the shirt was clean. Though the other men who came to visit had to pay for her services, the mulatto Jessie gave it to Clem free of charge. She even polished his boots and washed his shirts, despite the fact that he treated her like dirt. Puzzled me to pieces, it did. Jessie must be daft, too.

"Ain't you gonna speak?" he inquired.

"I ain't got nothing to say."

"What-ja doin', lollygagging about? Ain't you got chores to do?"

"I done 'em all earlier."

"You feed the boys breakfast 'fore they went to market?"

I nodded sullenly. My stepfather uncurled his arms and brought one hand up to his chin, the strong, blunt fingers resting on his jaw, the ball of his thumb slowly stroking his lower lip. Clem O'Malley was forty-five years old, yet he exuded a potent sensuality as strong as musk. Though fresh and clean, his thin white shirt was beginning to grow damp with perspiration. He smelled of leather and sweat and male flesh. The sunlight burnished his thick auburn hair, giving it deep coppery highlights. The intense, open desire smoldering in those blue-black eyes made me extremely apprehensive. I knew what he wanted—the same thing Jake and Randy and all the others wanted—and I tightened my shoulders, cool and defiant.

"You ain't scared-a me, are you, little Dana?"

"I ain't scared-a you, Clem."

"You oughtn't-a be. I wouldn't hurt you for th' world. You're growin' up mighty fast. Yeah, you're gettin' real ripe. I been noticin' that lately. Can't help noticin' it, the way you almost pop outta that dress-a yours. Real ripe. Real fetchin'."

I made no reply, gazing at him with level eyes. Truth is, I *was* scared of him, but I wasn't about to let him sense that. I vowed I'd claw his eyes out and kick him in the balls if he dared lay a hand on me.

"Jake and Randy tell me you've been real uppity lately," he said, thumb still stroking his lower lip.

"Indeed?"

"Figure it's 'cause you're nervous and high-strung, like your Ma. Figure it's 'cause you've got all that tension inside that ain't been released. You're mighty big to still be holdin' on to your cherry."

"That ain't none-a your business, Clem."

"I put a roof over your head, put food in your belly."

"And I work like a slave for it," I retorted. "Go stick it in Jessie or some other whore, Clem. If you know what's good for you, you'll leave me be."

His eyes grew hard, gleaming with anger, and his mouth tightened into an ugly line. Clem intimidated both his boys, intimidated Ma, intimidated everyone around with his brute strength and harsh manner, but I wasn't going to let him intimidate me. He had only stared at me before—he had never spoken to me quite so boldly or made his objective clear—and I knew I couldn't give an inch. Though I was trembling inside, I continued to gaze at him with cool defiance.

Clem O'Malley stood there before me, his large hands balled into fists, his mouth working at one corner. He started to say something but had second thoughts and held it back. He wasn't accustomed to defiance from anyone, and it must have galled him to have it from a mere snip of a girl. He glared at me for several long moments, struggling to control his anger, full of menace, and finally he gave a bull-like snort.

"Where've you been?" he demanded.

"I've been to see Mama Lou, to get medicine for Ma. She had another bad turn."

That gave him pause. He suddenly remembered he had a wife, remembered she was ill. It was something he rarely thought about.

"How is she?" he asked irritably. "I just come back. I ain't been inside the house yet."

"She was resting when I left her."

"I got some things to check on in the barn," he told me. "I'm gonna be wantin' some lunch 'fore long. See that you have it ready, and see that you watch that mouth-a yours, too, missy. I ain't havin' no uppity little slut talkin' to me like that! You understand?"

I didn't answer. My stepfather snorted again and turned and started toward the barn, heavy shoulders rolling beneath the damp white cotton. I took a deep breath, more shaken by the encounter than I cared to admit. Somehow I was going to have to get away from here. Somehow I was going to have to get Ma well and get her away from here, too. Her family . . . maybe we could go to her family. Surely they wouldn't turn her away. We had to leave this awful place before . . . I refused to think any further. Squaring my shoulders, I went into the house.

Something was wrong. I sensed that immediately. The hallway was dim, and the house was very still, too still. The hot, muggy air seemed to be permeated with an ominous quality, and the silence was ominous, too. It was as though the house had a life of its own and was holding its breath. I felt an instinctive panic, for I knew, already I knew, in my bones, in my blood.

I could feel the color leaving my cheeks. For a moment I was frozen, unable to move, held fast by the panic. I felt a wave of dizziness and feared I might faint, but I didn't. I dug my nails into my palms and prayed for strength, and then I hurried down the hall to Ma's room.

She was sitting up in bed. Her face was as pale as white candle wax. Her damp hair was smoothed back, and her beautiful eyes were wide open, gazing wistfully at something only she could see. The sheet covering her glistened bright red, literally soaked with blood. My knees went weak. I thought I would fall. I let out a sob and Ma heard me and peered intently through the mist, finally able to see me. She smiled. It was a lovely smile, tender and warm.

"Dana," she whispered.

"Ma. Oh, Ma!"

"He came back," she told me. Her voice was barely audible. "The redbird came back and—and he brought his family. A—a whole flock of redbirds. See them, darling?"

The pain and panic I felt was almost unendurable, and then it seemed suddenly to cease. I know not where the calm came from, but it came when I needed it, saving me, giving me the strength to do what I must do. I seemed to be in a dream, far removed, and nothing was quite real. The small, shabby room with its bare hardwood floor and dingy walls, the dilapidated furniture, the faded patchwork quilt at the foot of the old brass bed, the wet scarlet sheet: none of them were real. As though in a dream, I removed the soiled sheet and discarded it and replaced it with a fresh one I took from the bureau drawer. The panic was numbed, yes, the pain at bay, but tears spilled over my lashes nevertheless.

I bathed Ma's face with a damp cloth and moistened the lips still curved in a smile. The springs creaked noisily as I sat down on the bed beside her. Sunlight streamed through the open window, rays aswirl with dust motes. There was a sweet, cloying odor in the air—was it the smell of death? I took Ma's hand in mine and squeezed it, and she looked up at me, hazel eyes glowing with tender love.

"But—you mustn't cry, my darling," she said. "I am not afraid. You mustn't be afraid, either."

"I—I brought the medicine, Ma. You—I'm going to give you some, and you—"

"It's too late for medicine, darling," she whispered.

"Ma—"

"They came through the window, and I knew. It—it's for the best. I'm of no use to anyone anymore, and as long as I—you—you have your whole life ahead of you, and as long as I—"

She cut herself short, frowning, and then she began to shiver. I let go of her hand and pulled the fresh sheet up over her and got the patchwork quilt and spread it over her as well, festive squares and circles of blue and green and pink and yellow and gold sadly faded. I sat back down and gently stroked her cheek. I had an airy feeling of unreality, for this was still a dream, it wasn't real at all.

"You're going to be all right," I said, "you're going to be all right," but it was someone else speaking.

Ma looked up at me, her eyes full of tenderness, full of concern, and the gentle smile still rested on her lips. It seemed to be frozen there. I took her hand again, and it seemed colder, seemed lifeless. The anguish was there inside of me, but I couldn't feel it, I couldn't face it. The girl in the ragged pink dress was someone else, and I was observing her with a strange, light-headed objectivity.

A swamp bird called out, and the sound came through the window. The mote-filled rays of sunlight made misty patterns on the bare brown floor. My mother was leaving me, she had already begun her journey, and I could feel nothing at all. The emotions were locked inside, held close by invisible walls, and I knew it was a blessing. Objectively, I knew I couldn't give way, not yet, and so I held her hand tightly and the tears spilled over my lashes and I told myself this was really a dream. The sweet, cloying odor hung in the air like a miasma. It was indeed the smell of death.

"Dana?" It was the faintest whisper.

"Yes, Ma."

"Promise me you will be strong."

"I will be, Ma. I promise."

"Make—make something of your life. I wish I could be here to guide you, but . . ." The whisper faded way.

The smile faded from her lips and she closed her eyes, breathing in soft, short gasps. Her face was pale, waxen, coated with a faint sheen of perspiration, and her graying honey-blond hair gleamed with dampness. After a moment she opened her eyes again and saw me and the smile returned. Her eyes filled with joyous recognition.

"Robert," she said.

She thought I was someone else, someone named Robert.

"You never knew," she whispered. "If you had known—Oh, Robert, if you had known, you wouldn't have—I wanted to die then. I wanted to stop living, but I couldn't because—because I was carrying our little girl. They turned against me, turned me out, and I had no one—"

"Ma. Ma, it's me. Please—"

"Dana?"

"I'm here, Ma."

"But—Robert? Where is Robert? He was here. A moment ago he was—you mustn't blame him, Dana. He never knew, you see. If he had known—he wouldn't have left me. He—he was so handsome, so strong, like a young god. He wasn't our kind, I knew that, but he wasn't bad. I tried to tell them—I love him, I told them, but they didn't want me to have anything to do with . . ."

The words were coming with great effort, barely audible, and I could hardly see her through the tears brimming over my lashes. Everything was shimmering behind a glistening blur. I held on to that limp, cold hand so tightly I could feel the bones beneath the flesh. I could feel her slipping away. The room seemed to fill with an invisible force that lifted her, drawing her from me. I clutched her hand, desperately trying to hold her back.

"Ma," I pleaded. "Ma."

"Dana?"

"Yes. Yes—I—I'm right here, Ma."

"I did what I—I had to do," she whispered. "There was no one to turn to, and then—then there was Clem. He needed a mother for his two little boys and I—you were on the way, and there was nothing else . . ."

Her voice grew even fainter, and those sad, lovely eyes were full of anxiety. All my life there had been unanswered questions, and now she wanted to answer them. I could see that. She frowned, trying to find the strength, unable to do so.

"For—forgive me, my darling."

"Ma! There's nothing to forgive. I—"

"What will you do? It—it was wrong for me to—to keep it from you so long. I should have told—you should have known.

May—maybe they will—New Orleans—the family. Maybe they will forgive me and—you're blameless. Maybe they will—''

"Who, Ma? Who are—''

Her eyes widened, staring again at something I couldn't see. Moments before she had been tense, anxious, and now she relaxed. The gentle smile curved on her lips again, as though in greeting. Warm, salty tears bathed my cheeks, and a soft sob escaped my lips. Ma heard it. With great difficulty she tore herself away from the unseen and looked at me, trying to focus.

"Dana? Is—is that you?"

"It's me, Ma."

"I . . ." It was a mere breath.

"Yes? Yes, Ma?"

"I—I love you, darling."

"And I love you!" I sobbed.

She closed her eyes. She took a deep breath and exhaled and there was a soft, rattling sound and then silence. I clutched her hand, and I could feel life leaving her. The air seemed to stir ever so faintly with a mere suggestion of movement, and then it was over and Ma was gone. I released her hand and, ever so calmly, leaned over and kissed her cheek, silently saying goodbye. I stood up, still calm, looking around at the room without seeing any of it. Numb, blessedly numb, I shook my head and gazed at the emptiness. I knew I couldn't possibly go on without her.

Chapter Three

I STIRRED THE BATTER, wooden spoon weaving in and out, hitting against the side of the bowl, and then I poured the batter into two greased loaf pans. The oven was hot, coals glowing a bright red-orange when I opened the black iron door and placed the pans inside. I put the flour away and washed the bowl and began to wipe up the flour sprinkled on the counter. Late morning sunlight streamed in through the open kitchen windows and with it the barnyard smells of manure and damp hay and rotting leather. My ragged pink dress was damp with sweat under my armpits, and I could feel sweat trickling down my back. I paid no mind to it. Mess cleaned up, I checked the green beans cooking in a pot on top of the stove, adding a little more water, a generous pat of butter, some salt. They would be good and tender by noon. I noted that dully, not interested at all, not caring.

You go on, I had discovered. You go on living even though living is like death. The Negroes and some of the more superstitious folk here in the swamp believed in creatures they called zombies, men and women who had been called up from the grave by some voodoo spell. These creatures walked and moved arms and legs and tramped through the swamps like living human beings, but they weren't living at all. They were dead, merely going through the motions of living human beings, and that's what I felt like. I moved, yes, I fed the chickens and milked the cow and cooked the meals and did my chores like someone living, but I was dead inside.

Eight days had gone by since Ma drew her last breath, and I had been in a trancelike stupor the whole while. They had taken Ma away and put her into a crudely built pine box, and the next

35

day a wagon had fetched us and I had ridden to the tiny settlement on the banks of the river. The sky was a dismal slate-gray and filled with low, ominous black-edged clouds as the wagon let us out at the weed-infested cemetery. A motley crowd awaited our arrival, grim-faced men in shabby suits, slack-mouthed women in worn cotton dresses. There was no sympathy, no warmth. These people were past caring. They had come merely out of curiosity. I saw the hole in the ground and the mound of damp brown earth beside it, and I felt nothing, not even when they lowered the pine box down into the hole and began to cover it with the earth.

There was no church here, no preacher, and there were no words spoken for my ma. I stood there stiffly beside my stepfather. Clem was grim-faced, too, looking uncomfortable in the old gray frock coat that matched his breeches, and a threadbare emerald-green silk stock. My stepbrothers shuffled about uncomfortably, eager to be gone. Neither of them saw any reason why they should be here, for neither of them had cared a fig for Ma. Jake muttered a curse when it began to drizzle. As the earth was shoveled into the grave, slowly covering the coffin, Randy looked around at the women, finally spotting a lush slattern with moist pink lips and faded blond hair. He winked at her as another shovel of dirt hit the coffin. In my trance, I observed all this, and I wondered why I couldn't feel anything, why I couldn't cry. Salty tears had spilled over my lashes during those last moments with Ma, but I hadn't shed a single one since. The living dead don't cry.

The rays of sunlight coming through the kitchen windows were brighter now. It must be nearing twelve. I took the pork chops out of the larder and shucked three ears of corn and peeled silky brown threads from the hard yellow grains. I dropped the ears into a pan of boiling water atop the stove and, brushing an errant honey-blond wave from my cheek, trimmed fat from the pork chops. Nine should be enough. Nine? I vaguely recalled Jake saying he and Randy wouldn't be home for lunch, they were going crayfishing with the Anderson boys. I put six of the pork chops back into the larder, carefully wrapping them in cheesecloth. I never ate at the table with the men. My stepfather would be lunching alone today.

I put the skillet on top of the stove beside the two pots and dropped a generous pat of grease into it. The plump pink pork chops were soon sizzling and turning a satisfactory mauve-brown. I turned them with a long fork, then checked the bread. It was ready, a crusty golden brown. I removed both pans from the oven and set them on the windowsill to cool for a few minutes before turning them out. Pausing at the window for a moment, I stared at the moss-hung trees and the sun-speckled patterns on the ground. From the barn came a metallic clanging noise as my stepfather repaired some farm tool. The noise ceased abruptly, and a moment later Clem sauntered out of the barn, wiping a hand across his brow.

He stood there in the sunlight in brown work boots and snug tan breeches, his loose white cotton work shirt tucked carelessly into the waistband. His auburn hair gleamed with dark, coppery highlights, and there was a sullen expression on that brutal, rough-hewn face so many women found attractive. He reminded me of a bull, incredibly strong and muscular, full of surging energy he could barely repress. He glanced at the house, scowling, his hands balled into fists now and resting on his thighs. He seemed to be contemplating something, debating some course of action, the scowl deepening as he did so.

I turned away from the windows and checked on the pork chops and saw they were done. I took them out of the skillet and placed them on a plate, then I took the handle of the skillet with a thick cloth and poured the grease into a can, setting the skillet on the scarred oak countertop. I took the bread out of the pans and sliced one of the loaves, moving by rote, here in the kitchen but not here at all. Every feeling I had was deadened. I had been encased in total numbness ever since Ma's death, but my mind still functioned and I still saw and observed and took mental note of all around me.

Clem O'Malley had not been kind to me since the funeral—he was incapable of kindness—but he had treated me with a strange deference, speaking to me in a gruff yet courteous voice. Whereas before he had snapped orders in a surly growl, he now made requests in a manner that, for Clem, might almost be considered polite. The boys' manner had changed, too. There were no more rowdy jests, no more suggestive leers. Both of them were unusually quiet in my presence, seemed uncomfortable and slightly embarrassed, keeping their eyes lowered. Courtesy because of my loss? Hardly. Clem had spoken to them, telling them to mind themselves around me.

Leopards do not change their spots, I told myself, and people don't change overnight. Had I been capable of feeling, I might have been uneasy about this change of attitude toward me by my stepfather, but the numbness encased me, and I shuffled about doing my chores, blessedly free of feeling. I scooped buttery green beans onto the plate beside the pork chops, forked a tender ear of corn out of the boiling water and put it on the plate, too. The back of my dress was wet now, and the petticoat beneath felt limp and heavy. I heard my stepfather coming into the house, and a moment later I felt his eyes on me as I buttered slices of bread and placed them on a saucer.

He didn't say anything. He merely stood there in the doorway, staring at me with an intensity I could feel even though my back was turned. I buttered another slice of bread and, inside of me, something started to tremble, a tiny quiver of alarm that somehow managed to make itself felt despite the numbness. I turned around, holding the saucer of bread. Clem seemed to fill the doorway, not that tall, true, but so large, so sturdy and muscular. His presence was almost overwhelming, like some invisible physical force vibrating in the air. I set the saucer of bread on the table.

"I just see one plate, girl," he said. "You ain't eating?"

"I ain't eating," I said in a flat voice.

"You didn't have no breakfast, either."

"I wudn't hungry," I mumbled.

Clem tilted his chin down and lifted those dark blue eyes, looking at me with smoldering speculation. Broad shoulders leaning against the doorframe, arms folded across his chest, he raised one hand to his chin and began to rub his full, sensual lower lip with the ball of his thumb, his eyes continuing to devour me. Some of the layers of numbness seemed to fall away, and I felt another quiver of alarm, stronger this time.

"You gotta eat, girl," he said.

His voice was deep, and there was a husky catch in it, like a rough purr. Another layer of numbness fell away and then another, and deadened nerve ends vibrated with alarm. It was as though I were awakening from a long sleep, and instincts that had been dormant sprang back to life. I suddenly felt vulnerable and exposed. The kitchen seemed smaller, seemed to close in on me, and I was acutely aware that there was no escape except through the door he blocked with his sturdy bulk.

"I had some cornbread yesterday," I told him.

"That ain't enough. You gotta keep up your strength."

"Don't worry about it, Clem. Your food is getting cold."

Clem hesitated for a moment and then sauntered over to the table and sat down. The chair creaked a little from his weight. He smelled of wet hay and leather and sweat. I noticed that his auburn hair was slightly damp, and the white cotton shirt clung moistly to the musculature of his back and shoulders. Out in the yard the chickens squabbled. The noise seemed to come from a very long distance. Clem started to eat, looking up at me now and then as I took the corn and the beans off the top of the stove.

"Any applesauce?" he inquired.

"I shook my head. "I didn't have time to make any."

"You make tasty applesauce, Dana. I guess it's all that brown sugar and cinnamon you use. You're a right fine cook, come to think of it. You really know how to make a man's belly feel good."

I made no reply. Instincts were shrieking now. Get out, get out, leave at once. Run. Yet I knew I mustn't let him sense my uneasiness. I mustn't give him that advantage. How I wished Jake and Randy were here. Uncouth as they were, they would at least have dispelled this atmosphere of enforced intimacy. I didn't want to be alone with Clem. Ever.

"More green beans?" I inquired.

Clem nodded. I spooned more beans onto his plate. He watched me, those blue-black eyes taking in the full swell of my breasts, the smooth skin of my naked shoulders. I returned to the counter and set the beans down, trying to still the quivers of alarm.

"I have chores to do," I said.

I turned around and started toward the door. As I passed the table, his hand flew up and strong, sinewy fingers clamped tightly around my wrist. When I tried to pull away, he tightened his grip even more, brutally squeezing flesh and bone.

"What's your hurry?" he asked gruffly.

"I told you, I got chores to do."

"They can wait. I want coffee. You got coffee?"

"I haven't made any."

"Make some coffee," he ordered.

Our eyes met, Clem's dark with blue-black depths, my own cool and defiant. Those strong, warm fingers tightened a fraction more. I wanted to wince at the pain, but I stoically refused to do so. After a moment, he released my wrist. I rubbed it, still looking down into those hated eyes, and then I put water into the coffeepot, scooped coffee into it and set the pot on top of the stove. My wrist still throbbed painfully. I would have to brazen it out, I knew. If I backed down now, if I let him win, I would be at his mercy. I couldn't let him intimidate me.

"More corn?" I asked.

"Reckon I could use another ear."

I put it on his plate and turned back to the counter, wiping at it with a damp cloth, trying to keep occupied, aware of those eyes watching every move I made. Clem finished eating and wiped his mouth with a napkin. The coffee began to boil on top of the stove, its fragrant aroma wafting on the air. Clem pushed his plate aside and leaned back in his chair, well fed, looking rather indolent now.

"Yeah," he said, "you're a right fine cook. You're gonna make some man a good wife one-a these days."

"I ain't interested," I told him.

"No?"

"Not in the least."

"That's 'cause you don't know what it's like bein' with a man," he said. "Bein' with a man can be—better'n applesauce, better'n anything. You don't know what-ja been missin', girl."

I felt a warm flush tint my cheeks. Clem noticed it. The faintest suggestion of a grin curled on his full lips, and his blue-black eyes seemed to gleam with secret amusement. He enjoyed devilin' people, enjoyed making them feel uneasy. He was like a cat cruelly toying with a mouse, I thought, but I wasn't a mouse. I gave him a frosty look.

"You're gonna love it," he promised.

"I'm willin' to wait for the right man," I said.

"Yeah?"

"An' he ain't gonna be swamp trash like the men around here."

"Hold yourself pretty high, don't-ja?"

"Indeed I do."

"Think that cherry's some priceless jewel. You ain't no different'n any other wench, girl. Prettier'n most, maybe, but that don't make you no bloody princess. Tail's tail in the dark."

"You should know, Clem."

It was bold of me, but Clem didn't seem to mind at all. That faint suggestion of a grin flickered on his lips again. He shifted his position in the flimsy chair, broad shoulders rolling. He enjoyed his reputation with women. No man in the swamp was more successful with 'em, and no man treated 'em with more cavalier disdain.

"You look just like your ma," he suddenly observed.

A sharp pain seemed to thrust inside me. The protective numbness was completely gone now, and I was a prey to all the emotions I had managed to repress before.

"Yeah," he continued, "you're the spittin' image of her. Same honey-colored hair and hazel eyes. Same lush body. When I first seen her, I thought she was the fetchin'est woman I ever clapped eyes on. Wearin' yellow silk, she was, carryin' one of them yellow silk parasols trimmed with white lace. She was visitin' Miss Amanda at the plantation. Didn't even notice me, of course. I was a lowly overseer, shouldn't even-a been lookin' at two such highborn young ladies."

So it was true. My ma *was* quality. I had known it all along, even though she had always refused to discuss her life before Clem. He knew about her background. He could tell me all I needed to . . . If I could find out the name of her family, I . . . I might somehow be able to . . . Using the thick cloth as a holder, I took the coffeepot off the stove and poured the dark, steaming brew into a chipped white cup.

"I always knew Ma was a lady," I said quietly, setting the cup of coffee in front of him.

"Wudn't such a lady next time I seen her—two years must-a gone by, and I went to town to get some provisions one day and happened to go into one of them waterfront hotels for a drink. I seen her sittin' in the lobby, her bags beside her. They were throwin' her out. Seems her fancy man had gone off and left her all alone. Her folks back in New Orleans had already disowned her. She didn't have a penny to her name, didn't have no one to turn to. I went over to her and introduced myself, said I recognized her, asked if I could be of some kinda assistance. I never will forget them hazel eyes gazin' up at me, all fulla tears. I paid up her hotel bill and took her in to dinner, and three weeks later she became Mrs. Clem O'Malley."

"I—I see," I said.

"Your ma never told-ja anything about it, did she? Didn't

want you to know what really happened. Guess you thought she was married to your pa. Guess you thought he'd died, thought your ma was a widow when she married me. She wudn't no widow."

"My father—"

"Don't know anything about him. Just know he was some fancy man her family didn't approve of, know she ran off with him and lived with him for several months without th' benefit of clergy. He knocked her up and then did a vanishin' act. It's an old, old story—happens all the time."

He paused to take a sip of coffee, carefully observing my reactions to his words. I tried to show none. Ma had loved the man she called Robert. She hadn't married him, but . . . she had probably believed they would be married soon. I couldn't blame her for what she had done. They said love was an overwhelming emotion, said it made you do things you'd ordinarily never dream of doing, and I wasn't going to pass judgment. I might fall in love one day. I might do something even worse than what Ma had done.

"So you married her," I said in a flat voice.

"She needed someone to give his name to the bastard she was carryin' inside her, and I needed someone to look after my two motherless boys, so we made a bargain. She came back to the plantation she used to visit as a guest, this time as the wife of the overseer. It was humiliatin' for her, of course, but Clarisse wudn't in no position to complain. She was damned lucky to get me."

Clem didn't scowl, showed not the least sign of anger. He merely took another sip of coffee, looking at me with dark, thoughtful eyes. What desperation Ma must have felt to have married such a crude, sullen brute. What misery he had dealt her. I hated him with all my heart and soul, and I longed to claw his eyes out, but he had information I needed to know. I took his empty plate and the saucer of bread off the table, setting them on the counter.

"What was my mother's family name?" I asked, ever so casual.

"Whatta you wanna know that for?"

"I—I'd just like to know."

"Wouldn't do you no good. Whatta you think, think you might go to New Orleans an' track 'em down? That's rich, girl. Them

Creole families are haughty as royalty, think they *are* royalty, and they're totally unforgiving. Clarisse was brought up like a princess, and when she defied her folks, when she ran off with her fancy man, they disowned her completely. Think they'd have anything to do with her bastard?''

"I—"

"They'd have the servants throw your ass out, girl. You wouldn't even get past the front foyer. Any wild notions you might have, you might as well put out of your mind here and now.''

"I—I don't even know where New Orleans *is*.''

"And you ain't likely to find out," he told me.

Clem finished his coffee and set the cup down and rose slowly to his feet. He stood there looking at me for several moments, his eyes full of speculation again, and then he nodded to himself, a decision made. He flicked the tip of his tongue out and licked his full lower lip, and I could see the desire darkening in his eyes. I hated him, hated him, and that hatred was so strong now it left no room for fear. Nerves taut, body tightening, I braced myself like a cat, ready to spring.

"Yeah," he drawled, "you're just like your ma. Clarisse had that superior air about her, too, but I soon broke her of it. I'll break you, too. I've been patient with you this past week, girl, givin' you time to grieve, but now we're gonna settle things.''

"There ain't nothing to settle. I—"

"I've had my eye on you for a long, long time. You're gonna be my woman. You're gonna cook for me and see to my needs and—"

"Like hell I will," I said coldly.

"You're still a minor, an' legally you're my responsibility. You'll do as I say, girl, and you'll like it.''

"You ain't got no hold on me. You ain't even kin. I—I'm leavin' today, and—"

"You ain't goin' nowhere. We're gonna have us a real good time, an' when it's all over you ain't even gonna *want* to leave, girl. You've been holdin' on to that cherry far too long as it is. Ain't normal. Ain't healthy. I'm gonna take it. I'm gonna show you what life's all about.''

"Stay away from me, Clem," I warned.

"What-ja gonna do? You gonna beat me up?''

"I—"

"The little wildcat, they call ya. Me, I always like a bit of challenge. Fight me all you want, girl. That'll only make it more interestin'."

He moved slowly toward me with that loose, animal stride, his eyes gleaming darkly, his mouth curling in a grin of anticipation. A heavy auburn wave had fallen across his forehead. Closer and closer he came, huge and muscular and utterly confident, and I knew I couldn't possibly dart past him and reach the door. For a moment sheer panic threatened to overwhelm me. I felt weak, defenseless, at his mercy, and then something steely came to the fore. I wasn't going to let him do it. I'd kill him if necessary. Clem stopped a couple of feet from me—so close I could smell his hair, his skin, his sweat—and his eyes were alight with devilish amusement.

"Don't do it, Clem," I said.

"You're gonna love it," he murmured.

He reached for me. I moved back, stumbling slightly. Clem chuckled, enjoying himself immensely. The kitchen was hot, the air close and stuffy. The chickens were squabbling again. I was calm as could be on the surface, deliberately calculating each movement, but my heart was pounding, pounding, and I seemed to be having trouble catching my breath. I moved back another step, my thighs bumping against the counter. I was trapped, trapped, but I wasn't going to let him. I wasn't. I moved to one side and Clem chuckled again, taking his time, savoring my fear.

"I been waitin' for this," he told me. "I been waitin' for a long, long time. Seein' you bud, seein' you blossom, seein' you growin' up into the most beautiful woman I ever laid eyes on. Your ma was beautiful, too, but you got somethin' special about you, somethin' that makes a man's throat go dry, makes his palms sweat, makes him wanna—" He cut himself short, nodding, blue-black eyes agleam. "Yeah, I been waitin', girl, and now I'm gonna do what I've been wantin' to do since you was thirteen years old."

He moved quickly then, grabbing my arms, squeezing them tightly, slamming his body up against mine. He was as strong as an ox, his body rock-hard, solid muscle. His face was inches from my own, and his lips parted and he lowered his head, seeking my mouth. I struggled vigorously, shaking my head from side to side, his fingers digging into the flesh of my arms with brutal force, his breath hot on my cheek, my neck, my shoulder. My heart pounding, I managed to take a deep breath and make myself go limp. Clem was startled, and he loosened his grip on my arms as I seemed to succumb to his authority.

"That's more like it," he murmured hoarsely. "Yeah, you're gonna enjoy it as much as I am. This body-a yours was made for lovin'."

He curled one strong arm around my waist and leaned forward, forcing me to lean backward. I yielded, lowering my eyelids and letting a soft moan escape from my parted lips. Clem chuckled again, prepared to plunder as I tightened my calf muscles and drew my leg back. I brought my knee up suddenly, violently, with all the force I could muster, and he let out a howl of anguish as it made contact. He released me abruptly, staggered backward, and as he did I raked my nails viciously across his cheek, drawing blood. Clem howled again, his eyes wide with disbelief.

I was stunned by the enormity of what I had done, so stunned I was unable to move. I leaned against the counter with my bosom heaving, my legs curiously weak and watery. I stared at him with horror. His face was ashen, stamped with pain, four bright red streaks dripping across his right cheek. He weaved to and fro on wobbly knees, doubling over and groaning. I knew I must flee immediately, but there didn't seem to be a bone in my body. I was as weak as an infant, breathing in short, shallow gasps. Temporarily immobilized by shock, I could only listen to the pounding of my own heart and pray for the strength to run before it was too late.

"You—you—" he cried hoarsely. "I—"

Clem cut himself short and stood up straight, still in terrible pain but beginning to recover. I tried to move. My knees threatened to fold under me. The color slowly returned to his face. His blue-black eyes glared at me with venomous intent.

"You little bitch! I'm gonna show you. I'm gonna take you right here on th' kitchen floor. I'm gonna have you mornin', noon an' night till I've had my fill-a you, and when I get tired-a you I'm gonna turn you over to the boys and let them have a go at you. You're gonna pay—you're gonna pay dearly—"

He started toward me again and I was still immobile and in the middle of a nightmare, and in the nightmare I flung my arm back and my hand hit something hard and I winced and my fingers instinctively curled around cold iron which I vaguely realized was the handle of the skillet I had set aside earlier. Clem grabbed for me, and I gripped the handle tightly and lifted my arm and slammed the skillet against the side of his head with such force that my wrist seemed to snap. There was a hideous crunching sound and his eyes and his mouth flew open and for perhaps one full second he stared at me with stunned incredulity and then his eyes rolled upward and his knees gave way and he folded, hitting the floor hard with his kneecaps, then flopping forward with his arms outslung. His fingertips slapped against my bare foot.

My God, I thought, I've killed him. I've killed him, and I don't feel a thing. I don't care. He sprawled there limply at my feet like some gigantic rag doll, absolutely still, the hair on the side of his head damp with blood, blood drip-drip-dripping onto the floor and making a tiny red pool. I caught my breath, dizzy for a moment, and then I cautiously examined his body. Yes, he was still breathing. Barely. He wasn't dead yet, but he could die at any minute. I straightened up and backed away from him, horrified now. He might die, and the authorities would . . . and when the boys came back this afternoon they . . . I had to get away. Now. This minute.

I stepped into the hall, feeling dizzy again, feeling disoriented, and I paused there in the dim shadows for a moment, trying to think clearly. There was nothing to take with me, for I had nothing to take, no shoes, no clothes, no possessions. Where would I go? Mama Lou, I thought, Mama Lou will let me hide at her place, she'll help me get away, but . . . no, that would be the first place they would look for me. I couldn't go to town. I . . . I had to hurry, hurry, the boys could come tromping back at any time. I took another deep breath, acutely aware of that body sprawling on the floor in the kitchen, blood dripping onto the floor, and blind panic rose, almost overcoming me. I mustn't let it. I must stay calm. I must flee.

I rushed outside, the sunshine blindingly bright after the dimness of the hall. It splattered all around me in vivid yellow rays, and a bird was singing in a tree nearby. Everything was so peaceful, so normal, and inside the house Clem was . . . He could be dying. He could be dead already. Still disoriented and shaken to the core, I looked around me as though for an answer to my dilemma, and I felt terribly exposed. First they would clap me into jail, and then they'd hang me. The panic swept over me then, and I ran past the barn and the chicken coop and the pigsty, heading toward the moss-hung cypresses surrounding the property. In moments I felt the soft, ghostly gray tendrils brushing my face and arms, and I plunged ahead, running as fast as I could.

The swamp seemed to welcome me, and the farther I penetrated into the fetid green and gray world, the safer I felt. I kept running until I felt sure my lungs would burst, and then, panting, I slackened my pace only a little, moving deeper and deeper into the swamp, circling streams, wading across tiny rivulets and carefully avoiding the bogs. Mossy gray trunks surrounded me, huge roots exposed, tangled over the ground like great gnarled fingers. Spanish moss and vines dangled from the limbs overhead, some of the vines festooned with glossy purple and mauve blossoms. It was hot, hot, my dress plastered to my body, my face and arms glistening with perspiration, my hair damp, spilling to my shoulders in heavy waves as I forged on.

An hour passed, two, and finally I had to stop, I had to rest. I brushed damp waves from my cheeks and sat down on a log, breathing heavily, exhausted, still shaken by what had happened, what I had done. I couldn't rest long. I had to keep going. Jake and Randy might already have come home and found the body, might already have notified the authorities of my crime. Sometimes they turned the bloodhounds loose to track you down, and the bloodhounds often tore their prey to pieces before they could be stopped. I turned my head, listening intently, almost believing I could hear the bloodhounds' vicious bark. It was only a bird calling in the distance but, nevertheless, I was as frightened as I had ever been in my life. Pale with fear, I huddled there on the fallen log, trying my best to let common sense prevail.

I had hit Clem very, very hard with the skillet, true, but he had a very thick skull and he probably wasn't dead at all, despite the blood dripping onto the floor. He had been breathing when I fled. And Jake and Randy were usually gone all day when fishing with the Andersons. Sometimes they left their catch at the Andersons' shanty and sauntered into town to find a girl willing to take on all four of them for the price of a shiny hair ribbon or a pair of stockings. Most likely the boys wouldn't get back home till after sunset, if then. Common sense told me this, but fear prevailed. They could easily come home early today. The men could already be unleashing the bloodhounds, making them sniff one of my old handkerchiefs to pick up the scent.

I stood up. My lungs still hurt, and every bone in my body seemed to be aching. My wrist was sore from swinging the heavy skillet. My ragged pink skirt had caught on a thorn when I was running, and there was a bad tear, revealing the shabby petticoat beneath. Dirty, sweaty, bruised, I felt utterly defenseless. What was I going to do? Where was I going to go? I couldn't just wander around the swamps, waiting for them to catch me. I had to have a plan. I had to have a destination. New Orleans, I thought. Somehow I would get to New Orleans, and somehow I would find out who Ma's folks were and go to them. I had no idea where New Orleans was—it might be hundreds of miles away for all I knew—but someone would know where it was located and tell me how to get there.

Mama Lou had told me I had strength. Ma had, too. Some of that strength came to my aid now. I felt a steely resolve replacing the panic. I wasn't going to let them catch me. I wasn't going to give in, give up, let life defeat me. I was going to make something of myself. I was young and strong and healthy, and I could read and write, at least a little. I could work from dawn to dusk without complaining, had done so most of my life. Maybe I could get some kind of job, maybe as a cook or maid. I would do anything I had to do to get away from the swamps and the desolate life I had known here. Somehow I would earn enough money to get me to New Orleans, and then . . . I squared my shoulders, resolve strengthening inside.

Familiar with the swamp since early childhood, I had a keen sense of direction. West of the swamp, some thirty-five miles away, there was a town, I knew. I didn't know what it was called, had certainly never seen it myself, but I knew it was there, a proper town, situated on the river, with shops and houses and a busy waterfront. Clem had gone there once several years ago. I remembered him talking about it, complaining bitterly because he had to pay a whole dollar to spend the night at the waterfront inn. If I went west, I was bound to reach the town eventually, I reasoned, and maybe there I could find work and get some information about New Orleans.

Stepping over the log, moving around a gnarled gray cypress

draped with spooky moss, I headed west, moving with a purpose now, moving with hope. It would take me hours and hours to walk thirty-five miles. I wouldn't even be able to reach town before nightfall, I realized, and the thought of spending a night in the swamp wasn't at all cheering, but I would think about that later. Now I must make as good time as possible, get as many miles as possible between me and the farm. After a while familiar sights vanished and I was in a part of the swamp I had never seen before. I moved quickly but cautiously, avoiding the bogs, keeping my eye out for snakes and alligators, surrounded by the constant buzz of insects and a chorus of bird calls that echoed eerily among the treetops.

I wasn't afraid. Not a bit. I told myself that over and over again. I wasn't afraid and I wasn't lost, either. I was moving west and I was certain to reach the river eventually, and the town was on the other side of the river. There were far more streams and ponds in this part of the swamp, water everywhere, it seemed, trees as thick as ever, gray trunks coated with moss and lichen, limbs forming an impenetrable canopy overhead. The ground was damp and spongy beneath my bare feet. Once I stepped on a mossy rock and tumbled into a stream that was much deeper than I had judged it to be. An alligator sleeping on the bank opened its jaws and hissed nastily, slithering into the water. I climbed out quickly and, wet all over, moved down the bank until I found a spot narrow enough to leap across. Weak rays of sunlight wavered through the treetops, only intensifying the gloom as I moved on, and it seemed to me that the light was growing dimmer.

It must be nearing five o'clock, I thought, wading across another stream and brushing aside strands of moss. It would be dark before long. I had never been in the swamp at night—that was when the spooks and zombies prowled, when the wild creatures came out. Stuff and nonsense. I didn't for a minute believe in spooks and zombies, and any wild creature I might encounter would be every bit as scared of me as I was of it. There was nothing to be worried about, I assured myself. I would find a dry, secure place and curl up and go to sleep and continue on my way at dawn. I kept reassuring myself, but apprehension grew nevertheless. I was all alone and, yes, I was frightened, and I wanted to sit down and cry like a baby.

I was hungry, too, ravenously hungry. I hadn't paid any attention to it before, had staunchly ignored it, but the emptiness inside was now like an urgent demand, intensified by the roiling and rumbling I couldn't control. I'd been hungry before, but never like this. When was the last time I had eaten? Yesterday morning? Yes, I'd had a piece of cornbread then. One piece. Without butter. I'd had no appetite at all since Ma died, had eaten very little, but now I felt that if I didn't have something soon, I would actually pass out. Pay no attention to it, Dana, I scolded myself. Don't think about food. Keep on moving.

I kept on moving, and the light grew dimmer and dimmer and the air seemed to be tinted with mauve. Hazy blue-black shadows were gathering, and spiraling tendrils of mist were beginning to rise from the water, looking just like wraiths, looking spooky as could be. Soon I was going to have to find a spot to spend the night. Someplace dry. Someplace secure. Maybe up ahead there would be a clearing or something, I told myself. The ground was too wet here, like mud, and there were sure to be more alligators about with all the water. Shadows thickened, making dark nests, and the mauve air was deepening to purple. Night was falling, falling fast, and then, abruptly, it was upon me. I stopped, panic beginning to set in again.

You can only be strong for so long. I looked around me at the dark nests of shadow, the black shapes of trees, silvered only slightly by wavery rays of moonlight. Water gurgled, sounding sinister now, and the mists still swirled, more ghostly than ever in the darkness. I was afraid to move on and afraid to stay where I was. Every drop of courage I had mustered earlier on deserted me now. I was only seventeen years old and my Ma had died and I had no one and I wanted to die, too. I listened to the night noises and folded my arms around my waist, trembling, and it was then that I saw a light flickering in the distance. At first I thought it was a firefly, but fireflies weren't stationary, were yellow-gold, not orange. A campfire, I thought. Someone was camping out here in the middle of the swamp.

I hesitated only a moment and then moved slowly toward the light, taking each step cautiously. I stumbled on a tree root and almost fell, knocking my shoulder against a tree trunk. Moonlight faintly silvered a small stream, and I waded across it carefully, passed under more trees, trying my best to avoid the tangle of exposed roots. The light seemed as far away as ever, a glowing orange shadow at the end of a long black tunnel, but gradually it grew brighter. Yes, it was a campfire. I could see the flames leaping merrily, casting yellow-orange patterns in the darkness. Someone was moving about in the small clearing, a man, I saw, although I was still too far away to make out any details. I crept forward, extra cautious now, for I didn't want to alert him of my presence. It seemed to take me forever to reach the edge of the clearing. Stationing myself behind a tree, shielded by its thick gray trunk, I leaned my head to the left and peeked through a tangle of shrubbery.

The fire wasn't nearly as big as I had thought it was, and it had burned down considerably now, a few logs glowing bright orange inside a small circle of rocks. A coffeepot was setting on one of the rocks, steam wafting out of the spout and filling the air with a delicious aroma, and over the fire on an improvised spit some kind of fowl was turning a rich golden brown. Drops of grease splattered on the logs, making tiny tongues of red-gold flame shoot up. Near the fire was a thick bedroll of blankets, beside it three lumpy-looking bags made of some kind of heavy cloth. A curious tepee-shaped object made of wooden sticks stood a few feet away, a half-finished painting leaning on a narrow wooden ledge midway up the tepee. Funny contraption to set a painting on, I thought, and who'd want to look at a painting that wasn't finished? But I gave it only a moment's attention. I was much more interested in that fowl roasting over the fire. I could smell the meat cooking and, hungry as I was, it almost drove me out of my mind.

The man I had seen earlier was nowhere in sight. He had left the clearing for some reason or other. I quickly moved around the tree and parted the shrubbery, stepping into the clearing. The fowl wasn't fully cooked yet, and there was no way I could get it off the spit without burning my hand. Almost reeling from hunger, I hurried over to the heavy cloth bags. Maybe they would contain some other kind of food, beef jerky or cheese or even an apple. Kneeling on the blankets, I opened the first bag and pulled out an enormous leather folder full of watercolor paintings of flowers and plants. There was a box of watercolors, too, paintbrushes, a lot of other things, nothing to eat. Opening the second bag, I discovered a pair of boots, a mirror, shaving equipment, several neatly folded garments. The breeches were of the finest material, and the shirts were exquisite, soft and silky and as light as air, like woven cobweb, I thought. I was examining one of them when I heard a footstep behind me and an ominous metallic click. I froze.

"Make one move," a lazy voice warned, "and I'll blow your head off."

My blood literally seemed to have turned to ice, and I was indeed frozen. I couldn't have moved if I had wanted to. I was kneeling there on the pile of blankets, the soft, exquisite shirt still in my hands. My fingers were numb. The silk spilled from my hands, the shirt floating to the ground like an airy wisp. He was there, behind me. I could feel his presence, and I could feel the pistol, too, aimed at a point just between my shoulder blades. Was he going to pull the trigger? Was I going to die? Several moments passed, and my knees and the muscles of my legs began to ache. I couldn't maintain this position much longer. I tried to swallow. My throat was dry. A log in the fire broke in two, making a loud crackling noise, and I let out a little cry, expecting a bullet to smash into my spine.

"Looks like I've caught a thief red-handed," the man drawled.

"I—I wudn't—" My voice cracked.

"All right," he said. "Stand up."

I gnawed my lower lip and got slowly to my feet. My legs were trembling so badly I could hardly stand, and my heart was palpitating madly. I didn't dare turn around, not without his permission, and I stared at the trees a few yards away from me. The flickering orange glow of the logs made shadows leap over the ground like frenzied demons. I could still feel the pistol pointing at my back. He might as well shoot me, I thought. The smell of the roasting fowl was sheer torture. If I didn't have something to eat, I was going to die anyway. At that moment my stomach gave a terrific rumble so loud it startled even me.

"What was that?" he asked sharply.

"My—my stomach."

"Turn around," he ordered. "Very, very slowly."

Trembling, I obeyed.

Chapter Four

THE FIRST THING I SAW was the barrel of the pistol, long and sleek, the small black hole at its end pointed at my heart now, ready to send a bullet tearing through flesh and bone. I stared at it with horrified fascination. An elegant hand gripped the pistol, one long finger curled tightly around the trigger. I was still trembling, gnawing my lower lip, and tears spilled over my lashes. After a moment I raised my eyes and looked at my captor's face, and I let out a gasp. He was the most beautiful creature I had ever seen. Beautiful probably wasn't the right word, but to me he was like a vision from another world.

His hair was thick and glossy, rich chestnut-brown, silvering at the temples. His cheekbones were broad and flat, his nose Roman, his jaw strong and square. Beneath dark, finely arched brows, his eyes were a gentle brown, and his mouth was gentle, too, full and firm, a pale, delicate pink in color. He was terribly old, at least forty, I judged. His lightly tanned skin was like fine old parchment, and there was a soft roll of flesh beneath his chin. The faint double chin somehow made him all the more attractive. He lifted a brow and looked at me with inquiring eyes. His was a good-natured face, and there was a humorous curve to his mouth.

"What have we here?" he inquired.

"Please, mister—don't—don't shoot me."

He frowned. "What was that? I can't understand a word you say."

"I said please—please don't shoot me."

"Do you speak French?"

"I speak perfect French," I said in that language.

"Perfect is hardly the word, lass. Lord, what a dreadful

53

sound—exactly like a strangled duck. Where did you *get* that abominable accent?"

"I speak *good*," I protested.

"Never heard such a deplorable noise," he informed me.

I was mortally offended. No one had ever criticized my voice before. I knew I sometimes slipped and said "ain't" and used bad grammar, but my voice sounded perfectly all right to me. It certainly didn't sound like a strangled duck. His voice was deep and melodious, with a faint huskiness that was like a soft caress. He was wearing highly polished brown boots and a pair of snug brown kidskin breeches and, over a full-sleeved, silky white shirt, a marvelous vest of brown and bronze striped brocade. I'd never seen such beautiful clothes on a man before. He must be very rich, I thought, must be a blooming aristocrat. Maybe even a prince or something, even if he was so old. Kindly face notwithstanding, the pistol was still leveled at my heart.

"You—you gonna shoot me?" I asked.

"I might. What were you doing going through my bags?"

"I—"

"Planning to rob me, were you?"

"I—I was just—"

"Might as well confess it, lass."

"I was just lookin' for something to *eat*," I wailed.

To my complete horror and amazement, I started bawling then, bawling just like a baby in loud, heaving sobs, my whole body shaking, tears spurting from my eyes and spilling down my cheeks in a veritable flood. The man looked horrified, too, looked very uncomfortable. He jammed the pistol into the waistband of his breeches and sighed miserably and glanced around the clearing as though looking for some means of escaping this wretched exhibition. I fell to my knees, sobbing still, giving lavish vent to all the grief and heartache and fear I had kept locked inside since Ma's death. The man finally cleared his throat, pulled me to my feet and, holding me with one strong arm curled around my waist, dabbed at my face with a soft linen handkerchief he had pulled from the pocket of his vest.

"There," he said. "There, there—do stop crying."

"I—I cain't—"

"Can't, not cain't. *Can*. Stop it this instant, do you hear me? It's frightfully unbecoming."

"I—I'm sorry."

"Ah'm saw-ree. What kind of diction is that? Bears looking into by some phonologist. He'd be intrigued. Lord, what a filthy little swamp rat you are, covered with mud from head to toe. And the smell—I don't believe my nostrils have ever been assailed by such a noxious stench."

I let out another wrenching sob and more tears spurted and the man let out an exasperated sigh and, taking hold of my shoulders, sat me down on the blankets. He sat down beside me and wrapped an arm around me and pulled my head up against his chest and let me cry myself out. His arm was very heavy, very comforting. He was a total stranger and I didn't even know his name, yet for some reason I felt completely secure. He was a large man, tall and perhaps a trifle overweight, certainly not fat but not overly lean, either. He talked funny and used a lot of words I didn't understand, but I sensed warmth and strong compassion in him.

"There now," he said when my tears stopped falling. "Do you want to tell me about it? What are you doing in the middle of the swamp at this bizarre hour, and why are you so deplorably filthy?"

"I fell into a stream, it was all muddy, and there was an alligator on the bank and—I—I think I killed my stepfather."

"Indeed?"

"I hit him hard as I could with an iron skillet, hit him on the head, and then—then I decided to run away."

"Sounds like a sensible decision to me. Why, pray, did you bash him with the skillet?"

"He—he was trying to—to—"

I started sobbing yet again, and amidst the sobs I blurted out the whole story. I told him about Clem and Jake and Randy and about Ma seeing the redbird and her death and that terrible day at the cemetery with the wooden box and the grave and the mound of brown dirt. I told him about my being a bastard and about my unknown relatives in a place called New Orleans, and finally I told him about Clem's attempting to rape me in the kitchen. He listened with a solemn expression on his face, trying his best to follow my near incoherent ramblings.

"And—and I ain't had—haven't had anything to eat since I ate a piece of cornbread yesterday and—and that's why I was goin' through your bags. I thought—the fowl wudn't—wasn't ready yet and I was afraid I'd burn my fingers and I thought maybe there'd be something to eat in one of them bags. I wasn't plannin' to rob you, I—I swear it.''

"Call me an idiot if you choose, but—you know, I think I actually believe you, lass. You just sit here and rest up, child. I'll have something for you to eat quick as a flash.''

He climbed to his feet and opened the third bag, the one I hadn't looked into. I watched him as though through a shimmery fog, so weary after the crying and emotional outpouring I could hardly hold my eyes open. The third bag did indeed contain food, cutlery and utensils as well, and I watched him pull things out, my eyelids growing heavier and heavier. I felt dizzy again, like I was floating and not really here at all. The hunger pains I had felt earlier had vanished, and I just wanted to drift away. The man moved about briskly, rattling things, his shadow shifting over the ground in the dying glow of the fire.

"Here we are,'' he said.

He handed me a plate piled high with slices of roasted fowl and beans he had just heated and bread and a chunk of hard cheese. He handed me a glass, too, filled with a clear amber liquid that proved to be wonderfully tasty, if a bit peculiar when it slid down your throat. He stood with his arms folded, watching me eat, and I finally set the plate aside, half the food uneaten. I felt even dizzier than before, felt my head was actually spinning around, but there was a warm glow inside that made me cozy as a kitten.

"Finished?'' he inquired.

I nodded sleepily and held up the empty glass.

"Don't feel like eatin' anything else just now, but I'd sure like another glass-a this funny stuff.''

"That funny stuff is wine, lass—a very fine vintage, incidentally, best my cellar contains. From the look of you, I'd say one glass was more than ample. Feeling better now?''

"I feel like a kitten.''

"A kitten?''

"I just wanna curl up and purr.''

"Jesus,'' he said.

"Mind if I take a little nap on these blankets?''

"Feel free.''

I yawned, making myself more comfortable on the thick blankets, everything hazy and kind of blurry, like I was looking through a shimmery piece of glass. The tepee thing with the half-finished picture on it seemed to wobble a little, and the glowing orange logs seemed to separate and become two piles of logs and then become one again. Curious as hell, I thought, blinking my eyes. My head still felt like it was spinning, only spinning slowly now, and I felt a wonderful glow inside. Never felt anything like it before. Maybe I'm dying, I told myself, and that frightened me.

"Am—am I dying?" I asked him.

"No," he said. "you're just drunk."

"I couldn't be drunk," I protested.

"That was very potent wine. I shouldn't have given it to you. I should have given you coffee instead."

I sighed and pulled one of the blankets over my bare legs. I was glad I wasn't dying, glad I was only drunk. The man had put my plate down and held a glass of the very potent wine himself, sipping it as he looked down at me. He was so big and so beautiful in them, no, those elegant clothes, even if he did have silvery temples and a tiny double chin. The proud Roman nose and strong, square jaw inspired confidence, while the gentle eyes and full, humorous mouth made you feel real comfortable. Still, he was a man, and all men wanted to get into your drawers. Maybe it wouldn't be so bad if it was someone like him, I thought. He'd probably be real careful and tender and make it feel as good as they said it could feel.

"Are you going to take advantage of me?"

"I beg your pardon?"

"All the men, they wanna pop my cherry."

"Indeed?"

"I—I know I'm all dirty and wretched-lookin' right now, but when I ain't covered with mud and my hair idn't all tangled, I look kinda nice. A-course, my waist is too narrow and my teats are too big, but th' men don't seem to mind it at all."

"I shouldn't imagine they would," he observed.

"You ain't—aren't bad-looking yourself."

He took another sip of wine, smiling to himself.

"You *ain't*," I insisted.

"Thank you, child."

"You're plum appealin', even if you *are* so very old."

"Ouch," he said.

"I'll bet a lotta women'd *like* for you to get into their drawers. I betja a lot of 'em even invite-ja to do it."

"It's been a while," he confessed.

"If—if I *had* to lose my cherry, I guess I wouldn't mind losin' it with a great big man with warm brown eyes and a lovely mouth, 'ticularly if he was gentle and didn't get all grabby and rough. A man as old as you are would probably know what he was doin'."

"Jesus," he exclaimed, shaking his head. "One little glass of wine, just one, and you're babbling like a gin-soaked lush. Of course, you drank it on an empty stomach and you'd never had wine before, but—"

"What's your name?" I asked.

"Julian," he said. "Julian Etienne."

"Julian—that's a lovely name. It suits you. You kinda look like a Julian."

"Absolutely soused," he said to himself.

"I'm Dana," I informed him.

"Delighted to make your acquaintance, Dana, even under these rather bizarre circumstances. Go to sleep now, child, before you say something even more outrageous and offensive."

I obediently closed my eyes, snuggling my cheek against the soft blankets. I could hear the crackle of the smoldering logs and the stirring of leaves as a light wind sprang up. An owl hooted in the distance, and insects kept up a raspy chorus. They were all soothing sounds, and the rocking was soothing, too. I wondered why the ground should be rocking to and fro like this, like I was on a raft and the water was wavy. It didn't really bother me all that much, though. It was kind of nice.

"I wonder if you're the man in my dreams," I murmured, eyes still closed.

"What's that?"

"You could be him," I said, "or you could be one of the others. Mama Lou said there'd be four, but she wudn't real specific 'bout which one was which—couldn't see all that clearly. I'll bet you ain't the bad one, though, or you'd already-a done something unpleasant."

"Definitely soused," he said.

I sighed again, drawing my legs up and pulling the top blanket over me. My eyelids were as heavy as lead, layers of darkness swirling behind them. I heard the man moving around, his boots crunching softly on the ground. I drifted into the welcoming darkness, warm and snug, lulled by the night noises and the gentle rocking of the ground. I dreamed and I was running and they were running after me and the bloodhounds were baying and Clem wasn't dead, he was urging the bloodhounds on and I cried out and strong, warm arms held me close and a husky, melodious voice said, "There, there, it's all right, you're all right now, child," and I saw a flock of redbirds then and saw Ma and her face was white and she was trying to tell me something but I couldn't hear and then she began to fade away and I couldn't stop her, couldn't hold her. I sobbed and sobbed and called her name and the arms tightened around me and I felt a large, tender hand smoothing back my hair, stroking my head. It all seemed so real, so very real. I could actually feel warmth and strength in those arms and actually hear that voice telling me it would be all right, telling me to sleep, just go back to sleep.

Bright silvery yellow lights were dancing against my eyelids and a bird was making a dreadful racket and the ground was very hard and no longer rocking. I moaned, wishing the lights would go away, wishing the bird would shut up, wishing I could sleep and sleep and sleep and never wake up. A lovely smell filled the air, coffee, strong, hot coffee, and there was a tantalizing sizzling sound. I opened one eyelid and blinked. I moaned again and finally sat up and shoved deplorably dirty honey-blond waves from my temples. Every bone in my body was sore and my head felt awful and there was a queasy feeling in my stomach.

"Good morning," Julian Etienne said.

I gave another moan, frowning. He smiled and poured coffee into a big pewter cup and brought it to me. I accepted it silently, wondering if I was going to live or die. I felt a little better after drinking some of the coffee. The blasted bird was still singing, warbling lustily. I longed for a rock to chunk at it. My bare feet, my legs, my arms, every part of me I could see was coated with dried mud, and my torn skirt was streaked with mud and stained with greenish moss. He, on the other hand, was clean as could be, freshly shaved, wearing a new pair of breeches, soft gray fawn, and a new white shirt and a lovely gray vest striped with silky blue and purple stripes.

"I'm filthy," I said.

"Indubitably," he replied.

What kind of word was that? He spoke flawless French which

was clearly his native tongue, but he sure used funny words. He looked even better this morning than he had looked last night, his waist a bit too thick, his body a bit fleshy, a large man, just slightly overweight, big and comfortable with himself and elegant in his fine clothes. The faint double chin and silvery temples somehow added to his charm, made him even more appealing. I wondered what he was doing in the swamp with all them—those pictures and the tepee thing, still standing nearby with the unfinished painting perched on it.

"Want some breakfast?" he asked, indicating the fish slowly frying in the skillet. "I caught them this morning, deboned them, sliced them into fillets. They're going to be quite tasty."

"Yuck," I said.

He smiled again. It was a beautiful smile. Old as he was, as old as Clem, maybe even older, he was still the handsomest man I had ever seen. He might be big and strong, but there was something cozy and reassuring about him. I didn't for a minute worry about him trying to take my cherry. I stood up and stretched my arms, working the kinks out of my back and shoulders. Even if he did try to take it, I didn't think I'd put up too fierce a struggle.

"Would you like to wash?" he asked.

"I'd love to."

"There's a pond nearby. The water's crystal-clear, with a tiny waterfall feeding into it. I've no more soap left, I fear, but you can improvise. You'll feel better after you've removed some of that mud."

He gave me directions and I left the clearing and found the pond. Rays of silver sunlight danced on the water, making it sparkle, and a miniature waterfall spilled from a high, rocky bank on the far side. Willows and mossy plants grew all around. I stood on the bank for a moment, looking at my reflection in the shimmering water. Lord, my face was streaked with mud, too. I looked like a blackamoor. I took off my dress and petticoat and hauled them into the water with me and gave them a thorough rinsing, removing most of the stains, and then I spread them on the bank to dry.

The pond was only shoulder-high at the deepest point, the bottom of smooth white and blue-white stones, and the water was deliciously cool. I swam around for several minutes, letting the water massage my body, and then I gathered two large clumps of moss and crushed them and rubbed them together until I had made a rich, foamy lather. It was as smooth as satin, and I spread it all over me, savoring the luxuriant feel of it on my skin. I rubbed it into my hair as well and used my fingers to work it in. I swam under the waterfall and let the cool water splatter all over me, washing the lather away. I repeated the process all over again and then swam some more, feeling gloriously clean as I stepped out of the water.

The girl reflected in the pond now bore no resemblance to a blackamoor. I gazed at the shimmery image for several moments, intrigued. She looked like a tall, willowy water nymph with long, shapely legs and a slender waist and full, swelling breasts tipped with tight nipples as pink and tender as rosebuds. Her skin was a creamy tan, her expression bemused, her hair clinging to her head in damp, dark tendrils. I sighed and kicked a stone into the pond, shattering the reflection, and then I stretched out on the bank to dry. The sun was very warm already. I could feel its rays stroking my skin, causing my hair to turn light and feathery as I reclined on the soft, grassy bank.

I closed my eyes, enjoying the sensation of warmth on my body as the sun continued to bathe me with its rays. I must have drifted off to sleep again. The sound of footsteps approaching awakened me with a start, and I leaped to my feet and snatched up my clothes, which were already dry. My hair was dry, too. I held the dress and petticoat in front of me and watched with frightened eyes as the dangling willow branches parted. Julian Etienne stepped into view, and I stared at him. I couldn't speak for a moment. I was trembling, and my heart was pounding something awful. He frowned.

"Relax, child," he said. "I mean you no harm."

"I—I was afraid it might be *them*," I said hoarsely.

"You'd been gone for over an hour and a half, and I was beginning to worry about you—just came to see if you were all right."

"I—I guess I am."

I was still trembling, clutching the dress and petticoat in front of me to hide my private parts. He looked at me for a long moment, and his lovely brown eyes filled with compassion.

"You look like a frightened doe, child," he said quietly. "No one is going to hurt you, I promise. I won't let them."

"My stepbrothers—Clem—"

"No one is going to hurt you," he repeated. His voice was very firm now. "You go ahead and get dressed. I'll go back to camp and heat up the fish, make you some toast."

I nodded, and Julian left. I pulled on my petticoat, adjusting the tight, tattered bodice over the full swell of my breasts. I felt a curious peace inside. All the terror, all the apprehension, all the worry seemed to melt away, and I had a sense of security I had never experienced before. I believed him. He wouldn't let anyone hurt me. He would help me. I put on my dress, spreading the torn pink skirt out over my petticoat. All my life I had had to fend for myself, fight my own battles, and it was strange having a protector, made me feel real young, made me feel kinda soft and fluttery.

Julian Etienne was standing at the tepee thing with a paint-brush in his hand when I stepped into the clearing. He was finishing up the picture perched on the narrow wooden ledge. I stood very still, watching him. He was painting one of the wild-flowers growing on a vine that dangled from a tree nearby. It was a gorgeous flower, pale orange with delicate gold and bronze specks—I hadn't noticed the vine earlier, and of course it had been too dark for me to see it last night. He frowned, squinted at the flower, nodded, made another stroke with his brush, and stepped back to observe the picture.

And there the flower was on the stiff paper, as lovely as it was in life, hanging from the vine like a glorious bell, fragile petals opened to reveal the soft, deeper orange center with its stamen projecting like a golden fairy wand. I marveled at its beauty and at the magical gift that enabled this man to create anything as wonderful as the picture. He sighed deeply, put the brush down, and then turned. He saw me, and a peculiar look came into his eyes, as though he were marveling at the sight of me like I had marveled at the picture. It wasn't lust, like I'd seen in the eyes of a dozen other men, and it was far more than mere admiration. It was something like awe, I thought, and it made me extremely uncomfortable.

"My God," he said quietly.

"Is—is somethin' wrong?" I asked nervously.

"I hadn't realized—you were covered with mud, a wretched little creature with an awful, twangy voice—"

"My voice *ain't* awful!"

"Isn't," he corrected, "and I was preoccupied when I went

to check on you at the pond, saw nothing but the fear in your eyes. Up until now I haven't had a proper look at you without a mask of mud. I had no idea . . ."

He paused, shaking his head, still looking at me with an amazed expression in those deep brown eyes.

"Am I so ugly, then?" I asked.

"You're breathtaking, my child."

"Breathtakin'? What's that mean?"

"It means you're a veritable vision, even in those rags. You may well be the most beautiful woman I've ever laid eyes on."

"You're joshin' me," I said, "and it ain't polite."

"Isn't."

"Isn't. I ain't beautiful at all, not like—like that flower you painted."

"Far lovelier—and totally unspoiled."

"I still got my cherry, if that's what you mean. I ain't lettin' no man take it till *I'm* ready."

He shook his head again, amused now. I wasn't sure if he was making fun of me or not, but at least he was no longer looking at me like I had two heads or something.

"What's that tepee thing?" I asked him.

He smiled. "This 'tepee thing' is called an easel. A painter uses it to hold his work in progress."

"Are you a painter?"

"Heavens no, I merely dabble."

"That picture you done is mighty pretty dabblin'. If you ain't—aren't a painter, what are you?"

"I like to consider myself a botanist, though I fear my friends and relatives consider me merely eccentric."

"What's a botanist?"

"Botany is the study of plant life. A botanist is one who studies them. Tromping through the swamp, taking notes and gathering specimen and painting the flora and fauna is hardly a gentlemanly pursuit, according to my esteemed family."

"What-ja plan to do with all them notes and paintings and things?"

"Eventually I hope to assemble a book. I'd like to do for our plant life what Audubon has done for birds, but I fear that aspiration is quite beyond my humble reach."

"Who's Audubon?" I asked.

"A most distinguished ornithologist," he replied.

"Oh," I said.

Julian Etienne smiled and strolled over to the fire. It was merely a bed of coals now with a skillet setting on top. The skillet had a lid on it now, and he removed the skillet from the fire and took off the lid to reveal a small mound of scrambled eggs, two slices of buttered toast and several tasty-looking fillets of fish, everything still hot.

"Hungry?" he asked.

"Starvin'."

"You must learn to pronounce the final *g*, child. You are star*ving*, not star-vin'. Sit down on the blankets. I'll put everything onto a plate. Want some more coffee?"

"I—I'd like some of that funny stuff you gave me last night."

"I fear your tolerance of that 'funny stuff' deems that most inadvisable, particularly at this hour. Besides, I drank most of the rest of it myself after you went to sleep. I desperately needed it," he added.

"Oh. Guess I'll have to settle for coffee, then."

"Guess you will."

The food was delicious, the eggs soft, flavored with cheese, the toast of some kind of dark bread, wonderfully crunchy. The fish was tender and flaky, browned with butter, the best fish I'd ever eaten. Julian Etienne might be eccentric, whatever that meant, but he was a wonderful cook, better'n me, even. Imagine being able to produce a meal like this in the middle of the swamp. It was downright amazing.

"So," he said when I had finished eating. "what do you plan to do now?"

"I ain't—I'm not rightly sure," I replied. "I know there's a big town 'bout thirty miles from here—don't know the name of it, but I know it's on a river with a waterfront and lots of buildings."

He nodded. "I'm quite familiar with the place, although I'd hardly call it a 'big town.'"

"I'm gonna get there somehow and—and I guess I'll try to get some kind of job. I can cook real good—not as good as you—and I'm a dandy housekeeper. I can scrub floors and make beds and—there's not much I can't do around a house. Think one of them inns there might hire me?"

"It's possible," he allowed.

"I'll get a job and save all th' money I can, and then I'll go to New Orleans and—and maybe I can find my ma's folks. I don't even know their name or anything about 'em, but somehow—somehow I'll find 'em, and maybe they'll take me in."

Julian Etienne made no comment. His eyes were grave, and I got the feeling he seriously doubted this would ever come about. If her family kicked Ma out and refused to have anything else to do with her, why would they have anything to do with her bastard eighteen years later? And how would I ever find them in the first place? I realized how improbable it all was, but I couldn't let myself have doubts. I . . . I had to have some kind of purpose. I could feel salty tears welling up in my eyes again, and I staunchly held them back. I wasn't going to feel sorry for myself. I wasn't. I was going to be strong and I was going to *make* it.

"More coffee?" he asked.

I shook my head, handed him my empty cup and got to my feet.

"Thank you for—for all your kindness," I said. "If I hadn't run into you last night, I don't know what I'd have done. I—I guess I'd better be on my way now. I've got a lotta miles to—"

I cut myself short. My face went white. I heard heavy footsteps crashing through the swamp, accompanied by loud voices shouting back and forth. I recognized the voices. I began to tremble violently, and for a moment I felt I might pass out. My knees shook. I reeled. Julian Etienne took hold of my shoulder with a firm hand, steadying me. I looked at him with desperate eyes, my heart pounding.

"It's—it's—" My voice was a mere croak. "They—"

"Relax, child," he said.

"It's *them*, and they're gonna—they're gonna—"

"No one's going to do anything to you you don't want them to do," he informed me. "No one is going to hurt you. Stay behind me, do you understand? Stay behind me, and don't say a word."

He calmly fetched his pistol and cocked it. The large, amiable man with those warm brown eyes and that gentle, humorous mouth suddenly changed into a completely different person. He was cool and calm and remote and as hard as granite, looked utterly confident, looked frighteningly intimidating, too. I cowered behind him as the voices and footsteps grew louder, came nearer, and I gave a loud gasp as Clem came tearing into the clearing, Jake and Randy hot on his heels.

All three of them stopped when they saw Julian Etienne standing there so calmly with the pistol in his hand. Clem looked flushed, a soiled white bandage tied around his head. His boots were covered with mud, and his shirt was torn, one sleeve dangling at the shoulder. Jake and Randy were in little better condition, both of them disheveled and splattered with mud. Jake leered at me, his eyes full of greedy anticipation, and Randy smiled a lazy smile, extremely pleased with himself.

"I told-ja she'd head this way, Pa," he said. "I told-ja we'd find her if we just kept headin' west."

"I'm th' one who tracked 'er," Jake growled. "I'm th' one who spotted that patch-a pink skirt caught on th' branch."

"Shut up, both of you!" Clem thundered.

He looked at Julian and looked at the pistol, and there followed a moment of silence broken only by the distant cry of a bird and the buzzing of insects. I stood behind my protector, peeking around his broad back, my knees still weak and trembly. Clem's blue-black eyes were smoldering with anger, his mouth set in a determined line, but Julian's expression and the sight of the pistol made him cautious. So I didn't kill him, I thought. I wish I had. Oh God, how I wish I had.

"May I help you gentlemen?" Julian inquired.

His voice was cool, polite and absolutely chilling.

"I've come to get my girl. That's her, hidin' behind you. I don't know what she might-a told-ja, but—she run off. I intend to take her back home. This ain't none-a your affair, mister. If you know what's good for ya, you'll stay outta this."

"It seems we have a problem," Julian replied.

"Yeah? What's that?"

"Apparently I don't know what's good for me."

"Look, mister—"

Clem took a step forward. Julian leveled his pistol. Clem froze.

"Take one more step," Julian said, "and I'll put a bullet through your heart—quite cheerfully."

"I think he means it, Pa," Randy observed.

"Shut your mouth! Look, mister, I been prowlin' through this swamp for hours, since before daybreak—before that, I was too weak. The girl slammed a skillet 'gainst the side-a my head, damned near killed me. My boys wanted to get the authorities, call out the bloodhounds, but I told 'em that wouldn't be necessary. No need draggin' other people into family affairs.''

"Quite sensible of you. Considering."

"Considerin'?''

"Considering that the girl is legally a minor, was under your legal protection and that you attempted to rape her. I have no idea what the mores of the swamp might be, but I am thoroughly acquainted with the laws of the state of Louisiana. Assault on a female minor by an adult male is a criminal offense. A hanging offense," he added.

"I—I never—"

"The girl gave me a full account of the incident, sir. She was so shaken she could hardly speak. She has bruises on her arms. She told me you had forced yourself on her, that you planned to let your sons use her sexually as well."

"She's a goddamn liar! I—"

"She begged me to help her. I agreed to take her to the authorities and file criminal charges. As you've so conveniently turned up, perhaps you will accompany us. It'll save everyone ever so much trouble."

"He's bluffin', Pa!" Jake cried.

Clem's face had been flushed when he entered the clearing, but as Julian spoke so calmly about assault and the law and criminal charges, the color had slowly drained from my stepfather's face. Randy had plucked a twig from one of the bushes and was idly picking his teeth, his eyes full of sardonic amusement. Jake stood with fists balled, belligerent, spoiling for a fight. Julian was completely unperturbed.

"On the other hand," Julian continued, "I might just go ahead and put a bullet through your heart. That would save everyone even more trouble and is, I understand, a far more pleasant way to die than hanging."

"He's bluffin', I tell ya!" Jake insisted. "We can take him, Pa! There 're three-a us and only one-a him. You ain't gonna— you ain't gonna back down an' let that little slut get by with what she did! We can rush him. He cain't shoot all three-a us."

"Indeed I can't," Julian agreed. "I'll be content enough merely to shoot your father."

"He's serious, Pa," Randy said.

"Utterly," Julian drawled.

He lifted the pistol a bit higher, his arm perfectly steady, his index finger curled snugly around the trigger. Clem's face was entirely bleached of color. He took a step back, then another, bumping into Jake. Jake cursed. Randy gripped his arm, pulling him back.

"She ain't worth it, Pa," Randy said. "She ain't worth gettin' shot for. We don't need her. Lots-a other tail around. Maybe Jessie'll move in with us. That'd be real cozy."

"You cain't let—" Jake began.

"You open your mouth one more time, boy, and I'm gonna knock th' teeth outta your mouth," Clem said, his eyes never leaving Julian and the pistol. "Your brother's right. Th' gal ain't worth it."

"But—"

Clem whirled and slapped Jake across the face with such vicious force that Jake reeled backward, crashing into the bushes and falling to the ground. Julian sighed, growing impatient. Clem faced him again, trying hard to control his anger and fear. He took a deep breath, his broad chest heaving, and finally he managed to speak.

"You—you still goin' to the authorities?" he asked.

Julian nodded, grim.

"No need—there ain't no need causin' a lotta ruckus," Clem said. "Th' gal ain't hurt. You take her. Yeah, you take her. Do anything you want with her. You got my blessin'."

"Clear out," Julian ordered.

Clem needed no encouragement. He helped Randy pull Jake to his feet, and then the three of them stumbled through the bushes and disappeared from sight. We heard their footsteps retreating noisily, heard a splash as one of them fell into some water. Julian sighed again and finally lowered the pistol. Neither of us spoke until the sound of their retreat died away completely.

"Is—is what you said about the law true?" I asked. "Is what Clem did really a hangin' offense?"

"I've no idea, child. I was merely improvising."

"Would you really've shot him?"

"Unquestionably," he replied.

"You ever shot a man before?"

"I've never even fired the pistol, actually."

"*Never?*" I was incredulous.

"I'm much better with words than I am with firearms. I just

carry this thing around with me in order to emphasize a point now and then. Works admirably," he added.

"You're daft," I told him.

"But I do have a certain aplomb, you must admit. I suggest we pack up and leave now before your charming kin have second thoughts and decide to pay us a return visit. I have a large canoe tied up nearby."

"You—you'll take me to that town on the river?"

"Unless you keep on asking questions in that deplorable whine and I decide to throttle you instead. Hurry now, lass. It's well after noon, and we have a long way to paddle."

Chapter Five

THE LAKE WAS HUGE, surrounded by very tall cypress trees draped with moss. Sunlight reflected on the muddy brown-green water, making shimmery golden patterns on the surface. The canoe was indeed large, with plenty of room for the two of us and all the bags, but Julian handled it with ease, paddling with no apparent effort. I leaned back, resting my shoulders against one of the bags, watching him dip the paddle in and out, from side to side, the soft splash of water making a soothing sound. He really was in very good shape, I thought, quite muscular and surprisingly strong for a man of his advanced years. He had been paddling for over three hours and he didn't even look tired, though his fine white shirt was damp with perspiration.

"I never seen this lake before," I said. "It's mighty big."

"It leads into a smaller lake, and that leads into a narrow river which, in turn, leads into another wider river which takes us out of the swamp and to the waterfront."

"You know an awful lot about these parts."

"I've spent an awful lot of time here."

"Paintin' watercolors?"

"And collecting specimen and taking notes."

"Seems a mighty peculiar occupation for a grown man," I observed.

"So family and friends constantly remind me."

"You do it for a livin'?"

"It's an avocation," he explained.

"Oh," I said.

He grinned, knowing full well I didn't understand the word.

"It's something I do to occupy my time," he explained. "Fortunately I don't have to make a 'living.' "

"You rich?"

"Solvent," he said. "That means there's enough to keep body and soul together but not enough for inordinate luxuries. There used to be quite a lot of money, but I fear the family fortunes have been considerably reduced."

"I'd like to be rich," I said.

"Indeed?"

"I'd like to have a pair of nice shoes with high heels and two dresses and a—a real silk petticoat."

"That doesn't sound too unreasonable."

"And—and I'd like to have a parasol," I said wistfully. "I know it's silly of me, but—I've always wanted a parasol."

I sighed, lounging against the bag, watching a heron wading at the edge of the lake, its long bill dipping into the water in search of fish. Julian dipped the oar into the water, studying me with bemused brown eyes. A lock of chestnut hair had fallen across his brow, giving him a curiously boyish look. He studied me for some time, silent, and I wondered what he was thinking. Did he like what he saw? Did he want to pop my cherry, too, like all the other men? Genteel and kindly he might be, but there was undeniable virility in that large, strong body, in the lines of that handsome face.

"Just how old *are* you?" I asked suddenly.

He looked surprised, then amused. "I'm forty-one," he told me.

"*That* old?"

A grin played on his lips, and his brown eyes were full of amusement. "I know it's ancient," he confessed, "but I figure I have a few good years left. How old are you?"

"Seventeen."

"Goodness! Seems you're getting on, too."

"Most girls my age're already married, already have a couple-a kids hangin' on to 'em. Bessie Barker got married at thirteen— had to, her pa had a shotgun handy—and she's got *four* kids. Bessie ain't but two or three months older'n I am."

"Gracious," he said.

"Are *you* married?"

"I've managed to avoid that fate so far," he replied, "despite innumerable lush candidates shoved my way by meddlesome friends and matchmaking relatives.''

"If you ain't married, I suppose you've gotta mistress, then?''

"Really, child, you do ask a lot of questions.''

"Do you?''

"Have a mistress? On occasion I greatly enjoy the company of an attractive and companionable woman, but I do not— ahem—I do not currently have one stashed away in an apartment.''

"You're so good-lookin', I imagine a lotta women'd like to marry you, imagine a lot of 'em would like to be your mistress, too.''

"A moment ago I was seriously contemplating tossing you overboard,'' he informed me, "but you have just redeemed yourself. You must learn not to ask so many questions, though, child, and you mustn't be quite so outspoken. Another man might—uh—misinterpret you.''

"He'd get a knee in the groin if he did,'' I promised. "No man's goin' to misinterpret me unless I *want* him to.''

Julian Etienne chuckled, though I failed to see anything to chuckle about. I decided he was probably making fun of me, and I didn't like that one bit. He might be a real swell gent in those fancy clothes and he might be real educated and read a lot of books and things, but that didn't give him the right to make fun of a girl. I might not-a been to school, but I wudn't—*wasn't* dumb, and I gave him a very frosty look and the silent treatment as he continued to paddle across the lake.

The canoe glided smoothly over the water, moving toward a line of cypresses with enormous, exposed gray roots. Was he going to steer us right in to shore? I wondered. No, he moved right through a narrow opening between the roots, and we were moving now down a narrow finger of water leading out of the lake. The land on either side of us was soggy with mud and covered with tall grayish-tan grass. Cattails grew in profusion, and the cypress trees grew very close, gnarled roots projecting into the water. It was dim and shadowy here, very little light penetrating the gloom. I kept an eye peeled for alligators.

"Sure you know where you're going?'' I asked nervously.

"Quite sure.''

"Looks like we're goin' to run out of water any minute now.

That ground is all muddy, wouldn't hold a person's weight, and—look out, you're gonna run into that tree.''

"Trust me," he said.

Gradually the finger of water grew wider, deeper, and the cypresses weren't so thick. Insects buzzed loudly, flying about us in swarms, and birds cried out noisily. Shafts of sunlight began to penetrate the gloom, and soon we were moving across the surface of yet another lake, just as he had promised. Water lilies spangled the water close to shore, pink and pale orange, floating on splayed dark pads. Beginning to grow uncomfortable, I sat up straight, shoving long honey-blond waves back over my shoulders. The sunlight wasn't nearly as strong as it had been earlier. It seemed hours and hours since we had left the campsite. Julian patiently dipped the paddle in and out of the water, seemingly tireless. I would have offered to take over, but I had never handled a canoe before, and I felt sure I'd capsize us immediately.

"How long before we reach that town?" I asked him.

"Two or three more hours—around sundown. Tired?"

"I ain't complainin'."

"What do you plan to do when you reach town?" he inquired.

"Get a job," I told him.

"Just like that?"

"Like I told you before, I'm a very good worker. I can keep any house as clean as can be, and I'm also a wonderful cook. My greens are the tastiest you ever tasted. I use a bit of vinegar, you see, gives 'em a special flavor, and my cornbread is—you're laughing at me again."

"Not *at* you, child. I'm sure your cornbread is delicious."

"It is. I can bake pies, too. I can feed chickens and milk cows. I can churn butter. I—there's not much I *cain't* do. Anyone willin' to work hard as I'm willin' to work is bound to get a job. I ain't worried one bit."

"Ah, the optimism of youth. I had forgotten how stirring it can be. And where do you plan to sleep tonight?"

"I—I don't rightly know, but I'm sure something will turn up."

"Likely it will," he said.

The canoe rocked and bobbed on the water, and the soft splashing sound as he paddled was curiously lulling. It was very warm, and I was growing sleepy, my eyelids drooping. He steered the canoe toward an opening between the mournful cypress trees, and water lilies were all around us now, swaying and swirling as we passed through them. I leaned over and plucked one, pale pink, fragrant, toying with it as we passed through the cypresses. We were soon moving down a narrow river with a current so strong he barely had to paddle. I rested against the bag again, trying to make myself comfortable, and Julian smiled at me as my eyelids grew heavier and I yawned.

It was almost dark when I opened my eyes again. The sky was a misty violet-gray, smeared with pink, and the water was pewter-gray, inky-looking. The cypresses were gone, so was the fetid smell of the swamp. I sat up, stretching my arms, throwing my head back, and the canoe rocked. We were moving down a very wide river, the banks on either side shadowy with trees and shrubs. Up ahead there were many boats, all shapes and sizes, tied up around wooden piers that extended into the water. Beyond them were many buildings, lights in windows making cozy yellow-gold squares against the gathering darkness. The town looked enormous to my eyes. I had never seen so many boats, so many buildings. It was overwhelming.

"We—we're almost there," I said.

"Sure are. You slept like a baby."

"I guess I was kinda tired," I admitted.

Shadows were falling fast as we reached the waterfront, Julian skillfully steering the canoe around a labyrinth of boats and finally toward a flight of wooden steps that led down from the pier. I could hear voices now, boisterous laughter and the sound of tinkling music. there must be a party going on nearby, I thought as Julian carefully moored the canoe. A husky, gruff-looking man in old clothes and a battered cap came down the steps. He greeted Julian warmly and loudly and looked surprised when he saw me in the canoe.

"Figured you might be pulling in 'bout now," the man said roughly. "See she got you there'n back again. Uh—let me help you with them bags, Monsieur Etienne. I'll carry 'em on to the inn for you."

"Thank you, Hawkins. This is Miss O'Malley. She made the trip back with me."

"Me, I ain't askin' no questions," Hawkins retorted. "It ain't none-a my business."

"Hawkins owns the canoe," Julian told me. "He rents it to me whenever I take a jaunt into the swamp."

Looking extremely embarrassed, Hawkins unloaded all three of the bags and carried them up the steps. Julian helped me out of the canoe, holding my hand firmly as the craft rocked. Hawkins had already disappeared with the bags when we reached the top of the steps. We were standing on a pier made of wide wooden planks with cracks between them, boats rocking on the water on either side. My legs were a bit unsteady after being confined in the canoe for so long, and the pier seemed to sway. The air was laced with the pungent odors of fish and tar and rotting hemp, and the noise was much louder up here, voices shrill and coarse, laughter raucous, rowdy music coming from half a dozen different establishments.

Brave and determined I might be, but I suddenly felt very, very vulnerable, and I felt afraid, too. What if he just left me here? What would I do? Where would I go? I had no money. I had no clothes. I knew not a soul in this huge, bewildering place. I felt confident I would eventually find some kind of work, but what was I going to do tonight? Where was I going to sleep? How was I going to find food? All the spunk and spirit drained out of me, and I could feel my lower lip trembling. Julian Etienne wrapped his fingers around my elbow and gripped it tightly. My knees were shaking.

"Stick close to my side," he ordered. "The waterfront's full of undesirable types, even at this early hour."

"You—you're takin' me to the inn with you?"

"I intend to see that you have a solid meal and a decent place to sleep tonight, of course. Did you think I was going to abandon you?"

"You don't owe me nothin'," I said.

"That's quite true. I do, alas, have a conscience. It causes me ever so much inconvenience. I frequently try to be a cold, heartless cad, but it rarely works. I fear I'm a soft touch."

"What's that?"

"Never you mind. Just stay close to me and keep your eyes down."

We left the pier and passed stacks of barrels and piles of ropes and then moved up a cobbled street lined on either side with brightly lighted establishments full of rowdy people. A din assailed our ears, coarse voices and laughter drowning out the music of pounding pianos. Burly men in rough attire swaggered along the pavements, looking formidable indeed. Several of them gave me close scrutiny, but Julian's stern expression discouraged any overtures. There were women, too, fascinating creatures with painted faces who wore very colorful gowns and feather boas and leaned provocatively against the walls, calling out friendly greetings to the men, including Julian. He ignored them, holding my elbow so tightly I winced and marching me along as though I were a felon he had just arrested.

"You don't have to be so rough," I protested.

"I thought I told you to keep your eyes down."

"I cain't help lookin'. It's terribly interestin'. That lady back there was mighty taken with you."

"That was no lady," he retorted.

"I loved her gown. Think I'd look good in bright red like that?"

"Keep moving," he said sternly.

The inn was on a wide, tree-lined street beyond the water-front. It was a large, rambling place painted bright yellow with white shutters at the windows and tall white columns around the verandah. It was almost completely dark by the time we got there, and light spilled out of the windows onto the verandah with its cozy, plump-cushioned chairs and tall green plants. Julian led me up the steps and into the main room, and I tried hard not to gape.

I have never seen such a room in my life. The polished hard-wood floor was covered with a lovely gold and white patterned carpet as soft as grass and almost as deep, and from the ceiling hung a crystal waterfall. There were large gold chairs and elegant little tables and in the center of the room a big gold sofa shaped like a circle. There was a long counter of dark, gleaming wood, a long row of boxes behind it. Several people milled about, all of them dressed in handsome attire, and I was acutely aware of my bare feet and tattered dress as Julian led me over to the counter. The man in charge there was taken aback by my appearance, but he managed a nervous smile nevertheless.

"Ah, Monsieur Etienne—nice to have you back with us again. We've sent your bags on up to your usual rooms. I—uh—did you want to take a separate room for the young lady?"

Julian nodded, completely at ease. The man checked the boxes on the wall behind him and discovered that there was a single room available right next to Julian's. Julian said that would be fine, accepted the keys the man held out, then scribbled his name in the leather-bound ledger open on the counter. Everyone in the lobby was carefully pretending not to stare, all except one woman who was staring quite openly. She had glossy black hair worn in long ringlets that spilled down her back, and her deep blue eyes were full of wry amusement. A smile curved on her lovely red mouth. She was wearing a rich blue gown with a very full skirt adorned with ruffles of black lace, as was the extremely low-cut bodice. Long black lace gloves covered her bare arms. Catching Julian's eye, she nodded and moved to intercept us as we headed toward the stairs.

"It looks like you had quite an interesting trip, Julian," she observed. "Collecting a new kind of specimen now?"

"What are *you* doing here?"

"I'm with a friend, darling. He owns quite a bit of property hereabouts and came down to inspect it. Who is your charming companion?"

"I—uh—I'll explain later, Amelia."

"That should be very interesting," she said.

She had a low, melodious voice and smelled of magnolia blossoms. She was quite the loveliest creature I had ever seen, and she seemed to know Julian extremely well. Her blue eyes examined me, not unkindly, and then she looked up at Julian and shook her head.

"You *are* full of surprises, darling," she said lightly. "I would never have expected it of you."

Julian gave her an exasperated look. He was holding my elbow again, gripping it so tightly I felt sure there would be bruises.

"Look, Amelia, could you—uh—could you wait for me down here? I want to take this child up to her room and order her a bath, and—and then I think I may well need your assistance."

"Oh?"

"I know now why I dumped you," he said grumpily. "You always were a sarcastic wench."

"You didn't 'dump' me, darling. I moved on to greener pastures, and I was absolutely enchanting to you every time we were together. I even helped transcribe those wretched notes of yours, *quite* a novelty for a lady like me, you'll have to admit."

"Meet me here in ten minutes?"

"I wouldn't miss it for the world," she told him.

He led me up the stairs and down a wide hall with a golden rug and gleaming white walls with doors on either side. I was a little breathless and very much in awe of the plush surroundings, but I still couldn't control my curiosity about the gorgeous brunette. I asked Julian who she was, and he told me in no uncertain terms that it was none of my business. Stopping in front of one of the doors, he released my elbow and inserted a key into the lock. I rubbed my elbow, not willing to give it up so easily.

"She's very beautiful," I said.

"She is indeed."

"I'll bet she was your mistress."

"You're pushing it," he said.

"Pushing what?"

"Your luck. I have a very strong urge to turn you over my knee and spank your bottom, and it's all I can do to control it."

"You wouldn't do that. You're a gentleman."

"At the moment I'm quite willing to forget that."

I couldn't help but smile. Julian opened the door and gave me a forceful shove. I stumbled inside the room, not at all resentful of such rough treatment. He liked me. I knew that. I liked him, too. He was the nicest man I had ever met, and he did use the funniest expressions. The lady called Amelia had been lucky indeed to have such a man, and I couldn't imagine how she could possibly have wanted to move on to 'greener pastures,' whatever that meant. I wouldn't mind having a man like Julian Etienne, even if he did have silver temples and a faint double chin.

"I'm going to order a bath for you," he said. "A tub and water will be brought to your room, soap and towels as well. Wash yourself thoroughly, and be sure to scrub behind your ears."

"I ain't a child," I told him.

He gave me a look. "We'll eat downstairs in the dining room," he continued. "I'll be back to fetch you at eight o'clock."

"But—"

"No arguments. I'm very tired and I'm very irritable. Do as you're told and we may possibly get through the evening without my committing murder. You be ready, you hear?"

I nodded obediently, even though I knew I couldn't possibly

eat downstairs in these rags. I had seen how everyone stared at me and I had pretended not to care, but I had. Despite my seeming indifference, I had been deeply humiliated, and I wasn't going to subject myself to that again. Julian gave me a final exasperated look and left, closing the door behind him, and I sighed and examined the room for the first time.

It was ever so large, roomy as could be, the walls covered with pale white wallpaper printed with tiny blue and purple flowers. The floor was polished to a high golden sheen, a gray and purple rug covering much of it, and fancy white curtains hung at the window. The bed had a blue silk counterpane, and the dressing table and wardrobe were of glossy white wood. I studied everything in wonder. Imagine sleeping on a bed as big and comfortable-looking as that one. Imagine sitting at such a grand dressing table, looking at yourself in such a silvery mirror. I could hardly believe such luxury existed.

Was it only yesterday morning that I had awakened in my shabby attic room, numb with grief over Ma and full of dread about Clem? So much had happened in the past two days. I already felt like a different person. I was beginning a whole new life, and I must never look back. I must always move forward. I was a swamp girl, I couldn't deny that, and although I could read some and print my name, I knew I was ignorant. There was so much to learn, so much, but I was going to learn, and I was going to make something of myself. One day I would walk into a place like this with my head held high, and people wouldn't stare, people wouldn't whisper or struggle to hide their distaste. One day I would fit right in with those elegantly attired folk downstairs, I vowed, and no one would ever suspect that I grew up in the swamp.

A plump, cheerful maid not much older than I brought my bath a few minutes later. First she brought the white tin tub, with little blue and green flowers painted on the sides, and then she returned with buckets of steaming hot water. The tub filled, she dumped some funny-looking oil into the water, grinned at me, and returned a few moments later with big, fluffy white towels and a clever little tray with sponge, a white washcloth and a tiny basket of soap. She told me to have a nice wash and then departed, leaving me alone once again. I looked at the tub of water with a skeptical eye. Although I would never have admitted it to a soul, I had never bathed in a tub before. When I

was a very little girl I had sometimes bathed in the big wooden
rain barrel behind the house, but all of my other bathing had
been done in the pond. The tub looked mighty small to me. Did
you sit up in it? Yes, there was a little seat built right in, I saw,
real low so you'd be submerged to your shoulders.

Hesitantly, I dipped my hand into the water. It was wonderfully warm, and the oil she had dumped into it made it as soft
as silk. A delicious fragrance wafted the air, like lilacs, I thought.
Quickly I undressed and climbed into the tub, and the silky
water seemed to caress me all over. I arched my back in pleasure, slipping farther down into the tub and reaching for the
sponge and a piece of soap on the tray beside the tub. The soap
was scented with lilacs as well, and it made a gloriously thick
lather. What luxury this was. What bliss. I felt exactly like a
queen. I might just spend the rest of the evening here in the tub,
I thought, but half an hour later I finally climbed out and wrapped
myself in one of the big towels, glowing all over.

I looked at my tattered pink dress and the soiled white petticoat with disdain. There was no way I was going to go back
downstairs to dine wearing them. I was growing extremely hungry, true, but it wouldn't hurt me to miss a meal. I might miss
a number of them in days to come, I admitted to myself, at least
until I found work, but I was tough. I doubted it would kill me.
A knock on the door startled me. I cautiously opened it a crack
to see the plump maid's skirt and feet. The rest of her was hidden
by the stack of boxes she was carrying in her arms. She edged
carefully into the room and, sighing heavily, put the boxes down
on the bed. They were lovely boxes, glossy white with thin
golden stripes. The maid grinned.

"The gentleman sent 'em," she informed me, "though I've
no idea where he got 'em. There idn't no shops open at this
hour. Idn't none around here packs things in such fancy boxes."

"Really?"

"Beats me," she said. "Oh, by the way, I brung you a brush
and a comb to use. I noticed you didn't have none."

"Why—thank you."

"The gentleman, he gave me a great big tip and told me to
be sure and take extra good care of you. You need anything else,
just let me know."

She placed the brush and comb on the dressing table, gave
me another merry grin and left. Still wrapped in the towel, I

opened one of the boxes and gave a little gasp when I saw the beige silk petticoat. It was absolutely sumptuous, resting in a nest of soft, thin paper that made a crinkling noise when I lifted it out of the box. I held the garment up, and the cloth rustled softly, shimmering in the candlelight. A real silk petticoat. I couldn't believe it. My hands trembled as I opened the other boxes. There were silk stockings as frail as cobwebs, two beige lace garters, a pair of pale orange kidskin slippers with elegant high heels. The dress I discovered in the largest box was beige linen, with gold and orange and deep tan stripes, the cloth thin and as fine as silk. The last box contained a fancy parasol of the same striped linen, the thin, delicate handle of polished golden wood.

I couldn't hold back the tears that brimmed over my lashes. They streamed down my cheeks, and I made no effort to restrain them. I sat down on the bed, surrounded by all my new finery, my heart so full of gratitude and happiness, I felt it might actually burst. What a wonderful man he was, so kind, so considerate, so thoughtful. If . . . if he had the least hankerin' to pop my cherry, I vowed I would let him. Not just because he had given me the clothes, but because I was, already, genuinely fond of him. He was big and virile and ever so refined, and he gave me a cozy, secure feeling. It wasn't that pleasant, itchy feeling like I had in the dream, like warm, sweet honey flowing in my veins, but it was nice just the same. I owed him so much, and I was quite prepared to pay my debt.

Wiping the tears away, I stood up, feeling much better now, feeling cheerful and buoyant. I had just started my new life, and already I had shoes and a beautiful dress and petticoat and my very own parasol, and I had a handsome and charming new friend who might become more than a friend. Smiling, I wadded the old pink dress and ragged petticoat into a ball and dumped them into the pretty white wastebasket beside the dressing table. They symbolized the past, and the past was behind me, the future awaiting. As I reached for the stockings, I was convinced the future was going to be glorious indeed.

The silk stockings felt heavenly on my legs, clinging to and caressing every inch of my skin, and it was strange wearing garters. I had never worn them before. The petticoat was just a little snug at the waist, and the bodice was cut daringly low, barely concealing my nipples. The skirt was very, very full, swelling out in luxuriant folds that swirled and rustled as I moved. The shoes were a bit tight, too, but the kidskin was soft and pliant, and it didn't bother me. Took me a few minutes to get used to the high heels. You had to walk just a bit slower, and you had to adjust your balance, back arched slightly, breasts quite prominent. Almost popped out of my new petticoat several times before I finally got the hang of it.

The linen dress was sumptuous. It had small puffed sleeves worn off the shoulder and a heart-shaped neckline almost as low as the petticoat. It, too, was snug at the waist, not a proper fit but not at all uncomfortable, and the exquisite skirt belled out over the petticoat, sweeping to the floor in splendor. The creamy beige with its gold and orange and deep tan stripes seemed to make my skin a darker, creamier tan, and there was quite a lot of skin exposed. What if I sneezed? Did fashionable ladies really go around showing so much bosom?

I stepped over to the mirror, examining myself with some amazement. After combing and a thorough brushing, my hair fell to my shoulders in rich, lustrous honey-blond waves aglow with golden-brown highlights, and my hazel eyes seemed to sparkle. My cheekbones were still too high, my mouth too full and too pink, but I looked . . . I looked different. I didn't look like Dana. I looked like a fine lady. Reaching for the parasol, I opened it and rested the handle on my shoulder, twirling it around. No one would ever guess I came from the swamp if they saw me now. They'd think I was as swell as could be, a real aristocrat on my way to take tea with the other blue bloods.

I was still admiring the stranger in the mirror when I heard someone knocking on the door. I opened it with a gracious smile, the parasol still propped on my shoulder. Julian stood there in the hallway, clean and brushed and looking magnificent in shiny brown boots and tobacco-brown breeches and frock coat. His waistcoat was white satin, embroidered with tiny brown fleurs-de-lis, and a white silk cravat was folded neatly at his neck. I continued to smile, waiting for him to say something, but he just stared at me in consternation.

"It's eight o'clock on the dot," I said cheerfully, "and, as you can see, I'm all ready."

"I see," he said.

"You don't like the dress?"

"It's—uh—hardly the thing I would chose for a seventeen-year-old girl, but I didn't have much choice in the matter. Do you think you might pull it *up* a few inches?"

"I tried," I told him. "This is as high as it goes."

"Jesus," he whispered. He shook his head, resigned. "When we get to the dining room, don't you dare lean over," he cautioned. "Not for *any*thing. Damn Amelia! I should have known the treacherous wench would do something like this, but then I don't suppose she *has* anything more conservative."

"This is her dress?"

"I explained the situation to her, and Amelia generously contributed some of the things she had purchased for the trip—she hadn't even taken them out of the boxes yet. Leave the parasol, child. Ladies rarely carry them inside."

"Do—do I look bad?" I asked as we walked down the hall.

"You look quite fetching," he informed me. "Of course, I'll probably have to challenge every man in the room to a duel, but—Lord, how do I get into these situations?"

"I don't *have* to eat," I told him.

"Don't get snappy," he retorted.

The dining room downstairs was beautiful, all done in blue and gray, with a splendid crystal waterfall hanging from the ceiling and snowy white linen cloths on all the tables. The waterfall, Julian informed me, was called a "chandelier," and I made a mental note of it. Almost all of the tables were occupied with elegantly attired people like those I had seen earlier. They all watched as Julian and I followed a man in a fancy black uniform to a table Julian had reserved for us. I saw Amelia sitting with a distinguished silver-haired gentleman even older than Julian. She was wearing a magnificent purple silk gown with black polka dots and a pair of long black gloves, and she was showing even more skin than I was. She gave Julian a friendly nod, the wry smile playing lightly on her lips. He scowled at her and muttered something very unflattering under his breath.

"That wasn't very nice," I said. "After all, she did give you the clothes for me."

"Slut knew exactly what she was doing, too. She knew everyone in the place would see you in that dress and think I— assume you—" He cut himself short.

"Assume what?" I asked innocently.

"Never you mind," he snapped.

Julian ordered for both of us from the large gold and white menus and, giving me a meaningful look, told the man we would do without wine tonight. While this was going on, I was busy feasting my eyes on the splendors of the room: the plush blue brocade curtains, the deep gray carpet with its tiny blue and purple flowers, the chandelier with its dozens and dozens of crystal pendants glittering with rainbow hues in the candlelight. Who would have thought such a palace existed so near the swamp? Julian told me the inn was merely adequate and hardly grand by any standards. I told him it still looked like a palace to me. He sighed and shook his head, looking rather testy, perhaps because of Amelia, perhaps because of all the attention I was getting.

There must have been two dozen men in the dining room, and all of them kept stealing glances at me. A dashing blond youth was sitting at a table across the room with a husky companion, both wearing handsome frock coats and cravats. The blond raised his glass to me, grinned and said something that caused his friend to chuckle. I had a pretty good idea what he had said. They had better manners and wore much better clothes, but they weren't all that different from the louts in the swamp, I thought. Horny as could be. Always on the lookout for another piece of tail, and not just the young men either. Amelia's gentleman friend was looking at me, too. She finally had to tap his wrist with her fan to get his attention back. I smiled to myself as our food arrived.

"Know the proper fork to use?" Julian inquired.

"I ain't a—I'm not a savage," I said airily. "Ma taught me proper table etiquette. Did-ja think I was goin' to eat with my fingers?"

"Nothing would surprise me at this point."

"Why are you being so nasty all of the sudden?"

"Am I being nasty?"

"Very," I said. "I—I can't help it if all the men are lookin' at me. I can't help it if—if this dress don't meet with your approval."

"*Doesn't* meet with my approval," he corrected.

"And I can't help it if I—if I don't always use the proper words or speak with a tony accent. Not all-a us had the advantage of a fancy education. Some of us had to—" My voice started to tremble.

"If you start bawling, I swear I'll throttle you."

"I ain—I'm not going to bawl!"

"Don't," he warned.

"*I* have feelin's, too, you know."

"Indeed?"

I longed to stab him with my fork.

All around us was the soft hum of polite conversation, the tinkle of crystal and china, the light clatter of silverware, but Julian and I ate in silence. The food was so delicious I quickly forgot his bad mood, eating with relish. We had hot turtle soup and a wonderful salad of lettuce and artichoke hearts, slices of tender pink ham, small new potatoes cooked in butter, tasty asparagus. There were hot rolls, too. I had three, buttering each generously. Best meal I ever had, no doubt about it, and it wasn't even over yet. After the man cleared our places, he brought bowls of rice pudding with a thick, hot sweet sauce with raisins. Julian didn't touch his, and I looked at it longingly after I had finished my own. He pushed it across the table to me, and it was soon gone, too.

"It was a lovely meal," I said. "Thank you."

"It was my pleasure. Coffee?"

"I don't think I could hold any," I replied.

"One cup," he told the waiter.

The waiter poured Julian's coffee and left, and Julian sipped it thoughtfully, his mind on something else. He might as well have been alone at the table, I thought resentfully. Amelia and her gentleman friend had departed some time ago, and the good-looking blond youth and his friend were just leaving. They were in their mid twenties, I judged, virile lads with the confident swagger of the well-to-do. Planters' sons, probably. The blond nodded at me and gave me an exceedingly roguish smile as they left the room. Julian didn't notice it. He was still lost in thought, and several minutes passed before he finally looked up and remembered my existence.

"Sorry," he said. "I didn't mean to be rude."

"Do you often go off like that?"

"When I'm tired, when I have a lot on my mind. It's been a very long day."

"I—I guess I'll start lookin' for work tomorrow," I said. "In a town as big as this one, I'm bound to find something."

"I'm sure you will," Julian said, "but I'm going to leave

some money with you just the same, enough to keep you here at the inn for a couple of weeks."

"You—you don't have to do that," I protested.

"I have a conscience," he reminded me. "I couldn't just leave you stranded with no funds."

"You're a—a very good man," I said quietly.

"But nasty," he added.

"Sometimes. I—I'll miss you."

"I imagine I'll miss you, too," he confessed. "This has been quite an adventure. It's getting late, Dana," he added. "I'd better take you back up to your room."

Julian signaled to the waiter, signed a slip of paper and then escorted me out of the room. Only a few people were in the lobby, the clerk behind his desk scribbling in a ledger, a middle-aged couple sitting on one of the sofas, talking quietly, the blond youth and his husky friend who, hovering over a giggling, flashily dressed young woman and playing her with persuasive words, didn't notice us moving toward the stairs.

"What will you do now?" I asked Julian. "Go back home?"

He nodded. "Tomorrow, at noon, a boat leaves for New Orleans. I intend to be on it."

"New Orleans? You live *there*?" I could hardly keep the excitement out of my voice.

"I live in a rather decrepit old house in the Quarter. The Etienne Mansion, it's called, but I fear that's a misnomer. It's something of a landmark, one of the first houses built there, but the grandeur has long since disintegrated into crumbling brick and rusting wrought iron."

Holding my elbow firmly, he led me up the stairs. My heart was palpitating rapidly.

"Take me with you," I begged.

He looked nonplussed. "What?"

"Take me with you. To New Orleans. I've gotta get there, you see. That's where my ma's folks live. I told you about that last night, didn't I? Didn't I tell you I was plannin' to go to New Orleans and find my ma's folks? I originally planned to get a job and earn enough money to get me there, but—if you took me with you, I'd be *way* ahead."

"Out of the question," he said.

We reached the landing and started down the hall. I wasn't about to accept defeat so easily.

"I'd work for *you*. You ain't—aren't married, and I'm sure you need a woman to look after you. I'd keep that decrep—that old house-a yours sparklin', and I'd cook for you and take care of your things and—"

"I have an aunt who does all that," he informed me. "Rather, she supervises the servants. My life is quite complicated enough as is without my taking on the responsibility of—of a headstrong and much too nubile young woman."

"I wouldn't be no responsibility. I—I'd be *help*ful."

"Forget it," he said.

We stopped in front of my door. I looked up at him, and I could see he was absolutely implacable. His expression was that of a tolerant adult dealing with a charming but irrational child.

"*Why* won't you take me?" I asked.

"It would cause a major scandal, for one thing. I'm already considered eccentric and suspect, a shiftless dreamer who spends his time journeying into the swamps, studying plants, failing to uphold the family name. If I showed up with a seventeen-year-old girl, the entire Quarter would be abuzz with talk, my ultra-conservative family leading the chorus. They would believe the worst, and nothing would persuade them differently."

"But—"

"For another, my life is very calm, very well organized, and you, my child, would cause major disruptions. I'm terribly boring and terribly set in my ways. When I'm not collecting specimen and data, I'm in my study, surrounded by notes, scribbling, and—" He shook his head. "I couldn't take you to New Orleans and turn you loose—it's no place for a young girl on her own—and I couldn't take the responsibility of seeing to your welfare."

I didn't say anything. I couldn't, nor could I meet his eyes. Bright hope vanished and disappointment swept over me. Of course he couldn't take me to New Orleans with him. He . . . he had his own life, and he didn't owe me anything. He had been kind and very generous, and I couldn't expect . . . I lifted my eyes, giving him a brave smile. Julian frowned, looking uncomfortable.

"You do understand?" he said.

"Course I do," I said with false cheerfulness. "You—you've done plenty enough for me already. I ain't—I'm not your responsibility. I can take care of myself. I'll find a job and—and I'll get along just fine."

His frown deepened. He took both my hands in his and held them very tightly, looking into my eyes. He seemed torn, seemed about to say something, but he merely squeezed my hands and, after a moment, sighed and released them. When he spoke, his voice was carefully matter-of-fact.

"I'll leave the money in an envelope for you at the desk," he told me. "I have to organize my papers and label some specimen in the morning, so I won't be having breakfast with you. I've ordered some to be brought up here to your room at eight o'clock."

"That—that was very thoughtful of you."

"I'll stop by to see you before I leave to board the steamboat."

I merely nodded. Julian patted my arm.

"Good night, Dana."

"Good night," I said.

He left, and I went into my room. The bath things had been removed, and the bedclothes had been turned down. Only one lamp was burning on the bedside table, the flame flickering a hazy yellow-orange inside the glass globe. Shadows brushed the walls. Trying to ignore the sadness, trying to ignore the fear and the loneliness, I undressed and put all my new things away in the wardrobe, and then I climbed into the bed and turned off the oil lamp. Darkness swallowed me up, it seemed, and gradually a silver mist of moonlight sifted through the window and began to make patterns on the walls and ceiling. The bed was heavenly, so soft, and the sheets smelled of verbena, but I knew I wouldn't be able to go to sleep.

I was wrong. Embracing my sadness, I drifted off to sleep almost immediately and woke up several hours later as early morning sunlight streamed languorously through the window, making hazy yellow-white pools on the carpet, and the sadness was still there, greeting me like a tangible thing. He's leaving today, I thought, and I will never see him again. The thought was more painful than I could have imagined. I had known Julian Etienne for only two days, and yet . . . and yet it seemed that I had known him forever. I stretched my legs, the soft sheets rustling and caressing my nude body, and then I clutched one of the pillows to my bosom and stomach, trying to rid myself of the depression that settled around me like a heavy cloak.

You got everything to be happy about, I told myself. You're

finally free of the swamps, free of Clem and Jake and Randy, and you're going to find work. You'll be on your own, sure, but you knew that from the beginning. He doesn't mean nothin' to you. He's just a very kind stranger who came to your aid, and there ain't no use frettin' because he won't take you with him. Why should he? He's been wonderful, and he's going to leave you some money to tide you over until you get a job. That's more'n you have any right to expect. You'll miss him for a while, yes, but you'll get along. You'll get to New Orleans, too, eventually, and everything will work out and . . . and there's no excuse for you loafin' here in bed, feelin' sorry for yourself.

I finally climbed out of bed and donned my new clothes and brushed my hair, still feeling listless and glum, determined to fight it. Breakfast arrived, and it was lavish indeed: fluffy eggs, tasty sausage, grits, a rack of buttered toast, peach preserves, a whole pot of coffee. Although I had little appetite, I forced myself to eat every bite. Heaven only knew when I'd have another meal like this. I sipped a second cup of coffee, watching the pools of sunlight spread lazily on the floor. It was after nine now, and there was nothing to do but sit here in this room and wait for Julian to come and say good-bye. I felt I would go mad if I did that.

I decided to explore the town a bit, get the lay of the land, maybe get some idea about where I might find work. Fetching my parasol, I left my room and went downstairs, and I received several stares as I passed through the lobby. I suspected the low-cut striped linen dress wasn't quite appropriate for this hour of the morning, but it was all I had and certainly better than the rag I had thrown away. I ignored the stares and, head held high, parasol open and resting jauntily on my shoulder, I moved on out onto the verandah and down the steps.

The sky was a misty white with the merest suggestion of blue, and the morning sunlight was misty, too, silvery white, streaming down in lazy rays. It was already warm, and not a breeze was stirring. A lethargic feeling seemed to permeate the air, and the town itself seemed drowsy. There was a small park across from the inn, leafy chinaberry trees spreading hazy blue-gray shadows over the grass, the beds of pink and yellow daisies looking listless. Two wooden benches with peeling gray paint faced a sundial in the center of the park. A drab brown sparrow perched wearily on its rim, not bothering to fly away as I strolled past. I could smell the mushy, rotting chinaberries that littered the ground under the trees and also the smell of parched grass. Leaving the park, I sauntered slowly down the street, parasol atwirl.

The street was lined on either side with large, comfortable-looking houses with spacious verandahs. Though lovely and, to my eyes, grand indeed, they all looked slightly mellow, weathered by the elements and in need of a fresh coat of paint and minor repairs. A large, shaggy, rust-colored dog wagged its tail at me and shambled after me for a short while until he finally lost interest and, yawning, turned back toward home. A plump Negro woman in a faded blue dress, a white apron and bandanna was shaking a rug out on one of the verandahs, flapping it without enthusiasm over the wooden banister, and she was the only person I saw until I reached the business district.

Only a few people strolled up and down the pavements, mostly middle-aged women with open-net shopping bags or Negro servants on their early morning errands. Shops and businesses lined the street, a stationers', a pharmacy, a grocery store with stalls of fruit and vegetables in front, a bakery, a small bank and, farther along the street, a large emporium with plate glass windows displaying wearing apparel. A trim black surrey with black silk fringe stood in front of the emporium, a glossy chestnut standing patiently in harness. A nattily attired Negro man was sitting on the front seat, holding the reins loosely in his lap while waiting for his charge to return. I paused in front of the windows, gazing at the gloves and reticules and bonnets and lovely dresses. I planned to buy another dress just as soon as I could, like that fetching yellow cotton, perhaps, or that mauve linen with thin purple stripes. Both had modest necklines, and Julian would undoubtedly consider them "suitable" for a seventeen-year-old. He called me "child" and thought of me as a little girl, but I had been a woman for a long time.

As I was admiring the dresses, a remarkable-looking middle-aged woman came out of the emporium. Comfortably plump and well padded though not actually fat, she had very bright copper-red hair worn in long sausage curls and emerald-green eyes. Her chubby cheeks were well powdered, her mouth a vivid red. She wore a dress of black and green checked silk with a black velvet bodice, a pair of long black gloves and, slanted atop her coiffure, a wide-brimmed black velvet hat absolutely aswarm with black and emerald feathers.

The Negro leaped off the surrey to take the packages from her and stow them in back of the vehicle, and, sighing heavily, the woman adjusted the tilt of her hat, fussed with one of her gloves and prepared to climb into the surrey. When she happened to look up and see me standing in front of the windows, she paused, examining me with considerable interest. After a moment she said something to the Negro and strolled over to me, silk skirts rustling crisply. She was wearing a wonderful if rather strong perfume.

"Mornin', honey," she said. "New in town?"

She had a warm, very friendly voice. I smiled.

"I just arrived last night," I told her.

"Didn't think I'd seen you around before. I'm Mrs. Williams, hon, but all my friends call me Lorena. See you're admirin' the dresses—not your style at all," she confided. "Too prim and proper. You need something with a bit more dash, like that rig you're wearin'."

I was surprised. "You like this dress?"

"Real class, hon, and you certainly got the body for it. Betcha it's from New Orleans—Corinne, I'd wager. She's the best, learned her craft in Paris, I understand. Gonna be in town long hon?"

"I imagine so. I'm looking for work."

Mrs. Williams's emerald-green eyes gleamed with even more interest. She was an amiable soul, I thought, quite motherly, the first person I'd encountered who didn't stare at me as though I were some kind of freak.

"What—uh—what kind of work do you do?" she asked.

"Most any kind. I can cook or clean house or milk cows or— I can do washing or almost anything."

One eyebrow shot up at this, and she looked rather startled, but she quickly recovered. She tugged at one of her gloves, smoothing it over her arm, thinking all the while.

"I—uh—I just might be able to help you out, hon," she said.

Now I was startled. "Really?"

"I can always use an extra hand in—uh—in the kitchen. Why don'tja come with me and let me show you my place: I'm sure you'll like it. I can even give you a room to stay in."

"Why . . ."

Mrs. Williams gave me a motherly smile. "I've been lookin' for a new girl to help out, hon, and I think you'd fit the bill perfectly."

"I—I can't come with you just now," I told her. "I've got to go back to the inn. A—a friend is expectin' me."

"Oh," she said, disappointed. "You're *with* somebody?"

"He—he's leavin' for New Orleans at noon," I said. "That's why I've gotta get back—to tell him good-bye."

She looked relieved. "I see," she said. "We—uh—wouldn't want him to worry about you."

"Maybe—maybe I could come to your place later on," I suggested.

"That'd be perfect, hon. It's just outside-a town, at the end of Jeffers Road—you can't possibly miss it. You keep goin' down the road, pass the pecan grove, and there it is. A big pink house."

"Pink?"

"Always did think pink was a happy color. Tell you what, hon, why don't I send Henry here to pick you up—it'd save you a lot of trouble. You can bring your bags and settle right in."

I didn't have any bags, but I thought it best not to mention that. I told her that would be very nice and she said Henry would pick me up in front of the inn at one o'clock, and then she patted my arm, looking quite pleased with herself. We said good-bye, and Henry handed her up into the surrey. Mrs. Williams settled herself on the seat, checked to make sure all her packages were aboard, and then gave me another smile, waving as Henry clicked the reins and the surrey pulled away. I couldn't believe my good fortune. Hadn't left the inn more than an hour ago and already I had a job working in the kitchen of a nice, cozy lady like Mrs. Williams. I'd even have my own room. Who would've believed it'd be so easy to find work?

My spirits were considerably higher as I started back to the inn. I dreaded the thought of telling Julian good-bye and seeing him leave, but at least now I had a place to go. Mrs. Williams and I hadn't discussed money and I had no idea what she would pay me, but I intended to save as much as possible. I'd be going to New Orleans myself one day before too long, and I'd find work there, too, and somehow I'd find my ma's folks and . . . and wouldn't Julian be surprised when I came to call on him, lookin' all elegant and refined? The orange kidskin shoes were beginning to hurt my feet a little as I turned down the street of old houses that led to the inn, and I longed to pull them off, but that wouldn't be ladylike. I *was* going to be a lady one day, I vowed.

The rust-colored dog wagged his tail at me again and padded along after me to the park, where he sniffed at the rotting china-berries, wrinkled his nose and finally rolled lazily in the grass before going back home. I paused at the sundial for a moment and, after I had figured out how to read it, was surprised to discover that it was after ten-thirty. I wondered if Julian had finished labeling his specimen and organizing his papers. Fancy someone devoting so much time to wildflowers and plants. Funny way for a grown man to spend his time, but Julian seemed to think it was very important.

Strolling on through the park, I crossed the street to the inn and moved up the steps and across the verandah, dying now to get upstairs to my room and take off the shoes. As I stepped into the lobby, I was surprised to see Julian leaning across the counter and gripping the clerk's arm, glaring at him with an angry expression as he demanded some information. The clerk shook his head nervously and, spotting me, looked relieved indeed and pointed to where I was standing. Julian released his arm and, trying his best to calm himself, marched over to me and took hold of my elbow. He was wearing the same handsome attire he had worn last night, but the clothes looked a bit rumpled, frock coat creased, cravat coming undone. He didn't say a word, he merely jerked my elbow and led me back out onto the verandah and walked me briskly around to the side, me tottering precariously on the unaccustomed high heels. He finally stopped in front of two wicker chairs with plump cushions, plants stationed on either side and dangling from hanging baskets.

Julian let go of my elbow and took a deep breath and leaned against the banister, his brown eyes dark with anger. What could possibly be the matter? I wondered. This wasn't like him at all. Still trying to calm himself, he didn't say anything, merely scowled, so I sat down in one of the wicker chairs and took off my shoes. It was a great relief.

"I've been looking all *over* for you," he informed me.

"Oh?"

"For the past hour and a half I—no one had seen you—the

maid, the clerk. I was growing frantic. I thought something had—dammit, child! Where the hell *were* you?''

"I went for a walk," I said, rubbing the sole of my left foot. "I strolled downtown to see the shops.''

"In that dress?" He was horrified.

"It was all I had," I reminded him.

He shook his head. "Jesus," he whispered.

"I thought you were goin' to be in your room organizin' your papers and labelin' your specimen and things.''

"I couldn't concentrate," he told me. "I couldn't sleep last night, either. I kept thinking about you, about the way the men kept staring at you—that blond pup, for example. Oh yes, I saw him nodding at you, smiling, sending signals. Up to no good, that one. If I hadn't been there to watch over you . . .'' He paused, looking grim indeed.

"That ain't—isn't anything to get riled up about," I told him. "Men are always starin' at me, sendin' signals. I can take care of myself.''

"Sure you can," he said.

"I *can*," I retorted. "I ain't a child, despite what you think, and I—I don't *need* anyone to watch over me.''

"No?"

"No," I said testily, rubbing my right foot now. "You—you just go on to New Orleans and don't worry about me. I'll be fine. I ain't your responsibility, remember?''

"I keep telling myself that.''

"Besides," I added, "I already got work.''

"Indeed?"

"I met a very nice lady this morning, a Mrs. Lorena Williams. She was real friendly to me, and when I said I was lookin' for work, she said she'd been lookin' for a new girl to help out, said I'd fit the bill perfectly. She has a big pink house just outside-a town, and she's goin' to give me a room and—''

"Jesus!"

He didn't whisper it this time. He thundered it so loudly I almost tumbled out of the chair. I looked up at him in amazement and decided that he might not be quite right in the head. Lots-a tetched folk seemed perfectly all right when you first met 'em, seemed sane as anyone till something set 'em off and you discovered they were loony as a bat. Julian looked at me in total disgust and said I was a babe, a mere babe, so green I'd grow if you stuck me in the ground, said I was hopelessly naive, a hazard to mankind. I sat very still and nodded at everything he said, not about to disagree. Best to humor him, I thought. Finally running down, he gave an exasperated sigh and ordered me to put my shoes back on. I tried. I couldn't. My feet were swollen.

"I—I can't," I sobbed.

"What difference does it make?" he asked wearily.

He pulled me out of the chair and led me back around the verandah, me holding the orange kidskin shoes in one hand and treading along apprehensively in my stockinged feet. He seemed quite calm now, seemed utterly resigned.

"Where—where're we goin'?" I asked nervously.

"We're going to fetch my bags and then we're going to hire a cab and go buy you a decent outfit and then we're going to go board the steamboat for New Orleans. I've taken complete leave of my senses—I'm fully aware of that fact—but I'd never be able to live with myself if I left you to the mercy of . . ." He shook his head once again.

"Why me, Lord?" he asked.

I thought I was going to burst with joy.

Book Two

The Ward

Chapter Six

NEW ORLEANS WAS COMPLETELY OVERWHELMING, and as we left the steamboat, a porter following behind with Julian's bags, I couldn't believe I was actually here. I held on to Julian's arm, in awe, sad, too. This was where Ma had grown up, and this was where she had known such happiness, such heartbreak. Ma . . . I didn't want to think about her. I wanted to keep the grief locked up inside where it couldn't harm me. Julian tilted his head and glanced down at me, and I managed to smile a feeble smile. He seemed to sense that I didn't want to talk, seemed to sense the reason why. He gave my arm a little pat and guided me past a huge stack of cotton bales.

The docks were vast and very crowded and full of activity, but there was a curiously lethargic atmosphere nevertheless. Perhaps it was the rather oppressive blue-gray sky looming overhead, or perhaps it was the sultry heat, but although everyone seemed to be busy, no one seemed to be in any hurry. Passengers arriving and departing strolled along leisurely, as though they had all the time in the world, and the Negro slaves loading and unloading huge crates and barrels or yet more bales of cotton did so at a shambling pace. There seemed to be dozens of sailors, some of them in foreign uniforms, and they lounged about, eyeing the women who sauntered about the docks in colorful and provocative garments. A number of these women were very beautiful and some of them quite dark, obviously mulattos or quadroons. They were the most beautiful of all, coyly twirling fancy silk parasols.

My own parasol had been returned, along with the dress, the silk petticoat and the orange kidskin shoes. Julian had instructed the woman at the emporium to wrap them up and send them back to Amelia at the inn, and I was now proudly wearing the mauve linen frock with thin purple stripes I had admired in the window. It had short puffed sleeves worn slightly off the shoulder, a modest neckline and a narrow purple waistband, the very full skirt belling out over the beruffled white petticoat beneath. I was also wearing a new pair of shoes, purple kidskin this time. They fit much better, but the heels weren't nearly so high. We had purchased everything hastily before boarding the steamboat. Even though I was now "suitably" attired and my bosom was no longer so exposed, the sailors eyed me, too. I pretended not to notice.

As we continued through the crowded labyrinth, Julian informed me that New Orleans was one of the busiest ports in America. Cotton from the South was exported all over the country and overseas as well, most of it leaving from right here, and in the city one could buy goods imported from all over the world. New Orleans was the most cosmopolitan city in America, he continued, the most sophisticated as well. I didn't understand what some of those big words meant, but I agreed that it was certainly a fascinating place.

"I can't believe I'm here," I said.

"I can't either," he said dryly.

"I—I'm a little scared," I confessed.

"Whatever for?"

"It's so big and I—I don't know anything. I've spent all my life in the swamps. I—I'm afraid everyone will laugh at me."

"You need a bit of polish," he agreed, "but I imagine we can take care of that."

Reaching a line of carriages, he helped me climb inside one of them, tipped the porter for carrying the bags and gave directions to the driver. The interior of the carriage was dusty, the seats upholstered in brown leather cracking at the seams. Julian settled in beside me, closed the door, and we were on our way, wheels spinning noisily, horse hooves clomp-clomp-clomping on the street. I sat up very straight, clutching the handle on the side of the door as we rumbled and rocked along. My stomach felt a little queasy, and I hoped I wasn't going to be sick.

"Why are you sitting like that?" Julian asked.

"I—I ain't never been in a carriage before. Are—are you sure we ain't going to tump over?"

"We aren't going to tump over, I assure you. Sit back and relax."

"We're going awfully fast," I said nervously.

"We're barely moving. You've really never been in a carriage before?"

"I've been in a wagon, but it wudn't closed-in like this and it didn't shake so much."

"You'd never been on a steamboat, either, and that didn't frighten you."

"Yeah, but I'm used to water."

"Lord," he said wearily, "you really are a primitive. What am I going to do with you?"

"Put me to work," I replied. "I can earn my keep, I promise ya. You won't be sorry you brung me along."

"Brought," he corrected.

"See, I—I don't even use the proper words at times. People *will* laugh at me."

"Not in my presence, they won't."

"Will your family really be upset when you show up with me?"

"Delia will be no problem. She's a dear, if somewhat absentminded. Charles will raise hell when he finds out—fortunately he's in Europe on business at the moment. Lavinia will undoubtedly come charging over with fire in her eyes. Lavinia is my uncle's wife and only an Etienne by marriage, but she considers herself the matriarch. A most unpleasant woman."

"I—I don't want to cause you any trouble."

"Oh, I can handle Lavinia. She may be a dragon, but Charles and I still control the family business—and what little money remains. That has always been a thorn in her side. Lavinia feels she should be in charge and frequently believes she is. Her offspring, my cousins, are deplorable snobs, and poor Andre, their father, spends most of his time at his club, drinking bourbon and losing at cards. There are various other relations scattered throughout the Quarter, but they only appear for handouts—or at family gatherings where there is a generous outlay of food."

"Who are Delia and Charles?" I asked.

"Delia is my father's sister, and she's lived at the house ever since I was a boy. She came to stay with us after her young husband was killed in a boating accident—and somehow she never got around to leaving. She runs the house and clucks and fusses over Charles and me and forgets things and mutters to herself, and just when you think the old dear's completely dotty, she'll fix those eyes on you and startle you with some remarkably astute observation. Delia may spend an inordinate amount of time gathering wool, but in a crisis she's the very soul of strength.''

Julian shook his head, a faint smile on his lips as he considered his aunt, and then his eyes grew serious and a frown creased his brow.

''Charles is my brother,'' he informed me. ''He's twelve years my junior and quite good-looking and nothing at all like me. He's sober, dedicated, driven, a very hard worker. I fear Charles doesn't get much fun out of life, but he certainly accomplishes a great deal. He runs the business and handles all the family's affairs and is tactful enough to consult me every now and then to maintain the fiction that I have equal authority. Business is not my forte. I'm perfectly content to let Charles manage everything. He does so with great efficiency.''

''Is he married?'' I asked.

''Charles is far too busy keeping the business afloat to make such a serious commitment. There have been women, of course—Charles has been known to attend more than one Quadroon Ball—but, as yet, no wife. Well-born belles wring their hands in frustration, even though the Etienne wealth is mostly a memory.''

''And—and he won't be happy about me?''

''He'll be incensed,'' Julian said, ''but, as I told you, he's in Europe and won't be back for several months. Happily for us. No doubt he'll learn of his big brother's latest folly as soon as Lavinia can put pen to paper, but there's not a lot he can do about it with an ocean between us.''

He didn't seem to be particularly worried about it, so I decided not to worry either. I had gotten accustomed to the movement of the carriage now and was no longer frightened. I leaned forward, peering out the window. We had passed a lot of warehouses and ugly brown buildings, and now we were moving down a street lined with mellow old buildings with fancy wrought-iron galleries. Gentlemen in handsome frock coats and women in lovely outfits strolled along leisurely beneath the galleries, many of them followed by Negro servants carrying their parcels. I caught glimpses of some of the strange and wonderful goods displayed in shop windows, and Julian leaned forward to point to a particularly impressive shop on the corner. Its windows were filled with beautiful and ornate furniture and exquisite vases and screens and other marvelous items.

"That's Etienne's," he informed me. "Grandest and most exclusive purveyor of imported goods in New Orleans."

"You sell furniture?"

" 'Furniture' is hardly the appropriate word. You want a Boulle cabinet, a Giovanna Bologna bronze, a bedroom screen painted by Boucher for Madame Du Barry, a set of Sevres china once used by Catherine the Great, a crystal chandelier that once graced a ballroom in Versailles, you come to Etienne's with a wagonload of money and leave the proud possessor of the desired item."

"People actually have money to buy them things?"

"Not as many people as we would like," Julian confessed, "and each things costs *us* a great deal, plus shipping costs. The profit for Etienne's isn't all that large, but the shop was established by my great-grandfather over a hundred years ago and it's something of an institution, so we hold on to it—albeit shakily. The real profit is in cotton."

"You sell cotton, too?"

"We import luxury items for the shop. We export cotton which Charles buys at auction or, more recently, in advance."

"How can you buy cotton in advance?" I asked.

"You strike a deal with the plantation owner, agree to buy his entire crop as soon as it's planted. It's an idea Charles came up with himself, and he was able to buy at a bargain price, much less than we'd pay at auction. Belle Mead and Ravenaugh are currently growing for us. Cleaned out the coffers, but we've got the jump on all our competitors and will clear a huge profit once the crops are harvested."

It sounded risky as hell to me. Sounded like buyin' a pig in a poke. What if something happened to the crops before they could be picked? Course, I didn't know anything about business, didn't know that much about cotton, either. I did wonder, though, if this Charles was quite as shrewd as his brother seemed to think he was. He sounded bossy and thoroughly unpleasant. I was glad he wasn't going to be here for a while.

We had left Etienne's far behind by this time and were driving through a series of narrow, twisting streets. The shops here were shabbier, the people not as well dressed, but there was a mellow charm nevertheless. I wondered how a person would ever learn their way around a place as vast and confusing as this. Turning a corner, we drove past a huge area completely filled with stalls, dozens of people milling about, examining baskets of plump pink shrimp and barrels of eel and mounds of apples and limes and oranges. There were racks of meat, too, carcasses hanging on hooks, cages of live chickens and geese as well. Julian told me that here at the market you could buy every kind of food imaginable, from the most exotic spices to freshly baked bread. It was a festive blur of color and slow movement, and the smells as we passed were heady indeed. I longed to leap right out of the carriage and spend hours examining those fascinating stalls, mingling with those unhurried matrons who rubbed elbows with stout men in leather aprons, those Negro women in bandannas who idly squeezed melons and filled their wicker baskets with produce and fish wrapped in newspaper.

"I've never seen so much food," I said.

Julian smiled. "New Orleans is famous for its food. Our cuisine is rivaled only by that in Paris."

"Makes you hungry, just seein' it all."

I sat back against the worn leather cushion, wearied and a little bewildered by all the wonderful new sights and impressions. Life in the swamp with its never-changing routine and bleak sameness hadn't prepared me for all this color and variety. I felt like a child who had been given so many presents I couldn't fully appreciate any of them. I was aglow with happiness, yet the sadness was there as well, and I found myself wanting to cry. Ma . . . this was her city. How dear she had been, how gentle and loving, and . . . and now she was gone. The anguish and grief would always be inside, would always come upon me unawares, despite all my efforts to keep it contained. Julian studied me closely, his brown eyes full of understanding.

"Tired?" he asked quietly.

"Not at all, but I—I'm awfully nervous."

"There's no need to be. No one is going to harm you."

"I know, but—it's all so strange."

"I imagine it must be. You'll feel better after we get home and you've had a little rest."

"Are we almost there?" I asked.

"Almost."

"I—I want to thank you for bringing me with you."

"I'll undoubtedly rue the day," he replied.

The market behind us, we were now driving slowly through a beautiful district of old brick houses festooned with intricate wrought-iron balconies and columns. Purple bougainvillea spilled over crumbling gray brick garden walls, and through wrought-iron gates I caught glimpses of gardens abloom with camellias and azaleas and roses and all sorts of exotic greenery. The air was heavily perfumed, and one could hear the gentle splattering of hidden fountains. A sleepy, almost dreamlike atmosphere prevailed, as though life lived beyond the weathered walls and all that wrought-iron lace was somehow removed, set apart. Everything seemed strangely familiar to me, and I had the curious feeling that I had been here before, that I belonged, that I was coming home. I wasn't able to define the feeling, it didn't really make sense, but it was very strong nevertheless, something Mama Lou would understand.

Julian sighed and sat up straight, adjusting his neckcloth as the carriage slowed down, finally stopping before a set of wide, slightly rusty wrought-iron gates. Julian climbed out and pulled the chain of a tarnished bell hanging beside the gates, and then he turned to help me out of the carriage, squeezing my hand tightly as I stepped down. Footsteps approached, and the gates were opened wide by a plump, cheerful Negro boy in black knee pants and a rather shiny black frock coat he had begun to outgrow. He grinned broadly, shoving the gates even wider.

"Welcome home, Mista Julian!" he exclaimed. "We's happy to have you back again."

"Hello, Elijah. It's good to be back."

"Don't stand there wasting Mister Julian's time with your chattering, Elijah. Get them bags down, carry them into the house."

This order was issued by a stern-faced Negro man who appeared at the boy's heels. He wore a black broadcloth suit as shiny as Elijah's, an embroidered maroon waistcoat that had seen much better days and a crumpled white linen neckcloth. His skin was a shiny black, his eyes a haughty brown, his fuzzy hair a peppery gray-black. He gave Julian a cool nod, gave me a look of instant disapproval and then devoted all his attention to the unloading of the bags. Julian hooked his arm through mine and led me into the garden.

"You mustn't mind Pompey," he said. "He's always been an officious bastard and became even more so after he was elevated to the rank of butler. I was about twelve years old at the time."

I was surprised to find that he kept slaves. Julian saw it on my face.

"Pompey and Elijah aren't slaves," he informed me. "They are free men of color, with papers to prove it. They work for us by choice and for a salary, as do Jezebel, Kayla, and all our other devoted and exorbitantly expensive family retainers."

"I'm glad," I said. "Glad they ain't slaves, I mean. I don't think it's right for men to own other men, like they was cattle or something."

"You'll find a lot of people here in New Orleans who agree with you. We've a large population of free people of color, a whole community, in fact, many of them with lighter skin than yours. Unfortunately, you'll also find thousands of slaves and monthly auctions. It's an imperfect world."

"Is—is your aunt at home?" I asked nervously.

"I imagine she is. She doesn't bite," he added.

I was extremely apprehensive now, hesitating, and Julian paused to give me time to gather myself together and look around before we went inside. We moved to one side of the flagstone walkway so that Pompey and Elijah could pass. Julian thrust his hands into his pockets, watching me with his head tilted to one side as I examined my surroundings.

The garden was filled with strange, unfamiliar plants, feathery ferns, tall, fan-shaped greenery, beds of flowers badly in need of attention. Magnolia trees towered overhead, studded with huge, waxy white blooms, and the dusty pink-gray walls were espaliered with fruit trees. There were two fountains, both of them abrim with coral lilies, water spilling from basin to basin with a quiet, tinkling music. The house itself was enormous, twice as large as any of its neighbors, of the same ancient pink-gray brick. Sprawling the full length of the garden, it was two stories high with a slanting blue-gray slate roof. The galleries above and verandahs below were adorned with a dazzling profusion of ornately patterned wrought iron that really did look like lace. Old white shutters hung at all the windows, sagging here and there, and a graceful fanlight spread over the blue-gray front door.

"It—it's beautiful," I said in a hushed voice.

''Weathered with age, worn at the edges, a majestic old relic that desperately needs overhauling—but I suppose it does retain a certain patina of charm. I only wish it weren't so costly to maintain.''

Julian took me firmly by the arm and led me up the front steps. An expressionless Pompey held the door open for us, and I could have sworn he sniffed with disapproval as I passed. We were in a spacious foyer with high, domed white ceilings and paneled walls painted a soft white. A worn pink and gray carpet covered most of the parquet floor, an immense and rather dusty crystal chandelier dangled overhead, and, at the other end of the room, a lovely white spiral staircase rose gracefully to the second floor. The room was dim, the natural light softly diffused and wavering as though reflected from water. Pale lilac-gray shadows shifted and stirred, even at this hour of the afternoon.

I heard a rustle of skirts, a clatter of heels, and Julian's Aunt Delia came tottering into the room, halting abruptly when she spotted me standing beside her nephew. In her late fifties, she was not quite as tall as I, and admirably thin. Her face was lightly powdered, her lips painted a pale coral-pink, and her eyes were a clear light green. Her soft, silvery gray hair was cut short and floated out all around her head like the fluffy cap of a dandelion, an eccentric but curiously appropriate coiffure that suited her perfectly. She was wearing a lilac silk frock and a white organdy apron, and she twisted the latter in bewilderment as she looked at her nephew and then looked at me and then back at her nephew, a delicate frown creasing her brow.

''You've brought a guest, Julian?'' Her voice was lovely.

''In a manner of speaking. This is Dana, Delia. She is an orphan. She is going to be staying with us.''

''Well, I'm sure that will be charming, dear. We've plenty of room. Where did you find her?''

''In the swamp. It's a long story. I'll tell you later.''

Delia examined me more closely, her clear, lovely green eyes alight with curiosity. I needn't have been nervous about meeting her, I saw. There was a fragile, otherworldly quality about Delia and a childlike innocence that was immediately endearing. Vague she might be, but she radiated goodness and gentility, and I sensed at once that she hadn't a mean bone in her body.

''She's absolutely breathtaking, Julian,'' she observed, ''but—she's only a baby.''

"Seventeen," Julian told her.

"You're not thinking of—you know I'm tolerant, dear, I never raise an eyebrow at anything you or Charles do, but—well, in this instance it really wouldn't do, dear. I hope you haven't already—"

"It's not like that at all, Delia," Julian said patiently.

Delia was visibly relieved. "I'm pleased to meet you, dear," she told me.

"I'm pleased to meet you, too," I said.

Delia blinked, frowned again, and looked at her nephew.

"What's wrong with her voice?" she inquired.

"It can be fixed," he said. "Elocution lessons. In fact, we're going to have to hire a whole fleet of tutors. The child can barely read and write. We're going to have to start from the ground up."

Delia was unperturbed. "I'm sure that will be very interesting," she observed. "Where are her things?"

"She hasn't any—only the clothes she is wearing."

"That will never do. I'll have to take her to Corinne's tomorrow and make arrangements for a complete wardrobe. What fun it will be, dressing her. It's been quite dreary around here of late, Julian, with Charles gone and everything. I'm sure I'll be enchanted to have her stay with us, but—what will Lavinia and the others say?"

"God knows."

"She and Raoul are going to be here tonight."

His handsome face registered shock, exasperation and, finally, weary resignation.

"I suppose I'll just have to deal with it," he said.

"I suppose you will, dear. I could never deal with Lavinia, even when I was younger. She does try one's nerves, and her children . . ." Delia shook her silvery cloud of hair. "Magdelon is impossible, of course, and I fear Raoul is the worst sort of heartbreaker. The boy is much too good-looking, and he has no scruples at all when it comes to women."

"Any idea what she wants?" Julian inquired.

"A more responsible position for Raoul," his aunt replied. "It's embarrassing to the lad to work at the shop like a common clerk, selling furniture."

"He's rarely there," Julian said. "He's damned lucky to get a salary. If he weren't an Etienne—"

"I know, dear, I know. *You* put in your time at the shop, Charles did, too, both of you working without complaint on the floor for your dear father, charming all the customers, I'm sure, but Lavinia feels it's demeaning for her Raoul. You know Lavinia . . ."

Delia sighed and, dismissing the problem from her mind, came over to take my hand. Her own was like soft old parchment.

"Poor child," she said gently. "I'm sure you must be all tuckered out after the trip. I'll just take you up to your room—let me see, the yellow room, I think. Pity there wasn't time to have it properly aired."

Before I could say anything she led me toward the spiral staircase, chattering pleasantly the whole while. As we started up the graciously curving stairs, I looked back at Julian. He stood there in the foyer, watching us with a bemused look in his eyes. I felt I was in the middle of a dream as his aunt led me on up the stairs and down a wide, shadowy hallway lined with lovely old chests. Still holding my hand, she guided me around a corner and down another hallway, explaining that the yellow room had been her own when she was a girl, before she left to marry Mister Beauregard.

"There's a gallery that looks out over the courtyard and a flight of steps leading down to it. The entire house is built around the courtyard," she continued, "all the French windows downstairs opening out onto it. The carriage house and the servants' quarters are in the back. We're in the west wing now. The east wing, facing this across the courtyard, is, alas, closed up, all the furniture covered with dustcloths. The house is far too large, you see—I do fear it's an albatross, but one does one's best to keep everything tidy."

Delia opened a door and led me into a small room with walls hung with faded old yellow silk, very pale. Bed, dressing table and wardrobe were of exquisite golden wood with fancy patterns inlaid in darker gold and brown wood, curlicues and garlands of old brass adorning each piece. A heavy yellow satin counterpane was spread over the bed, matching draperies at the set of French windows, and a worn but still lovely yellow, white and pale blue rug covered much of the floor, its floral patterns sadly fading. A pale blue silk screen with sprays of equally fading white apple blossoms stood in one corner. Delia tactfully informed me that behind it I would find pitcher, ewer and "all the necessities," and then she opened the French windows.

"Now you just rest up, dear, you hear? I'll send Kayla up with fresh water and a little something to tide you over till dinner. If I were you, I'd slip off those shoes and that frock and have myself a little nap. You must be thoroughly exhausted."

"I—I am just a little tired," I confessed.

"Dear me," Delia said, speaking to herself. "I'm sure I don't know what Julian can be thinking of, but—" She looked at me and smiled. "We'll cope," she said.

"I—I hope I'm not—I don't want to cause any—"

"I, for one, think it will be *nice* to have someone young around the place," she told me. "It gave me quite a turn at first, but Julian is entitled to his little whims. Although this time—"

She left the words dangling in air and examined me again.

"It'll be all right, dear," she said.

Delia came over to me and took my hand again and squeezed it, and then she sighed and shook her head and released my hand and drifted out of the room like a wraith, closing the door soundlessly behind her. Wavering rays of late afternoon sunlight drifted languorously through the windows, gliding the smooth gloss of varnished wood, making pale gold pools on the carpet. I thought of my shabby attic room with its bare board walls and corn husk mattress, and it was hard to believe that I was actually here. I gazed in awe at all the lovely things, running my hand over the polished wood, cautiously fingering the frail blue silk of the screen and the lustrous yellow satin of the drapes, and then I moved through the French windows.

A wrought-iron gallery wound all the way around the second floor like intricate, ornate lace, supported by lacy iron columns. Nearby a flight of steps led down to the courtyard, a matching flight across the way. The courtyard was completely enclosed and paved in glazed tile, an elaborate three-tiered fountain in the center. There were strange, exotic green plants and wonderful flowers—pink, purple, deep red—and two mimosa trees, one dusty mauve, the other a pale yellow-gold, the silky blossoms filling the air with a heady perfume. Shadows were beginning to spread in blue-gray layers, gradually darkening as the sun waned. It was incredibly beautiful and somehow mysterious. I seemed to receive strong impressions of time past. What dramas had unfolded in this courtyard during the past hundred years? What emotions had been expelled, leaving subtle traces that lingered still?

Hearing a noise behind me, I turned around to see a Negro girl entering the room with a heavily laden tray. Thick black hair fell to her shoulders in glossy waves, and her large brown eyes were full of sparkle. The wide, flat nose and overly full red lips her only Negroid features. Her complexion was a deep, creamy café au lait, in truth not much darker than my own. The girl smiled, gave me a pert nod and set her tray down on the dressing table. Pert, vivacious, she promptly began to turn back the yellow satin counterpane.

"I be Kayla, Miz Dana," she informed me. "Miz Delia, she says I's to make you real snug and comfy and see if you's wantin' anything. I brung up water for the ewer so's you can wash yourself and I brung somethin' to eat, too, some crabmeat paste spread on l'il pieces of bread, some cheese, an apple, a glass-a lemonade. These sheets is fresh, by th' way. I changed 'em only a couple-a-days ago."

She plumped up the pillows with merry little pats, frankly examining me with those lively brown eyes.

"I hopes you don't mind me sayin' it, Miz Dana, but you's the most beautiful woman I ever did see."

"Why—why, thank you, Kayla."

"Is you a buffalo gal?" she inquired.

I shook my head. Kayla spread a beruffled blue and mauve wrapper over the bed, arranging it in graceful folds.

"I hope you ain't offended, my askin', but your skin ain't that much lighter'n mine and—well, you never can tell. Some-a them gals paradin' at the Quadroon Balls are whiter-lookin' than you. Ain't none of 'em as beautiful, though. Mister Julian done hisself fine, he did. Took us all by surprise, him bringin' you here 'stead-a settin' you up in an apartment, but then Mister Julian's never paid no mind to what people thunk."

"I believe you have the wrong idea, Kayla," I said.

The girl looked surprised. "You ain't his lovin' gal?"

"I—I'm just his friend," I told her. "I'm not anyone's lovin' gal, never have been."

"You mean you's still *intact*?"

I nodded, not at all offended. Kayla shook her head.

"Gal as beautiful as you is—it don't figure. Me, I ain't been intact for years. I was thirteen when I gave my cherry to a fine-lookin' stableboy. White, he was, a rogue with a wicked grin and twinklin' eyes. Took my cherry an' broke my heart. Been lots-a fellas since then. I *tries* to be good like Miz Delia says I should, but I got this weakness for lovin'. Makes you feel so tingly and cozy an' all. Reckon I can't help myself when I sees a fine-lookin' fellow who wants to tumble. They all does, a-course.''

I was at a loss for words in the face of this candid admission. "How pleasant for you," I finally observed.

"Oh, it's pleasant—long as they don't get too rough and long as you's th' one pickin' an' choosin'. Mister Raoul now, him I steer clear of. He's as handsome as can be an' randy as they come, but to him I's just a nigger gal he thinks he can tumble any time he pleases.''

"Raoul? He—he would be Lavinia's son.''

"Yes'um. Trapped me in the broom closet, he did, had his pants down and was ready to start plungin', would-a had me, too, if Mister Charles hadn't come along an' heard me screamin'. Beat th' tar outta Raoul, Mister Charles did. Said he'd kill him if he ever tried any-a that again in this house. Mister Charles, him I wouldn't *mind* takin' me, but he ain't never showed th' least interest.''

Kayla sighed regretfully and stepped behind the screen to fill the ewer. I found the girl enchanting, if a bit too forthcoming. She arranged the food on a platter and put it on the bedside table.

"Miz Delia said you'd probably be wantin' to take a nap," she informed me. "Dinner'll be served at eight-thirty. I'll come up round eight to help you get ready.''

She paused at the door, giving me a long, appraising look.

"Mister Julian's a fine gentlemen," she said. "A gal could do a *whole* lot worse, take my word for it. Spoiled that Miz Amelia to pieces, he did, gave her th' moon. Older men—they's th' best. They takes their *time*.''

Kayla left with a brisk rustle of skirts, and I sighed, feeling bone-weary now. I hadn't intended to nap, but the bed looked terribly inviting and it was a long time until dinner. I removed shoes and stockings and frock, slipping the ruffled blue and mauve wrapper over my petticoat and tying the sash at my waist. I wasn't really hungry now, but I sipped the lemonade and ate a few of the snacks Kayla had brought up. Lethargy stole over me, my eyelids growing heavier by the minute, and I stretched out on the bed, the mattress so soft beneath me, sheets a soft, sweet-smelling yellow linen. Older men are the best, Kayla had said, and I felt sure she spoke from experience. How free and easy she was about matters of the flesh, totally unfettered by bothersome conventions. I had guarded my cherry like a treasured jewel, but . . . yes, gladly would I have given it to the man who had rescued me from Clem and the swamp. Out of gratitude . . . or because he was so warm, so handsome, so wonderfully appealing? I closed my eyes, thinking about all that had happened, and sleep quickly claimed me.

Soft rustles and whispers awakened me, and I stirred, feeling rather groggy, aware at once that the sultry heat hadn't abated even though the room was full of velvety black shadows, all color faded. The drapes made silken music as a gentle breeze stirred them, bringing with it all the heady scents of the courtyard. The fountain below splashed and splattered, softly pattering, making another kind of music, and the sheets rustled as I got out of bed, pulling the wrapper more closely around me, adjusting the sash. Ruffles fluttered on the full skirt as I moved over to the French windows. The sky above was a deep opal, gradually darkening to black, the moon a thin silver disk. The courtyard was a nest of shadows, broken here and there by golden blurs of light fanning out from the windows downstairs.

It had only been dark a short while, I could tell that from the color of the sky. I had plenty of time before Kayla returned, I reasoned, so I decided to explore the courtyard. Moving down the gallery to the stairs, I descended slowly, my bare feet making no noise whatsoever. Tall green plants rustled all around me, and soft fronds touched my cheek as I moved toward the fountain. The air was so heavily scented it was almost dizzying, and heat seemed to shimmer in the violet-gray semidarkness. The fountain was indeed a marvel, water spilling from tier to tier, a plump cherub with a dolphin in its arms perched on top, large lilies floating in the wide bottom tier.

''—absolutely unthinkable!'' a harsh voice exclaimed, and I whirled around, startled.

''—really none of your concern, Lavinia.''

''None of my concern! The family—the family name! It might not mean anything to you, Julian, but it means everything to me. I won't be able to hold my head up. I won't be able to face any of my friends. What will people say when they hear you've—no, it won't do, Julian. It simply won't do. I forbid you to let that creature stay in his house."

"It isn't your place to forbid anything, dear aunt," Julian said.

The voices were coming through a partially opened set of French windows, and I moved through the courtyard toward them, unable to help myself. Standing just beyond the hazy fan of light, concealed by the shadows, I peered in at the brightly lighted room, a parlor of sorts, it seemed, the walls hung with pale lime silk patterned with white, sofas and chairs covered in varying shades of lime, emerald, and white. A somewhat dusty chandelier hung from the ceiling, and candles burned in ivory wall sconces. Julian was standing in front of a white marble fireplace, a tall glass in his hand, his expression utterly indifferent as the thin, bony woman in black glared at him, seething.

"All of us have tolerated your eccentricities, Julian. Going off to those god-awful swamps, collecting plants, holing yourself up in your study, filling notebook after notebook with scribbling while Charles runs the business—that's bad enough. But this! I've no objection to your taking another mistress, but I will not stand by and see you bring ridicule to—"

She cut herself short, trying hard to contain her outrage. She was standing beside one of the sofas, tall, imperious, frighteningly grand. A good fifteen years older than Julian, she had a very thin face with sharp cheekbones and a long nose and thin, pursed lips painted a bright scarlet. Her eyes were dark brown, almost black, glittering now with icy rage, and her hair was as black as a raven's wing, piled atop her head with a plump roll dipping down to midtemple on either side. No woman that age had hair that black, I thought. She must dye it. Long garnet earrings hung from her lobes, and a garnet brooch was fastened at the throat of her long-sleeved, high-necked black gown. Ugly as sin, she was, like a gaunt, haughty scarecrow.

"We are Etiennes," she reminded him in her crisp, icy voice. "We have an obligation to the community. There are standards we must uphold. Minor transgressions are one thing, they're expected of the aristocracy, but this—this is outright defiance of every precept of—"

Julian's weary sigh interrupted her. I noticed then a shiny black boot and a deep plum trousered leg stretched out from a large white chair that was turned at an angle from my line of vision. The leg moved, and a man stood up, his back to me. He was wearing a superbly tailored plum-colored frock coat that accentuated his broad shoulders and narrow waist, and his hair was thick and glossy and startlingly black. He walked across the room to a liquor cabinet and poured himself a drink, turning then. Raoul Etienne, for that was who he must be, was lean and sleek and polished. His skin was deeply tanned. His dark brown eyes seemed to glow. His full pink mouth was undeniably sensual. As Kayla had said, he was as handsome as could be, but I sensed something crafty and dangerous just beneath the surface. He reminded me of a beautiful panther.

"I'd like to see this girl," he said.

His voice was deep and melodious, like a husky caress. His mother shot him a warning look, and he grinned, leaning back against the liquor cabinet, clearly amused by all the uproar. Lavinia Etienne drew herself up haughtily, glaring at her nephew-by-marriage, every inch the formidable grande dame.

"What precisely do you intend to do with her?" she inquired.

"I intend to see Emil Moreau in his offices first thing tomorrow. I intend to make her my ward, become her legal guardian. The child has no one."

Lavinia gasped and slammed a palm to her heart. Both men ignored her dramatic gesture.

"I intend to hire tutors," Julian continued, "and see that she is given a chance in life. She's an intelligent child. I have no doubt she'll come around splendidly."

"An illiterate swamp girl! A bastard to boot! You've lost your mind, Julian! You've quite plainly lost your mind. Charles will— if Charles were here, he would never allow this to happen!"

"This does not concern Charles," Julian said calmly, "and I might remind you that *I* am the elder brother, Lavinia. I have taken this child in and that is that. I need not justify my actions to you, dear aunt, or to anyone else. People can think what they will. I couldn't care less."

"She must be something," Raoul observed.

"You're both welcome to stay to dinner. I'm sure you'll find her as charming and guileless as I do."

"She's obviously a clever and conniving little trollop who has you completely hoodwinked! You've always been a fool, Julian, but I never believed you could be so—so—" Lavinia's icy voice seemed to crack. "Come, Raoul," she commanded. "I don't intend to stay in this house one minute longer!"

Raoul arched an eyebrow, took a final sip of his drink and, giving Julian an amused look, reluctantly followed his mother as she marched haughtily out of the room. Julian watched them leave, lifted one hand to run his fingers though his hair and then moved over to the liquor cabinet to pour another drink. I slipped back through the shadows to the staircase and hurried back up to my room, arriving just as Kayla tapped on the door. I quickly lighted candles and then opened the door.

Kayla insisted on helping me dress, then insisted I sit at the dressing table and let her do my hair. She brushed it skillfully until it shined with rich golden-brown highlights, then fluffed the waves and let them tumble in a gleaming cascade about my shoulders. She chattered blithely all the while, mostly about men and the delights of loving. Finally satisfied, she stepped back to examine her work.

"Oh, you's a real beauty, Miz Dana," she declared. "Th' men are gonna go wild for you. New Aw-leans is fulla dashin' bucks, an' all of 'em are gonna be bustin' their breeches to win you."

"Nonsense."

"You got lovin' in your blood," she continued. "I can tell. You's still a virgin, still unawakened, but when you becomes a woman—oh, lawdy, Miz Dana, they ain't gonna be no stoppin' place. You's gonna have all-a th' men at your feet."

"I ain—I'm not interested in men," I said primly.

"You just *thinks* you ain't," she informed me.

I stood up, adjusting the folds of my skirt. Kayla led me out of the room and down the hall to the backstairs, which, she explained, were much handier and quicker. I was bewildered and disoriented, quite certain I would never find my way around in this large, rambling house. Downstairs we moved through a series of short, narrow hallways, finally turning under the grand staircase and arriving in the main foyer, where Delia was waiting. Kayla gave me a grin and made a pert curtsey, then scurried away.

"I do declare, that girl beats all," Delia sighed. "She's a hard worker, and she has very winning ways, but she simply refuses to learn proper decorum. Always larking about."

"She's charming," I said.

"Come, dear, Julian will join us in the dining room. Jezebel's cooked a very special meal tonight—I believe we start with buttered escargots."

"Escargots?"

"Snails, dear."

"I—I'm sorry, but I ain—I'm not eatin' no snails, ma'am."

"You'll adore them dear. Jezebel uses just a touch of garlic in the butter."

"Even so . . ."

Delia smiled and led me down a wide hall leading off the foyer and then into the dining room. The long mahogany table was draped with fine old linen and set with wonderful gold-rimmed white china and crystal glasses. Candles burned in ornate wall sconces, and massive silver pieces set on a huge mahogany sideboard, most of them in sad need of polishing, I observed. Rich dark wood covered the lower half of the walls, rather depressing faded maroon wallpaper with pink, white and brown flowers above. The chandelier hanging over the table had round and pear-shaped crystal pendants, all of them shimmering and throwing off rainbow spokes of reflected light. Like the other rooms I had seen, this one was elegant indeed but slightly worn at the edges.

Julian joined us a few moments later, sporting a new neck-cloth and looking distracted, his mind clearly on other things besides food. How handsome he was in his frock coat, his thick chestnut hair a bit rumpled, as though he had been running his fingers through it again. He remained distracted during the meal, speaking little, although he did chuckle when Delia insisted I eat a snail and showed me how to employ the tiny silver fork. Tasted surprisingly delicious, it did, particularly when you dipped it into the little dish of melted butter. The snails were followed by asparagus with hollandaise sauce and filet of sole cooked in wine, tiny green peas and baby carrots on the side.

The meal was served by a grinning Elijah, under the stern supervision of Pompey, and after dessert of cream custard with melted brown sugar sauce, an exceedingly plump Jezebel waddled in to ask if the meal had been satisfactory, although her real purpose was plainly to get a good look at me. Dressed in a voluminous purple dress, a white apron around her waist, a white bandanna atop her head, she had a round black face, a wide grin and friendly brown eyes. I liked her immediately.

"You's too skinny, chile," she told me. "We's gonna hafta fatten you up some. Leave it to Jezebel. She'll see you gets some flesh on dem bones."

Julian informed us that he had some things to attend to in his study, and he left, patting me absentmindedly on the shoulder as he passed. I was disappointed and a little hurt. It seemed that now that he had me here in the house, he had lost interest in me, although I realized I was probably being too sensitive. He had certainly stood up for me to that dreadful Lavinia and her sleek, too good-looking son.

"I suppose he's eager to sort out his specimen and get to his notes," Delia said. "He's always preoccupied when he returns from one of his trips, but I should think this time he would . . ." She shook her head, letting the rest of the sentence drift away. "We'll go to my sitting room and visit for a while, dear."

I obediently followed her down the hall again, Delia chattering about our forthcoming visit to the dressmaker Corinne, who, she assured me, would create a marvelous wardrobe for me. Her sitting room was near the back of the house, a small, comfortable room done in shades of ivory, peach and pearl-gray, the furniture French, elegantly gilded. There were several pieces of gorgeous porcelain—Sevres, she informed me, dusty, I observed—and candles burned in magnificent silver candlesticks lightly spotted with tarnish. The nap of the embroidered peach silk covering the sofa was worn, and the low table in front of it was pleasantly littered with magazines and books. I noticed these things as she led me into the room, but my attention was caught and held by the portrait hanging over the light gray mantel.

I had a curious feeling of déjà vu, although I knew for certain I had never seen the man before. He had rich chestnut hair and dark blue eyes and a full mouth held in a firm, resolute line. His face was lean with high, broad cheekbones and a perfect Roman nose. He was extremely handsome, extremely virile as well, like . . . like a younger, leaner version of Julian, I thought, although Julian could never look so stern and formidable. The artist had done a superb job in capturing those strong, chiseled features and the character behind them. One could sense strength and impatience and steely determination. The dark blue eyes seemed to stare at me with accusatory wrath, while the mouth tightened in disdain. It was a disturbing portrait yet strangely compelling, too. I couldn't seem to look away.

"My nephew Charles," Delia said lightly. "He hates that portrait, wanted to destroy it. I rescued it and brought it in here."

"It's—quite unusual," I remarked.

"Charles to the life. He's a dear, dear boy, but he can be a mite intimidating—usually unintentionally. He demands so much of himself, you see, and he expects other people to have the same drive, the same integrity."

"I—I can see the family resemblence, but—somehow he isn't like Julian."

"You'd scarcely believe they were brothers," Delia admitted. "Charles is twelve years younger, but you would think he was twelve years older. He is the guiding force, the strength. Julian is casual, compassionate, unhurried, something of a dreamer. Charles is a doer, often brusque and sometimes overbearing, though he doesn't mean to be. Do sit down, dear."

I sat down in the pearl silk chair, trying to keep my eyes averted from the portrait, but even when I wasn't looking at it I seemed to feel those eyes taking stock of me, dismissing me with cool superiority. Delia arranged herself on the sofa, looking as fragile and insubstantial as some dream creature in her lilac gown, her corona of silvery hair floating softly about her head.

"They're very close," she said.

"Julian and his brother?"

She nodded. "You wouldn't think so—they being so different. Julian respects Charles's business acumen and judgment, his ability to make decisions and his strength under pressure. Charles respects Julian's remarkable intelligence, his kind heart, gladly tolerates his charming eccentricities. Julian wasn't always so absentminded, you understand, but after the tragedy . . ." Delia again let the rest of the sentence drift away.

"Tragedy?" I prompted.

"Maryanne, his wife. She died of the fever—it must be over fifteen years ago. She was a lively, vivacious creature, full of love, full of laughter. Julian was utterly crushed. After Maryanne passed away he seemed to lose interest in everything but his plants and that book he's been compiling."

"I—I didn't know he'd ever been married," I said.

"He never talks about it. Over the years there've been other women—he's male, after all, and still in his prime—but they were merely pretty creatures to amuse himself with. He's never allowed himself to care deeply about another woman after he lost Maryanne."

That explained a great deal, I thought.

"Is his brother married?" I asked.

"Charles is devoted to the business, to restoring the family fortune. He's much too sober and serious for anything as frivolous as courtship. He's extremely eligible—Julian is, too, for that matter—and half the belles in the Quarter have tried to snare him. To no avail. When Charles needs a woman, he—I needn't go into details, dear. Certain types of women are very available in New Orleans."

In the swamp, too, I thought, recalling Jessie. Delia seemed to accept her nephews' sexual activities quite casually. Men will be men, her attitude seemed to be, so why make a fuss about it?

"Julian said his brother is in Europe," I remarked.

"There are to be several important estate sales. Charles hopes to pick up some bargains for Etienne's, and he's also exploring new markets for our cotton. I believe he'll be spending a couple of months up North when he returns from Europe. He hated to be away so long, but he felt the trip was necessary if we are to remain solvent."

Delia picked up a palmetto fan and began to fan herself, changing the subject back to Corinne and my new wardrobe, interrupting herself now and then to insert family anecdotes, her mind drifting from fabric and cut and color to memories of days gone by when Julian and Charles were boys. It really wasn't that difficult to follow her once you got used to the sudden shifts. Candles flickered, bathing the room in soft light, and all the while I was aware of that portrait, those eyes, as though there were another living presence in the room with us. It was most unsettling, and I was relieved when Delia finally suggested we retire early.

"Do you want me to show you back up to your room?" she asked.

"I think I can find my way."

"Here, take one of these candles. I'll see you in the morning, dear. We'll have a nice breakfast and then go straight to Corinne's. She'll be thrilled to create a wardrobe for someone as lovely as you.''

"I—I can't tell you what your kindness means," I said, and my voice trembled.

"Oh dear—you're not going to cry, are you?''

"I—I don't think so. It's just—no one's ever been so kind to me before and—''

I cut myself short, gnawing my lower lip.

Delia smiled, squeezed my hand tightly and led me back to the main foyer. I told her good night and started up to my room, wondering what Julian was doing, still feeling a bit neglected. Most of the candles had been extinguished, and my own flame danced, casting wavering golden patterns on the dark walls. The house was full of soft, whispering noises—the gentle flutter of drapes, the rustling of leaves from the enclosed courtyard—and there were creaks and groans as well, as though, like an aged being, it was settling down for the night.

I found my room after only one wrong turn. The yellow satin counterpane and thin yellow linen sheets had been neatly turned back. A single candle burned beside the bed. There was a carafe of water, a glass of milk, a plate of tiny iced cakes. I smiled, thinking of Jezebel and her promise to fatten me up. Removing my clothes, I placed them carefully in the wardrobe and, completely nude, slipped on the wrapper someone—Kayla?—had draped across the bed. Sipping the milk, nibbling one of the cakes, I felt I was in the middle of a dream. Four days ago I had been living in the swamp, my emotions numbed by Ma's death, Clem a constant threat, life a bleak expanse of endless days, and now here I was in New Orleans, in this marvelous old house, with people who genuinely seemed to care about me. I was still overwhelmed, still disoriented, not at all certain I wouldn't wake up to discover it was all a product of my imagination.

Removing the wrapper, slipping under the covers, I blew out the candle. The room was immediately filled with violet-black shadows that gradually lightened as moonlight sifted in hazy rays through the opened French windows. I listened to the splash-splatter-splash of water in the fountain and the raspy crickle-crackle of leaves in the breeze, and I smelled the heady perfumes of the garden. Was I awake, or was I dreaming? I closed my eyes and velvety darkness slowly engulfed me and time passed, time had no meaning, and I saw the mist and the man, and the great river was there nearby, I could hear its murmur. He came to me and looked searchingly into my eyes, and then he took my hands and squeezed them and pulled me to him, as always. That wonderful feeling began, warm and kind of itchy, and sweet, flowing through my veins, delicious, tormenting. The dream was the same, but this time I could see his face.

It was the face in the portrait in Delia's sitting room.

Chapter Seven

EVERY SINGLE CRYSTAL PENDANT of the huge chandelier glittered, sparkling with a shimmering diamond brightness, shooting off rays of rainbow color as the morning sunlight touched them. It hung at waist level, and I moved around it with a critical eye, looking for the least little smudge or speck of dust. Finding none, I nodded, and Elijah scampered away to pull the concealed rope that would lift the chandelier back up to the ceiling. I stepped back, watching it slowly rise. The pendants swayed, tinkling loudly, and I gave a little gasp as Elijah heaved too violently and the whole chandelier swung wildly, threatening to come crashing down.

"Gently!" I called. "*Care*fully!"

"Yes'um!" he shouted back.

"Fasten the rope securely!"

"Yes'um!"

Finally in place, the chandelier swayed gently for a few moments before it finally steadied and grew still. Elijah scurried back into the foyer, grinning merrily, quite pleased with himself.

"I told-ja I could do it, Miz Dana. I told-ja we didn't need Pompey helpin' us."

"You did an excellent job, Elijah. For a moment there I—I thought you were going to let it fall, but—"

"I jerked th' rope too hard," the boy confessed, "but I never let loose uh it. Tied it real right, too, with that special knot Pompey learned me."

"Taught," I corrected, "not 'learned.' "

"Taught me," he said, testing the words. "Lawdy, Miz Dana,

123

since you've been havin' all dem lessons, we's *all* gettin' smarter. Whatta ya want me to do next?"

"You can help with the rugs. They've all been carried out behind the carriage house, and I want them properly aired and dusted."

"I gets to beat 'em with dat big swatter?"

"You can take turns with Job and Elroy."

"Dem boys, dey ain't worth much, Miz Dana. Dey's older'n me, sure, but dey ain't got *der* heart in it. Shore am glad dey's just helpin' out and ain't part-a th' family."

I smiled. Elijah and the other servants were openly resentful of those we had employed to help out with the major cleaning. Jezebel refused to have them in her kitchen and resented cooking for them, and Kayla was haughty as could be when she had to deal with any of them. Pompey resented their presence most of all and resented me even more. Since I had taken over the house-keeping shortly after I arrived, he somehow felt I was trying to usurp his position. No amount of kindness on my part could make him unbend.

"You want me to carry dem cleanin' things back?" Elijah asked. "We's all finished with all th' chandyleers, ain't we?"

"This was the last," I said. I had elected to clean all the chandeliers myself, and I never wanted to polish another crystal pendant as long as I lived. "Yes, Elijah, you may take the things away, then run on out and help with the rugs."

"Yes'um."

He gathered up the bucket of suds, the rags, the polish.

"And don't get into any scraps with Job and Elroy," I warned.

"I won't, Miz Dana, but I ain't takin' no sass from 'em either."

Elijah left, and I sighed, looking around at the foyer. Everything seemed to shine, not a speck of dust in sight. The faded, mellow charm was still very much in evidence, but now the parquet floor had a rich, dark sheen, and the white paneled walls had the gleam of old satin. The graceful white spiral staircase gleamed, too, each banister individually polished, the faded pink runner covering the stairs newly cleaned and tacked back into place. I savored the smell of lemon oil and polish, and I took pride in my handiwork. The entire house had a new sparkle, and I intended to see that it stayed that way. It was the least I could do in exchange for all Julian and Delia had done for me.

"*Here* you is!" Kayla exclaimed. "I thought you was out back, supervisin' the rug cleanin'."

"I wanted to finish the chandeliers this morning."

"My, that one sure looks different. Dazzles you, it does."

"What did you want, Kayla?"

The girl made a face, looking petulant.

"Well, Miz Dana, I saw that *all* the silver was brought out and carried into the dinin' room and put on the table, just like you told me to, and I herded them girls into the dinin' room and put them to polishin', like you said, but *I* ain't supposed to help polish it. I'm supposed to supervise."

"That's right."

"That Ruby, she keeps givin' me lip. Says I can get my black ass to work, too, or she ain't polishin' a piece. I told her I was a ladies' maid and I was just supervisin' as a special favor to you 'cause you were busy elsewhere, an' I told her if she didn't watch her mouth, I'd have *her* black ass booted out without a penny of pay."

"Oh dear," I said.

"I ain't havin' any lip from th' likes of that Ruby, I can tell you right now. Trash, they is, havin' to hire out by the job. Lucky to *get* work. Me, I got my position to think of."

"Be generous, Kayla," I said, humoring her. "They're just jealous of you because—because you have such an important position with such a fine old family."

"Reckon they could be," she said thoughtfully.

"And because you're so pretty and have so many beaux," I added.

"Reckon you're right."

"You can afford to be tolerant."

"Reckon I can," she said, "but I still ain't polishin'."

"I'll speak to the girls," I promised.

"You're gonna have to speak to Jezebel, too. She's balkin' at cookin' for that lot, says she ain't got the provisions to make lunch for twelve extra niggers."

No wonder Delia couldn't handle them, I thought ruefully. They're all as temperamental as those opera singers in that novel Delia loaned me. Prima donnas? Yes, they're all prima donnas.

I went to the dining room and chatted with the girls and sat down and polished a candlestick myself and told them how grateful I was to have them helping out. When I left they were all smiling and all working industriously with nary a complaint. It was a bit more difficult to win Jezebel over. She was fussing and fuming mightily, slamming things around in the kitchen and carrying on just like one of those silly opera singers. I agreed that it was a terrible imposition on her, that it wasn't fair for her to have all this extra work and said I certainly wouldn't want her to waste her great skills on hired help. Why, simple stew and cornbread would be good enough, and I could make that myself. Jezebel said she wasn't about to let *me* get all hot and sweaty slavin' over an oven, and reluctantly agreed to make the meal.

"You're a darling, Jezebel," I told her.

"An' you thinks you is pretty smart, don't-ja, missy? Think you done hoodwinked ole Jezebel an' got th' best of her. I'se on to your tricks, an' the only reason I gives in is 'cause you is such an angel."

"I'm hardly an angel, Jezebel."

"You is, too, an' don't try to tell me different. You is still too skinny, missy, after all dis time, an' you is workin' too hard. You is supposed to be a proper young lady, learnin' things from all them tooters Mister Julian hired for you, an' you works like a nigger yourself."

"I have to make myself useful," I told her.

"You is supposed to make yourself smart, an' Mister Julian's gonna have hisself one fit when he learns you is polishin' furniture an' cleanin' window glass 'stead of readin' them books."

"Mister Julian rarely leaves his study except for meals," I reminded her, "and the house was in terrible shape. I wanted it to look—to look especially nice when his brother returns."

"An' Mister Charles is due back in just a few days, ain't he?"

"Next week," I said.

"I'se gonna hafta make some of them almond cakes he likes so well. Mister Charles—now there's a man who has a real appetite."

"What—what is he like?" I asked cautiously.

"Mister Charles? Thorny as one of them cactus plants, he can be at times, an' stubborn as a mule, but I don't take nothin' off-a him. I smacked his behind when he was a toddler, I did, and I gave him what for and chased him outta my kitchen when he was a boy. He don't fool me none with them mean looks a-his. I'se on to him, have been for a long time."

"What do you mean?"

"I knows his secret. See, *some*one has to be strong in this crazy family, someone has to keep things goin'. Mister Charles realized that a long time ago an' elected hisself to be th' one. I knows that underneath all that thorniness he's really sweet as a lamb, only he can't afford to let on. It'd be a sign of weakness."

"You—like him a great deal, don't you?"

"I loves him," she confessed, "but I wouldn't hes'tate to smack his bottom again iffen he got too smart. I'd do it, too, missy, an' he *knows* it. He don't try to 'timidate ole Jezebel, no-sir."

Jezebel dumped cornmeal into a huge bowl and added milk and eggs, beating vigorously. I longed to linger in the kitchen with its glazed redbrick floor and huge old black iron stove. Gleaming copper pots and pans hung on the wall, strings of peppers and onions and bunches of herbs hanging from the ceiling. I loved the smells and the warmth, and I loved the huge, bustling black woman who ruled her domain like a tyrannical queen.

"Won't take me no time to make th' stew," Jezebel informed me. "I gotta pan of broth already and all them meat scraps from last night. I'll add vegetables and seasonin' and water, an' that'll hafta do for them shiftless niggers you an' Miz Delia brung in. I'se fixin' a delicate lunch for you an' Miz Delia and I'se sendin' some food to Mister Julian's study, an' if he don't eat it, I'll smack *his* bottom."

"Thank you, Jezebel."

"Get on outta here now, missy. I got work to do."

Unable to resist it, I gave her a hug, folding my arms around her considerable girth and squeezing tight. Jezebel gave an exasperated sigh and pushed me away, but I could see that she was pleased. I left the kitchen and crossed the courtyard and went out back behind the carriage house to check on the boys. Heavy lines had been strung up, rugs draped over them. Elijah was busily beating one of them with a giant swatter, dust flying, while Job and Elroy brushed spots from the rugs yet to be dusted.

"I want them to hang out in the sunshine after they've all been cleaned," I told them.

"Yes, Miz Dana," Elroy said.

"And they'd better all *be* clean."

"We's doin' a good job," Job drawled.

"See that you do, and if I'm really pleased, I'll see that Jezebel makes a batch of honey cakes just for you this afternoon. Lunch will be ready in just a little while. You'll eat in the servants' hall with the others.''

Strolling back through the courtyard, I paused by the fountain for a moment to enjoy the late morning sunlight. The crepe myrtles were in full bloom, great masses of fuchsia and mauve and purple-red, and the mimosa trees made soft shadows. How peaceful it was here. How restful. I'd had precious little rest since I arrived at the Etienne mansion. Lessons, lessons and more lessons. No less than six tutors had been instructing me all these months. Professor Jobin taught me how to speak properly. Madame LeSalle gave me lessons in deportment, taught me how to walk properly, how to conduct myself at a dining table, how to act like a proper young lady. Monsieur Vidal taught me reading, although he no longer came now that I was greedily devouring several novels a week on my own, and Mademoiselle Latour had taught me penmanship, finally declaring that I had a ''lovely hand'' and required no more lessons. Dreary Mister Howard instructed me in history, geography and math—how I dreaded those sessions—and the dapper Monsieur Augustine with his pixie mannerisms and pointed goatee gave me delightful lessons in dancing, which usually ended with both of us in giggles.

The swamp and the life I had lived there seemed like a distant dream to me now. I wasn't ''educated'' yet, far from it, but I was learning, learning, learning, and I loved every minute of it besides those tedious hours with Mister Howard. I could now read any book I chose, learning new words by the score by using the dictionary whenever I was stumped, and I could write a perfectly decent letter with very few grammatical errors. I could eat an artichoke with confidence, daintily stripping off the leaves and dipping them into a dish of melted butter, and I could walk into a room with graceful poise, the very picture of a demure young maiden. I wasn't a proper young lady, of course—I could never be that with my background—but I no longer went barefooted, and I no longer spoke in a voice that made fine folk cringe.

I was still the same Dana, inside, in my heart, but I no longer resembled the awkward, ignorant little swamp girl Julian had brought to New Orleans over five months ago. I was Mademoiselle O'Malley, and Julian Etienne was my legal guardian until

I reached the age of twenty-one. His good friend Judge Emil Moreau had handled everything, even though, according to the judge, it was "highly irregular" for a bachelor gentleman to take on a female ward my age. People in the Quarter might well be scandalized, but Julian didn't give a damn. After all the papers were finalized and I was "as good as his daughter in the eyes of the law," he turned me over to Delia and the tutors, retreated to his study and promptly forgot all about me, totally immersed in his work. He had returned to the swamp twice during these past months to gather more specimen and take more notes for that bloody book. I rarely saw him except for the evening meals, for no one dared intrude on him in his study. Interrupted at his work, the usually genial and easygoing Julian had been known to snarl like a tiger and hurl heavy objects at the intruder.

He did spend one day a week at Etienne's, going over the books and checking on the business, a task he deemed "utterly bothersome and infuriating," and he longed for his brother's return. After these days we were generally treated to a long tirade at the dinner table about the arrogance and total inefficiency of his nephew, Raoul, who considered himself too good to work at the store, was rarely there and expected the other employees to cover for him while he racketed about town with his wealthy and well-born but disreputable friends or chased after the painted hussies on Rampart Street.

On those occasions when I happened to encounter him somewhere in the house during the day, Julian was friendly and made polite inquiries about my progress with the tutors, but he always seemed a bit startled to see me, as though wondering who I was and what the blazes I was doing in his house. He was wrapped up in his work, true, but no one could be *that* absentminded. He never noticed my lovely new clothes or my new social graces or the poise I had acquired, and I couldn't help but resent it. He had rescued me from the swamp and brought me to New Orleans and made me his ward, and then, for all practical purposes, simply forgot all about me.

"My dear," Delia said when I entered her sitting room a few minutes later, "this simply won't do."

After all these months, I was quite used to these statements that seemed to come out of the blue. Delia was on her chaise lounge, looking particularly fragile in a beige silk wrapper trimmed in old ivory Valenciennes lace. Her silver hair billowed about her head like a soft cloud, and there were faint mauve shadows beneath her eyes. A French novel was open on her lap, a cup of herbal tea and a plate of tiny iced cakes on the table beside her. She had been suffering from one of her headaches for two days, and I had come in to check on her.

"What won't do?" I asked.

"Look at yourself, child. You hair's all atumble and you've got a smudge of dirt on your cheek. That fetching yellow dress is deplorably soiled. I appreciate your helping out—you have *such* a way with the servants, dear, and I could never control them properly—but you're a young *lady*, and young ladies do not work alongside the nigras."

"I enjoy it," I told her. "It makes me feel useful."

"Young ladies aren't supposed to be useful, dear. They're supposed to be ornamental."

"What a silly idea," I said.

I stepped over to the mirror and saw that I did indeed look frightful. I wiped the smudge of dirt from my cheek with a handkerchief and smoothed back my hair. As always when in this room, I was acutely aware of that portrait, those strangely magnetic blue eyes that seemed to watch my every movement. I knew it was foolish and unreasonable of me to feel this way, but I couldn't help it. I turned back to Delia, trying to pretend the portrait wasn't there.

"How's your headache?" I asked.

"Better, I think. I feel so guilty, lolling about in here and letting you supervise everything. I *do* appreciate all you do, dear. I only wish you didn't feel it was necessary."

"It is," I said, "for my own well-being. I'd go mad if I just sat around being 'ornamental.' I'm used to work."

"You work hard enough at your studies."

"That's different."

"The progress you've made is amazing. You're reading book after book, raiding the shelves every week, and you have better penmanship than *I* do. Madame LeSalle says you're already more refined and have better deportment than most well-born young ladies she knows, and Monsieur Augustine says you're a natural dancer, the personification of grace."

"I stepped on his foot only last week."

"And your voice . . ."

Delia shook her head, unable to find words to express the miracle Professor Jobin had wrought. There was nothing miraculous about it. Months and months of grueling, frustrating elocution lessons had finally eliminated all traces of the swamp and the shrill screech Julian had found so distressing. I now spoke in a low, softly modulated voice Professor Jobin declared quite satisfactory, and after all this time, it came naturally. I no longer had to concentrate on my diaphragm and stomach muscles and breathing before I spoke.

"Jobin is a wizard," she declared.

"He's a cruel, unfeeling tyrant."

"He's quite pleased with you. He says you're one of the best students he's ever had."

"And what does Mister Howard say?"

"I fear he says you're a hopeless dolt, dear."

"I'm not surprised."

"You really must spend more time on your math. He says you don't even know the multiplication table yet and that your addition and subtraction is wretched. I never cared for figures myself," she added.

"I'd much rather be reading than doing those silly problems he gives me, although I don't mind coloring the maps for geography. He's terribly dull, Delia. When he teaches me history, its as dry as math, all dates and things. I find out much more about history from the novels I read. Julian says they are frivolous, but they're more interesting than the books *he* recommends."

"I should think so," she said.

"He gave me a book on plants—put me right to sleep. I struggled through it anyway, just to please him, and then he never even asked me about it."

"That's Julian, dear."

"Is he *ever* going to come out of that study?"

"He will this Friday," Delia said. "Not even Julian would dare refuse to attend the Lecombs' annual ball. It's *the* social event in the Quarter. People have been known to kill for an invitation, to commit suicide when an invitation wasn't received. Julian will grumble and complain something awful, but he'll be in his best attire and he'll be there, all right."

"Is it really so grand an occasion?"

"It's a tradition, dear. The Lecombs have been holding an

annual ball for over thirty years now—they're both creaking, I'm afraid, but still a power in society. He's from the Lyons branch of the Lecombs, a second cousin, I believe, and she was a lady-in-waiting to Marie Antoinette, barely got out of France with her head intact during the Reign of Terror, eventually emigrated to New Orleans. Of course," she continued, "the Etiennes' credentials are every bit as good as the Lecombs', if not better, though we may lack some of the glamour. Guy Etienne had already established himself here in New Orleans thirty years *before* the revolution."

"Must *I* go the ball, Delia?"

"We have to introduce you to society sometime, dear, and what better occasion than the Lecombs' ball?"

"I—I'd really rather wait a while," I protested. "A few more months. I wouldn't embarrass you then. I'd be prepared, and—"

"Nonsense. You'll do beautifully, child. In fact, I've no doubt you'll be the belle of the ball."

"I doubt that," I said dryly.

My becoming Julian's legal ward made everything perfectly respectable in Delia's eyes, and she had not given another thought to the admittedly unconventional arrangement existing here at the Etienne mansion, but I doubted that the rest of New Orleans was going to be quite so accepting. I kept remembering the thin-lipped Lavinia, her outrage, her accusations, her opinion of me, and I was willing to bet that was the opinion shared by most of the Quarter. Delia was a dear soul and something of an inno-cent, despite her casual acceptance of her nephew's peccadillos. She hadn't a mean bone in her body nór an evil thought in her mind and saw no reason why I should be the least apprehensive about meeting the cream of New Orleans society.

"You mustn't forget about Corinne's, dear," she reminded me. "You have an appointment at three for the final fitting on your ball gown. Corinne's a perfectionist, and she wants to make certain everything's just right before she delivers the gown."

"I hadn't forgotten," I said.

"It's going to be a lovely gown, dear. I can hardly wait to see you wearing it."

After lunch I checked on the various projects afoot—the boys were almost finished with the rugs, doing a fine job indeed, and half of the silver was already polished—and then I took a leisurely bath and changed into an afternoon frock of pearl-gray linen with narrow rose stripes, one of the many lovely garments Corinne had designed for me. The carriage was waiting for me in front of the house, a hastily spruced-up Elijah sitting proudly up beside the driver. He hopped down to open the door for me, handed me inside and then scrambled back up to his perch. I leaned back against the cushions as we drove away, rather tired after the morning's activities and in no mood for another tedious fitting and Corinne's vivacious chatter.

It was a warm, lovely day, hazy sunlight brushing the mellow old walls and wrought-iron lacework of the Quarter with pale gold. As the carriage drove slowly through the streets, I gazed out at those worn, gracious old houses with their courtyards and gardens, and I wondered if my grandparents and perhaps some aunts and uncles lived in one of them. I hadn't forgotten about finding my ma's folks, not for a minute, but thanks to Julian's incredible generosity, I had an opportunity to improve myself, and I knew they would be far more likely to accept me if I spoke properly and had at least a smattering of the social graces. Was I deluding myself? How could I even begin to go about locating them when I didn't even know their name, and if by chance I *did* locate them, why would they accept the bastard child of a daughter they had disowned almost twenty years ago?

I wasn't nearly as naive as I had been five months ago. I knew now that my chances of finding them were small indeed, and the chances of their welcoming me with open arms were even smaller. I didn't intend to worry about it. By an unbelievable stroke of good luck, I had a whole new life. I had a home, a guardian, people who cared about me, even if Julian was rarely out of his study long enough to show it. He *did* care, or he would never have brought me here and made me his ward. Besides, *who* I was wasn't nearly as important as what I was, and I intended to be everything he wanted me to be. I intended to make him proud, and one day, I vowed, I'd find a way to repay him for his great kindness.

We were passing the elegant shops now, and the carriage slowed down, finally stopping in front of Corinne's. Elijah leaped down to open the carriage door for me, and I smiled, resisting an impulse to pat him on the head. He was a delightful boy, good-natured and eager to please, if not always as efficient as he might be. Gathering up my skirts, I stepped out of the carriage, told the driver I would be about an hour and then went on into the shop. A bell tinkled discreetly over the door as I entered.

The spacious front room of Corinne's salon was done in shades of soft gray, sky-blue and rich sapphire, two crystal chandeliers suspended from the elaborately molded white ceiling. Up front, white shelves held bolts of cloth for customers to examine, and there was a purple velvet sofa and matching chairs where they could sit and be served coffee while studying patterns. The tasteful grandeur of the place had overwhelmed me the first time Delia had brought me here, but now I felt completely at ease. How quickly we adapt to new circumstances, I thought. Only a few months ago I wouldn't have believed so grand a place existed.

Corinne herself dashed forward to greet me, taking both my hands in hers and squeezing them exuberantly.

"Mademoiselle O'Malley! *Ma chère*, it's almost finished, merely a few minor adjustments here and there, and—I must say, it's the loveliest gown I've ever created."

"You say that about all of them."

"Ah, but this one *is*!"

Corinne released my hands and smiled that toothy smile of hers that unfortunately brought a horse to mind. Tall and skinny, with an elongated face and gray hair stacked atop her head in an untidy pile of waves constantly slipping out of place, she was nevertheless a striking figure, chic and vitality triumphing over ugliness. Her withered cheeks were generously brushed with pink rouge. Her heavy lids were coated with tan-mauve shadow. Her thin lips were painted, too, and her blue eyes sparkled vividly. In her late fifties, Corinne always wore a highnecked, longsleeved silver-gray silk dress with narrow waist and a full, crackling skirt. Long coral earrings dangled from her lobes, a matching coral brooch on her shoulder. Garrulous, vivacious, as exuberant as a child, Corinne was genuinely enthusiastic about her work and took great pleasure in creating sumptuously beautiful clothes for her exclusive clientele.

"You're looking radiant today, *ma chère*!" she exclaimed. "Oh, to be eighteen again with the world at your feet."

"The world is hardly at my feet," I pointed out.

"It soon will be," she promised. "When they see you in my new gown—you're going to create a sensation, *ma chère*!"

Corinne always spoke in superlatives, and I paid very little attention. As we started toward the fitting room, the bell over the door tinkled again and two women came in, a plump brunette in blue and a slender, attractive blonde in lime-green silk. In their early twenties, they were clearly affluent and spoiled and very conscious of their superiority, the blonde in particular. She had a haughty tilt to her chin, a petulant curl on her pink lips. Corinne left me for a moment to go speak to them, explaining that one of her assistants would help them. The young ladies were not happy about it. They stared at me with open curiosity and, at least on the blonde's part, an ill-concealed hostility. I ignored their stares, my head held high. I had as much right to be here as they did, and I was not at all intimidated by their superior airs.

"Tiresome creatures," Corinne said a few moments later, leading me on into the fitting room. "Mademoiselle Cautier, the fat one, always makes my creations look like potato sacks— she *will* go on stuffing herself with pastry—and Mademoiselle Belleau, the blonde, is the only daughter of one of the wealthiest men in the Quarter, who never pays his bills on time. She owes me for several expensive gowns and seems to think her condescending to frequent my place is payment enough."

She shook her head, gray waves slipping and spilling, coral earrings swinging to and fro.

"These aristocrats! Of course, Monsieur Etienne always pays his bills, and on time, too, but most of them—*zut*! The actresses and the ladies of the demimonde are much more reliable. They're pleasant, punctual, they pay without complaint and have much better manners than the wellborn belles."

The fitting room was large and comfortable but far less grand than the showrooms. The walls were a pale pearl-gray, a rather worn dark gray carpet covered the floor, and four big blue silk screens concealed cubicles for changing. Stepping behind one of the screens, I removed my frock and petticoat and then, wearing only a thin chemise, joined Corinne in front of the huge three-sided mirror. Two assistants, both in black silk, entered, one carrying the petticoat, one the gown Corinne had created for me.

"Exquisite!" Corinne exclaimed. "Just exquisite! Here, *ma*

chère, slip on the petticoat—eight skirts! Like butterfly wings! See how they stand out and float. Now the gown—Adele, help me with these hooks. There! Now, *ma chère*, if you will just step up onto the little stool . . ."

I obeyed and, waving the assistants away, Corinne began to pat and pull and make minor adjustments, pincushion in hand.

"Yes!" she declared. "We were quite right to select this topaz satin over the melon pink. Pink is too girlish. The topaz is—it's much more sophisticated, *ma chère*. You look gloriously grown-up, ever so provocative, and the color is perfect with your light, creamy tan, those hazel eyes and that marvelous honey-blond hair."

On her knees, Corinne stuck a final pin in the hem and then stood up to adjust the modestly low-cut bodice and fluff up the full, off-the-shoulder puffed sleeves. In the mirrors surrounding me on three sides, I watched her fluttering about like some gigantic silvery gray butterfly, and I gazed in amazement at the poised, demure young lady who stood on the low stool in the gorgeous topaz satin gown, its extremely full skirt belling out over the eight cream gauze petticoats. Can that really be me? I wondered. Corinne moved back several steps in order to properly examine her handiwork.

"Simplicity!" she enthused. "Simplicity and elegance. You, *ma chère*, have no need for fussy frills and laces and adornment. Exquisite cloth—see how it shimmers with just a hint of gold— and clean lines. Yes! We've created a masterpiece."

"It's lovely, Corinne."

"It's sheer delight working with you, *ma chère*," she confided. "That slender waist needs no whalebone stays, and that bosom—it's quite magnificent, perfect for décolletage. We've cut it just low enough to intrigue and tantalize the men without being immodest."

"I hope Julian approves," I said.

"You look like a goddess, *ma chère*. When I think of that gauche, frightened little girl Delia first brought to me—can it be only five months ago? It seems so much longer. The transformation is simply amazing."

"It took a lot of work. I'm still working."

"Monsieur Julian must be very proud of you."

"I wouldn't know. I rarely see him, and when I do, he's preoccupied with his work."

"Something about plants, isn't it? What a waste—a great big handsome male like that, loaded with charm and appeal, spending his time closed up in his study when he could be driving the ladies wild."

"I—I don't think he's interested in that," I told her.

"*Zut!* Don't you believe it for a minute."

"After his wife died he—he decided to devote all his time to his researches."

"He was crushed, poor man. I remember it well. I designed Maryanne's wedding gown—she was a vision. He was twenty-five, a charming, good-natured lad, very much in love. When she died it took him a long time to recover, and he did indeed devote himself to this plant project of his, but he did *not* lose interest in women, *ma chère*. During the past fifteen years there have been any number of little affairs—nothing serious, granted, but that's because he hasn't encountered the right woman. One of these days she'll come along and knock him off his feet and he'll forget all about flora and fauna. I know men, *ma chère*."

I didn't doubt it. In her youth, in France, she had cut quite a swath, with lovers by the score, one of whom, an older man, conveniently passed away and left her enough money to come to New Orleans and set up the business she had longed to have since her days as apprentice seamstress to a famous dressmaker in Paris. At past fittings Corinne had regaled me with chatty, amusing stories about her early days. Despite her vast experience and worldly wisdom, I still felt she was wrong about Julian and told her so.

"Ah," she said, moving behind me to unfasten the tiny, concealed hooks. "I sense something, *ma chère. You* would like to be the woman to make him forget the plants, *n'est ce pas?*"

"I—"

"You are attracted to him. It is only natural. He is a delicious man, even if he is remote and preoccupied with this silly book of his."

"He—I'm very fond of him, of course," I replied. "He's much older than I am—and he's like—like a very kind uncle."

"La!" she clacked. "Age does not matter in affairs of the heart. He is, I think, attracted to you, too, though he may not be fully aware of it. One day he will wake up and—*zut!* We will see some interesting developments."

"Nonsense," I said primly.

Corinne finished unfastening the hooks, and the bodice fell forward. I eased the sleeves down, freeing my arms.

"In the meantime," she said, "I hear the younger brother is returning home next week. *That* one—a cold fish, he is, though it has never prevented him from savoring the ladies. I dressed Lorine, the lovely quadroon he kept for a spell. Charles brought her here a number of times—dangerously, devastatingly good-looking, he was, but utterly heartless, I sensed. Poor Lorine swallowed a whole bottle of laudanum when he dumped her."

"You really are an outrageous gossip, Corinne."

"Of course, *ma chère*—one of the reasons my establishment is so popular. I am indiscreet, but never about people I like. I would never gossip about you. I won't even answer their questions."

"You-you've been questioned about me?"

"Naturally. Everyone wants to know all about this most curious arrangement. I say only that you are a very charming young girl."

"What happened to Lorine?" I asked, unable to resist it.

Corinne smiled, helping me step out of the gown. "The curiosity is stronger than the disapproval of my gossip, *n'est ce pas*? She almost died, but she recovered and eventually found another protector. Her spirit was broken, alas, and to this day she pines for the man who broke her heart."

"That's—terribly sad," I said.

"Lorine is not the only one whose heart was broken by the devilishly attractive younger brother. He has attended many a Quadroon Ball and always left with the prize beauty on his arm. He is a superb lover, one hears, but he knows nothing about *love*. No heart. When he has had his fill—*zut*! It's back to the office until he happens to feel randy again."

Corinne carefully folded the vast skirt over her arms. The topaz satin shimmered with golden highlights and made soft, rustling music. She held the gown as though it were some priceless treasure.

"It will be delivered tomorrow," she promised. "I've indicated a minor adjustment at the waist, a few stitches only, and, of course, the hem must be done. I'll put Adele on it immediately. The petticoat is perfect. You can leave it in the changing cubicle, *ma chère*."

"Thank you, Corinne."

The dressmaker left for the workroom with her precious burden, and I stepped behind the screen again. The frail cream gauze skirts billowed as I took off the petticoat and hung it carefully on a rack. I dressed slowly, thinking about what Corinne had told me about Charles Etienne. I was indeed curious about him, and I was nervous about his return. He was a total enigma. He was strong, he took the responsibility of the family business on his shoulders, the rock, the capable one who kept everything going, the patriarch at the age of twenty-nine. He was a womanizing cad, utterly heartless, according to Corinne, yet Jezebel "knew" that beneath this thorny exterior he was "sweet as a lamb" but couldn't let on lest it be taken as a sign of weakness. Hard and driven he undeniably was, but maybe it was because he *had* to be, I thought. From what I had seen of the family, keeping the Etiennes afloat and solvent couldn't be an easy task.

And now he's coming back home to find yet another person on hand, I thought, smoothing my rose-striped gray linen skirt over the ruffled white petticoat I was wearing beneath. Julian had spent an enormous amount of money here at Corinne's on my wardrobe—the ball gown alone was costing a small fortune—and none of the tutors he had hired had come cheap. Even if Charles wasn't outraged to find that his brother had become my guardian, he wasn't going to be pleased at the expenses it incurred. He had every right to resent my presence. I was a drain on the coffers, and, from all that I had gathered, the coffers were already pretty well depleted. Behind the screen, I fluffed the sleeves of my frock and rubbed my hands around the narrow waist, arranging the line.

I had had the dream again that first night in the Etienne mansion, and I had seen the man and his face, and his face was the same as that in the portrait hanging in Delia's sitting room. The feeling had been there, too, stronger than ever, delicious torment, a languorous ache in blood and bone, and I had awakened wanting something I couldn't quite define. The face had been Charles Etienne's, yes, but . . . but that meant nothing, I told myself. The portrait had made a strong impression on me, and when I went to sleep I had transposed those features on the man in the dream. I hadn't had the dream since, not in all these months, probably because my mind was so worn out each night after all the reading and studying that I dropped into a deep sleep immediately and didn't dream at all.

Running my fingers through my hair, shoving the thick waves back from my temples, I sighed and started to move around the screen when I heard rustling skirts and the hum of voices. Someone was coming into the fitting room and, for reasons I couldn't explain, I stayed where I was, concealed by the tall blue silk screen. The voices grew louder, and I leaned forward to peer through a tiny slit where two sections of the screen joined together. The plump brunette in blue and the tall blonde in lime-green I had seen earlier came on into the room, the brunette holding a red velvet gown and in a state of moral outrage.

"—shocking that she would allow a creature like that to come here and mingle with respectable people," she declared in a girlish voice. The words were slurred together with a thick southern accent. "Why, my daddy'd have a *fit* if he knew I was even in the same *room* with someone like her."

"Your daddy sends all his mistresses here," the blonde replied. Her voice was a cool, lazy drawl, considerably more cultivated. "It's a wonder we haven't run into one of them."

"They couldn't be as bad as her, Regina. Daddy's very discreet. He doesn't bring his women into his own *house* like Julian Etienne. I'm shocked that Corinne would agree to dress that—I forget her name."

"They call her Dana," Regina drawled, "and everything's quite respectable, Bertha. He *adopted* her, at least made her his ward. I should think it might set a whole new trend. Whenever one of our men find a pretty slut they want to fuck, they simply go to Judge Moreau and become her guardian—saves the expense of setting her up in an apartment."

I was shocked to hear that word on the lips of a young woman who was supposedly well-bred, and I was stunned at the implication she had made. I stood there behind the screen, numb, a cold rage slowly mounting.

"Do you really think she's pretty?" Bertha asked.

"Passable, I suppose. Some of those buffalo gals *do* have nice features."

"Buffalo gals? You mean—"

"She's bound to have nigra blood with that complexion of hers."

"I wouldn't call her *dark*," Bertha said, "but she does have a large mouth. That makes it even worse! Poor Lavinia—she's absolutely distraught, has been ever since that creature arrived, and Magdelon is so humiliated she's ashamed to show her face in public.''

"So that's why I haven't seen Magdelon lately? I just assumed Reginald Vandercamp had gotten her pregnant. They've been screwing in his aunt's gazebo ever since April.''

"Reggie has moved to Memphis. Magdelon's been seeing Pierre Dorsay.''

"I wish her luck,'' Regina said. "He gets it up at the drop of a hat, gets it off before a girl even gets started. A great lay he isn't.''

"He's gorgeous. *I* wouldn't mind trying him.''

"You'd try anything, pet. Not that you get that many offers. If your daddy weren't so wealthy, you'd still be a virgin.''

"You're wicked, Regina!''

"I wonder what Magdelon's brother is up to these days. Raoul Etienne is undoubtedly the most exciting man in the Quarter. I'd give a pretty penny to have *his* shoes under my bed.''

"There's not much chance of it,'' Bertha said snidely. "Raoul likes a *challenge*, not a pushover.''

Why, they're no better than the girls in the swamp, I thought, trying to control my anger. Bloodline and background and money don't mean a thing. They've got the morals of alley cats, and they say nasty things about *me*. I may come from the swamp, may have fed chickens and pigs and gone without shoes, but I'm as good as those two strumpets any day of the week. My anger under control now, I walked from behind the screen and glanced at them with cool hauteur. Bertha blushed furiously. Regina turned pale, and then her green eyes began to flash angrily.

"I suppose you've been eavesdropping!'' she snapped.

"I haven't been eavesdropping,'' I said politely, "but I couldn't help hearing what you said.''

"You heard—''

"I heard enough to know that you're a malicious shrew with the instincts and appetites of the basest whore.''

Bertha gasped. Regina turned even paler, trembling with outrage.

"Why—why, you filthy little slut. How dare you speak to me like that! How dare you speak to me at *all*!''

I looked at her ashen cheeks and her blazing eyes and then

walked calmly toward the door. Regina spluttered. Bertha's cheeks were still a fiery pink. At the door I turned and gave them another frosty glance.

"I don't intend to stand for this!" Regina cried. "I don't intend to let a piece of trash from the swamp call *me* names!"

"I would tell you to go get laid," I said sweetly, "but you'll undoubtedly do that anyway."

Regina was shocked speechless. Bertha was leaning against the wall, clutching the red velvet gown she had yet to try on. I gave the two ladies a polite nod and left the establishment with perfect poise. You really *have* changed, I told myself. Five months ago you'd have gone after them with claws unsheathed. Apparently everyone in the Quarter was talking about me. I was a shameless creature from the swamp who probably had Negro blood as well. Tongues would wag even more after today. Let them. I had nothing to be ashamed of, and I vowed I was going to make Julian very proud. People could talk all they liked. I was going to show them exactly what being a lady was all about.

Chapter Eight

I LOOKED AT THE ELEGANT CREATURE IN THE MIRROR, and I saw a little girl with a dirty face and tangled honey-blond hair, wearing a ragged pink dress. I felt a tremulous feeling inside, remembering, trying to forget. It seemed I could hear the chickens and smell the pigsty and I saw Ma's face and heard her soft voice and I thrust the memory aside. The pain was still too great. The dirty little girl shimmered in the glass, vanishing, gone now, and I coolly inspected the woman in the sumptuous topaz satin gown. I couldn't believe she was real, much less that she was me. She was indeed elegant, the gorgeous gown complimenting her creamy tan complexion, short puffed sleeves worn off the shoulder, bodice cut low enough to reveal the full swell of bosom, waist snug, the skirt spreading out luxuriantly over the underskirts.

Kayla had performed miracles with my hair, pulling it back sleekly like a tight cap, leaving three long sausage ringlets to dangle on the right, just below my temple. Above the ringlets she had affixed the lovely creation Corinne had designed especially for me, three short cream-colored ostrich feathers fastened to a cream velvet bow. Instead of standing up, the feathers curled delicately around the right side of my head. It was a gorgeous creation that went beautifully with the satin gown and long velvet gloves. At Kayla's insistence I had applied a bit of rouge to my lips, just slightly darkening their natural pink, and I had used a bit of blush, which emphasized my high cheekbones and, on my lids, a faint golden-brown shadow. The makeup was subtle and merely highlighted my own coloring, but I felt it made me look older and far more sophisticated. Why, I could pass for twenty or twenty-one, I thought.

"I cain't believe it, Miz Dana," Kayla declared, looking at me with something like awe. "I just cain't believe it's *you*."

"Thank you," I said.

"Oh, I didn't mean you ain't always fetchin', but tonight—tonight you's downright dazzlin'. I ain't never seen any gal so beautiful, and I ain't joshin'. I 'spect it has somethin' to do with th' way I done your hair."

"I 'spect it does. You did a marvelous job, Kayla, even if it did take a good two hours."

Kayla beamed and continued to chatter about my hair and my gown and what a sensation I was going to cause, and I took a deep breath and willed myself not to scream. All day long I had kept my nerves at bay, convincing myself that I wasn't at all nervous, but now as the time drew near for me to go downstairs, to leave for the ball, I could feel panic mounting inside. I am not afraid of those people, I told myself. I am every bit as good as they are, and I intend to hold my head high and be cool and polite and gracious, no matter what. They can stare and whisper all they like, but it won't bother me in the least. I'm not going to *let* it bother me. I know that none of those things they are saying about me are true and . . . and I don't care what they think.

"—when they sees you tonight, them handsome young gents're gonna all be flockin' round. You's gonna have so many beaux we won't be able to *count* 'em all."

"I doubt that, Kayla," I said.

"An' one of 'em will sweep you off your feet. That's how it happens. Me, I've been swept off my feet so many times I's still dizzy. Ain't nothin' like it."

I took a deep breath and made a final adjustment of the sleeves, the panic jangling inside. Kayla seemed to sense the way I felt. She looked at me with warm brown eyes full of understanding and genuine affection.

"Don't you worry none, Miz Dana," she told me. "They's just people like you an' me. They ain't gonna *eat* you."

"Maybe they'll just tear me from limb to limb."

"They's gonna *love* you."

"Don't count on it," I told her.

I seemed to be numb as I started down the hall, the full satin skirt making rustling music. I had the feeling I was on my way to face a firing squad, and I wasn't at all sure I wouldn't prefer that to going to the ball and being on display all evening. Was I showing too much bosom? Was I wearing too much makeup? The woman in the looking glass was beautiful—I couldn't deny that—elegant, too, and superbly composed, but that was all an act. I had acquired polish and poise, but inside I was still Dana and—I might as well admit it—absolutely terrified. You can whistle in the dark all you like, but the terror is still there.

I moved slowly down the gracefully curving white staircase, my hand resting on the smooth banister. Hearing voices below, I paused, peering down into the foyer. Julian and Delia were waiting for me, Julian looking wonderfully handsome in beautifully tailored black breeches and frock coat. His shirtfront gleamed white, his white silk neckcloth perfectly arranged. In her pale opal satin gown, with her silver cloud of hair, Delia looked like some fragile porcelain figurine.

"Do stop grumbling, Julian. You know you can't miss the Lecombs' ball, so be a *man* about it."

"I'd rather be drawn and quartered."

"You haven't been out of the house even once since you got back from your last trip to the swamp. You can't spend your entire life shut up in your study. It'll do you good to see people."

"They bore the bejesus out of me. Idle, narrow-minded men, haughty matrons, impudent young rakes, flirtatious, empty-headed belles—all of 'em ever so superior. The Creole aristocracy!"

"They're our people, Julian, and they're not all like that. Do try to be civil tonight, and please, dear, for my sake, don't start babbling about plants and things. No one's interested."

"They're not interested in anything but bloodlines and the next party and their tawdry little love affairs."

"That's not so, dear, and you know it. You *are* a grouch tonight. I wish Charles were here. He might not en*joy* these gatherings, but at least he doesn't carry on like a spoiled child and make everyone else miserable. I for one intend to have a marvelous evening."

"It's almost eight. Where's that blasted girl?"

That blasted girl? I felt my cheeks flush. I swept on down the stairs, skirts swaying. Delia gave me a warm smile. Knowing I had overheard, Julian looked sheepish, and then, when he had had a good look at me, looked completely stunned.

"Jesus," he whispered.

"I'm sorry if I've detained you," I said coldly.

"You haven't, dear," Delia assured me.

"What have you *done* to yourself?"

"Done?"

"You look—you look—"

"She looks enchanting, Julian."

"That child I brought back from the swamp—"

"I'm not a child! I haven't been for some time."

"There's no need to get snippy. I merely meant—My God, you're—maybe it's the gown. How much did it cost me, by the way?"

"Plenty," I retorted.

Julian looked amused. I glared at him, still offended by his referring to me as "that blasted girl." I longed to tell him exactly what I thought of him, longed, in fact, to give him a sharp kick in the shin, but I was a proper young lady now and proper young ladies didn't do such things. Being "civilized" definitely had its disadvantages.

"The surface is smoother," he said, "but the spirit is still there. Why haven't I noticed these changes before?"

"You've been too bloody busy with your blasted book," I snapped, and that particular sentence was quite a test of my newly acquired vocal skills. Professor Jobin would have been proud of me.

"It's amazing," Julian said thoughtfully. "I could swear the last time I saw you you still had a dirty face and pigtails."

"I never had pigtails!"

"And now—lo and behold, you stand before me the very epitome of gracious young womanhood. You're cool, refined, beautifully poised, although I fear you're as lippy as ever, even if the sound is more soothing. All those tutors putting me into the poorhouse have apparently done an excellent job."

"Dana has worked very hard," Delia said.

"I certainly have."

"Can you read and write now?"

"I read all the books I can—" Seeing his grin, I cut myself short. "You're teasing me!"

"It's a deplorable habit I have," he confessed.

"I even read that horribly long book you gave me—all about the evolution of ferns and the sex life of hydrangeas."

"Oh? How did you find it?"

"Tedious. I prefer Balzac and George Sand."

Julian elevated one eyebrow. "Balzac? George Sand? I see Delia's influence at work. Looks like I'm going to have to start supervising your reading. I didn't spend all that money on tutors so that you can fill your head with the plots of frivolous French novels."

"They're quite educational," I informed him. "I've learned a lot."

"About the wrong subjects," he countered. "Well, ladies, shall we depart for the ball? Unless, of course, you'd rather skip it? I'd just as soon start making up that reading list—"

"We'll depart," Delia said firmly.

Julian grinned again, looking positively jovial now. He linked his arm in hers and hooked his other arm around my shoulders and led us out to the waiting carriage, a disapproving Pompey holding the front door open for us. I was very aware of his arm on my bare flesh. It rested heavily, warm, pulling me closer, giving me a delicious feeling of security. He looked down at me, eyes full of warmth, and I wondered how I could ever have harbored nasty thoughts about him. I felt a wonderful glow inside. Affection? Gratitude? Something more? I was disappointed when he removed his arm to help Delia into the carriage. When she was settled in, he took my hand and performed the same service for me, settling me on the seat opposite her. I smoothed my skirts down, and he climbed inside, plopping down beside me and closing the door. He was so large, and although he appeared indolent and low-keyed, he had such great vitality.

"So," he said as the carriage pulled away, "your first ball. How do you feel?"

"Terrified," I admitted.

"No need for you to be," he said. "They're just a group of silly, boring people who happen to believe they're better than anyone else in the city—or in the country, for that matter."

"You're being very unfair, Julian," Delia scolded. "*We* happen to be part of that group."

"More's the pity."

"It's called reverse snobbery," Delia explained to me. "Julian disdains them and, therefore, feels superior to the people *he* thinks feel superior to everyone else. . . ." She hesitated, frowning. "Does that make sense?"

"None whatsoever," Julian said.

"I'm sure I know what I meant to say, but somehow it—you've confused me, Julian. I intend to ignore you for the rest of the evening."

Julian chuckled and patted my arm, settling back against the cushions, taking up more than his share of room. The carriage moved slowly through the labyrinth of streets. It was a lovely evening, pleasantly warm, the air perfumed as always by the multitude of flowers growing behind mellow brick walls. The Quarter was cloaked in a hazy violet-black darkness and awash with silver moonlight. We rode on in silence, and I could feel panic rising anew as we slowed down even more, falling into a line of carriages that were entering an enormous courtyard, stopping in front of a gracious portico.

"Actually the Lecombs' house isn't any larger than ours," Delia said. "It is similar in layout and design, but they have reception rooms and a huge ballroom where our east wing would be."

The line of carriages creeped forward at a snail's pace. We finally turned through a pair of crumbling stone portals and stopped on the semicircular drive to wait for the three carriages in front of us to unload their passengers. Julian gave a weary sigh and sat up straight, smoothing the lapels of his frock coat and looking very resigned. We inched forward a few more yards. Delia brushed at her pale opal skirt. I felt numb with apprehension. Sensing this, Julian took my hand, squeezing it so tightly I winced. In a matter of moments we had pulled up before the portico and the carriage door was being opened by a Negro footman. Julian scrambled out and helped us alight, and our carriage moved on as we started up the wide steps toward the front door.

"You'll find the Lecombs rather unusual," Delia confided to me. "They're quite charming, but he, alas, is somewhat hard of hearing, and she, poor dear, has never gotten over being part of the French court—she still dresses in the mode of Marie Antoinette, complete with wide paneled skirts and towering, befeathered headdresses."

"They're both barmy," Julian said.

Delia gave him a warning look as we entered a huge foyer done all in shades of pale blue and white. I could hear music and voices coming from another part of the house. I felt icy cold. I felt my feet would not work. Another Negro footman greeted us and led us down a long corridor, and my feet were working and I was perfectly poised and I didn't turn and run, I didn't faint. The music and sound of voices grew louder, and then we entered a large, lovely reception room. Gold gilt patterns adorned the white walls. Three huge crystal chandeliers hung from the molded ceiling. The room was filled with gorgeously attired people who chattered and laughed and then suddenly they were no longer chattering, no longer laughing. They were whispering, staring. The music continued to swell, coming from the adjoining ballroom. I heard a loud, shocked gasp and saw Julian's Aunt Lavinia across the room beside her son Raoul and a lovely, haughty young woman I assumed was his sister Magdelon. An eternity seemed to pass, but actually it was only a few seconds, and then people began to talk again, in lower voices, staring more discreetly now, pretending not to. Julian missed not a beat, leading Delia and me over to the bizarre couple who were greeting their guests.

The old man was gray-haired and stooped and held an enormous ear trumpet to his ear. He wore a brown velvet frock coat and a white satin waistcoat embroidered with silver thread. He was nodding happily and seemed about to break into a lively jig. The woman beside him was much taller and had a haunted, withered face heavily coated with powder and paint, a heart-shaped black beauty mark pasted on one cheekbone. She wore a strange silver and white gown with a skirt that spread out a yard on either side of her waist, parting in front to show off the ruffled gold underskirt. Atop her head stood a powdered white wig with a pompadour that towered two feet high, white and gold feathers pinned to one side with a dazzling diamond clasp. Diamonds sparkled at her throat and on her wrists as well, and several strands of pearls adorned the bodice of her peculiar gown.

"Dipped," Delia confided in a whisper, "and the gems are paste."

"Julian!" Monsieur Lecomb shouted in a hoarse croak. "You look more like your father every time I see you."

"Thank you, sir. I take that as a compliment. You know my Aunt Delia, of course, and allow me to present my ward, Mademoiselle Dana O'Malley."

"Card?" he shouted. "Card, you say?" He adjusted his ear trumpet. "Present your card if you like, but I'd much rather meet this ravishing creature you brought with you."

Julian presented me again and Monsieur Lecomb cackled and said I was indeed a card and asked if I was a relation of some kind and Julian gave up and said he was happy to be here and left Delia to deal with our host. From across the room Lavinia was giving us outraged looks while whispering furiously to her daughter. Julian presented me to Madame Lecomb who smiled a sweet, tremulous smile and examined me with misty blue eyes that were kind and sad. I had the feeling Madame Lecomb lived in a vague, hazy world neither past nor present. A delicate frown creased her brow as she continued to examine me.

"It's so pleasant to see you again—but, no—you remind me of—I must be thinking about—please forgive me."

She looked both pained and embarrassed. There was something very touching about this outlandishly dressed old woman with her heavily painted face and tremulous smile.

"I'm delighted to be here tonight, Madame Lecomb," I said quietly.

"It's been much too long," she said. "I haven't seen your parents for a while, either. Are they here tonight?"

"I—I'm afraid not," I told her.

"Do give them my best. Enjoy yourself, child."

Julian took my elbow and led me aside, explaining that our hostess was frequently confused. People were still staring, still whispering, and, with a mischievous gleam in his eye, Julian took me over to where the outraged Lavinia was standing with her two children. The color drained from her face. She was wearing a black silk gown and a ruby necklace. Her daughter wore peach-colored satin. With her lustrous black hair and large brown eyes, Magdelon was lovely indeed, if glacial at the moment. In his formal attire, her brother was as sleek and handsome as I remembered, an amused smile on his lips as we approached.

"Aunt Lavinia!" Julian said cheerily. "Fancy seeing you first thing! Let me introduce my ward, Dana O'Malley. Dana, this is my Aunt Lavinia, of whom you have heard so much, and her children Raoul and Magdelon."

"How *dare* you!" Lavinia whispered hoarsely. "How dare you humiliate the family this way!"

She gave him a venomous look that would have reduced a lesser man to ashes. Julian merely smiled. Magdelon might have been carved from ice. She stared at me with pure, unadulterated hatred. I remembered what Regina had said about her and Reginald Vandercamp, and I suspected that she knew I knew about those trysts in his aunt's gazebo. Her nostrils flared. She longed to scratch my eyes out. Spoiled, petulant, sexually promiscuous, this haughty young woman certainly wasn't *my* superior. I smiled and gave her a polite nod that caused her nostrils to flare even more. Livid, she turned to her mother.

"Let's leave at once, Mother," she said frostily. "I will not be in the same house as this trollop. I told you what she said to Bertha and Regina. I'm not going to—"

"Hold on, Magdelon," Raoul said mildly.

"I would love to leave," Lavinia said, "but we must remember who we are, Magdelon. We must maintain a front. I hope you're satisfied, Julian. I hope you realize you've affronted everyone in the Quarter with this—this outrage to decency."

"Lavinia, dear," said Delia, who, having stopped to speak to a friend, had just joined us. "How lovely to see you."

"You're in this, too! I'll never forgive either of you!"

Lavinia took her daughter's arm and the two of them marched away toward the ballroom, chins atilt, skirts arustle. The amused smile still played on Raoul's beautifully chiseled lips. He shook his head and explained that his mother had been under considerable strain recently, apologizing for her conduct. It was in his best interest to stay on Julian's good side, I thought. He kissed Delia on the cheek, shook Julian's hand and then gazed at me with velvety brown eyes that could easily make many women grow weak at the knees. Tall, lean, glossy, he was undeniably handsome, spectacularly so, with tremendous allure. I could feel the pull of that allure, even if I failed to respond to it.

"We meet at last," he said in that husky, melodious voice. "I've heard an awful lot about you."

"I feel sure you have," I replied.

Raoul chuckled softly. It was a very sensual sound. "She's enchanting, Julian," he said "and not at all what I expected."

And what did you expect? I asked silently. He turned to me, another smile curving on those full lips that seemed even pinker because of his deep tan. His brown eyes seemed to glow, seemed to promise future delights. Oh yes, he was a womanizer. He exuded sensuality and animal magnetism, and I could see why women vied for his attention.

"I suppose I should call you 'Cousin,' " he said.

"Cousin?"

"You're Julian's ward. He is my cousin. So, in a sense, you're my cousin, too. Once or twice removed. What *shall* I call you?"

"Mademoiselle O'Malley will do nicely," I said.

That amused him. He chuckled again and turned back to Julian.

"I'd better go see about Mother," he said. "I look forward to seeing you all later on."

He nodded to us all and strolled away in a loose, confident stride, looking as though he owned the place, I thought. "Insufferable young ass!" Julian muttered. Delia shushed him, then went over to speak to a friend who had just arrived. Julian sighed and took my arm, leading me on into the ballroom. People were watching us. I held my head high, pretending not to notice. The ballroom was wondrous to behold with a huge, gleaming golden oak dance floor and pale yellow walls with delicate panels adorned in gold gilt designs. Six glorious crystal chandeliers hung from the domed white ceiling, and all around the floor were bowers of yellow and white roses with gilt chairs and small tables for guests to use. To the left was a bank of French windows opening onto the large courtyard, and to the right were doors leading into another large reception room where buffet and bar had been set up. Long drapes of thin yellow silk hung at the opened French windows, billowing gently to and fro, and the musicians were concealed behind yet another bower of roses at the end of the ballroom. The dance floor was aswirl with couples moving gracefully to the melodic strains.

"Impressed?" Julian asked me.

"It—it's like something out of one of those novels. It's like— like being inside a jewel box."

Those guests not dancing were sitting at the tables or moving about, visiting, chatting, drinking champagne. I saw Raoul surrounded by a bevy of admiring young belles in lovely pastel gowns. Magdelon was dancing with a tall, redheaded youth, and Lavinia was sitting at one of the tables, looking quite distraught as she spilled out her woes to a plump matron in purple silk who patted her hand in commiseration.

"Feeling better now?" Julian inquired.

"A—a little, I suppose."

At least there wasn't a mass exodus when I arrived, I added to myself.

"You handled yourself beautifully," he told me. "Perfect

poise. The little girl from the swamp has come a remarkably long way in a very short time.''

''I may have been ragged,'' I retorted, ''and I may have spoken with a terrible accent, but my—my ma was gentry, and she brought me up properly. I was never the—the ignorant urchin you seem to think I was.''

''There's no need to be so defensive. I was merely trying to pay you a compliment. Apparently I'm out of practice.''

''Apparently you are.''

''My, we're very testy.''

''We—we're just very nervous,'' I said.

Julian smiled. It was such a lovely smile. It was like sunshine, full of warmth. I *had* been defensive, but I was indeed very nervous. His smile helped. What did it matter what any of these people thought? What did it matter if they continued to stare discreetly? Julian was beside me, large and strong and handsome, and no harm could come to me.

''Sorry about Lavinia and Magdelon,'' he said. ''Who, incidentally are Bertha and Regina and what *did* you say to them?''

I told him about the encounter at Corinne's, eliminating only those details about his cousin Magdelon and her lovers, and Julian chuckled as I repeated that parting remark of mine. The music continued to swirl, lovely and melodic, as he led me over to one of the tables. The scent of the roses was heady, blending in with the smell of candle wax and powder and, already, the musty odor of perspiration.

''I suppose I shouldn't have said it,'' I told him. ''I'm sure it's all over the Quarter by now.''

''Undoubtedly. You're an original, my dear, and considerably more interesting and amusing than any of these simpering society belles.''

''Is that another compliment?''

He nodded, smiling again. Goodness, he was actually being gallant, in his way. Was it my gown? Was it the ever so subtle makeup? I felt a curious exhilaration as he helped me into one of the gilt chairs and let his hand linger a moment on my bare shoulder. I loved that faint suggestion of a double chin, the full curve of his lower lip. I loved the mischief and amusement that danced in those warm brown eyes. There were dozens of handsome young men in the ballroom tonight, a few, like Raoul, dazzling indeed, but none was as handsome, as virile, as this genial, oft absentminded man who had given me a new life.

"Champagne?" he inquired.

"Do you think I dare?"

He chuckled, remembering that night in the swamp when I had been very under the influence after drinking the wine he produced. That seemed a lifetime ago. Julian signaled to one of the liveried Negro footmen and plucked two glasses of champagne from the tray he was carrying. Delia entered the ballroom with two elderly ladies, all three of them talking at once. She waved gaily as she sauntered to a table across the way with her friends. I sipped the champagne, relaxing a little, though still acutely aware of the attention we were receiving from the other guests.

"They keep staring," I said. "They pretend not to, but—"

"The men in particular," Julian observed. "You're quite the loveliest woman here tonight—bar none."

"If you continue with these compliments, I fear it'll go to my head."

"I'll keep you in line," he promised. "I can't understand it. Last time I looked you were a wretched waif with a clacking voice, then suddenly—voilà! Confounding, to say the least."

"You don't like me this way?"

"On the contrary, I find you distressingly enchanting."

"Distressingly?"

"Drink your champagne, Dana," he ordered.

I smiled to myself, feeling a particularly feminine triumph. Julian took a sip of his champagne and sat back in his chair, looking around with lazy contentment. Although he had vehemently protested coming, I could tell that he was enjoying himself. He nodded occasionally to friends of his, but none of them came over to the table to visit. I knew the reason why, of course. Julian looked at me. He seemed to be reading my mind.

"They'll come round eventually," he said. "Maybe not tonight, but eventually they'll see we have nothing to hide, and— all this talk will end."

"You knew they were going to stare and whisper, didn't you?"

"Of course. I fully expected it. I knew it would be rather uncomfortable for you, but—it was important we come tonight."

"To *show* them we have nothing to hide."

"Precisely. Not that I give a damn what they say, but I have the family to think about."

"I've caused you an awful lot of problems, haven't I?"

He nodded. "I should have dumped you out of the canoe and let the alligators get you, but, being the idiot I am, I decided not to. Now, alas, it looks like I'm stuck with you."

"Looks like you are," I said. "Thank you, Julian. Thank you for—everything. You—if it hadn't been for you—"

My voice trembled. He gave me an exasperated look.

"If you cry," he said, "I fully intend to spank you."

"You probably would, too."

"Unquestionably."

He grinned and finished his champagne. The music stopped for a moment, and the dancers applauded politely. A few of them left the floor, moving toward the tables and the reception room where food was being served, but most of them waited for the music to begin again, which it did almost immediately, slow, lilting, lovely. I saw Regina dancing with a tall, handsome blond youth. She was wearing a gorgeous pink satin gown trimmed with white lace, a large pink-white camellia in her hair. She saw me, too, and shot me a venomous look. I nodded politely as she swirled past. Julian arched an inquiring brow.

"Regina Belleau," I said. "The girl I didn't tell to go get laid."

Bertha was on the dance floor, too, looking even plumper in mauve satin and dancing with a dashing red-haired youth. I longed to dance myself, to swirl and sway to that enchanting melody. Monsieur Augustine and I had executed our steps to the flat, tinny notes banged out by the pianist who accompanied him, but this music was so rich, so fulsome, it would catch you up and propel you along. Julian must have seen the longing in my eyes, for he gave a resigned sigh and got to his feet.

"I suppose," he said, "I really should see if all the money I've been paying that fop Augustine has been well invested."

"I suppose you should," I agreed.

"I'm rather out of practice," he confessed, "but—we'll see if Augustine has done his job."

He took my hand and led me onto the floor and curled his arm loosely around my waist and, I swear, whispered one-two-three under his breath and then twirled me around and we were moving to the music. It seemed to possess me, and my body melted and moved to the melody, held back only by Julian's grip on me. Were he to release me, I felt I would soar and spin like a butterfly, completely carried away. He was not nearly as good a dancer as Monsieur Augustine. He was not, in fact, any good at all, executing each step cumbersomely and by rote and frequently losing count even then.

"I told you I was out of practice," he said.

"That's all right."

"You dance divinely, though."

"Ouch!"

"Sorry. Did it hurt?"

"I think you crushed a couple of toes, but I'll survive."

"Dancing's not my specialty."

"Don't keep talking, Julian. You'll lose count again."

"Lippy minx."

"One-two-three, one-two-three, turn, begin again. One-two-three—"

"I *should* have let the alligators get you."

He grinned and tightened his arm around my waist, pulling me closer, and we moved around the floor without crashing into anyone and his ineptness didn't matter at all. It was wonderful to be held so closely, to feel his strength, to be led around the floor, however inexpertly. I felt a curious delight, a delicious sensation welling up inside me, and it continued to glow even when he stepped on my foot again. When, finally, the music ceased and he led me off the floor, the exhilaration was still there. Julian took me into the reception room, and we had our plates filled with beautiful food and went back to our table. The aspic was wonderful, the lobster salad divine, and the tiny pastries filled with meat were absolutely marvelous

"I've never had such food," I said.

"The Lecombs always put on a lavish spread," Julian informed me. "They've got the best cook in the city."

"I liked them a lot. She—Madame Lecomb apparently thought I was someone else, someone she knew."

"The old dear's daft. So's her husband. They're still a power in the Quarter, though. She actually helped Marie Antoinette into her laces and velvet, and unloosened her stays when that royal personage had had too much cake. You can't get much more exalted than that."

"Poor Marie Antoinette. I read a novel about her only last week."

"One of Delia's infernal romances, no doubt. I'm glad to see you reading, though, even if it is historical romance."

"I can't get enough of it," I confessed. "Reading, I mean. It's like I step into a whole new world with every book I read. Each time I finish one book, I'm eager to begin another immediately."

"I *will* have to do a bit of supervision. Madame Campan's memoirs, for example, are far more interesting than any novel about the unfortunate Antoinette. She was First Lady-in-Waiting and the queen's intimate friend. Her memoirs are full of fascinating details about daily life at the court."

"I'd love to read them."

"We've got them at home, I'm sure."

"How is *your* book coming along?" I inquired.

"Rather well, actually," he told me. "During these past five months I've completed the entire text and now I'm working on the footnotes—they're hellishly difficult, but I should be done in a few more months. After all of these years, all those hundreds of thousands of notes, I've finally managed to put it all together."

"I had no idea you were actually—writing. Delia said—"

"Delia has always considered my work a rather amusing hobby—as, indeed, does everyone else. Absentminded old Julian, trekking through the swamps, taking notes, picking plants, scribbling, scribbling. No one ever believed I'd actually *do* anything with all that material I've been compiling. When my book is printed, they'll see."

"I think it's wonderful, Julian."

"It's going to be splendid. I've been in touch with an engraver who's going to do the plates. He'll reproduce all my paintings— in full color, too. Frightfully complicated process, frightfully expensive as well, but I want this book to be a *land*mark."

"Like Audubon's bird book," I said.

Julian looked surprised. "You remembered. Yes, I want this to do for native flora and fauna what Audubon's book did for ornithology. I want to make a contribution, Dana. I want to—"

He cut himself short and gave me a little smile. "No wonder people think I'm barmy. Here I sit with my lovely young ward on the night of her very first ball and what do I do? I bore her to death with dreary talk about a dreary project that couldn't possibly interest her in the least.''

"I'm not bored at all!" I protested. "I think it's fascinating."

"You're very kind, but—you're eighteen years old. You should be enjoying yourself."

"I heartily agree," Raoul said.

Immersed in talk, neither of us had noticed him approaching our table. He gave Julian a patronizing smile and turned to me with a gleam in those dark, attractive eyes. He looked for all the world like one of the heroes in those novels I'd been consuming so avidly: smooth, elegant, wickedly handsome.

"I saw you dancing earlier," he said. "You deserve a partner who can show you off properly."

"Not a doddering middle-aged man," Julian added.

Raoul smiled again, not denying the implication. "Come, Cousin," he said to me, "honor me with this dance."

"I—"

"Go ahead, Dana," Julian told me. "I'll just sit here nursing my arthritic old bones. Maybe someone will bring a rug to put over my knees."

I hesitated. I really did long to dance again, even if it was with Raoul, but I didn't want Julian to think . . . He saw my hesitation, laughed and got to his feet.

"Dance," he said. "It'll give me an opportunity to talk with a couple of my old cronies who are, I'm sure, dying to learn all about the cross-pollination of wild orchids."

He patted my arm and sauntered off, and Raoul swept me onto the floor, holding me firmly, whirling me into the dance. It was a lively, melodic waltz, and I really did seem to soar this time, so caught up by the music it seemed to be a part of me. Raoul was a superb dancer, strong, energetic and masterful yet moving with a lithe, athletic grace it was impossible not to respond to. I matched my movements to his, forgetting my dislike of him, forgetting everything but the sheer bliss of the dance.

"You've caused quite a sensation," Raoul informed me when the music finally stopped.

"Oh?"

"All my friends are fascinated. They've bombarded me with questions about you."

"Indeed?"

"They think you're positively enchanting, the most beautiful creature they have ever seen. They all want to meet you. Ah, here comes Zack—I figured he would be the first to break the ranks.''

A robust, healthy-looking youth with floppy blond hair and twinkling brown eyes approached us across the crowded dance floor. He was quite attractive with that wide grin playing on his lips, and he looked resplendent in his formal attire. Raoul greeted him with a grin of his own and introduced us. People were watching, one young lady in particular. Her eyes blazed with fury as the youth executed a cocky bow and gazed at me with unabashed admiration.

''And what do you want, Rambeaux?'' Raoul inquired.

''I wanna dance with this little lady. You don't mind, do you? I mean, I wouldn't wanna encroach on someone else's territory.''

''The territory's wide open, but you'll have to ask my cousin. I'm not her keeper, alas.''

I ignored the double entendres, all innocence. The clothes were much finer, the manners smoother, the accents much more refined, but I had been dealing with bucks like these since I was thirteen. Zackery Rambeaux asked if he could have the next dance and I smiled demurely and said I would be delighted and the music started again and we danced and he wooed me with his eyes and with pretty words and asked me if I would like to go riding with him and I politely refused and he looked quite surprised, obviously accustomed to having any girl he wanted at the snap of his fingers.

I smiled to myself as Zack retreated, quickly replaced by the dashing red-haired youth I had seen dancing earlier with Bertha. He introduced himself and said he'd been admiring me all evening and told me he would blow his brains out if I refused him the next dance. I said I certainly wouldn't want to be responsible for such a violent demise, and he chuckled and gave me a sleepy, seductive look and pulled me into his arms and, as we danced, wooed me even more ardently than Zack had. He had his own boat, a dandy little craft, and he would love to show it to me, maybe we could sail up the river and dock in a delightful little spot he knew, real private, and I sweetly informed him that I always grew dreadfully sick on boats. He looked nonplussed, and, across the room, plump Bertha looked positively livid, fanning herself viciously and speaking emphatically to the befrilled belle standing beside her. I was clearly not making a great many friends tonight.

I was enjoying myself immensely. It seemed I was very much in demand, and during the next hour and a half I must have danced with over a dozen of Raoul's friends, including Pierre Dorsay who, I knew, was currently seeing Magdelon and, according to Regina, got it up at the drop of a hat and a great lay was not. I could attest to the first part, for he was holding me much too close, and I had no doubt about the rest. Pierre told me he was an amateur wrestler and said he would like to show me a few holds. In a voice like honey, I suggested he get a certain hold on himself. The youth actually blushed, literally fleeing as the music stopped. That was very naughty of you, Dana, I told myself, but I hadn't been able to resist it. I was still smiling at his dismay as Raoul came up to me again.

"You're the belle of the ball," he said. "No question about it. You've got them all clamoring for you."

"And all their girlfriends ready to hack me to pieces. Your sister looks as though she'd love to drive a knife through my heart."

"Does that bother you?"

I thought for a moment. "Not really," I replied.

"I imagine you could hold your own," he said.

"I rather imagine I could."

I felt a curious sense of power. It was extremely flattering to be showered with such attention by all these attractive young bucks, even though I was fully aware of what they thought of me and what they wanted, and it was satisfying, too, to feel I had somehow bested the snobbish Regina and her like. I had no illusions about the reasons for my success, but the success was genuine nevertheless. I had done my reputation no good—my detractors must hate me even more now—but I was indeed the belle of the ball.

"May I have this next dance?" Raoul inquired.

"I'm really rather tired," I said, "and I should get back to Julian. He must think I've abandoned him."

"Cousin Julian hasn't missed you at all," he informed me.

He nodded toward the other side of the room, and I saw Julian sitting at a table with two older gentlemen, all three of them deeply immersed in an intense and rather heated conversation. Julian nodded his head emphatically and raised his hand to make a point, undoubtedly discussing his favorite subject and clearly having a wonderful time. He was certainly not pining for my company. Raoul smiled and lightly gripped my elbow.

"You do look a bit tired, Cousin, and it's rather warm in here. Why don't we step out into the courtyard for a few minutes."

I looked into his eyes, quite sure of myself and not the least bit worried by this smooth, glossily handsome, arrogant young buck. I had cut my eyeeteeth on men far more dangerous than Raoul Etienne could ever be, and I could certainly handle myself. The little wildcat was still very much alive beneath the demure, ladylike new facade.

"Very well," I said. "I could use some fresh air."

The courtyard was awash with silver moonlight and full of velvety shadows, and the night air was cool, scented with all those perfumes that made this part of New Orleans so enchanting. I sighed, reveling in the touch of the cool air on my cheeks and bare arms and shoulders. Leaves rustled all around us in the gentle breeze and water made soft splattering noises as it spilled from tier to tier in the fountains. I felt a glowing elation inside, scarcely aware of Raoul's presence at my side. It was wonderful to be young and alive, to be wearing a lovely gown, to be pleasantly weary after dancing with a bevy of healthy, attentive youths.

"Pleased with yourself?" Raoul inquired.

"Very," I said.

"You've certainly proved something tonight."

"And what would that be?"

"You've proved that you could have any man you wanted."

His voice was husky and melodious, a beautiful voice, persuasive and quite seductive. Raoul knew that. He was all too aware of his remarkable good looks and his virile allure. That very awareness negated both in my eyes. I for one was not going to swoon and melt into his arms. The very thought of it brought a smile to my lips.

"It's true," he murmured. "Any man you wanted—"

"But I don't want any of them," I said.

"I find that hard to believe."

"I know this will undoubtedly come as a shock to you, Cousin, but I couldn't care less what you believe."

Raoul chuckled quietly, enjoying the fencing match, convinced it would ultimately end in triumph. I imagined there weren't many young women who failed to respond to that potent allure. We strolled beneath a tall magnolia tree and paused beside one of the ornate fountains. The music began again inside, drifting out into the courtyard in muted, melodic waves. It was supremely romantic, and I felt a yearning inside me, a taut, not unpleasant ache, but it wasn't for this man who gazed at me with dark, glowing eyes, his handsome face sculpted in silver and shadow.

"Yes," he said, "Cousin Julian has done very well for himself. It surprised the hell out of me. A man his age winning a trophy like you—it defies all logic."

"You think so."

"You could do much, much better," he crooned. "He's twice your age. His hair is graying. He's overweight. He's a lethargic, ineffectual dreamer without a shred of backbone."

"If you lived to be a hundred," I said coldly, "you'd never be half the man Julian is, and—I'm not anyone's trophy. Despite what you and the rest of them might think, Julian is my guardian, nothing more."

He smiled, clearly not believing me. He moved closer, his eyelids drooping heavily, his chiseled lips half-parted. I stood quite still, knowing what was to come, braced for it. When his hands rested on my bare shoulders, I spoke in a voice like chipped ice.

"Don't, Raoul."

"You need a man," he murmured, "a real man—someone worthy of that incredible body. The moment I laid eyes on you I knew I had to have you. I knew we were destined for each other."

"Don't," I repeated.

"I'll set you up in the finest apartment. You'll have servants, clothes, a carriage all your own. You'll have everything you could possibly want—and bliss, Dana, such bliss. I'm going to make you feel things you never imagined it possible to feel—"

He pulled me to him and curled his arms tightly around me and held me very close and covered my mouth with his own, his lips firm and warm, pressing, probing, demanding. Sensations exploded inside me despite myself, for I was human, and I was hungry, too, so hungry. The sensations swelled, urging me to yield, to respond, and I stiffened myself, trying to pull away. Raoul moaned deep in his throat, pulling me even closer, crushing me against him. I caught his hair in my hands and tugged at his head, but my struggles seemed only to spur him on more. I didn't want to do what I knew I had to do but after a few more moments I knew I had no choice. I let go of his hair. I placed my palms flat against his thighs and shoved, lifting my knee at the same time, lifting it swiftly and with considerable force.

He released me abruptly. He stumbled back, doubling over, gasping. His face was ashen with pain, locks of hair spilling over his forehead. I smoothed my skirt down, cool, calm, thoroughly poised.

"You—you—"

"You're lucky I didn't scratch your eyes out as well."

"You—"

He stumbled back another step and lost his balance, plopping down onto the outer rim of the fountain. He groaned, trying to sit up, unable to manage it. He leaned forward, resting his hands on his knees, grimacing as the pain continued to agonize him. He didn't look polished and glossy and arrogant now. He looked very young, like the petulant boy he was. As the music wafted out into the courtyard in melodic waves, as moonlight gilded shrubbery with soft silver, I felt utter disdain for this spoiled, pampered, dissolute youth who thought he and his kind owned the earth.

"You'll live," I told him.

"You little whore—" he whispered.

I brushed my skirt and adjusted one of my sleeves. The music stopped, replaced by polite applause and subdued chatter. Raoul looked up at me, his face sculpted in silver, etched in pain. Locks still splayed over his forehead, and his dark eyes were aglow with venom.

"You little whore," he repeated, and his voice was a hoarse croak. "You're going to regret this. I swear it. If it's the last thing I do, I intend to see that you—"

He groaned again, unable to continue. He brushed the locks from his forehead and closed his eyes, pressing his lips tightly together. He was in great pain, but I'd done no permanent damage. The wanton belles and women of Rampart Street need fear no loss of attention. He'd be right as rain ere long, if considerably uncomfortable. He opened his eyes, looking at me again. I had never seen such concentrated venom, such hatred.

"No woman has ever—"

"This one just did," I told him.

"You're going to pay—I swear it."

"Thank you for the dance, Cousin Raoul," I said sweetly.

I went back inside. It would be some time before Raoul would be in shape to face his friends. His threat bothered me not in the least. What was he going to do, ruin my reputation? I didn't intend to say anything to anyone about the incident, and I seriously doubted that Raoul would either. He would hardly want his cronies to know he'd been so thoroughly rejected by his cousin's swamp girl mistress. And I realized that was exactly what they all thought I was. I moved across the dance floor past couples patiently waiting for the music to begin anew, and they shunned me, turning away, pretending not to see me. It hurt deeply. I wanted to cry. I wouldn't. I was too proud. To hell with them. I held my head high, forcing a pleasant smile onto my lips.

I reached the tables across the room. I didn't see Julian anywhere. The music began again. Couples began to sway and swirl, a shifting kaleidoscope of color under the golden glow of candlelight, and I waited beside the table Julian and I had occupied earlier, smiling still, and everything seemed to blur. I was much more upset than I cared to admit. The smile, the cool poise, were pure pretense. An eternity seemed to pass, and I stood there in my elegant gown and fancy coiffure and tried to look like I belonged, though I realized now I never would, never could.

"Here you are, dear," Delia exclaimed.

She took my hand, smiling, so warm, so genuine. Thank God for Delia.

"I—I didn't see you," I said.

"I've been looking all over the place for you, dear," she told me. "Julian has bored everyone he could buttonhole with dreary talk about pollen and petals and such and no one else will listen to him. He's growing restive."

"Oh?"

"It *is* late, dear, and—I may as well confess it, I'm beginning to feel my age. I hate to drag you away when you've having such a grand time, but—"

"I'm a bit weary myself," I said.

"Then you don't mind leaving?"

"Not at all."

We joined Julian in the foyer, where he was chatting with the Lecombs. We made our farewells, and I thanked them both for a lovely evening. The old woman in her outdated gown and preposterous hairstyle gazed at me with perplexed eyes, frowning, as though trying to place me, then shook my hand and told me to be sure and give Mathilde her best. Who was Mathilde? Madame Lecomb lived in a foggy haze of past and present and obviously believed I was someone else. Ostrich plumes waving, she nodded and turned to speak to Delia. Julian took my arm and led me outside. He had already called for our carriage, and it was waiting for us in front of the portico.

"It was ever so nice to catch up on all the news," Delia said as we drove away. "Julian, dear, did you know that Natalie Aumont's little daughter Alicia married one of the Martineau boys from St. Louis? You remember Alicia, surely? She and her cousin Celeste used to—"

"Delia, my love, it would be virtually impossible for me to care less than I do now about little Alicia Aumont, or her cousin Celeste, either. Wretchedly insipid creatures, I seem to recall."

"Lottie Devereaux told me that Cerise is having trouble with her gall bladder. Cerise is her daughter, you know, fifty-five if she's a day, a spinster, alas—that dreadful Randall boy left her waiting at the altar lo those many years ago—and Lottie's *got* to be over eighty. Still as bossy as ever. Still as large, too. I *don't* know how she gets around—"

"Delia," Julian said patiently.

"You're not interested, dear."

"You're right, my love."

"You've no manners whatsoever, Julian. No consideration for your elders, either. You can put everyone to sleep with interminable talk about *your* favorite subject—and no one cares, dear, I may as well enlighten you—but when someone else wants to discuss—"

Julian sighed wearily, looking quite sulky, and Delia sighed, too, shaking her head in fond disgust. Delia might scold and nag and sweetly put him in his place, but she clearly believed her large, often lethargic nephew hung the moon and would have gone to the stake in his defense. He gave her hand a little pat and she smiled in contentment.

"It *was* a successful evening, though," she observed. "Particularly for you, Dana dear. Why—you danced and danced. There wasn't another girl there who received such a rush.''

I made no comment. Delia brushed her pale opal satin skirt, giving another sigh.

"A pity Charles couldn't have come home a few days earlier. He'll be sorry he missed it.''

"Charles thinks just about as much of these affairs as I do," Julian told her.

"Dear, you *do* know how to put a damper on things. I really can't imagine how I've managed to abide you all these years.''

Julian grinned and gave her hand another pat. When we arrived home, Delia stiffled a yawn, declared she could hardly keep her eyes open and, after giving us both a hug, wandered off to her room. Julian and I stood in the foyer, soft candlelight bathing the walls. He looked slightly rumpled, his handsome black frock coat creased, his white silk neckcloth askew, but he had never looked any more appealing. His hair gleamed rich and dark in the candlelight, a bit unruly now, and a faint, thoughtful smile curled on his lips as he gazed down at me with those warm brown eyes.

"Tired?" he asked.

I nodded.

"I'm not surprised. You did receive quite a rush tonight. Oh yes, I saw, even if I was busy talking. Every randy young buck at the ball had to have his turn with you. I suppose they all made advances?''

I nodded again.

"Young scoundrels! Any of them start trying to hang around you, I'll take a horsewhip to him.''

"Would you?"

"Believe it."

"Most of them are quite eligible," I informed him. "Almost any one would be considered a fine catch.''

"It isn't marriage they're interested in," he informed me.

I smiled. "I know," I said.

"Did any of them make—"

"They all extended invitations. You'll be happy to know I refused all of them.''

"Good," he said gruffly.

I smiled again, feeling unreasonably pleased. Could he possibly be jealous of all the attention I had received? Could he possibly be seeing me as the woman I was instead of the girl he believed me to be? I looked at him and felt warm, wonderful feelings inside and longed to touch his cheek and have him fold me in his arms. I didn't know if it was merely affection or gratitude or something altogether different, but the urges I felt were extremely hard to resist. Looking into his eyes, I sensed he felt similar urges and was finding them just as difficult to control.

"I—I'd better get to bed," I said.

"I'll walk you to your room."

There was a husky catch in his voice I hadn't noticed before. He took my elbow and guided me slowly up the stairs. My skirt rustled quietly in the silence. Julian sighed when we reached the landing and casually slipped his arm around my waist. Only a few candles were burning in the wall sconces, and they cast flickering gold patterns that only intensified the shadows. I was acutely aware of his strong arm holding me, of the bulk of him beside me, the warmth of his body, his smell. I felt weak, and my feet hardly seemed able to work properly. I was glad of the support of that arm.

"Here," he said, stopping in front of my door.

"I—I really am tired," I murmured. "I suppose it was all that dancing, or—or maybe it was the champagne."

Julian released me. I stood with my back to the door and Julian stood in front of me. So close. So large. So warm. I loved him, but I wasn't sure of the nature of that love. There was so much hunger inside me, so many feelings pent up and longing for release. Raoul had aroused them, even Raoul, whom I detested. Julian looked at me with dark eyes full of affection . . . or was it something else?

"I've been neglecting you," he drawled.

"Neglecting me?"

"So bloody wrapped up in my work I haven't paid the least bit of attention to—to the changes going on right under my eyes."

"Changes?"

"You've developed into a—into a very lovely young woman."

"Thank you, Julian."

"I'm very proud of you," he said.

"I—I'm glad."

"Very proud," he repeated.

I leaned against the door, feeling weak and confused, waiting. The house was so silent, so still. Everything seemed to be suspended. Several long moments passed as he continued to look into my eyes, his own glowing darkly, full of conflict now. He reached for me, his big hands curling around my upper arms and drawing me to him. He started to say something, hesitated, frowned, and my knees trembled. Our eyes held for perhaps a moment more, his frown deepening, and then Julian shook his head.

He released me. He kissed me on the brow.

"Good night, Dana," he said quietly.

He turned then and walked down the hall, and I listened to the sound of his footsteps, leaning back against the door, too weak to turn the doorknob and go inside. The sound receded and finally there was silence again, broken only by the rapid beating of my heart. I closed my eyes, the prey of a dozen different emotions. I heard a door shutting in the distance as Julian went into his bedroom, but it was a long time before I stepped into my own.

Chapter Nine

DELIA WAS IN A FLUTTER. It wasn't often that she went out socially, and having lunch with her friend Natalie Aumont was a big occasion. Several other ladies were going to be there as well and they would spend a delightful afternoon continuing the gossip-fest begun at the ball three nights ago. Wearing a gown of watered gray silk accentuated with mauve silk bows, she fussed and fidgeted as the carriage was brought round. Where was her mauve silk reticule? Should she carry her smelling salts? Really, it was just too much trouble, she would stay home. It was going to rain, anyway. I fetched her reticule and saw to it that her smelling salts were put in and told her that she was going to have a wonderful time. Delia sighed, lifted her eyes heavenward and wrapped a purple lace shawl around her arms, informing me that she had no idea when she would be back but it was bound to be late.

"When those old biddies start telling family tales and tearing reputations asunder, there's no stopping them."

"And you'll love every minute of it," I told her.

"Of course *I* never gossip, but I may as well confess it, I do love listening. It's so amusing. And what are you going to do today, dear?"

"I've no lessons, thank goodness. Mister Howard has taken ill and won't be coming to drill me in math. I thought I might explore the east wing. I'd like to see those Boulle cabinets you told me about."

"They're covered with dustcloths, alas, along with everything else."

"Julian said there were two Fragonards, a Watteau, too, I believe."

"Shrouded in sheets. They'd fetch a fortune at Etienne's, but they've been in the family for decades and I wouldn't allow Charles to take them to the shop. One has to hold on to something."

"I'm very eager to see them."

"You've taken an immense interest in such things." Delia remarked, fussing with her shawl. "You already know more about furniture and paintings and porcelain—the things we sell at Etienne's—than most people I know. You've spent hours poring over those weighty old volumes, studying the plates. Raoul couldn't tell the difference between a Sevres vase and a Meissen if his life depended on it, and he *works* at the shop."

"When there isn't something better to do," I said dryly.

"I fear Raoul isn't the most reliable employee—Julian's always in a rage about it—but he *is* family. We can hardly toss him out on his ear, although I must admit Charles has been tempted to do just that any number of times."

"I'd love to see the shop sometime," I confessed.

"Yes," she said vaguely. "Perhaps Charles can show it to you when he returns. Oh dear, here's Pompey. Is the carriage waiting? It is? This is a bad idea—I'm beginning to get one of my headaches. Do I look all right, dear?"

"You look enchanting, Delia."

"At least I've kept my *waist*line, which is more than I can say for the rest of them. They *do* envy me for it. Have a pleasant time, dear." she said as I stepped out onto the portico with her, "and don't get too dusty. Gracious! It *is* going to rain—look how dark the sky is. I'd better not go."

"You wouldn't miss it for the earth," I told her.

Delia denied it vehemently, and she made protesting noises as Pompey opened the carriage door, but her step was as light as a girl's as she climbed into the carriage and she couldn't quite conceal her excitement. Eager to feast on macaroons and the gossip she adored, she gave me a merry wave as the carriage pulled away. I lingered on the front steps a few moments, looking at the sky. It was indeed dark, an ugly pewter-gray tinged with purple and heavily laden with swollen rain clouds, but nothing short of a hurricane could have deterred Delia from her visit. Thunder rumbled in the distance as I stepped back inside. Kayla met me at the foot of the stairs, an exasperated expression on her face.

"Jezebel's havin' another one of her spells," she told me. "She's already broken a cup and two plates and chunked a perfectly good rice pudding out of the back window."

"Whatever set her off?"

"You all," Kayla informed me. "She had a lovely lunch planned for today, clear soup, lobster salad, them little finger sandwiches Miz Delia likes so much an' first Miz Delia tells her *she* won't be lunchin' today an' then Mister Julian goes gallivantin' off an' says *he* won't be lunchin' either, an' Jezebel says you don't eat enough to keep a bird alive."

"Lord," I said.

"The rice pudding was gonna be you all's dessert," Kayla added.

"I guess I'll have to go speak to her."

"Guess so. Me, I ain't goin' near the kitchen till she simmers down."

"You—you say Mister Julian went out?"

Kayla nodded. "He said he was goin' to go talk to some printer man about plates, though what a printer'd know about plates beats me. Said he'd probably be gone all day as they were going to test inks or somethin'. First time he's left his study in months."

"It would be a wonderful opportunity for us to clean it."

"No, ma'am. Mister Julian don't want *no* one in his study *no* time. If even a paper's outta place he throws a tantrum."

I didn't doubt it, but I longed to snoop about nevertheless. Good judgment prevailed, however, and I bypassed Julian's study and went into the kitchen to pacify the distraught Jezebel. I assured her that she was the best cook in the city and said that Miss Delia wouldn't be having anything nearly as delicious as her lobster salad and finger sandwiches and added that Julian would be terribly upset when he discovered he'd missed her famous rice pudding. Jezebel calmed down considerably but wouldn't let me leave the kitchen until I had eaten a luncheon large enough to satisfy any field hand.

It finally began to rain as I started to the east wing, huge drops pelting down on me as I crossed the courtyard. I darted under the overhanging gallery and unlocked the French doors with the key Delia had given me earlier. As I opened them, there was a loud blast of thunder, a blinding flash of lightning, and the rain began in earnest, splashing noisily on the tiles in the courtyard, pounding on plants and leaves. Closing the doors behind me, I gazed around at the gloom, hardly knowing where to begin. Everything was murky and gray, dustcloths covering the furniture and making ghostly shapes that seemed to hover in the semidarkness, ready to leap on the unwary. I had recently read one of Mrs. Ann Radcliffe's scary gothic novels, but I wasn't at all unnerved. Spooks and goblins held no terror for me, never had.

I found a candelabra under one of the dustcloths, several candle stubs in the holders, and once I had lighted these a golden glow slowly began to diffuse the gloom. There was dust everywhere, cobwebs in profusion and the unmistakable smell of mildew. I'll have to get a fleet of servants in here, I thought. Closed up or no, the east wing should be thoroughly cleaned and the dustcloths washed. Some of the furniture under them was undoubtedly valuable and shouldn't be allowed to ruin for lack of polish. I welcomed the idea of the project. It would give me something to occupy myself with besides reading and the interminable lessons, and it would also help keep my mind off other things.

I had hardly seen Julian since he said good night to me at my bedroom door. He had been closed up in his study during the day, and during the evening meals he had been preoccupied and distracted, paying no attention to Delia or me, returning to his study as soon as dessert was finished. I sensed that it was deliberate. I sensed that he had been as disturbed by those few minutes in front of the door as I had myself. During the meal last night, as Delia chattered on about nothing in particular, I had looked up from my plate to find him studying me intently, his brown eyes bothered. He looked away quickly and I gave no indication that I had noticed, but I felt certain I knew what was bothering him—the same thing that was bothering me.

Holding the candelabra high, I started down the hall toward the small parlor where, I knew, the Watteau and one of the Boulle cabinets were kept. Shadows flickered on the walls, and the sound of the pouring rain echoed strangely here inside, creating a muted, monotonous background. Cobwebs floated from the ceiling like ghostly silken threads. The sour smell of mildew and dust was almost overwhelming. Yes, I would have to get the servants in here. It was in a shocking condition. Good hard physical work would help me sort things out in my mind.

Julian was an extremely attractive man, warm and appealing, and I did love him. There could be no denying that. I loved him, but . . . but did I really want to sleep with him? Was it that kind of love? No, I decided. I was eighteen years old and I knew the facts of life and knew about the needs blossoming inside me, but Julian wasn't the one to relieve them. I admired him, respected him, wanted to please him and make him proud of me, but, even though I might be attracted to him in a purely physical sense, I didn't want things to change. I wanted to love him as I loved him now, as my savior, as my mentor, as the man I could always rely on for warmth and wry teasing and protection. That would all change were I to become his mistress.

And Julian . . . He had considered me a child, had treated me as he might treat a bothersome, amusing kitten. This had irritated me, and from the first I had endeavored to make him see me as a woman. Three nights ago, I had finally had my wish . . . only to discover that it really wasn't what I wanted at all. I felt I had unleashed something that could easily get out of control. Julian saw me as a woman now, all right, a highly desirable woman, and it was going to be difficult to keep things the way they had been. There was a new tension between us. Never again would there be that playful badinage, that give and take such fun for both of us. The jaunty camaraderie was gone, I knew. Never again would either of us be completely at ease with the other.

It was all so bewildering and confusing, and it was all my fault. It was as though . . . as though I had been carelessly playing with some weapon I wasn't even aware of as such. Now I had spoiled things and upset Julian and made him feel things he didn't want to feel, couldn't help feeling now. Maybe they were right after all. Maybe I really was wicked. I loved Julian in a special way, would always love him, and I wouldn't have him hurt for the world. Where would it all end? I had a lot of thinking to do and, I realized, several decisions I must make. Time. I needed time, but right now I just wanted to put it out of my mind.

Finally reaching the parlor Delia had described to me, I set the candelabra down in the center of the dusty hardwood floor. The carpets had been rolled up and stored away, I was glad to see, but a set of heavy golden brocade drapes hung over the small room's one set of windows. Clouds of dust flew in the air when I pushed the drapes apart, revealing a set of deplorably dirty French windows overlooking the narrow strip of garden and high stone wall on this side of the property. It was raining furiously, waves of it slashing against the windows, and the constant flashes of lightning made the candelabra almost superfluous.

I waved my hand in front of me, coughing at the dust and thankful I had on the simple pink and tan striped cotton frock instead of something nicer. I was already dusty, my face undoubtedly smudged, and the rain had done little to lessen the sultry heat. I could feel the perspiration running down my spine and moistening my armpits. Oh well, it made no matter. No one was going to see me. I began taking off the once white cloths, causing more clouds of dust to fly in the air. Maybe I wouldn't have to worry at all, I thought wryly as the dust billowed around me. Maybe I would simply die of asphyxiation here in the east wing. When the dust finally settled, I gazed around at the pieces I had uncovered and, oh yes, they were superb, much too lovely, much too valuable, to be drying up and gathering dust in this abandoned room.

There was a lovely, delicate sofa of intricately carved rosewood, upholstered in faded wine-colored brocade richly embroidered in a deeper wine. Running my hand along the top, I saw the royal sunflower motif carved in the wood and knew from my studies that the sofa must be Louis XIV. The rich red-brown gloss of the varnish was there beneath the dust, begging for polish. I longed to give it the attention it needed here and now. Beside it stood a small table, also of rosewood, inlaid with floral patterns in different woods and lavishly festooned with brass garlands, sadly tarnished now. Although I couldn't properly date it, I guessed that it was Louis XIV, too. And there across the room was the Boulle cabinet, incredibly beautiful with its intricate brown and gold marquetry and its smooth, graceful lines. From my reading I knew Boulle had died in 1732, and his pieces had never been equaled in beauty and craftsmanship.

I got down onto my knees to examine the cabinet more closely, running the palm of my hand over the satin-smooth curves of wood, banishing the thick layers of dust, and so rich was the patina beneath that it seemed to catch all of the candlelight and reflect it from within. The cabinet was banded and ornamented with thin, delicate strips of metal engraved with tiny flowers, and the metal was gold, I realized. Neglected though it had been, the gold dim with dust, the rich woods thirsty for proper oils, the cabinet was still even more beautiful than any of those I had seen pictured in the book I had studied. It might have belonged to a king, I thought. Imagine growing up with things like this in the house.

Standing up, massaging the small of my back, I caught a glimpse of myself in the blurred, murky glass of the tall, oval-shaped standing mirror I had uncovered as well. The mirror stood in a carved rosewood frame embellished with garlands of brass flowers. The glass was indeed murky, speckled with spots as well, but in the glow of the candlelight I could see the reflection of a slender young woman with dust-smudged cheek and thick, honey-blond hair that tumbled to her shoulders in unruly waves. I ran my fingers through the waves and brushed the dust smudge from my cheek. My pink and tan striped frock was dusty, too, and there were perspiration stains as well. I pulled at the off-the-shoulder puffed sleeves and adjusted the rather low-cut bodice that emphasized my too full bosom. Corinne claimed it was a great asset that should be shown off to advantage, but I still longed for less in that particular area.

Sighing, I shoved an errant wave from my temple and examined the sadly faded gold and ivory damask that covered the walls. It was tattered in places, and cobwebs festooned the corners. How lovely the room must have been at one time. There, over the soot-stained white marble fireplace, hung what must be the Watteau, shrouded with a dust-layered sheet. Flashes of lightning illuminated the room as I pulled the sheet off, and there was a great rumble of thunder that seemed to shake the house. Sheets of rain still slashed against the windows and gave no signs of lessening. I prayed it would be over by the time Delia was ready to return, and then I gave my attention to the painting in its ornate and flaking gold gilt frame, setting the candelabra up on the mantel to provide more light.

It was gorgeous, the rich colors still aglow after all these years. Sitting on what appeared to be a stump, against a background of green-gold forest and vivid blue sky, a young woman in eighteenth-century attire gazed pensively into space, eyelids lowered, a faint smile on her lips. Slender and graceful, she had rich chestnut hair worn in the elaborate coiffure of the time, and her half-veiled eyes were a deep violet-blue. Her gown was of gleaming ivory brocade lavishly adorned with beige lace ruffles and small gold velvet bows. The tip of one beige satin slipper was visible beneath the voluminous skirts, part of her beige lace underskirt showing, and in her lap she held a delicate ivory silk fan with gold patterns. The painter had captured not only a person but a mood as well, and I knew that the pensive young woman must be thinking about a young man who was, perhaps, betrothed to another.

I knew very little about painting, only what I had picked up from reading those heavy art volumes in the library and studying the plates, but I did know this painting was superb, if not a masterpiece at least a perfect example of a master's work. The blue sky shimmered with sunlight, the green-gold treetops feathery and full, seeming to to stir, while hazy violet-brown shadows spread beneath them, making patterns on the grass. The young woman was alive, so real I could read her mind, feel what she was feeling. I gazed at her in the flickering glow of the candlelight, wondering if she had lost her young man, if she had finally found happiness. Several long moments passed, and I began to have the curious feeling that someone was studying *me* as intently as I was studying the portrait. The feeling persisted, quite unsettling. I could almost feel a pair of eyes boring into my back.

I whirled around. I gave a little gasp. He was standing in the doorway, one hand resting on the frame, the other resting on his thigh, and the doorway was hazy with shadow and he was little more than a tall, lean silhouette dimly seen against the gray. My heart began to pound. There were no ghosts in the east wing, and I didn't believe in ghosts anyway. The man continued to stand there, filling the doorway, and then he straightened up and walked on into the room, stepping into the circle of light spread by the candles. My heart continued to pound. He continued to study me, taking in every detail, making no effort to conceal his disapproval and disdain, and after a moment he looked up at the portrait.

"She was my grandmother," he said.

"You—you're Charles," I whispered.

"And you are the young woman I've been hearing so much about from my Aunt Lavinia—and others."

His voice was a lazy drawl. His manner was calm, deliberate. His very dark blue eyes were cool, his wide, beautifully shaped mouth was held in a stern line. He was like a younger, leaner version of Julian in many ways, the Etienne features clearly pronounced, but he wasn't at all like his older brother. No warmth, no humor softened those perfectly chiseled features. He was a hard man, and I sensed he could be utterly ruthless if the need arose. Not as glossily handsome as his cousin Raoul, he was even more attractive, mature and virile. The skin was stretched tautly across his high, broad cheekbones, and his lower lip was full and sensual. His rich chestnut hair was slightly damp, and I realized he must have dashed across the courtyard to get here.

"You weren't supposed to be here until day after tomorrow," I said, and I was horrified to discover that my voice trembled.

"My ship docked this morning, two days early."

"I see."

"I stopped by the shop, then came home to discover that both Delia and my brother were out. Pompey informed me that you were prowling about here in the east wing, so I came on over."

"How long were—were you standing there?"

"Long enough," he said.

He was wearing brown boots, snug tan breeches and a thin white lawn shirt damp from rain. As tall as Julian, with slender waist and broad shoulders, he had a lean, powerful build with superb musculature. That body might have been sculpted by Michelangelo, I thought, remembering the plates I had seen in one of the art books. Charles Etienne was a gorgeous male with a commanding presence and, as well, potent sexual magnetism that was like a palpable force. I was acutely aware of that force, and my knees seemed to grow weak. Few women would even try to resist a man like this one, I thought, and I was scandalized by the sensations stirring inside me at the mere sight of him.

"What are you doing in the east wing?" he asked.

"I—I wanted to see the Boulle cabinets and the Watteau. Julian told me there are two Fragonards as well."

"You're interested in valuable things, then?"

I caught the implication immediately. "No," I said coldly. "I'm interested in beautiful things. There's a difference."

He nodded, as though acknowledging my score, and then he looked around at the things I had uncovered. "Christ, I haven't seen this stuff in years. I'd forgotten all about that cabinet."

"It's far too lovely, far too precious, to be gathering dust in this abandoned room. It needs to be hand-rubbed with polish, and the gold bands should be cleaned.''

''You're right. It would fetch a princely sum at Etienne's.''

''You—surely you wouldn't sell it?''

''I'd sell it in a minute—all the rest of this stuff as well—if I didn't think Delia would have a heart attack.''

''Even the Watteau?''

''Even the Watteau. Sentiment is all well and good, but money in the bank is far more reliable. Our family account was pitifully low when I left . . .'' He gave me a long, meaningful look. ''I imagine it's considerably lower now.''

I knew what he was implying, and I could feel my spine stiffen. He moved over to the mantel to examine the portrait more closely, his back to me. The damp cloth of his shirt clung loosely to his back and shoulders, and his chestnut hair gleamed darkly in the candlelight, several wet tendrils curling up at the back of his neck. The room seemed suddenly much smaller, the rain seemed louder, and I felt as though my knees might give way at any moment. Never had I felt this kind of physical longing for any man, an urgent ache inside, and I found it intensely unsettling, frightening as well. He turned around, folding his arms across his chest.

''Lavinia wrote to me about you,'' he said.

''I know she did.''

''She wrote me several letters, in fact—keeping me abreast of the situation.''

''Giving you her version of it.''

''My first impulse was to grab the first ship home, but common sense told me Julian was far too sensible to do anything really disastrous. I was wrong, as it turned out. Lavinia's next letter informed me that he had made you his legal ward.''

He spoke in a matter-of-fact voice that had a husky rasp and that drawling accent of the South, though his was not as pronounced as many. He looked at me with cool assessment.

''I must say,'' he added. ''you're not at all what I expected.''
''No?''

''From Lavinia's letters, I expected a vulgar corn husk slattern who still smelled of alligator oil.''

''I'm sorry to disappoint you.''

''I didn't expect to find someone who admired fine furniture, who appreciated Watteau and Fragonard and could pronounce their names properly.''

"I don't image you did.''

He raised one hand to stroke the cleft in his chin. He was my enemy, I knew that, yet the physical desire I felt for him continued to ache inside, a totally unreasonable thing under the circumstances. I was perfectly poised, facing him with icy composure, and he, of course, hadn't the least inkling of his effect on me, but had he taken me into his arms, I would have succumbed to him immediately, without the least hesitation.

"Apparently you're very clever,'' he told me. "You'd have to be to take my brother in so completely. Julian is something of a dreamer, I'll concede that, but, contrary to what many believe, he's no fool.''

"You're quite right.''

Charles frowned. My composure bothered him. It was the only weapon I had, and it was growing more and more difficult to maintain it. He looked at me with half-shrouded eyes, chin tilted, examining me again with that intense scrutiny so rude and disdainful. After a moment, he nodded.

"I can see how it happened,'' he admitted. "Julian's always had exquisite taste in women. He doesn't stray from his study often, but when he does, it's usually with a woman who makes him the envy of his peers.''

"Is that supposed to be a compliment, Monsieur Etienne?''

"You're a very beautiful woman. You know that. You've used your beauty to climb up in the world, and you'll undoubtedly continue to do so in the future.''

"I'm not a whore,'' I said.

"A rather unpleasant word, but I'm sure it applies well enough.''

"Your brother—''

"My brother has taken temporary leave of his senses,'' he said sharply, "but I'm here now to extricate him from this mess. I know exactly what you are, Mademoiselle O'Malley, and I have no intention of letting you wreck Julian's life. God knows you've done enough harm already.''

"I—''

"I told you I stopped by the shop before I came home. My cousin Raoul was there. He told me about your disgraceful conduct at the Lecombs' ball—apparently the whole Quarter's talking about it. Not content with ensnaring my brother and taking him for all you could, you had to make him appear even more ludicrous by flirting outrageously with every young man at the ball and attempting to seduce his own cousin right on the premises. Oh yes, he told me about the episode in the courtyard."

"I'll bet he did," I said dryly.

"I've no use for Raoul—he's a leech and a knave and I'd boot his backside out of the shop if he weren't family—but at least he had enough judgment to resist your blandishments. He wanted you, he admitted that, but for once he thought of the family name."

His dark blue eyes held mine, full of accusation, full of distaste, and I didn't look away, nor did I say a word in my defense. Charles Etienne had already made up his mind about me, and anything I might say would be futile. I realized that. He was convinced I was a clever, conniving whore, and nothing was going to change his mind. Several brilliant flashes of lightning illuminated the room as we stood there, facing each other, and then, abruptly, the rain ceased, still dripping from eaves and plants.

The accusation was there in his eyes, the distaste as well, but as long moments of silence passed, I realized there was something else, too. He despised me, of that there could be no doubt, but he also wanted me as I wanted him. His features were stern, his mouth tight, and he was in perfect control of his emotions, but the desire was there, a purely physical thing that had nothing to do with his opinion of me. My dress was dusty and there were perspiration stains, my hair fell to my shoulders in an unruly tumble and my face was dirty, but still he desired me. The muscles of his jaw tightened. A tiny vein throbbed at his temple. He despised me, but he wanted to throw me down onto the floor and take me here and now, roughly, savagely.

"Have you nothing to say for yourself?" he asked finally.

"Anything I said would be useless. You've already summed up the situation and reached your decisions about me."

"Are you telling me I'm wrong?"

I didn't reply. I had too much pride. My tightly held composure was beginning to slip. I prayed this would end soon. I could feel tears welling up inside, and I didn't want him to see me cry. I didn't want to give him that satisfaction.

"Are you telling me Lavinia was misinformed? Are you telling me Raoul was lying?"

"I'm not telling you a goddamn thing," I said.

"Ah, the ladylike demeanor begins to crack."

Two bright pink spots burned on my cheeks, and I welcomed the anger. I longed to slap his face. Anger was better than tears. The son of a bitch had decided I was a whore out to wreck his brother's life long before he returned to New Orleans, and nothing was going to change his mind. These past months had been like something out of a fairy tale, too good to be true, and I should have realized it would end like this.

"You're going to throw me out," I said.

"Indeed I am. You needn't worry, Mademoiselle O'Malley. I'll see that you are well provided for. I'll give you enough money to pay your expenses until you can ensnare some other hapless male."

"Keep your bloody money," I told him.

I turned then and left the room with all the dignity I could muster, my back straight, my chin held high, and it was only after I had journeyed halfway down the dim, murky corridor that my step quickened. I hurried on down the corridor and through the dusty labyrinth of rooms until I finally reached that front room with the French doors. He had left them open. Rain had swept in through them, making large puddles on the fine hardwood floor. It should be mopped up at once. To hell with that. To hell with everything. I dashed through the doors and out into the courtyard. Rain dripped noisily from leaves, splattering onto the tiles, and the fountain was still gurgling merrily. There was a fine mist in the air. It stung my cheeks as I hurried across the courtyard and moved up the iron staircase that wound up to the second-floor gallery.

Moments later I was in my bedroom, leaning against the French windows I had closed behind me. My heart was palpitating, and my breath was coming in short gasps. I closed my eyes, fighting the tears, stubbornly willing them not to fall. Crying was for weaklings, and I wasn't weak. I was strong. I was a survivor. I was on my own once again, but at least I was in a better position than I'd been in when I hit Clem over the head with the skillet and fled through the swamps. I stayed there against the windows for several minutes, trying to gain control of the emotions raging inside, and finally, a curious calm came over me.

First things first, I thought. I summoned Kayla and asked her to prepare a bath for me and told her about the water that had blown into the room in the east wing and asked her to see that it was mopped up, and fifteen minutes later, in the small room down the corridor, I was soaking in a tub full of hot, scented water, rubbing my arms and shoulders with a rich lather from the French soap as smooth as satin. I spent a long time bathing. I washed my hair as well, toweling it dry afterward. Back in my bedroom I donned my petticoat and brushed my hair until it fell in thick, lustrous waves shining with rich highlights.

I selected my gown carefully. Why? Why did I want to look especially fetching tonight? I wasn't going to see Charles Etienne again. I wasn't going to see anyone if I could help it. Nevertheless, I took down one of Corinne's loveliest creations and put it on. Of thick, creamy beige silk, it had pencil-thin stripes of gold and brown and bronze. The heart-shaped neckline was low, the full puffed sleeves worn off the shoulder, and there was a narrow waistband of bronze velvet. The skirt belled out over the underskirts in gleaming folds. Ridiculous, dressing like this, but . . . I would need to look nice when I checked into the hotel.

Seeing the stack of books piled on my bedside table, I decided to return them to the library downstairs. It wasn't necessary, of course, but I wanted to see the library one last time. I encountered no one on my way downstairs, but I could hear Delia talking to one of the servants in her sitting room. I was relieved to know she had gotten back safely. She must be in a flurry of excitement after she learned of Charles's early return. Lamps were burning in the library, but there was no one there. How many hours had I spent prowling around the shelves, pulling down weighty volumes, perching on the window seat to study the plates? How many times had I whirled that huge bronze and green and gold globe, trying to locate some country or other to complete my geography lessons? How many exercises had I done at that old desk with its embossed leather top, dipping my pen into the ink pot, scribbling my answers carelessly, eager to be finished? How many delightful, enthralling novels had I taken down and carried upstairs to read until the wee hours of the night? It seemed a hundred memories swarmed in my mind as I put the books I had brought down back into their proper slots on the shelves.

"Here you are dear," Delia said, stepping into the room. "I thought I heard someone moving around. My, you look ravishing tonight, child. I suppose you heard that Charles is back?"

"I heard," I said.

"I almost fainted when I got back and Pompey told me he was here. Jezebel will throw a fit, I thought—she likes to be prepared, likes to know exactly how many will be to dinner—but, on the contrary, when I went into the kitchen she was happily cooking all his favorite things, including her chocolate nut cake with marshmallow icing. He always loved it as a boy. She hasn't baked it since he left."

Delia was beaming, so elated she could hardly contain herself. She had changed into a lovely pale pink silk gown adorned with beige lace ruffles and deeper rose-pink velvet bows. Her eyes sparkled. A radiant smile played on her lips. Her hair billowed about her head like a silvery cloud. I realized that I loved her dearly. No one had ever been so kind to me. I was going to miss her dreadfully.

"For some reason or other, Charles was in a wretched mood. He gave me a quick hug and demanded to know where Julian was—I had no idea, it seems he went out today, too. Anyway, Julian got back about ten minutes after I did, and Charles gave him a surly hello and drug him off to the study. They're in there still. I stuck my head in to tell them dinner would be served at eight o'clock on the dot, and Charles almost bit my head off. Poor dear, he's probably exhausted from the trip."

"He probably is."

"It's wonderful having him back," she confessed. "He can be a terrible bore at times—so stern, so sober, such a grouch—but deep down he's really a darling. I always feel so much more *secure* when he's at the helm."

I put the last book in place and turned, wanting to tell her good-bye and knowing I hadn't the courage. Instead, I took her hand and squeezed it.

"I—I won't be coming down to dinner tonight, Delia," I said.

"But—oh dear . . ." She looked alarmed. "Is something wrong?"

I managed a smile and shook my head, giving her hand another squeeze.

"I just—just have a headache," I lied. "I spent quite a long time in the east wing, and there—there was so much dust. I bathed and changed, hoping I'd feel better, but—I think I'm just going up to my room and go to bed early."

Her clear light green eyes were full of concern. "You must

take one of my headache powders, dear. I'll run fetch it immediately."

"I—I've already taken one. It's made me a little drowsy."

"I wish they'd make *me* drowsy. Nothing seems to help when I have one of my migraines. I just suffer, suffer, suffer, hours on end—but, my dear, you must have something to eat. I'll have a tray sent up to your room. Nothing heavy, of course. A bowl of soup, perhaps, and some—"

"I'll be fine," I assured her. "Delia, I—I love you very much."

Delia was immensely touched by my admission. She smiled a lovely smile and tightened her fingers around mine.

"Why—what a lovely thing to say. I love you, too, my dear. You've become the daughter I never had."

I fought the tears. I couldn't cry now. I couldn't. I let go of her hand and pushed a wave back from my temple.

"I just wanted you to know," I said.

"You run on up to your room and rest, dear. Charles will be disappointed when you don't come down for dinner, but the two of you can meet at breakfast."

"Yes," I said.

I gave her a hug and clung to her for just a moment, and then I released her and quickly left the library. Julian I would not see at all. I couldn't face that. Later, perhaps, I would send him a letter. I moved up the gracefully curving staircase to the second floor. Julian and Charles were cloistered in the study, and I had a good idea what they were talking about. Charles was telling Julian what a fool he'd been, what a clever, manipulating little harlot I was. I wasn't going to give Charles Etienne the satisfaction of throwing me out. I was going to leave of my own volition, tonight, as soon as I could pack.

Several old traveling bags were, I knew, kept in a storage closet at the end of the hall—I'd seen them during my house-cleaning project. I walked to the closet and took out two of them, large, rather unwieldy bags of worn, supple brown leather with tarnished brass buckles on the straps. Charles would be able to call me thief now, as well as whore, for the bags weren't mine and I intended to take them with me. Carrying them to my bedroom, I put them on the bed and opened the wardrobe door and then the tears came, abruptly, spilling over my lashes in salty rivulets.

I didn't want to cry. I hadn't meant to. I was tough. I was a fighter. I could take care of myself. The tears came nevertheless, and I felt a wrenching sadness inside that was every bit as bad as that I had felt when Ma died, perhaps worse. I sat down and let the tears spill and let the sadness possess me, and a long, long time passed, soft candlelight bathing the bedroom, only darkness inside. An hour must have passed before I finally stood up and moved numbly over to the stand behind the screen and washed my face. I felt no better, but the tears were behind me now.

Stepping over to the wardrobe, I began to take down clothes and, folding them carefully, put them into the bags. I couldn't take them all, and I selected only the most serviceable. The sumptuous topaz ball gown remained on its hanger, as did the pink velvet and the bronze and silver striped taffeta. I had fled through the swamps without a single possession, with only the ragged dress I wore, but I would be leaving here with a substantial wardrobe and a little money as well. Delia had insisted I be given a small weekly allowance for spending money. It was only a few dollars, and I had spent most of it on little gifts for Delia and Kayla and Elijah, but I had saved over thirty dollars nevertheless, intending to buy Delia's birthday gift with it. It was enough to pay for a hotel room for a few days until I could find a job of some kind. I was far better qualified to seek employment now than I had been when I tore out of the shanty and raced into the swamps.

Shoes, stockings, underclothes, brush and comb, the small cosmetics case I was so proud of. Almost finished. I would go out the back way and I would walk until I found a hotel. I remembered seeing one on the way to Corinne's. The Quarter at night held no terrors for me. It would be tiring, lugging the bags, but I wasn't worried about that. There. Finished. I closed the bags and buckled the straps. Glancing at the clock, I saw that it was after nine-thirty. Kayla would be with her new boyfriend. Elijah would be helping Pompey clear the dining room table, and Jezebel would be in the kitchen. No one was likely to see me as I crept down the back stairs and out of the house.

He must have moved very quietly. I didn't hear him coming up the staircase outside, nor did I hear him walking down the gallery toward my room. My heart gave a leap when I heard rapping on the windows, I froze. Charles stepped into my bedroom, bold as brass. I gasped and turned pale, and Charles looked at me and looked at the bags and slowly arched one fine dark brow. He had changed for dinner and looked resplendent in shining black knee boots and breeches and frock coat of dark blue broadcloth. His waistcoat was white satin with narrow black stripes, and a sky-blue silk neckcloth was folded neatly at his throat. His thick chestnut hair was smoothly brushed, shining with dark luster. That shock of purely physical desire swept through me once more despite my dislike and resentment.

"All packed, I see," he said.

"Perhaps you'd like to open the bags to see that I'm not stealing any of the family silver."

"I don't think that will be necessary. Where had you planned on going?"

"I intend to find a hotel."

"At this time of night? On foot?"

"I'm leaving, Monsieur Etienne. That's all that need concern you."

"And after you find a hotel?"

"I'll get some kind of job."

His full lips curled into a faint half smile, and his dark blue eyes held a hint of amusement. Mocking amusement, I thought, longing to slap his face. I had every reason to hate this man, and I did hate him, intensely, yet still my knees seemed to turn to water as I looked at those broad shoulders and the stern planes and angles of that handsome face. His incredible magnetism was like an irresistible force, drawing me to him and making me experience a wild variety of unreasonable sensations. Never, never had I been drawn to any man like this. I wanted things I had never wanted before and felt utterly wicked for wanting them.

"Respectable jobs are scarce for young women in your circumstances," he told me.

"I'll find something. I'll wash dishes, scrub floors. I'll do anything I have to do, and—and if that doesn't work I can always find some other hapless male," I added defiantly.

"Julian is right," he said. "You are a spunky little thing."

I made no reply. He moved closer, resting his hands on his thighs, that half smile still curling his lips. His hands, I noticed, were very large, strong, palms wide, fingers long and sinewy. Hands that could caress gently or squeeze with brutal force. I looked away from him, trying not to blush at the wicked thoughts that sprang to mind. I had been lightly attracted to Julian, yes, wouldn't have minded if he had taken me into his arms after we returned from the ball, but I had felt nothing like this, like I was completely helpless, pulled to this man by some invisible force I couldn't resist no matter how I might try.

"I had a long talk with Julian," he informed me.

"I know you did."

"He told me all about you. He assured me that there had been nothing improper between you, that he thought of you as a daughter and intended only to do a Christian deed in bringing you here, giving you a home. I believe him. I believe his intentions were strictly the most honorable."

"But you don't believe mine were," I said.

"Julian informed me that, for all your background, you are as pure as the driven snow, a thoroughly charming and engaging young woman with a remarkable intelligence and a driving determination to make something of yourself. You have made incredible progress, he says."

I was silent, simmering. How could you long to kick someone in the shin and long to melt into his arms at the same time? I was pleased I had chosen this particular, fetching gown, that my hair had been brushed to a high honey-blond gloss, that my skin smelled of delicately scented French soap. Charles Etienne studied me with lazy insolence, and I knew instinctively that he wasn't immune, knew that he would like to do all those things that I so unreasonably longed for him to do.

"You are his legal ward, he says, and he couldn't care less what anybody says or thinks. Lavinia is a vicious, snobbish busybody, he claims, and her son is a goddamn liar. He wants to horsewhip Raoul."

"Indeed?"

"He says your conduct was impeccable at the Lecombs' ball. He says both he and Delia were inordinately proud of you. What *did* happen between you and Raoul out in the courtyard?"

"I'd rather not discuss it."

"I can guess," he said. "It seems I owe you an apology."

"I don't want an apology from you, Monsieur Etienne. I—I want to leave."

"At dinner, Delia could do nothing but sing your praises,"

he continued, ignoring my words. "You are, it appears, a positive treasure. You've taken the servants in hand and they've never been so efficient. You've worked your fingers to the bone, cleaning, organizing the household, trying to make yourself useful. You've brought incalculable joy to Delia, who can't imagine how she ever got along without you."

"She exaggerates," I said.

"Perhaps she does, but the fact remains that the house has never been so clean, nor can I ever remember Delia being so focused and looking so content. She feels she has found a beloved daughter."

"Nevertheless—"

"I may be a hard man," he told me. "Many say I am, and it may well be true—I don't know. I do know that I am a just man. It would appear I have done you an injustice, and I've come to make amends."

"It would 'appear,' " I said. "You're not certain."

This time he failed to reply. He still thought I was a clever, conniving trollop who had pulled the wool over the eyes of his gullible brother and endearingly foggy-minded aunt. I could see that. You might fool them, those dark blue eyes seemed to say, but you haven't fooled me for a minute. I took a deep breath and picked up one of the bags. It was quite heavy.

"I still think I'd better go," I said coldly.

"It would break Delia's heart, I fear."

"I'm sorry about that."

"And it would put my brother to ever so much trouble. You are his ward, and he has legal control over your actions until you turn twenty-one. If you leave, he will only come after you and bring you back, and that will be quite exasperating for him."

"Julian—"

"Julian took on the responsibility of you because he has a tender heart, because he is as good as any man I've ever known, and my brother is not a man who shirks his responsibility. Put down that bag. You're not going anywhere tonight."

"I beg to differ with you. I'm leaving. I—you don't want me here. I can tell that. You think—"

"What I may or may not think has no bearing on the case. You are legally in my brother's charge, and by God, you'll stay right where you are. I'm not going to have him upset by some—"

He cut himself short, scowling.

"Put the bag down," he repeated. His voice was quite stern.

"Go to hell," I said.

He stepped over to me in three long strides and seized my wrist and gave it a brutal twist and took the bag from me and then emptied its contents onto the floor, and then he took the other bag off the bed and emptied it, too. I rubbed my wrist, my cheeks burning as skirts fluttered and rustled, spreading over the carpet like so many giant, multicolored petals. Charles threw the bag down and glared at me, his jaw tight, his mouth a resolute pink line. He silently dared me to defy him. I stepped over to him and slapped his face as hard as I could, so hard I thought my wrist might snap.

Charles Etienne was thoroughly stunned. He didn't say a word. He stood there looking at me, a bright pink mark burning on his cheek, the rest of his face ashen. My palm stung viciously and my wrist hurt even more than it had after he twisted it. Several long moments passed. I could hear a bird singing in the courtyard. Candles spluttered beneath their glass globes. After a while he reached up and rubbed his cheek, and then he sighed.

"I suppose I had that coming," he said. "Do you feel better now?"

"Not really," I replied.

"Pick up these things," he ordered. "Put them back into the wardrobe."

"I—"

"Do as I say!" he said sharply.

I longed to defy him again, but I didn't dare. I reached down and picked up a yellow linen frock and held it crumpled against me. Charles Etienne nodded and then sighed again, looking weary now, looking exasperated.

"Am I going to have to lock you in your room?" he asked.

"I don't think that will be necessary."

"Good. If you're not at the breakfast table in the morning, if you have run off as you planned, I'll come after you myself, and when I find you, I'll beat the hell out of you. Do you believe me?"

I nodded. Charles looked at me for a moment longer and turned and left the way he had entered, closing the doors behind him. I held the yellow dress tightly, unconsciously twisting it in my hands, a whole bewildering array of emotions sweeping over me, anger and hurt and humiliation and piercing disappointment and sadness and shattering need. When, finally, I began gathering up the clothes and putting them back into the wardrobe, I faced a truth impossible to deny.

Things would never be the same again.

Chapter Ten

CHARLES WAS ABSOLUTELY LIVID, and not even Jezebel's wonderful *crème brûlée* could restore his good humor. We were at the dining table, six days after his return to New Orleans, and the candles in their ornate silver holders shed a soft golden glow over the fine damask cloth, the priceless, paper-thin white bone china, the sparkling crystal glasses. It had been a superb meal, one of Jezebel's usual triumphs, but Charles had sulked through the turtle soup and frowned at the salad of lettuce and white truffles and artichoke hearts with its special mayonnaise dressing, and he had finally exploded during the lobster thermidor. Raoul was lazy, undependable, irresponsible and impossibly cavalier about his job, and this was the last straw, this was inexcusable, the young scoundrel was going to have his ass kicked from one end of the city to the other as soon as he saw fit to return. All the goods Charles had purchased overseas had come in and he had had to unpack every last item himself because Raoul had jaunted off for a holiday at a friend's plantation house upriver.

"Do simmer down, dear," Delia said kindly. "I'm sure Raoul didn't *think*, or he wouldn't have gone off like that. He would have realized you needed his help."

"We pay the little varlet a perfectly good salary, and he goes off without even telling anyone. I'd never have known if Magdelon hadn't come by the store and casually mentioned his departure."

"Jezebel's going to be very upset if you don't eat your *crème brûlée*. You know how touchy she is, dear. You did get all the things unpacked, after all. No real harm's been done."

"And now I have an inventory!" he thundered. "It's abso-

191

lutely impossible for me to do it without assistance. I have to itemize every single piece in the shipment, with detailed description of each, the price I paid for it and a suggested resale price.''

''My, that does sound like quite a task,'' Delia agreed, delicately dipping her spoon into her gold-rimmed bowl of *crème brûlée*. ''Perhaps it can wait until Raoul returns.''

Charles shot her a murderous look. He was wearing a dark gray frock coat, a white satin waistcoat with navy blue stripes, a spotless white silk neckcloth expertly arranged at his throat. He looked wonderfully virile, gloriously handsome, charged with an energy that seemed to crackle in the air around him. He had brushed his hair, but one heavy chestnut wave had dipped over his forehead, giving him a strangely boyish appeal.

''I think we should fire him,'' Julian said idly. ''I've longed to for over a year now. Just because he happens to be—''

''Oh, dear,'' Delia exclaimed, ''you couldn't do that. Lavinia would never give us a moment's peace.''

''She never gives us a moment's peace as it is,'' Julian drawled. ''Firing Raoul might well make her so angry she'd refuse to speak to us at all. Imagine the bliss.''

He pushed his empty bowl aside, contemplating that nirvana. Like Charles, he wore a frock coat, dark brown, rather rumpled, and his yellow silk neckcloth was rumpled as well, carelessly tucked into the top of the splendid white satin waistcoat embroidered with tobacco-brown patterns. Julian found it tedious to dress for dinner each night when he was so immersed in his book, but there were certain standards one must uphold, and Delia, lovely tonight in pale peach silk, would have been outraged had he failed to uphold them.

''Poor Lavinia,'' Delia said. ''She never knows when to desist. She was in a frightful snit when she left day before yesterday. What *did* you say to her, Charles?''

''I refused to give her son a raise in salary and a more important involvement in family affairs. The same old argument.''

I kept my eyes lowered, ever so demure in my pale salmon-pink linen frock. I had seen Lavinia departing, black skirts crackling, garnet earrings swinging, her thin face as pursed and sour as a lemon. She and Charles had gone into the parlor and remained there behind closed doors for almost two hours. One couldn't help hearing their voices rising now and then even if the exact words weren't quite audible. I knew full well that Lavinia had demanded I be thrown out at once, and Charles had been put in the uncomfortable position of having to defend someone he really had no inclination to defend.

We had been very polite to each other these past six days, meeting only at mealtimes, both of us wary behind the polite facades. Charles spent almost all of his time at Etienne's, and I had initiated the east wing cleaning, supervising a small fleet of servants hired especially for the job, trying to keep them on the job and trying to keep the uproar down so as not to disturb Julian, busily working on his book and testily sensitive to outside noise. Charles and I both pretended that the scene in my bedroom hadn't taken place, and I pretended that the overwhelming, unreasonable attraction I felt toward him had been merely a temporary aberration, even though it stirred anew every time I saw him. I knew that he desired me, too—a woman always knows—and I wondered if he denied it as I denied my own desire.

"I'm going to have to have some help with the inventory, Julian," he said grimly.

"Hire someone," Julian told him.

"I need someone who knows something about furniture and paintings and porcelain, someone familiar with antiques. God knows Raoul doesn't know much, but at least he's picked up a smattering. I could throttle him for going off like that."

"You'd hear no objections from me."

"You're going to have to help out," Charles told him.

Julian looked appalled. *"Me?* Totally impossible, brother dear. I couldn't possibly take time away from the book. I'm at a very tricky point, trying to compile all the footnotes, juggling hundreds of cards, tracking down obscure references. There's no *way* I could leave it, even for a day."

"I know you're very immersed in your blasted book," Charles said wearily, "but this is important."

"And my 'blasted book' isn't! You're an insufferable hypocrite, Charles! You pretend to be interested, pretend to be supportive, but you're every bit as bad as the rest of them! You think I'm a dreamer and a fool! You think I'm wasting my time! I'll have you know—"

"There's no need to raise your voice!" Charles interrupted, raising his. "I had no intention whatsoever of slighting your all-important endeavor to satisfy the world's great curiosity about unknown weeds growing in the Louisiana swamps. I merely meant that our family *livelihood* depends on—''

''Go ahead, be sarcastic! One of these days—''

''Goddammit, Julian, you're as unreasonable as—''

''Boys,'' Delia said, tapping on her glass with a spoon.

They both looked at her. They both fell silent, sulking like intractable children. Delia sighed and shook her head.

''You haven't changed a bit, either one of you. You're still as unruly as you were as boys, always scrapping at the dinner table. I used to be able to send you to your rooms without dessert, but now—well, my dears, you may both be all grown-up, but I simply will *not* tolerate these shouting matches. I can feel one of my migraines coming on already.''

''Sorry, Delia,'' Charles told her.

''Sorry,'' Julian said grumpily, ''but he can be such a—''

''Julian,'' she warned.

''Oh, all right,'' he grumbled.

''They really love one another dearly,'' Delia informed me, ''but brothers *will* be brothers. It's always been like this, I fear. They might scrap like cats and dogs at home, but just let some outsider try to come between them and they're like the Two Musketeers.''

''The Three Musketeers,'' Charles corrected.

''Whatever. Julian's work *is* important to him, Charles, and I can see why he doesn't want any distraction just now. By the same token, I know how important it is for you to get your inventory done properly, and I have a perfectly brilliant suggestion.''

''What's that?'' he asked.

''Let Dana help you.''

''Out of the question!'' he snapped.

''That *is* brilliant,'' Julian said.

''I couldn't possibly,'' I told her.

''Dana knows much more about fine furniture and such than Raoul ever will, Charles. She's examined every piece in the house, asked questions, fascinated by the history. She's pored over all those dreary old books in the library, learning all sorts of facts. Why, only last week she was telling me all about Madame de Pompadour and the Sevres factory Louis XV set up for her and informed me that that vase we have sitting on the hall table—the pink and gold one with those chubby little cupids and blue flowers—was especially designed for Pompadour. She showed me the markings on the bottom of the vase and the date, told me—"

"I'm sure she's very clever," Charles said.

He gave me a look. He probably thought I planned to steal the vase. I wanted to give him the finger.

"And that little table I have in my sitting room, the one I pile my magazines on, she recognized it at once as—"

"You've made your point, Delia."

"I'm sure she would be an invaluable assistant, dear. You couldn't find anyone better for the job."

"I agree," Julian said eagerly.

I gave *him* a look.

"I would love to help out," I said sweetly, "but I'm in the middle of cleaning the east wing. All the floors still have to be waxed, I have to supervise the washing of all the dustcloths, three of the chandeliers have not been cleaned yet and there are several pieces of furniture I wouldn't let any of the servants touch—I'll have to polish them myself. It's going to take me at least another week to—"

"All that can wait," Julian airily informed me. "Getting the inventory done is far more important than—"

"You don't care *who* helps do it as long as it isn't you," I said testily. "It should be perfectly clear to you that your brother doesn't want me to help, doesn't think I'm capable of it, and I'm damn sure not going to make both of us uncomfortable so that you can—"

"Now, now, don't *you* two start!" Delia exclaimed. "Really," she added with a weary sigh, "I don't know what all the fuss is about. Dana has wanted to see the shop for ages, Charles—Julian's never taken her—and she can certainly do a better job than Raoul—than Julian, either, for that matter—and, Dana dear, the east wing *can* wait. It's the perfect solution."

"Perfect," Julian seconded.

"Then it's settled," Delia said happily.

I started to protest. "But—"

"It's settled," Julian said firmly. "Isn't it, Charles?"

"I suppose it is." He wasn't at all pleased. "Meet me in the front foyer at eight o'clock," he told me, "and wear something sensible, not one of those—those fancy rags that silly dressmaker ran up for you that leave most of your bosom bare."

"Charles knows nothing about fashion, dear," Delia pointed out.

And so it was that I stood waiting in the foyer early the following morning, nervous as hell but determined not to show it. My hair was brushed to a high sheen, I had taken a bath, and I was wearing a frock of pale apricot-colored cotton. It had narrow elbow-length sleeves and a square-cut neckline not quite as low as most of my other garments. The bodice was form-fitting, snug at the waist, and the very full skirt belled out over half a dozen ruffled underskirts.

The clocks were just striking eight when I heard footsteps and turned to see him moving briskly toward me, looking very brusque and businesslike. He wore highly polished black knee boots, snug dove-gray breeches, and a loosely fitting shirt of thin white lawn, open at the throat, the tail tucked casually into the waistband of his breeches, the bell sleeves gathered at the wrist and billowing as he moved. Although he had brushed his hair, it was already beginning to flop a little, that heavy wave spilling over his brow. He gave me a curt nod, frowned slightly and led me to the door.

"I hope this dress is suitable enough," I said as we stepped outside.

His blue eyes swept over me. "It'll do. You might go upstairs and wipe that paint off your face, though."

"I'm not wearing paint. This is my natural coloring."

He seemed just slightly taken aback but said nothing, leading me instead down the steps to the small open carriage waiting for us on the drive, a pair of gleaming bays stamping impatiently. The Negro driver, whom I hadn't seen before, sat perched up front in a neat black uniform, and the passengers' seat was upholstered in plush gray velvet. My skirts rustled as Charles handed me up into the seat and I settled back. He swung up lithely and sat down beside me and gave the driver a nod. In moments were were moving down the street at a nice clip. It was a lovely morning, sun-spangled, the sky a bright, silvery blue, the air fresh and invigorating. Charles was every bit as uncomfortable as I was, staring straight ahead, his profile stern and oh so handsome. The silence between us became more and more strained, broken only by the spinning of wheels and the merry clop of horse hooves on the cobbles.

"Did you have breakfast?" he asked after a while.

"Just coffee," I said. "I rarely eat anything in the morning."

"I noticed that."

"Oh?"

"The other morning you had only half a sweet roll."

"But I was at the breakfast table," I pointed out. "As directed."

We turned down another street. The Quarter was very quiet at this hour, no one to be seen but a few Negro women with baskets of laundry. The gardens behind their stone walls and wrought iron gates were cool and shady, gorgeous red and purple bougainvillea spilling over the walls. How mellow and sleepy the old houses looked with their elaborate lacework of wrought iron. The silence was becoming strained again. I tried not to look at those strong, muscular thighs so tightly encased in gray kidskin, at the large, powerful hands resting on his knees. We were sitting quite close out of necessity, and when the carriage rocked our bodies touched and I could feel the weight of him and the warmth of his skin. He was very tense.

"Look," I said, "I don't like this any better than you do. It wasn't my idea."

"I know it wasn't." His voice was curt.

"Why don't you just stop the carriage. I—I'll walk back to the house. I'll tell Delia I've developed a splitting headache. That's something she'll understand. Julian will never know I've come back."

"I still need help with the inventory," he told me.

"And I suppose mine is better than nothing."

"Right."

"You know, you really are a miserable sod."

He seemed delighted that I had lost my composure. A faint smile played at the corner of his lips, and he seemed to relax for the first time. How I detested him. How I wished those thighs were clamped around mine, those arms holding me imprisoned, that full pink mouth plundering my own. I quickly banished such wicked thoughts, a blush tinting my cheeks.

" 'Miserable sod,' " he repeated. "A description you picked up from your years in the swamps?"

"It fits, believe me."

"I've never heard it expressed quite that way, but I can assure you that there are any number of people who would agree with you. I'm not supposed to get out and fight the world and keep the family afloat. I'm supposed to club around with like kind and drink mint juleps and discuss the glory of the family name and squander what little money is left on cards and women. It's the done thing in our crowd.''

"People resent you because you work?"

"It's demeaning to be in trade—particularly if your name happens to be Etienne. It's far more honorable to sit back gracefully and helplessly watch the decline like half the families in the Quarter. Many still have money, of course, but the majority have seen better days and will eventually see worse, clinging to their honor and describing past glories even as they starve.''

"Then they're bloody fools," I said.

"I couldn't agree more.''

"You're still a miserable sod, though.''

"I won't argue the point," he said.

We had left the residential district now and were passing rows of small, exclusive shops: a bakery where you could buy fancy French pastries at exorbitant prices, a salon that sold Parisian perfumes in beautiful crystal bottles with gold-encrusted stoppers, a plush bookstore with all the latest magazines and books from the City of Light, a florist's with banks of heavenly pink and orange blossoms in the windows. Corinne's wasn't far from here, and Etienne's was just around the corner, on the main thoroughfare. The streets all sparkled in the early morning sunlight, nests of hazy blue shadows lingering under striped awnings. At this hour the shops were still closed and there were only a few carriages abroad. Ours pulled up in front of Etienne's, and Charles helped me alight.

"We'll be here all day," he told the driver. "You can come back for us around five.''

The driver nodded, snapped his whip and drove away, and Charles took the door key out of his pocket and stepped over to unlock the front door. Built of light gray brick, with large plate glass windows on either side of the ornately carved white door, Etienne's was impressive indeed, an awning of white and gold striped canvas stretching across the front, shading the windows full of magnificent, casually arranged furniture and objets d'art. I could easily have spent half an hour admiring them, but Charles held open the door and impatiently waited for me to follow him in. He shut the door behind us, locked it and checked to see that the CLOSED sign was still in place.

"We won't be open to the public until the inventory is finished," he informed me. "the storeroom is—"

"It—why, it's like Aladdin's treasure cave," I exclaimed, interrupting him.

To my eyes, it was indeed. A gorgeous old gray and gold Aubusson carpet covered most of the floor space, and the walls were hung with dull gold moiré. Exquisite tapestry screens stood against the walls, and ornately framed paintings were expertly hung—Fragonards, Bouchers, Watteaus, a collection of magnificently detailed watercolors by Lancret. Shelves and tables held beautiful sets of china and porcelain figurines, and the remaining space was taken up by the furniture, each piece more sumptuous than the next, and all, I noticed, in need of a good dusting. My eye was caught by a delicate commode, surely Louis XV, and I moved over to examine it while Charles assumed a look of weary forbearance.

"I've never seen anything lovelier," I said in a hushed voice. "Look at the detail."

Delicately carved legs that curved in, then curved out, held the superbly designed octagon-shaped top with intricately inlaid patterns of ebony and cherry wood, and the lid was a masterpeice of similar marquetry. There were four beautifully painted porcelain ovals, framed in brass garlands, that might have been done by Bouchet, and the whole piece was lavishly adorned with brass lace and narrow brass strips etched with tiny flowers. The brass was beginning to tarnish, the porcelain ovals were dusty, and the wood was deplorably dry, crying out for polish.

"It's criminal to let a piece like this get into such condition," I said testily. "It looks as though it hasn't been polished for years, and the brass is almost green."

"Waste of time to clean it," Charles informed me. "I've been thinking of throwing the damned thing out."

"Throwing it out!" I was appalled. "Why, it—yes, it's Louis XV, and Bouchet might have done those ovals. It's priceless."

"It's a very clever fake—one of my few mistakes. I bought it in a lot over three years ago. People who patronize Etienne's *really* know their furniture and can quickly spot a copy."

"Even so, it's still incredibly lovely. It may be a copy, but it's wonderfully made. I don't see why—"

"It's unsalable, a useless piece of junk that merely takes up space. Remind me to toss it out when we're finished today.

Come along," he said curtly, "we've got work to do—though I doubt if you're going to be much help to me."

I was smarting as he led me through an archway hung with dark gold drapes and into the back. I didn't know furniture at all, he had implied. I couldn't even spot an obvious fake and was going to be useless. We walked past two offices and into the storeroom in back, a vast area cluttered with empty wooden boxes and furniture and stacks of dishes and table loads of porcelain figurines and bronzes. Some of the boxes were broken, slats littering the floor, and packing straw was everywhere. What an incredible mess it was, I thought, trying not to let myself be distracted by the sumptuous objects on every side. Charles placed his hands on his thighs and looked around in disgust.

"We can't possibly work in all this mess," I said practically. "I suggest you do something with all those boxes—is there an alley out back? Perhaps you could carry them out there. I'll sweep up all this hideous straw and gather up all that wrapping paper, then we can start taking inventory."

"I give the orders around here," he informed me.

"I wasn't ordering you to do anything," I replied. "I was simply making a suggestion."

He hesitated, scowling, then gave an exasperated shrug and began to carry the empty boxes out, gathering up the broken slats as well. I located a broom and started sweeping, and half an hour later the job was done. Charles disappeared into one of the offices and returned a moment later with a leather-bound ledger and a huge bundle of receipts. He explained to me that each piece must be checked against its sale receipt, then listed in the ledger with price paid and price to be charged and a brief description. We would start with the porcelain. I would bring each piece over and he would sit at the desk and do the listing after he located the appropriate receipt.

"If you drop one, you're dead," he told me. "Some of those pieces are worth a great deal."

"Don't worry about it," I said.

We started to work, and after he had listed one or two pieces I found myself waiting while he completed the listing and located a receipt for the next piece. I simplified matters by locating the receipts myself and providing him with a brief description of each piece I brought over. Meissen box, blue and gold court figures on lid. Sevres vase, white porcelain with gold etching and pink and orange flowers. Dresden figurine, lady in sedan chair carried by two page boys in gold and green livery. Charles was both surprised and pleased by my efficiency and my ability to identify each piece correctly and find the receipt for it. Work progressed much more smoothly. As each piece was listed I placed it on one of the empty shelves provided for that purpose, and I was always ready with another before Charles had finished making his entry. An hour passed, two, three, and we had finished with the porcelain and listed half the china when we were interrupted by loud knocking on the back door that led into the alleyway.

"Jesus!" Charles snapped. "Who could that be?"

He stood up and threw his shoulders back and flexed his arms, stiff after sitting at the desk so long. His hair was decidedly unruly, and his fine lawn shirt was moist with perspiration, the sleeves rolled up to his elbows now. I had perspired myself, for it was very warm back here with no windows to let in a breeze, and I was weary, too, glad for a little respite. Charles moved angrily to the door and threw it open, and a beaming Elijah grinned up at him, his arms laden with two large baskets.

"What on earth are *you* doing here?" Charles demanded.

"Jasper, that new driver, he brung me in the carriage. Jezebel said Miz Dana didn't eat no breakfast an' you all needed a hearty lunch if you was gonna be workin' an' told me to bring these here baskets. They're fulla goodies. She said you was to eat every bite of 'em or she'd know the reason why."

"Give them to me."

Elijah handed over the baskets and stood there grinning, and Charles gave him a mock fierce look and Elijah grinned all the wider. Reaching into one of the baskets, Charles took out a small iced cake, gave it to the boy and closed the door. I ran my fingers through my hair, my back sore, my feet aching from being on them so long. Charles set the baskets on the desk, pulled over a superbly designed Henry X chair and told me to sit down. I hesitated, reluctant to sit on so fine a piece. He saw my hesitation, frowned and gave me a little shove, then started taking things out of the basket.

"Let's see—cold fried chicken, slices of ham, slices of turkey, a loaf of dark brown bread, cheese, apples, grapes, honey cakes, tiny chocolate cakes with white icing—Jesus! There's enough here to feed an army. Knives, forks, and two crystal glasses, a container of lemonade—she hasn't forgotten anything.''

"The lemonade sounds wonderful.''

Charles filled both glasses, ice tinkling as he did so, then gave me one. I drank it with relish and took the piece of chicken he handed me along with a white linen napkin.

"We've made great progress,'' he remarked. "We should finish the china and the bronzes this afternoon, and we can easily do all the rest tomorrow. I thought it would take half a week. You—uh—you're quite efficient, and you do know your porcelain.''

"That hurt, didn't it?'' I said.

"What hurt?''

"Admitting I wasn't a dunce.''

"I didn't say you weren't a dunce. I just said you know your porcelain.''

"Sod.''

"Eat your chicken, Dana.''

It was delicious, and so was the turkey and bread and cheese. Both of us were starved. I watched him tearing meat from a drumstick with his teeth, and I lowered my eyes, not wanting those wicked thoughts to start anew. He seemed quite relaxed and pleased now and not at all resentful of my company. I drank another glass of lemonade, sipping it slowly.

"Want a cake?'' he inquired.

"I really shouldn't.''

"Jezebel will be upset if they're not eaten. She'll have another one of her spells, and you'll have to go humor her. Delia tells me you do it beautifully. She says Jezebel thinks you hung the moon.''

"I get along well with all the servants.''

"You have a way with them. Delia never did. She let them run all over her. You've made life much easier for her.''

"I—''

"We got off to a bad start, Dana. What do you say we call a truce?''

"That—that's fine with me,'' I said.

"I'm very protective of my family, you see. Someone has to look out after them. I've been doing it since I was in my teens.''

I accepted a small chocolate cake. Charles ate two of them and wiped his mouth with his napkin and then looked at me with dark blue eyes that were full of lazy curiosity. I lowered my own eyes.

"You really do like beautiful things, don't you?" he said.

I nodded. "I—I suppose it's because I grew up with—without any beauty around me at all."

"Julian told me all about that."

I didn't reply. I finished my cake, remembering, feeling sad.

"He told me about your mother, too—told me the whole story. You wanted to come to New Orleans to find her people, he said."

"I—I don't even know their name," I said. "I still hope to find them, though. I haven't pursued it because I've been so busy with lessons and everything. When—when I do find them, I want to be a lady—I want them to think I'm a lady."

Charles didn't say anything for a while. He stood up and started putting things back into the baskets. He was so tall, so lean and muscular, exuding a marvelous confidence and that potent magnetism. I handed him my empty glass. Our fingers touched.

"Give it up, Dana," he said.

"Give what up?"

"This idea you have about finding your mother's people. If, indeed, she did come from one of the Creole families here in the Quarter, they would never accept you. You'll never be a lady, Dana. Not to people here. No matter what you do, what you achieve, you'll always be that creature from the swamps Julian Etienne brought back and made his ward."

"You—don't believe in mincing words, do you?" I said quietly.

"I know these people. I should. My name is Etienne and I'm one of them, even if they consider me a rebel. They're close-knit, inbred, arrogant and incredibly exclusive. Their doors are closed to any and all outsiders. If your mother's people disowned her because she ran off with an outsider, they're not likely to take in her bastard daughter."

I could feel my cheeks coloring. I could feel the pain inside. I wasn't going to cry. Charles looked at me and frowned, and when he spoke again, his voice was almost gentle.

"I say this only for your own good," he told me. "If you pursue it you'll only be setting yourself up for a great deal of disappointment and a lot of hurt."

"But—"

"Where you come from—who your family is—doesn't matter. All that matters is what you are. You no longer need your mother's people. You're no longer an orphan. You have a place now. You have a home. You're Julian Etienne's ward."

"And you're not happy about that, are you?"

"I love and respect my brother. I may not be happy about what he did, but I stand behind him. Always. You're one of the family now, whether I like it or not, and that means I stand behind you, too. I won't allow anyone to defame you, and I don't want to see you hurt."

I didn't reply. Charles finished packing the baskets and set them on the floor beside the desk. I stood up and moved the Henry X chair back into place, and we resumed our work. I thought about all that he had said. He didn't understand. How could he? How could he understand how it felt not to know your mother's name, not to know who your father was? It was something I wasn't prepared to explain to him. I found the receipt for a gold-rimmed tea set with a deep pink border with tiny gold stars. Charles casually told me it had once belonged to Maria Theresa of Austria, the mother of Marie Antoinette. I handled the dishes carefully, with something like awe.

"Where did you get all these things?" I asked.

"The Gerard family in France has fallen on very bad times. I was able to acquire some of their possessions before they went to public auction. I paid a fair price, far more than they would have fetched under the gavel."

"Why didn't you wait until the auction?"

"I wanted to be sure I got the items, and I wanted to be sure the Gerards got a fair price. I could've obtained them cheaper if I'd waited for the auction, perhaps, but the Gerards would have been the poorer for it."

"You—you have your own honor, don't you?"

"I'm not a scavanger, fattening off the misfortunes of others. I'm a legitimate dealer with, I hope, a modicum of integrity, which is more than can be said of some of our competitors. I may have paid too much, but I can face myself in the mirror each morning and, believe me, Etienne's will make a generous profit from each item."

"You overcharge your customers?"

"Outrageously."

"And you find nothing wrong with that?"

"Customers of Etienne's can afford to be overcharged. The more they pay, the happier they are. Enough chitchat, Dana. We've got work to do. Be careful with that sugar bowl.''

We finished with the china an hour later and began on the bronzes. I wasn't nearly as well versed in bronzes. It took me much longer to find the receipts, and I made couple of errors that caused Charles to scowl. It was very warm back here. His hair was damp now, and the lawn shirt clung moistly to his back and shoulders, his skin visible beneath the thin cloth. I was growing extremely weary and longed for a break, but hell would freeze over before I would ask for one. I picked up another heavy bronze, stumbled on my way to the desk, and almost dropped the piece. He gave me a murderous look as I set it down and began to search for the receipt.

"Uh—French bronze, man and woman embracing, by P. Bertrand," I said uneasily.

"Italian bronze," he corrected, "*The Rape of the Sabines*, after Giovanni Bologna. You've made another error. Find the *right* receipt.''

"I never said I knew everything there is to know about bronzes," I retorted. "I'm doing the best I can!''

"Snap it up," he ordered.

At that point there was noisy banging on the front door, and Charles threw his hands up in disgust and said it was a would-be customer and told me just to ignore the noise, they'd go away. I found the right receipt and gave it to him, and he began to scribble furiously. Not only did the banging not stop, it grew even noisier. Charles's pen skipped and splattered ink all over the page, and he looked as though he would love to commit murder. He grabbed a blotter and began to blot and ordered me to go see who it was and get rid of them at once. I brushed damp waves from my temples and hurried to the front of the shop.

Through the windows I could see a stout, middle-aged man in a plum-colored frock coat and a gray silk neckcloth with a diamond stickpin. He stood smoking a fat cigar while the woman with him continued to bang lustily on the door, clearly determined to be allowed inside. Fearing the door might actually break down, I hastily unlocked it and opened it, and the woman came tripping eagerly into the shop, grabbing her husband's arm and dragging him in after her. She was a good half head taller than he, a robustly built matron with merry brown eyes, a plump red mouth and hair an improbable shade of gold. She was wearing a garish dress of red, green, black and white plaid taffeta, eye-catching to say the least, and vividly red false cherries dangled from one side of her wide-brimmed black straw hat. An enormous diamond sparkled on her wedding finger, quite the largest gem I had ever seen, and a diamond sunburst was pinned to her lapel.

"I just *knew* someone was here!" she exclaimed in an accent so thick I was barely able to make out the words. "I told Herbie, Herbie, I said, I just *know* someone's here an' I'm gonna keep right on knockin' till I get results. Didn't I, Herbie? Didn't I say just that?"

"You said just that," Herbie said patiently.

"Louella, honey, you just can't go to New Orleans without stopping by Etienne's, my friend Junie Summerfield told me. Last year Junie bought a pair of candlesticks here, real steep, they was, cost her a mint, an' she hasn't talked about anything else—you've gotta look at them candlesticks every time you go see her. Well, I said to Herbie, Herbie, I said, I'm not gonna let Junie Summerfield get the jump on *me*. I'm gonna buy me somethin' that's gonna make her bloomin' candlesticks look plum puny."

"I—I'm very sorry," I said when I could finally get a word in edgewise, "but we're closed today. We're taking inventory, you see, and—"

"Oh, now, honey, you're not gonna break my *heart*? We're leavin' tomorrow, goin' back home to St. Louis, and I'd pine plum away if I didn't have somethin' from Etienne's to carry back with me. Somethin' special. Look at them chairs, Herbie! Ain't they grand?"

"Kinda big, Louella," Herbie observed.

"We're the Kramers from St. Louis, honey. I'm Louella and this here's Herbie. Kramer's Emporium—perhaps you've heard of it. It's the biggest store in the city, but we don't sell stuff like *this*! I just gotta buy somethin' to take back with me, and I just won't take no for an answer. You can sell it to us yourself an' we'll pay cash. Herbie's got a bundle in his pocket. Oh, what a gorgeous screen! Look at them cupids cavortin'. That's real tapestry, ain't it? Whatta you think, Herbie?"

"I'm not particularly fond of cupids, Louella."

"Talk about hard to please!"

Louella began to examine various pieces, darting here and there, her plaid taffeta skirt crackling noisily. Herbie took a puff on his cigar and gave me a long-suffering look as though to tell me there was no controlling her once she'd made up her mind to have something. He had a plump, pleasant face with sleepy-looking gray eyes and heavy lids. The top of his head was bald and shiny, with a sleek black fringe around it. The diamond in his stickpin, I noticed, was almost as large as the one on his wife's finger.

"Might as well sell her something," he said. "You're not gonna get rid of her 'less you do."

The idea came to me all at once, and I knew I wasn't going to be able to resist it. I brushed my hair back again and, leaving Herbie to his cigar, joined Louella, who was critically examining a Louis XV side chair.

"We have a great many beautiful pieces," I told her, "but, of course, if you want something really special, there's the Josephine commode."

"Commode? Where is it, honey? Let me have a look."

I led her over to the commode Charles had denigrated earlier. I could see that Louella was not at all impressed.

"It needs dusting," I said. "It needs a good polish, too, but it's quite the finest thing we have in the store."

"Hmmmm," Louella murmured, eyes wandering.

"Of course, it's a copy," I confessed.

"A copy! Honey, I ain't payin' Herbie's good money for any copy, no matter how old it looks."

"Josephine didn't know it was a copy. They say it was her favorite piece of furniture when she was living on the isle of Martinique."

"Josephine?"

"Josephine Bonaparte," I said reverently, "Napoleon's first wife and the empress of France. This commode belonged to her when she was a girl growing up on Martinique. They say she was especially fond of the Bouchet ovals and polished all of the brass with her own hands, dreaming of some grand future as she did so."

"You don't say! Herbie! Herbie, come on over here and look at this!"

Herbie sauntered over and gazed at the commode with about

as much interest as he would have shown an ant crawling across the carpet. Heavy lids drooping, he puffed on his cigar and listened patiently as Louella enthused over the commode.

"It belonged to Josephine—you know, the empress of France, the one who slept around so much Napoleon divorced her. Junie Summerfield will bust a gut! I gotta have it, Herbie. I don't care *how* much it costs!"

Herbie gave me a weary look. "How much does it cost?" he asked in a martyred voice.

"Well—" I began.

"Money's no object!" Louella told me.

"The asking price is fifteen hundred dollars," I said calmly, "but it *is* a copy, after all, and—I really couldn't sell it for over a thousand and have a clear conscience."

You're going to go straight to hell, I told myself.

"We'll take it!" Louella exclaimed. "Just wait'll Junie Summerfield sees it. Wait'll I tell her how Josephine polished all the brass herself, dreaming of marryin' an emperor. A mere thousand bucks! It's a bargain, Herbie."

"It is indeed," Charles said gravely.

None of us had heard him come into the front of the shop. He had brushed his hair back from his brow and tucked his shirt in more securely and wiped the sweat from his face. His face was grim. Oh Lord, he's going to throttle me, I thought.

"I'm Charles Etienne," he told the Kramers. "I'm the owner. May I be of some assistance?"

"No assistance needed," Louella said happily, "this little girl here has already sold us this marvelous commode. Herbie's gonna pay cash. Give him the thousand bucks, Herbie."

"If you will just step back into my office with me, Mr. Kramer, I'll write out a receipt for you, and we'll make arrangements to have the piece shipped to you."

"Shipped, my eye! We're gonna carry it with us!" Louella exclaimed. "We have plenty of room in the carriage—our man will help carry it out—and they can put it on the steamboat tomorrow morning. I ain't lettin' no one *ship* it. Might get lost on the way."

"Very well," Charles said smoothly. "There are some crates and packing straw in back. I'll pack it up for you myself."

"That'd be lovely, honey. Hurry up and give him the money, Herbie. I wanna stop by that fancy dress shop before it closes—

Corinne's. I saw a cunning hat in the window, pink straw with the sweetest velvet bows on the brim. It'll be smashing with my purple satin gown."

Charles smiled at her and gave me a very severe look that said we had much to talk about and then led Herbie to one of the offices in back. Louella chatted nonstop while we waited. Herbie had made a bundle with Kramer's Emporium, she informed me. Everyone thought he was crazy, buying that tacky little store that was going out of business, no one wanted it, you're gonna lose your shirt, everyone said, but Herbie knew a good thing when he saw it and went right ahead and bought it and began to expand and first thing you knew it was making a mint and now it was the biggest store in town and the Kramers were rolling in money. Herbie had a genius for business, no doubt about it, he was thinking of opening branches all over the South.

"Ten years from now we're gonna be an *empire*!" Louella enthused.

"I'm sure that will be lovely for you," I said.

Charles and Herbie came back, Herbie thrusting the receipt into the pocket of his frock coat. He stepped to the door and summoned his man inside, and the strapping Negro in green livery carried the commode into the back of the store, Charles and Herbie following. Herbie paused to grind his cigar out in a Meissen dish sitting on a table. Charles pretended not to notice. Louella continued her monologue, and after a while we heard banging as a lid was hammered onto one of the crates Charles had carried out into the alley earlier. The men returned shortly thereafter, and the Negro carried the crate out to the carriage. Herbie took Charles's hand and pumped it vigorously.

"Clever idea you have here," he said, "having a beautiful young woman to wait on your customers. You gotta real gem. I never saw anyone make a sale so smoothly. Knows her stuff, this little girl does."

"Yes," Charles said. He had to force the word out.

Herbie turned to me and gave me a big grin. "If you ever wanna leave this place, ever wanna get yourself another job, you just come to St. Louis and look me up. I promise ya I'll pay you double what you get here, even more if I have to. Kramer's could *use* a lass like you."

"Why—thank you very much," I said politely.

Charles showed the Kramers out and returned a few moments

later and closed the door and locked it and heaved a heavy sigh. He gave me a long, thoughtful look, and I braced myself for the outburst.

"I—I suppose you're angry," I said nervously.

"Not really. Mildly irritated, perhaps."

"I couldn't resist it," I said in my defense. "She wanted something she could show off to her friends, and—well, they're going to be very impressed. I *did* tell her it was a copy."

"I heard."

"What else did you hear?"

"Everything. How Josephine polished the brass with her own hands—that was a nice touch."

"It made her happy."

He nodded lazily, unfolding the arms he had folded across his chest, resting his hands lightly on his thighs. Bright afternoon sunlight slanted through the front windows, making restless pools on the carpet.

"Mr. Kramer could afford it," I said.

"I've no doubt he could afford to buy the whole store."

"At any rate, you're a thousand dollars richer."

"A hundred of it is yours," he told me.

I was startled. Charles nodded slowly.

"Our salesmen—that's Raoul at the moment—make a very small salary, but they get ten percent commission on every item they sell."

"That's wonderful!" I exclaimed. "Why, I'll bet I could sell a tremendous lot of things. It would be lovely working in a store like this, surrounded by beautiful things. It would help you out—Julian says Raoul's a lousy salesman—and I—I'd be earning my keep."

Charles smiled, genuinely amused, and it was a lovely smile. I didn't see what was so bloody amusing.

"You can't work at Etienne's, Dana, though I've no doubt at all you'd be a whiz. Julian has spent an inordinate amount of our money trying to turn you into a proper young lady, and proper young ladies do not become shopgirls. Come along now, we have work to do in back."

"Don't forget my hundred dollars," I said peevishly.

"I wouldn't dream of it," he drawled.

We resumed our work on the inventory, and Charles was as testy and demanding as he had been before, and I wasn't a bit better-versed on bronzes, making a number of mistakes that irritated him no end. Dripping with perspiration as I lugged yet another heavy bronze over to the desk, I suggested that he pull open the back door so we might have a little air, and he informed me that good honest sweat never hurt anyone. I shot him a look that should have felled him on the spot. We continued to work, and I carried over a pair of firedogs representing Jupiter and Juno by M. Anguier—French bronze, not Italian. I had the distinct impression it pleased him to see me straining under the weight of them. I was young and healthy and strong, true, but there were limits. Proper young ladies didn't work like galley slaves. I told him so. He told me to find the bloody receipt and stop whining.

"Well," he said two hours later, "that's the last of the bronzes."

"Thank God for that," I snapped.

"I can't believe we've accomplished so much in one day. We should easily be able to finish the whole lot tomorrow." He stood up and arched his back, and I could hear tiny bones popping. "We just have the furniture and the paintings left."

"If you think I'm going to move heavy furniture—"

"No moving involved, you'll simply tag each piece after I've listed it. I imagine you can handle that. Tired?"

"Exhausted," I complained.

"You did a commendable job," he told me, "better by far than Raoul would have done. The mood I've been in, I'd probably have killed him, but then he's responsible for the mood I've been in. I'll kill him when he gets back."

He rubbed the back of his neck and brushed a spray of moist chestnut locks from his brow and smiled again. His smile was every bit as nice as Julian's, I thought. What a beautiful mouth he had. What a beautiful man he was, however stern and formidable. I no longer detested him. I was no longer the least bit intimidated by him. He could actually be almost nice when it suited him, I reflected.

Charles glanced at a lovely ormolu clock. "It's almost five. Jasper will be arriving any minute now. Shall we call it a day?"

"Gladly," I said.

He gave me a look that was—well, not fond but not at all hostile either. Had I won him over? Did he no longer resent my presence in his house? Did he no longer consider me a conniving little harlot? I couldn't tell for sure, but I did know that both of us were more relaxed, more at ease with each other than we had been before. Charles stretched, throwing his shoulders back, a healthy, magnificent animal. He looked tousled and weary, and I decided not to tell him about the tiny smudge of ink on his jaw.

Leaving the desktop a shambles with ledger open and papers scattered everywhere, he led the way to the front of the store. I brushed my skirt and adjusted my sleeves as he unlocked the door. How lovely it was to step out into the fresh air. There was a light breeze I found very welcome. Only a few carriages moved down the street. Jasper hadn't arrived yet. Charles sighed, shoving errant chestnut locks from his brow yet again. His blue eyes were thoughtful, but he wasn't thinking about me. He was thinking about business. A frown suddenly appeared, making a furrow over the bridge of his nose, and he snapped his fingers.

"The records of last month's sales—I meant to bring them home with me to go over tonight. I'll go fetch them. You wait here."

"We forgot the baskets, too," I said. "You'd better bring them."

He didn't answer. He unlocked the door again and went back inside, and I peered down the street, looking for Jasper and our carriage. A few moments later a bizarre sight appeared, a grand and very ancient gold and white open carriage with a sturdy milk-white horse in harness. The horse had a bobbing golden plume fastened to its head, and the driver perched on the high seat in front wore very grand and very old livery of gold and white velvet. It was like something from an era long since passed, as was the passenger who sat on the tufted white velvet seat. She wore a gown of sky-blue satin much adorned with frothy cascades of beige lace and pink velvet rosebuds, a gown that must have been in the height of fashion sixty years ago. Her hair was done up in a towering powdered white pompadour, pink and white plumes affixed to one side with a diamond clasp, three long sausage curls dangling over her shoulder. Her withered face was heavily painted, and a black satin beauty mark was pasted on one cheekbone. I recognized her immediately, of course.

Seeing me standing there alone in front of the store, the old woman leaned forward and said something to her driver. He slowed the horse down, pulling to a stop only a few feet away.

"Good afternoon, Clarisse," the old woman said. "How charming you are in that frock. Do you need a ride?"

"No, thank you, Madame Lecomb," I said pleasantly. "And it's Dana O'Malley, ma'am, not Clarisse."

As I spoke that familiar name myself, realization dawned, and I could feel a cold chill inside. I remembered how she had mistaken me for someone else the night of the ball, and I understood why now. I knew I must look very much like my mother had looked twenty years ago.

Madame Lecomb frowned, looking foggy and bewildered.

"O'Malley? But I've never heard that name before in my life. Don't tease me, child. It isn't polite. You're Clarisse DuJardin. Your mother, Mathilde, is—was—one of my dearest—but that was such a long time ago." She looked very distressed. "What has happened to Mathilde? I haven't seen her in years. She used to come to all my Sunday Afternoons, and then . . ."

She shook her head, plumes waving.

"There was some scandal . . ." she said, squinting, trying to remember. "The daughter ran off—none of us ever knew what became of her—and then Theophile was involved in some unpleasant business at the bank where he was a partner. I seem to recall—embezzling? But Theophile was such a gentleman. He—yes, he died—suicide. Poor Mathilde—all the money gone. She would have been penniless if her brother hadn't . . ."

Madame Lecomb frowned, and I could almost see the memories dissolving into a haze. After a moment she sighed and motioned for the driver to move on.

"Lovely seeing you, Clarisse," she said in that cracked old voice. "Tell your mother I'm expecting her next Sunday. Martineau is going to play Mozart, and we'll have champagne and tiny iced cakes and that delicious goose liver pate she likes so well."

The carriage drove away. Charles came back out with the baskets, and I was so lost in thought it was several moments before I realized he was standing beside me. He looked at me with questioning blue eyes.

"You're pale," he said. "Is something wrong?"

I shook my head. He wasn't convinced.

"I—I'm just tired," I said.

"You'll feel better after you've had a hot bath and a good

meal," he told me. "Ah, here's Jasper at last. Been a long day, hasn't it?"

I nodded. I was barely aware of his hand on my elbow as he helped me into the carriage. I was silent as we drove back home. Charles made a few remarks about the inventory, but I didn't reply and he didn't press me. My mind was on other things.

Chapter Eleven

DELIA WAS FEELING THE EFFECTS of the oppressive heat and was in her sitting room suffering from one of her headaches. I entered that small, comfortable room two mornings later to find her reclining on the embroidered peach silk sofa, holding a cologne-soaked handkerchief to her temples. I had no doubt Delia's headaches were genuinely bad, even though both Charles and Julian slighted them, but Delia *did* make much of them, carrying on with high drama like an aging actress milking a scene for all it was worth. She sighed mournfully as I entered, dabbing at her brow with the handkerchief. Wearing a sky-blue silk frock trimmed with antique ivory lace, she looked up at me with miserable eyes that had faint mauve shadows beneath them. Her face was slightly pale, her forehead moist with a faint film of perspiration. The room was stifling. I set down the tray of lemonade I had brought her and, parting the pearl-gray velvet drapes, opened the windows to let in some air. Delia sighed again, throwing an arm over her eyes as though to protect them from the blinding rays of the sun which were nonexistent. The courtyard was full of blue-gray morning shadows.

"I've brought you some lemonade," I told her.

"Oh, my dear, I don't mean to be unappreciative, but nothing will help. I simply can't endure this heat. It's worse than ever this summer, although I remember one summer when I was a girl when it was so hot every plant in the courtyard simply withered away. I thought *I* was going to wither away, too."

"Jezebel put ice in the lemonade," I said.

"So sweet of you to bring it to me, dear. Perhaps I'll have just a sip."

She managed to stir herself into a sitting position and weakly

215

accepted the glass of lemonade and drank half of it with considerable relish, ice tinkling as she did so. I looked at the portrait hanging over the light gray marble mantel. As always, those dark blue eyes seemed to watch my every move.

"Alicia Duvall has invited me to spend a couple of weeks with her at Grande Villa, and I've decided I simply must go. It's right on the river, with a wide, shady verandah and the loveliest rose gardens—I always find a stay there wonderfully reviving, even if Alicia is a dreadful chatterbox—never stops talking for a minute, my dear, and rarely says anything worth remembering."

I had come to the sitting room with a definite motive in mind, and I knew I was going to have to use all my guile to allay any suspicion on Delia's part. I took the now empty glass of lemonade from her and refilled it from the pitcher I had also brought on the tray.

"Charles was so pleased with your help with the inventory," Delia informed me. "He told me last night you'd finished it in half the time it would ordinarily have taken."

"I'm glad I could help," I said.

"And you're almost finished with the east wing."

"Kayla did a wonderful job supervising things while I was at Etienne's, and everything is done but a few pieces of furniture I want to polish myself. I intend to get right to them. Delia—"

"Such industry!" she exclaimed before I could change the subject. "I just don't know how you do it in this heat. I just know it would give me a dreadful headache. . . ."

Remembering that she had one, she picked up a palmetto fan and began to fan herself weakly, refusing the refilled glass I offered. I set it on the table in front of the sofa.

"The Duvalls are a very fine old family, aren't they?" I inquired.

"One of the oldest, one of the finest—though not, of course, anything to compare with the Etiennes. The Duvalls came to New Orleans a good ten years later, and Pierre Duvall had made his fortune as a trapper in the Northwest, trading with the Indians for furs or something equally as distasteful. No class at all, I fear, though his children managed to acquire a little polish."

"You know all the old families, don't you?"

Delia nodded. Abandoning the palmetto fan, she picked up the glass of lemonade and took a big gulp.

"I know the genealogies of all the families in the Quarter, dear, it's been a hobby of mine for decades. I know most of the family skeletons, too—people *do* gossip, though of course I'd never stoop to such a thing myself. It's so very undignified."

"Of course," I agreed.

"You must send Jezebel my compliments on this lemonade, dear. It's ever so refreshing—though nothing could help this wretched migraine," she added mournfully. "I just suffer and suffer and suffer for hours on end. No one *knows* the agony of it, dear."

"Let me get you a headache powder."

"I've taken two already. I'll just have to suffer. I'm definitely leaving for Grande Villa—Alicia's chatter won't help my migraine a bit, but those wonderful cool breezes off the river will be most welcome, I'm sure. I wonder what clothes I should take—there's bound to be a summer ball. That pale rose taffeta Corinne did up for me should be all right—I'm certain Alicia hasn't seen it—and I can use the gray tulle wrap lightly spangled with sequins. The buttercup-yellow silk, of course, and . . ."

Delia paused, looking torn.

"Tell me, dear—and please do be honest—do you think the white silk with the mauve velvet bows is a bit too girlish for a lady of my years?"

"I think it's lovely, perfect for you. Delia, I wonder if—"

"Then I'll take it, and some light morning frocks, of course, and perhaps a sprigged muslin or two for strolling in the rose garden, and I mustn't forget my wide-brimmed garden hat, white tulle with trailing ribbons. Oh dear, there's so much to remember. . . ."

"I'll help you pack," I said, beginning to feel quite frustrated. "Delia, I—I wonder if you've ever heard of a family named DuJardin? I don't remember meeting anyone by that name at the Lecombs' ball."

"You wouldn't have met a DuJardin at the ball, dear—although I seem to remember that Mathilde DuJardin was one of Madame Lecomb's regulars years ago, before the scandal. Why are you so interested in the DuJardins, dear?"

"I—oh, I just heard the name mentioned," I said quickly, covering, "and I wondered if you knew them."

"*Such* a scandal," Delia declared, warming up. "Theophile DuJardin was one of the most respected men in the Quarter—very old family, very best lineage, a considerable fortune. The DuJardins and their two daughters lived in a perfectly beautiful house, one of the grandest in the Quarter, and their gardens were a marvel. Mathilde had an absolute passion for azaleas and camellias, and in season they were a perfect blaze of pink and white and red and mauve. Mathilde introduced the garden party to the Quarter—she gave the very first one, and they caught on immediately. Everyone started giving them—I gave several myself. I remember one in particular—oh, it must have been thirty years ago. I was *much* younger, of course, and I remember I wore white and yellow muslin. . . ."

Delia remembered at great length and in considerable detail. I wore an interested expression and tried my best not to scream. She rambled on and on, her headache quite forgotten.

"—and that was the party where Therese Delys first met Beau Gabin, *such* a handsome boy he was, though a complete rogue. They married a few months later, and poor Therese never could learn to accept his infidelities. She took to gin, eventually took to laudanum, finally swallowed a whole bottle of it. Beau broke up at the funeral, actually threw himself on the casket. He loved her, you see, even if he couldn't resist a pretty face."

"And it was Mathilde DuJardin who started the vogue for garden parties?" I said, hoping to lead her back to the subject.

"They were all the rage. Poor Mathilde, she doesn't even have a garden at that tacky little house her brother bought for her—number four Conti Street, I believe, gray brick, *green* shutters, my dear, the front steps leading right down to the sidewalk. There could be a garden in back, but of course no one from the Quarter has ever been there. Mathilde might have weathered the storm—she wasn't responsible, after all—but she chose to turn her back on the Quarter and live in seclusion."

Number four Conti Street. I committed the address to memory.

"Actually, people felt very sorry for her. Theophile was vice president of one of our biggest banks, handled the finances of half the families in the Quarter, and he'd been using some of their money for personal investments and embezzling on the side. Everyone was horrified when he was finally exposed—quite a few families lost their savings. Jail was inevitable, but before that could happen Theophile strolled into Mathilde's lovely garden and blew his brains out. I remember well the sensation it caused—''

Before she could remember at length, I asked her what had become of the two daughters.

''Solonge was still living at home—a tall, plain girl, unfortunately, old maid written all over her. She moved to Conti Street with her mother. The other girl, Clarisse, had already left home. The DuJardins claimed she had gone to a fancy finishing school up East and married a Yankee, but there were rumors she ran off with some good-looking scoundrel from out of town. I could give no credence to such rumors. She was a shy thing, as pretty as Solonge was plain, with such lovely manners. Mathilde had hoped to make a grand match for her. It wasn't to be, alas. Clarisse never returned to New Orleans, not even to attend her father's funeral.''

I didn't say anything. I was finding it difficult to contain my emotions. Delia mustn't suspect my interest was anything but casual.

''Mathilde's brother came to her rescue,'' Delia continued. ''He wasn't one of *us*, you understand, although he was a perfectly respectable man. He owned a number of warehouses down on the docks, and several of the men in the Quarter did business with him. Anyway, Guy Chevrier bought the house for Mathilde. He made some very bad investments several years ago, lost most of his money and lost the warehouses as well. I understand he moved into the house with Mathilde and Solonge and now makes a living supervising cargo on the docks.''

Delia shook her head. ''Pity,'' she said, and then she glanced at the clock. ''My, it's almost eleven. Dana, dear, please tell Jezebel I've changed my mind. I'll have a bite to eat, after all. Charles said he'll be home for lunch today, and that'll make four of us if we can pry Julian out of his study. A nice nourishing lunch might help this wretched headache.''

Lunch was an ordeal. I had an aunt, a great-uncle and a grandmother living right here in the city and not too far from here— I knew that Conti Street was near Exchange Alley, where the fencing academies were located, and close to both Royal and Bourbon. I could hardly contain my impatience. I longed to rush over to number four immediately, but I had to sit at the table with Charles and Julian and Delia and maintain a calm demeanor. Jezebel had outdone herself—cold, tender asparagus with white cheese sauce, sliced ham, lobster salad, popovers—but I had no appetite at all and barely touched my food.

"Raoul reported to work this morning," Charles remarked, buttering one of the golden-brown, light-as-air popovers. "He gave no explanations and made no apologies, merely said he'd had a dandy time."

"Is he still alive?" Julian asked.

"He's alive, but he got a severe dressing down. I told him in no uncertain terms that his ass was out if he pulled a stunt like that again."

"Language, dear," Delia said.

"He had the temerity to ask for a raise in salary. Can you believe it? He said it would make his mother very happy."

"You didn't give it to him," Julian said.

"On the contrary, I told him I was docking him for the days he missed. He sulked a bit, but he didn't dare complain—he saw the mood I was in. The young varlet was lucky I didn't kick his—"

"Language," Delia warned.

"Backside. I wanted to, believe me. Incidentally, you'll never guess who came into the shop this morning, Julian."

"I never will. Who?"

A half smile curled on Charles's chiseled pink lips, and he gave his brother an amused look. "The lovely Amelia," he said.

Delia looked surprised. "Amelia Jameson?" she asked.

"The same."

"Oh dear," she said.

I remembered the lady well. She was the gorgeous brunette with violet-blue eyes who had loaned me the gown and slippers and parasol when Julian and I finally reached the inn and I had nothing but the rags I was wearing. How I had envied her sumptuous clothes and worldly poise.

"I wonder what *she*'s doing back in town," Julian remarked, helping himself to more lobster salad. "Last time I saw her she'd taken up with some rich property owner who was keeping her in style."

"Really," Delia protested, "I'm not sure this is a suitable subject for the lunch table."

Charles and Julian both gave her looks.

"She was looking extremely well," Charles continued, grinning. ''Lovelier than ever, in fact. She was wearing crimson silk and long black lace gloves and a wide-brimmed black hat with crimson plumes and ribbons. A veritable vision, I must say.''

''I never realized you were so observant, dear,'' Delia said.

''What did she buy?'' Julian asked.

''She wasn't buying, she was selling. It seems she's a little short of cash and wanted to know if I'd be interested in a silver filigree box she brought in. Late seventeenth century, fine craftsmanship, superb detail.''

''You give her a good price for it?''

''More than I should have, but we'll still turn a nice profit. I felt sure you'd approve. The rich property owner is apparently out of the picture,'' he continued, ''and the lady is unattached.''

''That won't last long,'' Julian said dryly.

''She asked about you,'' Charles told him.

Julian looked highly disinterested. ''Yeah?''

''I told her you were working on your book. 'It figures,' she said. 'He always was.' ''

''That's quite enough, Charles,'' Delia said. ''Did I tell you boys I'm leaving for Grande Villa tomorrow morning? Alicia's been begging me to come visit, and this dreadful heat is *so* oppressive. I've had a terrible migraine for days. I just suffer and suffer and—''

Julian lifted his eyes heavenward. Charles buttered another popover and reached for the platter of ham. Delia continued her monologue until dessert was served—chilled chocolate pudding with whipped cream on top—and then Julian informed us that he, too, was going to be away.

''I thought I'd made my last trip to the swamps, but in working on the footnotes I discovered that I need more information on certain soil conditions. I'm leaving day after tomorrow— shouldn't be gone for more than a couple of weeks. The bronze orchids grow only in damp soil, you see, while the purple orchids are found only in a certain kind of flaky gray clay. I should've brought soil samples back with me last time, but I was so intrigued with those new ferns I found I forgot about everything else. The ferns grow only at the edge of the water in muddy soil, they're a peculiar shade of yellow-green and have unusually soft and feathery—''

''Really, dear, I don't mean to be unkind,'' Delia said, ''but we're not at all interested. You go on and on about the most boring things. Some of us prefer *stim*ulating conversation at the table.''

Charles and Julian exchanged looks.

''Why hasn't one of us murdered her before now?'' Charles inquired.

''Miraculous restraint,'' Julian replied.

''You boys,'' Delia said fondly.

Julian retired to his study after lunch, and Charles went back to spend the rest of the day at Etienne's. Delia declared that a nice long nap might do wonders for her headache, she would pack after dinner. She went up to her bedroom, and I gave a sigh of relief. I found Kayla and asked her to prepare a bath for me, and forty-five minutes later I was in my bedroom wearing a petticoat and trying to select the right dress to wear. I rejected several, finally selecting a demure frock of thin, leaf-brown linen. It had elbow-length puffed sleeves and a square-cut neckline higher than most. I adjusted the snug waist and smoothed the folds of the very full skirt over my petticoat. Examining myself in the mirror, I wasn't satisfied with my hair. I spent another fifteen minutes brushing it, pulling it back from my face and fastening it into a French roll on the back of my head.

Kayla tapped on my door and stepped inside, looking surprised at the change in my appearance.

''Why, Miz Dana!'' she exclaimed. ''You look—why, in that dress an' with your hair done up like that, you look plum prim''

''That's how I want to look,'' I told her.

''I come up to see if you needed anything. You plannin' on goin' to a prayer meetin' or somethin'?''

''Kayla,'' I said, ignoring her impertinence, ''has that new man Jasper come back yet from taking Mister Charles to the shop?''

''He got back half an hour ago,'' Kayla replied, ''came into the east wing where I was workin' and pinched me right on the rear, he did, then tried to take liberties. What sauce! I told him I wudn't havin' none of that, not from the likes-a him. He *is* good-lookin', I have to admit that. Don't you think so, Miz Dana?''

''I—I really hadn't noticed, Kayla.''

''Very well built and such roguish eyes. Of course, he's rather *dark* for a gal light as me, but those muscles—to tell you the truth, I wouldn't mind all that much if he *did* take liberties.''

"Kayla, I want you to do a favor for me. I want you to ask Jasper to meet me on the street in ten minutes—on the street, not in front of the door—and I want him to use the closed carriage."

"Don't want no one seein' you, is that it?"

"That's it," I said impatiently.

"You ain't goin' to meet a lover, that's for sure. Not wearin' that dress. Guess you've got a secret errand."

"Exactly. And I'd like to *keep* it a secret. Please don't tell anyone else about it, and—and ask Jasper to keep quiet about it, too. Will you?"

Kayla nodded, clearly intrigued. "Sure thing, Miz Dana. I'll tell him if he blabs he ain't gettin' any of this. The closed carriage will be waiting for you on the street in ten minutes, I promise you."

She scurried out of the room, and I turned to the mirror again. I did look a bit too prim, I thought, and, to remedy it, decided I would carry my green velvet reticule and fasten a green velvet bow at the side of the French roll, above my temple. That helped considerably. I looked demure and well-bred, but not as if I were on my way to a prayer meeting.

I slipped out of the house without being seen and hurried down the drive to the wrought-iron gates. I was pleased to see the closed carriage waiting a little way down the street, Jasper standing ready to help me inside. He *was* a handsome chap, I noted, with a trim, muscular physique, skin like polished ebony and strong, rather stern features. The eyes Kayla described as roguish were a very dark brown, discreetly impassive now. He nodded curtly when I greeted him, then handed me into the carriage.

"Do you know where Conti Street is?" I asked.

Jasper nodded again. I asked him to drive me to number four, a gray house with green shutters, and he closed the carriage door. I leaned back against the padded velvet cushions, spreading my skirts out as the carriage started to move. Everything had happened so quickly, I hadn't had time to make any plans or think about what I was going to say, what I was going to do. I peered out at the gray brick walls spilling with bougainvillea, at the greenery beyond and the lacework of wrought iron that adorned the houses, and I tried to tell myself I wasn't being impulsive, tried to tell myself I wasn't nervous at all. Mathilde

DuJardin was my grandmother, my own blood kin, Solonge my aunt, Guy Chevrier my great-uncle, and blood had to mean something. I found myself gripping my skirt tightly, bunching up the thin brown linen with my fingers, my knuckles white. I stopped immediately.

You should have waited, I told myself. You should have sent them a letter first. You should have prepared them. What are they going to say when you appear on their doorstep, out of the blue, claiming to be their kin? What if they don't believe you? These and other questions plagued me as the carriage gently swayed, as the horse hooves clop-clopped on the cobblestones. I should wait. I should tap on the roof of the carriage and ask Jasper to turn around and take me back home. I didn't. I took several deep breaths. I forced myself to relax. It's going to be all right, I assured myself. You're no longer a ragged little waif from the swamps. You're a respectable young lady.

We passed the market, a riot of color and activity at this hour. Negro women with huge baskets examined piles of oranges, barrels of eels, mounds of plump pink shrimp, piles of crisp pale green lettuce. Children darted about merrily, and fashionably dressed ladies strolled together, twirling their parasols, chatting in front of stalls selling delicious pastries or the mouth-watering praline candy for which the city was famous. I could smell the wonderful exotic spices and freshly baked bread, the salty smell of raw fish and, too, the acrid odor of droppings from the chicken pens, all of it somehow blending together to create a tangy perfume. I had come here several times with Jezebel, amused by her sharp eye and her ability to drive a hard bargain. Woe unto anyone who tried to sell her a slightly bruised melon or a bucket of oysters less than fresh. I wished I were shopping with her now. I wished I were doing anything else but what I was doing now.

I wondered if Ma had loved the market as much as I did. Ma . . . She had been a lovely young girl, growing up in this city, very much a part of the snobbish, exclusive society of the Quarter, the daughter of one of its most respected members. She had lived in a grand house with lovely gardens, gardens ablaze with azaleas and camellias, and there had been an older sister, a sister she had never mentioned to me, plain, perhaps jealous of her beauty. It had been a luxurious life, gracious and full of gentle splendors. There had been parties, and beaux, too, of course, probably a great many beaux, dashing, handsome young blue bloods who longed to capture Theophile DuJardin's beautiful daughter. Ma would have none of them, though. She wanted someone else, and because of him she had given up that luxurious life and . . . and ended up in the swamps with Clem O'Malley.

I repressed a sob and forced back the tears. The grief was still there inside, as strong as ever, and it threatened to break free and sweep over me anew. No. No, I wouldn't let it demolish me. Deliberately, with great effort, I controlled it, forced it back into that dark place inside where it would always remain, a part of me for as long as I lived. Ma was gone. I had resigned myself to that a long time ago. Ma was gone, and I must go on. That was what life was all about, going on—no matter how hard it sometimes might be. I brushed the moisture from my lashes and sat up, composed now and much calmer than I had been since I left the house. I had lost Ma, but I had found her people, thanks to the ramblings of a pathetic yet touching old woman who could no longer differentiate between past and present.

We turned into Exchange Alley, where at least fifty *maîtres d'armes* operated fencing academies for the young bucks of the city. Fencing was the fashion, and duels at dawn were much too frequently held in the grove of giant live oaks outside the city called, simply, the Oaks. I saw several young men on the street, some with fencing masks and swords in hand, most of them simply lounging together and exchanging tales of their prowess at today's practice. I recognized Zackery Rambeaux and Pierre Dorsay and one or two others I had met at the ball. How pleased with themselves they all looked, idling about with nothing to fill their days but wenching and dueling and gambling and other mischief. They laughed at Julian and called him a dreamer, but at least Julian was striving to make a contribution, and they looked down on Charles because he worked and refused to conform to their ideas of "aristocratic" behavior. No wonder Raoul resented working at Etienne's. These were his close companions, and they must ride him mercilessly about being "in trade."

Exchange Alley turned in to Conti, and a few moments later the carriage came to a stop. Jasper climbed down and opened the door for me, and my skirts made a soft rustling noise as I stepped down. We were in front of a tall, three-story house that was one of an attached row, all of them flush with the sidewalk.

Number four was of old gray brick, as were most of the others, and it had the worn, mellow patina of age. No wrought iron here, only a short flight of dirty white marble steps, a white door with fanlight above it and green shutters at the windows. The green paint was peeling, I noticed, and the heavy glass panes of the windows needed a good washing. A tarnished brass Four was affixed to the center of the door, and there was a heavy brass knocker over the doorknob.

"I don't know how long I may be, Jasper," I told him. "You may go on back to the house. You'll be needing to go pick up Mister Charles in a little while, anyway."

"I ain't to wait for you?"

I shook my head. Jasper looked dubious. He looked stubborn, too.

"How you gonna get back?" he asked.

"I—I'll stroll down to Canal and hire a cab."

"It ain't fittin' for a young lady like you to be traipsin' around the city without a chaperone, Miz Dana. I'd better wait for you. Mister Charles'd have my hide if somethin' happened to you."

I gave him an imperious look. "I'll hire a cab, Jasper," I said firmly. "There is no need for you to wait."

"But—"

"Don't argue with me."

Jasper hesitated, still dubious, but he finally scowled and climbed back up onto his perch and picked up the reins. I waited until the carriage was driving down the street before moving up those soot-stained white steps. Now that I was actually here, panic swept over me. My body seemed to turn ice-cold and my heart seemed to leap and I knew I couldn't do it, knew I hadn't the courage, was going to turn and flee. It must be after four o'clock now, and the street was spread with soft purple-gray afternoon shadows. It was too late. I would come back in a few days, after I had written them a letter, after I had prepared them. I was terrified. I realized that, and I knew I couldn't let it get the best of me. I waited another few moments, trying to compose myself, and then lifted the knocker and rapped on the door.

The sound seemed to echo in the empty hall beyond. The street was empty at this hour, and I felt terribly vulnerable and exposed standing there in front of the door. There was no answer. I waited. I knocked again, and again the sound seemed to echo inside. Maybe no one is home, I thought hopefully. I can leave without feeling like a coward. It's better this way. I'm not ready to see them just yet. This was a very foolish idea. I was far too impulsive. Then I heard the sound of footsteps approaching the door from within. I caught my breath. I felt frightened and resigned, and then, strangely, the fear vanished and a peculiar calm came over me.

The door was opened by a handsome, rather heavily built man who appeared to be in his early sixties. Although completely silver now, his hair was thick and had a healthy sheen. Although lined and worn, his face with its strong jaw and broad, flat cheekbones bore the vestiges of extreme good looks. His complexion was deeply tanned, and his hazel eyes were sad, full of disillusionment. He was wearing a superbly tailored gray frock coat that had clearly seen years of wear, as had the silver-gray satin waistcoat and black silk neckcloth. He looked weary, looked resigned, looked as though life had dealt him one too many hard blows and he had given up the battle. He gazed at me with questioning eyes, as though to ask why in the world I would be bothering him, and then recognition flickered in those eyes and he blinked, stunned.

"Clarisse . . ." he whispered.

"Not Clarisse," I said. "Her daughter."

He stared at me, holding the door open, his hand gripping it tightly, and I feared the shock might be too much for him. The handsome face seemed to sag, and the hazel eyes gazed at me and saw the past and grew even sadder. It was several moments before he was able to speak again.

"Cla-Clarisse's daughter. Yes—yes, there can be no doubt. I—none of us ever knew she—"

He cut himself short, unable to go on. I stood there on the doorstep, full of conflicting emotions, superbly composed on the surface. A carriage passed on the street behind me. Guy Chevrier, for it must be he, finally managed to pull himself together. He straightened up, and his expression grew guarded. When he spoke, his voice was guarded, too.

"I'm Guy Chevrier," he said.

I nodded. "My great-uncle. I'm Dana O'Malley."

"If it's money you want—"

"I didn't come here for money," I said.

"Then—"

"I came to see you—and my grandmother and aunt."

Guy Chevrier looked at me closely, suspiciously now, I fancied, and finally he stepped back and asked me to come inside. I moved into a small foyer with a faded blue and gray rug on the dark hardwood floor and cheap flowered blue wallpaper on the walls. The paper was faded, too, the pink and gray flowers almost white now. My great-uncle led the way down a narrow corridor toward the back of the house, and I could smell something cooking. Cabbage? Corned beef? A skinny Negro girl in a calico dress stuck her head out of the kitchen, peering at us as we passed. I had the impression visitors were rare indeed at number four Conti Street.

The parlor he showed me into was at the very back of the house, French windows looking out over a small, unkempt walled garden. There were no azaleas, no camellias, only a few pathetic rose bushes and what looked like a patch of vegetables. I found it very sad, depressing. The parlor was done in shades of gray and blue and mauve, a purple carpet on the floor. Most of the furniture was old and shabby, but there were two or three sumptuous pieces—a magnificently gilded white cabinet, a gorgeous mauve silk screen, a pair of very ornate silver candlesticks with amethyst wax candles. These relics of a grander time served only to emphasize the genteel shabbiness of the rest of the room. A basket of knitting sat beside a large blue velvet chair with worn nap, and religious pamphlets were stacked untidily on a table in front of the matching sofa.

"My niece is at church," Guy Chevrier said. "A group of ladies are packing baskets of food for the needy or something of the sort, and Solonge is supervising. My sister is in her room, resting. I hesitate to disturb her. This is very distressing, Miss O'Malley."

"It wasn't my intention to distress anyone," I said.

There was a catch in my voice. I was losing courage fast.

"Then why did you come?" he asked.

"Because—because you're my kin."

Guy Chevrier frowned and examined me with suspicious eyes, debating whether or not he should inform his sister of my presence in her house. He was my blood kin, and yet he looked at me as though I were some kind of criminal, as though I had blackmail in mind or planned to run off with the silver candlesticks. I was still cool and poised on the surface, but I knew I couldn't maintain that facade much longer. Frown deepening, my great-uncle examined me for a while longer and then, decision reached, gave me a curt nod.

"I suppose I might as well alert my sister," he said. "We might as well get this over with and be done with it. Mathilde has not been well, but—if you will wait here, Miss O'Malley . . ."

He left the room. I could hear his footsteps moving back down the corridor and up a flight of stairs. I waited. I didn't sit down, I was far too nervous. Several long minutes passed. Shadows were spreading in the back garden, stretching across the dusty yard like hazy blue-gray fingers. This was what my grandmother looked out upon every day. How sad she must be when she remembered that glorious blaze of azaleas and camellias, when she thought about those garden parties for which she had been celebrated. Was she sad when she thought about her daughter, too? How could anyone disown a child? It had probably been done in the heat of emotion. She had probably regretted it all these years, longing to see Ma again, but Ma had had too much pride to contact her folks again after she had been abandoned and left with child.

I wandered restlessly around the small room, idly examining things. A set of hand-embroidered samplers hung on one wall, all neatly framed, all with a religious motif, the messages grim and not at all uplifting. One depicted a gravestone with a weeping mother placing a flower on the mound of earth in front. In His Arms Now, the embroidered message read, and in the upper right-hand corner a chubby infant could be seen resting on clouds. Hardly a cheerful thing to spend weeks working on. The others were as morbid. I suspected that my aunt Solonge had done them. The religious pamphlets on the table were pretty morbid, too, I discovered, all about hellfire and doom and the perils besetting those who dwelt in this vale of tears. *Solonge DuJardin* was printed on the flyleaf of each pamphlet. She must not be a very happy person, I thought.

At least twenty minutes passed. I was even more restless, my nerves on the verge of snapping altogether. Had my grandmother refused to see me? Were they just going to leave me waiting here? When, finally, I heard footsteps descending the staircase, I caught my breath and tried valiantly to compose myself. I heard low voices, my uncle's soothing, the other a harsh grumble, and then footsteps moved down the corridor, moved slowly, and I heard the unmistakable thump-thump of a wooden cane. My heart seemed to stop. My uncle entered the room and turned to give his sister some assistance. She waved him away impatiently, moving into the room on her own, leaning heavily on her ebony cane. She gave me a long, cold look that betrayed no emotion whatsoever, then moved with regal stiffness over to the large blue chair.

Dressed in black broadcloth with a black lace shawl wrapped around her arms and shoulders, she had a stout, solid body and steel-gray hair worn in two tight braids twisted into a coronet on top of her head. She had her brother's square jaw and his broad, flat cheekbones, but there the resemblance ended. There were no vestiges of beauty in her face. It was harsh, hard, the lips thin and disapproving, the eyes dark brown, bitter. There was no warmth, no softness, nor was there any of Ma's sweet gentility. Gripping her cane with both hands, she lowered herself into the chair, again disdaining her brother's assistance. Leaning the cane against the side of the chair, she adjusted the black lace shawl to her satisfaction and gave me another cold look.

"Well, young woman," she snapped, "what is it you want?"

"I—I wanted to meet you," I said. My voice trembled.

"If your mother thinks she can use you to wedge her way back into the family after all this time, she's sadly mistaken."

"My mother is dead," I said quietly.

Guy Chevrier took a step forward. His face seemed to crumple. I could see that he was shocked, that he had been fond of his niece. Mathilde DuJardin displayed no reaction at all. I might have been commenting on the weather.

"How?" my uncle asked. "When?" His voice was weak.

"Ma died earlier this year—in the swamps. She had had consumption for a long time. I—I was with her when she passed on."

He shook his head, staring into the past again, and then he stepped over to the gilded white cabinet, opened it and took out a decanter and glass. Mathilde DuJardin pursed her thin lips as she watched him pour a strong brandy.

"Really, Guy," she said. "It's barely five o'clock. Must you start quite so early?"

"I've just received some very upsetting news, Mathilde."

He downed half the brandy. His face was still crumpled. He toyed with the glass and looked at his sister.

"I loved the girl," he said.

"I know you did. So did her father. Clarisse had a way with men, even as an infant. They could never resist her charm."

I was appalled by her attitude, her lack of emotion. "You—you don't *care* that she's dead?" I asked.

"My daughter died for me the day she ran off with that dreadful man. I had plans for her. She could have married Jacques Cartier. He was mad for her, and he was the greatest catch in the Quarter. He inherited two plantations and over a million dollars when his father died."

"She didn't love him," Guy Chevrier pointed out.

"Love! What did an empty-headed slip of a girl know about love? That man beguiled her. I told her he was no good. I told her if she didn't give him up I would disown her. If she had married Jacques, there would have been money and her father could have—put back what he borrowed. Everything would have been different."

My great-uncle finished his brandy. He no longer looked broken. He merely looked resigned and very, very sad.

"You can't blame Clarisse for all that, Mathilde."

"I told her we needed money. I didn't go into detail, but I told her that her father was having problems at the bank and it was imperative she bring money into the family. Jacques would have done anything for her. She wouldn't listen to me. She was in *love*. Her family didn't matter."

"She was only a girl," my uncle said.

"A selfish, willful girl. Her father spoiled her dreadfully. So did you, Guy. All the men spoiled her. She was pretty and capricious and they all wanted to make her smile. She could have had anyone—anyone—and she chose to run off with that *nobody*."

Mathilde DuJardin pressed her lips together, her eyes burning with terrible bitterness. This woman was my grandmother. I had nourished foolish fancies of a joyous, loving reunion, of intimacy and days spent together in warm companionship. My grandmother may have loved her azaleas and camellias, but she had never loved my mother. She gave me another cold look, still the haughty aristocrat despite her present surroundings.

"I suppose you're *his* daughter?" she said.

I nodded. "I—Ma never told me who—"

"I don't suppose he married her, did he?"

I shook my head. She looked triumphant.

"I told her that would happen. I told her he'd leave her high and dry and in serious trouble. Your name is O'Malley, Guy said. I suppose she found another fool man to give her bastard a name."

"Who was my father?" I asked.

"I vowed his name would never pass my lips," Mathilde DuJardin said stiffly. "I have no intention of breaking that vow now."

"But—"

"If you've come here to blackmail us, young woman, you've wasted your time. Everyone in the Quarter believes my youngest daughter went to school up East and married a Yankee. At one time the knowledge that she ran off with a good-looking charlatan and bore his bastard would have ruined the family name, but shortly thereafter her father ruined it so sufficiently that nothing people found out now could possibly matter."

"Do you actually believe I came here to blackmail you?"

"Of course you did."

"Not—not everyone is venal and cold hearted, madame," I informed her.

Mathilde DuJardin caught the implication at once. Her mouth flew open and her brown eyes widened. She was outraged that anyone had the temerity to speak to her that way. What a dragon she must have been before her fall. The old Creole families of the Quarter were notorious for their snobbery and arrogance, but she must have given new meaning to those words. Perhaps because she wasn't born into the society, I thought unkindly. Guy Chevrier wasn't "one of us," Delia had said. Before her marriage to Theophile DuJardin, my grandmother would have been an outsider, too.

"How dare you—" she began and cut herself short when she heard the front door slamming. She shot a look at her brother. "Solonge," she said. "You'd better go prepare her."

Her brother nodded and left the room. My grandmother adjusted the folds of her black lace shawl again and looked at me with those cold eyes. I could hear voices in the front hall, a muted background. I felt trapped in the middle of a very bad dream. I wanted only to leave.

"You look exactly like her," Mathilde DuJardin said.

"I consider that a compliment, madame."

"Coming here was a grave mistake, young woman."

"I realize that," I said.

"I don't know what you hoped to gain, but—"

"What I hoped to gain is something you're quite incapable of providing," I told her.

She had no idea what I was talking about. Reaching for her cane, she propped it between her knees and rested her hands on top of it, looking at me with a total lack of feeling. Was it possible for a mother to hate her daughter, to be unmoved by news of her death? I found that hard to believe, but it seemed to be true in this instance. Mathilde DuJardin clearly blamed my mother for all those misfortunes that had befallen the family. I stood there in front of the shabby blue velvet sofa, amazed and appalled. The voices in the corridor grew somewhat louder, accompanied now by the sound of footsteps, and a moment later my aunt Solonge stepped into the room.

She was tall and extremely thin, almost emaciated, wearing a drab puce dress with long sleeves and a high neck. Her face was an elongated version of her mother's, the features pinched and sour, the eyes a lighter brown, almost amber, full of self-satisfaction and superiority. Her mouth was pursed, sanctimonious, and her mousy brown hair was pulled back and worn in a tight bun on the back of her neck. She had the officious, self-important air of the professional do-gooder, and no warmth. No warmth whatsoever. Everything about her was dry and brittle, as though the saps inside had long since turned into dust. She was clutching a Bible, I noticed. I suspected that she was rarely without it. When she saw me, she stopped and her face went a little white, but she did not lose a jot of her frigid composure.

"So," she said, "it's true. At first I thought you might be an impostor, but I can see that isn't the case."

"The resemblance is remarkable," her uncle said, stepping into the room behind her.

"Quite," Solonge DuJardin said. She looked at her mother. "I hope this hasn't distressed you too much, Maman."

"I'm fine, daughter."

"What a pleasant day *this* has been. The dear ladies I recruited did everything wrong, and I had to repack all the baskets myself—*one* apple to a basket, one orange—and I'll probably have to distribute them myself as well. I had to dress down Mrs. Ashbury for being inexcusably tardy, and Father Phillipe had been at the sacramental wine again—I'm going to have to write a letter to his superiors, one is long overdue—and then I come home to find this charming situation confronting me. I don't know how I cope."

Admirably, I'm sure, I thought. Solonge DuJardin turned those piercing amber eyes on me, her mouth twitching with distaste.

"My uncle informs me that you are named O'Malley."

"That's right."

She nodded, a wintry smile now curling on those thin lips. She looked extremely pleased with herself.

"I know who you are," she said. It was an accusation, not a statement. A muscle twitched at the side of her left eye. "We may no longer be a part of the Grand Society, but we hear about everything that goes on in the Quarter. You're the girl Julian Etienne brought back from the swamps."

I nodded. Solonge DuJardin turned to her mother.

"He brought her out of the swamps and installed her in his house," she informed her. "*Then* he made her his 'ward.' The entire Quarter was scandalized. She's nothing but a little whore."

She was still clutching the Bible.

"Like mother, like daughter, I suppose. Oh yes, I can see the resemblance. The same face, the same body, the same guile—" She was addressing me now. "My dear sister could always twist the men around her little finger—starting with Daddy. I—I tried my best to please him in every way I could, but she was his favorite. Always. Daddy never caught on to her wiles. Darling Clarisse could do no wrong. She took after him, had his features, his coloring. *I* was the dutiful one, but she was the one he loved."

"I'm glad someone loved her," I said.

"The men flocked around her, all of them, vying for her favors, plying her with flowers and presents and attention—how she reveled in it. She could have married a fortune, could have saved the family. I would have done anything for my father, anything, but Clarisse chose to enter into a—a thoroughly disgusting illicit relationship with a scoundrel. He got her pregnant. He abandoned her. She bore his bastard and ended up in the swamps. She got exactly what she deserved, and I'm *glad*."

"What a fine Christian lady you are," I said.

She didn't miss the irony. She recoiled, incensed.

"I'm not a whore," I told her, "and neither, thank God, am I a dried-up, frustrated, brittle old maid consumed with jealousy and hate. I pity you mademoiselle. I pity all of you. I can understand now why my mother ran away. How terrible it must have been growing up with a mother and a sister like the two of you. My mother was gentle and compassionate and caring. I may be a bastard, as you pointed out with such relish, but I was raised with *love*—something my mother had to find outside her home."

Mathilde DuJardin gasped, looking like some outraged duchess. Her daughter puffed up like an adder, ready to explode. Guy Chevrier had sunk down onto the sofa, ashen, broken, spineless, as bad as they were in his way. I marched over to the door and then turned to face the three of them.

"When my ma died, I had but one thought—to get to New Orleans somehow and find her family. I wanted to have a place. I wanted to—to be a part. I wanted to belong. I came to the city, and I *did* find a place. A man not related to me at all took me into his home and made me his ward, not for the reasons you believe, dear Aunt, but because he is kind and good and caring, because he actually practices those virtues found in the Bible you're clutching. He and his aunt and—and his brother have made me a part of their lives, and I belong."

I paused for breath. All three of them were speechless.

"Coming here was indeed a mistake. I thought I might find people like Ma, kind and Christian and good, but I see that I was wrong. We have the same blood flowing in our veins, but—thank God I'm not like any of you. Thank God Ma got away from you all and found some happiness with the man she loved, however brief it may have been, and—and thank God I don't have to see any of you ever again. How lucky I am to have a *real* family."

Mathilde DuJardin was still gasping. Her brother looked at me with woeful eyes, wanting to say something to me, too spineless to do so. My aunt was ashen with outrage and looking more than ever like an adder with head thrust forward on her scrawny neck and amber eyes blazing.

"You—you impudent little tramp!" she spluttered. "How dare you speak to people like us in that manner. You—why, you act as though you think you're better than we are—you, the

bastard offspring of a highborn slut and her penniless paramour!
You're your mother's daughter, all right.''

"I am indeed," I said, "and I'm so very proud of it."

I turned then and left the room. I could hear my grandmother
and her daughter burst into exclamations of outrage as I moved
down the corridor. The skinny Negro girl peeked out at me from
the kitchen door as I passed, her eyes as large as saucers. She'd
undoubtedly overheard everything. I felt numb as I walked to
the front door. I hadn't broken down. I had maintained my
dignity throughout, despite the insults to me and to Ma. I was
pleased with that much. I had been dignified, a lady. I hadn't
cried . . . Oh God, please let me get out of here before I start
sobbing.

I opened the front door and stepped outside and pulled the
door shut, and I could feel all the emotions I had repressed
welling up inside. I could feel the tears, too. I stood there on
the shady doorstep for a moment, gnawing my lower lip, willing
myself to be strong. It was over. It didn't matter. It didn't matter
at all. Home. I must get home. I was trembling inside now,
trembling badly, though I was still cool and calm on the surface.
I closed my eyes, praying for the strength to go on, and then I
went down the steps and started toward Canal. I still seemed to
be in the middle of a dream. The girl in brown linen with the
green velvet reticule swinging from her wrist reached the corner,
moved across the street, moved on, and another me seemed to
be watching her with curious objectivity.

Bastard . . . Whore . . . Tramp . . . It didn't matter what they
said. It didn't matter what they thought. I was a good girl. I was.
I wasn't a whore. I was . . . I wanted to be a lady. I wanted to
make Julian and Delia and . . . and Charles proud of me. I had
been raised in the swamps and, yes, I was illegitimate, born out
of wedlock, a bastard, that much was true, that I couldn't deny,
but Ma . . . Ma had raised me right and she had loved me and
oh, how I had loved her. I mustn't let go. I mustn't. I couldn't
fall apart out here on the street. I must move on.

Canal was very busy. Vehicles of every description rumbled
up and down the street, and the banquettes were thronging with
pedestrians, fine-dressed folk and rowdy sailors and flashy
women and Negro servants, all moving along with purpose and
talking and laughing loudly and carriages clattered and horses
neighed and I was in a daze, in a dream, moving against the

colorful flow and trying to remember why I was here. A cab. Yes, yes, I must hire a cab. A burly sailor leered at me. I started. The brassy blonde in pink velvet on his arm burst into gales of shrill laughter. I stumbled. A plump Negro woman with a kind face took hold of my elbow and kept me from falling. I thanked her with my eyes and stepped to the edge of the street, searching for something. What? Why was I here? Dozens of vehicles clattered past and a closed carriage halted a few yards away from me and the driver looked familiar and the carriage door flew open and Charles moved toward me at a brisk stride, his expression furious.

"What in hell do you think you're *do*ing!" he thundered.

He seized my arm and yanked it savagely and I stumbled again and then I was in the carriage and the door was closed and we were moving and he was yelling at me and I finally started to cry. I sobbed wretchedly and the tears spurted in a salty flood and he looked appalled and pulled me to him and held me and demanded to know what was wrong and somehow I managed to babble through the sobs and tell him about my visit to Conti Street and what they had said and how they had treated me and his strong arms tightened around me and held me closer and I rested my head on his shoulder and he murmured soothing words, holding me tightly, tenderly, and I managed to stop sobbing and whimpered quietly instead and finally grew silent and still. We rode on, down quiet streets now, and Charles Etienne still held me tight.

"Are you better now?" he asked finally.

I raised my head from his shoulder and nodded. "Don't— please don't tell anyone," I pleaded. "I don't want Julian and Delia to know."

"I won't tell."

"I—I feel so humiliated. I—"

"Forget it, Dana." His voice was stern. "I suppose it was something you had to do. It's over now."

"I—"

"It's over. You don't need them. You have Julian and Delia— and you have me."

He held me, and I felt the strength in his arms and the warmth in his body. Gradually the hurt and humiliation receded and I felt something else, a tautness inside, a delicious torment, that same languorous ache I felt when I woke up after the dream. He held me, and I made no effort to free myself from that tight circle of arms. He was wearing a thin lawn shirt and I could feel its soft texture against my cheek and feel the smooth muscles of chest and shoulder beneath. The carriage rocked gently, moving slowly now. My eyelashes were moist, and an occasional tear still spilled down my cheek. Charles sighed a disgruntled sigh and shifted his position, tilting me slightly.

"They mustn't see you like this," he said gruffly.

"Charles—"

"Be quiet," he ordered.

Keeping one arm curled around me, he began to brush the tears from my face, his fingertips blunt, rough, rubbing my skin. He looked down at me and I looked at his face and his expression was stern and his eyes were bothered, and I knew. He knew, too. Unable to stop myself, I reached up and ran my index finger along the full, smooth curve of his lower lip. His eyes held mine. His fingers rested on my cheek and then slipped down to curl around my jaw, tilting my head back even more. His lips parted. He grimaced then. He released me, even sterner now. I sat up straight and moved away from him and smoothed down my skirts, and we rode on in silence. Both of us pretended that nothing had happened, yet the knowledge was there between us. It was going to happen. We both knew that. It had been inevitable from the first. Now it was simply a matter of time.

Chapter Twelve

CHARLES GAVE JULIAN A MANLY EMBRACE, pounded him on the back, told him to stay out of trouble and departed for Etienne's. I had another cup of coffee while Julian finished his breakfast, and then he went into his study to make sure he wasn't leaving anything important behind. I joined him in the foyer a few minutes later. Julian told Pompey to let him know the moment Jasper returned, and Pompey nodded and left to locate Elijah. Julian sighed, resting his hands on his thighs, just as Charles did. During these past weeks of isolation in his study, he had lost weight, I noticed. In his black knee boots, gray breeches, and silky white shirt, he looked leaner, I thought, looked like an older, more mellow version of Charles. How I loved those silvering temples and that plump little roll of flesh beneath his chin, those compassionate eyes and that smile that curled so amiably on his full lips.

"That's a fetching blue dress you're wearing," he said.

"It isn't blue. It's turquoise."

"Not much *of* it on top," he observed.

"Don't be silly. It's the latest fashion—and everything is nicely covered up."

"Barely. That bloody dressmaker should be run out of town."

I smiled. Julian smiled, too. The dress was really quite modest even if it did leave my shoulders and the swell of my bosom bare. Julian, as his aunt had observed, knew nothing about fashion. I had the feeling he would be much more comfortable if I had no bosom at all, wore pigtails and had freckles scattered over my cheeks.

His bags were by the door, the same bags he had been carrying the night I had spied on him in the clearing in the swamps.

Well-worn, battered, they had seen many a trip, and they were bulging now. Julian put on his black and emerald striped satin waistcoat and, standing before the mirror in the foyer, began to adjust the emerald silk neckcloth under his chin, folding it carefully, tucking the loose ends into the top of his waistcoat. What a beautiful, gentle man he was. How grateful I was for all he had done for me. I helped him slip on the superbly tailored frock coat with its long tails and told him that I was going to miss him.

"Indeed?" he inquired.

"Of course," I said. "I won't *pine* every moment, but I'll miss you just the same."

He arched one brow. "You won't pine? I'm crushed."

"The house won't seem the same with—with you and Delia both gone."

Delia had left for Grande Villa yesterday morning in a swirl of hatboxes and parasols and breathless last-minute instructions. Neither she nor Julian knew of my visit to Conti Street, and they never would know, at least not from me. The hurt and humiliation of that visit still smarted inside, but I wasn't going to let it get the best of me. My blood kin wanted to have nothing to do with me, but I had been taken in and given a home by this wonderful man, and I could only thank God for bringing him into my life. What would have happened to me if I hadn't run into Julian in the swamps? I shuddered to think of it. Still standing before the mirror, he smoothed down his waistcoat and made a final adjustment to his neckcloth, then turned and sighed. I rested my hand on his arm for a moment, looking into those gentle brown eyes.

"I really will miss you, Julian," I said.

"I'm touched," he confessed. "You *will* keep up with your lessons," he added sternly.

I nodded. "Mister Howard's due this afternoon," I said wearily. "He'll bring a set of math problems for me to solve and a set of maps for me to color and he'll drone on and on about long division and the climate of Southern Rhodesia and I'll count the minutes until it's time for him to leave. He's really frightfully dull, Julian."

"Have you learned your multiplication tables yet?" he asked.

"Almost."

"How's your long division?"

"Dreadful," I confessed.

"Fractions?"

"What are they?"

He grinned. "It looks like Mister Howard will continue to come for quite some time."

"Why do I *need* to know long division? I speak beautifully now. I have lovely manners and perfect deportment. I use good grammar and write a legible hand and read dozens of books every month. Mister Howard says I'm a dolt. He says he's never had a slower student. He makes me feel—"

"Mister Howard is the best there is," Julian told me. "When I get back, I fully expect you to be able to recite your multiplication tables and startle me with your prowess at long division."

I made a face. Julian smiled again.

"Did you pack everything you need?" I asked.

"I think so—even an odd bottle of champagne or two."

"What about your pistol?"

"I packed that, too. One of these days I might actually have to fire it. Most disconcerting thought."

"Do be careful," I said, quite serious now. "I—you could run into a wildcat or an alligator or—any number of things. I know the swamps, and I—I'll worry about you."

"Will you?"

There was a husky catch in his voice, and there was a curious thoughtfulness in his eyes as he looked at me. I remembered the night of the ball and the emotion-fraught moments in front of my bedroom door. Julian was remembering it, too, I sensed, and I knew he wanted to say something, wanted to stroke my cheek, touch my hair. He did neither. He merely looked at me, silent. It was an eloquent silence, and I waited, afraid, so afraid of what he might say.

Pompey came into the foyer then to inform Julian that the carriage was waiting, and Elijah came prancing in to carry the bags out. The moment was lost. I was vastly relieved, and I think Julian was, too. He sighed again and told Elijah to be careful with the bags and started toward the door, all bustle now. I followed him out to the front steps. Morning sunlight splashed all around us in brilliant pools. Julian checked his pocket to make sure he had his tickets and his wallet. I took his hand and squeezed it tightly.

"Watch out for the alligators," I said.

"I intend to."

"Snakes, too."

"I will, " he promised.

"You'd better hurry now. The steamboat leaves at ten."

"Ten sharp. You're right. I'd better hurry."

He frowned, checked his pocket again and hurried down the steps and climbed into the carriage and scolded Elijah, who had dumped the bags into an untidy pile on the seat. Elijah hung his head and looked properly chastened and then peeked up and asked if he could go to the docks, and Julian put on a look of weary forbearance and told the rascal to climb on. The lad bounded up onto the seat beside a sternly disapproving Jasper, who had just returned from taking Charles to work. I stepped to the carriage door, resting my hand on the open window.

"Do be careful, Julian," I said.

"Dana—"

"Yes?"

"When I get back, there—there's something we're going to have to discuss. I think you know what I mean."

I nodded. I knew. We were both uncomfortable.

"Behave yourself," he said.

"I'll try."

"And—and study that math."

Jasper clicked the reins and I moved back and the carriage pulled away, Elijah waving merrily from his perch. I stood in front of the steps with sunlight splashing brilliantly all around and watched the carriage move slowly around the drive and disappear through the front portals, and I gently gnawed my lower lip, far more disturbed than I cared to admit. Julian Etienne was a wonderful, wonderfully attractive man, and I owed everything to him. I loved him, but I wasn't *in* love with him. I was in love with his brother, and Julian was very definitely in love with me. He had fought it, had tried to deny it, I knew, but he had finally acknowledged the truth to himself, and when he got back he planned to declare his love . . . What was I going to do then?

I gazed at the flowers and plants in the front garden and felt the sunlight on my cheeks and arms. How complicated it all was. I knew that I couldn't hurt Julian, nor could I disappoint him, not after all he had done for me, and I knew as well that I couldn't quell my feelings for his brother. I had been attracted to Julian in the beginning, but it was nothing like what I felt for Charles. It was as though . . . as though part of me had been completely dormant before and had sprung vibrantly to life all at once, changing my whole being. In the romances I read, love was frequently called a "great awakening," and I understood now what that meant. I felt newly alive to sight and sound and sensation, and I was filled with heady exhilaration that, at any moment, could turn to bleak despair. I didn't want to feel this way, but I had no choice in the matter. Remembering the dream, I could almost believe I was destined to love Charles Etienne even before I laid eyes on him.

I went inside. The house seemed strangely quiet and empty. I missed Delia already, and I would indeed miss Julian, too. I wandered around the rooms, hoping to find some task to be done, but everything sparkled, everything was in order. How different it had been when I first arrived. Delia was a darling, but she wasn't a housekeeper. Restless, I went into the library and browsed through half a dozen books, but I could find nothing that interested me. The novels of George Sand and Jules Sandeau and Alexandre Dumas that I had read with such relish seemed strangely unappealing now, the fictional emotions eclipsed by those I felt inside. I browsed through a volume on porcelain and finally, more restless than before, went upstairs and began to sort out the linens. It was there Kayla found me forty-five minutes later.

"There you are, Kayla," I said. "The linens in this pile need to be mended, and these need to be laundered. Such fine linen, as soft as silk. The pillowcases over there need to be laundered, too, and do you think we can match the lace that is torn?"

"I'se sure we can, Miz Dana. I'll get right on it, but you'd better go see Jezebel. Mister Charles went off and forgot his lunch, and she's madder'n a wet hen."

"Oh dear," I said, but actually I welcomed the distraction.

Leaving the linens to Kayla, I went down to the kitchen. Jezebel was pouting among her pots and pans, angrily poking a wooden spoon into the pan of gumbo simmering over the fire. Cut okra and plump shrimp bubbled up temptingly, and I could smell a wonderful array of spices. Jezebel put down her spoon and pointed to the basket sitting on the edge of the butcher block table.

"Mister Charles, he's gonna poison hisself. Dem places down

there where he goes to eat lunch, dey don't know nothin' 'bout proper cookin'. I told him so. You jest stay out of dem places, Mister Charles, I told him, you let Jezebel fix you up a lunch basket to take with you, and dat's what he's been doin'. I worry 'bout dat chile, an' now he's gone off an' forgot his basket an' he'll be eatin' dat poison dey serve in dem eatin' places.''

Jezebel began to chop up parsley, her round black face a study in exasperation. "I packed dat basket special for him,'' she continued, "put in all th' things he likes, includin' a huge chunk-a angel cake with sugar frostin'. He'll eat in one of dem places down dere where dey fry everything in hog fat an' he'll come home with a bellyache an' won't want his dinner either—an' me fixin' my special chicken breasts stuffed with spices and butter tonight. You ain't never had 'em yet. You stuff 'em an' bread 'em an' bake 'em till deys real tender an' juicy and you serves 'em with white wine sauce.''

"They sound delicious,'' I said.

"He ain't gonna be in no shape to 'preciate 'em iffen he fills his belly up with dat poison dey serve. I reckon I might jest as well feed you all corn pone an' greens tonight.''

"Why—why don't I carry the basket down to him,'' I suggested. "I'm sure Jasper is back from taking Mister Julian to the boat. He could take me and we'd get there before Mister Charles has time to go to one of those places you disapprove of.''

Jezebel beamed. "Dat's what I was hopin' you'd suggest, only dere ain't no need you goin' yourself. Elijah can deliver de basket.''

"I—I don't mind going,'' I said, perhaps a little too quickly, I thought. "I—I'm kind of restless with—with Miss Delia being gone.''

"Her bein' away don't seem natural,'' Jezebel said. "Seems like de heartbeat's gone outta de house. You be sure you'se back in time for your own lunch, missy,'' she added.

"I will be,'' I told her. "I can hardly wait to taste that gumbo.''

Jezebel looked horrified. "Dis stuff! It's for de servants. You I'se makin' a *real* lunch.''

Ten minutes later I was on my way to Etienne's with the lunch basket on the seat beside me. Jasper was certainly earning his keep this morning, I reflected as the carriage rumbled over the cobbles. Jezebel was right. There really was no need for me to be taking the basket to him myself, it would have been far more appropriate to send it by a servant, yet I had jumped at the opportunity to see him, if only for a few minutes. I had taken time to brush my hair and apply just a suggestion of blush to my cheeks, and I was glad I was wearing this flattering turquoise dress with its low-cut bodice and very full skirt.

My heart seemed to sing with joyous anticipation as the carriage moved down the street. Was it wicked to feel this way? Ever since he had held me so tightly in his arms, I had scarcely been able to think of anything but Charles, and I ardently yearned to feel those arms around me again, to feel those muscles tightening, drawing me closer, to feel his strength and his warmth and smell his hair, his skin, his sweat. That yearning was like an obsession in my blood, tormenting me constantly. It was tender torment, a not unpleasant ache that craved to grow and swell until it possessed me completely. I had never felt anything like it. Charles and Charles alone could assuage that ache, with his arms, with his mouth, with his body.

All this was inside, yet I knew I must control it, must let no one suspect, not even Charles. I wanted him, I wanted him urgently, but deep inside I knew I must not let it happen. I must fight. I must resist. I was a good girl, and I knew it would be disastrous to give in to this urgent desire. It would complicate things even more. I could exercise control, yes, but in the meantime I saw no reason why . . . why I shouldn't warm myself in his glow of glory. Just to be near him was joy enough. I had seen precious little of him since he held me in the carriage. He had been cool and remote, avoiding me as much as possible. I knew the reason why. I knew it was because he felt the same way about me. He wanted me every bit as much as I wanted him, and he, too, knew it would be disastrous.

I was playing with fire, I realized that, yet I couldn't resist the opportunity to see him and give him the basket and perhaps chat for a few minutes, savoring the rich, husky sound of his voice. I would warm myself by the fire, yes, but I wouldn't get burned. I would be dignified. I would be demure. I would smile pleasantly and ask him about things at the store and I wouldn't stroke his lean cheek or rub my thumb along the full pink curve of his lower lip or beg him to hold me, hold me close. I caught my breath as the carriage came to a halt in front of the store. A faint, rational voice inside warned me to beware, told me to let Jasper take the basket in and then drive straight back home, but I didn't listen. I stepped out of the carriage, that joyous anticipation swelling inside until I could scarcely contain it.

"I will only be a few minutes, Jasper," I said, and my voice was perfectly normal, betraying none of what I felt.

I reached into the carriage and took out the basket and went into the store. Sunlight streaming through the two front windows stroked richly varnished woods, gleamed on gilt and glittered on crystal and porcelain. Beautiful furniture and objects of art exuded a rich, opulent atmosphere. There was no one in the front of the store. Charles must be in the back or in his office, I thought, and then the heavy gold drapes over the archway parted and Raoul Etienne came in, arching one brow in surprise when he saw me.

"Cousin Dana," he crooned, "what an unexpected pleasure."

I was startled. I had forgotten all about Raoul. Of course he would be at the store. He worked here—not very satisfactorily, from all reports. He smiled a smooth, professional smile that wasn't quite a leer but wasn't at all friendly either. His dark eyes gleamed as they took in every detail of my dress and person. How sleek and handsome he was in his deep wine-colored breeches and frock coat, his white and wine striped satin waistcoat and white silk neckcloth. His thick, luxuriant hair had a healthy gloss, and his skin was lightly tanned, like pale, creamy coffee. He was a splendid creature, all right, the answer to every maiden's prayer, but the maiden would be despoiled, greedily used and ruthlessly abandoned when he had had his fill. Perhaps he wasn't actually evil, but he was spoiled, selfish, superior, a pampered young lord who believed the world was his to plunder.

"It's been a long time," he said.

I hadn't seen him since I drove my knee into his groin. "Not long enough," I retorted.

I stood where I was, clutching the handle of the basket. Raoul slowly approached me, and I remembered the story of the spider and the fly. I stiffened. He smiled again, stopping a few feet away. His eyes seemed to undress me. The smile lingered at the corners of his mouth.

"Surely you're not nervous," he said.

"Not at all. I believe I proved I could take care of myself."

"You surely did," he agreed. "I haven't forgotten that, Cousin dear. You might have done some serious damage. Women all over New Orleans would have been dressed in mourning, bewailing their loss."

"I don't doubt it," I said dryly.

"You don't know what you're missing," he told me. "I could provide excellent references."

"I—I don't intend to stand here sparring with you, Raoul. I came here to see Charles. Where is he?"

"Out, I'm afraid. The lovely Amelia Jameson came in earlier and wanted him to come look at a pair of chairs she's thinking of selling. I volunteered to go myself, but neither of them would hear of it."

"I'm not at all surprised."

"Is there anything *I* can do for you?" he inquired smoothly.

I shook my head, discomfited and disappointed. "I—I brought his lunch," I said. "I'll just leave the basket in his office."

"How very thoughtful," he observed. "So one brother isn't enough? You've got them vying for you now. Most interesting, though I must say I'm surprised. I shouldn't have thought noble Charles would encroach on the property of his beloved Julian."

"I have no idea what you're talking about," I said crisply.

"Haven't you?" He moved closer. "A word of advice, Cousin dear. Those two are very, very close and inordinately loyal to one another. Don't come between them. If you do, they'll both turn against you."

I didn't deign to answer. Ignoring him completely, I moved purposefully to the archway and parted the heavy gold drapes and, stepping into Charles' office, placed the basket on top of his desk. It was piled high with papers and account books, I noticed, and Charles' frock coat and neckcloth were hanging on the back of his chair. Apparently he hadn't deemed it necessary to don them when he went to examine Amelia Jameson's chairs. He would be wearing his striped satin waistcoat and fine lawn shirt, and his hair would probably already be unruly, with an errant wave slanting over his brow.

"You needn't worry about the lovely Amelia," Raoul said.

I whirled around, startled to find him behind me.

"She's a delectable creature," he continued, "but his trip to her apartment was strictly business. He's purchased several things from her of late. It seems the lady is down on her luck."

"If you'll excuse me," I said, "I'll go now. Please inform Charles that his lunch is on his desk."

Raoul made no effort to move. He was standing between me and the door, effectively blocking my way. I would have to move around him to get to the door, and I wasn't about to get that close. The office seemed suddenly much smaller. The four walls seemed to close in on me like a trap. I stood my ground, my chin held high. Raoul sensed my apprehension and he smiled, his dark eyes aglow with amusement.

"You needn't worry," he said. "I shan't attempt to rape you here and now. I'll get my own back, Cousin dear—no woman treats me the way you did and gets away with it—but I'll do it in my own sweet time."

"Don't fool with me, Raoul," I warned. "You're likely to get hurt again."

His smile broadened. He chuckled softly.

"You caused quite a sensation at the ball last month," he observed. "All of my friends were thoroughly captivated— they've been bombarding me with questions about you. They all want to get to know you much, much better."

"Please step out of my way, Raoul."

He ignored my request. "Speaking of friends," he continued, "a couple of the lads saw you on Conti Street the other day. You rode past the fencing academy and then turned on Conti and stopped in front of number four."

I didn't deny it. I looked at him with a cool, level gaze.

"I wonder why," he mused. "A clandestine rendezvous with a secret lover? We all assumed so at first, then we found that number four belongs to the DuJardin family. Now what could you possibly be going to see *them* for?"

"That's none of your bloody business," I said.

"I'll find out," he promised. "You intrigue me, Cousin. I intend to find out everything I can about you."

I didn't say a word. I continued to stare at him with that level gaze, and the mocking half-smile continued to play on his lips. Finally, after what seemed an eternity, he gave me a cocky nod and stepped aside. I longed to slap that smirk off his lips, but I didn't. I moved past him with icy composure and left the office, stepping outside a moment later.

"Is you all right, Miz Dana?" Jasper asked.

"I'm fine," I retorted.

"You looks upset 'bout somethin'."

"Take me home," I ordered.

The afternoon seemed interminable. I even welcomed Mister Howard with his dour expression and his dreary lessons. At least they helped pass the time. He stood over me as I attempted to do my long division, shaking his head in dismay. No one, he seemed to be saying to himself, could be *that* dense. He corrected my paper and informed me that math was definitely not my forte. I readily agreed. We did our geography lesson next, and I colored a map of Spain and learned about the Alhambra and he suggested I read Washington Irving's recently published book on the subject. I promised to order it and showed him out with considerable relief.

Charles came home shortly before six. I was in the front parlor. I heard him in the foyer, heard him speaking to Pompey, and my first impulse was to rush out and welcome him back and bask in his presence, but common sense prevented so impulsive an action. I would see him at dinner. I went upstairs and took a hot bath, lingering in the tub, luxuriating in the warmth and the rich scented suds. I washed my hair as well, brushing it afterward until it fell in a thick, glossy tumble. The sun had already gone down, and the courtyard was a nest of misty violet-gray shadows as Kayla came in to help me dress. Candlelight created soft golden patterns on the walls and floor.

"I declare," Kayla sighed, "it's sultry tonight."

I nodded, going through my wardrobe, trying to select a gown. The windows were open, and I could hear leaves rustling and a bird warbling and smell a dozen fragrant perfumes. The air was warm and slightly moist. A gentle breeze stirred the curtains and seemed to caress my skin. Kayla stepped to the gallery and took a deep breath, gazing up at the sky.

"There's gonna be a quarter moon," she said. "Know what kinda night it's gonna be? It's gonna be a night for love."

I looked at her sharply. Was there a double meaning to her words? Did she suspect something? Was my feeling for Charles so obvious? The girl sighed once more and stretched and smiled a contented smile.

"Reckon I might just let Jasper have his way tonight," she confided lazily. "He's done everything *but*, an' I must say, he's a master with his mouth an' his hands. Makes me plumb crazy—

kissin' me all over, feelin' me up. Reckon it's time to let him explore th' rest of me.''

I said nothing. Kayła looked concerned.

"Is you shocked, Miz Dana?"

"Not—not at all," I replied.

"Lovin' ain't bad. Lovin's good. It makes you feel—I cain't rightly explain how it makes you feel, but you'll know what I mean when it happens to you. You get an achin' in your bones and your blood seems to boil and then your bones seems to melt an' you gets all frantic an'—"

"That will be quite enough, Kayla."

"You'se tense, Miz Dana. I been noticin' it for a while now. I reckon you need a little lovin', too. It's a splendid tonic for what ails you. It ain't natural to keep everything all pent up an' pressin' your insides."

"Damn you, Kayla!"

"I didn't mean to up*set* you, Miz Dana."

"I know. I—I'm just a little edgy."

"Reckon it's th' weather," she said. "When it gets all sultry like this, you cain't help feelin' a stirrin' in your blood. When that quarter moon's sailin' in the sky tonight, I'll be wigglin' in Jasper's arms, moanin' like a she-cat as he loves me. Reckon you'll be readin' another one of them books."

"If you'll just help me put this on, you can go on about your business," I said crisply.

"You'se gonna wear *that* dress?"

"What's wrong with it?"

"Ain't nothin' wrong with it—reckon it's right sumptuous. It just looks like th' kinda dress you'd wear to a ball or somethin', not just for dinner, an' no one but Mister Charles to see you in it—"

Kayla cut herself short, her eyes widening as realization dawned. I cursed silently. Kayla grinned then, pleased and approving. I longed to push her over the balcony. I started to tell her that she was completely wrong, but I doubted she would believe me and it would only make matters worse. Silent now but still grinning, she helped me into the gown and told me I looked like a vision, said I could cast a spell over any man, lookin' like I looked now, and then, grin widening, she finally left.

I stepped over to the full-length mirror, examining myself

carefully. The gown was of rich rose brocade, embroidered all over with flowers in deeper rose. It had full, off-the-shoulder puffed sleeves, a very low-cut neckline and a form-fitting bodice that accentuated my slender waist, the extremely full skirt belling out over half a dozen tissue-thin red silk underskirts. It *was* a sumptuous garment, far too opulent and formal for dinner at home, but it made me feel older, made me feel very much a woman. I might not look like a vision, but I knew I had never looked better. All traces of the girl had vanished. I was looking at the reflection of a woman, sensuous, voluptuous, created for love. It wasn't just the dress, I knew. Without realizing it, I seemed to have passed over some invisible threshold into full-blown womanhood, leaving the girl behind. I wondered if others noticed it as well.

Sitting at my dressing table, I smoothed faint mauvish-tan shadow on my eyelids and applied a subtle pink blush to my cheeks. I used lip rouge, too, sparingly, the cosmetics merely pointing up my natural coloring. I brushed my hair some more until it gleamed with rich honey-blond highlights and decided to let it fall to my shoulders in natural waves. I removed the stopper from the crystal bottle of perfume I had bought at Corinne's and smelled the scent. It was a subtle, tantalizing smell evoking sun-drenched fields of poppies, extremely sensual, and I hesitated a moment. I had never used it before. Was it too tantalizing, too sensual? Perhaps my regular lilac perfume would be better. No, that was a proper young lady's perfume. Tonight I was a woman. I applied the poppy-rich perfume to my wrists, my throat, behind my ears. I felt like . . . like one of Balzac's courtesans preparing for an assignation and, in a sudden crisis of nerves, almost decided to skip dinner entirely.

My nerves were still on edge as I went slowly down the graceful white staircase, full rose brocade skirts rustling. The house seemed still and quiet, dozens of candles bathing it in a pale golden glow. Windows were open, and curtains billowed with the sound of soft whispers. I could smell night-blooming jasmine and rich loamy soil and, in the stillness, hear the soft patter of the fountain. Moving across the foyer, I stepped into the front parlor where we always met before dinner. Charles had not come down yet. I ardently longed for one of the mint juleps he and Julian sipped before meals. I ardently wished I weren't wearing this dress, wished I had never laid eyes on Charles Etienne, wished life were not so hellishly complicated. My nerves were so taut I thought they might actually snap when I heard his footsteps in the foyer.

He stepped into the room. He was wearing his dark blue breeches and frock coat and a sky-blue satin waistcoat embroidered with white silk leaves and a perfectly folded white silk neckcloth. His hair was brushed to a high chestnut sheen, but already that errant wave was beginning to tilt forward. His lean face was all hard planes and angles, his mouth set in a full, firm pink line, and his eyes were so deep a blue they seemed black in the candlelight. I looked at him, and I seemed to feel a shock going through me. My knees felt weak. I actually thought I was going to faint. It seemed impossible that another person could stir emotions so completely overwhelming.

Charles seemed as ill at ease as I was. He didn't look at me at first. He stepped over to the liquor cabinet and made himself a mint julep, taking ice out of the silver bucket sitting atop it. He turned then and sipped his drink, and his eyes darkened even more with disapproval. He didn't like my gown. I felt like a fool. I felt like a little girl playing dress-up. Balzac's courtesans were worldly, opulent creatures who would have laughed heartily at my pretenses. Charles was probably laughing to himself at this very moment. Perfume and a low-cut gown could not take the place of experience. I felt as gauche and naive as a newborn colt under his stern gaze.

"Did—did you find your lunch basket?" I asked.

He nodded. "Raoul told me you brought it by. It wasn't necessary, Dana."

"Jezebel was afraid you'd have lunch at one of the places nearby where they fry everything in hog fat."

"Jezebel thinks no one can cook a decent meal but her."

"Did you enjoy the angel cake?"

"It was delicious," he said.

He took another sip of his mint julep. He seemed disinclined to talk. He seemed bored and indifferent to me. I sensed that this was because he was every bit as uncomfortable as I was, and I cast around for something else to say before the silence grew even more unsettling.

"Did you buy the chairs?" I inquired.

He shook his head. "They were fakes. Amelia was crushed when I told her. She roundly cursed the dealer who sold them to her. I did, however, purchase an eighteenth-century writing desk from her, an exquisite piece.''

"It's a pity she has to sell her things.''

"It's an occupational hazard for women in her profession. She's lucky she has nice things *to* sell. Amelia is too amiable, too casual, too easygoing and too kind to be truly successful. She lacks the venality and the killer instinct of the true professional.''

"You—you like her very much, don't you?''

"She is a charming, sophisticated woman, and she was very good to my brother during their time together. She was genuinely fond of him. For that matter, she still is.''

I wished I had some of her sophistication and charm. I could think of nothing else to say, and Charles made no effort to keep the conversation going. He finished his mint julep and set the glass down. The curtains stirred. The air was warm, laden with heady fragrance. I was relieved when, a few moments later, Pompey stepped in and announced that dinner was served. Charles condescended to escort me into the dining room, holding my arm stiffly, helping me into my chair with cool formality.

The table seemed much larger with only the two of us at it. The fine damask cloth was gleaming white, and there was a centerpiece of delicate purple and mauve iris. Silver and crystal and fine china sparkled in the candlelight. How I wished Delia and Julian were here to ease the tension. I had looked forward to this all day, and now I was acutely uncomfortable. Pompey served the soup from a white porcelain tureen. It was turtle soup, rich and savory. I hardly tasted it. The silence dragged on and on. Charles was utterly remote. We might have been complete strangers who just happened to be eating at the same table.

Pompey removed the soup bowls and, with assistance from Elijah, brought the main course in, Jezebel's special chicken breasts served on a bed of brown rice, with steamed artichokes on the side. The chicken was delicious, butter and spices flowing out as you sliced the meat, but I still had no appetite. I stripped a plump leaf from my artichoke, dipped it into the dish of melted butter sitting beside my plate. I looked up. I caught Charles studying me, his dark eyes full of conflicting emotions. He frowned and looked away and continued to eat, taking no more pleasure in the wonderful food than I did. Tension seemed to crackle in the air, and I could see that it was getting to him, too. When, finally, he broke the silence, it took a visible effort.

"I hope you're feeling better," he said.

"I—I'm fine."

"I know you were terribly upset over what happened at Conti Street, but you should never have gone there."

"I realize that, but—at least now I—I know where I stand, and I can get on with my life."

He nodded curtly and sliced his chicken.

"I don't suppose I'll ever know who my father was," I added.

"It's not important," he told me.

"I—don't suppose it is. I don't intend to try and find out. I—I don't want to be hurt again."

"A wise decision," he said.

"How—how are things going at the store?" I asked, frantic to avoid another long stretch of silence.

"We're doing well enough. Raoul's precious little help, but—."

He frowned and shook his head. "Speaking of business, Dana, I'm going to be away for a few days myself."

"Oh?"

"I need to go inspect our cotton crops. I've been putting it off too long as it is. As Julian might have explained, our real income is from the cotton we buy and export."

"He said something about your purchasing crops in advance."

"Instead of waiting for auction, I purchased the entire output of Ravenaugh and Belle Mead before the crops were even planted. My competitors thought I was insane to take such a risk, but in the long run I will have saved a great deal of money."

"I see."

"I need to visit the plantations and see how the crops are doing. I'll be leaving first thing in the morning."

I didn't say anything. I toyed with my rice.

"I'll have to spend several days at each plantation," he continued, "and I don't know just how long I'll be gone. I would imagine I'll be back a day or so after Delia returns from Grande Villa."

Pompey came in and I motioned for him to remove my plate. Charles was finished as well. I folded my napkin and placed it on the table and told Pompey I would have neither coffee nor dessert. He scowled, knowing he would face Jezebel's wrath when he delivered the message. I would apologize to her later. I couldn't take any more of this. I stood up and started toward the door, afraid I might break down if I didn't escape immediately.

"Dana . . ."

I didn't turn. I didn't answer. I hurried out of the room and turned into the foyer and hurried up the stairs. Tears were spilling down my cheeks when I reached my bedroom. What a fool I had been. What an ass I had made of myself, wearing this red gown, painting my face, using the exotic perfume. I knew nothing about seduction, nothing about love, nothing about men. I knew only that I was utterly miserable and that I would never be able to face Charles again. How foolish I had been to . . . to think that he wanted me, too. He couldn't stand to be alone in the same room with me. He was going to go away and leave me here with the servants because he couldn't bear being in the house with me. Charles despised me. He had every right to despise me. I was a complete ninny to think I could interest him.

I brushed the tears from my cheeks and sat down, nursing my misery. A long time passed, and the candles were beginning to burn down and splutter when I finally stood up, stiff and sore now, feeling empty inside. I moved out onto the balcony and rested my hands on the wrought-iron railing and gazed up at the sky. The quarter moon was sailing like a ship of silver amidst a sea of ashen clouds. It was still warm and sultry and the night air seemed to caress my bare skin and the fragrance of flowers was dizzying. Kayla was in her lover's arms, writhing and moaning and relishing delight forbidden to me, and I had rarely felt so desolate, so alone.

I heard a low rumble of thunder in the distance. It was followed by a sudden rush of wind that caused leaves and plants to shiver in the courtyard below. We were going to have an evening shower, one of those light, pattering rainfalls that lasted an hour or two and lessened the heat not at all. I stepped back inside as the first warm drops began to splatter. Four or five of the candles had already burned out, the others spluttering wildly and throwing frantic gold shadows on the wall. I saw by the clock that it was after eleven. I was bone-weary, so weary I scarcely felt like undressing. The rain was falling faster now, making loud splattering noises. Another candle spluttered out, only four burning now. Wearily, I slipped off my shoes and kicked them aside, then lifted my skirts and rolled down my stockings.

I didn't hear him coming up the metal staircase outside, nor did I hear him walking down the gallery. I heard only the monotonous splatter-splatter of the rain. I sighed and, barefooted, stood up, and I saw his shadow stretching over the floor and I whirled around, gasping. He stood between the open French windows with his hands resting lightly on his thighs. He had removed his frock coat and waistcoat and neckcloth. His tall black boots were shiny with wetness, and his snug blue breeches were spotted with rain. The thin white shirt, opened at the throat, clung damply to his skin, and his hair was a cluster of dark, wet curls. Rain dripped from his brow and down his cheeks. He didn't say anything. He looked at me, unhappy, hesitant, burning with desire.

"I shouldn't be here," he said. His voice was tight.

"I suppose you shouldn't."

"I couldn't stay away."

"You're wet."

"I tried to stay away."

"You're here, Charles."

"You knew I'd come."

"I—I hoped."

Another candle spluttered out, leaving the room in semidarkness. The rain blew over the railing, wetting him even more. He didn't seem to notice. I felt resigned. I felt defeated. I felt afraid, too, and beneath it all a wild elation began to surface, eclipsing everything else. He had come. He wasn't able to stay away. The desire burning in those dark eyes was like some savage force, devouring him from within. I saw the bulge swelling between his legs, pressing against the blue broadcloth of his breeches. I knew and I was afraid and I was delirious with joy.

He stepped inside. I took a handkerchief and dried the raindrops from his face and he didn't speak, he just held my eyes with his own. More drops spilled down his face from the wet tendrils of hair on his forehead. I smoothed the wet hair back and dried his face again and rested my palm on his lean cheek, fingertips touching one broad cheekbone. I stood up on tiptoe then and touched that full pink mouth with my own, and his arms flung around me and crushed me to him, holding me so tightly I thought I might snap in two, but I felt no pain. I felt only that wild elation, surging through me now, soaring, singing in my blood. I clung to him, my palms running over the strong musculature of his back and shoulders as he kissed me with passionate urgency.

When, finally, his mouth freed mine, I gasped for breath, trembling inside, my knees so wobbly I could hardly stand. Rain continued to splatter noisily and sweep over the railing, making damp spots on the edge of the carpet, but neither of us cared. I ran the ball of my thumb along his lower lip, feeling the moist, firm flesh. My body rested against his. I could feel the throbbing pulses of his manhood through the layers of cloth. The ache and the honied warmth I felt when I awakened from the dream were a living torment now, demanding surcease, and I knew I would swoon any moment now, knew I couldn't endure much more. He took hold of my upper arms and held me away from him, looking down into my eyes.

"I want you, Dana," he murmured hoarsely.

"I know."

"I've wanted you from the first moment I laid eyes on you. I hated you because I wanted you, because I knew I wasn't going to be able to help myself, no matter how I tried."

"I love you, Charles," I whispered.

"I wanted you to be everything I first believed you to be. I wanted you to be a scheming little hoyden, a clever trollop who had taken in my gullible older brother. When I discovered you weren't, I hated you even more because I couldn't throw you out and—remove the temptation."

"Charles—"

"I've fought it. God knows I've fought it. Tonight was sheer agony. I know I was cold and remote, but—I was still fighting it, still telling myself I could find the strength."

Another candle spluttered wildly, casting frenzied shadows before it finally went out. The room was filled with a blue-gray haze broken only by the weak, flickering golden glow of the three remaining candle flames.

"It's all right," I said softly.

"You don't know how I've suffered."

"I—I've suffered, too. I—even before I met you, I felt—I knew—this was meant to be."

He didn't say anything. He lifted his hand and stroked my

throat and moved his palm up over my jaw and along my temple, then smoothed my hair back, fingers entwining in the silky strands. I tilted my head, my lips parting, and he made a moaning noise in his throat and kissed me again, tugging gently at my hair and crushing me to him with his free arm. I felt the honied warmth flowing, spreading throughout my body, and the torment was divine and impossible to endure much longer. He kissed me for a long, long time, his mouth working over mine, eager, demanding, and when he finally stopped my head was reeling and I was faint, felt sure I couldn't stand were it not for the support of that steel-strong arm holding me up.

Reaching behind me, he slowly began to unhook the bodice of my gown, and it loosened and fell forward, my breasts swollen and straining against the frail red silk of my petticoat. He caught hold of the full puffed sleeves of my gown and pulled them down over my arms and, leaning forward, shoved the gown down. I wiggled, helping him, and the gorgeous rose brocade crackled and made rustling music and finally fell to the floor like a huge fallen petal. I stepped out of the circle and kicked the dress aside with my bare foot. Charles caught one of the thin straps of my petticoat and tugged it, and my right breast popped free of its silken prison, full and round, the nipple extended and pulsating with sensations like tiny pinpricks. He spread his hand over my breast, his fingers squeezing, kneading the flesh, and I cried out, reeling.

He caught me before I could fall. He freed my other breast and, frowning, struggled to free me of the garment. I wanted to help him. I couldn't. I was in a sweet, tormenting delirium, unable to move, barely able to stand. He lifted my arms and I heard the delicious rustle of half a dozen thin silk skirts and felt silk sliding over my flesh and covering my face and then I was free and the petticoat was floating to the floor like a crimson cloud. Another candle spluttered out and more hazy shadows danced over the walls and Charles kneeled, freeing me of the final garment, and I stood naked in the pale golden haze of the two remaining candles.

I moaned, and across the room I saw the mirror and the hazy reflection of a naked woman, honey-blond hair tumbling down her back, her skin bathed soft gold by the candlelight, a man, fully clothed, kneeling in front of her, wrapping his arms around her legs, and it was like some beautiful, misty painting executed by a master, a Bouchet canvas come to life. I closed my eyes, arching my back, and another moan escaped my lips as he began to kiss my thighs, his lips brushing my skin, and when, finally, they reached the soft center of me I cried out and felt myself falling and then I was in his arms and he was carrying me over to the bed and I was writhing atop the satin counterpane, its smooth, silken surface caressing my back and buttocks and legs.

The rain was still splattering softly, a muted music in the background, and one of the two remaining candle flames leaped in a frenzied dance and made spluttering noises and finally expired, and Charles was standing beside the bed, looking down at me as though in awe, as though unable to believe what he saw. I was writhing, floating, falling into an abyss of splendid, tormenting sensation. My limbs seemed to be tied with velvet cord and someone was stretching me on a rack and the ache grew and grew and I would expire at any moment if I wasn't released, if I wasn't complemented, completed, the aching void inside me filled with flesh and made whole. Moans formed in my throat and softly escaped my mouth. My eyelids were so heavy I could barely keep them open.

Charles moved away from the bed and slowly removed his damp white shirt and tossed it aside, and the last faint glimmer of candlelight burnished his muscular chest, his strong shoulders and powerful arms. He sat on the edge of the chair and tugged at his boots, removing first one, then the other. He peeled off his stockings and stood, tugging at the waistband of his breeches, and the last candle flame fluttered and leaped and went out and the room was engulfed in shadowy blue-gray darkness and I could see the white blur of him bending, straightening, moving across the room. He stepped in front of the windows and I saw him standing there, his tall, lean body like a Greek statue seen through the mist. He shut the windows and came slowly toward the bed, a moving white blur in the semidarkness. I saw him leaning over me and felt a burst of anticipation that seemed to shudder throughout me, and when I felt his hands on my flesh I gave a quiet sob, shuddering still.

He gathered me up in his arms and swept the bedclothes back and gently lowered me down onto the mattress, cool, crisp linen caressing my skin now. He was there, looming over me, and it was real, it wasn't the dream, the dream had never been so intense. I raised my arms, drawing him to me, and he lowered himself carefully. When I felt the weight of him atop me I gasped and he crooned softly to me and adjusted my body beneath his and instinctively I spread my legs, wrapping them around his, my hands moving up and down his back, finally clasping his rain-damp hair and tugging violently as I felt the velvety tip of that hard, warm rod touch, part, probe. I thought I would explode inside as it moved in, moved deeper, flesh meeting, massaging, melting together.

It was bliss. It was beauty. Sensation followed sensation and I let go of his hair and gasped again as I felt tremors of pain amidst the pleasure. I felt his surprise as he met the unexpected obstacle, felt his hesitation. I gripped his buttocks with my hands and arched my hips, letting him know he must continue despite the pain. Arms at my sides now, I clenched my fists and felt the tearing inside and felt white-hot stabs of pain that seemed to shoot through my body and then miraculously melt into shimmering waves of ecstacy violently surpassing all that had come before. They swept over me, mounting, mounting, higher, higher, drowning me in delight. I felt him tense, poised, felt him shudder and fall limp and heavy atop me even as I went soaring into a shattering oblivion.

I opened my eyes and the room was awash with silvery moonlight and the rain was no longer falling. It still dripped from the eaves, though, slowly dropping with soft, intermittent plops. There was a delicious languor in my blood, a delicious ache in my bones. I sighed deeply and stretched and he stirred beside me, moaning sleepily, reaching for me, gathering me to him. I nuzzled against him, savoring the scent and feel of him, gloriously, gloriously happy, and he shifted his position and warm ashes inside stirred into flame and it began anew, wonderful this time, even better, no pain, only lazily prolonged pleasure that mounted as before and filled me with the same shimmering bliss. Charles yawned mightily afterward and dropped off to sleep immediately, his arms still enfolding me. I cradled his damp head to my bosom and watched the moonlight make shifting silver patterns on the ceiling, asking myself if it was really possible to be so blissfully content.

A bird warbled in the courtyard, I opened my eyes. The moonlight was gone now, replaced by a hazy pinkish-gold glow. Charles was moving around the room, completely naked, gathering up his clothes. I stirred, the bedclothes rustling. He looked at me and I smiled, but he didn't smile back. He seemed bothered, his blue eyes dark and moody, and he was frowning, a deep furrow above the bridge of his nose. Silently he put on his breeches, pulling them up and over those lean, muscular flanks, then he sat down and began to put on his stockings. Why was he frowning? Why hadn't he returned my smile? Was he sorry? Did he feel guilty? The cheerful warbling of the bird continued as he thrust his right foot into his boot and pulled it up to mid-calf. He put his left boot on next and then stood, shifting his weight a little as his feet eased down into the boots.

"Good morning," I said.

He didn't answer.

"Is—is something wrong?"

"Why didn't you tell me you were a virgin?"

"I—I assumed you knew."

"My mistake," he said grimly.

"I told you I was a good girl. I told you none of—none of what you believed was true. That day in the east wing I—"

I cut myself short, looking at him. He pulled on the thin white lawn shirt and tucked the tail loosely into the waistband of his breeches. I sat up on the edge of the bed, holding the satin counterpane up over my bosom. The back of my throat felt tight. He hadn't believed me. He had thought there had been other men. He brushed the errant wave from his brow and looked at me, the frown still making a deep furrow. Last night we had been as close as it was possible to be, and now it was as though we were strangers.

"I'm glad you were the first," I told him.

"The harm is already done."

"Charles, I love you, and—"

"I'm sorry, Dana."

"Sorry?"

"I take full blame for what happened."

He stepped over to the windows and opened them. It was six o'clock in the morning. He planned to slip back to his room before any of the servants were up and about.

"Are you still going to go visit the plantations?" I asked.

"That can wait," he said. "I suggest you either burn those sheets or wash them yourself. Those bloodstains are a dead giveaway. The maid will know immediately what took place here last night."

My throat seemed to tighten even more. The bird stopped warbling. I could hear the splash of the fountain below.

"Will—will you be coming back to my room tonight?" I asked.

"Oh yes," he said. "I'll be back. As I said, the harm has already been done, and I haven't the strength nor the inclination to stay away. You've cast your spell over me completely."

He stood there in front of the windows, cool and remote, looking at me with silent accusation, and then he turned and left the room.

Chapter Thirteen

DELIA WAS IN FINE FORM, wonderfully refreshed and full of delicious gossip with which she regaled us at breakfast the morning after she returned. I sipped my coffee, trying my best to pretend an interest in the goings-on of the gentry on the River Road, and Charles was frankly bored. With a captive audience, Delia continued to chatter on with great vivacity, looking charming in her pale lilac frock. Her cheeks were flushed a delicate pink, her eyes all asparkle, and her hair was a soft, silvery cloud framing that aged but piquant face. I was glad she had had such a good time, but her enthusiasm was rather hard to take so early in the morning.

"—and then the ball, my dears! I'll say this for Alicia, she spared no expense. The food, the champagne, the flowers! Huge bunches of lilies wherever you turned, all tied up with blue and silver ribbon. I wore my buttercup-yellow gown and, I might as well confess it, I was rather a *hit* with the elderly set. You'd never believe how many arthritic old men shuffled me around the dance floor. One of them even proposed! Poor dear, eighty-five if he was a day, and with only one kidney—"

"You should have grabbed him," Charles said dryly.

"Don't think I wasn't tempted," she retorted. "His father made a fortune in tobacco and indigo before we even *grew* cotton in Louisiana. He has a palatial town house in Baton Rouge, a famous collection of Ming porcelain and investments amounting to three million—still, there's that missing kidney." Delia sighed and helped herself to more apricot preserves. "Did I tell you all about Alicia's cousin Jessica?"

"Her horse fell on her," Charles said.

"They had to amputate a leg," I added.

"I guess I did. It hasn't stopped her from enjoying herself one bit. She sat on the sofa, painted like a doll, fanning herself with an exquisite fan and flirting outrageously with any male who came within range. Later on, at cards, she cleaned *up*. Everyone was vying to be her partner. Of course, with those full skirts she wore, you couldn't *tell* her leg was amputated."

"How did she get around?" I inquired.

"I understand she uses a crutch at home, but at Alicia's she had a perfectly enormous Negro in white velvet livery who *carried* her to and fro. Very dramatic. Jessica always was theatrical, Alicia tells me, even before she lost her leg. I for one think it's splendid how she copes. I must say, Charles, you've been very quiet and solemn this morning."

"Who's had a chance to get a word in edgewise?"

"I know you don't really mean that, dear. I know you're positively delighted to see your old aunt again. Confess it—you missed me?"

"The peace and quiet almost drove me mad."

"Eat your ham and grits, dear. I feel altogether too good to let you get a rise out of me this morning, even if you have spent the entire meal looking like you were staring into an open grave. Julian, I trust, will be a little more enthusiastic about seeing his aunt back safe and sound. I understand he's returning this afternoon. No doubt he'll bring a bag full of plants and muddy roots, all wrapped up in paper, and painstakingly describe each one to us. Still, it's nice to have a hobby."

Charles rose. "If you'll excuse me, I really must be getting to the store now," he said.

"You haven't finished your plate," Delia pointed out.

"Delia, darling. I am no longer twelve years old."

"One would never guess it from the way you act, dear. Your manners are as bad as they were back then—every bit as bad. Have a nice day, dear, and when you get home I expect you to be a little more at*ten*tive."

Charles moved around the table to her chair and leaned down, kissing her on the cheek. Delia shooed him away in mock exasperation, but I could see that she was utterly enchanted with this moody nephew of hers. Charles left without even glancing at me. I felt a sharp pang, but I told myself it was because he didn't want to give anything away. Our nights together in my bedroom were intensely intimate and swollen with passion, but during the day and in front of others Charles affected a cool indifference toward me I couldn't help but find hurtful. I poured another cup of coffee, giving Delia a warm smile.

"He *was* awfully solemn this morning," she observed, buttering another one of Jezebel's wonderful biscuits. "I know that boy like the back of my hand and I can read him like a book. Something's preying on his mind. I can tell. He never was one to conceal things with any success."

"Per—perhaps he's worried about business," I said lightly.

"Could be," she replied. "I know he's terribly displeased with Raoul and resents having him at the store, but that situation has been going on for a long time. No, it's something else. Hmmmm."

Delia frowned, musing about it.

"I'm so glad you enjoyed yourself," I told her, changing the subject. "It is nice to have you back. You look marvelous."

"I haven't had one of my headaches in days," she confessed. "I must say, though, my dear, *you* certainly seem to have bloomed during the time I've been away. There's a new glow about you, and you seem—well, curiously older. More grown-up."

"It must be your imagination."

"Perhaps my being away has merely given me a new perspective. You've been changing all the time, of course—when I think of the gawky, screechy creature Julian first brought home . . ."

Delia shook her head. I forced a smile.

"That seems such a very long time ago," I said.

"I did enjoy myself tremendously," Delia confided, "and I'm sure it did me a world of good, but I felt strangely out of touch. I missed you all, and I missed the house and—well, I have the feeling things have been going *on* while I was at Alicia's."

"Everything's fine," I assured her.

"I do hope Charles isn't having more financial difficulties. He tries to keep these things from me, doesn't want me to worry about them, but I worry all the more when I don't *know*. I'm going to have to have a talk with him."

I finished my coffee and carefully set the cup in the saucer.

"All through dear?" Delia asked.

I nodded, folding my napkin beside my plate.

"I'd love to have another one of those biscuits with some more of the preserves, but I dare not, not if I want to keep this willowy waistline. I missed Jezebel's cooking, I can tell you for sure.''

"What are you going to do this morning?" I asked.

Delia smiled a smile that could only be called mischievous.

"I'm going to pay a call on Lavinia," she told me. "I hate to go visit her, but I can't resist the opportunity to crow about my social conquests. Lavinia has never been invited to Alicia's, and I shall probably rub it in. When I tell her about the ball and all my dancing partners and the marriage proposal she'll turn green. I don't intend to mention the missing kidney."

"You're awful, Delia."

"Actually, dear, I am, rather," she agreed.

Delia went up to her room to change for her visit. Kayla and I were going to mend some curtains this morning, and I started down the back hall toward the sewing room. As I passed a narrow corridor branching off the hall, an arm flew out, seizing me. A hand clamped over my mouth, smothering my cry. I had a moment of sheer terror until I heard Charles's voice speaking quietly into my ear, telling me to be calm, there was nothing to fear. Slowly he removed his hand from my mouth and turned me around.

"You scared the life out of me!" I exclaimed.

"Keep your voice down."

"I thought you'd already gone."

"I waited. I wanted to speak to you."

"My heart is still pounding. Really, Charles, you—you're lucky I didn't stomp on your foot and drive my elbow into your stomach and—and then do some real damage."

A smile flickered on his lips. "It seems to me I've won all the wrestling matches we've had."

"That's because I *wanted* you to win."

He brushed a wave from my cheek and let his hand linger for a moment on my hair. Little sunlight penetrated this part of the house, and the corridor was dim and hazy. His handsome face was softly brushed with shadow, his cheekbones prominent, a heavy wave dipping over his brow. His eyes glowed darkly. I saw desire smoldering in them, but I could not see love. There was a vast difference. I loved him with all my heart and soul, but after all our nights together, I still wasn't sure how he felt about me. He never spoke of his feelings, was reserved and rather withdrawn except in the actual act of love, and then he was splendidly abandoned.

"What—what did you want to speak to me about?" I asked.

"I wanted to warn you. We must be even more careful now."

"I—I realize that."

"You looked hurt when I left the breakfast table. I—don't want to hurt you, Dana, but no one must suspect. Delia is much shrewder and far more observant than anyone gives her credit for being."

"I know."

"If I had any sense at all, I would give you up," he said, and he seemed to be speaking to himself. "I'm not very happy with myself or with what's happened, but . . ." He hesitated, frowning.

"I—I'm glad it happened."

"You're eighteen years old, Dana. I don't expect you to understand what I feel."

We heard footsteps coming down the back hall. Charles stiffened and then quickly drew me into the shadowy recess of a doorway farther down the corridor, cupping a hand over my mouth again. We saw Pompey pass by a few moments later, and Charles didn't let me go until the sound of his footsteps had died away completely. I hated this furtiveness. I hated this deception. My heart was full of love, and I wanted the whole world to know, but I knew that wasn't possible. I knew we must keep it a secret, at least . . . at least for the present.

"He—he didn't see us," I whispered.

"I must be out of my mind taking a risk like this," he said, and again he seemed to be speaking to himself. "I must go now, Dana. Jasper is waiting out front. Remember what I said—we must be very careful."

I nodded. I hoped he would kiss me. He didn't.

Later on, in the small sunny sewing room in back of the house, I sat with Kayla, diligently trying to help her with the mending. A luscious yellow satin drape was spread over my knees and flowing over the floor like a glossy pool as I worked with needle and thread, tacking the hem. I wasn't very good at it, and my mind really wasn't on the task. Kayla hummed to herself as she mended a linen tablecloth, her stitches so tiny and neat you would hardly be able to tell it had been patched. Sunlight streamed in through the windows, and there were a number of potted green plants which created a pleasant atmosphere. The large worktable was piled high with various things that needed to be mended, a vivid magpie's nest of whites and colors.

I thought about Charles, and I thought about love. How little I had known of life before. How naive I had been. During these past months I had devoured dozens of romantic novels, but how little I had actually understood as I turned those turbulent pages. In a love affair, George Sand wrote, there was one who loved and one who is loved. I had thought that a clever, rather cynical observation when I read it, but now I knew the truth of it. I loved. Charles was loved. For a woman, Madame Sand continued, love is everything, her reason for being. For a man, love is but a pleasant diversion from his main concern, making a living. Charles certainly gave more thought to business matters than he did to me.

Madame Sand, I knew, was a notorious creature who elected to live her life with the freedom of a man, taking lovers as freely as men took mistresses, sometimes even donning trousers and top hat in order to gain entry to cafés open to her male friends but closed to women. Scandalous she might be, but no one knew the human heart so well, and no one wrote of it with such insight. The worldly wisdom in her books might give me guidelines and help me understand the mysteries of the heart, but nothing could still the doubts and fears that so frequently besieged me when I was not in his arms. Love was a glorious awakening, yes, but it almost made you extremely vulnerable.

"Damn!" I exclaimed.

"You'se pricked your finger, Miz Dana!"

"It's my own fault. I wasn't paying attention."

"It ain't easy, is it?"

"I never was good with needle and thread."

"That ain't what I mean. I mean it ain't easy bein' in love."

I looked at her. Kayla made another neat stitch, deftly drawing the needle through the fine white linen.

"You know," I said.

"Course I does. Them sheets you cleaned, Miz Dana—you didn't do a very good job on 'em. I had to use lye soap and lemon juice to get them bloodstains out completely. I ain't *told* no one, Miz Dana."

"I'm almost glad you know. At least now I can talk to someone about it."

"I'd a knowed even if I hadn't seen them sheets. You got that bloom lovin' brings. Your hair's all glossy an' shiny, your skin's as smooth as a magnolia petal, an' there's a new grace in th' way you move. Lovin' does that every time."

Kayla finished with the tablecloth and took the drape from me, yellow satin slipping and flowing over our knees.

"You'd better let me finish this. You got th' will, but you ain't got th' skill. Guess I'll just pull them stitches you done out an' start all over. It ain't easy lovin' a man. Makes you all skittish an' jumpy. When you is with him you worry 'cause you wanna please him and fear you ain't, and when you is away from him you worry even more 'cause you start thinkin' he don't love you as much as you loves him. Men don't," she added.

"Are you in love with Jasper?" I asked.

Kayla laughed, shaking her head. "Lawsy no, Miz Dana. I lets him pleasure me 'cause I like it, but I shore ain't in love with him. I'se only been in love once—'member that white boy I told you about, th' one who took my cherry? Him I loved, an' he broke my heart. Figured once was enough for me, an' I promised myself I wudn't gonna fall in love no more."

"But—you were only a child. You were barely thirteen."

"Reckon age don't mean all that much when it comes to lovin'. Your heart ain't keepin' track-a th' number of years you been on this earth. I was thirteen, yes'um, but th' hurtin' was grown-up hurtin'."

"It must have been—very bad," I said quietly.

Kayla had been tearing my stitches out of the yellow satin hem, and now she began to sew the hem up again with those neat, precise stitches she had used on the tablecloth.

"When you gives yourself to someone," she said, "gives yourself entirely an' with no holdin' back, you gives them the power to hurt you. Jest a glance, jest a word, jest a tone-a voice, can cause a stabbin' pain, can cause new doubt an' make you lie awake worryin' all night."

Her voice was soft and serene. Her lovely eyes were downcast, looking at the satin she continued to stitch but not seeing it, seeing instead a time gone by. She was not French nor a celebrated novelist, but there was wisdom in her words. I told her so.

"Reckon it ain't nothin' every woman don't learn eventually,'' she said in that soft voice. "You'se got it bad for Mister Charles, ain't you?''

"I'm afraid I do.''

"Reckon he ain't an easy man to love, him bein' so moody an' all. With a man like that, you ain't never gonna know where you stand, Miz Dana. You jest has to hang on, hopin'.''

"I don't know how it's going to end.''

"A woman don't never know that,'' she told me. "It ain't no use thinkin' 'bout how it's gonna end—or when. You jest resigns yourself an' takes your pleasure an' takes your knocks an' thank th' Lawd you gotta fine-lookin' man in your bed.''

"I wish it were that simple,'' I said.

Kayla finished hemming the drape and stood up, folding the yellow satin into a neat square.

"It *is* that simple,'' she said. "Leastways for us it is. White folks are always complicatin' things. Mister Charles is smitten an' he's tormentin' hisself 'cause he dudn't think he should be. You'se head over heels in love with him and worryin' yourself sick because he ain't talkin' tender to you an' tellin' you how much you mean to him.''

"He—he does love me, Kayla.''

"I'se sure he does, Miz Dana, in his way. Only his way ain't th' way you'd like. Man like Mister Charles ain't never gonna woo you with roses an' fine words. Man like that's gonna keep it to hisself 'cause that's his way. Either you accepts it or you drives yourself crazy.''

"You *are* wise,'' I said quietly.

"Reckon I knows th' ways of men. Lawd knows I'se had enough experience.'' Kayla put the folded drape on the work-table and took up a pale blue pillowcase with a small tear. "Me, I don't want nothin' more to do with love. I takes my pleasure an' takes my time, shoppin' around. One-a these days I'm gonna find a man I think worth marryin' an' he ain't gonna have a chance.''

"Jasper, perhaps?''

"No way,'' she said, "but he sure is good at pleasurin'.''

I felt much better after talking to Kayla. We spent the rest of the morning mending, Kayla doing most of the work, and then I went up to my room. The frock I was wearing was wrinkled and damp under the armpits. I removed it and, wearing only my thin white petticoat with its five ruffled skirts, poured water into the ewer and sponged myself off. I brushed my hair until it shone and applied a little of my lilac perfume, examining myself in the mirror as I did so. Kayla was right. There was a new bloom. Lovin' caused that.

And it was wonderful lovin' indeed, I thought, turning to look at the bed. The golden headboard with its fancy darker gold and brown marquetry had a rich, glossy patina, and the heavy yellow satin counterpane gleamed lushly in the sunlight. It had been a virgin's bed before, the repository of dreams, but now it was the field of amorous combat. I had no basis for comparison, of course, but Charles was a magnificent lover, passionate, patient, demanding, fulfilling. I felt a flush of pleasure as I thought of those prolonged bouts between the linen sheets. He was quite masterful, and there was a carefully controlled brutality in his lovemaking, yet there was tenderness, too, and, always, concern that I experience bliss equal to his. At first I had worried that I might conceive a child, but Charles stilled that worry, assuring me he was taking precautions. Relieved on that score, I achieved even greater pleasure as our limbs entwined, as flesh welcomed flesh and we two became one.

Sometimes, afterward, he held me close and I nestled in the prison of his arms and he stroked my back, my arms, my hair, tenderly, so tenderly, and I was sure that he loved me, even though he never spoke the words. As Kayla pointed out, that was not his way, and . . . and I would just have to be content with what I had. He was a complicated man, moody, often withdrawn, carrying a burden of responsibility that frequently made him seem hard, even ruthless, but he could be wry and charming and, on occasion, almost boyish. A perfect lover he wasn't, but he was mine and I loved him passionately and longed for that magical hour when the house was dark and still and he crept into my room and I could melt into his arms once again.

I donned a pale yellow frock sprigged with small brown and dark gold flowers. I adjusted the off-the-shoulder puffed sleeves and smoothed down the snug bodice. It was a girlish garment, but little of the girl remained. My breasts strained full and proud against the low-cut neckline, the line of cleavage distinctly, if modestly, defined. I did feel older, felt wise and experienced and full of wonderful secrets, and I reminded myself that I must continue to be the demure young lady for Delia and Julian and the others. Our secret must remain a secret, and I must remain a dutiful ward.

Delia and I had a light but lavish lunch of chilled lobster soup and fresh green salad with artichoke hearts and tiny shrimp and Jezebel's wonderful dressing. There were popovers, too, as light and delicious as always. Delia told me all about her visit to Lavinia and Lavinia's envy and inward fury when Delia described her triumphs at Grande Villa. A bit tired after we finished eating, Delia said she thought she would go up to her room and rest for a while. I confessed that I needed to spend some time at math.

"How dreary," she observed.

"I'll never get the hang of long division," I complained.

"*I* never did, dear."

I dutifully spent two hours at the desk in the library covering pages with numbers and trying to figure them out. Two into four went two times, sure, anyone could figure that out, but six into twenty-five was another matter altogether. I finally figured that it went four times and that made twenty-four, but I hadn't a clue what to do with the one left over. It was all a useless waste of time, I decided, perfectly silly. I had been a dutiful schoolgirl all of these months, diligently doing all my lessons, striving hard to please my tutors, but I was ready to rebel.

Closing my math book and pushing the papers aside, I deserted the desk and stepped through the open French windows into the courtyard beyond. The sky was high overhead, a clear, hot blue, and afternoon shadows were already spreading, making cool blue-gray pools on the tiles. Deep green fronds spread, and lighter green ferns were like cascades of frothy lace. Pink, purple and deep red blossoms filled the air with exotic perfume, and the mimosa trees were like two huge umbrellas, one dusty mauve, the other pale yellow-gold. How peaceful and beautiful it was here, I thought, strolling toward the three-tiered fountain. The splash and splatter of water spilling from rim to rim made tinkling music.

I looked at that winding wrought-iron staircase that led up to the gallery running outside my second-floor bedroom. Every night since that first time, he had slipped out into the courtyard when the moon was high, silvering the tiles, intensifying the darkness, and he had silently climbed that staircase and moved along the gallery to my opened French windows. How impatient

I was, waiting in the darkened bedroom, longing to hear his step, yearning for his touch, craving the splendid gymnastics that made us one.

Dipping my fingertips into the cool water of the fountain, I thought about the changes in my life. I was happier now than I had ever been, in one sense, but I was also more insecure. What you do not have, you are not afraid of losing, and now that I had this beauty, this bliss, I didn't know how I could possibly live without it. I remembered the dream, and somehow I knew I was meant to love Charles Etienne. How disconcerting it all was. How much simpler life had been before I stepped over that invisible threshold and discovered my reason for being.

I heard a step behind me. I turned. Julian smiled.

"Good afternoon," he said.

"Julian—"

"Kayla told me you were in the library. I found a math book on the desk, a clutter of wretchedly scratched-over papers, but I didn't find you. I looked out. I saw you standing here."

"You—you're back."

"Just got in a few minutes ago. Haven't even changed. You—my God, you look beautiful. I paused at the French windows, watching you. You looked like a vision, standing here by the fountain in your yellow dress, the sunlight gilding your hair."

That made me nervous. I changed the subject.

"I'm through with math, Julian," I told him.

"Oh?"

"It drives me crazy. It makes my mind all a muddle. I don't intend to try to learn any more."

"Very well," he said fondly.

"You—you aren't even going to argue?"

"I want you to be happy. I've come to the conclusion that that's about the most important thing in the world to me—making you happy."

He smiled again, a lovely, tender smile. He was wearing brown leather knee boots and dark tan breeches and a pale beige lawn shirt open at the throat, full sleeves gathered at the wrist. The boots were dusty, the breeches snug, and the shirt was not at all fresh. He looked even leaner, looked trim and fit and brimming with robust good health. He had acquired a tan, which made him look younger, while his chestnut hair was lightly sun-streaked, golden glints showing amid the dark brown.

"Did—did you have a good trip?" I asked.

"Marvelous trip. Got everything I needed. Spent a lot of time in the sun. Didn't encounter a single alligator."

"You look wonderful, Julian."

"I need to change. I've been traveling in these clothes."

He was in an exuberant mood, exuding energy and vitality, and he seemed far more at ease than he had been when he departed. Those gentle brown eyes looked into mine and I saw what was in them. It was something I had never seen in Charles' eyes.

"Did you hear what I said?" he asked.

"I heard."

"Making you happy—that's my main priority. You know what I'm trying to say."

I nodded. I knew. I wished it weren't this way.

"I love you, Dana. There, I've said it at last. Never thought I'd be able to come right out with it. I think I've loved you for a very long time, perhaps from the first."

His voice was husky and gentle and sincere. How beautiful his words were. I was very touched, so touched I could feel my eyes grow moist. If only he were the one.

"I knew it was happening, Dana, but I fought it. I fought it valiantly. I told myself it was wrong. I told myself I was too old for you. I told myself society would disapprove. I told myself I'd get over it, and I tried, I really did try, but it was no use. That night after the ball, in front of your bedroom door, how I wanted to take you into my arms."

I didn't say anything. Julian shifted his weight, legs spread wide, hands resting lightly on his thighs.

"It bothered me. I tried to avoid you. I tried to put you out of my mind. I couldn't Dana. I decided to take this final trip and try to sort things out in my mind. I did quite a lot of soul-searching."

He paused, smiling at me and looking at me with eyes that made no secret of the love inside him. How I wished this weren't happening. How I wished I were someplace else. I loved him, too, though not the way he wanted, and I couldn't bear to hurt him.

"I decided age didn't matter," he told me. "I'm older, yes, but you make me feel young again. I'm old enough to protect you, take care of you, give you the security a younger man couldn't. Do I seem terribly ancient to you?''

I shook my head, loving him.

''I decided I didn't give a damn what people might say. Let them talk. I'm not going to sacrifice happiness for fear of a few wagging tongues. People are going to talk no matter what you do.''

I nodded, afraid my voice would betray me.

''I—I never thought I would feel this way again, Dana,'' he continued, his voice quiet, full of sincerity. ''This is difficult to say, but—after I lost my wife I shut myself off from—from any kind of emotional entanglement. There were women, of course, but they were mere amusement. When I lost Maryanne I was so crushed I vowed I—I'd never allow myself to love again.''

''I—understand,'' I said.

''Then you came charging into my life and turned everything upside down. My comfortable old routine was unsettled. Peace and quiet was disrupted. I suddenly had new concern, new responsibility, and, I might as well confess, it was extremely aggravating at first. Something started happening to me, and I tried my best to deny it. After the night of the ball, I could no longer even try to deceive myself. I knew I loved you.''

He took my hand in both of his and squeezed it.

''I love you, Dana. I want to marry you.''

I was startled, so startled I pulled my hand free.

''You—you want to *marry* me?''

''Of course I do,'' he replied. ''I love you, and I'm an honorable man. I wouldn't dream of—any other kind of arrangement.''

Your brother would, I thought.

''I want to make you my wife. I want to give you the world. I'll be completely finished with the book in six weeks, two months, and then—then I want to take you to London, to Paris. I want to show you a world you've never seen. I want to make you the happiest woman on earth and—I swear I'll try.''

He would try. I knew that. No woman could ask for a finer man than this. No woman could ask for love stronger than that shining in his gentle brown eyes. Why, why, why did it have to be this way?

''But—'' I hesitated. ''I—you're an aristocrat, Julian. You come from a fine old family. I—I come from the swamps. I'm a bastard. I'm—people already believe I'm a trollop. If you married me—"

"Those things don't matter, Dana."

"Your family—"

He took my hand again, holding it tightly.

"I love you," he said. "That's all that counts."

"I—don't know what to say."

"I realize you—well, you're very young and I—I don't expect you to feel the same way about me, but—" He looked suddenly afraid, doubtful. "I believe you—you could learn to love me."

I couldn't bear that look in his eyes. I rested my free hand on his cheek. "I love you already," I said quietly.

"But—not in that way?"

I didn't answer. I couldn't bring myself to wound him. Julian let go of my hand and sighed, and then he smiled that beautiful, gentle smile that touched my heart every time I saw it.

"I know this must all come as a great surprise to you," he said. "I never thought I'd have the courage to—speak my piece. I was scared spitless you'd laugh at me."

"I'd never do that."

"I realize you'll need time. I just—I just want you to think about it. Will you do that, Dana? Will you think about marrying me? You needn't make up your mind right away."

"I'll think about it," I said gently. "I—I'm very honored, Julian."

"We—uh—we won't say anything about this to the others," he said. "It will be our secret."

"I think that would be best," I agreed.

Julian let go of my hand and stepped back, looking relieved now and looking suddenly shy and awkward as well. He grinned boyishly and then said he'd better go wash and change. I said I would see him at dinner. He nodded and turned and moved back toward the French windows in a long, brisk stride. The fountain continued to splatter merrily. Afternoon shadows continued to spread, darker now, purple-gray. I stood there for a long time, facing this new dilemma, wondering how I was going to handle it, and then, finally, climbed thoughtfully up the outside staircase and moved along the gallery to my bedroom.

Jezebel outdid herself that evening in celebration of Julian's return. We had a marvelous lobster bisque to start with, savory and thick with meat, then a delicious cucumber salad. For the main course we were each served an individual oyster loaf, a small, flaky, piping hot loaf of buttery bread stuffed with baked oysters cooked in a sauce and a variety of wonderful herbs and spices. Delia was radiant in an ivory silk frock with mauve velvet bows, chattering nonstop about her visit to Grande Villa. Charles wore his dark blue frock coat and a sky-blue waistcoat embroidered with sapphire leaves, looking splendid and neat and irritated as his aunt continued to babble charmingly. Julian was wearing a dark brown frock coat and a handsome waistcoat I had never seen, light tan satin with brown and gold stripes. Leaner than ever, with his new tan and the sun-streaked hair, he did indeed look younger. When, finally, Delia paused for breath, he told us about his trip, about his experiments with soil, about the plants he couldn't resist bringing back with him.

How warm and genial he was, wry and witty and full of good humor, an honorable man indeed. I sat there in my pale apricot silk frock, watching him, loving him, wishing he were the one. Charles, to spite Delia, I suspected, asked a number of questions about the soil, about the plants, egging his brother on, and Julian grew even more expansive. Pompey and Elijah cleared our places and then brought in dessert, vanilla ice cream with pecans and hot praline sauce, a rarity as ice was so very expensive. Delia clapped her hands in delight, declaring it a wonderful surprise, and I saw Jezebel peeking through the door, a wide grin on her round black face.

"And how is business?" Julian asked. "Have you gone to inspect the cotton crops yet?"

"Uh—not yet," Charles replied. "I thought I'd wait a little while longer. There are a few business matters I do need to discuss with you, though."

"Not at the dinner table," Delia insisted. "We've had to endure all that dreary talk about mud and roots and such. I positively refuse to listen to business talk. You boys can go into the study after we finish."

"Yes, ma'am," Charles said.

"We wouldn't want to bore you," Julian agreed.

"Heaven forbid," Charles added.

"I'm in much too festive a mood to let you boys rile me," Delia told them. "It's wonderful to be back, and it's wonderful to have you back, too, Julian. I must say, all that tramping around in the swamps seems to agree with you. I've rarely seen you looking so hale and hearty."

"Thank you, Auntie."

"Don't be disrespectful!" she cautioned. "You know I detest that appellation. I do hope, dear, that you can pull your brother out of the mopes. Charles has never been the most amenable person I know, but ever since I returned, he has been downright somber. I suspect it has something to do with business."

"Business is fine," Charles said.

"Perhaps it's a woman, then. Oh my word! *You* haven't gotten involved with that dreadful Amelia Jameson, have you?"

"I haven't," he replied, "and Amelia is not dreadful at all. She's a delightfully charming, sophisticated woman who happens to still be carrying a huge torch for Julian."

"Really?" Julian inquired.

"God knows why," Charles replied.

The men retired to Julian's study after dessert, and I took coffee with Delia in her sitting room, conscious as always of the stern scrutiny of those eyes in the portrait hanging over the mantel. Running out of gossip, Delia recounted the plots of two delicious new novels straight from France she had read while at Grande Villa. Really, she confided, that M. de Balzac was getting a bit too racy even for *her* taste, but I would love *Eugenie Grandet* and she would get a copy as soon as the stores here had it.

It was after ten when I escorted Delia to her room and told her good night. Charles and Julian were still in the study. I went to my own bedroom. The bedcovers were turned down and candles were burning. I put most of them out, preferring a hazy semidarkness. Still wearing my apricot frock, I walked out onto the gallery and stood there looking at the moonlight and shadows. It was a warm night, though not nearly as sultry as it had been two weeks ago, and a gentle breeze stirred the greenery below. A single window was lighted in the servants' quarters. Was that Jasper's room? Was Kayla with him? Kayla was shopping around for the right man to marry, and the finest man in New Orleans wanted to marry me. He was ready to face the wrath of society, perhaps even ostracism, in order to do so.

What was I going to do? He loved me as every woman wants to be loved, sincerely, utterly, exclusively, and I had no doubt he would be as passionate a lover as his brother was, but therein was the rub. I loved his brother. I didn't want to, I realized that now. I didn't want to love him as I did, I didn't want anyone to have that kind of power over me, but love him I did, and there was nothing I could do about it. I stood there on the gallery for a long time, thinking about my problem and wondering how I could possibly find a solution. I watched the moon sail lazily behind a bank of clouds, watched silver pools vanish below, and the clock struck eleven as I went back inside.

I put the rest of the candles out. I was sitting in the darkness when, almost an hour and a half later, I heard his soft step outside. I hadn't known if he would come or not. I stood up, my apricot skirt rustling. He stepped into the room, silhouetted dark against the moonlight that now streamed down in brilliant rays. He was still dressed, too, although he had taken off his frock coat and neckcloth. How tall he was, how lean and muscular. How my blood stirred at the sight of him. I almost resented that hunger inside. If I were free, if I were my own person again and not a captive of these emotions, everything would be much easier. Because he stood in front of the silvery blaze, I couldn't see his face, only the shape of him, but I could feel those eyes studying me.

"I didn't know if—if you'd come or not," I said quietly.

"I started not to. I couldn't stay away."

"You're not—happy about that, are you?"

Charles didn't answer. He stepped toward me and took me in his arms, and I submitted to that kiss. When, finally, he drew back, I knew I must tell him before it went any further. I brushed a wave from my cheek. I could see his face now. His eyes were dark with desire. His mouth was tight. He hungered for me, but hunger wasn't love. Did he love me? What would his reaction be when I told him about Julian's proposal?

"You're strangely unresponsive tonight," he remarked.

"Do you love me, Charles?" I asked abruptly.

The question took him aback. I could see that. I hadn't wanted to ask it, but I felt I must. He scowled, not at all pleased.

"I'm bewitched by you," he said finally.

"That isn't an answer. Or—perhaps it is."

"What is all this, Dana?"

"Would you marry me?" I asked.

"Marry you? No, Dana. I wouldn't. I'm an Etienne. When I marry, it will be to a woman of my own background."

"Julian would," I said.

"Would what?"

"Marry me. He wants to. He told me so this afternoon."

Charles was stunned. He stepped back. Even in the moonlight I could see the color drain from his cheeks. He didn't say anything for a long time. I was silent, too, sad, for I knew I had made a dreadful error. I could feel him withdrawing from me, could feel his anger, his disapproval, his suspicion.

"Have you slept with him, too?" he asked at last.

"You know that's not true."

"Then how did you trick him into—"

"There was no trickery, Charles. He loves me. He wants me to become his wife."

He looked at me, not wanting to believe it, knowing it was true, and I felt a terrible pain inside. I loved him with all my heart and soul, but Charles didn't love me, not really. He made love to me, but that was something altogether different. He had disapproved of me from the first and had wanted to get rid of me, and then . . . he had accepted me only because of Julian and Delia, only to keep peace in the family. I was good enough to visit furtively, to love in secret, in the darkness, but I wasn't good enough to marry an Etienne. I accepted all of these truths, yet I loved him still. I didn't want to. I wanted to hate him. I couldn't.

"What do you intend to tell him?" he asked.

"I—I don't know what I'm going to tell him. He promised not to press me. He doesn't expect an answer right away. I—don't want to hurt him, Charles."

"Nor do I," he said solemnly.

"What are we going to do?"

"I don't know," he said. "The fool!" he exclaimed then. "The goddamned fool!"

He turned and moved back to the French windows, back into the silvery blaze of moonlight. He stopped, looking at me, and it was a long while before he finally spoke.

"I won't allow it, Dana," he told me.

He left. I knew that I had lost him.

Chapter Fourteen

CHARLES LEFT TO INSPECT THE COTTON CROPS at Belle Mead and Ravenaugh the following morning, to be gone ten days. He left immediately after breakfast, avoiding my eyes throughout the meal. I didn't have an opportunity to speak to him, nor did I want to. I was completely devastated by what had happened, but somehow I managed to put on a front for Delia and Julian during the days that followed. I went to Corinne's with Delia to refurbish her wardrobe, helping her decide which fabrics, which styles were most flattering and suitable. More intent than ever to complete his work, Julian spent a great deal of time in his study, but he was wonderfully warm and attentive when he wasn't working, his eyes aglow with those tender emotions he found difficult to hide. If Delia noticed anything, she made no comment, merely observing that she was delighted he was no longer so grouchy. Day followed day in smooth progression, and I managed to get through each of them without betraying the desolation inside.

Charles had been gone for almost a week when, at breakfast one morning, Julian informed us that he was going to the printer's to look at some sample plates and asked if I would like to accompany him, adding that we could go to lunch afterward. I didn't really want to go, but he was clearly so eager for my company that I hadn't the heart to refuse him. I changed into a bronze taffeta frock, and an hour later we were on our way to the printer's, Julian looking splendidly handsome in his brown breeches and frock coat and another new waistcoat, dark burnt orange with narrow brown stripes, his neckcloth creamy tan silk. He chatted pleasantly about his work as we rode and, to my relief, made no reference to our conversation in the court-

281

yard. He was a gentleman, and he was going to give me plenty of room, plenty of time. He did squeeze my hand as he assisted me out of the carriage, holding it perhaps a moment or two longer than necessary.

The printer's shop was large and incredibly cluttered with strange machines, stacks of paper and pamphlets, boxes of lead type, dusty shelves filled with bottles of ink and more paper and various tools. Monsieur Delain, the printer, was small, stooped, ancient and bearded, wearing a black broadcloth suit as dusty as the shelves. A young blond assistant in shirt sleeves and a thin leather apron was busily setting type, a process I found fascinating. Monsieur Delain greeted Julian in a cracked, hoarse voice, nodded curtly when introduced to me and scurried into a back room, stumbling over a stack of freshly printed pamphlets as he did so. He came back a few minutes later bearing a large, bulky portfolio, his watery old blue eyes full of pride. Sweeping a long wooden worktable clear of its clutter of paper and type, he put the portfolio down, untied the strings and began to pull out the plates one by one.

Printed on large sheets of heavy, creamy paper, they were absolutely exquisite, details perfectly executed, color bright and glowing. There was the swamp lily, pale pink and ivory, resting on its rubbery dark green pad, and there the wild bluebell blossoms, dangling from a slender green vine. I caught my breath as I recognized the painting Julian had been working on that day in the swamp, a gorgeous pale orange flower with delicate gold and bronze specks. The reproduction was remarkably exact, the fragile petals spreading open to reveal the deeper orange center, stamen projecting like a golden fairy wand. There were twenty plates in all, each more breathtakingly lovely than the one before. While I exclaimed over their beauty, Julian and the printer discussed ink and engraving techniques and processing and a whole lot of technical jargon I couldn't even begin to comprehend. I learned that a renowned but impoverished French artist had done the actual engravings from Julian's paintings, and Monsieur Delain himself had experimented until he perfected a process that would allow each color to come through in vivid, natural shades.

"It's costing a fortune," Julian confided when we left the shop, "but Delain is a genius. I wouldn't trust anyone else with the plates."

"They were glorious."

"Those were just samples to test the process. The final plates will be even finer. Charles is going to croak when he finds out how much this is costing, but I've spent over a decade working on this book, and I will settle for nothing but the best."

"Is Monsieur Delain going to print the text, too?"

Julian nodded. "There's no one better. The sheets will be bound in Baton Rouge by Clarkson Brothers, best bindery in the South. I'm thinking in terms of dark leaf-green leather, with marbled endpapers, of course."

"The book is going to be wonderful."

"It's going to be a landmark in the field of botany," he said confidently. "The restaurant is only a few blocks away. Let's walk. Jasper can follow after us in the carriage."

We did so, Julian holding my arm as we strolled down the covered esplanade. I had never been in this part of the city before. It wasn't nearly as grand and elegant as the neighborhood around Corinne's and Etienne's, all the shops rather shabby, needing a new coat of paint, the front windows dirty, and there were not any costly items displayed. Here one bought hammers and nails, not perfume, and here one picked up a leather harness, not a bouquet of expensive hothouse flowers. The pedestrians were not nearly as grandly dressed, a number of burly workmen and stevedores among them, and while some fancy carriages bowled up and down the street, there were far more drays and wagons loaded with big wooden barrels. There was vitality here, a sense of purpose, a reminder that New Orleans was not just the playground of pampered aristocrats but a vital, thriving city.

Near the waterfront, the restaurant was large and spacious and simple, with white walls and ceiling, a polished golden oak floor and tables and chairs painted white. Yellow curtains hung at the windows, and brass lanterns hung from the ceiling. Despite its lack of pretensions, the place was crowded with richly attired gentry, and the prices, I later discovered, were high enough to insure its exclusivity. The maître d' recognized Julian and showed us to one of the better tables. People stared discreetly as we passed, and a buzz of whispers followed us. I pretended not to notice, but I was glad I was wearing the bronze taffeta. Julian ordered our lunch and nodded to a few acquaintances nearby, then gave his full attention to me.

"Like it?" he inquired.

"It's very nice, but—I'm surprised to see all these swells having lunch in this neighborhood."

Julian smiled at my use of the word 'swells.' "Alain's is another New Orleans institution. Originally it was frequented by workmen from the docks. The food was good, the prices reasonable. Soon the wealthy planters moved in to conduct their business deals over lunch and before long, for some inexplicable reason, the place became chic. The food is still good, but the prices are no longer reasonable."

"It seems a pity the workmen can no longer afford to eat here."

"Oh, they have other eating places. The 'swells' come and eat bouillabaisse and cornbread sticks and feel delightfully democratic because they're not dining on pheasant."

The bouillabaisse was served in large brown bowls, the cornbread sticks in a wicker basket, and while both were delicious, neither could compare to what Jezebel prepared. All around us was the hum of polite conversation, the sounds of refined laughter. There was a special atmosphere, as though this were a private club for members only, and I felt out of place. I didn't belong to this world. I never would. When bowls and basket had been removed, Julian informed me that Alain's was famous for its coffee and fried pies and said we must have some. He gave the order and smiled at me.

"You're rather subdued today," he remarked.

"Subdued?"

"Very much the proper young lady. Sometimes I miss the saucy waif with the wicked tongue."

"Blame Madame LeSalle. She's the one who gave me lessons in deportment and taught me how to conduct myself at the dining table."

"The transformation is remarkable. One would never know you weren't to the manor born."

I indicated our fellow diners. "They know," I said.

"Does it bother you?" he asked.

"Not any longer," I said truthfully.

"You're worth a dozen pampered belles."

"I fear you may be—just a little prejudiced," I told him.

Julian chuckled quietly. How many women would give anything to have a man like this look at them with such adoration? Why couldn't I love Julian Etienne instead of his brother? Love him I did, of course, but in a filial way. How was I going to tell him I couldn't possibly become his wife? The pies and coffee were served. The pies had been fried to a crisp golden brown, then generously sprinkled with powdered sugar. Mine was peach. The coffee was so strong, I had to use half the small pitcher of cream. As I was sipping it, I saw Julian's expression change. He was looking across the room and seemed suddenly ill at ease. Turning slightly in my chair, I saw the reason why.

Amelia Jameson had entered the restaurant on the arm of an attractive middle-aged man in cream-colored breeches and frock coat and a dark tan waistcoat. His longish blond hair was beginning to gray, and he looked rather apprehensive as they were shown to a table, Amelia clinging to his arm. She wore a spectacular violet silk gown, long black velvet gloves and a wide-brimmed black velvety hat festooned with violet ostrich plumes. She was as glamorous, as gorgeous, as I remembered, a wicked twinkle in her eyes as she observed her escort's unease. Hardly had they been seated when she spotted Julian. She murmured something to the blond man, got back up and came toward us, wide skirts swaying.

Julian slipped down a little in his chair and looked like he would like to slip through the floor as well, but, gentleman that he was, he stood when Amelia reached our table. He nodded nervously. She treated him to a wry smile.

"Fancy seeing you here," she said. "I thought you never left your study, darling."

"Only on occasion."

"You're looking positively yummy."

"You're looking well yourself, Amelia. You remember Miss O'Malley?"

Amelia gave me the briefest of glances and nodded. I gave her a brief nod in return. I knew I should dislike her intensely, but I found her fascinating and curiously engaging.

"Your taste in clothes has improved considerably," she said.

"Yours remains the same."

"Touché, darling."

"I hear you've fallen upon hard times," Julian told her.

"It's only temporary, darling. I've sold a few of my things to your brother, true, but I'm getting by."

"Who's the man you're with?"

"He's only temporary, too. A planter from upriver, in the city for a few weeks to do business. He's afraid someone here might recognize him and report back to his dragon of a wife. How's the opus coming, darling? Are you still working night and day?"

"As a matter of fact, I'm almost finished."

"Really?" She seemed genuinely pleased. "Somehow I knew you'd finish it. I always believed in you—I suppose that's why I spent so much time transcribing all those notes and copying pages for you. I probably know more about botany than any other woman in the South."

"You probably do," he agreed.

"Lovely seeing you again, darling," she said sweetly. "Should you ever grow tired of children and decide to play with the grownups again, look me up. We'll discuss old times and plan some new ones."

She gave him a radiant smile, nodded to me again and then sashayed back to her table. I had never seen a grown man blush, but Julian's cheeks were decidedly pink as he paid the bill and led me out of the restaurant. Amelia Jameson must have meant more to him than he cared to admit, I thought. She was certainly still able to get a strong reaction from him. I wondered how long they had been together and why he had left her. At the inn, when I had first seen her, Amelia had responded to his remark about "dumping" her by reminding him she had moved on to "greener pastures." Even at the time I had had the impression she was still extremely fond of him, and I suspected Julian still wasn't completely immune to the lady's considerable charms. As we rode home I longed to question him about her but, of course, I didn't. Good breeding definitely had its drawbacks, I thought wryly.

When we arrived home, Kayla met me in the front foyer, and I could tell she had something important to tell me. She contained her excitement, however, until Julian retired to his study, and then she took me by the hand and led me into the parlor. Checking first to make sure that no one was within earshot, she gave me a conspiratorial look and then pulled a small envelope out of her apron pocket.

"This came while you was gone, Miz Dana. Thank heaven Pompey was in back, didn't hear the door. I answered it myself an' there was this boy an' he said this note was for you an' it was real important an' I wudn't to let no one have it but you."

"I—I wonder who it could be from."

"I don't know, but that boy was real smart-alecky, wudn't going to give it to me till I promised I wouldn't let no one else see it."

"Thank you, Kayla," I said.

But Kayla wasn't about to be dismissed so easily. She lingered, watching as I opened the envelope and read the brief note. It was from Guy Chevrier, my mother's uncle. He asked me to meet him at number eighteen, Rampart Street, at three o'clock Sunday afternoon and added that it was imperative that absolutely no one know about our meeting. Puzzled, I read the note again, then slipped it back into the envelope. Kayla waited expectantly, and I felt almost guilty as I told her I would not be needing her for anything else. I went up to my bedroom and, slipping the note into the small drawer in my bedside table, wondered why Guy Chevrier could possibly want to see me after all this time and why such secrecy was necessary.

I was relieved when, after lunch Sunday, Delia declared that she was going to have a little nap in her room, and Julian decided to do some more work in his study. Charles was due back sometime this afternoon, but I would be safely out of the house long before he arrived, as he wasn't expected until after four. I went upstairs and quickly changed into a ruffled beige petticoat and pale beige muslin frock sprigged with tiny gold and brown flowers. I brushed my hair, letting it tumble loosely around my shoulders. No severe hairstyle this time; no dull brown dress either. I could not care less what kind of impression I made on Guy Chevrier. I was only going to meet him out of curiosity, I told myself. I left my bedroom and started downstairs.

Kayla was in the foyer, a light feather dust mop in her hand, and although she pretended to be dusting a vase, I had a distinct impression the little hussy was deliberately waiting for me. I did adore her, of course, but she was altogether too nosy.

"Where-ya goin', Miz Dana?" Her voice was ever so casual.

"That's none of your business, Kayla," I said coolly, "but if you must know, I—I'm going for a walk."

"At this time-a-day? In this heat?"

"It isn't that hot," I retorted, "and I feel the need for a little exercise after that huge lunch."

"Miz Dana, you—you ain't doin' somethin' you oughten, is you? Does this have somethin' to do with that note you put in your bedside table?"

"How did you know I left it there?" I asked sharply.

"I—I was cleanin', an' I just happened to see it."

I was indignant, but I realized no real harm had been done. Kayla couldn't read, of course, and she couldn't possibly know where I was going. I gave her a stern look that informed her I would tolerate no more questions, and then I swept past her and went on outside, opening my parasol on the front steps before proceeding.

It was a lovely day and not really that warm. With the parasol shading my face and shoulders, I strolled slowly. It wasn't quite two o'clock, and I had plenty of time, even if I couldn't get a cab farther on and had to walk all the way. The Quarter was drowsy and silent this Sunday afternoon, and as I passed stone walls awash with bougainvillea the only sounds I heard were the splashing of fountains and the lazy buzz of insects. The air was heavily laden with the perfume of flowers, and I could smell moist soil and sun-warmed stone and rusting iron, a peculiar smell unique to the Quarter with its profusion of fanciful wrought iron.

I wondered anew why Guy Chevrier had requested this secretive meeting. He had certainly seemed more sympathetic toward me than either my aunt or my grandmother, but he was too ineffectual, too spineless, to defy them and accept me as kin. Perhaps . . . perhaps he intended to apologize for the reception I had received at Conti Street in order to salve his conscience. He wouldn't want his sister or her daughter to know about our meeting, of course, and that would explain his request for secrecy. Perhaps he intended to answer the question that his sister had refused to answer. Perhaps he intended to tell me who my father was. That didn't really matter to me anymore, I told myself, turning a corner, leaving the residential district behind. What good would it do for me to know? I knew who *I* was, and that was all that mattered.

The streets here were almost deserted of pedestrians, but several vehicles passed up and down. I kept my eye out for one of the sturdy brown cabs, as the carriages for hire had recently been designated as they transported both customers and bags. Several rumbled past during the next ten minutes or so, but all were occupied. Finally, after I had walked several more blocks, I spotted one sitting idle near the corner and hurried to hire it. The horses were two heavy chestnuts, the driver a grizzled old character in a dirty black coat and a tall black top hat. He opened the door for me and looked askance when I told him to take me to number eighteen Rampart Street.

As I settled in I noticed another cab coming down the street, and my heart gave a leap when I recognized Charles as its occupant. He was peering intently in my direction. I leaned back out of sight, praying he hadn't recognized me. The boat that brought him back from the plantations upriver had evidently come in early. I wasn't going to think about Charles now, I promised myself as the driver cracked his whip and the carriage lurched forward. How much sleep had I lost, going over in my mind every detail of our last encounter? How many tears had I shed? No more, I vowed. I had my pride. He would never know how much I had suffered.

Rampart Street, at least certain sections of it, had a shady reputation, I knew, and I expected to see gambling houses and taverns. Instead, I saw houses painted in pale pastel colors, many with spacious front porches. Flower boxes were in profusion, but there was very little wrought iron. Several dandily attired young men strolled the street, some in groups, others with attractive women on their arms. We passed a house with several young women idling lazily on the front porch, rocking on the porch swing, fanning themselves with fans, turning the pages of fashion journals. All wore light, frilly dresses. I wondered if it might be a finishing school for young ladies. Number eighteen was farther down the street, a tall house painted pale lime-green.

I climbed out of the carriage and paid the driver. He gave me another peculiar look, shook his head and then climbed back onto his seat and drove away. Number eighteen had no front porch. Four dingy gray marble steps led directly to the front door. I lifted the heavy brass knocker and rapped several times. After what seemed a long while the door was finally opened by a young Negro woman in a blue calico dress, a purple bandana tied around her head. Sullen and thin as a rail, she seemed slightly nervous as she led me into the large, dimly lighted corridor. The place smelled of tobacco and sweat. A narrow staircase to the right led up to the second floor. There was no furniture, only a shabby purple carpet on the floor and hideous gray wallpaper on the walls, with red and purple flowers that had faded deplorably. I realized that, like many old residences, number eighteen had been divided into apartments.

"I'm Dana O'Malley," I said. "I've come to see Monsieur Guy Chevrier."

The girl looked me over with dark, resentful eyes and then nodded sullenly and led me up the staircase and down the hall to a door with a brass 4 fastened above it. I supposed the apartment belonged to one of my great-uncle's friends, who had loaned it to him for this meeting. If the other apartments were occupied, one would never know it, for the house was as quiet as a tomb. As musty, too, I thought. The girl looked even more nervous than she had below, glancing over her shoulder.

"Has the gentleman arrived yet?" I inquired.

The girl didn't answer my question. She opened the door and showed me into a large sitting room, then left, pulling the door shut behind her. I heard a curious metallic clicking noise but paid little attention to it as I gazed in wonder at the room. Someone had an inordinate fondness for pink. Faded pink fabric covered the walls, and tattered pink rugs were scattered over the floor. A large divan and two side chairs were upholstered in fraying pink velvet. Dirty pink curtains hung at the windows through which brilliant silvery white sunlight spilled in profusion. There was much gold gilt, too, on picture frames, on the frame encircling the large oval mirror, on the wall sconces, and most of it was beginning to peel. I could smell stale face powder and old cigar smoke and whiskey. A closed door to my right, beyond the divan, led into what I assumed would be the bedroom.

No one was waiting for me. I felt a twinge of alarm, and it began to grow rapidly as I looked more closely at the pictures on the walls and realized what they depicted. The men and women in them were definitely not strolling through flowery glades. Holding the furled parasol, the brown velvet reticule dangling from my wrist, I took a step backward, every instinct telling me to run. Something was wrong. Something was very wrong. I realized that this was a house of assignation where men rented rooms to bring their fancy women, and Guy Chevrier would never have asked me to come to a place like this. Hearing the deep rumble of male laughter coming from the next room, I took another step backward, my heart pounding.

The door opened. Raoul Etienne strolled casually into the room, a taunting smile on his lips.

"So the ruse worked," he said pleasantly. "The bastard daughter showed up after all."

"You—" I whispered.

"Yes, Cousin dear, I sent the note. It took a trifling amount of investigation to discover why you went to Conti Street. Guy Chevrier has a very loose tongue when he's in his cups—and he's in his cups several nights a week."

He was wearing black leather knee boots and snug plum-colored breeches and a loosely fitting white silk shirt opened at the throat, the full sleeves gathered at the wrist. His glossy dark hair was tousled, his lean cheeks flushed. He had been drinking. He strolled toward me, smiling, stopping a few feet away from me and resting his hands on his thighs in the Etienne manner. I faced him with icy composure even though my pulses were leaping and my heart still pounding. I wasn't about to let him know how terrified I was. I backed toward the door, reaching for the knob behind me.

"It's locked," he informed me. "Cleo is well paid to obey orders."

There was more rumbling laughter from the next room, and then two more men came stumbling into the room. I recognized both: Zackery Rambeaux, the hearty youth with floppy blond hair and twinkling brown eyes who had danced with me at the ball, and Pierre Dorsay, the amateur wrestler who was seeing Raoul's sister. Zackery still wore his leaf-brown frock coat and a canary-yellow vest, his dark tan silk neckcloth rumpled. He carried a half-full bottle of champagne and had a lopsided grin. Pierre, dark brown curls spilling over his brow, had on tight gray breeches and a white lawn shirt open to his navel, the full sleeves rolled up to his biceps. Brawny and baby-faced, he tripped over one of the pink rugs and grabbed Zackery to keep from falling. Both men laughed uproariously. Raoul looked at me with malicious satisfaction.

"We're going to have a little party," he told me, "and you're going to be the guest of honor."

"You'll never get away with this."

"When the party's over," Raoul continued, "you're going to take a little trip. A boat's leaving tonight for Cuba—you'll be on it. You'll love Havana, Cousin dear. A room has been reserved for you at one of the biggest houses. I understand they're a bit strict with their women, but you'll undoubtedly please the clients.''

''I—I don't believe this.''

''Believe it. All the arrangements have been made. You'll be delivered to the boat bound and gagged—and it's good-bye forever. No one'll ever know what happened. Good riddance to trash from the swamps. There'll undoubtedly be rejoicing throughout the Quarter.''

I saw that he was serious. He was really that evil. I stared at him in shocked amazement. He was so beautiful on the surface, so corrupt within, far more corrupt than I could possibly have imagined.

''Let's get this party rollin'!'' Pierre cried.

Zackery took a swig of champagne and nodded in eager agreement. My blood seemed to run cold. Raoul wasn't nearly as drunk as the other two. He watched me closely, an anticipatory smile on his lips as he waited to see me cringe and beg. He was going to be disappointed, I vowed, tightening my grip on the parasol handle.

''Which one of you boys wants to be first?'' Raoul inquired.

''Me!'' Zackery exclaimed, waving the champagne bottle.

''You're always first!'' Pierre thundered, shoving him roughly aside. ''I'm gonna be the first to plow *this* field.''

''Watch her, '' Raoul warned. ''She's not the fragile flower you're used to. This one's got moves.''

''I got moves, too! Can't wait to show 'em to her.''

He lurched toward me, grinning a baby-faced grin, and as his muscular arms lunged out to grab me, I slammed the parasol across his head with all my might. He yelled in agony, doubling up, and even as he did so I delivered a sharp kick to his shin. He roared again, buckling, then crashed to the floor with a tremendous thud. The demure young woman had vanished. The little wildcat of the swamps was fighting for her life. Raoul came toward me. I swung the parasol again, hitting him on the side of the arm. He managed to seize the handle and pull it out of my grasp, hurling it aside.

I turned and pulled frantically at the doorknob. It was securely locked. I whirled back around. Raoul was smiling. Pierre was on his hands and knees, shaking his head. Zackery was finishing the bottle of champagne, enjoying himself immensely as he watched the show. My breath was coming in short, painful gasps.

Pierre clambered to his feet, weaving a little as he stood. He started toward me again, moving slowly, blue eyes enraged.

"Go get her, Dorsay!" Zackery shouted.

"Watch her, " Raoul warned again. His voice was flat.

Flattened against the locked door, watching him approach, I had a sense of total unreality. None of this was happening. This dreadful room with its garish pinks and peeling gold gilt was something out of a nightmare and the brawny youth with the baby face and angry blue eyes was part of the nightmare. I felt I was far, far away, watching it all happen, even though my heart still pounded and I was gasping. Pierre Dorsay reached for me and I seized his hand and bit it as hard as I could, tasting blood, and he roared in agony and managed to get his hand free and seized my shoulders and swung me, hurling me across the room. Raoul caught me before I could fall, slinging his arm around my throat, holding me so tightly I thought I would pass out.

"I told you to watch her," he said, his lips not inches from my ear. "It looks like you're going to have to wait your turn, Dorsay."

"Yeah!" Zackery taunted. "The big guy can't handle her!"

Raoul's arm tightened even more and I could feel my consciousness slipping away, dark clouds beginning to shadow my brain, but my instincts were still unimpaired. I raised my right foot knee-high and slammed it down on his instep, the heel of my slipper digging in like a spike. I swung my elbow back into his stomach at the same time, knocking the breath out of him. His grip went slack, and I pulled free, whirling around to face him. His face was white with pain, his dark eyes afire with fury. He swung his arm back and slapped me across the face. I felt an explosion of pain, even as I fell to the floor.

"Jesus!" Zackery exclaimed. "I've never seen anything like it. She's a regular hellion!"

Huddled on the floor, barely conscious, my cheek on fire, I tried to catch my breath. I turned, panting, and, looking up, I saw the three of them standing over me, looking incredibly tall from this angle, a forest of booted calves surrounding me. I saw thighs and bulging breeches and chests and three peering faces, Pierre's bruised, Zackery's grinning, Raoul's cold and expressionless, a beautiful mask. The black clouds were shadowing my brain again, and I felt curiously airy, as though I had no weight, no substance. I looked up at the men, and they seemed to have no substance, either, seemed foggy, unclear. I moaned. The clouds thickened and blackness swallowed me for a moment. When I opened my eyes, the men were standing as before, talking, and their voices seemed to come from a great distance.

"You really shipping her to Cuba?" Pierre asked.

"I told you. Everything has been arranged. All we've got to do is get her to the boat before midnight."

"I—uh—we've been in a lot of scrapes, Raoul, but we've never done anything like *this*. I mean—shipping a girl off to a whorehouse! What if someone found out?"

"No one's going to find out. The guy I contacted on the waterfront is going to pay in cash. We'll split it three ways."

"You don't do things in half measures, do you?" Zackery said, full of admiration.

"The little bitch has it coming, and I'm doing my family a favor."

"Pity we have to ship her off tonight," Zackery said. "Couldn't we keep her here a few days?"

"Don't worry, Rambeaux. There's plenty of time for you to get your fill. Let's get on with it."

I tried to sit up. I hadn't enough strength. Arms reached down for me. Hands grasped me, jerking me to my feet. My knees were so weak I could barely stand, but still I fought, or tried to. Pierre seized my hair, jerking my head back, at the same time pinning both my arms behind me. Raoul stood by, watching calmly, and Zackery, champagne bottle abandoned, clapped his hands in glee, eager to begin.

I tried to struggle, tried to resist, but it was futile. Pierre forced me to move forward, jerking my hair and gripping my arms savagely, marching me into the adjoining bedroom, and I saw that it was pink and gold, too, even more hideous. Pierre let go of me and shoved me brutally onto the bed with its sleazy pink satin counterpane, and when I tried to get up he shoved me again. I hit my head against the bedpost. Zackery and Raoul came into the room, Raoul calm and without expression, Zackery grinning and rubbing his hands together like a little boy.

"Looks like I'd better take first crack at it," he said. "It'll give you two time to nurse your wounds."

"Be our guest," Pierre growled.

I wasn't going to let it happen. I wasn't. I would fight to the death if necessary. A voice inside me assured me of this, but that voice was weak, fading. I wasn't going to pass out again. I mustn't. I lay very still, the back of my head throbbing where I had hit it, and the black clouds hovered for a moment and then dissolved. Everything was still slightly hazy and the pink walls seemed to weave in and out, but I saw Zackery removing his frock coat as Pierre and Raoul moved back, prepared to watch. I turned my head and closed my eyes, and when I opened them again, I saw the bedside table and the bottle of whiskey sitting atop it. I prayed for strength.

Zackery tossed his frock coat aside, tore off his neckcloth and, too impatient to take off anything else, lunged toward me. I rolled to one side, grabbing the neck of the whiskey bottle as I did so, swinging it like a club, slamming it forcefully against the side of Zackery's head. The impact of the blow was so powerful, my wrist almost snapped, but the bottle didn't break. His eyes widened and his mouth flew open, but he didn't yell. He simply stared blindly for half a second and then crumpled to the floor at the side of the bed. There was a splintering crash as the door in the next room was knocked off its hinges, and, sitting up now, still holding the bottle, I saw Raoul and Pierre jump, saw Charles come charging into the room.

Raoul was too startled to react, but Pierre, the fighter, flew into action immediately, leaping toward Charles with fists flying. Everything seemed to be happening all at once. The two men moved to and fro, exchanging vicious blows, and then Raoul leaped into the fray and both men were pounding at Charles as he defended himself superbly. I managed to get to my feet and stood there shakily with fingers still tightly wrapped around the neck of the bottle. Charles delivered a blow that caught Raoul on the jaw and sent him reeling backward, even as Pierre slammed Charles against the wall and grabbed his throat, his enormous hands tightening around Charles's windpipe. Hardly aware of what I was doing, I rushed over and swung the bottle a second time, crashing it against the back of Pierre's head. The bottle broke this time and glass and liquor flew everywhere and I was left holding the neck. I dropped it and moved aside as Pierre staggered backward and toppled to the floor, almost directly beside Zackery.

Raoul, genuinely terrified now, rubbed his jaw, looking at his cousin with beseeching eyes. Chest heaving, Charles shoved a heavy wave from his brow, and then, his face as hard as granite, he smoothed down the lapels of his dark blue frock coat and straightened his silk neckcloth, his eyes never leaving Raoul's. The bodice of my muslin frock was torn, one breast almost exposed. I pulled up the cloth, adjusting it.

"She—it was her idea," Raoul stammered. "She—she asked me to set everything up. She's a whore! We were going to pay her."

"I ought to kill you," Charles said, and his voice was frighteningly cool and level. "If you say one more word, I just might do it. You're finished at Etienne's, Raoul. From this moment on, not one penny of money will you receive from the family."

"You can't—"

"You will also leave New Orleans. Tonight. I don't care where you go or what you do, but if you're in the city tomorrow, I'll hunt you down and call you out and blow your head off at the Oaks."

He turned calmly and asked me if I was all right. I nodded and he took my hand and led me out of the room. Raoul watched us, his face completely drained of color. The door to the sitting room had indeed been knocked off its hinges, had broken into several pieces. We stepped over them and out into the hall. I was perfectly clearheaded now and remarkably calm. Perhaps I was merely numb. Charles had let go of my hand and was gripping my elbow so tightly I winced. I realized that I had dropped my reticule sometime earlier. It didn't matter. I let him lead me down the stairs, and I was surprised to see Jasper in the foyer, his arm wrapped tightly around the throat of the Negro girl, Cleo. Her lip was bloody. They had clearly had to persuade her to tell them where I was. As we moved toward the door, Jasper released the girl and shoved her aside brutally.

I didn't say a word until we were in the carriage and on our way home. I took a deep breath then, numbness dissolving, a delayed reaction setting in.

"How—"

"I saw you climbing into a cab as I was on my way home. As soon as I got there I asked Kayla where you had gone. She said she didn't know and then told me about the note you received. I went to your bedroom, got the note and read it. Julian and Delia weren't even aware that I'd come in."

"If—"

"We will drive around back," he told me. "You will go

through the servants' quarters and up the back stairs to your bedroom without anyone being the wiser. I will then ride back around front and 'arrive.' My aunt and my brother will undoubtedly learn about this eventually—I've no doubt Raoul will make up some story for his mother—but I don't want either of them to be unduly upset.''

''But—''

''You will clean up and compose yourself,'' he continued, ''and at the appropriate hour, you will come downstairs for the evening meal as though nothing had happened. Later on this evening I shall call on young Dorsay and Rambeaux and give them an alternative: complete silence and long holidays beginning immediately, or separate appointments at the Oaks. I'm a dead shot. Everyone in the city knows it.''

He didn't look at me. His voice was flat, without emotion. I could tell that he blamed me for what happened. Even though he knew Raoul had been lying, he blamed me. I didn't try to say anything else. I sat there in silence until the carriage finally stopped, and then I got out and went through the servants' quarters and up the back stairs to my bedroom, filled with steely resolve. If that was the way he wanted to play it, that was the way we would play it. Maybe in time I could actually grow to hate him as he hated me.

Kayla was waiting in my room, literally wringing her hands.

''Oh, Miz Dana! You—I didn't mean to tell Mister Charles 'bout the note, but I was so worried an' he—Lawd! Your dress is torn and your cheek is—oh, Miz Dana, your cheek is swollen! What happened to you? I—''

''I'm perfectly all right, Kayla,'' I said calmly. ''Please prepare a bath for me.''

''I should never-a let you leave th' house. I had a feelin' somethin' was wrong. When you came down them stairs, I just knowed—''

''A bath, Kayla. Immediately.''

Three and a half hours later, I moved slowly down the grand staircase with superb composure. I had applied an ice pack to my cheek, and the minor swelling was gone. There were no visible signs of my experiences this afternoon. I was wearing a lovely satin gown with narrow silver gray and emerald-green stripes, the full skirt belling out over half a dozen rustling underskirts. My hair was arranged on top of my head in sculpted honey-blond waves, with three long ringlets dangling down in back, and I was wearing long gray velvet gloves. I could hear voices in the sitting room as I reached the foyer. I hesitated a moment, steeling myself, and then I joined the others.

Charles and Julian, both splendidly attired, already had their mint juleps in hand, and Delia was wearing a lovely new gown of pale lime-green silk. As I entered the room, all three of them looked up. Julian smiled warmly. Charles gazed at me without expression. Delia beamed with delight.

"My dear! Why—you look every day of twenty-three and absolutely scrumptious in that gown. Corinne is a genius. No question about it. Did Kayla do your hair?"

I nodded. "She's quite gifted."

"Look who's back, dear."

I glanced at Charles. "Did you have a good trip?" I asked.

"Satisfactory," he replied.

"Thank goodness you're here, my dear. They've been boring me to tears for the past fifteen minutes—nothing but cotton, cotton, cotton, this crop, that crop, potential yield per acre. Quite maddening."

"Both Ravenaugh and Belle Mead are going to yield admirably, all top-quality cotton," Charles informed her. "You should be glad to know we're going to turn a huge profit. We might actually get out of debt."

"I'm positively ecstatic, dear. I just don't want to hear all the dreary details. You could at least have brought back a *tiny* bit of gossip. Didn't it occur to you I might want to know all about Janette Duprey? She and I grew up together, though I never really liked her. I haven't seen her since she became the mistress of Ravenaugh."

"She was quite gracious," Charles told her.

"Pooh," Delia said.

"She's gained an awful lot of weight," he added. "She must be well over two hundred and fifty pounds now."

"Really?" Delia was delighted. "Why didn't you *tell* me? It doesn't surprise me at all. She always was a prissy, affected little thing, forever putting on airs, and when she snared Claude Duprey of Ravenaugh you'd have thought she'd nabbed the king of England. Her engagement ring was an absolutely vulgar diamond, big as a walnut, and she flashed it around like—" Delia

hesitated, a frown creasing her brow. "Is that someone at the door?"

"Sounds like it," Julian said.

"I wonder who it could possibly be. If it's Lavinia, I positively refuse to see her. She calls at the most inopportune times. She knows full well we dine promptly at eight, and—"

Pompey opened the front door and we heard a loud, urgent voice, though actual words couldn't be discerned, and then we heard the front door closing. A moment later Pompey stepped into the doorway of the sitting room. He looked extremely upset.

"What is it, Pompey?" Charles demanded.

"Mister—Mister Charles. That was Mister Danton, th' gen'leman what owns th' shop down th' street from Etienne's. It—he's done on his way back there, said there wudn't time to speak to you hisself."

"What is it, man!"

"Dere's a fire, Mister Charles. Mister Danton, he said Etienne's was done goin' up in flames, and—"

The old man's voice broke, and Charles and Julian exchanged looks and then rushed out of the room immediately, followed by Pompey. Delia sat down on the ivory velvet sofa, her face positively white. She had taken out her fine lace handkerchief and she was quietly tearing it into shreds, not even aware of what she was doing. I went to her and put my arm around her, and she looked up at me with huge, worried eyes. I patted her shoulder.

"Per—perhaps it isn't so bad," I said, trying to reassure her. "Perhaps the fire brigade will be able to—"

My voice was trembling. I cut myself short. Delia gazed at the shreds of lace in her lap and saw what she had done and shook her head. She sighed then and brushed the shreds aside and stood up.

"I shan't go to pieces, my dear," she informed me. "I am an Etienne, and for some peculiar reason we're always at our best in the face of a crisis. I'm sure I can't explain it, but it's a fact. I'll have to inform Jezebel that dinner will be postponed, of course, and—"

"I'll do that," I said quickly.

"And then I must tell Pompey to have the carriage brought round. The boys will have saddled their own horses. We must go, naturally. I don't intend to sit around waiting to hear. I suppose I'll need a wrap."

Twenty minutes later Delia and I were in the carriage, driving through the night-shrouded Quarter to Etienne's. She was admirably calm, silent, too, sitting beside me with back ramrod-straight and chin held high, a pearl-gray shawl around her frail shoulders. Although she didn't speak, she held my hand tightly, so tightly I felt my fingers might break. Jasper drove rapidly, the sound of clopping hooves and clattering wheels echoing in the perfumed silence of the night. My heart seemed to be racing along with the carriage.

We could smell the smoke and burning wood long before we turned the corner. There was a huge crowd gathered in the street in front of the shop. They stood back, speaking in hushed voices, watching as the men in the fire brigade continued their work. Jasper stopped the carriage, and Delia and I climbed out. Only a few flames spluttered now, lazily licking already blackened lumber, and these were quickly extinguished. Fortunately, the fire had been contained—no other buildings on the block had suffered serious damage—but Etienne's was a yawning, smoking black hole, completely gutted from within, roof gone. The air was still hot, filled with wisps of smoke and ashes, and the night sky seemed to retain a pale orange glow.

"Please make way," I begged as Delia and I tried to get through the crowd of people. "Please let us through."

"—dead," someone was saying. "They brought him out just a few minutes ago. He's under that blanket."

"Oh God," Delia whispered. "Oh dear God—"

"Please!" I begged urgently. "Please make way."

"Etienne—yeah, that's who he is. Name's same as the store. Burned to a crisp, though Alan—he's my cousin, he's with the fire brigade—Alan said he musta been overcome by the smoke and already dead before the flames—"

I stopped begging. I started shoving, forcing my way through the tightly packed mass of people, using shoulders and elbows and hips, panic swelling inside, gripping me with icy fingers. I stumbled, falling against a burly stevedore. He grabbed me and gave me an angry look. I shoved him aside, knocking him against a redhead with painted face and flashy green dress. She called me a name. I forged ahead, finally reaching the front of the crowd. Delia was right behind me. The heat was intense, but I seemed to be freezing, icy cold fingers gripping me as I stared at the scattered pieces of smoke-stained furniture that had been salvaged, at that mound stretched on the ground with a heavy blanket covering it.

The fire brigade was still busily at work, hurrying to and fro, moving in and out of the smoking ruin that had been Etienne's. They passed huge buckets of water and wielded large axes and shouted orders and warnings to each other, faces soot-stained and pouring with sweat. Some sections of burned wood were still glowing a fiery red-orange, popping and crackling and sending up showers of sparks, sizzling loudly as buckets of water sloshed over them. A partially standing wall of black charcoal tumbled, crashing loudly as the men scrambled. Delia stood beside me. Her face was waxen. She didn't move a muscle. People behind us murmured, whispered, pointed.

One of the men working wore a badly singed frock coat. He passed a bucket of water and turned, and I saw that it was Julian. I cried out. I rushed toward him. His hair was wet with sweat. Sweat poured from his brow, and one cheek was completely black with soot. He looked startled when he saw me tearing toward him. He hurried forward, catching me before I actually entered the smoldering ruin.

"Thank God!" I cried. "Oh, thank God you're all right!"

"You shouldn't be here," he said. "It's still extremely dangerous. How did—Jesus! I see Delia's here, too. You shouldn't have come. There's nothing—"

"You're all right! Oh, Julian, I was so—"

Julian put his arm around me and held me tightly, leading me over to where Delia was standing. His face was very grave. Delia looked up at him, and when she spoke, her voice was hollow.

"Charles," she said.

"He's all right, Delia."

"They said—" She took a deep breath. "They—someone said—an Etienne. In the fire—the—under the blanket."

"Raoul," Julian said gently.

He released me and took his aunt's hands in his.

"Apparently he'd come to the store for something—we'll never know what—and the fire started accidentally—perhaps he left a cigar burning. He tried to put it out himself, apparently, and—"

He cut himself short, squeezing her hands.

"He—he can't have known what was happening," he said gently. "He can't have had any pain."

"Someone will have to tell Lavinia." Her voice was still hollow. "I suppose I'd better go to her—"

."Charles and I will take care of that, Delia." He gave her hands another squeeze. "We'll take care of everything. Did Jasper bring you? I'll take you back to the carriage. You and Dana go on back home. I—Charles and I probably won't be back until late tomorrow morning. We'll have to finish here, then see Lavinia and make—arrangements. You don't worry, love. Everything is going to be all right."

Delia didn't reply. He put his arm around her shoulder and started leading her through the crowd. People stepped aside, making way. I didn't go with them. Turning, I happened to see Charles coming out of the blackened ruin carrying a still-steaming metal box, using his frock coat as padding. He set the box on a scorched table and dropped the ruined frock coat onto the ground. His face, like Julian's, was streaked with soot. His neckcloth was gone, his white lawn shirt wet with sweat and plastered to chest and shoulders, one sleeve badly torn. Damp, dark locks spilled over his brow, and his eyes were filled with stoic resignation. He looked ten years older.

I went to him. I touched his arm.

"I'm sorry," I said.

He looked at me as though I were a stranger.

"It wasn't an accident, was it?"

"It wasn't an accident," he said. His voice was flat. "He set the fire deliberately. You and I know that. You and I know why. Apparently it got out of control before he could get out."

We had to step aside to make way for four men in the fire brigade who carried more buckets of water. There was a crash as another section of wall fell. Ashes swirled in the air like gray snowflakes. Charles shoved damp locks from his forehead and looked at me with weary, desolate eyes.

"Everything—everything gone," I said. "All those priceless paintings, the porcelain, the furniture—what will you do?"

"The family will survive," he said.

"Charles—"

"Go away, Dana. Just go away. There's nothing you can do here. You've already caused enough damage."

He turned and walked back into the ruin. I watched him for a moment, and I felt dead inside. I stood there in my silvery-gray and emerald striped satin gown and long gray velvet gloves, ashes floating around me, the air filled with the acrid smell of smoke and desolation, and finally I turned and moved blindly through the milling crowd toward the carriage. Delia was already inside. Julian was waiting for me with a worried expression.

"Here you are," he said.

He took my hands and looked into my eyes.

"We must all be very strong," he told me.

I nodded. He let go of my hands.

"See that Delia gets to bed."

"I will."

He opened the carriage door for me. I didn't climb in.

"Julian—"

He looked at me, waiting.

"I—I do love you," I said. "There will never be anyone else in my life as—as fine as you are. I'll always be grateful for all you've done for me. I—want you to know that."

I stood up on tiptoes and kissed him on the lips and clung to him for just a moment, and then he helped me into the carriage, smiling a gentle smile. He squeezed my arm and closed the carriage door, and as we drove away I looked out the window and saw him standing there with his soot-stained face and damp hair. Tears welled up, but I refused to let them fall. I took Delia's hand and held it tightly. She gave me a brave smile. Both of us were silent during the ride back home.

"I think I'll go right up to my room, dear," Delia said as we entered the house.

"I'll go with you," I told her.

"No—no, I don't want you to fuss over me, dear. I'm going to be perfectly fine. Tomorrow is going to be a difficult day for everyone, and they're all going to need me. I intend to be a paragon of strength."

"I'm sure you will be," I said.

"Good night, Dana dear."

"I love you, Delia. I—I'll always remember your kindness, and I'll always remember how you took me in and treated me like—like a daughter. You'll always have a place in my heart."

"And you'll always have a place in mine, dear."

I kissed her on the cheek and took her arm and walked with her to the foot of the stairs. Kayla came into the foyer, and I signaled for her to go up with Delia. She nodded, understanding. I watched the two of them go up the stairs, and then I went into the library and, sitting at the desk, wrote two brief letters. I asked Delia to forgive me. I told her that I was doing what I was doing for the good of everyone, and I repeated that she would always have a place in my heart. I told Julian that I would always remember him and I would always love him in a very special way. I told him that I would always be honored that he had asked me to marry him and that one day, perhaps, he would understand and be grateful to me for leaving. I sealed both letters and left them on the desk, and then I went upstairs.

The old worn leather traveling bags were still in the storage closet where I had replaced them weeks ago, a lifetime ago. The brass buckles were a little more tarnished, the limp, supple leather covered with a fine layer of dust. I carried both of them to my bedroom and dusted them and put them on the bed, and I spent a long, long time packing, carefully selecting the clothes I would carry with me, those I would leave behind. I stood for over five minutes holding the embroidered rose brocade gown I had worn the night Charles first came to my bedroom. I didn't cry. I couldn't. I couldn't feel anything but the emptiness inside. I hung the gown back up and sat down on the bed, carefully folding undergarments, placing them in one of the bags. It was after three o'clock in the morning when I finally finished packing.

I had taken off the long gray velvet gloves earlier, and now I removed the elegant striped satin gown. It smelled of smoke and soot. So did I. I washed myself thoroughly and put on a white petticoat with several ruffled skirts, and then I undid the coiffure Kayla had so artfully styled. I shook my hair loose and brushed it until it gleamed. I still felt empty inside. I felt incapable of emotion. I took down a simple, beautifully made frock of thin yellow linen and put it on, spreading the skirt out over the underskirts. I put out all the candles and sat down, staring through the open French windows at the night sky. When the first streaks of pink and amethyst dimly appeared, I stood up and took the bags and left the house.

It was a long, long walk to the waterfront, but no one molested me, no one paid the least attention to me. Even though it was not quite seven, the waterfront was bustling with noisy activity. I located the ticket office, and there I was lucky indeed. I discovered that a steamboat was leaving for St. Louis at eight o'clock. I was able to get a cabin. It was quite expensive, but I had over $130, the majority of it my commission for selling the commode to Mrs. Louella Kramer. I prayed her husband would remember his offer of a position at his emporium when I arrived. I found my way to the steamboat and boarded it. Forty minutes later I was standing at the railing of the lower deck as it puffed and chugged and pulled away, the huge paddle wheel turning slowly.

I watched the wharves grow smaller as we pulled out into the river. I had arrived in New Orleans a girl, a child really, innocent and naive despite my experiences in the swamps. I was leaving the city a woman, sadder and much wiser about the ways of the world and how the world treated people who didn't belong. I didn't belong to Julian's world. I didn't belong anywhere, not yet, but as I gripped the railing and the great wedding cake of a boat turned and started upriver, I vowed I would make a place for myself. I would belong, and I would *be* somebody. I would show Charles Etienne and his kind. I would show the blood kin who had turned me away. One day, I promised myself, Dana O'Malley was going to look down her nose at the whole bloody pack.

Book Three

The Woman

Chapter Fifteen

I NOTICED HER THAT VERY FIRST MORNING on the boat. I was standing at the railing, watching the churning water and the far bank, listening to the slosh-slap-slosh of the paddle wheel. It was nearly eleven o'clock. Several people were sauntering on deck, chattering with great animation, but I paid no attention to them. Lost in thought, lulled by the motion of the boat and the sound of the water splashing, I might have been completely alone. An hour must have passed, and I finally turned, thinking about lunch. I couldn't face the dining salon. Maybe that nice steward could arrange to have a light lunch brought to my cabin. The deck was almost deserted now. I sighed and started toward the narrow stairwell that led down to the cabins, and it was then that I saw her.

She was walking in my direction on the arm of a tall, slender, dark-haired man in gleaming black boots, gleaming white breeches and frock coat and a white Panama hat. He wore an emerald-green stock with an enormous diamond stickpin, and a gold watch chain dangled from the pocket of his black brocade vest. Gambler, I thought, one of the flashy, flamboyant rogues who were a permanent fixture on the riverboats, fleecing wealthy lambs foolish enough to play cards with them. I judged him to be in his late thirties, handsome if a little too smooth and glossy. His dark eyes were much too sincere, and the thin black mustache couldn't quite minimize the venal curl of his full lips. His head was slightly turned and he gazed down at the woman as they walked. He seemed to be totally enraptured with her, and no wonder.

She was incredibly, amazingly beautiful. No, not so beautiful, I decided. Not really. Her cheekbones were too prominent, her nose just a fraction long, and her lips were too full. She was striking, dramatic, rivetingly attractive, with that sparkling vitality and indefinable allure that was far more arresting than mere beauty. Her eyes were a dazzling sapphire-blue. Her hair was a deep raven-black, gleaming with blue-black highlights, piled on top of her head in a gorgeous arrangement of waves, long ringlets spilling down her back. A diamond spray was fastened to one side. She wore a stunning taffeta gown with blue and white and garnet stripes, the extremely low-cut bodice and snug waist accentuating her remarkable figure.

As the couple neared, I stepped to one side to let them pass. The man in white had eyes only for the glamorous creature at his side and didn't even know I was there. The woman looked up and caught my eye and smiled. It was perhaps the warmest, friendliest, most engaging smile I had ever received. It was both greeting and acknowledgment and came straight from the heart. Hello there, it seemed to say. We don't know each other, but I'm sure we would like each other if we did. She gave me a little nod as they passed on, and I heard the musical crackle of her taffeta skirt and smelled her subtle yet wonderfully tantalizing perfume. I stood there for a few moments, watching them move down the deck, and I felt a curious sense of loss, as though I had been bathed in sunlight and it had suddenly been taken away.

The steward did indeed bring lunch to my cabin, arranging everything neatly on the small round table. I tipped him generously and he bowed himself out. I wondered how many of Magdelon's haughty friends knew that Doctor Samuel Johnson had begun the custom of tipping in a London coffee house over seventy years ago, giving his waiter a gratuity "To Insure Prompt Service." None of them, no doubt. A lot of good such trivial knowledge did me, I mused as I unfolded the spotless white linen napkin. I might be brighter than the whole pack—better-mannered, too—but I was a bastard from the swamps and I would always be their inferior. In their eyes. One day Charles would undoubtedly marry one of them, a magnolia-skinned belle with impeccable lineage and a head as empty as a gourd. To hell with him . . . Oh God, let me be strong. Let me forget. Let me begin a new life and put the past and its pain behind me.

While the cabin was roomy and comfortable and nicely appointed, I realized I couldn't spend the entire trip hiding away from other people. After lunch I took a short nap and freshened up, and then I decided to explore a bit. I hadn't wanted to lunch in the dining salon, but around four o'clock I found myself strolling into the main salon, very grand with thick red carpet, mahogany paneling and a plethora of potted plants. There were overstuffed gray velvet sofas and chairs and at least a dozen leather-topped tables. The woman I had seen on deck earlier was at one of them, shuffling a pack of cards while the gambler in white and four other men watched. The cards seemed to fly in her slender white hands with their bright pink nails, and they flew ever faster as she dealt them. The gambler in white did not look particularly happy, I observed.

There were few other people in the salon. I lingered for a moment by one of the potted plants, and the woman looked up and saw me and gave me a pleasant little wave, as though we were already friends. I nodded somewhat stiffly, and although I would have loved to stay and watch the game, I strolled out of the salon and spent the next hour or so wandering around the deck. Not too long ago, I knew, the Mississippi had been filled with keelboats and flatboats, bringing trade goods downriver. It had been the haunt of vicious river pirates and marauders and, in its way, had been as perilous for the unwary as the notorious Natchez Trace. The coming of the big steamboats had changed all that. Although keelboats and flatboats could still be seen, the river pirates and marauders had been replaced by gamblers, con men and fancy women who used more subtle means to separate fools from their gold. Was the woman in striped taffeta a fancy woman in league with the gambler? I hated to think so, but the way she had handled the cards clearly suggested it.

I finally retired to my cabin, wishing fervently I had brought a book with me. Time hung heavily on my hands, and that was dangerous. I wasn't worried, I told myself, and I wasn't afraid either. If Herbie Kramer didn't remember me and I didn't get a job at his emporium, I would find some other job and I would survive. I would *succeed*. You're not going to sit around this cabin worrying, I promised myself. You're making a new beginning, and you're going to move forward with strength and courage and determination. You fended for yourself all those years in the swamps, and you can bloody well fend for yourself now.

At six I washed up, brushed my hair and changed into a

simple frock of tan and gold striped silk, and then I braved the dining salon. It was a bit early for the majority of passengers, and there were few people at the tables. I was thankful for that. Even so, I received a number of speculative stares as I ate my meal. Proper young women did not travel without a chaperone, and as I occupied a single table I was the subject of much curiosity. An ancient dowager in black lace and dusty garnets examined me through her lorgnette, lips pursed. A trio of middle-aged planters gazed at me and whispered. A handsome youth with sleek bronze hair tried to flirt with me. I ignored them all. I *looked* proper enough, but, traveling alone, I must either be an upstart poseur or some clever adventuress. Finishing my meal, I left the dining salon with my head held high and a frosty look in my eyes.

It wasn't dark yet, but thick twilight shadows shrouded the bank and shimmering orange reflections from the sinking sun danced on the murky brown water. I walked slowly along the deck, feeling low, feeling lonely, trying to convince myself I was as brave and self-sufficient as I wanted to be. Although I could hear the sound of voices drifting from other parts of the boat, I seemed to have this section of the deck all to myself. The boat rocked gently. The huge paddle wheel turned slowly, water sloshing with a monotonous music. A giant white smokestack loomed up ahead, and as I moved around it I was aware of someone huddling in the shadows behind it. Startled, I paused, and a vague alarm began to grow. There was a rustle of taffeta, and the woman I had observed earlier came out of the shadows, gripping the handle of a large, unwieldy carpetbag.

"Hello," she said. "We meet again."

"You—you startled me."

The woman smiled and then glanced nervously up and down the deck. "Sorry, love. I heard someone coming and I thought it might be him, so I darted behind the smokestack."

"Are you in some kind of trouble?" I asked.

"You might say that. I haven't done anything really wrong, mind you, but I could use a place to hide for a while. I thought about crawling into one of those lifeboats, but that seems terribly melodramatic."

"I'm sure it would be terribly uncomfortable as well."

"Got any other ideas?"

"You could come to my cabin," I said.

"You'd let me do that?"

"I've plenty of room."

"Marvelous! I can't tell you how grateful I am. Do let's hurry. If he finds me, there will be a *very* unpleasant scene. I'm not a criminal or anything like that, but—"

"It's the gambler, isn't it?"

"However did you guess? I was a little short of money, you see, and I met him yesterday in New Orleans and I have to be in Memphis day after tomorrow and he kindly offered to pay for my ticket and I discovered I was expected to share his cabin and well—"

"You don't have to explain anything to me," I said, leading her down the narrow stairwell.

"Oh, but I *want* to, love. I'm not an angel, but I really don't sleep with just anyone and he wears the most dreadful-smelling hair pomade and, anyway, he decided to fleece some suckers this afternoon and I sat in on the game and just couldn't help myself—I beat him at his own game, won a *bundle*, and there wasn't anything he could do without letting the suckers know *he* was cheating, too. The cards were marked, you see. Not very cleverly. I spotted it at once and I insisted on dealing myself."

I unlocked the door to my cabin and ushered her inside. She looked around appreciatively, setting her bag on the floor.

"This is charming, love—I'll just sleep on that couch, won't put you out at all. Mr. Lance Sherman was *livid* when he kept losing and I kept winning—I let the other men win a few hands, too, just for the sake of appearances. They insisted we keep on playing, and I finally gathered up my winnings, excused myself, dashed to his cabin, grabbed my bag, and—here we are. Do you think I'm just *terrible*?"

"Not at all," I told her.

The woman smiled again. It was as friendly, as dazzling, as the smile she had given me on deck when she was with the gambler.

"It's strange," she said. "but when I first saw you this morning, looking so sad, looking so lonely, I said to myself—there's someone I'd like to know."

"I—I felt the same way," I confessed.

"It's fate, love," she declared. "We were *meant* to be friends."

She reached for my hand and gave it a gentle squeeze, and

never had I felt such immediate closeness, such rapport. It was as though we already *were* close friends and had been for some time. With her gorgeous clothes, her provocative perfume and low-pitched, musical voice, she was a fascinating creature, full of vitality and perfectly natural charm. There was worldly sophistication as well and a breezy self-confidence I longed to emulate.

"How did you become so expert at cards?" I asked, genuinely interested.

"In my profession, you have lots of time on your hands and the men are always playing cards backstage and—well, you pick things up."

"Backstage? You—you're an actress?"

"I'm on the stage, love. There's a world of difference, as my dear cousin constantly reminds me. Were it not for the family connection, he'd have booted me out of the company ages ago. I'm not that good, I confess, but I'm not that bad, either, and I'm extremely ornamental. Even Jason admits that. I'm Laura Devon, by the way."

"What a beautiful name," I said.

"It's a damn site better than Mabel Utterback, the name my parents gave me. Don't *ever* tell anyone I told you that. Jason's the only one who knows the awful truth, and he's as eager to forget it as I am."

"I'm Dana O'Malley," I told her.

"That's a nice name, too. What do *you* do?"

"I—I don't do anything yet," I replied. "I hope to find a job in St. Louis. A man I once met said that if I ever came to St. Louis he'd be happy to put me to work at his emporium."

Laura studied me for a moment, as though trying to discern something.

"You're running away from home," she said.

"I—I don't really have a home."

"Family?"

I shook my head. I felt like bursting into tears. Laura sensed that, and she squeezed my hand again.

"I have an idea, love. I'm loaded. I mean, I've got a whole bundle in my bag—more money than I've ever had at one time. I can't leave the cabin until we reach Natchez—he is getting off the boat at Natchez, has a big game set up there—but you could dash down the hall to the steward's post and order us a bottle of champagne and some food."

"I've already eaten."

"I'm ravenous, love, and champagne is always lovely. Tell him you want a bottle of the *best*."

Thirty minutes later we were both sitting on the couch, drinking champagne and talking. I had already learned that Laura was twenty-three years old, had been with her cousin's theatrical troupe for four years, had been visiting a retired actress friend in New Orleans when she met the gambler and that the "diamond" spray in her hair was really paste. How stunning she was with that shining black hair, those sparkling, good-humored sapphire eyes, that smooth, creamy complexion. The prominent cheekbones and slightly long nose made her face all the more interesting, I thought, and the full pink lips were beautifully shaped and seemed designed to smile. She helped herself to more of the pâté the steward had brought, spreading it on a thin sliver of toast.

"Sure you don't want some?" she inquired.

I shook my head.

"It's delicious. The fillet of sole was, too. I don't know when I've had such a meal. When you're traveling all over the South with a third-rate theatrical company, the food you get is hardly first-rate."

"Your cousin's company is third-rate?"

"Second-rate, perhaps. Jason's very ambitious and has dreams of becoming a great theatrical entrepreneur, but the plays he produces—well, let's just say they're crowd pleasers. The crowds we get are rarely very discriminating. Jason writes most of the plays himself, and most of them are flagrantly cribbed from sensational French novels and English penny dreadfuls."

"Still," I said, "it must be a fascinating life."

"Life upon the wicked stage is frequently hazardous to your health and always stressful—but it's a living and, I must confess, quite a lot of fun if you don't mind towering temperaments and constant backstage feuding. Jason is not the most amiable of men—though he's a dear, actually. You just have to know how to handle him."

"Did you grow up with him?" I asked.

Laura nodded, pouring herself another glass of champagne. "I was sent to live with my aunt and uncle when my parents died—I was five years old at the time. Aunt Megan was an actress and Uncle James managed the theatrical company—just as Jason does now. I grew up on the road, so to speak, living out of a trunk, traveling from one town to another, staying in wretched hotels and frequently sleeping in train stations. I loved it, of course, even though my aunt tried to keep me from the other actors and wouldn't dream of letting me go onstage. Jason is ten years older than I, and he was already taking an active role in the company. He considered me an insufferable pest. I was always tagging after him, and he was always pulling my pigtails or locking me up in a closet.''

"How dreadful," I said.

"I worshiped him," she confessed. "He was dashing and devilishly handsome even as a teenager. The women in the company spoiled him rotten. Those who didn't want to mother him wanted to get into his pants—a great many did. We lost so many ingenues because of Jason, a number of leading ladies as well. He was an unprincipled young rogue—still is, for that matter.''

"Your aunt finally let you go onstage?" I asked.

Laura shook her head. "She was a dear, straight-laced lady, even if she was in the theater, and she was determined I was not to be corrupted by the riffraff backstage. Jason she couldn't do anything about, but *me* she was going to give a proper upbringing. I was sent away to a number of schools—I hated every one of them, missed the company dreadfully. I finally ended up in a very refined finishing school in New England. It cost the moon, but Aunt Megan managed to pay the tuition. I hated it worst of all.''

She smiled a wry smile, remembering.

"I'm afraid I had already been corrupted by the riffraff. I was 'fast' and not at all 'refined.' The other girls, prim, prissy blue bloods that they were, looked down their patrician noses at me. I was constantly rebelling and defying authority. I was miserable, but there was some consolation. A man, of course. I was sixteen and quite mature and rather pretty and much more sophisticated than the other girls. He was twenty-seven, our music teacher, and I thought he was the most exciting man I'd ever met. He was handsome and sensitive and moody and, I thought, wonderfully sympathetic.''

"You fell in love with him?"

"As only a naive sixteen-year-old can. I was convinced it was love everlasting. We would run away together and get married and I would be his inspiration and he would compose great symphonies and we would live happily ever after. It didn't work quite that way," she said ruefully. "I let him have his way with me and it was utterly divine and I thought I was ever so grown-up, ever so superior to the other girls, smug little ninnies who didn't know beans about 'real life.' *I* found out about real life a couple of months later. We were discovered."

"What—what happened?"

"My handsome, moody, gifted Knight in Shining Armor informed the authorities that *I* had seduced him. He lost his job anyway. He left without so much as a polite good-bye to me. I was expelled, in total disgrace and terrified I might be pregnant. I wasn't, fortunately."

"Did you go back to your aunt?"

"I was too humiliated to face her," she said. "I ran off and managed to get a job with a rival theatrical company, even shabbier than Jason's—he was already managing it by this time. My uncle was in poor health, had handed the reins over to Jason."

Laura finished her champagne and set the glass down, a thoughtful look in those lovely sapphire-blue eyes. A faint smile lingered on her lips. After a moment she sighed, refilled her glass and gave me a wry look.

"So I was on the stage at last, in a rival company. I was dreadfully inexperienced, but I learned. I did dozens of small parts, gradually improving, going from abysmally bad to fairly competent. I still hadn't learned my lesson about men," she continued. "There was another one—an actor, God help me. Whatever you do, love, never, ever, under any circumstances, get involved with an actor. They're totally irresponsible and completely incapable of any genuine emotion, a pack of posturing egomaniacs who spend all their free hours admiring themselves in the mirror."

I couldn't help but smile at her vehemence on the subject.

"I had been with the company for over a year when our new leading man arrived. He was even handsomer, even more exciting than the music teacher. I was eighteen by that time, extremely ornamental and receiving considerable attention from the eager chaps who hang around the stage doors. I ignored them all. Once burned, you stay away from the fire. Right? Not me, love. Like an idiot I went rushing straight into the flames. Oh, I was really in love this time—at least that's what I told myself.

The son of a bitch could charm the birds off the trees, and he had me eating out of his hand.''

''How did it end?''

''It ended with me out on my ass, love. His wife arrived. He hadn't mentioned a wife. Wifey dear was nobody's fool. She saw what was going on immediately. She marched into the manager's office and informed him that I was to be dismissed instantly or she'd haul hubby back to Tuscaloosa, Alabama. Guess what? I was dismissed instantly. The company moved on to the next stop, and I was stranded in Macon, Georgia, without a cent to my name and owing two weeks' rent for my room in the fleabag boardinghouse we'd been staying in. The manager was supposed to take care of that. He didn't.''

''What did you do?''

''I charmed the landlord and wrote to Jason. My uncle had died of the flu the year before, and Aunt Megan had passed on a few months later. I'll always believe she died of a broken heart. I wasn't at all sure Jason would be willing to help me.''

''Did he?''

Laura nodded. ''He came to Macon, paid my bill, called me every kind of a fool and shook me until my teeth literally rattled. Then he tracked down the company, bloodied the nose of the manager who had fired me and beat the bejesus out of the leading man who had so heartlessly despoiled me—Jason didn't know about the music teacher. Violence dutifully done and my honor revenged, my dear cousin took me back with him to Jackson, Mississippi, where his company was performing *Lord Roderick's Revenge*, a thundering melodrama he'd penned the previous summer. The ingenue came down with the hives. I took her place, and I've been with the company ever since.''

''And—you got over the leading man?''

''In record time, love. One does. I learned my lesson, though. There've been other men, of course, but I haven't been burned again. A girl soon finds out how to handle such matters.''

I stood up and stepped over to the porthole, peering out into the night. The bank was shrouded in velvety black shadow, tiny pinpoints of golden light glimmering here and there. The Mississippi was dull pewter gray now, spangled with silvery flecks of moonlight. The boat seemed to be standing still as the river and bank went drifting by.

''Want to tell me about him, love?'' Laura asked.

I turned. "How did you know?"

"I saw the sad, lost look in your eyes this morning. I saw the tremulous smile. I've been there. I know all the signs."

"It's a long story," I said quietly.

"We have nothing but time, love. I've babbled on and on, telling you all about me. I'd like to hear about you, but—I don't want to pry, love. If you'd rather not talk about it, I'd certainly understand."

"There was a man," I said.

And I told her my story. I told her about the swamps and Ma and Clem and Julian, about Delia and the Quarter and how the people there thought me a harlot, an adventuress. I told her about Raoul and my reception at Conti Street, and finally I told her about Charles. Laura sat quietly, her eyes filled with sympathy and understanding as she listened to my tale. My voice broke once or twice, but I carried on, telling her about the house on Rampart Street and the fire and Charles' final words to me.

"So you see, I—I had to leave," I said.

Laura nodded in agreement. "There was nothing else you could do, love," she told me.

"I didn't want to hurt anyone, but—the situation was impossible. Julian must have read my letter by now and he must be desolate, but—I couldn't have married him, Laura. Not after sleeping with his brother."

"Of course you couldn't."

"I know he won't understand—Charles won't tell him. He'll think me ungrateful. He'll think I—" I cut myself short, staring across the room without seeing. "He'll get over it," I said finally.

"So will you, love. I promise."

"I—I'll go on."

"I'll tell you a little secret," Laura said. "That's what life is all about—going on. Coping. Forging ahead. We're brought up on fairy tales, love, and we believe in them, we believe life is that way, too. It isn't. We all find that out eventually. The weak give up and accept defeat. The strong face facts for what they are and—make the best of things."

I looked at my new friend, and I knew what she said was true. Her illusions had been lost at an early age, too, as had mine. She had had her share of sorrow and disappointments, yet she had managed to retain her vitality, her warmth, her strength and good humor. She was strong and she was a realist. I admired

her for that. I wished I could be like her. Laura sighed and
pointed to the bottle of champagne resting in its bucket of melting ice.

"We might as well finish it," she said.

"We might as well."

"I'll pour. Here you are, love. Goodness, the bottle's almost
empty and you've only had the one glass? There, that's the last
of it. You know, love, we really should have a toast. Don't you
think?"

"By all means."

Laura lifted her glass and smiled again. "To the men in our
lives—may they all rot in hell. No, that's too negative. To Going
On. Too self-consciously dramatic. How about—to friendship?"

"To friendship," I said.

We clicked glasses and drank. Laura finished her champagne
and stood up, striped taffeta skirt rustling. She picked up her
bag, set it on the bed and, opening it, began to pull things out:
a lovely garnet satin gown, a black velvet shawl, a frock of
expensive brushed sky-blue cotton printed with tiny sapphire
and black flowers.

"Mind if I hang some of these things up in the wardrobe? I
understand we have a charming Irish woman down below who
does laundry and presses things for an exorbitant fee. This cotton could use a good pressing, and this taffeta I'm wearing will
definitely need a going over."

She opened the wardrobe door and began to hang the garments up, examining some of my frocks when she had finished.

"What workmanship. Corinne's, I'll wager. Am I right?"

I nodded.

"I could never afford to go to a dressmaker like her. Dulcie
makes most of my clothes. She's our wardrobe woman, an absolute wizard with a needle and thread and a bolt of velvet. She's
sixty, built like a dumpling and takes absolutely no guff from
anyone. Jason's terrified of her."

"She sounds delightful."

"I—I have a confession to make," Laura said.

"Oh?"

"I've never had a girlfriend near my own age, love. Older
women like Dulcie and Melinda—she's the retired actress I was
visiting in New Orleans—I get along well enough with them,

but women my own age don't like me. They seem to find me threatening.''

"I shouldn't wonder," I said. "You're so incredibly beautiful, you probably make them feel like drab little sparrows. You certainly make me feel that way.''

Laura looked stunned. ''*You?* To begin with, love, I'm not all that beautiful—ornamental, as I've said. I make the best of what I've got. But you're the loveliest creature I've ever laid eyes on. Breathtaking is the word, I believe.''

"Nonsense.''

"Anyway, love, you're the first woman roughly my own age who hasn't wanted to scratch my eyes out the moment she saw me.''

"I—I've never had a girlfriend either.''

"Like I said earlier, love—it's fate.'' There was a merry sparkle in her eyes as she took out a purple velvet gown and hung it up. "We were meant to be friends. I already feel like I've known you for ages.''

"I feel the same way.''

She looked delighted. "Really, love?''

I nodded. I smiled. I no longer felt lonely and lost.

The sky was a vivid blue the next morning and the sun was shining brightly as I stood on deck in a soft peach muslin sprigged with tiny white daisies. We had docked before dawn and the gangplank had just been lowered. Passengers strolled leisurely along the deck, enjoying the sunshine, some leaving here at Natchez, chatting with shipboard friends before moving down the gangplank with bags in hand. I moved over to the railing. The docks here at Natchez weren't anything like those in New Orleans. They were much smaller and there was none of the bustling activity, none of the exotic color. Negro men lolled idly on bales of cotton waiting for cargo to be unloaded, and a plump Negro woman in a ragged pink dress was selling coffee and hoecakes at a wooden booth. A sleepy, serene atmosphere prevailed. A number of expensively dressed people, obviously gentry, had come to meet the boat, and they stood around in clusters, talking in lazy drawls as they watched the gangplank for friends or relatives.

I watched for Lance Sherman, and, sure enough, he left the boat, carrying a black leather bag and looking quite disgruntled as he walked down the wooden gangplank. His fine white suit was slightly rumpled, his emerald stock not so neatly folded now. I smiled to myself as I thought of how Laura had taken him in, fleecing him as he had fleeced hundreds of others. He had probably stayed up all night trying to win back the money she had taken from him. Two gentlemen stepped forward to meet him, and the three of them sauntered toward a waiting carriage. I watched it drive away. The coast was clear now. Laura would no longer have to hide out in my cabin. I started to turn away from the railing and go deliver the good news when I spied the open carriage and its exquisite passenger.

The carriage was elegantly crafted of shiny black ebony, with powder-blue velvet upholstery and two magnificent black horses in harness. Its passenger was a woman in her midtwenties with a dark, creamy complexion and large, luminous brown eyes that gazed demurely at the hands folded in her lap. Her hair was blond and she wore an extremely low-cut white silk gown with huge puffed sleeves, the skirt awash with ruffles of the same white silk and spreading out over the seat.

As I studied her, a man walked over to the carriage. His back was to me, so I couldn't see his features, but I could see that he was tall and lean, with the trim, muscular build of an athlete. His hair was thick and neatly brushed, a deep, coppery brown, and he was wearing gleaming brown leather knee boots and superbly tailored light tan breeches and frock coat. He said something to the woman and she nodded. He climbed into the carriage and took up the reins, and he turned and glanced toward the boat, and I saw that he wasn't nearly as young as I had assumed him to be. His lean, ruggedly handsome face had the weathered, lived-in look of a man who must be at least in his early forties, perhaps older.

He tightened his grip on the reins, preparing to drive away, and he raised his eyes and saw me looking at him. I didn't look away. Somehow I couldn't. Recognition seemed to flicker in his eyes and he parted his lips, a frown creasing his brow. He let go of the reins. He stared. I still couldn't look away. Something held me. I had a curious feeling inside, as though I recognized him, too, though I had never laid eyes on him in my life. During those few brief moments of direct eye-to-eye contact, it was as though he and I were the only two people in the world, as though everything else had melted away. His smoke-gray eyes held mine.

Time seemed to stand still and his eyes communicated to me and I felt disconcerting emotions sweep over me, and even though I realized it was totally absurd, I couldn't turn away. People moved slowly along the deck and marched down the gangplank and strolled on the wharf, but they didn't exist, nothing existed but this strange force joining us together. The lovely woman sat beside him, but she didn't exist either, he wasn't even aware of her. Only those few brief moments passed before I was finally able to pull myself free, but each one seemed frozen, each seemed to last an eternity. I turned away from the railing, and it took a great physical effort, as though I had to tear loose from invisible bonds restraining me. I had never experienced anything remotely like this before, and I was deeply shaken.

Laura was amused when I told her about my experience later that afternoon. We were strolling slowly along the shady upper deck as the huge boat cruised on up the mighty river. The water wasn't so muddy now, blue instead of brown and silvery with sunlight, and the banks were covered with moss-hung oaks and other trees, fields of cotton and sugarcane visible in the distance. Now and then I caught glimpses of one of the plantation houses that stood along the River Road, redbrick walls faded to soft pink, tall white columns adding a touch of serene grandeur.

"It—it was very disturbing," I confessed. "It was almost as though we *had* known each other. In—in some other lifetime, perhaps."

"Chemistry," Laura said.

"Chemistry?"

"Physical attraction. I don't believe in love at first sight, but physical attraction is another matter. He looked up and saw you and was immediately drawn to you, wanted you—strongly and forcefully. Apparently you were drawn to him, too."

"It—it didn't feel like that."

"You said he was attractive, love."

"He was, very, but—there was something else, Laura. I can't explain it. It was as though—as though we were bound together."

I looked at the sunlight reflecting on the river, remembering those sensations I had felt, and then I sighed.

"I don't suppose it matters. I'll never see him again. He's not likely to come strolling into Kramer's Emporium in St. Louis to buy himself a new pair of gloves.''

A handsome gentleman in blue frock coat and tall gray top hat was approaching us on the deck. He slowed down, smiled, lifted his hat to Laura. She gave him a lovely smile. Every man on the boat seemed to find her fascinating, but she wasn't interested in shipboard flirtations just now.

"I've been thinking about that, love," she said as we moved on.

"Thinking about what?"

"St. Louis. Kramer's Emporium. Somehow I just can't see you standing behind a counter, selling ribbons."

"I have to work," I reminded her.

"I know, but—selling ribbons. It sounds terribly dreary, and it would be a shameful waste, love. Beauty like yours should be seen, should be properly displayed."

"Indeed? What do you suggest I do?"

"Get off the boat at Memphis with me," she said. "Go on the stage."

I was so startled I stopped in my tracks.

"You must be out of your mind," I told her. "I've never even been *inside* a theater. I've never seen a play. I have no experience, no training, no talent, no—"

"Training and experience you can get on the road. Talent you don't need—not when you look like you look, love. I happen to know for a fact that Maisie Barlow isn't going to be back this season, and Jason will be needing a new girl to replace her."

"It isn't going to be me," I assured her.

"I could arrange everything, love. Jason pretends to be a bear, but actually he's quite fond of me—we're all the family either of us has—and I can usually wrap him around my little finger. He'll be grateful to me for bringing you into the company."

"It's out of the question, Laura."

Laura didn't press me, but I soon discovered she didn't give up easily. A few hours later we were sitting at a table, the best, in the main dining salon, selected for us by the maître d', who would probably have gladly leaped through hoops had Laura requested it. She was wearing her garnet satin, I was wearing my bronze, and we were dining on oysters on the half shell, pheasant, asparagus with hollandaise sauce, the best. Laura thought it a pity not to spend some of the money she'd won at cards yesterday. The maître d' hovered nearby, eager to refill our crystal wineglasses with the sparkling white wine he had personally chosen for us.

"I think he's in love with you," I told her.

"He's a pet." She took a sip of her wine and sliced a piece of the moist, marvelously tender pheasant. "Really, love, I do think you're being very unreasonable. You'd love the theater. Here we've just become the best of friends, and you're already planning to desert me and spend the rest of your life behind a ribbon counter."

"I'm not an actress," I told her.

"Neither am I," she confessed, "not if you believe the reviews I usually get, but I have a following and lots of admirers just the same. It's interesting work, it's always challenging, and we have a marvelous time—even when the going gets rough. The company is—we're a *family*, love, and I want you to be part of it."

"Your cousin would never hire me."

"He'll hire you, I promise."

"He'd boot me out the minute he saw me attempt to act."

"The season doesn't start for three weeks. We've all been on hiatus during the summer months. Jason's reassembling the company in Memphis, and we'll have three weeks to get things organized before we tour. Jackson, our advance man, has booked theaters throughout the South. Ollie and I will help you with your parts and teach you all the tricks you need to know before we actually go on tour."

"Ollie?"

"Mrs. Helena Oliphant, our character actress. She's British, seventy-one years old, an outrageous old ham with flaming red hair, a ruined, sagging face covered with garish makeup, and a voice that could shatter glass. Everyone on the road adores her."

"She sounds wonderful."

"She's touchy, temperamental and dictatorial, with a heart as big as Montana. Ollie's a real trouper, the one who keeps us all together. She's like a testy den mother, scolding us, giving us encouragement and giving us comfort and aid when any of us need it."

I could feel myself beginning to weaken. It was her use of the word "family" that had done it. Sensing this, Laura quickly pressed on.

"You'll love the rest of the company, too. There's Bartholomew Hendrics, our character man, fifty-four, silver-haired, blue-eyed, a darling. He speaks in a deep baritone, has courtly manners and always wears a top hat and a flamboyant black cape lined with red satin. Nothing ever ruffles Bart. He always keeps his head, a perfect pro."

I severed the tip of an asparagus, weakening.

"And there's Billy Barton, our juvenile. He's twenty-seven years old but looks about nineteen. He has perfectly chiseled features and merry brown eyes and a roguish grin, and the ladies on the road are *mad* for him. They're always flocking around him and he's always leading them on. Billy's a scamp, I fear, but he's lovable. He dons a mustache and lowers his voice and doubles as our resident villain—he's strangled me to death dozens of times, once pursued me over the ice floes with a crackling whip. You think *that* wasn't tricky!"

"You had ice floes on stage?"

"Clever illusion, love. Chunks of papier-mâché on a moving platform with snow machines offstage. I'm the resident femme fatale, and Maisie was our ingenue—you'll be taking her place. When I was in New Orleans Melinda told me Maisie eloped with a Yankee banker three weeks ago and was afraid to let Jason know about it. He probably hasn't heard yet. Your arrival will be most providential."

"Laura, I could never—"

"Trust me, love. Our leading man left at the end of last season, and Jason will have hired a new one while I was in New Orleans. Our leading lady is the only thorn. Carmelita Herring. You'd *think* she'd have had the good sense to change that name. Carmelita's thirty-seven and overripe and fancies herself the chief attraction. She's spoiled and demanding and hot-tempered and a pain in the ass, but we pretty much ignore her. She's the 'star' and keeps to herself, snubbing everyone but Jason and God."

"Is she a good actress?"

"She is, actually, though a bit too grand for some tastes. Audiences in the sticks admire her. I've already told you about Dulcie, our wardrobe woman who looks like a dumpling, and finally there's Jackson, our advance man, who's also treasurer, assistant manager, jack-of-all-trades. He's the rock, the one who handles all the money and most of the business affairs and keeps my cousin in line. Jackson looks like a battered prizefighter, wears loud checked suits and smokes huge, smelly cigars, but for all his gruffness and angry scowls, he's the softest touch in the world—always ready to give you an advance on your salary when you find yourself flat.''

''That's the company?''

''There's a crew who handle the scenery and set everything up at the various theaters, but they travel separately. Supernumeraries—extras, bit players and such—Jason picks up on the road. The world is full of amateurs eager to don costumes and go onstage sans salary. Actually, we're like a band of gypsies, trouping from town to town—never the big cities—performing our melodramas and then moving on. There's a new crisis every day and a lot of frustration and a lot of discomfort, but the camaraderie is marvelous.''

''You make it sound very appealing,'' I confessed.

''No matter what happens, you know that you belong, love. You know you're part of a group and have support behind you—Carmelita notwithstanding. It's not all roses, far from it, but you're never bored. It beats selling ribbons, believe me.''

People stared as we left the dining salon—*two* women traveling without chaperones, one of them decidedly flashy in garnet satin—but I didn't mind the stares with Laura at my side. We decided to walk around the deck awhile to work off the large meal, and Laura left me waiting at the railing while she went down to the cabin to fetch a light wrap. It was a beautiful evening, the moon riding high in a hazy purple-black sky full of mottled silver-gray clouds. The boat cruised serenely up the river, the paddle wheel turning slowly, water spilling, splashing. Again I had the sensation that we were standing still as the river and shadowy banks flowed past.

The hurt, the sadness and grief swept over me, try though I might to hold it at bay. I thought of Julian and Charles and all that I had left behind me, and I didn't feel I could bear it. I had loved Charles with all my heart and soul, and he had turned me away. He blamed me for Raoul's death. He blamed me for everything. It was all right for an Etienne to slip into my bedroom in secrecy as he had done night after night, but I wasn't good enough for an Etienne to marry. Charles wouldn't even consider such an unlikely alliance, nor would he allow his brother to do so. I was a bastard, trash from the swamps, and that's what I would always be in his eyes. Charles had never loved me, he had used me. I realized that, but it didn't make the loss any easier. Julian had loved me sincerely, with all the goodness of his heart, and I had hurt him badly. That was the worst thing of all.

"It's bad, isn't it, love?" Laura said quietly.

I hadn't heard her approach. She moved over to the railing to stand beside me, a gauzy black lace shawl wrapped around her arms. Moonlight and shadow played over the deck. The boat rocked ever so gently.

"It's bad," I agreed.

"Time helps," she said.

"I—I was such a fool," I told her. "I loved him and I thought—I believed—"

"I know. We always do."

"I don't ever want to fall in love again."

"Would that we could control these things. We can't. All we can do is learn from our experiences and try not to make the same mistakes when the next man comes along."

"There'll never be another man in my life," I vowed.

I believed that. Laura didn't say anything. A wise, sad smile played on her lips. We passed a small town, a sprinkling of golden lights strewn across the night-dark bank, disappearing as the boat moved on. We heard footsteps on the deck. A man in top hat and frock coat approached us, and as he drew nearer I recognized him as the handsome gentleman we had seen on deck earlier this afternoon. His features were just discernible in the moonlight. He stopped, smiled, removed his top hat.

"Evenin', ladies," he drawled.

"Evenin'," Laura replied.

"You ladies look like you could use a little company."

"We're doing fine," she informed him.

"It's a lovely evening," he persisted, "much too lovely to spend all by yourselves."

"Sweetheart"—her voice was bored—"we're not interested."

"Let me take you to the main salon. There's music. I'll buy us a bottle of champagne and we can get to know each other. Later on we—uh—we might get to know each other even better."

"Do me a favor, love," she said.

"What's that?"

"Go take a flying leap at the moon."

Affronted, the man scowled and moved on, muttering something quite uncomplimentary under his breath. Laura sighed, not in the least perturbed. I had the feeling she had fended off dozens of similar advances in the past with the same cool aplomb. We stood at the railing for a few moments more and then began to stroll, skirts rustling, a cool, gentle breeze sweeping over the river. Laura adjusted the black lace shawl around her arms. How wonderful it was to have a friend. We had known each other such a short time, yet in some ways I felt closer to her than I had to anyone. I felt I could tell her anything, share anything with her. This must be the way you felt when you had a sister, I thought.

If I went to St. Louis, I would be entirely on my own. I wasn't sure Herbie Kramer would remember me. I had no guarantee he would give me a job at his emporium. If I got off the boat at Memphis, at least I would be with Laura. I wouldn't be alone. She seemed to be reading my mind.

"Live dangerously, love," she said. "You weren't meant to languish behind a ribbon counter."

"Do—do you really think I could go onstage?"

"I know you could," she replied. "I'd help you. So would Ollie. Who knows, love—you might really be *good*. You're sensitive and intelligent and gorgeous. You might put us all to shame."

"If it doesn't work out, I—I suppose I could find work in Memphis as easily as I could in St. Louis."

"You'll do it? You'll come with me?"

I nodded. Laura reached for my hand and squeezed it.

"We're going to have glorious times, love," she promised.

I prayed I had made the right decision.

Chapter Sixteen

THE SKY WAS LADEN with ponderous gray-black clouds swollen with rain, and everything below looked gray, too. Although it was barely ten o'clock in the morning, it was almost as dark as night as Laura and I walked down the gangplank at Memphis, she in blue, me in my yellow linen, followed by a single gentleman she had conned into carrying our bags. I was so nervous I felt certain I'd lose my footing on the tilting, serrated wooden plank and fall crashing into the people in front of us, but I reached the safety of the dock without mishap. There was a huge crowd and there was bustle, everyone in a hurry to be gone before it began to pour. Only Laura seemed calm. She smiled warmly at the gentleman as he set our bags down. He asked if we were going to be in town long. She gave him an evasive answer and brushed him off politely. She handled men with the expertise of a veteran, I thought admiringly.

Thunder rumbled ominously. There was a shattering, blinding flash of silver-blue lightning. People hurried even more, scrambling toward the carriages waiting beyond the dock area. I caught glimpses of old brown warehouses yawning open and dirty bales of cotton and untidy stacks of wooden boxes. Memphis had a distinct smell, like soot and old smoke, I thought, combined with the mossy, muddy smell of the river which was more pungent than it had been elsewhere. A wind began to blow, causing our skirts to flutter. Laura glanced around calmly, unperturbed by the scurrying, jostling crowd or excited voices or the imminent threat of deluge. It might have been a sunny spring day. Her cousin was to meet us. She searched for him, an expectant smile on her lips. I wanted to flee. What madness this was. I should still be on the boat, preparing to move on to

St. Louis. Jason Donovan would take one look at me and see I was a fraud and shove me into the river. I should never have let Laura talk me into this. It wasn't too late. My passage was paid to St. Louis. I could still snatch up my bags and rush back to my cabin.

"Here he comes," Laura said, waving. "Oh dear, he looks awfully grumpy, but then he usually *does*. Don't be alarmed, love. He stamps and roars and carries on like a surly bear, but he's really a pet."

"Laura, what—what if he—"

"Relax, love. It's in the bag."

"I'm terrified," I admitted.

"Nonsense. He's going to love you."

The man who moved toward us in a loose-limbed, impatient stride was lanky, well-muscled but much too thin, every bit as tall as Charles. He wore scuffed dark brown knee boots and shabby tobacco-brown breeches and frock coat, the latter flapping open in the breeze. He wore no waistcoat. His white shirt looked threadbare. A disreputable forest-green scarf was knotted around his throat in lieu of a neckcloth, and his hair, as black as Laura's, was poorly cut and much too long, tumbling over his brow in unruly locks. My God, I thought. He looks like an escaped criminal or . . . or a mad poet. He was scowling. He exuded a frightening vitality, seemed charged with energy and impatience he could barely contain.

"Here you are, darling," Laura said.

She gave him her dazzling smile. He was immune to the smile. He scowled even more when she stood up on tiptoes and kissed him on the cheek. He looked as though he wanted to strangle her on the spot. His hands were big, with broad palms and long, blunt fingers, the nails chewed down to the quick. Hands quite capable of seizing a throat and squeezing, I thought, moving back a step or two. What a horribly unpleasant person he was. His face was lean, with a wide, surly slash of pink mouth and a long nose that had been broken and was slightly twisted and gray-green eyes that seemed to burn with intensity. His cheekbones were too broad, too flat, and he was anything but handsome. He was almost ugly, in fact, yet . . . what a fascinating face it was. I could see why women would be strongly attracted to him. Jason Donovan was no well-bred southern gentleman. He had a rough-and-tumble aura that was curiously exciting.

"I've been waiting for two bloody hours," he snarled. "I'm using a hired carriage. It's costing me a fortune."

"Really, Jason, you can hardly blame us for the boat being late. I understand there were some sandbars they had to navigate around. Anyway, we're here now."

He gave her a suspicious look. "We?" He seemed to notice my presence for the first time. He glared at me. "Who's she?"

"My discovery, darling. I want you to meet Dana O'Malley."

"Discovery? What's this all about?"

He had a peculiar voice, light, almost soft, but with a scratchy, guttural quality nevertheless. A fascinating voice that could bark a command or croak a husky endearment. I had never heard anything quite like it, and it suited Jason Donovan perfectly.

"Dana's an actress," Laura explained. "I found her in New Orleans, and I knew you were going to need a new ingenue, and—"

"Maisie! That ungrateful little slut! She left me in the lurch without a word of warning. I got a letter from her yesterday—*yesterday*, mind you, and the company already assembling. How the hell am I supposed to find a new ingenue in—" He paused, glowering. "How did *you* find out about her defection?"

"She wrote a letter to Melinda. Melinda told me. I knew you were going to need a new ingenue and—"

"Married! Why the hell would she want to get *married*? And to a Yankee to boot!"

"He's a banker, love. Loaded, I understand. Maisie's done quite well for herself, considering that unfortunate overbite. I don't want to distress you, Jason, but it's going to pour any minute now. Don't you think we might possibly continue this conversation in the carriage?"

He glared at me again. His eyes were more green than gray, I noticed, and smoldering with emerald fire. Deeply set, heavily lidded, they were surmounted by unusual, quirky eyebrows as dark and smooth as sable. They rose into a high arch, then swept down and flared winglike at the corners. Jason Donovan might not be handsome, not with that twisted nose and mobile, too wide mouth, but his was a face you would never forget. A pirate might have a face like his, I fancied, or some western desperado. One would hardly expect to encounter it in polite society.

"So you're an actress?" he rasped.

"I—"

"She's marvelous, darling," Laura said quickly. "Better than Maisie ever hoped to be."

"Yeah?" His eyes never left me.

"When I saw her in—in *A Rose for Angelina*, I knew she was just what the company needed."

"*A Rose for Angelina*? Never heard of it."

"A huge success, darling. Ran for three months at the Court Theater."

"Court Theater? Never heard of it, either."

"It's new," she said glibly. "They just built it last year."

"She played the ingenue?"

"Brilliantly," Laura lied. "I just felt a raindrop, Jason. Do let's get to the carriage."

Jason Donovan ignored his cousin and studied me intently, as though searching for hidden imperfections. I saw no masculine appreciation in those critical eyes, only rude examination. He might have been inspecting a horse. I half expected him to ask me to show him my teeth. I could feel a blush coloring my cheeks. I could also feel the raindrops.

"At least she doesn't have an overbite," he snapped.

"Thanks for nothing," I said crisply.

"Why'd you leave the play?"

"It closed," I replied.

"Every manager in New Orleans was after her, Jason, but I persuaded her to come to Memphis. I knew you'd be in a bind with Maisie leaving like that, and I knew you'd love Dana."

"I could kill the little trollop!"

"Me?" I asked.

"Maisie," he said.

"It's going to pour, Jason," Laura reminded him.

"What are you dawdling for? Come along!"

He turned and marched away, leaving the two of us with our bags. His cousin shook her head, gave an exasperated sigh and lifted her bag. I picked mine up, too, and we hurried to catch up with him. There was another deafening rumble of thunder, another bright flash of lightning, and it began to pour in earnest, heavy raindrops pounding down in sheets, splattering all around. People shouted. Horses neighed. We were running now, lugging the heavy bags, finally reaching the carriage Jason had already

climbed into. The driver had opened up a huge black umbrella.
The horses were stamping. Laura threw her bag into the carriage
and scrambled inside and took my bags. I climbed in hastily,
stumbled and fell sprawling across Jason Donovan's lap. He
gave me a look.

"You've already got the job," he said dryly. "I don't demand
extra favors."

I longed with all my heart to punch him in the nose. I didn't.
I wiggled across his knees, straightened myself up and, with all
the dignity I could muster, moved across to sit down beside
Laura on the opposite seat. Jason reached over and pulled the
door shut and we began to move. Rain lashed at the windows
and pounded on the roof. The carriage shook and jiggled. It
smelled of tobacco juice and damp wool.

"You all right, love?" Laura asked.

"I'm fine," I said bitterly.

She smiled, clearly amused. I wasn't feeling any too generous
toward her at the moment, either. My hair was damp, tumbling
limply across my cheeks. My yellow linen was spotted with
raindrops, and my arms ached from running through the crowd
carrying the heavy bags. I smoothed my skirt down, brushed
the limp waves from my face and took a deep breath, willing
myself to maintain some semblance of calm.

"Where are we staying?" Laura asked her cousin.

"Birdie's," he replied.

"*Again?*"

"It's cheap," he told her.

"The food's abominable," she protested.

"Birdie's happens to be one of the very few boardinghouses
that will take actors, and she gives us free run of the house."

"There's that," she admitted. "has everyone arrived?"

"Everyone but Carmelita and the new man. Carmelita's arriving by train at six o'clock. New man's supposed to get in
sometime this afternoon."

"Who is he?"

"Big strapping fellow named Michael Prichard. Had a stroke
of luck there. He was with Bradshaw's company—best company
in the South, I don't need to remind you—got fired for pulling
a six-shooter on the boss."

"A six-shooter!"

"He was raised in Texas. Old habits die hard, I suppose."

"You've hired a *bandit*?"

Jason allowed a wry smile to play across that wide slash of mouth. "Mike grew tired of the territory—too many Comanches, too many Mexicans imposing too many new laws—so he pulled up stakes and journeyed to Alabama. He caught the eye of Doreen Falkner, Bradshaw's leading lady. She persuaded Bradshaw to take him into the company. Apparently the fellow had a natural flair for acting. In less than a year he was a bigger draw than Doreen, idol of all the ladies. Got decent notices, too."

"What about the six-shooter, Jason?" she asked patiently.

"According to Mike, Bradshaw refused to pay him his full salary, said there were 'expenses' that had to be deducted. Mike refused to accept the deductions and demanded the full amount. Bradshaw wouldn't bend, so Mike whipped out his gun."

"Did he *shoot* him?"

"No, but he collected his full salary."

"Charming," Laura observed. "Just what the company needs."

"Good leading men are hard to come by," Jason told her. "Mike's a pleasant fellow, natural and unassuming, down-to-earth. You'd never take him for an actor. No temperament whatsoever."

"Just quick on the trigger," she said.

The wry smile widened on his mouth, and amusement actually sparkled in the gray-green eyes. Loose-limbed, lanky, he lounged there across from us in those disreputable clothes, and although I disliked him intensely, I had to admit that he was utterly intriguing. Laura had told me that he wrote all the plays they performed himself, so he must be very gifted, I thought. You would never guess it from the looks of him.

"Has Jackson done all the booking?" she inquired.

Jason nodded. "Everything's set up. He did unusually well for us, got us three full weeks in Savannah this time."

"What about Atlanta?"

"Afraid not."

"It figures," she said.

"One day we'll play Atlanta," he promised her. "One day we'll take over the National Theater for the entire season. I'm going to write a play that'll bowl them over. They'll be clamoring to have us. One day Donovan's is going to be the most famous company in the country.''

"And one day pigs will undoubtedly sprout wings and fly. What are we doing this season?''

"Sweetheart of the West, The Captive Bride—it's new, I just finished the last act three weeks ago, marvelous part for you, a wicked courtesan determined to marry the heir, poisons all the competition, gets impaled in the last scene. We're also doing *Purple Nights, Lord Roderick's Revenge*—''

"That old turkey?''

"Audiences love it. It's a very well-made play. *Lena Marlow, The Three Musketeers*—''

"The Three Musketeers?" I interrupted. "I read that novel. I loved it. Alexandre Dumas must be very pleased to have it on the stage.''

"Alexandre Dumas doesn't know anything about it,'' he informed me, "and *you* keep quiet about it.''

"You mean you—you just *stole* his book and turned it into a play?''

"I prefer not to use that word. My version is much better than his, more passion, less swordplay. Milady de Winter seduces *all* the musketeers.''

"It sounds like a winner,'' I said dryly.

"Everyone's a critic,'' he grumbled.

Laura and Jason continued to discuss business, and I looked out the window at the rain-swept streets. Memphis seemed vast, much more spacious than New Orleans, with wider streets, the houses and buildings not so crowded up. Through the swirling gray sheets of rain I saw lots of greenery and lofty trees and old frame houses set back behind lawns with picket fences in front. Life here must be more casual, more neighborly, I thought. It was hard for me to believe that I was in Tennessee, even harder to believe that I had just been accepted as the new ingenue in Jason Donovan's theatrical company. What would he do to me when he discovered I couldn't act? I preferred not to think about it.

The rain hadn't slackened a bit when, ten minutes later, the carriage came to a halt in front of one of the large frame houses with a wide verandah. The house was painted yellow, I saw through the rain, with white trim. Shrubs grew around the verandah, and two tall trees shaded the currently sodden front lawn. The driver climbed down from his perch and, holding the huge black umbrella up, opened the door and hurriedly escorted Laura and me to the safety of the verandah. The umbrella protected us from most of the rain, although our skirts were splattered. Jason Donovan was left to bring in all our bags, and it served him right, I thought, following Laura into the house. We found ourselves in a cozy front foyer with mahogany wainscotting and a faded wine-colored carpet. Lamps glowed pleasantly despite the hour, revealing archways leading into other rooms and, at the rear of the foyer, a wide staircase with mahogany banister leading up to the second floor.

An excessively handsome, very young man was tripping nimbly down the steps, humming to himself. Seeing us, he stopped, slammed a hand to his heart and pretended to swoon. He had thick, floppy blond hair, merry brown eyes and a beautifully shaped pink mouth. His features were clean-cut and almost too perfect. Young men weren't supposed to be so absurdly good-looking. He wore black leather slippers, gray breeches, a white shirt and, over them, a maroon satin dressing robe with black satin lapels and cuffs, this outlandish garment tied loosely at the waist with a maroon satin sash. Recovering from his false swoon, he waved, blew kisses and tripped on down the stairs, hurrying toward us. He reminded me of a naughty seraphim. He couldn't be all of twenty.

"Laura!" he exclaimed in a surprisingly deep voice. "You're back! Have you any idea how I've missed you? All the long, lonely nights I've spent pining, with only my pillow for company. Quick! To my bedroom! We must recapture the splendor at once!"

"Your ardor overwhelms me," she said.

"You look ravishing, poppet, even if you are drenched."

"You look outrageous. Where'd you get the robe?"

"A lady friend gave it to me. Splendid, isn't it?"

"Blinding."

"How was our Melinda?"

"Sassy as ever. Running her own hat shop. Divinely happy to be away from Jason Donovan and company. Billy, I want you to meet Dana O'Malley. She's our new ingenue. This is Billy Barton, Dana. I told you about him."

"Lies," he said, "all lies. Don't believe a word she said. I'll marry you if I must, but I'd much rather have a mad, passionate affair, beginning immediately. Let's haste to my bedroom. I'll help you out of those wet clothes and teach you the real meaning of bliss.''

"I never sleep with men who haven't started shaving," I told him.

"I've been shaving for over a decade!" he protested.

"You started at age seven?"

Billy Barton grinned. "She's sharp, Laura. I like her. Welcome to the company, poppet," he told me. "I really should hate you, you know. Jason has finally managed to hire someone prettier than I am.''

"That's debatable," I said.

"I *do* like her," Billy declared. "What fun to have someone lively to romance and terrorize onstage. Maisie had no wit whatsoever, and there was that unfortunate overbite. She managed to nab herself a rich banker, nevertheless. You, my lovely, will probably capture a king.''

He gave Laura an exuberant hug and then, to my total amazement, hugged me, too, as friendly and inoffensive as a puppy. Theater people were certainly demonstrative and free with endearments, I thought.

"I'm on my way to the kitchen," he confided. "I hope to steal a snack before lunch. Breakfast was inedible, children. Soggy scrambled eggs and stewed mushrooms. Guess what we're having for lunch.''

"Corned beef and cabbage," I said.

He arched a brow. "You're psychic?"

"I have a keen sense of smell."

At this point the front door flew open and a thoroughly drenched, thoroughly disgruntled Jason Donovan staggered in with our bags. The three of us stood watching as he dropped the bags, shook himself like a wolfhound and shoved dripping wet black locks from his brow. He grumbled. He glared. Billy scurried off through one of the archways, maroon satin flapping, and Laura tactfully informed her cousin that he was dripping all over the carpet. He shouted a reply that should have brought a blush to my cheeks. I had heard worse in the swamps, though not often. Laura merely smiled at his obscenity.

"Temper, love. So sweet of you to bring in our bags. You'd better run up and change into some dry clothes. Can't have our resident playwright and manager coming down with pneumonia.''

Jason spluttered another reply almost as obscene and marched past us, shaking water with every step. Laura followed him with fond eyes as he went up the stairs with, I thought, an unnecessary amount of stomping. I doubted seriously that any of his "artists" possessed a more volatile temperament than he did himself. I had the curious feeling that I had stepped into a madhouse.

"What *was* all that ruckus about?" a tiny, squeaking voice inquired.

I turned to see a tiny, round-cheeked, drab little woman standing in one of the archways. She wore a drab brown dress and had drab gray hair worn in a severe bun, but the blue eyes twinkling behind a pair of thick spectacles were unusually lively and filled with good humor.

"Jason," Laura said.

"Oh dear, look at my carpet."

"Jason," Laura repeated.

"What a relief. I feared it might be Theodore. I happen to know Bartholomew hasn't let him out since it started raining."

"Theodore is Bartholomew's dog," Laura explained. "This is Birdie. Birdie, I'd like for you to meet Dana O'Malley, our new ingenue. She's come with me from New Orleans."

"Enchanted, I'm sure," Birdie squeaked. "No overbite," she added, studying me closely. "I do hope you're comfortable here, Miss O'Malley. I'm afraid we're a bit short of help at the moment. My best girl quit last week. 'I came here to sweep floors and make beds, Miss Birdie, not to be pinched on the backside every time I turn around,' Adele told me as she handed in her apron."

"Billy?" Laura asked.

"Bartholomew," Birdie replied.

"Who would have thought it?"

"The new girl is built like an ox and unfortunately moves like one, too. She's terribly slow, but she has yet to complain of untoward behavior from one of the guests. You have your old room, Miss Laura. The one right across the hall from it was reserved for Miss Maisie. I'll have Bertha bring your bags up."

"The big one is mine," Laura said. "The other two are Dana's."

"Both of you could probably use a nice hot bath. I'll make arrangements."

"You're a darling, Birdie."

"I do try. I don't know why everyone objects to theatrical folk. It's a bit taxing, I'll admit, but so much more interesting than taking in dull spinsters and fussy old bachelors. I'm rarely bored."

She made a vague gesture and wandered away, and Laura and I went upstairs. The house was large and sprawling and redolent of camphor and beeswax, face powder and cooking, corned beef and cabbage prevalent at the moment. Blue wallpaper with faded purple flowers covered the walls of the upstairs corridor, and a shabby purple-gray rug covered the floor. The floorboards squeaked. The place was anything but grand, I mused, but it was surprisingly pleasant, particularly with the rain pounding on the roof. As we moved past an open doorway, a crisp, cracking voice called out to us, and we stopped. Laura smiled warmly as an old woman in a flamboyant purple frock came out into the hall.

I tried not to gape. Imposingly tall and as skinny as a bean pole, the woman had blazing red curls stacked untidily on top of her head and a ruined, sagging face garishly painted: eyelids deep mauve, cheeks bright pink, lips a vivid scarlet. The curls couldn't possibly be real, and the paint couldn't possibly conceal the cruel inroads of time, but there was something vital and youthful about her nevertheless. Her emerald-green eyes were shrewd, witty and intelligent, and although she might look like a painted old scarecrow, she exuded authority and a striking presence. Commanding was the word for her, I thought. There was no way you could possibly ignore her.

"You're back, I see," the woman said.

"Hale and hearty," Laura replied.

"I feared you'd succumb to the temptations of New Orleans, duckie. I was afraid you'd decide to abandon us and live in lovely sin with a handsome Creole dandy or some wealthy planter with a mustache. Knowing Melinda, she tried her best to match you up with someone."

"She tried," Laura confessed. "The Creole dandy had a wife and two children. The planter had a paunch. I passed."

"Very sensible of you," the woman declared "Don't despair,

duckie. One day your knight in shining armor will arrive right on cue.''

Her voice, while cracking, had unusual resonance and, had she wished it to be, could have been heard all the way across the street. It was crisp and dramatic, despite the shaky tremolo, with an undeniable British accent. This must be Mrs. Helena Oliphant, Laura's beloved Ollie.

''And who have we here?'' she asked, examining me with those brilliant emerald eyes.

''This is my friend Dana O'Malley,'' Laura said.

Ollie extended a thin, wrinkled but elegant hand. ''Mrs. Helena Oliphant,'' she said. ''Delighted to meet you, duckie.''

I shook her hand, slightly intimidated.

''We're going to need your help, Ollie. Dana has never even been inside a theater and—well, I lied outrageously to Jason and he has taken her on as our new ingenue.''

Ollie slowly arched one caustic brow. ''There's a story behind this, I assume.''

''I'll tell you everything later, love.''

Those shrewd emerald-green eyes swept over me again, taking in each detail of my dress and person.

''So you want to go on the stage?'' she asked crisply.

''Not really,'' I confessed. ''This was all Laura's idea. I was prepared to go to work at an emporium in St. Louis, selling ribbons or gloves behind one of the counters.''

''And a shocking waste it would have been,'' Ollie declared. ''You have incredible beauty and a very good voice. We'll have to work on projection, but I can foresee no problems there. No presence, not yet, too timid, unsure of yourself, but that can be fixed, too.''

''In three weeks?'' Laura asked.

''Shortly after I arrived in America with Sir Cyril Hampton-Croft's company and that rogue absconded and left us stranded in Washington, I opened a school for the spoiled, empty-headed daughters of diplomats who were always doing amateur theatrics. I taught 'elocution' and 'expression' and I turned a number of them into competent thespians—it was uphill work, children, believe me. We have much more to work with in this instance.''

''You think we can do it?''

''Give me three weeks,'' Ollie said grandly, ''and I could teach a block of wood to act. We'll do it, duckie. After all, our

Maisie was no Sarah Siddons. Any chit of a girl who can memorize lines and make herself heard onstage could do as good a job.''

''My sentiments exactly, love.''

''The company rehearsals don't begin until next week. We'll begin tomorrow morning—in the back parlor, I think. No one ever goes there, and we wouldn't want Jason to know what's afoot.''

''Definitely not,'' Laura agreed.

Ollie gave me a firm look. ''You'll have to work very, very hard, duckie,'' she informed me, ''and, I must warn you, I'm a tyrant. I brook no nonsense. I demand complete obedience.''

''Yes, ma'am,'' I said, thoroughly intimidated now.

She continued to skewer me with that firm look for another moment and then she smiled, mischief twinkling in her eyes. She touched my cheek. ''Don't look so frightened, ducks. Actually, we'll have *fun*. You'll be fine—I can sense it—and what a lark it will be putting one over on Jason. Run along to your rooms now, children. I'll see you both at lunch.''

I felt dazed as we moved on down the hall. Laura was smiling to herself, amused by my reaction to her friend.

''We'll do it, love,'' she assured me. ''Ollie's really a wonderful teacher. You'll be in fine shape before Jason ever sees you emote.''

''She mentioned being stranded in Washington,'' I said. ''I—I wonder why she never returned to England.''

''Politics,'' Laura said.

''Politics?''

''Intrigue. Romance. Ollie has a *past*, you see. You'll hear all about it ere long—you'll hear about it constantly, I fear. Ollie was a famous beauty several decades ago and the toast of the London stage and had several important lovers, and one day the Prince Regent spied her and was immediately infatuated. He swept her off the Royal Pavilion at Brighton and Mrs. Fitzherbert was insanely jealous and Parliament was appalled and secret meetings were held. Ollie was advised to leave the country if she wanted to stay healthy. According to her, she was the great love of Prinny's life—though naturally it was kept very hush-hush.''

''Goodness, she does have a past.''

''Or a very vivid imagination,'' Laura said wryly. ''Anyway, she's remained in America all these years, and we're lucky to have her in the company. Here's your room, love. Mine's over there. After you've had your bath and everything, come on over and we'll visit before we go down to lunch.''

The room I entered was large and comfortable-looking with faded blue wallpaper and heavy, rather battered furniture. A flowered counterpane was spread over the large four-poster, and curtains with matching floral print hung at the windows. The mirror over the dressing table was murky silver-gray, and the mahogany veneer of the immense wardrobe had tiny networks of weblike cracks. Behind a threadbare lilac silk screen I found pitcher, ewer, chamber pot, all the necessities. It was a welcoming, womblike room, shabby and snug, a perfect retreat. But you didn't come here to retreat, I reminded myself. You came here to forge ahead, to forget. That's what you're going to do. You're going to immerse yourself in a new life and . . . and put the pain behind you.

I was startled when the door banged open and a large, lumbering woman with flat brown eyes and lifeless blond hair came shambling in with my bags, dumping them beside the bed and giving me a sullen look. Bertha, I assumed. She did rather resemble an ox. She departed without a word and returned fifteen minutes later carrying a huge tin tub, followed by a skinny, skittish girl in mobcap and apron who carried towels, soap and sponge. Bertha set the tub down in the middle of the room and muttered something about water coming soon and left. The skinny girl, surely no more than thirteen, grinned shyly, dropped a nervous curtsey and scurried out after Bertha. I had scarcely finished hanging up my clothes in the wardrobe when they came back with buckets of water. Steam rose as they poured water into the tub. I thanked them profusely. Bertha grunted. The girl giggled. I was relieved when they left.

I'm dreaming all this, I told myself. I must be.

Half an hour later, refreshed, smelling of perfumed soap, hair brushed to a glossy honey-blond sheen, I donned my pale apricot gown and went across the hall to knock on Laura's door. ''Come in!'' she called, and I was surprised to find her still sitting in her tub, rich mounds of bubbly white suds rising all around her. Her hair was piled atop her head and fastened with a ribbon. Her sapphire eyes gleamed with contentment as she squeezed her sponge and let rivulets of water spill over her arms and shoulders.

"Sorry, love. I've been looking forward to this for so long I just couldn't drag myself out of this delicious water. We have plenty of time. Did you meet Bertha?"

"She's a charmer," I said.

"But efficient. You look radiant."

"I don't feel very radiant."

"Still nervous?"

I nodded, sitting down on the dressing table stool. Laura smiled and began to rinse herself. Her arms and shoulders were as smooth and creamy as satin, and she had a beautiful body, her breasts full and firm, with rosebud-pink nipples.

"So what do you think of my cousin?" she inquired.

"He's—different," I said cautiously. "I—I've never met anyone quite like him."

"And you never will, love. He's brilliant, mercurial, often impossible, but he's honest and strong and extremely protective. He watches after his own with fierce vigilance, his own being every member of the company. You'll long to kill him several times a week, but you can always depend on his being there for you when you need him. Behind all that bluster, he's a brick."

"You really admire him, don't you?"

"He's the genuine article, love. He's rough at the edges and unpolished and outspoken, but there's no pretense and absolutely no hypocrisy. What you see is exactly what you get, and a great many women have tried their very best *to* get him. Jason has the morals of an alley cat where women are concerned, I fear, but you can hardly blame him for that. It seems he's irresistible."

"Oh?"

"Women *will* keep throwing themselves at him, and he's always happy to oblige them. He never lies and never leads them on, always lets them know just where he stands, but they all keep right on adoring him until he finally dumps them. No strings, no entanglements, that's Jason's creed. Just glorious, uncomplicated coupling—and lots of it."

I was shocked. I tried not to show it.

"What about love?" I asked.

"Oh, Jason's never been in love. He treats his ladies with rough affection, very fond of them while they last, but he's never been seriously smitten with any of them. When he *does* fall in love, God help us all. He'll probably be even more impossible.''

Laura reached for the large white towel, stood up, stepped out of the tub, and began to dry herself.

''He's pleased to have you with us, incidentally. He came in here to tell me so, that's why I was late getting into my bath. He was worried no end when he received Maisie's letter, wondering how on earth he was going to get another ingenue on such short notice. He actually thanked me for solving his problem.''

''He won't be so thankful when he sees me try to act.''

''By the time he sees you, you'll be fine. Ollie and I will make sure of that. There's really nothing to it, love. You learn your lines, you pretend, you project.''

''I think I'd rather sell ribbons,'' I said.

''Nonsense. You'll love it. Every girl dreams of going on the stage.''

''I never did. I didn't even know what a stage *was*,'' I added.

''You've come a long way,'' she said merrily. ''Think of it as an adventure. You're going to have a wonderful time.''

It was at this point that the door flew open and a very big, very attractive man strolled casually into the room, carrying a large leather bag. Laura let out a little cry, clutching the towel in front of her. The man gave her a long, lazy look and calmly set his bag down. He seemed completely unperturbed and not the least surprised to find a naked woman in what he obviously assumed to be his room.

''Who the hell are *you*!'' Laura demanded.

''Name's Michael Prichard, ma'am. Who might you be?''

''I'm Laura Devon, and—''

''Mighty pleased to meet you,'' he drawled. ''Go right ahead with what you were doing. Don't mind me a bit.''

Laura gasped. Michael Prichard looked at me, nodded. I nodded back. He removed the wide-brimmed brown western hat he was wearing, and a tumble of sun-streaked golden-brown hair spilled over his brow.

''Dana O'Malley,'' I said. ''The new ingenue.''

''Mighty pleased to meet you, too, ma'am.''

''What are you doing in my room!'' Laura cried.

'' 'Fraid there's been some error. The lady downstairs told me this was my room. Third door on your left, she said, plain as could be.''

"This happens to be the fourth door on your left, you big lummox! Didn't anyone ever teach you to *count*?"

He didn't answer. He grinned. It was a delightful grin, both boyish and slightly wicked. He was indeed a strapping fellow, powerfully built and solid with broad, rough-hewn features that were somehow reassuring. His clear gray eyes were hooded by heavy, drooping lids that gave him a lazy, nonchalant look, and the sun-streaked golden-brown hair was unusually thick and luxuriant. He wore tooled brown leather boots, snug tan breeches and, over a silky tan shirt open at the throat, a loose, rather battered tan kidskin jacket that looked as though it had seen many years of service. He was supremely masculine, rugged as granite, yet there was a breezy wholesomeness about him that inspired immediate confidence.

At least in me. Laura didn't look at all confident. She looked furious, her sapphire eyes flashing.

"You weren't supposed to be here till this afternoon," she snapped.

"Got in early," he said lazily.

"On horseback, I assume."

"Train. Never been too fond of horses. High-strung creatures, too easily spooked. Have to pamper 'em just like you'd pamper a woman. No, give me a train every time."

"Where's your six-shooter?" she asked sarcastically.

"It's in my bag. Wanna see it?"

Laura didn't deign to reply. She stood there gripping the towel tightly, absolutely indignant. Intrigued, too, I could see that. She found the actor from Texas immensely intriguing, though she would undoubtedly have gone to the stake before admitting it. For all her experience and devil-may-care sophistication, she was as susceptible as any other woman to masculine charm. Michael Prichard had charm in abundance and, with those sleepy eyes and that lazy, low-key manner of his, sexual allure that was potent indeed. Laura looked at him with visible disdain.

"You're an *actor*?"

"Yes, ma'am. One of the best in the South, I'm told. I could show you my clippings. I could also give you personal references."

"I'm sure Doreen Falkner would vouch for you."

"I'll betcha she would, come to think of it."

Their eyes held. I might as well have been invisible. He

grinned again and reached up to brush the thick hair from his brow, and then he examined his hand, frowning.

"Hair's still a bit damp from all that rain," he said. "Think you could loan me that towel for a minute?"

"Get out of here!" Laura snapped.

"No need to get all riled, ma'am. I'm not gonna bite you, not unless you ask me to. Just bein' friendly."

"Out!"

The grin continued to curl on his wide, full lips, and there was a decided twinkle in those clear gray eyes. He looked at her for a moment longer and then, sighing with sad resignation, plopped the wide-brimmed brown hat back on his head and picked up his bag. "See you girls later," he drawled and nodded to both of us and sauntered out of the room, leaving the door wide open. Laura stormed across the room and slammed it with a resounding bang. I smiled to myself. Sophisticated she might be, but she was also transparent, even to one as inexperienced as I was. I couldn't resist making a few sly thrusts as she finished drying off and dressed for lunch.

"What a friendly man," I remarked.

"Friendly! The man's an oaf!"

"I found him quite amiable. Attractive, too."

"Attractive! He's as big as a grizzly bear. He's got to be at least six five, and those shoulders—they're as wide as—"

"You noticed," I said. "He's big, but he's magnificently proportioned, like—like a statue of Hercules I once saw in a picture book. He has wonderful hair, like sunshine blazing on a field of wavy brown wheat, and those eyes are a lovely clear gray."

Laura pulled on her ruffled white cotton petticoat. "He does have rather nice eyes," she admitted, "but they're entirely too fresh. Did you see the way he was looking at me?"

"I saw," I said. "I loved his voice."

"I can just imagine him playing Porthos with that lazy, burr-filled Texas drawl."

"He's the leading man," I reminded her. "He'll undoubtedly be playing d'Artagnan."

"And Milady Carmelita will undoubtedly be crawling all over him. She has the libido of a Pekingese in heat. It'll take her no time at all to appropriate the new leading man."

"Why should you care?" I asked.

"Me? I couldn't care *less*. She's welcome to him."

I smiled. She saw it. It didn't improve her mood one bit.

Laura was still in an irritable mood when we went downstairs. Wearing a lovely blue linen frock, black waves tumbling in a rich cascade, she had a visible chip on her shoulder and snapped at Billy when he greeted us in the foyer. She led me into a large parlor with a profusion of potted plants, dusty purple velvet drapes and a large gray rug with green and purple floral patterns. An elderly, distinguished-looking man with a long, oval face and silvery hair sat on a plush purple sofa, a large brown standard-size poodle sitting beside him. The man was perusing a volume of Shakespeare. The poodle was gazing contentedly into space. A stocky man in a loud checked suit stood at the window, holding the drape back and staring morosely out at the rain. All three looked up as we entered. The poodle wagged his fluffy ball of tail. The silvery-haired gentleman put down his book and stood up, smiling benignly.

"Laura, my dear," he said in dulcet tones, "so pleased to see you back. And this must be Miss O'Malley, the new ingenue Jason was telling us about. I am Bartholomew Hendrics, child. Delighted to meet you."

"I'm delighted to meet you, too."

"What's this about you and Adele?" Laura asked. "I hear you caused her to hand in her apron."

"The girl viciously maligned me," he protested. "There's not a word of truth in anything she said. Would *I* do something like that?"

"It wouldn't surprise me at all, love," she told him.

The man in the loud checked suit made a disgruntled noise, let the purple drape fall back in place and came over to greet me. He had a battered, belligerent face that reminded me of a bulldog's. His small black eyes were full of perpetual suspicion. He smelled of cigar smoke and cheap hair oil. He sized me up, scowled and then took my hand, pumping it vigorously but with a noticeable lack of enthusiasm.

"I'm Jackson," he growled. "Advance man, assistant manager, you name it, I get it done. Jason was right. You *are* gorgeous, too bloody gorgeous for an ingenue. Carmelita's not going to like it a bit. You're gonna make her look like hash. Jason says you were appearing at the Court Theater in New Orleans. I thought I knew all the theaters in the city. Never heard of the Court."

"It's new," I replied.

"You're gorgeous, I grant that, but can you act?"

"I've never had any complaints," I said truthfully.

"We'll see," he told me.

Jackson didn't intimidate me at all. I saw through him immediately. Besieged by problems, burdened by tremendous responsibilities, and no doubt constantly put upon by the demanding, temperamental members of the troupe, he had, I suspected, assumed the gruff, disgruntled manner as protective armor. I had the curious feeling that we were going to be friends, and I smiled at him. He scowled, thrust his hands into his pockets and stalked back over to the window to glare out at the rain. I'm going to win you over, Mr. Jackson, I vowed. Just you wait and see.

"And we mustn't forget Theodore," Bartholomew Hendrics said. "Say hello to Miss O'Malley, Theodore."

Theodore wagged his tail, gave two barks, one high, one low—it really did sound like a canine hello, I thought—then leaped from the sofa, squatted in front of me and raised one neatly clipped brown paw. I shook it solemnly. Bartholomew looked enchanted. Theodore looked expectant. Bartholomew told me he expected a cookie. I said I'd try to have one for him next time. Jackson snorted. Laura casually asked where the new leading man was.

"He hasn't come down yet," Bartholomew said. "He's a frightfully intelligent chap. We were discussing *Macbeth* earlier on. He knows the play backwards and forward. Seems he read a lot of Shakespeare when he was out there on the plains."

"I'm surprised he knows *how* to read," Laura said acidly.

"He's quite good, Laura. I saw him when he was with Bradshaw's company. They were doing *She Stoops to Conquer*, and he was playing Marlow. He has tremendous stage presence and a remarkably effective technique. I was delighted when Jason said he was going to become part of our little troupe. We're lucky to have him."

"I'm starving," Laura said. "Let's adjourn to the dining room."

I followed her into the foyer, Bartholomew and Jackson and Theodore close behind. Jason Donovan had just come downstairs. He had brushed his hair and changed into gray breeches and frock coat and a black silk waistcoat and would have looked almost respectable had it not been for his dark red neckcloth. He was with a short, enormously fat woman with sharp brown eyes and yellow curls, her girth covered by a long, tentlike garment of lime-green linen. Seeing me with Laura, she gave an exclamation of delight.

"Exquisite!" she cried. "Absolutely exquisite! That glorious coloring! That divine body! It's going to be sheer enchantment dressing *her*. You realize, Jason, that none of Maisie's costumes will even begin to fit her, and the colors would be wrong anyway. We'll have to start from scratch, new patterns, new materials—and only three weeks. I do adore a challenge!"

"Jesus," Jason groaned. "What's it going to cost us?"

"Plenty," she said as she marched over to me. "I'm Dulcie, sugar. Jason told me we had a new ingenue, but I had no idea you'd be such a treat. You and I must get together right after lunch to discuss costumes—I'll have to take measurements as well. I see you in pink for Cora, very pale pink, a layer of tulle over satin, perhaps, embroidered with delicate white flowers. And for Evelina—"

"Later, Dulcie!" Jason snapped.

Dulcie gave me an enormous hug and told me how pleased she was to have me with the company. Overwhelmed by her effusion, I thanked her and told her Laura had said several nice things about her. Billy Barton came tearing into the foyer, blond wave flopping, brown eyes snapping, face white with outrage. He raised one fist in the air and began to wave it.

"Do you know what that bloody woman has *done*? She's burned the cabbage! And the corned beef's so tough Theodore wouldn't even touch it. Know what she plans to serve for lunch? Ham? *Last night's* ham!"

"Out of the question," Ollie said, coming down the stairs on the arm of Michael Prichard. "I don't know what she did to it, but that ham was so salty, I almost died from indigestion. You'll have to do something, Jason. I have a delicate stomach, as you very well know, and I refuse to eat any more of her ham."

"Theodore can't eat ham, either," Bartholomew put in. "Ham isn't good for him, particularly Birdie's ham."

"Hello there," Michael Prichard said, sidling up to Laura.

"Get stuffed," she told him.

The front door burst open. A very grand woman in a very damp gray satin gown and long pink velvet gloves stalked furiously into the foyer, followed by a black-clad cabbie who held a huge black umbrella over her. A very wide gray hat with now limp pink ostrich plumes was slanted atop her glossy blond coiffure. She took us all in with one blazing blue glare and then focused her attention on Jason Donovan. He turned pale. Carmelita Herring, I thought. It couldn't be anyone else.

"You son of a bitch!" she shrilled. "Why didn't you meet the train!"

"I thought—Jesus, Carmelita, I didn't think you were due to arrive until four-thirty."

"That was my *original* schedule. I wrote and told you I was going to take an *earlier* train that arrived at eleven-thirty. Sharp. I arrive at the station and there's no one to meet me and I have to find a carriage myself in the pouring rain and those bastards lost one of my bags and—"

"Have that man close the umbrella, Carmelita," Bartholomew said. "You know it's bad luck to have an open umbrella inside the—"

"Go to hell!" she shouted. "I've had just about enough, Jason! I'm an *artist* and I expect to be treated like one! It's bad enough having to stay in this god-awful dump because you're too cheap to put us in decent lodgings, but if you expect me to —" She paused, fuming, looking as though she were planning a particularly gruesome murder. "I won't stand it!" she shrilled. "Do you understand me! *I won't stand it!*"

Theodore started barking. Ollie raised her eyes heavenward. Bertha lumbered in to announce that lunch was served. Laura caught my eye.

"Welcome to the theater, love," she said.

Chapter Seventeen

I WAS NUMB WITH TERROR and knew I would never be able to go through with it. I was going to be violently ill, I could feel it coming on, and I wouldn't remember a single line and I would make an absolute idiot of myself and disgrace the entire company and it would be much better if I just slipped out of the theater right now. I hated to leave them in the lurch, particularly since everyone but Jason and Carmelita had been so kind to me, making me feel a part of it all and making me feel important, a member of the family. Jason hadn't really been unkind, just snappish and distracted, and Carmelita was bitchy to everyone. Ollie and Laura had worked with me until I was ready to drop, and I hadn't really been that bad in company rehearsals. Billy and Bart had been very supportive, helping me through the scenes, giving me advice and showing me little tricks to make my performance more effective. Michael had been a dream, like a teasing, affectionate older brother, constantly encouraging me. They were all in on my secret and thought it was a lark, pulling the wool over Jason's eyes. Carmelita didn't know, of course, nor did Jason, and Dulcie couldn't have cared less as long as the costumes were right and "moved" onstage.

We had left Memphis three days ago and arrived in this little town in Alabama whose name I had already forgotten in the confusion, and yesterday had been spent blocking everything out on the stage of this rickety, dusty theater, and I had felt the terror coming on then. Jason had been in a fury because the crew hadn't arrived on time and the set hadn't been ready and one of the painted canvas backdrops had been damaged in transit. Confusion reigned. Tempers flared. Nerves were on edge. Carmelita threw a fit. Laura and Michael got into a loud shouting match. Ollie was testy and out of sorts. Billy was more interested in the girls who had been following him about ever since we arrived than in doing his job and threw away all his lines during rehearsal. Bartholomew was upset because Theodore had turned down his food, and Dulcie still wasn't completely satisfied with the fit of my pink ball gown and kept dragging me away whenever I wasn't actually onstage in order to make yet another adjustment. Somehow we managed to get through the block-out and, late last night, the dress rehearsal, and now—I glanced at the clock—in forty-seven minutes they expected me to step out onstage as Cora and fend off the advances of the wicked Hugh Northcliff, and I couldn't do it.

The play had already started. Even as I sat here in this cramped and dingy dressing room staring stony-eyed at my reflection in the mirror, Michael as the widowed Lord Roderick was wooing Carmelita as the poor but aristocratic Angela Hampton and telling her that his pure young daughter Cora would be leaving the convent and returning in time for the engagement ball, even as, unbeknownst to either, Billy as the wicked Hugh Northcliff was plotting with Laura as femme fatale Lorena to kidnap Cora the night of the ball and hold her in hiding until Lord Roderick handed over the priceless Manners-Croft rubies which had once belonged to Good Queen Bess. Thank God I didn't appear in the first act. I wondered what they would do when the curtain came up on Act Two and the lovely and virginal Cora didn't wander into the antechamber where Hugh was lurking. Cora would already be on her way back to the hotel to pack her bags and head for the train station as fast as her feet would carry her.

The dressing room door opened. Laura came in, looking very exotic in dark brown velvet and blue egret feathers. Her face was heavily made-up, eye shadow and black liner and dark lip rouge giving her a look of wicked sensuality suitable for the scheming Lorena.

"My word, love!" she exclaimed. "Act One is almost over and you haven't even put on your ball gown."

"I'm not putting it on," I informed her. "I'm not going on tonight. I'm sick. I'm going to throw up any minute now. I've forgotten every single line. I'm leaving. I'm leaving the company. I'm leaving town. If I'm lucky, I can still get that job in St. Louis."

Laura wasn't at all alarmed. She plucked the arrangement of

egret feathers from her head and removed the fake sapphire jewelry that adorned her wrists and throat.

"Nonsense," she said. "You're going on and you're going to be fine. You were wonderful in rehearsal."

"I was awful. Everyone said so."

"Carmelita is the only one who said so, and she's a rotten bitch scared to death you're going to steal her thunder. Michael said you have a natural flair for acting."

"You two are speaking again?"

"Barely. And Ollie said you were the best student she'd ever had. You're just experiencing first-night nerves, love. All of us do. I played Cora when I first joined the company, as you know, and you're much better than *I* ever was. It's hard to believe I was ever an ingenue," she added wistfully.

"I—I can't do it, Laura."

"Of course you can. Let me help you dress."

I stood up like a zombie, and Laura took down the exquisite ball gown Dulcie had done up for Cora. It was pale pink satin, overlaid with a paler pink tulle embroidered with delicate white and silver flowers. I stepped into it and put my arms through the puffed sleeves, and Laura fastened it up in back. The bodice still didn't feel right. It felt loose on the left side. Dulcie had let it out twice. The last time she had let it out too much, I thought. My bosom was half-exposed, and the cloth didn't cling to my left breast as it should have done.

"The dress doesn't fit," I said.

"If fits fine. You look positively glorious."

"If Cora is so sweet and virginal, why would she be wearing such a low-cut gown?"

"For the paying customers, love. Here, let me put your hair up. Sit down and hand me the hairpins. Really, Dana, you should already have done this. If Jason knew you weren't ready he'd have conniptions."

"He'll have conniptions anyway when I ruin his rotten play."

"It *is* rather rotten, I've always said so, but the yokels do love thundering melodrama. There. Perfect. Let me just fasten this spray of white flowers above your temple."

"What—what's that terrible noise?"

"The audience, love, applauding the end of Act One. They adored it. Carmelita was so grand and affected you wanted to boot her backside, but they like her that way. Michael was good—I hate to admit it, love, but he really *is* good, he really can act. I was marvelous, of course, and you should have heard them hissing Billy.''

"Was he that bad?"

"He was that good. They always hiss the villain. He's in fine form tonight, has three local belles meeting him at the stage door after the show. I have no idea how he's going to manage all three.''

"He's young," I said dryly.

Laura stepped back, looking at me admiringly. I stood up and tried to adjust the bodice of my gown. It didn't *look* wrong, I saw in the mirror, but it still felt loose on the left side.

"You might apply just a touch of lip rouge," Laura said, "You don't need any other makeup. Dark pink. Here, use this.''

I applied it, feeling like death. She wasn't going to let me get away. I finished rouging my lips and looked at her with stoic resignation.

"We'd better get out to the wings," she said. "I have plenty of time to change. I don't appear again until the middle of Act Three when Hugh discovers I'm double-crossing him and stabs me to death. How's the stomach?''

"Still doing cartwheels."

"You'll be fine once you go on."

"Sure," I said.

We left the dressing room and moved down the narrow, dusty corridor toward the wings. I was still numb with terror. Marie Antoinette must have felt like this on her way to the guillotine, I thought, stepping over a coil of rope. My heart seemed to have stopped beating. I seemed to be walking in my sleep. The backstage area was dimly lighted. The curtain was down, and on the stage several brawny crew members were quickly, efficiently moving scenery and pulling up a new backdrop showing the antechamber in Lord Roderick's castle. Jackson was supervising things, a cigar clamped between his teeth, and Jason Donovan was in the wings, talking to our leading lady in a low voice. Neither of them looked up as Laura and I approached.

Carmelita was tall and statuesque—just short of stout—with very glossy pale blond hair and heavy-lidded blue eyes and a small, petulant mouth. Rather lovely with her high cheekbones and straight nose and creamy smooth complexion, the thirty-seven-year-old actress born in Biloxi, Mississippi, had the hau-

teur and arrogance of an English duchess. She kept herself aloof
from everyone else in the company and was disliked by all, but,
as Laura grudgingly admitted, she was a strong drawing card.
Begowned now in pale gold satin, false pearls about her throat
and woven through her elaborate coiffure, she told Jason in no
uncertain terms that she would not *abide* something or other and
then stalked grandly past us and across the stage, almost collid-
ing with a crewman who was setting up one of the towering
"marble" columns. Her dressing room, the only decent one,
was on the other side of the theater. Jason looked as though he
longed to whip out a gun and shoot her in the skull.

"Problems?" Laura asked sweetly as he came over to us.

"She wants curtains and a carpet in her dressing room. I told
her we were only going to be here four nights and it was out of
the question. She says she won't go on tomorrow night unless
she has them."

"So where are you going to find the curtains and carpet,
love?"

"Jackson will see to it. He always manages somehow."

"One day you'll get smart and get a new leading lady instead," Laura told him. "She's not *that* big a draw."

Jason ignored her and scrutinized me carefully, looking for
flaws. I felt the same resentment I had felt toward him from the
first. The man didn't like me and treated me like I was a pariah
whose presence he was forced to tolerate. He hadn't spoken a
civil word to me in all this time. Come to think of it, he had
hardly spoken a civil word to anyone. Quirky black eyebrows
hovering above those intense, critical green-gray eyes, his mouth
curling up at one corner, he finished his scrutiny and gave an
exasperated sigh.

"You look scared to death," he rasped.

"I am," I said.

"An actress with your extensive experience should be accustomed to opening nights." There was undeniable sarcasm in his
light yet guttural voice. "They aren't going to stone you. Even
if you botch it, they'll get their money's worth just looking at
you."

"I have no intention of botching it," I said icily.

"Good. You do and *I'*ll stone you."

He marched off then, leaving me incensed. I longed to whip
out a gun and shoot *him* in the skull. It was a good thing Michael

kept his six-shooter safely packed away. Laura observed my anger and smiled.

"Jason does have a way of riling people when he's under pressure," she remarked, "but he's much nicer once we're really under way. Don't let it get to you, love. He *did* pay you a lovely compliment."

"That was a compliment?"

"They'd get their money's worth if you didn't do anything but stand out in front of the footlights. He knows it. He admitted it. Even if you couldn't act, you'd still be an asset to the company."

"If I'm going to *do* this, I want to do it well."

"And you will, love. Just remember what Ollie taught you."

"Did I hear my name?" Ollie inquired, joining us in the wings.

She was still wearing the plum velvet gown and glittery paste diamonds she wore in Act One as Lord Roderick's imperious mother. A paste tiara was affixed atop her blazing red coiffure. Her sagging old face was vividly painted, rouge covering the withered cheeks, heavy mauve shadow on the paper-thin lids.

"I've only a moment," she said. "I have to change. I go on again right after Billy abducts you, and that black lace ball gown is hell to get into. You look sublime, duckie."

"I feel wretched."

"Perfectly natural," she informed me in a crisp voice. "I'd be worried if you *weren't* nervous. You were excellent last night at dress rehearsal, just a mite too self-effacing. Make them *aware* of you, duckie. Presence! That's the key."

"Presence," I said.

"Remember to speak in a natural voice but loud enough for them to hear you in the last row of the balcony. Pro*ject* your voice. Fascinate them, duckie. Make them love you."

"That should be a snap," I said.

Ollie chuckled and gently patted my arm. "And remember, duckie, it's only a silly melodrama in a backwater town, and no one out there is going to know if you're good or not. These simpletons actually believe *Carmelita* can act, and we all know she's a deplorable ham. Give it your best, duckie. You're going to dazzle them."

She gave me a tight hug and then moved off toward the dressing rooms. The crew had finished setting everything up, and the backdrop was in place. Beyond the mothy old purple velvet curtain with its tarnished gold fringe the audience had returned to their seats and were making restless noises. Jackson came over to us, looked me up and down with stern eyes and then nodded his approval. Removing the cigar from his mouth, he told me I was going to be fine, just fine.

"Thank you, Jackson," I said.

"Carmelita would like to see you fall flat on your ass."

"I know."

"Disappoint her," he ordered.

"I—I'll try."

Billy joined us then, looking very unlike Billy in dark makeup, black wig and sinister black mustache, but his brown eyes were as merry as ever. A grin spread on his lips as he looked me over.

"Hey, you look scrumptious in that gown. Why didn't I notice last night?"

"You weren't noticing much of anything last night," Laura told him. "You were preoccupied with your belles."

"Charmin' lasses, but I'd throw 'em all over for you, Dana. Why don't you and I forget this wretched play and slip off and make mad, passionate love?"

"If I believed for one minute you were serious I'd actually take you up on that offer."

"My irresistible charm has finally gotten to you?"

"I'm terrified," I confessed.

"No need to be, poppet. I'll be there to help you out. Three minutes before curtain. I'd better take my place."

He sauntered blithely across the stage in his handsome formal wear and the long, swirling black cape lined with white satin, gave us a wave and stepped behind one of the four fake marble columns. They were turning down the lamps out in front. The audience grew quiet. Jackson gave a curt nod. One of the stage crew stepped over to the huge ropes, ready to lift the curtain. I froze. Laura gave my hand a tight squeeze. This is it, I told myself. I can't remember a single line. I can't *move*. I'll never be able to do it. The man began to pull the ropes. The curtain slowly raised with a creaking rumble. The stage extended out in a semicircle, footlights burning brightly, revealing the backdrop and the huge columns and Billy crouching behind one of them. Laura let go of my hand.

"Good luck, love," she whispered.

I couldn't move. She gave me a little shove. I walked onto the stage and I was aware of the flickering footlights and a large moth fluttering around one of them and the yawning blackness beyond filled with small, blurry moons, faces, people staring. I stopped. I was going to faint. I could feel the force of hundreds and hundreds of eyes on me and I heard whispers. Out of the corner of my eye I saw the moth singe itself against the hot glass and drop. Time stood still. You can't let them down, I told myself. You can't. You're not Dana. You're Cora, pure and virginal, and you're in the antechamber of your father's castle. Move your *ass*. You're Cora. My heart was pounding, but I moved slowly past the first column, pure and virginal, just back from the convent. Billy stepped out from behind the second column, long cape swirling, and I managed to look surprised.

"Who—who are you?" I inquired.

Pro*ject* your voice. Make them *aware* of you.

"Are you one of my father's friends?" Cora asked.

Her voice was mildly curious, and it could be heard in the last row of the balcony. Presence. Presence. A curious transformation came over me. I could feel the magic happening. I *was* Cora. Fear melted. Confidence came. Billy stroked his waxed black mustache and gave a deep chuckle.

"I'd hardly say that, my beauty," he rumbled.

Cora stepped back, vaguely alarmed by his manner. She was as innocent as a lamb and as naive as they came, but she sensed something evil in this man and trembled slightly. Hugh moved closer, stroking his mustache again. The audience hissed.

"I—I'd better join the others," Cora said tremulously.

"Not just yet, my little beauty. You and I have an engagement."

He told me who he was and what he planned to do and I told him he was mad, told him he would never get away with it, and Dana was entirely forgotten and I was Cora, feeling what she felt, reacting as she would react, and Billy grabbed my wrist and he was the evil Hugh and I cried out and tried to pull away and it was going beautifully and I felt cloth slipping, sliding and my left breast was suddenly exposed, full and firm and bathed with light, the nipple extended like a small pink rosebud. I heard gasps from the audience. Billy turned pale beneath his makeup. I thought *he* was going to faint. There were more gasps and a titter of laughter and, from the back of the house, a loud whistle.

I looked at the audience, shook my head and calmly tucked my breast back into my bodice. Silence. Then thunderous applause filled the theater.

"You've got 'em, poppet," Billy whispered. "From here on out, they're in the palm of your hand."

The applause died down at last and Cora struggled and Hugh overpowered her and she pleaded and Bartholomew came rushing onstage as Lord Roderick's butler and shouted, "Unhand her, you villain!" and Hugh shoved Cora aside and delivered a powerful blow to the butler's jaw and the butler reeled and almost fell, then recovered and delivered a blow himself. Cora leaned against one of the columns breathing heavily as the two men fought. The audience seemed to be more interested in her breathing than in the fight. The butler was finally felled with a vicious kick and Cora cried out and tried to flee and Hugh caught her and slapped a palm over her mouth and drug her off the stage.

"Good *show*!" Michael whispered, grinning broadly.

He was standing in the wings with Laura and Jackson and Jason and Carmelita and a horrified Dulcie. He gave me a quick kiss on the cheek and then hurried out onstage to discover his fallen butler and sound the alarm. Carmelita was glaring daggers at me. She started to say something, but Jason gave her a warning look. She was wearing peach satin now, false diamonds in her hair and around her throat. She fumed and drew herself up and then moved grandly out onstage to ask her fiancé what all the commotion was about. Jason gave me a long, thoughtful look but made no comment. Billy gave a sigh of relief and wiped his brow, than hugged me so tightly I thought my ribs would crack. Dulcie and Laura led me away to the dressing room, Dulcie clucking and fussing and telling me she'd have to take at least three more tucks in the bodice.

I removed the ball gown and stood in my petticoat while Dulcie made the necessary tucks and Laura changed for her next scene. I felt a curious sense of triumph. I had done it, I had become Cora, and there had been an accident and I hadn't fallen to pieces, I had handled myself with aplomb. The audience hadn't turned on me, they had been on my side, and I had felt their approval pouring over the footlights along with the thundering applause. I could do it. I could act. Ollie rushed in to congratulate me and said Carmelita was in a rage and vowing to get me, and Dulcie helped me back into the ball gown, and Ollie hurried back to the wings for her next scene.

"I wonder how Carmelita intends to 'get' me?" I inquired.

"The last act," Laura said, "the final scene when you have been rescued and you and Angela are in the antechamber and you give your little speech telling her all your reasons for deciding to return to the convent. She plans to upstage you, love. She'll pull every trick in the book."

"Oh?"

"She'll do everything she can to distract the audience. They'll be watching *her* and won't hear a word you say."

"We'll see," I said grimly.

The audience applauded when the curtain rose on Act Three to find me wringing my hands and pacing up and down in a basement room in Hugh Northcliff's London house. They hissed and booed when Hugh came in with a tray of food which I refused. Hugh stroked his mustache and leered and I pleaded with him to let me go and he laughed and leered some more and told me I was a tasty little beauty, he just might have himself a bonus. I turned pale, realizing what he meant to do. I told him about the convent and my life there and told him there was good in everyone and there must be good in him too and he must give up his evil ways and not do this. He laughed and lunged at me and said the world was wicked and I might as well stop prattling and give in. He caught me up in his arms, swung me around and kissed me and I pounded on his chest with my fists and he carried me over to the single cot and threw me down and loomed over me and the basement door burst open and Lord Roderick came charging in with a pistol and Hugh tried to wrest it away from him and it went off and Hugh crumpled to the floor with a dramatic swirling of his cape. Lord Roderick folded me to him and I sobbed and he led me out the door and into the wings.

"Fantastic, sugar," Michael said. "Real tears, too. You're a natural. I knew you could do it."

"It isn't over yet," I said dryly, thinking of Carmelita.

Onstage the wicked Hugh writhed on the floor and finally managed to stand up just as Lorena came into the basement, a triumphant smile on her rouged lips and the Manners-Croft rubies around her throat. She informed him that Sir Roderick had given her the rubies in return for telling him the whereabouts of his daughter and said she planned to live a life of luxurious sin on the Continent. Hugh staggered and spluttered, calling her a treacherous hussy. Lorena laughed and then widened her eyes in horror as Hugh pulled a dagger out and stumbled toward her. She screamed and died quite dramatically and Hugh stood over her and reeled back and forth and then fell to the floor beside her as the curtain came creaking down.

Laura and Hugh hied themselves offstage, and the cot and tray of food were quickly removed and the backdrop yanked up and the antechamber backdrop pulled down. Michael and I stepped aside as a crewman hurried past us with one of the huge columns under his arm. The scene was changed in less than three minutes, and Michael hurried off to change into his elegant smoking jacket and Carmelita joined me in the wings, wearing a gray silk morning gown trimmed with blue velvet ribbons.

"You treacherous slut!" she whispered. "I saw what you did. You did it deliberately! No pie-faced little upstart is going to steal a play from *me*, I can assure you. I'm going to destroy you."

"Indeed?"

"Just you watch!"

The curtain came up and Ollie and Bartholomew strolled onstage and the butler told Lord Roderick's mother that the villain and his paramour were dead and the rubies reclaimed and Cora safely returned, shaken but unharmed. Lord Roderick's mother sniffed her smelling salts and said Thank God and added that she assumed the wedding would still take place that afternoon, she must tell everyone to proceed with their plans. Carmelita and I moved onstage, her arm around me, she very grand, me dejected and downcast but smiling bravely. My grandmother seized my hands and told me I must forget this terrible nightmare and get on with my life. I nodded. She kissed my cheek, and she and the butler left. Angela removed her arm from around my waist and moved around to face me.

"She's right, you know," she said. "You must forget all this horror."

"I—I'll never be able to forget it. Life—life outside the convent is wicked and . . ."

I continued my noble speech and Carmelita listened attentively and gradually moved upstage so that I would be forced to turn my back to the audience if I continued addressing her directly. I didn't turn. I paused, leaving her standing upstage and at a loss. Silence. I touched the spray of white flowers fastened in my hair and gazed pensively into space, thinking about the convent and the joys of solitude. Carmelita looked like an absolute fool.

"You—you had something else to say?" she inquired.

"When you are prepared to listen, dear Angela."

She moved back down and stood in front of me, and I went on with my speech. She fussed with the ribbons on her gown. She brushed her skirt. She spotted a bit of lint on her sleeve and plucked it away. She managed to distract the audience quite successfully. They were watching her instead of listening to me. A smug little smile played on her lips as I spoke the final words of my speech. Very well, you bitch, I thought. Two can play this game. I maintained a pure and noble stance, but I was steaming inside.

"You may be right, child," Carmelita declared, launching into *her* speech. "The world is cruel—I myself have suffered, I have suffered more than anyone could possibly know, and . . ."

I wandered over to one of the columns and leaned against it. I arched my back slightly and my bosom rose and my bodice slipped precariously low. I made a surprised "O" with my mouth and adjusted the bodice and kept fooling with it, trying to straighten it and contain my breasts, and there wasn't a person in the theater who heard a word Carmelita was saying. She finished her speech, cheeks burning a bright pink with anger, and Lord Roderick came onstage in his splendid gray velvet smoking jacket. I told him of my decision to go back to the convent. He took my hands. He looked into my eyes. He folded me to him.

"You little minx," he whispered. "Where did you learn such tricks? Carmelita is going to explode the minute the curtain's down."

"Let her," I whispered back.

"I have had my revenge," he declaimed. "I have defeated my archenemy and I have saved the Manners-Croft rubies, but, alas, I have lost the dearest thing in my life—my beloved daughter."

"You haven't lost me, Father. You have gained an advocate in Heaven. And you have Angela."

"Ah, yes—my darling Angela."

He extended his hand. Angela came to him and clasped it.

"I will be married to Angela," he declared, "and my daughter will be married to Christ."

"It is a very happy ending," I said.

Michael curled one arm around Carmelita's waist and the other around mine, and we both looked up at him with beatific expressions as the curtain came slowly down. Carmelita tore free, her cheeks a vivid pink, her blue eyes flashing venomously. Michael restrained her.

"Curtain calls," he reminded her.

Billy and Laura and Ollie and Bartholomew joined us onstage, and we stood together in a line and the curtain came up. The applause was rousing. Each of us stepped forward to receive individual acknowledgment—first Bartholomew and then Ollie, then Laura, then Billy—and when I stepped forward the applause was absolutely deafening. I bowed, careful with my décolletage. The applause grew even louder. The theater seemed to shake with it. There were several cheers and a number of whistles. I moved back into line. Carmelita's face was white. Michael took his bow, and then the leading lady swept grandly to the footlights and made a regal curtsey. The applause was moderate. She nodded, waiting for more. People began to leave their seats. Carmelita rejoined the line, and the curtain came down.

"*You bitch!*" she shrieked.

"Now hold on—" Ollie began.

"Let me at her!"

She whirled toward me. Billy and Michael tried to restrain her, but Carmelita shook them off, blue eyes ablaze. I stood my ground, as calm as could be in the face of her fury. She was a bully, I sensed, and I knew all about bullies. I had learned about them in the swamps. If you ever let them intimidate you, if you ever let them get the upper hand, they would never leave you alone. You had to deal with them from a position of strength.

"No one upstages Carmelita Herring! Do you hear me? *No one!* You wretched little whore! You come from nowhere and try to usurp me, try to steal my play and steal my applause— you're not getting away with it! You couldn't act your way out of a gunnysack, and those teats you're so fond of displaying aren't going to make you a star, either! I don't know what Jason had in mind hiring you in the first place, but as of now you're *finished* in this company!"

She hauled off and slapped me across the face as hard as she could. Ollie and Laura cried out. Michael shouted. I stood very, very still, my cheek burning. Carmelita smirked, very pleased with herself. Jason and Jackson hurried toward us. I tightened my right hand into a fist and drove it into her stomach with all the power I could muster, knocking the breath out of her. She grunted and her eyes flew wide open and she doubled over. As she did so, I clipped her on the jaw and sent her sprawling. She landed on her backside, skirts atumble, coiffure spilling down, her eyes glazed now. I placed my hands on my hips and looked down at her with cool disdain.

"Don't fuck with me, sister," I said, and Bartholomew almost fainted from shock. "You might push other people around, but you're out of your league with me. You're an aging, empty-headed trollop who gives new meaning to the word affectation, and if you know what's good for you you'll stay out of my way. Next time you pull something like you pulled tonight I'll not only upstage you, I'll tear your hair out by the roots as well."

"Bravo!" Billy shouted.

Laura, Ollie and Michael applauded. Bartholomew was still recovering from shock. Jackson looked at me with an expression of admiration on his battered, bulldog face. Jason had no expression at all. He reached down for Carmelita's hand and pulled her to her feet. She was dazed, her blond pompadour spilling into her eyes. She sobbed hysterically. Jason led her offstage and toward her dressing room. Everyone was looking at me.

"Are you all right, Dana?" Laura asked.

"I'm fine," I said. "I suppose he'll fire me now."

"Oh no he won't," Jackson told me.

"You *bet* he won't," Billy exclaimed. "If he even thinks of it, the rest of us will mutiny."

"We certainly shall," Ollie declared. "That dreadful creature has had it coming for a long time. You were grand, duckie. I doubt *seriously* she'll fuck with you again."

Bartholomew gulped and turned pink. Billy pounded him on the back. Michael grinned. Laura slipped her arm around my waist and led me toward our dressing room. The stage crew, every last one of them, applauded me lustily as we passed through the wings. By felling the detested and demanding leading lady, I had won their approval, their loyalty as well. I felt little triumph. I felt, instead, shame that all my fine polish had melted away and I had become the little wildcat of the swamps again.

Jason had taken the hotel dining room for the evening and planned a lavish party for the company—lavish for Jason, Laura noted wryly. Everyone looked forward to it, and I had been looking forward to it, too, but now, after all that had happened, I was less than enthusiastic. As we changed, I told Laura that I would just go on up to my room and skip the party. Stage makeup removed, hair brushed to a gleaming blue-black gloss, Laura slipped into a white taffeta gown with blue and purple stripes, spreading the full skirt out over her petticoats. I fastened it in back for her while she adjusted the full puffed sleeves.

"You can't skip the party, love. You're the heroine of the evening."

"I—I'm really not up to it," I said.

"Nonsense. Carmelita won't be there—I doubt she'll show her face again until curtain time tomorrow night, and she'll probably be sporting a tremendous bruise."

"It's not that. It's—I'm ashamed," I confessed. "I don't ordinarily use that—that kind on language, and I rarely use my fists. Everyone—they must think I'm—"

"They think you're marvelous," Laura assured me. She smiled and took my hand, squeezing it. "This is the theater, love. High color and high drama are the norm. Everyone's liked you from the very beginning, but tonight you proved you're one of *us*. It's going to be a festive party."

"I don't feel very festive."

"Nonsense. You'll come and you'll drink some champagne—*cheap* champagne, if I know Jason—and you'll feel much better. You look glorious in turquoise, love. Another Corinne creation?"

I nodded, adjusting the low-cut bodice.

"You're going to dazzle everyone. Ready?"

"I suppose. Laura, I would really much rather just skip the party and go on up to my room."

"Not a chance, love. Come along. We'll be late."

The hotel, large and ramshackle, was on the edge of town, a large verandah surrounding it. Lights glowed in several windows, despite the late hour, while from the dining room sounds of great merriment drifted out into the night. The party was apparently already in full swing, I thought as Laura and I climbed up the creaking wooden steps to the verandah. I was still feeling a little apprehensive as we passed through the shabby but comfortable lobby, and then we went into the dining room and I was immediately surrounded. Ollie gave me a welcoming hug. Billy thrust a champagne glass into my hand. Bartholomew waved from the table where he was sitting with Theodore. Theodore had his own chair, and he contentedly lapped champagne from his own glass.

"You're right, duckie," Ollie informed Laura. "It *is* cheap champagne, but deliciously bubbly just the same."

She was wearing deep opal velvet, dangling jet earrings and a jet necklace, her blazing curls caught atop her head with a black velvet bow. How outrageous she looked, how theatrical, and how very endearing she was. She told me I had surpassed her fondest hopes. I had been positively wonderful, had such amazing presence. I had dominated the stage, she assured me. A natural-born actress, no question about it. She gave me another hug, clearly already a bit the worse for champagne.

The room was quite crowded. All the stage crew were here, several of them with local girls, and Billy's trio of belles fluttered around him, feeling wonderfully wicked to be in such fast company, no doubt. Dulcie was at the buffet table, helping herself to oysters and boiled shrimp and green salad. Our leading man was beside her, looking rugged in his battered tan kidskin jacket and a red bandanna. They were both laughing, and Dulcie gave him a playful nudge. He turned and saw me and, brushing a sun-streaked golden-brown lock from his brow, sauntered over to wrap his big arms around me and squeeze.

"Hello, beloved daughter," he drawled. "How're you feelin'?"

"I think you just broke a rib," I told him.

He grinned and hugged me again, even tighter this time, then looped an arm around my shoulders, his clear gray eyes full of brotherly affection. Michael Prichard was indeed like a brother already, and I felt wonderfully secure with him. His breezy charm and casual manner and lazy drawl had made him an immediate success with everyone in the company, and his potent virility and rough but wholesome good looks had caused a stir in the hearts of two of the women. Carmelita had made immediate advances but had been politely rebuffed. Laura still pretended to find him an uncivilized lummox, but I suspected she was weakening. Michael was determined to win her over.

"We'd better get you some food before Dulcie eats it all," he said. "You like oysters?"

"I love them."

"By the way, that was quite an impressive one-two you delivered back there onstage. I could have used you back when I was fighting Comanches. Where'd you learn to punch like that?"

"I grew up in a tough neighborhood," I replied blithely. "Did you really fight Comanches?"

"Plenty of times. Rather face a whole band of 'em than our Carmelita when she's riled. You were terrific, sugar. I'd have knocked her flat myself if I weren't such a gentleman."

Dulcie gave me a hug, too, and told me the oysters were wonderful and said she had never dressed a lovelier Cora and planned to swathe me in honey-gold velvet and golden-brown fox fur for *Lena Marlow*, and Jason would cough up the money for the costume or lose himself the best wardrobe woman in the South. She intended to spring the news on him this very night.

"If he ever gets his ass down here to the party," she added, spearing another oyster. "He's still upstairs, nursing our leading lady. I hear you gave her a good clobbering—I'd have paid good money to see that."

"It was something to see," Michael assured her.

"I was busy hanging up costumes—as usual. Try some of the shrimp, Dana. They're marvelously tasty."

"You mean you've left some?" Michael inquired.

"Get out of here, cowboy. I'm taking none of your lip."

Michael filled a plate for me and led me toward Bartholomew's table.

"Your girlfriend's still giving me the cold shoulder," he said with mock sadness. "Tell me the truth, sugar—what is it about me she detests so much?"

"You're an actor," I replied.

"I'm an *actor*? That's it?"

"Laura swears she'll never get involved with another actor. One broke her heart a long time ago."

"Hmmm," he mused. "Looks like I'm going to have to work on that prejudice she has against actors. We're not all heartbreakers."

"No?"

"Some of us are pretty nice guys."

"Convince Laura of that."

"I'm trying," he said. "I'm trying."

Bartholomew stood up and executed an elegant bow and then wrapped his arms around me and informed me that I had made them all proud. Theodore barked and wagged his tail. I said I was pleased to see Theodore was feeling better now. Bartholomew beamed. So did Theodore. Ollie joined us, waving another glass of champagne, and Billy came over, followed by his three giggling admirers. Laura sat down beside me, ignoring Michael, who was leaning over my chair. A scowling Jackson sauntered over and grumbled that this bash was costing a mint, then looked at me and brushed the lapels of his yellow and brown checked jacket, his scowl deepening. Dulcie, a heavily laden plate in her hand, gave him a friendly nudge.

"Cheer up, Jackson. We were a smash. They *loved* the costumes."

"They loved our ingenue," he growled. "Never heard such applause. For a minute there I thought the rafters were gonna cave in."

Billy grabbed a bottle and jauntily filled every glass that wasn't already full, then lifted his own. "To Dana!" he cried. "To Dana!" they echoed, and I felt a great rush of emotion sweep over me. Laura squeezed my hand. Theodore licked my cheek. Michael curled his arm around my shoulders again. I was one of them. I was accepted. I was part of the family. Tears glistened in my eyes as Jackson twisted his ugly mouth into a grin and Dulcie and Ollie applauded and Billy looped an arm around the neck of one of his belles and gave a rousing cheer. I felt wanted. I felt loved. For the first time in my life I felt I truly belonged. I had been an outsider in Clem's home, was there on sufferance because of Ma, and I had been an outsider in New Orleans, too, would never have been accepted, as Charles had so clearly pointed out. Tears brimmed over my lashes and trailed down my cheeks.

"Thank you," I whispered.

Champagne continued to flow profusely, and Andy and Joe and Frank, three of the stage crew, brought out banjo, accordion and drums, respectively, and began to play loud and lively music, and tables were pushed back to make a dance floor. Ollie doing a tipsy polka with Billy was a sight indeed, but no more remarkable than Dulcie waltzing with a stiff and dignified Bartholomew. I danced with all the men except those playing and had another glass of champagne and smiled when Michael pulled a protesting Laura onto the floor. Finally, well after midnight, I slipped out through the French windows and strolled along the verandah, pausing after a while to savor the beauty of the night.

Pine trees surrounded the yard in back of the hotel, and I could smell the sharp tang of pine needles. A creek rushed along behind the trees, and I heard the gurgle of water and the deep croak of frogs and smelled mud and moss. Thin scraps of ash-gray cloud drifted across the surface of the moon and made shifting patterns of moonlight and shadow below. A cricket rasped nearby, and fireflies floated in the shrubbery, pale gold lights glimmering on and off. Wispy tendrils of night mist were beginning to rise from the ground and swirl like benign ghosts. Although my tears had long since ceased, my heart was still swollen with emotion. I felt warm elation still, but there was sadness as well. I stood at the railing, watching the shifting shadows and slowly curling mist and hearing the throaty croak of frogs and the muted sound of music coming from the dining room on the other side of the hotel.

I thought of New Orleans and Delia and Julian . . . and Charles. Almost a month had passed since I slipped away from the house in the middle of the night and made my way to the docks. There would have been a grand funeral for Raoul, everyone in mourning, and I doubted seriously that the rest of the family would ever know the true story behind his death. Charles would keep that to himself, even as he blamed me for it. He would be working night and day rebuilding Etienne's, borrowing money against the cotton crop to finance it, robbing the east wing of its treasures to replace those destroyed in the fire. The family would survive. Charles would see to that. There might be hard times, but he would take all responsibility on his capable shoulders and see them through. I wondered if he ever thought of me. Somehow I doubted it.

Julian would be crushed by my desertion, my ingratitude, but he would finish his book and that would help and one day, perhaps one day soon, he would be able to see that I had done him a favor by leaving. He would see that he could never have married me . . . I would always be touched that he had wanted to do just that. He would see the folly of it and be grateful I had gone, and perhaps he would eventually meet someone who would bring him the happiness he deserved. I missed him. I would always love him in a special way. I missed Delia, too, perhaps most of all. She would have been distressed by my disappearance and my letter, but Delia was very wise, very perceptive, too. She had sensed undercurrents, and in her heart of hearts she would have realized that my going was the best thing for all concerned.

"Why so sad?" Jason asked.

I turned around. He was standing a few feet away, watching me. Lost in thought, I hadn't heard him approaching. I didn't answer at once, and he moved closer, a tall, shadowy figure all sculpted in silver and black. I could tell that he was wearing a neat suit and a flowered waistcoat, but there was no color. His lean face was all sharp planes and angles, the dark eyes looking at me intently.

"I was—thinking about other times," I said quietly.

"New Orleans?"

I nodded, and he continued to look at me. Perhaps it was the silvery semidarkness or perhaps it was the circumstances, but he seemed different, far more relaxed, neither snappish nor indifferent.

"I suppose there was a man," he said.

"There was a man," I told him.

"I figured as much. With a woman as beautiful as you are, there'd have to be a man. He broke your heart, I suppose."

"That—that really isn't any of your business, Mr. Donovan."

"Right. I was out of line. You are very, very, beautiful, you know."

He spoke matter-of-factly in that light, scratchy voice that still managed to be guttural. Such an unusual voice, I thought. Not at all unpleasant. The frogs were still croaking, and the floorboard creaked as Jason moved even nearer. I realized that I had never had a private conversation with him. He had paid very little attention to me since my arrival in Memphis. I wondered why. I had been convinced he didn't like me.

"I finally made it down to the party," he said. "I didn't see you. Billy told me he'd seen you slip out onto the verandah. Thought I'd come looking for you."

"And you have found me," I replied. "I suppose you're going to fire me now."

He shook his head. "Carmelita had it coming. High time someone put her in her place. I've been altogether too lenient with her."

"How is she?" I asked coolly.

"Still ranting and raving when I left her. I had to call in a doctor. He put an ice pack on her jaw and gave her some medicine—hoping it would put her out. I slipped her an extra dose before I came down. I imagine she's sleeping by now."

"I—I don't usually act like that," I said. "I don't usually use words like that, either. She—"

"I saw the whole thing, Dana. You needn't apologize. I didn't come out here to jump you or fire you or dress you down. I came to compliment you on a superlative performance. You were tremendous. Those lessons Ollie and Laura gave you really paid off."

"You—knew about that?"

"From the beginning. I'm always distracted, always in an uproar before we begin a season, but I'm not blind. I peeked into the back parlor one afternoon and watched for a few minutes. I'd already spoken to a friend of mine from New Orleans. He assured me no new theater named the Court had been built, no play called *A Rose for Angelina* had been produced, and no actress named Dana O'Malley had ever appeared on the boards."

I could feel a blush coloring my cheeks. So he had been on to me from the first. That explained why he had been so distant and snappish. But why hadn't he fired me then? I took a deep breath, then asked him. A wry smile curled on his lips.

"I needed an ingenue," he told me, "and I figured you couldn't be much worse than Maisie. Too, there was your remarkable beauty. I figured audiences would forgive you almost anything just for the pleasure of looking at you. You don't need to rely on your beauty, though. You've got a gift. You're the best Cora we've ever had."

"I was terrified."

"You got over it. You recovered yourself quite nicely when you had—uh—when the accident occurred. You won them over completely. Nice bit, that. If I thought we could get by with it, I'd keep it in every night."

"That's very cynical of you, Mr. Donovan. I can promise you I wouldn't go along with such a scandalous plan."

"As it is, we're going to have standing room only tomorrow night. Everyone in the whole county is going to come piling into the theater, hoping to see it happen again."

"It won't," I assured him.

"But *they* don't know that."

The mist was thickening rapidly now, a whole parade of ghosts swirling all around, and it had grown cooler. Jason suggested we rejoin the party. I told him I preferred to go directly to my room, and he said he would escort me. We started walking along the verandah, the floorboards creaking. The cricket had stopped rasping, but the frogs were croaking louder than ever.

"You studied the other parts yet?" he asked.

"I've read all the plays we're to perform. I've already learned my lines. Laura calls me a 'quick study,' whatever that means. You needn't worry, Mr. Donovan. I'll hold up my end."

"What do you think of 'em? The plays, I mean."

"They're—I suppose they're exactly what the public wants," I said.

"Which means you think they're rotten."

"I—I didn't say that, Mr. Donovan, and—why should what I think matter to you? I know nothing whatsoever about drama. I've only read Molière and a little Shakespeare and—"

"Bloody bluestocking," he grumbled.

"Hardly that. I found Molière stilted, and, I might as well confess it, I didn't really understand Shakespeare all that well. I prefer novels."

"An actress who reads books. Just what I need. So tell me, what do you really think of my plays?"

"I think you're a very talented man, Mr. Donovan."

"Jason. I'm your boss, but I don't mind a little familiarity. So I'm a very talented man?"

"Some of the lines are very clever, and some of the scenes—on occasion, they're genuinely touching, but most of the situations are—well, wildly contrived. I have the feeling you could write a *real* play if you really tried."

"Thanks!" he snapped.

"Now are you going to fire me?"

"I'm thinking about it!"

He gripped my elbow and led me into the lobby with its warm

golden glow of lamplights. After the stark black and gray and silver of the night, we seemed to be flooded with color. I saw that his breeches and frock coat were tan, his flowered waistcoat gold, pink and brown. His hair seemed an even richer black, and his eyes were undeniably green, faintly touched with gray. I wondered why it was that that long, slightly twisted nose should make him seem even more attractive. He did indeed look like a pirate with those quirky eyebrows and that wide slash of mouth, yet there was a certain sensitivity as well. For all the bravado and posturing, I sensed a boyish vulnerability about him. Perhaps that was why he maintained such a thorny facade—to protect what was behind it.

The party was still going on, although it was much more subdued now. The trio of musical crewmen were playing a quiet waltz, and through the open dining room doors I could see Laura and Michael waltzing together. Laura looked quite contented, I thought. Ollie was asleep in her chair, tilting precariously, and Theodore was curled up under the table.

"Want to dance?" Jason asked.

"I want to go to my room."

"At least have some champagne with me."

"I'm very tired."

"Spoilsport. Jesus, you're gorgeous in that dress."

I started toward the staircase. He followed me, taking my elbow again as we started up the steps.

"I agree with you," he said.

"About what?"

"I agree that I could write a *real* play if I really tried. I've been toying with an idea for a long time. At first I saw it as just another melodrama, but then I realized the subject deserved serious treatment."

"Why haven't you written it?"

"There's never been a play about miscegenation performed in the South," he replied, "and I could hardly visualize Carmelita playing a beautiful quadroon passing herself off as white."

"Miscegenation is a touchy subject, I'll agree, but if handled delicately, I see no reason why it wouldn't be acceptable. And Carmelita's not the only actress in the world."

"I'm beginning to realize that more and more."

We reached the upper corridor and turned. He released my elbow. My flesh seemed to tingle where his fingers had gripped it. I felt strangely stimulated, but then Jason Donovan was a very interesting and stimulating man. We came to the door of my room and stopped. He looked into my eyes, and his own were full of interest now, full, too, of that familiar male hunger.

"I'm glad we've finally gotten to know each other," he said.

"I enjoyed our talk."

"If—uh—if I seemed a bit cool and distant and—well, snappish before, it's because I'm always under pressure when I'm getting the company on the road again. And—I wasn't sure about you."

"You're sure about me now?"

"You're a natural-born actress. I'm proud to have you with us."

"Thank you, Mr. Don—"

"Jason."

"Thank you. I hope to be much better than I was tonight."

"You will be. You've got the magic already."

I made no reply. There was a long silence. He seemed very reluctant to leave me, seemed hesitant, too, as though he wanted to say something and couldn't decide quite how to go about it.

"Uh—about that man in New Orleans," he began.

"What about him?"

"I—uh—I'd like to help you forget him."

There it came. Inevitable, I supposed. Jason Donovan was an intriguing and attractive man, but he was just like all the others.

"That's very kind of you, I'm sure," I said, "but—I think not. I've heard all about you and your women, Mr. Donovan, and I'm not at all interested in becoming another of your many, many conquests."

"Damn that Laura! She's been blabbing, hasn't she?"

"She filled me in on things."

"I'm going to strangle the slut!"

"Good night, Mr. Donovan."

"Dana—"

I opened the door and stepped inside, and Jason looked startled as I closed the door in his face. I turned the lock and sighed. I wasn't in the least upset, nor was I offended. At least he knows I'm alive now, I thought. My experience with Charles stood me in good stead. I had been hurt once, badly, and I still hadn't recovered from it. I wasn't about to let it happen again. But Jason Donovan was indeed an intriguing and devilishly attractive man, and I was only human. I had been tempted. Oh yes . . . I had been tempted.

Chapter Eighteen

How luxurious to wake up in a decent hotel room, to see late morning sunlight streaming through the windows and making warm, silvery pools on a lovely dusty rose and gray rug. This hotel in Savannah was by far the nicest we had been in, as gracious and mellow and elegant as the town itself. Summer was almost upon us now, and Savannah was our last engagement of the season. We had been playing here two weeks, with one week left to go, presenting our entire repertory. How nice it was to remain in one place for such a long time. How nice not having to pack in a rush after the performance, hurry to the train station and spend the rest of the night trying to sleep on lumpy, miserably uncomfortable seats while the train chugged shakily through the darkness. I stretched, savoring the crackle of clean linen sheets and the rustle of a rose satin counterpane. Remembering some of the wretched dumps we had stayed in during past months made my pleasure all the greater.

There was a discreet knock on the door. I glanced at the clock. Was it already ten-thirty? It certainly was. I hurried out of bed and pulled on the ruffled daffodil-yellow silk robe Dulcie had given me, tying the sash securely, and then I opened the door for Freddie. He grinned shyly and wheeled in a cart and began to arrange things on the small round table near the window. He was a charming lad in his late teens, as friendly and efficient as the rest of the staff here. He was a great admirer of mine, I had discovered, and considered me a sophisticated woman of the world, although, in truth, he was actually a few months older than I.

"Are you coming to the theater tonight, Freddie?" I inquired. "We're doing *Sweetheart of the West* again. I wear flowered pink calico and flirt with all the officers in the regiment and prove my real merit when bloodthirsty Indians attack the fort.''

"I'd love to see it," the lad replied, "but there are no tickets available. I already checked."

"There will be two tickets waiting for you at the box office tonight," I told him. "You can bring a girlfriend, but only if you promise to come backstage after the show and tell me what you thought of it."

"I—gee, Miss O'Malley. Thank you."

"Thank *you*, Freddie, for taking such good care of me."

A blush colored the lad's cheeks as he left the room. I smiled to myself as I sat down at the table. A pot of coffee, a rack of toast, strawberry preserves, butter, several crisp curls of bacon and a single pink rose in a slender crystal vase. Freddie always brought a rose. I unfolded the crisp linen napkin, feeling wonderfully spoiled. Jason could well afford to put us up in a hotel like this after the season we'd had, rarely an empty seat in any house we played. He and Laura both claimed our success was largely due to the great notices I had received and the wide circulation of my picture, but I knew they were just being kind. Laura because she *was* kind, Jason because he was still trying to coax me into his bed.

Poor dear, he was having a very hard time of it. I had permitted him to take me to lunch quite frequently and to an occasional midnight supper, and he had been amusing and charming and, invariably, sulky when he failed to get any further. I liked him a great deal and found him wonderfully attractive, but I wasn't about to become romantically involved with so mercurial and temperamental a man as Jason Donovan. Laura claimed I was being terribly unfair to him, assured me he was genuinely smitten. She had never seen him like this before, she declared, he was actually *suffer*ing. Be that as it may, common sense told me to keep him at arm's length, and that was exactly what I had been doing.

Not that I wasn't still tempted.

It would be nice to feel those strong arms around me, to hear that light, scratchy voice murmuring sweet endearments, to have that lean, lanky body warming mine in the middle of the night. It would be very nice indeed. I wasn't immune to his charm and incredible physical magnetism. Far from it. He was a very exciting man. I couldn't deny that I was strongly drawn to him, nor that I wanted the same thing he did, but after being so badly burned I was extremely cautious. Too cautious, perhaps. There had been many sleepless nights and nights of disturbing dreams, but I wasn't ready to risk being hurt again. Our frustrated manager and playwright-in-residence would simply have to find other amusement, and I would continue to go to bed with a good book.

Leisurely finishing my breakfast, I performed my ablutions and brushed my hair and, opening the wardrobe, took out a white muslin frock with narrow yellow and gold stripes. It was certainly warm enough for muslin now in mid-May. It had been an unusually cold winter—I remembered freezing dressing rooms in Columbia, South Carolina, and huddling under blankets on dozens of chilly night trains—but spring had been lush and verdant, and summer promised to be sultry indeed. I had no idea how I was going to spend those summer months. The company would be disbanded after we finished our engagement here, to reassemble in September. I had managed to save quite a lot of my salary, so I had no financial worries. I could do as I pleased. I was smoothing the muslin skirt over my full white petticoats when there was a knock on the door. Laura walked in, looking radiant and windblown in a dark blue frock whose skirt, I noticed, was definitely streaked with grass stains.

"Lovely morning, isn't it?" she said.

"Lovely," I replied. "Your hair's all tumbled. Your cheeks are flushed. You're usually still in *bed* at this hour."

"I've been riding," she informed me.

I arched a brow. "On a *horse*?"

She nodded. "Michael pulled me out of bed at the crack of dawn and took me to the stables. I protested vehemently, of course, but there was no reasoning with him. Next thing I knew, I found myself mounted atop this gigantic beast and we were galloping through the park. I'd never been on a horse before, and I was *terri*fied, love."

"Judging from your skirt, it looks as though you took a spill."

"I was just getting the hang of it when the beast suddenly *bolted*. Michael yelled and tried to catch up and suddenly I was flying in the air. I landed behind a clump of bushes. The ground was soft and grassy and I wasn't hurt, but I was shaken up, love, I promise you. Any coffee left?"

"I think there's still some in the pot."

Laura poured herself a cup of coffee and stood there with a thoughtful look in her eyes.

"Michael was ever so concerned," she told me. "He pulled me into his arms and checked all over for broken bones and murmured soothing words and stroked my hair. He was very thorough when he checked for broken bones," she added. "We *were* behind the bushes, and—well—"

"Laura, you're outrageous!"

"It was divine, love. Michael is a remarkable lover—quite the best I've ever had."

"I thought you vowed you'd never get involved with another actor," I said.

"Oh, I'm not *emotionally* involved," she protested, "but—well, when the bonbon is right there beside your plate, why pass it up?"

"Michael is a bonbon?"

"Absolutely, love. I'm not ready for the main course—I've made that perfectly clear—but I see no reason to forgo the delight."

Laura sipped her coffee and smiled, looking gloriously content. I wished I could be as carefree and cavalier as she was about such matters. Life would be much easier—and Jason would be happier, too. I stepped over to the mirror for a final inspection of my hair, brushing a heavy honey-blond wave from my temple and sighing, thinking of Jason again. He had been in Atlanta on "company business" for the past ten days. I missed him far more than I cared to admit. Laura set her coffee cup down.

"You might take a leaf from my book, love," she said.

"Oh?"

"Charles Etienne hurt you very badly, Dana. You've been nursing that hurt all these months—don't try to deny it, love. That lost, pained look has been in your eyes all along, even at your brightest, even when you smile."

"I was hurt, yes, but—"

"The best way to get over a man is to get *another* man," she told me, "and a perfectly marvelous man is waiting in the wings."

"Oh?"

"Don't be coy, love. Jason's mad for you, and you're attracted to him, too. He's a rogue—I won't deny that—but he's handsome and intelligent and amusing and, I hear, superb in the sack. I'm not saying you should marry him, love. I'm just saying you should—well, treat yourself to a bonbon.''

I gave her a look. Laura smiled.

''I'm just thinking of your welfare, love,'' she said pleasantly. ''All that reading can't be good for you. Jason's been pining for you ever since you joined the company. He hasn't even *looked* at another woman, and Lord knows they've been throwing themselves at him.''

''I—I wonder when he'll be back from Atlanta.'' I said casually.

''No one knows. No one knows why he *went* in the first place. It's a mystery to Jackson—probably something to do with that play he's been writing. He's always writing a new play, hoping the National in Atlanta will mount it. No disrespect to my dear cousin, but I seriously doubt we'll ever play Atlanta. The National has very high standards, and thundering melodrama is not their cup of tea. We're doomed to tour the sticks, I fear.''

''Savannah is hardly the sticks,'' I pointed out.

''It's not Atlanta, love. It's not New Orleans, either. I'm not complaining, mind you. We've done wonderfully well this season. No thanks to our leading lady, I might add.''

Poor Carmelita. She had done her best to have Jason fire me, and when he refused, she grew more and more frustrated and discontent. Instead of hitting the bottle, our leading lady began hitting the chocolates, adding a steadily mounting poundage to a figure hardly sylphlike to begin with. Dulcie had been forced to make constant alterations, complaining vociferously all the while. ''I no longer dress her,'' she claimed. ''Now I up*holster* her!'' On more than one occasion there had been loud ''Moos!'' in the audience when Carmelita stepped onstage, and only last week here in Savannah one journalist had written an article declaring it was high time Donovan's leading lady be put out to pasture.

''She's undoubtedly in her room right now, stuffing more chocolates,'' Laura continued. ''She's going back to Biloxi as soon as we close here, and Jason isn't about to sign her up for next season.''

''I wonder what she'll do.''

''She can always get a job as a roadblock.''

''That's very unkind, Laura. I feel sorry for her.''

"You shouldn't, love. It all started that first night when you decked her—she blames you for everything."

"I—I never wanted to supplant her. I never tried."

"No, but you *did*, love. This is the first time in the history of the company that the ingenue has received twice the attention—and three times the adulation—as the leading lady."

"I can't help it if they like me."

"True. You can't help being absolutely gorgeous and marvelously gifted. If I had a competitive bone in my body, I'd hate you myself, you hussy. Like it or not, love, you're the star of the company."

"Nonsense. I'm still billed below Michael and Carmelita and Billy."

"And above *me*," she pointed out. "Jason doesn't want you to get a swollen head. That's the only reason you haven't received top billing. You've certainly received the lion's share of attention from the gentlemen of the press—and that bloody picture keeps right on selling."

I had to smile. Several months ago, when we were performing *Lena Marlow* in Montgomery, Alabama, a very gifted young artist had drawn sketches of everyone in the company. Jason had bought reproduction rights from the artist, and the picture of me in the sumptuous and low-cut fox-trimmed gold satin had been immensely popular. Newspapers used it frequently, and copies of it were hawked in theater lobbies during intermission along with pictures of the rest of the company. Laura was forever teasing me because my picture sold twice as many as all the others put together. Over the months, I must have signed hundreds of them for the gushing teenage girls and would-be swains who, after every performance, were invariably waiting at the stage door.

"It's a very flattering picture," I observed.

"It doesn't even begin to do you justice," Laura said kindly, and then she gave me a hug. "I'm so pleased, love. I knew the minute I laid eyes on you, you had something special. It's been a great eight months, hasn't it?"

"Just great," I replied dryly. "Wretched accommodations. Inedible food. Nights spent waiting in squalid railroad stations. Freezing cold dressing rooms. Backstage squabbles. Forging ahead through thick or thin—mostly thin."

"Adulation. Admiration. Applause. Stage Door Johnnies

flooding your dressing room with roses. Ardent fans clamoring for your autograph. Newspaper articles extolling your beauty and skill. You've loved every minute of it.''

"I've loved every minute of it," I agreed.

Laura smiled and brushed her grass-soiled skirt. "I really must get back to my room. Michael's taking me to lunch, and I have to bathe and change and see if I can do something with this hair. Care to join us?"

I shook my head. "I'm going to the bookstore."

"It figures," she said. "Think about what I said, love. You *deserve* a bonbon."

There were several people in the lobby as I made my way down the gracefully curving staircase. Two well-dressed matrons were sitting on one of the red velvet sofas, exchanging bits of gossip, and an attractive older couple were checking out at the mahogany front desk. Rubber tree plants stood in brass urns, and a rather worn red and gray oriental carpet covered the floor. As I reached the foot of the stairs, two teenage girls swooped toward me, giggling nervously and holding out pictures for me to sign. I did so graciously, chatting with them a few moments before moving on. It still amazed me that anyone would want my signature, that anyone would think me glamorous or exceptional. It wasn't all that long ago that I had been wearing rags and feeding chickens in the swamp.

Wavery sunlight streamed down from a pale blue-gray sky as I strolled slowly toward the bookstore I had seen earlier but, until now, had not had an opportunity to visit. Savannah was a lovely, tree-shaded town with mellow, slightly weathered old buildings and a genteel, leisurely atmosphere. No hustle and bustle here, I thought, but a great deal of charm. Carriages moved slowly down the street, horse hooves clopping, and the people I passed on the sidewalk seemed to have all the time in the world. Several of them recognized me and gave me shy, friendly smiles. Actresses might be considered exotic, immoral creatures little better than prostitutes by some, but that wasn't the case here in Savannah. The good folk here had given us a very warm reception, packing the theater each performance and treating us like honored guests in their town.

Flowers grew in neat beds in front of Gittman's Book Shop, and white wooden steps led up to a shady porch where tables of dusty bargain books invited browsing. It had obviously been a small private home at one time, I reflected, pushing open the front door. A bell tinkled pleasantly overhead. I found myself in a large, sunny room filled with book-laden tables and shelves, colorful rag rugs on the floor and an abundance of potted plants giving the place a homey, welcoming air. A plump gray cat drowsed atop a huge leather-bound dictionary, basking in a ray of sunlight. There was a wonderful selection of new novels, I noticed, many of them imported from England and France, and I was delighted to discover a new Balzac and a gothic novel by Mrs. Ann Radcliffe I had not read.

"The Radcliffe's frightfully spooky," a plump, rosy-cheeked woman informed me, entering from a back room. "I read it when I was a girl—a *number* of years ago—and I couldn't sleep without a night candle for weeks. There's a scene in the grave-yard that'll curl your hair. Hi, honey, I'm Sally Gittman. I see you have picked up the new Balzac, too. I don't read French myself, but I understand from some of my customers that this one's a scorcher. Old Lady Marceau said it jolted her right out of her rocking chair—she bought three more copies to give to friends."

She laughed and gentle nudged the cat off the dictionary. She had bright, intelligent brown eyes, a small pink mouth and shiny blue-black hair pulled into a neat bun in back. She wore a fresh gray cotton frock and a white organdy apron and looked efficient, industrious and slightly self-satisfied, the kind of woman who would belong to several clubs and dominate them all with jovial tyranny. Although her manner was a bit officious, she was warm and friendly and very likable.

"Balzac can be quite racy," I said, "but he's always interesting."

"Old Lady Marceau certainly thought so. Can't wait until they translate it into English. Enjoying your stay in Savannah, honey?"

"Very much," I replied.

"I know who you are, of course. I saw you opening night— last Tuesday as well. I'm president of the Ladies' Theatrical Guild, and we bought a block of tickets. You were enchanting, honey."

"Thank you."

"Much better than the fat lady. Herring? Is that her name? I don't mean to be unkind, honey, but when she waddled onstage in that gray velvet gown, she looked exactly like a hippopota-mus. I had to laugh when that handsome leading man took her in his arms and vowed eternal love.''

"Carmelita is—a very good actress," I said tactfully.

"Not a patch on you, honey. You want those two? I'll just take them over to the desk and let you browse a while longer. I've got the best stock in this part of the South—won't find a better bookstore anywhere around."

"I've not visited a better one," I told her. "You certainly have a—"

I had been eyeing various titles as I spoke, and I cut myself short when I spotted a handsomely bound, boxed two-volume set on one of the tables. I moved to the table, my heart fluttering. *Flora and Fauna of the American South* stood out in bright gilt letters, *Julian Etienne* in smaller letters beneath. My hand trembled as I took one of the volumes out of the box. So he had finished it at last. So it had finally been published. I opened the volume at random, and my breath seemed to catch as I saw the beautiful full-color plate of the flower he had been painting that day in the swamps, fragile pale orange petals delicately flecked with gold and bronze, opening to reveal the deep orange center with the tall stamen projecting like a golden fairy wand. It was a superb reproduction, and I remembered the fussy old printer, Monsieur Delain, and his cluttered, dusty shop. My heart filled with pride, with sadness, too. He had done it, and I had not been there to share his triumph with him.

"Are you all right, Miss O'Malley?" Mrs. Gittman asked. "You've suddenly gone pale."

"I—I'm fine," I said. I closed the volume and slipped it back into its box. "I'll take this, too," I told her.

"My last one," she said, carrying the set over to the desk. "Would you believe I've sold twenty sets—and it's a frightfully expensive item, too. Of course, all the girls bought copies when Monsieur Etienne talked to our Literary Circle. He came here to the store afterwards and signed all the copies—this one's signed, too, by the way."

"He—Monsieur Etienne was here in Savannah?"

"Three weeks ago. Quite the charmer he was, too. He's still a bachelor, you know—surely you've read about him in the papers?—and Mildred Drake made an absolute fool of herself. He was as polite as could be, so suave, so witty, so handsome. I'd have made a play for him myself if I'd-a thought a plump middle-aged widow like myself had a chance.''

''There—there've been articles about him in the papers?''

''Honey, where have you *been* the past two months? The book's caused an absolute sensation, and Julian Etienne is all the rage. He's been traveling all over the South, giving lectures, signing books, being interviewed by all the important papers. The book is already in its fourth printing—this is a first edition, incidentally—and he's wildly in demand everywhere.''

''Who would have thought a book on plants would be so popular,'' I said to myself.

''It's a prestige item,'' Mrs. Gittman explained. ''People buy it because it's the thing to *do*—every cultured home should have one. Very few of them *read* it, of course, but they display it in their parlors to show how *au courant* they are. Actually, it's delightful reading, beautifully written and extremely witty.''

''I'm not surprised.''

''All those newspaper articles have helped, too. Southerners are proud one of their own has penned what the critics are calling a monumental work, and the journalists have taken him up. He's his own best salesman, of course, touring all over, giving his talks, delighting the ladies. I read that he was in Washington last week and the president invited him to the White House. No doubt he charmed the First Lady right out of her leggings.''

''I think it's wonderful. No one deserves success more than Julian.''

''You *know* him?''

''I—met him in New Orleans,'' I said quietly. ''He's a wonderful person. Was—did he seem happy when he was here?''

''Beaming all over the place,'' she told me. ''Proud as punch, he was, but modest all the same. He published the book himself, you know. He told me in confidence that he hadn't even expected to make back his costs, and now it looked as though he was going to make a bloody fortune. The family could certainly use it, he added. Like so many fine old families today, the Etiennes are apparently experiencing financial setbacks.''

I made no reply. Mrs. Gittman added up the price of the books, and I paid her for them. She pulled heavy brown paper off a roll beside the desk and began to wrap them.

''It seems he's not spending *all* his money on the family,'' she added, tying the package with twine. "When he was here, Josie Laidlaw saw him in the hotel dining room with a gorgeous brunette. Her name is Amelia Jameson—Josie's a terrible snoop, she chatted up the desk clerk and found out everything. Monsieur Etienne and the Jameson woman checked in on the same day—not together, mind you—and she left the same day he did. They were very discreet, stayed on separate floors, but there's no doubt they're traveling together. Of course, a man as handsome and virile as Monsieur Etienne *would* have a mistress."

"Of course," I said.

"Here you are, honey." She handed me the books. "It's been nice talking to you. The girls and I plan to see the show tomorrow night. They'll be real impressed when I tell them you came in today."

I thanked Mrs. Gittman politely and left the shop with my parcel of books, a prey to conflicting emotions. I moved through patches of sunlight and shade and passed the other shops and returned the smiles I received, but my mind wasn't on what I was doing. I was surprised to find myself in front of the hotel, moving up the steps onto the spacious verandah. Great swirls of mauve and purple wisteria draped the white wood banisters, and beds of vivid blue larkspurs grew beneath. I didn't go inside. I didn't want to see anyone just now. I stepped over to one of the white wicker sofas with its plump pale blue cushions and sat down, gazing pensively over the railing. Several long minutes passed, and tears spilled down my cheeks as I remembered all that had been and all that I had left behind.

This is absurd, Dana, I scolded myself. You're much better off now. You're making your own way, beholden to no one. Julian is better off, too. He's finally come into his own and he's savoring every minute of his hard-earned success and . . . and he's not pining over you either. He's got Amelia. No doubt she's very good for him. I remembered her wry wit and sophistication and that breezy, insouciant manner. Yes, he needed someone like her. Society would not look askance at a lovely mistress—indeed, it was expected of men in Julian's world—but they would never have accepted the wrong wife. Even if Charles had not been in the picture, I could never have married Julian, no matter how grateful to him I may have been. It would have ruined his life. It would have made him an outcast in the only world he had ever known. He might pretend indifference to society's opinion, but he was an Etienne nevertheless. I couldn't have deprived him of all that that entailed. I had done him a good service by leaving New Orleans, no matter how it may have pained him at the time.

How thrilled I was for him. How pleased I was by his success. The ineffectual dreamer had showed them all. He had come into his own at last, and he was riding high, basking in all the attention and acclaim, as well he should be. The money was pouring in, too. How ironic it was that Julian should be the one to replenish the family coffers. Charles loved his brother and would be proud of him, I granted that, but nevertheless it must rankle that the brother he had fondly patronized all these years had achieved such a success. Charles had always been the superior one, the breadwinner, the one who held the reins, and it was Julian who had come through, Julian who had been invited to the White House to dine with the President and First Lady.

Julian was happy now . . . That was all that mattered. And Charles? I didn't want to think about him. Charles had never loved me. He had used me, yes, but I had let him, relishing those nights of passion every bit as much as he did. I had loved him, I had loved him with all my heart and soul, and that was my own mistake. I had paid dearly for it in heartache and pain, but . . . it was over now. Charles could go to hell. I was appalled to find more tears brimming over my lashes, and I brushed them away angrily. I took my books and went inside, moving through the lobby and going up to my room.

I unwrapped the books and put the novels aside and sat in the overstuffed rose silk chair and slowly turned through the pages of the first volume of Julian's book. I recognized many of the plates—he was a superb artist, his plants and flowers magnificently executed, as fine as any of Audubon's birds—and as I scanned the text I remembered many of those oft tedious table conversations when he had regaled Delia and me with botanical anecdotes we had found less than fascinating. Those same anecdotes were presented here in clear and lucid prose asparkle with wit. Thanks to the vitality of his writing, even the driest facts seemed interesting. I had no doubt Julian would, in time, become as famous as Audubon, for though their fields were different, his contribution was equally as important.

I finally closed the volume and sat watching a pool of sunlight lengthening on the rose and gray carpet. After a long while I stood up and tidied my hair and went downstairs. It was almost two o'clock now, and the dining room was empty, but perhaps I could get a cup of tea. One of the polite young waiters happened to see me and hurried over to show me to a table.

"I realize it's too late for lunch," I said, "but I thought I might be able to have some tea."

"Anything you want, Miss O'Malley," he said graciously. "The cook would be delighted to prepare something special for you."

"No, I—I don't want to be any trouble."

"You just sit here and relax. I'll bring your tea right away and see if I can rustle up a snack or two as well. It's an honor having you here, and we want you to be happy."

"You're very kind," I told him.

The youth smiled and disappeared, and I looked around at the large, empty room with its dark gold carpet and faded yellow silk damask walls. Heavy gold satin drapes hung at the windows, pulled back to let in lazy silver rays of afternoon sunlight. Filled with people and the muted clatter of silver and china, the tinkle of crystal, the hum of a dozen conversations, the discreet scurry of waiters and the delicious smells of food, the room was elegant and inviting, but now, deserted of its crowd, the atmosphere was curiously sad and lonely, matching my own mood. Lonely? Yes, I realized that I was lonely. I had tremendous friends, I was part of a merry, mercurial family, but when the play was ended and the footlights put out I had no one. No one to hold me. No one to turn long, empty nights into nights of splendor.

"Here you are!" Jason cried.

I looked up, startled. He came swaggering into the dining room, bursting with that magnificent energy and vitality, looking absolutely marvelous in his snug gray breeches and loose white shirt and multicolored silk waistcoat. His black hair was all unruly, his lean face exasperated, those gray-flecked green eyes all afire as he charged over to my table. My spirits lifted immediately. They seemed to soar. Until now, I hadn't realized just how much I had missed him since he left for Atlanta.

"Miss me?" he demanded.

"Miss you?" I asked dryly. "Why on earth should I have missed you?"

"Ungrateful wench! You certainly know how to needle a man."

"As a matter of fact, it's been remarkably peaceful and serene these past days. Everything has run with unusual smoothness and efficiency. Perhaps you should leave us more often."

"Just got back," he announced. "I've been looking all over for you."

He stood there in front of the table, one hand gripping a rolled-up manuscript bound in thick blue paper, the other resting lightly on his thigh. He was indeed a roguishly attractive devil with those quirkily slanting eyebrows, that crooked nose and the wide pink slash of mouth. Not handsome, no, but incredibly appealing. No wonder women threw themselves at him. During the past eight months I had seen several of them do just that, but here was one who had no intention of making a fool of herself.

"Why should you be looking all over for *me*?" I inquired.

"To feast my eyes on your astonishing beauty," he said.

I sighed wearily. He was, after all, the author of second-rate melodrama, and a glib scoundrel to boot. At that point the young waiter returned with a tray laden with silver teapot, a large platter of delectable-looking sandwiches and a smaller platter of iced tea cakes. He nodded to Jason, deftly placed the things on the table and set delicate china cup and saucer before me. The tea emitted a fragrant aroma and a spiral of steam as he poured it.

"There are two kinds of sandwiches, Miss O'Malley—sliced tongue and watercress. Cook made them up especially for you. Those little cakes with the white icing have raspberry spread between the layers, and the others are chocolate with almond paste. May I bring you something, Mr. Donovan?" he asked.

"No, this'll do nicely for both of us," Jason replied. "You might bring an extra cup, though."

"Certainly, sir."

The youth left, and Jason slapped the manuscript down on the table, took a sliced tongue sandwich and plopped down across from me, looking completely relaxed. The sandwich was small, the crusts daintily removed, and he ate it in two greedy bites, immediately reaching for another.

"Why so sad?" he asked.

"Sad? What makes you think I'm sad?"

"I saw it in your eyes. Before I made my presence known. You looked sad and lost and terribly lonely. A beautiful creature like you—ridiculous! I suspect you did miss me, wench."

"Don't call me that!" I snapped.

"Why not?"

"This isn't an—an eighteenth-century melodrama, and I'm not—I'm not a buxom barmaid or a lass fresh from the country."

"No, you're very demure, very well-bred, very self-possessed—when you're not slugging someone, that is."

"I haven't slugged anyone but Carmelita."

"And the sow certainly deserved it. You *were* sad."

"I was thinking," I retorted.

"Sad thoughts," he insisted.

"Go to hell!" I said testily.

"I don't know why you always give me such a hard time, Miss O'Malley. I want only to woo you. I want only to see those eyes full of stars, see those lips part with pleasure as I murmur tender words into those delicate ears."

"Purple Nights," I said. "Act Three. Carlo's speech to Jessamyn."

"Really?" He seemed surprised. "I'd quite forgotten. I'm utterly sincere, though."

"Of course you are. Does that line actually work?"

"Usually," he admitted.

The waiter returned with his cup. Jason nodded his thanks and poured the tea himself, waving the waiter away. He ate another sandwich, too. I watched with mounting irritation, and when he reached for his fourth sandwich I slapped his hand. He looked dismayed.

"What'd you do that for?"

"This happens to be *my* lunch."

"I told you, I just got in, and I didn't eat anything on the train. They sure make skimpy little sandwiches here, don't they? Try one."

"How was your trip to Atlanta?" I inquired.

"Very successful," he said casually, taking yet another sandwich off the platter. "Things look good. They look very good indeed."

"It—it has something to do with the play you've been writing these past months?"

He nodded, pushing the manuscript across the table to me.

''I want you to read it,'' he told me. ''I want you to read it this afternoon, in fact. We've got a lot of things to discuss.''

''Did you—''

''Not another word about it until you've read the play. We'll talk about it tonight, after the performance. I'll take you to dinner. I might even buy you some champagne.''

''Jason—''

''Drink your tea,'' he ordered.

I managed to get one of the sandwiches and two of the cakes before he ate them all. He drank the rest of the tea as well, then escorted me upstairs to my room and told me to read the play slowly and carefully—he intended to quiz me about it tonight. I gave him a look and shut the door in his face, feeling much, much better than I had earlier. For all his swagger and posturing, for all his quips, he was a very intelligent, very perceptive man. Being with Jason Donovan was always stimulating. My senses seemed to be curiously heightened, and I seemed to be—well, more alive. It was his vitality, I assured myself. One couldn't help but respond to it.

I settled down to read the manuscript, opening it at the title page. *The Quadroon*, by Jason Donovan. Another thundering melodrama, no doubt. He had been working on it for several months, very secretive about its plot, refusing to discuss it with anyone. I began it without any great expectations, anticipating the usual florid dialogue and larger-than-life characters. It opened in a squalid room in New Orleans where a Negro woman, Jessie, is keeping her eye on two rowdy young sons while washing a tub of clothes, looking defeated and worn-out by life. Not a typical opening. Did Jason expect to use real Negroes? I read on, caught up immediately when Rufus, Jessie's husband, entered.

Rufus was a carpenter, and he was finding it ever more difficult to get a job. Rufus, Jessie and their children had been given their freedom when ''Master Bartholomew'' died, and life here in New Orleans was grim indeed, much harder than it had been on the plantation. Rufus takes the boys out so that Jessie can finish her washing and ironing and take the clothes to ''Miss Amy Sue.'' Janine, Jessie's daughter, enters, and it is immediately obvious that she isn't Rufus' child. Janine is a quadroon, a ''buffalo gal'' who could easily pass for white. That is exactly what she has been doing. She informs her mother that ''Joe'' is going to marry her and they are going to St. Louis. Jessie begs her not to do this evil thing, it is wrong, dead wrong, and can only bring unhappiness to all concerned.

"He loves me. He wants to *marry* me," Janine insists. "I—I'm not going to end up like the rest of my kind, Ma. I'm not going to show myself off at the Quadroon Ball and get myself a rich white lover. I'm going to marry my Joe and lead a real life—a respectable life—where no one knows what—what I am."

"Not even Joe," Jessie says. "He doesn't know, does he, chile?"

"He doesn't know," Janine replies, "and he'll never find out, either."

"What you plan to do, chile—it ain't only wrong, it's against the law, too. White folks an' colored folks, they ain't allowed to marry. You'se colored, chile. In th' eyes of th' law, just one drop of colored blood makes you as black as me or Rufus or either of yore brothers."

Janine leaves and Jessie bows her head in grief. Scene Two finds Janine in St. Louis, deserted by the faithless Joe, who, of course, never married her. She is working as a milliner's assistant and confides to her lovely and worldly friend Lenore that she has met a wealthy young gentleman, Travis, who plans to introduce her to his parents. He is madly in love with her. He intends to marry her. Travis is charming, carefree, but essentially weak, and his parents bitterly oppose this most unsuitable marriage.

In Act Two, Catherine, Travis's mother, comes to visit a radiant, blissfully happy Janine, who is living in a small, pretty house with her husband. Catherine confesses that she and her husband feared the worst and begrudgingly admits that Janine has made a new man of Travis, who has given up drinking, taken on responsibility and is now working diligently in his father's law firm. Janine confides that she is expecting a child. Catherine is thrilled and gives her daughter-in-law a hug. A tearful Jessie arrives two months later, telling her daughter that Rufus and the boys have died in a terrible fire. Everything is gone. Jessie would have died, too, but she was out delivering laundry when the fire broke out. Janine vows to take care of her and tells everyone Jessie is her old nanny. A stubborn Travis informs his wife that he will not have a Negro woman staying under his roof. He distrusts and despises all colored people but finally agrees to let her stay in the shed out back, warning Janine to keep the coon out of his sight.

When Act Three opens, Janine is giving birth to a child off-stage. Travis is pacing the floor anxiously as a very worried Jessie, hiding behind a column, wrings her hands. There are sounds offstage, then silence. A grave-faced doctor enters. The child is dead, stillborn. The mother is recovering. There is something else, he adds, hardly knowing how to say it. The child is black. Travis turns pale as Jessie cries, "My chile, my chile," and rushes to her daughter. Travis leaves the room. A moment later a gunshot is heard offstage. In Scene Two, Catherine and her husband, who have managed to keep the reasons for their son's suicide a secret, harshly banish Janine and her mother, and in the final scene a gorgeously attired Janine, back in New Orleans, is preparing herself for yet another Quadroon Ball.

I closed the manuscript, gazing into space, deeply moved. It was a beautiful play, wonderfully written, getting its message across with subtle touches. Even the more dramatic scenes were underwritten, with simple and realistic dialogue and none of the purple passages that usually marked Jason's work. There was truth and compassion, and Janine, of course, was a dream role for an actress. I stood up, still in that world Jason had created so superbly. The play could never be produced, I realized. The public would never stand for a drama about miscegenation— *Othello* had never been performed in the South—and even if a producer did dare to put it on, it couldn't be done effectively without real Negroes in the cast. A Jessie in blackface would destroy the entire mood of the play. Even so, I was tremendously proud of Jason for writing it. It merely proved what he was capable of doing.

I was still thinking of the play that evening at the theater. Backstage was aswarm with Indians—locally recruited youths in breechcloths, feathers, black wigs and fierce war paint—and I was waiting in the wings in my flowered pink calico while, onstage, an obese Carmelita in purple taffeta was telling a handsomely uniformed Michael that she couldn't possibly endure another year at the fort, the engagement was off, she was leaving tomorrow. Michael told her no one was leaving the fort while there was danger of an Indian attack. Laura joined me in the wings, attired in low-cut blue and mauve silk as the commander's seductive and scheming daughter who hoped to steal the noble Michael from the even nobler Carmelita.

"One of those bloody Indians *pinched* me," she whispered. "I think he's the one who tomahawks me in the last scene."

"What did you do?"

"I pinched him back, love. He's never had such a thrill, believe me. I suppose you know Jason's back?"

I nodded. "He's taking me to dinner after the show."

"Oh?"

"We—there's something he wants to talk about."

"Don't waste too much time talking, love," she advised. "I hope you're wearing something provocative."

"The red silk Dulcie made for next season's *Lena Marlow*. He hasn't seen it yet."

"But *I* have, love. Good thinking. It's perfect!"

My cue came and I rushed onstage to inform my brother, Michael, that Indians had been sighted on the ridge beyond the fort and the commander needed him to rally the men. He hurried off and I took Carmelita's hand and told her she mustn't think of leaving, he loved her dearly, as did everyone else here at the fort, for, after all, she was the Sweetheart of the West. That particular line got laughs the author hadn't intended, and there was a very loud "Moo!" from the balcony. Carmelita bristled but carried on like the trouper she was. During the second act I flirted with all the officers at the Cavalry Ball, primarily to make Billy, the dashing young lieutenant, jealous, and during the third act I showed my true merit when Indians attacked and overran the fort. I shot the Indian who had just tomahawked the wicked Laura and, when the bloodthirsty savages were finally defeated, hurled myself into Billy's arms and vowed eternal love.

I got tremendous applause when we took our curtain calls. So did Laura, a favorite. Carmelita got only a smattering of applause and several more rude "Moos." She waddled hurriedly to her dressing room, steaming. Jason grabbed my arm as I stepped into the wings.

"You read it?" he demanded.

"I read it," I said.

"Good. I've got business with Jackson. Why don't I meet you in the lobby of the hotel in, say, an hour? No, make it an hour and a half. I want to count tonight's box office take."

"I'm very hungry," I said. "I don't know if I can wait that long. Why don't I go ahead and eat and then—"

"You can wait," he said sternly. "The hotel lobby. An hour and a half. Be there!"

I was still in my costume when, ten minutes later, a very nervous Freddie knocked on my dressing room door. I ushered him in, along with an even more nervous lass with rosy cheeks, large blue eyes and tumbling blond curls. The youngsters were both tongue-tied. I tried my best to put them at ease, asking them if they had enjoyed the play, relating backstage anecdotes, telling June, for that was her name, that Freddie took marvelous care of me at the hotel. I signed pictures for both of them and walked them to the front lobby, returning to my dressing room via the wings and waving to the stagehands who were busily disassembling the set.

An hour later I was dutifully waiting in the hotel lobby, wondering if I had made a mistake in selecting the deep red silk gown. I had loved it when I tried it on, thrilled with the off-the-shoulder puffed sleeves and snug waist, delighted with the very full skirt that spread out over red gauze underskirts, but I didn't remember it being cut quite so low. It would be wonderfully effective onstage, but . . . was it really suitable for a private dinner? Would Jason think I had worn the gown because I wanted him to find me alluring? In all honesty, that was precisely why I chose it, I admitted to myself, and if the sod got too frisky I'd give him what for and no mistake about it.

He was ten minutes late. He didn't even notice the gown.

"Sorry," he said, striding briskly toward me. "Jackson and I were discussing business and I forgot the time. Ready?"

"Ready," I said.

He gripped my elbow and headed toward the staircase. I dug in my heels. He looked surprised.

"What's the problem?" he asked impatiently.

"Where are we going?" I demanded.

"Upstairs. To my suite. I thought we'd eat there. We've got a lot to talk about, and I don't want to be constantly interrupted by hovering waiters and inquisitive maîtres d'hôtel."

"I see," I said.

"I made all the arrangements earlier, spread tips all over the place so I could have everything set up just right. Come along. If I get out of hand, you can slug me."

"Don't think I wouldn't," I warned.

"This is going to be a *business* dinner, Dana."

"Just so that's understood," I told him.

He led me up two flights of stairs and then along the third-floor hallway, stopping in front of the door to his suite. I had never been to his suite before. He unlocked the door and ushered me into a sitting room done in shades of blue, gray and purple, a deep blue carpet covering the floor, slightly worn gray silk on the walls, the sofa and matching armchairs upholstered in a rich purple velvet. Gray silk drapes hung at the window, plump mauve and gray silk pillows were piled on the sofa, and a small crystal chandelier hung over a table set for two, candlelight gleaming on china and fine silver and the elegant crystal glasses. Beside it stood a cart piled with silver-covered dishes and a silver bucket with a bottle of champagne nestling in ice.

"Very fancy," I observed.

"You were expecting beer and a sandwich?"

"I—I don't know what I was expecting."

"This is a celebration dinner. Look, would you mind if I slipped out of this jacket? I'd like to be comfortable."

"Go right ahead," I told him.

He smiled at me and stepped through a doorway into the adjoining bedroom, returning a few moments later with a glossy black satin dressing robe over his black trousers and white shirt. The robe had gray satin lapels and cuffs. He was tightening the gray satin sash as he entered, and he looked so wonderfully appealing I felt a tightness in my throat, weakness in my knees and wrists. I could feel the familiar honied warmth stirring below as well and I tried valiantly to ignore it, to remain cool and remote. He gazed at me with those gray-flecked green eyes. A grin spread on that wide slash of mouth. His hair was tousled. This is going to be a *business* dinner, I reminded myself, holding onto the back of one of the chairs. I feared my knees might actually give way.

"Let's see—what have we here?" Jason said, removing one of the silver covers from a dish. "Ah, scallops and mushrooms, cooked in white wine sauce. And here—giant prawn on a nest of wild rice, with champagne-butter sauce. I didn't know which you'd prefer, so I ordered both. You like prawn?"

"I love prawn. Scallops, too."

"There's also broccoli and baby carrots and, for dessert, cream and chocolate gateaux, which, I am told, have seven layers with a delicate cherry paste between each layer, whipped cream on top."

"You want me to leave this room looking like Carmelita?"

"I want you to leave this room completely sated," he said in that light, scratchy, utterly enchanting voice. "Champagne?"

"I—I'm not very good with champagne," I confessed. "It goes straight to my head."

"Live dangerously," he said, uncorking the bottle.

Ice rattled and tinkled as he lifted the bottle out of the silver bucket. He removed gold foil and carefully twisted wire and the cork flew out, popping loudly. I jumped. He poured fizzling amber liquid into the two tall crystal glasses and brought one of the glasses to me. Our fingers touched as he handed me the glass. He smiled again, a smile that managed to be both boyish and wicked. I loved that slightly crooked nose. I longed to touch it. I longed to trace the quirky slant of those dark black eyebrows with my fingertip. The honied warmth was spreading, sweet torment in my blood. It had been so long, so very long . . . I took a generous sip of champagne. Jason placed his hands on my bare shoulders and helped me into the chair, his fingers pressing heavily yet gently into my flesh.

"Sit. Relax. You're my guest. I'll serve you."

The fingers still pressed and I wanted to arch my back like a cat. I was trembling inside now. I took another generous sip of champagne. Jason moved around the table, the long skirt of his dressing robe making soft, silken music. He began to uncover the rest of the dishes, humming quietly to himself as he ladled food onto our plates. Heavenly smells wafted on the air. The food was steaming hot, looked delicious. I couldn't eat a bite. My throat was too tight. I sipped more champagne. Jason sat down across from me and looked at me with those marvelous eyes and slowly lifted his own glass.

"To *The Quadroon*," he said.

"To—to *The Quadroon*," I echoed. "It—it's a wonderful play, Jason. It's touching and true and very, very moving, but—"

"But?"

"I don't see how it could possibly be produced—at least not here in the South."

"It's going to be produced," he told me. "In Atlanta. In September, at the National Theater."

"They—"

"There was some resistance—quite a lot of resistance, in fact—but the managers of the theater felt pretty much the way you do about the play, touching, moving and so on. They realize it will be controversial—extremely controversial—but Atlanta prides itself on its sophistication and likes to believe it's every bit as advanced as New York. The managers finally agreed to let *The Quadroon* open at the National in September, to run as long as the public decides it shall. The National, as I'm sure you know, is the Mecca of every theatrical company in the South. Only the finest productions are allowed to grace its hallowed stage."

"That—it's wonderful, Jason, but—"

"Due to the highly controversial nature of the piece, the worthy managers wisely refuse to put a penny of their own money into the production, will, instead, merely collect an exorbitant fee for every week the play occupies their highly expensive boards. It's going to cost a fortune to mount the right production."

"You don't have a fortune," I reminded him.

"Alas, that's all too true," he agreed. "However, Robert Courtland *does* have a fortune, and he's going to finance the entire production."

"Robert Courtland?"

"Chap I met in the hotel bar in Atlanta. Businessman. Lumber. Cotton. God knows what else. Divides his time between Atlanta and Natchez, where he owns a palatial mansion and, I understand, half the real estate in Natchez-Under-the-Hill. He's quite interested in the drama and we had several drinks together and I told him about the play and he asked to read it. I really didn't expect anything to come of it, of course, but—a potential backer is a potential backer, and you never know. The next day he had his lawyer draw up a contract and, when I signed it, gave me a generous check to start things rolling. He wants a first-class production—first-class all the way."

Jason reached for the champagne bottle and refilled my glass, which I had emptied as we talked. A smile was playing on his lips, and he looked extremely pleased with himself, like . . . like a little boy revealing a particularly delightful secret. For all his bravado and bossiness, for all his theatrical posturing, there was much of the little boy in him. Deep sensitivity as well, I thought, yet he was undeniably virile, as masculine as canvas and incredibly appealing. I watched the smile curling lightly on those lips and wondered how they would feel caressing my own.

I took another very large sip of champagne. It was delicious and didn't seem to be affecting me at all. The candles glowed, making a warm golden haze in the air. The tension I had felt earlier seemed to vanish, but it had nothing to do with the champagne, I was certain of that. The tension was gone, but the warmth still spread through my body like thick, sweet honey, and the sound of his voice, that marvelously unique voice, was curiously titillating.

"This prawn is delicious," he said, "and the wild rice has a wonderful flavor—I suppose it's the champagne-butter sauce they poured over it. Great meal."

"Yes," I murmured.

"We'll spend the summer in Atlanta—the entire company, sans Carmelita, of course. It'll take the entire summer to get the production ready, sets and costumes, blocking everything out, rehearsing. I'll probably be impossible to live with. I want perfection in every detail, and I'll probably drive you all without mercy."

"You probably will," I agreed.

"You really should eat something, Dana. More champagne? You're sure you want another glass? There are parts for everyone. Billy will play Travis and Bart and Ollie will play his parents and Laura will be a perfect Lenore. The guy who appears in the last scene, the one who brings Janine diamonds as she's getting ready for the Quadroon Ball—I'm going to build that up for Michael. It'll still be small, he won't be a leading man, but I doubt he'll complain as long as he can be close to Laura. Chap's hopelessly smitten with her."

"They're having a glorious time," I said, and my voice sounded peculiar, as though it were coming from a long way. "Laura says I need a bonbon," I added.

Jason gave me a look, arched one brow and helped himself to more rice. I toyed with my champagne glass. It was almost empty again.

"Jessie presents a problem, of course," he continued, "but I'm determined to use a real Negro. Courtland was telling me about a small theater in New Orleans where free people of color give performances for their kind. Some of the people are extremely gifted, I understand. I intend to go to New Orleans and check it out—I'll find my Jessie, I'm sure of it, and I'll have real Negroes for Rufus and the boys, too."

"Will—will the public accept that?"

"We'll *make* 'em accept it. These scallops are fabulous. I didn't realize I was so hungry. Eat your carrots, Dana. I warn you in advance that I'm going to be very, very hard on you. You're going to give the performance of a lifetime as Janine, even if I have to *beat* it out of you."

"You—you want me to play Janine?"

"Of course I do, you silly bitch. Why do you think I wanted you to read the play right off? I wrote it for you."

"You wrote it for *me*?"

"That's what I said. No, I don't think you need any more champagne. Oh hell, there's just a little left in the bottle, you might as well have it. Do you remember the talk we had on the verandah after you wowed the paying customers in your first performance? After you slugged Carmelita and I had to spend hours calming the trollop down? You told me some of my lines were very clever and on occasion some of my scenes were genuinely touching but most of the situations were wildly contrived—Jesus! What a lippy little thing you were. I wanted to smack you in the mouth. Almost did, too."

"I—I probably deserved it."

"Then you added you had the feeling I could write a *real* play if I really wanted to. I agreed with you. I told you I had been toying with an idea and you asked me why I hadn't written it and—I knew the time had come. I knew I had found the perfect woman to bring my Janine to life. You've been my inspiration, Dana. Every line I wrote—I was thinking of you. I wanted to please you. I wanted to show you what I could do."

"I'm—touched."

"I wanted to show you I wasn't just a noisy scamp. I wanted to show you I had real stuff in me. I wanted to—oh hell, I happen to be in love with you, dammit, and—"

"You're in love with me?"

"Of course I am."

I stood up. I wasn't terribly steady on my feet. I gripped the back of my chair with one hand and gave him a disdainful look.

"You—you are just saying that," I informed him, carefully enunciating each word. Was my voice slightly slurred? "You—you just got me up here so you could ply me with champagne and get me drunk and have your way with me. I think that is perfectly despicable."

"Get you drunk?" He stood up, too, outraged. "You certainly didn't need any help from me. You've been guzzling down that champagne like the town lush ever since I opened the bottle."

"You, sir, are no gentleman," I said.

"I've never pretended to be. Gentlemen are boring as hell. I'm not one of your overbred southern aristocrats with prissy manners and blue blood and a fancy lineage going back to God. I'm a—I guess I'm a rough-and-tumble rogue with no breeding at all, but I happen to love you and—if you weren't so dense you'd *know* I'm telling the truth."

"You want to sleep with me," I accused.

"Of *course* I want to sleep with you. That's part of it."

I gave him another disdainful look and let go of the chair and started toward the door. My knees buckled. He scurried around the table and caught me before I fell. He held me in his arms and looked down at me with those lovely gray-flecked green eyes and I seemed to melt, seemed to dissolve, was completely incapable of standing without his support. I made a throaty noise that was very like a purr and raised my arms and curled them around his neck and rested my cheek against his shoulder, the satin of his robe cool and silky against my skin. He smelled delicious. His arms were holding me tight. He was extremely strong.

"I want a bonbon," I murmured.

"We haven't any. We've got gateaux—Jesus, you're smashed."

"I'm not. I'm just relaxed. I've been so very lonely, you see. I have wonderful friends and I love the theater and I—I'm so lucky, if it weren't for Laura I'd probably be selling gloves in St. Louis, but—there's no one to hold me, no one to—"

"I'm holding you."

"You're a cad, taking advantage of me like this."

"I'm a cad," he agreed.

"But glorious. Did anyone ever tell you you're glorious? I for one happen to *like* that crooked nose and those crazy-slanting

eyebrows and that mouth that is much too wide and—I'm beginning to feel a little dizzy.''

"We'd better sit down."

He led me over to the couch and sat down and pulled me
down with him, his arms still wrapped around me. My skirts
rustled. I placed my palms against his chest and pushed, moving
back.

"You didn't notice my gown," I said.

"I noticed your gown. Believe me, I noticed."

"You did?"

"I wanted to gnash my teeth and hurl you down on the floor
and ravish you right there in the lobby."

"Really?"

"It took superhuman control *not* to."

"It might have been rather interesting," I observed. I stood
up again. "The dress comes off quite easily. You'll have to help
me with the tiny hooks in back, though."

"You've no idea what you're doing, no idea what you're saying."

"Yes," I said, "I do."

I did. Jason looked shaken. He gripped the edge of the couch
and hoisted himself to his feet, the heavy folds of his satin robe
bunching up and then sliding back down his legs. He stood there
in front of me, his eyes questioning. He saw the answer in my
own eyes, but he still wasn't sure. He finally shook his head,
resolute.

"For eight months I've been trying to—uh—I've wanted you,
but I'll be damned if I'm going to—you're drunk, you'd hate me
in the morning. I'm not a complete cad. I don't take advantage
of ladies who've drunk themselves into oblivion. I mean, I have
some integrity."

"I'm not that drunk, Jason."

"No?"

I shook my head. I touched his cheek, rubbing my fingertips
lightly over his skin, finally slipping my hand around and entwining my fingers in his dark hair. It was soft, slipping through
my fingers like heavy black silk. He was still hesitant, looking
worried and uncomfortable, and I smiled, once again reminded
of a little boy. This great big gorgeous man was as skittish as a
colt and looked like he wanted to turn and run for his life. The
smile still curving on my lips, I stood up on tiptoes and kissed

him lightly on the mouth, and then I moved back, very pleased with myself.

"Jesus!" he muttered. "I'm the one who's supposed to be doing the seducing."

"So you *did* plan to seduce me?"

"I—well, I thought maybe—I hoped perhaps—and when I saw you in that red gown—look, Dana, uh—"

"I don't want to be lonely any longer," I whispered.

Still he hesitated and then, finally, he pulled me into his arms and held me loosely, tenderly. He was rowdy and bossy and volatile, but he was tender, too, comforting me now. That wasn't what I wanted. I moved my hands over his broad back, over the smooth satin, feeling the strong musculature beneath, and I rested my palms on his shoulders and tilted my head back and Jason kissed me tenderly and then urgently, and I wasn't drunk at all now, I knew exactly what I was doing as I clung to him, demanding more. He kissed me for a long, long time and finally raised his head, peering down into my eyes, his own questioning again.

"You're sure?" he asked.

I nodded. "I'm sure, but—I'm afraid. Don't—don't hurt me. I don't want to be hurt again."

"Hurt you? I love you. Didn't I mention that?"

It doesn't matter, I said silently. You're merely a bonbon. I'm not going to let myself care. I'm not going to be hurt again. Jason kissed me again and then he led me into the adjoining bedroom and he was passionate and strong and greedy yet tender and gentle and caring and it was wonderful, wonderful beyond belief, and afterward he kissed me and cradled me to him and I reveled in his warmth, his smell, his strength, his beauty there in the moonlight. Laura was right, I thought, nestling in his arms, his thigh covering mine. When the bonbon is right there beside your plate, why pass it up?

Chapter Nineteen

THE TOMATOES AND ROTTEN EGGS CAME FLYING across the footlights, pelting the backdrop, ruining my gown, and I stood there in stark terror as the audience shouted and jeered. Stern-faced ladies carrying placards came marching down the aisles, chanting, "Stop this play! Stop this play!" and then the audience rose en masse, fists waving, feet stamping. There was a mighty roar as they charged the stage, intending to tear me limb from limb. I was frozen, totally unable to move, and I desperately tried to scream. The scream was trapped in my throat. I tensed as great hulking men and flinty-eyed women scrambled up onto the stage, shouting, "Scandal! Disgrace! Outrage!" My heart was pounding, pounding, and finally I threw back my head and released the scream and opened my eyes and Jason snorted, his body jerking violently, his own eyes flying open.

"Jesus!" he cried. "What th' hell was *that*?"

"Nothing," I said calmly. "Go back to sleep, Jason."

"Did you *hear* something?"

"Not a thing," I told him. "You must have been having a nightmare."

"What time is it?"

"I've no idea. I just woke up myself."

Jason groaned miserably and grabbed the pillow in a lethal hold and flopped and twisted around until he was in the desired position, then snorted again. He managed to pull the bedcovers completely off me, twining them cocoonlike around his lower limbs. It was just as well. He always slept in the nude. I climbed out of bed, the skirt of my thin white cotton nightgown fluttering. The carpetless floor was cool to my bare feet. The windows

405

were all open, the pale yellow curtains billowing gently in an early morning breeze. The thin rays of sunlight streaming lazily into the room were still weak. It couldn't be much later than six-thirty.

Our final dress rehearsal last night had dragged on until after one o'clock this morning. No wonder I felt so groggy. Jason had been an absolute beast. No wonder I had such a nightmare. I wearily pulled on the thin white and yellow striped robe that went with my nightgown, the skirt aflutter with ruffles. As I tied the sash at my waist, Jason flopped around again, wrapping the sheets tighter around his legs. He groaned, wrestled with the pillow and finally lifted his head, peering at me with one slightly open eye. I remembered that I was furious with him. That wasn't unusual. Ever since we had started rehearsals here in Atlanta hardly a day had gone by that I wasn't furious with him.

"Do—uh—do you—uh—think you might—uh—bring me a cup of coffee?" he croaked.

"I'm furious with you," I reminded him.

"Jesus, Dana, don't start in on me. Okay? Just—uh—please don't start in on me. I feel wretched."

"Good," I said cheerily.

"*Please* bring me some coffee. Pretty please."

"Fetch it yourself," I said.

He sat up abruptly, both eyes open now, both blazing.

"Sometimes you can be an absolute *bitch*!" he thundered.

Damp, unruly locks of black hair tumbled wildly over his head and his lower body was tightly encased in twisted sheets and he looked so comical and so utterly endearing that I had to smile. He scowled dangerously.

"What th' hell are you *smiling* at!"

"You, darling," I said lightly.

I stepped over to the bed and rested my hand on his cheek and smoothed that wild tumble of hair from his brow and he became a little boy again, wounded, thoroughly misunderstood. I leaned down and kissed him on the lips, my heart full of affection for this exasperating man whom, when I didn't want to murder him, I wanted to pamper and please and coddle. He reached up and grabbed my wrist in a tight grip and pulled me back down onto the bed, his eyelids drooping seductively now, his mouth parting for a longer, more meaningful kiss. I struggled free, getting off the bed, smiling still.

"Go back to sleep," I told him. "I may bring you some coffee later on."

"You really *can* be a bitch, Dana," he complained woefully.

"I've had to learn to be, darling—for my own protection. If I weren't a bitch now and then, you'd run all over me."

"I resent that! I'm the gentlest, most amiable—"

I left the room, blowing him a kiss at the door, and it was not until I had gone halfway down the hall that I remembered that I had nothing whatsoever to be so cheerful about. They were going to crucify us tonight. My nightmare would undoubtedly come true. The whole city was in an uproar about *The Quadroon*, and I wouldn't be at all surprised if someone actually planted a bomb in the theater to prevent its opening. Oh well, I thought, moving down the staircase, we will have given it our best, and if they run us out of town, they run us out of town. We can always reprise *Lord Roderick's Revenge* in Dothan, Alabama. As I reached the bottom of the stairs, the front door opened and Bartholomew entered, leading a complacent-looking Theodore on a leash. Our silver-haired, rosy-cheeked character man looked as distinguished and dignified as ever in a handsome blue frock coat and pearl-gray ascot.

"Dana, my dear," he said in those familiar dulcet tones. "You're up early this morning."

"Apparently not as early as you."

"When you reach my advanced years, child, you find yourself getting up with the birds. Besides, Theodore likes to be out and at his business while the dew is still on the grass."

"You look very elegant this morning."

"One tries to keep up the facade," he said, sighing with theatrical resignation. "One tries."

"You were marvelous last night," I told him. "Thank God *someone* is sane and unflappable. It was a disaster, wasn't it?"

"Final dress rehearsals are always a disaster. Everyone is always keyed-up and on edge. Our esteemed playwright-director *did* rather try himself, but we're used to that, aren't we?"

"Aren't we ever. He was a beast."

"But he gets excellent results, my dear. He's pushed us hard, but we have all surpassed ourselves. None of us has ever been better. Young Billy is amazing. I never thought I'd see the day he would give such a performance. His Travis is perfection."

"Billy's wonderful," I agreed.

"And your Janine is going to make theatrical history. Jason may have bullied you unmercifully, but under his direction you've created a luminous character no one is likely to forget."

"If anyone ever sees it," I retorted. "Do—do you think they'll actually let us open?"

"The city fathers have read the play. They've given their approval."

"But—"

"Oh, don't bother yourself over all this flapdoodle and hoopla, child. The protests, the public demonstrations, the articles in the papers have just helped sell tickets. We're completely sold out for weeks in advance. The League of Decency ladies and the ministers condemning us from their pulpits are actually doing us a very good turn."

"I'm still terrified something will happen."

"There might be a small ruckus, but I've no doubt sanity will prevail. The majority of folks here in Atlanta pride themselves on their tolerance, open-mindedness and sophistication. They'll not allow the radical fringe to besmirch the civic image."

"I hope you're right."

"I am, child. Relax. Come along, Theodore. Your kind old master has some particularly tasty doggy treats waiting for you in our room. I'll see you later, Dana."

I could smell coffee brewing as I moved down the lower hallway to the kitchen in back. Someone else was up early, too, it seemed. It was lovely, all of us living together in this huge old rented house near downtown, only a few short blocks from the theater. With the largess so lavishly provided by the mysterious Mr. Robert Courtland, whom no one but Jason and Jackson had met, we could have stayed in Atlanta's grandest hotel, but there wasn't a hotel in the whole of the South that would take Corey and Adam and the boys. The rest of us had elected to stay here so that our new cast members could be with us. Even so, there had been problems. The man who had rented Jason the house refused to have "niggers" staying inside the house, insisted they stay in the quarters over the carriage house in back. Ever the peacemaker, Corey claimed this suited them nicely as she and Adam liked privacy and they'd actually be more comfortable where they could keep an eye on the boys.

The coffee had finished perking as I entered the roomy old kitchen with its red-brown tile floor and huge oak cabinets. Corey herself was bending over the stove, taking out a pan of heavenly smelling cinnamon rolls. She smiled a greeting at me, carefully set the pan on the drainboard and began to pour thick white icing over the rolls. Corey was a magnificent cook. She loved to cook, and she spent most of her spare time in the kitchen, an unexpected bonus for the rest of us. She and I frequently made meals for the entire company, with extremely inept help from Laura who meant well but couldn't tell a skillet from a baking pan if her life depended on it.

"Lord," I said, "those smell delicious."

"Reckon they are," Corey replied. "They're my specialty. Adam always did love my cinnamon rolls. Them and my peach pies."

"Don't mention your peach pies," I told her. "I can gain five pounds just thinking about them."

"Wouldn't hurt you to put on a few pounds, honey. You're too thin."

"You sound like Jezebel."

"That Jezebel must've been one smart woman."

"She was—is," I corrected myself. "Bossy, too, just like you."

Corey grinned and began to remove the rolls from the pan with a pie server, arranging them on a large blue platter. In her fifties, she had pale brown skin and gorgeous black-brown eyes and thick, frizzy hair that had gone entirely gray some years before. She had lovely bone structure with high, broad cheekbones, a thin nose and full, Negroid lips. A little taller than I was, she had the slender frame of a girl, and she was given to bright, showy clothes, like the purple frock she wore this morning. Corey wore dangling opal earrings, coated her lids with mauve shadow and used special rouge to emphasize her cheekbones. The leading actress at the Jewel Theater in New Orleans, she was proud of her collection of wigs and sorry she wouldn't be wearing any of them in *The Quadroon*. Makeup and earrings were also banned when she was in character as Jessie.

"There," she said, "the icing's thick and gooey, just like Adam likes it. I'll just let it cool for a minute or two and harden up a bit. Don't know what I'd do if I couldn't piddle around in a kitchen now and then. It's so relaxing after the tension of the theater."

Corey had a deep, throaty, beautifully modulated voice that

was quite theatrical. She was a superlative actress, and as Jessie she employed a raspy, broken half whisper that could be heard in the top row of the balcony and indicated a lifetime of defeat. All of us were dazzled by her skills.

"Is Adam up, too?" I asked.

"No, that man is still piled up in bed, snoozing away. Takes an earthquake to get him up—that or a bucket of water in his face. Thought I'd just let him sleep this morning. He's nervous about tonight."

"I'm absolutely terrified," I confessed.

"Isn't any need to be. It's just a play, honey. You white folks all get too hetup. Either they likes us or they don't. If they don't, Adam and I'll go back to the Jewel and you-all can hit the road again with them noisy melodramas Mister Jason wrote."

"God forbid," I said.

"Isn't anything wrong with melodramas. We put on lots of 'em at the Jewel, them and the classics. Sometimes it's a relief storming around in entertaining hokum, particularly after a heavy season of Marlowe and Congreve and Webster."

"You—you do Marlowe and Congreve and Webster at the Jewel?"

Corey gave me a knowing smile. "Guess that surprises you. Idn't too many plays written for colored people, honey. We just do what all the other companies do and pay no mind to skin color—no one but colored folk come to the theater anyway, and they see nothing unusual about it. My Duchess of Malfi is a big favorite. I'm always having to revive it."

"It seems—" I hesitated, groping for words. "It seems somehow unfair—I mean—"

"I know what you mean, honey," Corey said. "If I were white—but I'm not white, I'm colored, and don't you go feelin' sorry for me. I'm one of the lucky ones. I have my papers. I'm free, so's Adam. Us Free People of Color have our own section in New Orleans, our own customs and culture. Things is what things is, Dana, and if you're smart you make the best of 'em."

She looked at me and nodded, black-brown eyes full of sad wisdom.

"Idn't no sense frettin' about what isn't," she said. "Just get on with what is."

"I—I wish I could be as—as philosophical as you are, Corey."

"You got a lot of years to get that way, honey. I am almost

old enough to be your granny, though I'd deny it with my dying breath. Sit yourself down now, have some coffee.''

I poured myself a cup of coffee and sat down at the battered old oak table, resting my elbows on it and watching tiny curls of steam rise from the cup. We really were fortunate to have Corey with us, I reflected. She had been the main draw at the Jewel for almost two decades. Adam, her husband in spirit if not in law, acted at the Jewel as well, usually in flashy roles, Corey confided. Eighteen years her junior, Adam was a strikingly handsome Negro, very vain about his looks and constantly grumbling about the fuzzy gray wig and heavy makeup he had to wear to make a convincing Rufus. Adam and Corey had no children of their own but had appropriated her two young nephews to play my little brothers. The boys were a lively pair, a ''mettlesome handful,'' Corey declared, but, rambunctious as they were, both had quickly become pets of the company. Ollie spoiled them deplorably, clucking over them like a stern mother hen. The outrageous Englishwoman with her bright red wig and imperious manner was the only one who could keep them in line.

''Here, honey, try one of these rolls,'' Corey said, setting the platter on the table. ''Icing's good and firm now. Still warm, too.''

I wondered how she could be so calm and matter-of-fact about tonight. Much of the protest about *The Quadroon* was due not only to its shocking theme but because real Negroes were to appear in the production. A certain highly vocal segment of citizenry vehemently protested this seditious affront to white sensibilities, and one of the leaders claimed that if the play opened he and his cronies would march on the theater with tar and feathers for the whole company. Answering this threat in an interview in Atlanta's major paper, Jason said that no one would be permitted inside the theater without purchasing a ticket and he seriously doubted any of the ''redneck yahoos'' could afford the price. He added that he would personally beat the bejesus out of any lout who tried to disrupt his play or molest any of his company. The interview caused quite a stir and prompted a whole spate of letters to the editor, both pro and con. It also sold hundreds of more tickets.

Corey sat down with a cup of coffee and sipped it thoughtfully as I sampled one of the rolls.

"It's sinfully delicious," I told her.

"They always are," Corey said. "My cinnamon rolls can't be faulted. Have another one."

"I wouldn't dare, but I will set one aside to take up to Jason."

"You and him were sure going at each other last night," she observed idly. "For a while there I thought you might actually kill each other. When you threw that lamp at him—good thing he ducked."

"He deserved it," I said.

"And you deserved the shakin' he gave you afterwards. You make up yet?"

I nodded. "In bed," I confessed.

"Best way there is to make up. That there's one fine man, honey. If you were smart, you'd latch on to him good and make sure he never got away. You're altogether too casual about it."

"It—it's just a casual thing."

"For you maybe, honey, but it idn't for him. Man's in love with you. Oh, he pretends to be as casual as you are, but he's got it bad. Men like that one are few and far between. You let him slip through your fingers, you'll be mighty sorry one of these days."

"He—he's merely a bonbon, Corey. I'm fond of him, of course, extremely fond, and we have—what we have in the bedroom is quite marvelous—but I don't want—" I paused for a moment, reaching for the right expression. "It's a convenient and very satisfying arrangement for both of us, with no strings attached. I don't intend to—to become emotionally involved."

"You think you ain't already? Lordy, hon, you white gals sure does love to fool yourselves."

She shook her head, took a final sip of coffee and stood up.

"Reckon I'll cook some sausage and biscuits and cream gravy. That teasin' Mister Michael always comes down round seven-thirty, likes a good hot breakfast in the morning, something he sure idn't going to get from Miss Laura. She's another one foolin' herself. That cowboy's done lassoed her and got her hog-tied good—she just don't know it yet."

I carried hot coffee and a roll upstairs to our room, expecting to find Jason still in bed. He wasn't. He had already bathed and shaved and, wearing his best gray breeches and a white lawn shirt, stood in front of the mirror brushing his hair. I paused in the doorway a moment, watching him. He was so tall, so lean, rakishly attractive with those unusual features, those glorious gray-green eyes that could blaze with murderous rage or sparkle with merry humor or smolder with lazy sensuality or reflect the soul of a vulnerable boy, put-upon and ever so misunderstood. At the moment they were quite sober, reflecting the serious, dedicated, formidably intelligent artist and businessman he was at heart. What a complex creature he was, full of contradictions, full of moods, decidedly mercurial. During the past three and a half months a number of women here in Atlanta had tried their best to capture his interest. He had given them all the cold shoulder. A rogue he might be, but at least he was a faithful rogue.

Putting the brush down, running one strong hand over sleek, neatly arranged black locks, he turned and saw me standing there in the doorway. He nodded and reached for the black and emerald striped satin waistcoat he had tossed over the bedpost.

"I brought your coffee," I said. "One of Corey's cinnamon rolls, too."

"Thanks," he said curtly, pulling on the waistcoat. "Just set it down on the table there."

"Where on earth are you going at this hour?"

"Jackson and I have a meeting with the stage crew at eight o'clock—there are still some technicalities to work out. Too much time elapses between scene changes in Act One, we've got to figure out how to speed it up. Need to get on it early so there'll be plenty of time to work out any problems."

"For that you're wearing your best clothes?"

"We've a meeting with Courtland and the theater directors at ten, then I'll take Courtland to lunch."

"You mean Robert Courtland has finally come to Atlanta?"

Jason smoothed down the waistcoat and picked up his elegant gray silk ascot, turning back to the mirror. "You think he'd miss opening night? Of course he's in Atlanta. Been here a week, in fact."

"And none of us *knew*?"

"There was no need for you to know," he informed me. "You had enough on your minds without worrying about Courtland, trying to impress him. Besides, he didn't want to bother you at this crucial time."

"Very considerate of him," I said.

Ascot finally arranged to his satisfaction, the flapping ends neatly tucked into the top of his waistcoat, Jason reached for the full-tailed gray frock coat he had also tossed over the bedpost.

"He's quite pleased with everything, incidentally. He caught the play last night, thought you were all superb."

I could feel the color drain from my cheeks. "Robert Courtland was in the theater last night?" I spoke each word carefully, with lethal calm.

"Told me he wanted to sit in on the rehearsal. He was out front, in one of the seats near the back of the house."

"You didn't tell us," I said.

"No reason for you to know," he replied.

"He—he saw that *fiasco*. He saw me make an absolute fool of myself. He saw me throw a lamp at you—"

"He understands all about nerves and temperament. He—"

"He probably thinks I'm a *mad*woman!"

"He thinks you're a brilliantly gifted actress. He wants to see you before the performance tonight, extend his personal best wishes. Extremely nice chap. You'll like him a lot."

"You son of a bitch!"

Jason looked at me with puzzled eyes, shrugged into the frock coat and then stepped over to pick up the cup of coffee I had set down on the table. I glared at him, two bright pink spots blazing on my cheeks. He sipped the coffee, gazing at me calmly over the rim of the cup. It was obvious he saw no reason why I should be upset. He was that dense. He was that blockheaded. I longed to hit him with something very heavy. I told him so.

"You really must get hold of yourself, Dana. Opening night jitters can be bad, I know, but—"

"You let us all make fools of ourselves! If we'd known he was out there we would have been on our best behavior, we would have—"

"You're making far too much of this," he said in an infuriatingly calm and reasonable voice. "Courtland didn't want you to know he was out front. He was afraid it might inhibit you. It probably would have, too. You'd have been even worse than you were."

"Even worse? *Who* would have been even worse?"

"You, my pet."

"I happen to have been brilliant last night!"

"Billy was brilliant. Corey was brilliant. You were abysmally bad until I finally got a performance out of you. Mmmm, this cinnamon roll is perfectly delicious."

"I hope you choke on it!"

Jason grinned, finished coffee and roll and then sauntered out of the room, pausing to plant a perfunctory kiss on my cheek. I seized his empty cup, ran to the doorway and hurled it at him. It crashed against the wall, missing his head by a good two feet. He turned, waved and strolled on down the hall, disappearing into the stairwell. I felt much better after throwing the cup. I felt remarkably stimulated, as a matter of fact. Jason had a way of making me feel richly, gloriously alive, even when he was at his worst.

We had all been instructed to relax today, to rest up for tonight's performance, but that, of course, was totally out of the question. All of us were entirely too keyed-up. Immediately after lunch Dulcie went back to the theater to fuss over the costumes some more, and Billy went out for a drive with the Atlanta belle he was currently squiring. Ollie took the boys for an outing, promising Corey not to stuff them with too many sweets, and Corey was busy preparing headache powders and ice packs for Adam, who claimed he was sick and couldn't possibly go on in that fuzzy gray wig and awful makeup. Bartholomew elected to stay in his room, teaching Theodore a new trick, and Laura and I decided that we simply had to go shopping, something we had had precious little time to do.

Because of the unrest over the play, Michael insisted he come along, and he dutifully trailed after us from shop to shop, looking painfully bored and splendidly masculine in scuffed tan boots, snug tan breeches, a faded old salmon-pink shirt, and the familiar battered tan kidskin jacket. A wide-brimmed western hat slanted atop his sun-streaked golden-brown hair, and drooping lids half-concealed his clear gray eyes. His six-shooter, I knew, was jammed into his waistband and hidden by his jacket. We received a great many stares as we made our progress, but no wild-eyed redneck came after us with tar and feathers, nor did a League of Decency lady pummel us with a placard. When I pointed this out, Michael reminded me that it was early in the day. He clearly expected trouble tonight.

"I think it's all a tempest in a teapot," Laura said, gazing into the shop windows as we strolled down the sidewalk. "It wouldn't surprise me a bit if Jason has staged the whole ruckus just to sell tickets. The people here in Atlanta have been splendid to us. It's a wonderfully civilized and sophisticated city, and—''

"And there are a lot of hostile bigots," Michael interrupted, "even in a city as forward-thinking as Atlanta. Some of those threats were genuine. I want you both to be on guard tonight."

"We've got you to protect us, love," Laura said blithely. "Look at that hat, Dana. Wide-brimmed black velvet with blue egret feathers sweeping over one side. What do you think?"

"Perfect for you," I told her.

"I must try it on. Let's go inside."

As she was trying on the hat, Laura agreed with me that it was dastardly of Jason not to tell us that Robert Courtland was in the theater last night. She, for one, would have paid more attention and given more spark to her teeny, tiny, shockingly small role of Lenore, hardly more than a *walk*-on. As it was, she had been desultory and boring, with no animation at all, and he probably hadn't even *no*ticed her. He was frightfully wealthy, she understood, as rich as Croesus, in fact, and extremely good-looking to boot. A girl needed to keep her eye out for the main chance.

"What's that you said?' Michael inquired.

"Girl talk, love. Go back to your guard duty."

Laura and I agreed that Jason must have made a very good impression on Robert Courtland, for Courtland had given him a free hand and provided him with unlimited funds. We had a full crew backstage, all of them paid top salaries, and sets and costumes were of the very finest quality—Dulcie had been in heaven, using the most exquisite silks and velvets, the costliest linens and broadcloth. All of our dressing rooms had been refurbished, my own completely redecorated in white and gold with gilded white Louis XV wardrobe and dressing table and an antique mirror, all of this done, according to Jackson, at Courtland's specific instructions. He seemed determined to give us the best production, the most lavish accommodations, yet he had remained in the background, indeed a man of mystery.

"It'll be interesting to meet him at last," Laura said.

"It certainly will," I agreed.

"I wonder if he likes brunettes."

"He'd better not," Michael informed her.

Laura passed on the hat, deciding that the faux jewel clip on the crown was gaudy, but she tried on several more, as did I, until Michael finally manhandled us out of the shop. We bought long, creamy soft kidskin gloves in another shop, reticules and silk parasols at yet another. Laura made Michael try on a beautifully tailored dusty tan jacket of heavy corduroy at Atlanta's leading emporium. It was a perfect fit and he looked quite magnificent. She bought it for him despite his protests and told him in no uncertain terms that she wanted him to get rid of that disreputable jacket he'd been wearing ever since we'd met him. Both Laura and Michael protested when I insisted on going into the downtown bookstore, where I purchased nothing but learned that Julian's book had gone into its ninth printing and that he had been the toast of Atlanta when he lectured here in May. It was well after five when we finally arrived back at the house, Michael heavily laden with packages and grumbling most unpleasantly.

We were all edgy and apprehensive as the hour to leave for the theater drew near. None of us could eat anything, but Billy poured himself a very stiff whiskey. He'd had a miserable afternoon. The belle had accused him of being insincere and he had accused her of being a prude and they had fought bitterly. Ollie complained that both boys had been absolute terrors and made themselves sick on maple sugar balls and Andy threw up and it was the last straw, positively the last, she intended to have nothing else to do with the little buggers. Bartholomew said that Theodore was looking puny and had turned down his chopped chicken and he, Bartholomew, was in no mood to go on tonight, he was too worried. Corey came in looking resplendent in garnet taffeta and a black lace shawl and told us that Adam had fully recovered and would be joining us as soon as he could decide which fancy waistcoat to wear to the theater.

"Headache powders do the job?" Laura asked. "Or was it the ice packs?"

"Wudn't either of 'em. I just finally got tired of pampering him and told him he was going to get his black ass outta bed or I'd kick it from here to Sunday. He leaped right up, fit as could be."

Adam dutifully appeared, extremely dapper in shiny black pumps, dark maroon breeches and frock coat and a noisy orange satin waistcoat embroidered with huge black and maroon flowers. A diamond stickpin glittered in the folds of his carefully arranged orange silk neckcloth. Gaudy as it was, he carried the attire off with jaunty aplomb, preening like a peacock. Corey raised her eyes heavenward and shook her head, but I could see that she was proud to possess so handsome and virile a man. The boys came in behind Adam, looking angelic and benign after long naps. They promptly rushed over and curled their arms around Ollie's legs. She rested a hand on each fuzzy little head and emitted a heavy, martyred sigh.

Although we usually walked the few short blocks to the theater, it had been decided that, under the circumstances, we would take carriages tonight. Jackson arrived with them at seven, sporting his usual loud checked coat and brandishing a smelly cigar. It was dark when we stepped outside, Bartholomew carrying a patient and bored-looking Theodore wrapped in a blue wool shawl. Adam elected to ride with Billy, Bart, Theodore, Ollie and the boys, and the rest of us got into the second carriage, Corey acidly informing Jackson that she was an artiste, her voice was very important and she did not intend to start coughing because of his foul cigar smoke. Jackson scowled and tossed the cigar away. He and Corey sat across from us. Michael, in his new tan corduroy jacket, curled his arm around Laura. Sitting on his other side, quite close because of limited space, I could tell that he still had the six-shooter jammed into the waistband of his breeches. All of us were grim as the carriage pulled away.

"I suppose Dulcie is still at the theater," I said.

"Been there all day," Jackson replied, "fussing over the costumes, guarding them like they were gold."

"I shouldn't wonder," Laura said. "That gown Dana wears in the last scene cost over fifteen hundred dollars. In my one infinitesimal appearance onstage, I wear a blue serge skirt and a white cotton blouse with balloon sleeves."

"Hush your moanin', gal," Corey scolded. "Me, I wear faded gingham—ragged at that."

"You're a milliner's assistant," Michael told his inamorata. "That's what a milliner's assistant would wear. My part isn't all that large either, but do you hear me complaining? I just consider myself lucky to be in a major production like this one."

"Sod off, love," Laura said.

As it was a warm evening, the carriage windows were open, and we could hear the grinding of spinning wheels and the lazy clop-clop of horse hooves on cobblestones. Gazing out the window, I saw an ashy gray-black sky strewn with silvery chips of stars and, as we neared downtown, the yellow-orange blur of lights. We turned onto Atlanta's main street, the theater up ahead, and we could hear shouting then, hoarse and raucous. Michael tensed. Jackson sat up, scowling darkly. The carriage would let us off at the stage entrance in back, but we had to drive directly past the theater before we turned.

"There—there's a crowd in front of the theater," I said nervously. "Men with torches. Women with placards."

"Everyone stay calm," Michael said grimly.

The din grew louder as we drew nearer. The horses became skittish, and the driver had to tighten his hold on the reins. The carriage slowed down. A pack of twenty or more uncouth-looking men dressed like farmers swarmed over the pavements in front of the theater, many of them waving torches, all of them shouting obscenities, while a prim brigade of bespectacled, middle-aged women dressed in drab gray and brown dresses marched to and fro, holding up hand-printed placards denouncing our play and warning decent folk to stay away. Two large baskets and a cart of what looked like tomatoes stood near the curb, the entire scene bathed in the flickering, nightmarish glow of the torches. Michael pulled out his six-shooter.

"Lawdy," Corey whispered.

"Just stay calm!" Michael snapped.

"Anything you say, cowboy."

A husky lout in muddy boots, old brown trousers and a patched, coarse-woven white shirt with sleeves rolled up over his forearms stared intently at our carriage and recognized me. He shoved lank yellow locks from his forehead and gave a lusty hoot, running toward one of the baskets.

"That's them!" he bellowed. "That's that Dana-gal, and look! There's the nigger woman, too!"

He dove his hand into the basket and pulled out an egg and hurled it at the carriage. It flew right through the window and crashed with a loud splat directly over Jackson's head. The carriage was pelted with several more eggs as other men joined the leader, though no more came through the windows. The lank-haired lout urged his fellows on, reaching for a tomato now, holding it aloft, prepared to throw. Michael shoved me back, leaned across me and took careful aim. There was a deafening blast as he fired. The tomato exploded in the man's hand, soggy red pulp seeping over his palm and down his arm, his eyes widening with shock. "Jesus!" he cried. "They got guns!" Michael fired again, shattering the wheel of the cart. It toppled over, rotten tomatoes spilling into the street.

"Bravo!" Corey exclaimed.

"Show-off," Laura said dryly.

Michael scrambled over me and leaned out the window. "Get the hell out of here!" he yelled at the driver, and then the carriage moved briskly on down the street, turning a corner and eventually bringing us in back of the theater, where a single lamp hung over the stage door, illuminating the wooden steps and making a misty fan-shaped slur in the darkness. Laura and I were both shaken as we got out of the carriage, but Corey climbed out like a queen, wrapping her black lace shawl regally around her shoulders. The second carriage pulled up right behind us, it, too, covered with ugly splatters. Bartholomew alighted with great dignity, cradling a still-bored Theodore in his arms, and then the boys came spilling out, quite elated by all the excitement. Billy and an exasperated Ollie helped Adam out. His dark brown face looked ashen. He was trembling visibly and jibbering incoherently. Corey gave a weary sigh.

"He's a lover," she explained, "not a fighter. You aren't hurt, buster!" she informed him. "If you don't want a boot up your ass, you'll stop that snivelin' *right now*!"

Adam gave her a mournful look, sobbed and tried manfully to pull himself together. A stern-faced, agitated Jason was waiting backstage. Striped waistcoat and gray frock coat had been removed, the neckcloth was gone, and his thin white lawn shirt was soiled, one sleeve badly ripped and hanging down at the shoulder. His black locks were atumble, the skin on his right cheekbone scraped, as though he had received a blow. That he'd been in a fight was fairly obvious. Ignoring the rest of us, he took Michael aside, and the two men conferred in lowered voices for several moments. Michael finally nodded and started toward the front of the theater. "Everything's under control!" Jason announced to the nervous assembly of actors. "Go on to your dressing rooms. The play will begin at eight sharp, exactly as scheduled." Everyone started talking at once then, and Jason came over to me and took hold of my arm.

"Are you all right?" he asked.

"I'm a bit shaken up, but—you—you've been hurt."

"It's just a scrape."

"It needs to be cleaned. What hap—"

"There was a little set-to—nothing you need bother about. I'll tell you about it later. You're all right—that's the only thing that matters. When I heard those gunshots—"

"No one was harmed. Michael was wonderful. I wish you'd let me—"

"I knew Mike'd be with you. That's why I didn't go back to the house with Jackson. I figured there'd be trouble—I didn't expect anything like this. We have the front doors barricaded, and Courtland has hired some men who'll be here shortly to handle the mob. It'll be dispersed before the paying customers start arriving. Sure you're all right?"

I nodded. He squeezed my arm.

"See you later, then. There're a lot of things I still have to do. You're a trouper, Dana. You're going to be great tonight."

"That scrape—I wish you'd let me clean it and put—"

"It's nothing!" he said testily. "I'm *busy*, Dana."

An excited Dulcie waylaid me as I started toward my dressing room. Yellow curls disarrayed, brown eyes asparkle, she was wearing one of the familiar tentlike garments that only emphasized her girth, this one of apricot linen, and the familiar pincushion was strapped to her wrist. With great élan she told me how the men outside had tried to break into the theater when they first arrived, how Jason and the stagehands had battled them back and barricaded the doors, how Jason had felled three of the ruffians, ever so heroic, it was better than a play, how that Mr. Courtland—so nice, so gallant, so attractive—had pitched in, too, then left immediately to go fetch the men he had hired earlier for security tonight. No one had expected trouble to erupt so soon, which was why the men hadn't already been here.

"You're going to adore that Mr. Courtland—he's a real gentleman. Told me I'd done a magnificent job with the costumes, said he'd never seen finer. He planned on meeting everyone in the cast before the performance tonight, but with all this ruckus I imagine he'll be too busy."

"I imagine he will be," I said. "No doubt we'll meet him afterward."

A heavenly fragrance assailed my nostrils as I opened the door of my dressing room. Candles filled the room with a bright glow, and I was startled to see three enormous white wicker baskets of roses, a veritable bower of roses, velvet-soft petals a delicate pink. There was a floral bouquet on my dressing table as well, white and mauve hyacinths tied with a blue satin bow, but it was completely overshadowed by the roses. I reached for the small white card visible in one of the baskets. *You are going to be magnificent tonight* was written in strong elegant script, and it was signed *Robert Courtland*. The roses must have cost a fortune, I thought, touching one of the velvety petals. Our producer certainly didn't do things by half measures. I reveled in the beauty of the roses for several moments, then picked up the bouquet of hyacinths. There was a card with it, too. It simply read *Love, Jason*. I smiled and my eyes grew suspiciously moist. Those two words, that paltry bouquet with its tacky blue ribbon, meant more to me than all the roses in the world.

I had already applied my stage makeup and done my hair and was slipping into the frock in which I made my entrance when the door opened and Laura came in, looking unusually pleased. Seeing the roses, she arched a brow and pretended to be put out.

"I only got *one* basket," she complained. "A small one at that."

"Help me do this up in back, will you? I love this brushed cotton. It's almost as fine as silk."

Laura fastened the tiny hooks, and I turned to the mirror to adjust the low-cut neckline and small puffed sleeves. The creamy, extremely expensive brushed cotton was a rich, vivid buttercup-yellow, perfect with my skin and hair.

"Well?" Laura asked expectantly. "What did you get?"

"Get? I don't know what you mean."

"What was in the basket, love? Robert Courtland placed a small gift in the basket of roses he had delivered to each of the ladies in the cast. Ollie got an exquisite blue and gold eighteenth-century pillbox, and Corey got dangling ruby earrings—real rubies, love. I got a small sapphire pendant on a thin silver chain. What did you get?"

"I didn't get anything."

"You must not have *looked*."

She searched the first basket of roses, found nothing, searched the second, frowned, then reached into the third basket with a triumphant smile, pulling out a long, flat white velvet box and handing it to me. I was surprised at how heavy it was. I sat down on the dressing stool and opened the box. The brilliant, shimmering fire of diamonds dazzled us both. Laura gasped. I lifted the necklace out of the box, holding it in my palm. There were three looped strands of perfectly cut diamonds, large pear-shaped pendants suspending from the center of each loop. The jewels glistened in the candlelight, each icy-clear gem ashimmer with liquid fire, pale violet and mauve and blue and silver, rainbow flames leaping and gleaming. I had never seen anything so gorgeous in my life. Laura was as speechless as I was, but only for a moment. She reached into the box, taking out the card nestling on a bed of white satin.

" 'A small token of my admiration,' " she read. " 'Please wear these in the final scene tonight. The prop diamonds are not worthy of you.' A token of his admiration! Looks like you've landed yourself a big one, love."

My hand trembled. The strands of diamonds shimmered all the more, delicate, rainbow-hued flames blazing inside their icy prisons.

"I—I couldn't possibly accept this," I whispered.

"Don't be hasty," she said.

"It wouldn't—it wouldn't be proper."

"Who's worrying about propriety?"

"When a man gives a gift like this, he expects—it means—"

"String him along, love," she advised, "at least until you get earrings and bracelet to match."

I placed the necklace back into its nest of white satin and closed the box, a resolute expression on my face. Laura shook her head and said I was a stronger woman than she was and added that while she admired my character, she thought I was out of my mind. I stood up and smoothed the rich folds of buttercup-yellow out over my underskirts.

"I'll give it back to him after the play," I said.

"Demented," she sighed. "Definitely."

Twenty-five minutes later I was backstage, in the dimly lit wings, wringing my hands. Ten minutes to go. In ten minutes the curtain would go up. Ten more minutes and we would be booed and hissed and pelted with refuse, just like in my nightmare. The ladies with their placards were still marching to and fro out in front of the theater, but Courtland and his hired men had broken up the crowd of ruffians. According to Michael, there had been only minor damage, all of it suffered by the ruffians who had quickly cleared the area when Courtland's men went into action. We had only the audience to worry about now, and I could hear them filing into the theater, speaking in low voices, turning down their seats, rustling their programs.

I stepped over to the peek hole in the curtains and peered out to see Atlanta's most elite filling up the house, all of them in elegant attire, all of them rather smug and self-conscious about attending this "very important" opening. I watched a plump, silver-haired matron in pink satin and cream lace wave gaily to a dour gentleman in blue with goatee and silver-headed cane. Stout middle-aged couples, belles and their beaux, studious-looking gentlemen, proud spinsters and three or four beefy men in dark suits settled down, studied their programs, prepared to pass judgment. My stomach seemed to flip-flop and my skin felt chilled. I moved back into the wings. Five minutes. List in hand, a stagehand was checking to see that all props were on the set, the squalid room in New Orleans where Jessie took in washing, all done in grim shades of brown and tan, gray and black. When I appeared, my yellow dress would seem like a burst of sunshine in the gloom.

"You're as white as a sheet, honey," Corey said, joining me in the wings. "No need to fret, child. They aren't going to eat us. Forget about them. Forget about Dana, too. You're Janine, and I'm your poor old ma."

I was amazed by her transformation. The chic, sophisticated colored woman with her caustic wit and dry, sarcastic manner had become a broken-down, defeated old Negro with lined, weary face and stringy gray hair, her shoulders bowed, her thin, frail frame covered with a shapeless and ragged gingham dress. Those sad brown eyes had seen a lifetime of grief, and that cracked, apologetic whisper of a voice had offered up many an unanswered prayer. She squeezed my hand, then ushered the boys onstage, warning them in her natural voice that if either of them messed up or stepped on one of her lines she'd tan their black hides so hard they wouldn't sit down for a week. The boys tittered. For all their rowdiness, they were perfect pros onstage.

The house lights began to dim. I saw Ollie in the wings on the other side of the stage, her own transformation almost as amazing as Corey's. Garish makeup was gone, replaced by far more subtle paint that concealed most of the wrinkles and gave her a pink and white complexion. The bright red wig had been exchanged for one of silver-gray, sleeked back smoothly, a bun in back. The flamboyant Englishwoman was now a demure southern matron, a role she played with an impressive skill. She gave me a wave. I nodded nervously.

The house was completely dark now, only the footlights blazing. There was an expectant hush out front, whispers and scurrying noises behind me. Onstage, Corey gave a weary sigh, picked up the washboard and, placing it into a big tub of water, began to scrub a wet, soapy garment. A creaking, ringing noise broke the silence as the curtain slowly rang up. The set was bathed with light, and there came a collective gasp from the audience. Clearly, none of them had ever viewed a set so stark, so realistic, and none of them had ever seen a Negro onstage before. There were low murmurs. Corey continued to scrub, while in one corner of the squalid room the boys played soldiers with dried corn husks. From where I stood in the wings I could see the first few rows beyond the footlights and the expressions of those sitting there.

The plump, silver-haired matron in pink was fanning herself vigorously and trying to control her shock. The gentleman beside her was nodding in approval, making a great show of tolerance and superiority. There were scattered "Boos!" and protesting "Shhhs!" and then the beefy gentleman in brown in the fourth row sprang to his feet and waved his fist.

"Get that nigger off the stage!" he shouted. "This here's a theater for *white* folks!"

Three other men in various parts of the theater jumped up, too, yelling in angry voices, while others tried to quiet them. The agitators were obviously plants, obviously intended to stop the play, but they were quickly thwarted. Several men rushed down the aisles, seizing the protestors and manhandling them out. Michael, who didn't appear until the last scene and was still in his cowboy attire, grabbed the beefy man in brown in a hammerlock and stranglehold, dragging him up the aisle to the back of the theater. There were shocked cries and much scuffling, and then, when the last protestor had been evicted, a great round of approving applause. Atlanta's elite had clearly decided to make a public display of their advanced thinking and sophistication. Throughout the disturbance Corey had continued to wearily scrub, rubbing the garment vigorously, wringing it out, never once slipping out of character, and as the applause died down she picked up another garment and immersed it in the soapy water.

Adam was in the wings beside me now, the dapper, handsome young buck transformed into a grizzled, careworn Negro defeated by life. He took several deep breaths. His legs were trembling. He closed his eyes for a moment, sending up a silent prayer, and then he shambled slowly onstage. High-strung and temperamental he might be, but he was a superb actor and in their scene together gave a performance almost as fine as Corey's. He finally gathered up the boys, herding them offstage, and Corey shook her head and went back to her washing, looking even more dejected. It was time for me to go on.

My knees turned to water. My stomach lurched, and my heart seemed to stop beating. The chill I had felt earlier returned. My skin was like ice. I was paralyzed, totally unable to move. This is absurd, Dana, I told myself. You're an actress. You're going to go out there and give a performance. They're not going to throw rotten tomatoes and eggs. They're going to love you. You're going to *make* them love you. This is just stage fright. You've had it before and you'll undoubtedly have it again.

A frantic Jason materialized out of the shadows, seizing my arm.

"What the hell *is* this? You're *on*. Get out there!"

"I—Jason, I can't—I'm sick—"

"You'll be fine."

"I—I think I'm going to—"

"Get your ass *out* there!"

He let go of my arm, and somehow I moved. Somehow my legs carried me out onto the stage and I was in the bleak, colorless room and my yellow dress was like a vivid burst of sunlight and I heard applause, they were applauding my entrance, and I looked at Corey and she wasn't Corey, she was Jessie, and she looked at me with sad, worried eyes that told me I was foolhardy and asking for a lifetime of grief, and I became Janine. I forgot Dana, forgot the tension, forgot the audience, living my role now, the only reality that of the drama unfolding. When I embraced Corey and called her Ma there were audible gasps, but I paid no heed to them. I was Janine, a Negro woman who had been passing for white, who intended to deny her blood completely and run off with a white man.

The first scene ended and the curtain rang down and there was loud applause and Corey gave me a tight hug and we hurried offstage, stagehands rushing past us to change the set for Scene Two. Jason grabbed me and rocked me and told me I had been magnificent, bloody magnificent, and then I was hurrying to my dressing room to change. The next hour and a half seemed to pass in a blur. Scene Two went even better than Scene One, Laura marvelous in her role as Lenore, however small, Billy not Billy but Travis, absolutely brilliant and compelling as the weak, pampered but good-hearted southern dandy determined to make Janine his bride.

The audience was rapt during Act Two, completely caught up in the drama and utterly silent, spellbound. When, in Act Three, Travis has shot himself and Janine and Jessie are thrown out by his parents, there were loud sobs from some of the more sensitive ladies out front. I knew we had won them over. They loved us. Just one more scene to go. I was rushing to my dressing room once again, and Dulcie was waiting, a worried look on her face. The false diamond necklace I was to wear in the last scene was missing, no one could find it anywhere, what were we going to *do*? I told Dulcie not to worry as she helped me into the spectacular gown I wore in the last scene, heavy white silk completely overlaid with tissue-thin white tulle with tiny stripes of gold thread. The tulle had been imported from Paris. The thread was real gold. The gown was incredibly sumptuous with its off-the-shoulder sleeves, low-cut bodice and full, swelling skirt.

"I don't know what could have *hap*pened to it—" Dulcie was still fretting about the necklace. "You can't possibly go on without it—it's pivotal to the scene. You *have* to have a diamond necklace."

"I have one," I said.

The long white velvet box was still on my dressing table. I opened it, and Dulcie's eyes widened as I took out the glittering cascade of real diamonds. It was very clever of Mr. Courtland to appropriate the false necklace so I would be forced to wear the real. I had no time to think about that now. I fastened the necklace around my throat, the shimmering gems with their rainbow fires resting heavily against my skin and drawing attention to my near-exposed bosom.

"It—it's gorgeous!" Dulcie exclaimed. "Where did—"

"Later," I snapped.

I hurried back to the stage and took my place at the elaborate dressing table in Janine's dressing room in the luxurious New Orleans apartment paid for by her handsome and ruthless white lover who she feared was about to leave her. I closed my eyes for a moment, Dana vanishing, Janine looking into the mirror with weary, disillusioned eyes as the curtain slowly rose. There was applause for my gown and the beautiful set, but Janine couldn't hear it. She heard only the sad voice inside that told her there was no escape, she was doomed to the inevitable fate of her kind. Hearing a carriage outside, I stood and walked to the window, fighting back my fear, telling myself it wasn't true, Beau wasn't going to leave me for another woman.

Michael entered, elegant and stunningly handsome and icy-cold as Beau. He told me it had been an amusing six months, but he was weary now, it was over, and I gnawed my lower lip and tried to take it calmly. He told me I had nothing to complain about, he had given me those diamonds, he had given me a fancy wardrobe and kept me in style. I was to vacate the apartment in two days. Another woman would be moving in. I told him he couldn't just cast me aside like an old shoe, and he told me he could do anything he damn well pleased.

"What—what am *I* supposed to do?" I asked.

"You can always sell the diamonds—or yourself."

"You—you're a bastard!" I cried. "A bastard!"

"And you, my dear, are an uppity nigger slut."

He slapped me brutally across the face and I fell to the floor and he gazed at me with utter disdain for a moment and then left. I sobbed. I pulled myself up and stood rubbing my cheek, tears streaming down my cheeks. After a few moments I brushed the tears away and went back to the dressing table and sat down, looking at myself again, accepting my fate. When my mother entered, dressed in an elegant black taffeta maid's uniform with a white organdy apron, I was calmly repairing my makeup, but my eyes were hard, my mouth set in a resolute line. I told her what had happened, told her we had to be out of the apartment day after tomorrow. She was distraught.

"But—but, baby, we don't have no money. Dat man never gave you any money, jest things. We ain't got noplace to go. We—lawdy, chile, what are we goin' to do?"

"You're going to stay here tonight," I told her, "and—and

you're not to worry. There's a ball in the Quarter tonight, and there will be many wealthy men looking for amusement.''

''Baby, you—you ain't gonna put yourself on th' block. You ain't gonna become a fancy nigger whore—''

''What do you think I've been for the past six months?''

''Baby—''

''I'm going to take care of us, Ma. I—I tried to be something I'm not, and now I'm going to be what—what I was destined to be at birth. Fetch my wrap. I'm going to the Quadroon Ball.''

The curtain came down in absolute silence, the audience so stunned and moved they made not a sound. I was wrung out, physically and emotionally depleted, but there was a wild elation as well. I took Corey's hand, and she gave me a triumphant smile. The rest of the cast hurried out and we lined up for curtain calls, and when the curtain rose there was raging, thunderous applause, the sophisticated, cultivated audience berserk in their approval. The applause grew even louder as each of us took our bows. The building seemed to shake when Corey stepped to the footlights, and when I moved out to take my bow, there was such a roar I felt the floor tremble. I moved back. The curtain came up, went down, came up again, eight curtain calls in all, and then they were shouting, ''Dana! Dana! Dana!'' and the others left the stage and I was standing alone in front of the footlights and they were cheering still.

I smiled, deeply moved by this adulation, and there were tears in my eyes as I nodded to them, and then everything seemed to blur together and shift strangely and I was no longer in the theater, I was back in the swamps in a room with herbs hanging from the beams and savage African masks on the walls and an enormous marmalade cat curling at the feet of a wizened, ugly old Negro woman. The applause was still defeaning, but it became muted, a mere background to the raspy drawl of her voice. ''I sees you an'—an' you is behind a half circle of lights an' you is wearin' a lovely gown, it seems like silk, yes, gold and white striped silk an' you is wearin' sparklers, too, at your throat a necklace of sparklers . . . The lights are flickerin' an' people—people, lots of 'em, they is watchin' you, makin' a big commotion . . . but you ain't frightened at all. You is smilin'.'' Mama Lou, I whispered silently, you *were* right, and I saw her wise old eyes then, saw her nodding, and then everything blurred and shifted again and the vision was gone.

Men came marching down the aisles carrying huge white wicker baskets of roses, creamy white and sumptuous yellow-gold roses, and I knew who had ordered them at once. The baskets were brought onstage and one of the men handed me a large bouquet of white roses and I held them and smiled and listened to the cheers and, finally, after what seemed an eternity, stepped back as the curtain came down. I turned then, applause still thundering behind the curtain, and I saw him standing in the wings, tall and lean with the trim, muscular build of an athlete. He wore elegant beige breeches and frock coat and a rust satin waistcoat and a cream silk neckcloth, and his coppery brown hair was neatly brushed. His lean and ruggedly handsome face had the weathered, lived-in look I remembered so well. He nodded, looking at me with smoke-gray eyes filled with the same recognition, the same emotion that had filled them that morning in Natchez when he stood on the dock and I stood at the railing and that strange, strong force seemed to bind us together.

Chapter Twenty

I KNEW FULL WELL that Robert Courtland was in love with me, and I couldn't deny that I felt a strange, compelling attraction for him, but nothing had happened, and, I assured myself, nothing would. Robert had been a perfect gentleman each time I had seen him—warm, considerate, gallant—and he had made no advances, had said or done nothing the least bit forward or untoward, but nevertheless, I knew. A woman always does. He had visited Atlanta several times during those seven months of our run there, had come to Washington, D.C., when we had opened in that city, and now he was in New Orleans for our opening here. He had taken me out to dinner a number of times with Jason's complete approval—it was only natural for our producer to want to dine with the leading lady—and each time I had felt that unusual bond between us, as though we had known each other in a different lifetime. It was a curious feeling, something I couldn't even begin to explain, but it was undeniably there. Although we had never discussed it, I knew Robert felt it, too.

I dressed carefully for our afternoon together in a white silk with narrow gold, red and turquoise stripes. It had short puffed sleeves, a demure scooped neckline and a very full skirt that belled out over half a dozen white silk petticoats. I slipped on a pair of long, elegant white gloves, then gave myself a final check in the mirror. Honey-blond hair tumbled to my shoulders in luxuriant waves, and the faint suggestion of lip rouge and eye shadow I had used earlier merely emphasized my natural coloring. I might not be the glamorous femme fatale the newspaper articles claimed I was, but at least I would pass. Fetching my white velvet reticule, I left my hotel suite, thankful that, for

431

propriety's sake, Jason had his own suite on a different floor. I wasn't attempting to *hide* anything from him, but I saw no reason why he should know I was spending the afternoon with Robert. After all, Jason didn't *own* me.

He thinks he does, I told myself as I started down the hall. He thinks he invented me, that I owe everything to him, that if it weren't for him, I would be selling gloves behind a notions counter. He thinks I should jump at his command, do exactly what he wants, and he can't understand why I am not willing to sign another contract and spend the entire summer working on his new play. I'm tired, tired to the bone. I want a little time off, time to rest, and he wants to push, push, push. He will simply have to wait. He is *not* going to bully me into giving up my time off. As soon as we finish our run here, I fully intend to forget the theater for three full months. When September comes . . . we'll see.

Poor Jason, I thought as I turned the corner and started toward the staircase. Although he would never admit it, he was afraid that if he didn't get me signed and sealed for next season I might well leave the company and accept one of the many offers I had received since *The Quadroon* opened. Every theatrical manager in the country had come to Atlanta to see our play, it seemed, and they all longed to take over the career of its star. Mr. Conrad Drummond, producer extraordinaire, had offered me a fortune if I would sign with him and appear in his next production in New York. Under his management, he assured me, I would become the toast of two continents, I was wasting my time "here in the sticks." I had managed to smile charmingly before Jason bodily ejected him from my dressing room. Drummond's offer made him extremely nervous, as did all the others I had received. I was content to let the scoundrel suffer. I had shared his bed and his life for almost a year now, and if he doubted my loyalty and love—well, deep affection, anyway—he could just worry.

The Fontaine was New Orleans' newest, grandest hotel, all gleaming mahogany and plush red velvet. The vast lobby was a tropical jungle of potted palms, huge green ferns and lushly blooming plants. It was aswarm with fashionably attired people, and most of them turned to stare as I came down the graceful marble staircase. I was quite accustomed to that by now. After the opening in Atlanta, I had become the darling of the journal-

ists. Dana, star of *The Quadroon*, the most notorious play of
the decade. Dana, the seductive beauty whose every move was
of vital interest to a sensation-starved public. I'd learned to live
with the publicity, but I still cringed on occasion when I read
the outlandish, preposterous stories the gentlemen of the press
concocted. I had yet to serve champagne to a foreign prince
from my satin slipper, turn down a fortune in rubies from an
Eastern potentate or weep when a New York millionaire shot
himself after I turned down his proposal. It was sheer hokum,
but, as Jason repeatedly pointed out, the public loved to read
that kind of crap and it was terrific for the box office.

"Here you are," Robert Courtland said in that deep, rich
baritone of his. "Looking splendid, too, I might add."

He stepped forward, taking my hand, giving it a firm squeeze.
I looked into his smoke-gray eyes, eyes full of warmth and masculine appreciation, and the familiar feeling of kinship filled me
once again. How secure I felt with him, how comfortable and
at ease. The physical attraction was undeniably there, but there
was no sense of threat, none of the complex undercurrents usually present in male-female relationships. Laura claimed that
Robert was merely biding his time, that when he finally made
his move, it would be a dilly. That might well be true, but in
the meantime I thoroughly enjoyed his company.

"Thank you," I said. "You—you're looking rather well yourself."

His wide lips curled and lifted at one corner in a genial half
smile. Forty-four years old, he had thick, neatly brushed auburn
hair that gleamed with a rich coppery sheen and hadn't a hint of
gray, belying his age, but his ruggedly handsome face had the
worn, weathered look that added character and made him even
more attractive. Wearing leaf-brown breeches and frock coat, a
bronze and beige patterned satin waistcoat and beige silk neckcloth, he had the polish and poise that come with great wealth,
the assurance as well. Robert was said to be one of the richest
men in the South, one of the most powerful, too. Charming,
pleasant, polite, he nevertheless exuded great strength and authority, and I suspected he could be utterly ruthless if he needed
to be. Robert Courtland was a self-made man without a drop of
blue blood, and one didn't attain his position and power without
the killer instinct.

"I have a carriage waiting outside," he said. "Where would

you like to lunch? I can think of any number of wonderful restaurants."

"I—do you know where I'd really like to go?"

"Where's that?"

'I'd like to go to the market," I told him. "There's an area with little tables and chairs sitting out under umbrellas. You can buy all sorts of wonderful food at the surrounding stalls and eat out in the open. It's not very fancy, but—I've always wanted to do that."

"Do it you shall," he promised.

He smiled again and took my arm and we moved through the palms and plants, passing the long, elegant front desk and heading toward the door. Two journalists happened to be in the lobby and, spotting me, hurried toward us, much like hunters pouncing upon prey. Although I got along well with them, silently enduring their rudeness and uncouth manners, I found journalists as a breed thoroughly unsavory. They were, to a man, loud, aggressive, unscrupulous and amazingly self-important. Getting a story, truthful or not, was only slightly less urgent than the Second Coming to all of them. The pair who besieged us now was typical, one a husky black-haired chap in a checked suit, the other an untidily dressed youth with tousled brown hair and eager eyes.

"Miss O'Malley!" the man in the checked suit cried. "I'm Joe Clancy from *The New Orleans Picayune* and I've been hoping you'd come down—"

"Stevens!" the youth barked. "*The New Orleans Crescent*! Is it true you plan to perform in a nigger theater?"

"We are giving two special matinees at the Jewel Theater, yes," I replied in a cool voice. "Corey Washington, who plays my mother, has a huge following there, and we wanted to give them the opportunity to see their favorite actress in—"

"The Jewel is in niggertown. How do you feel about going down there, performing for an audience made up entirely of—"

"I feel quite honored to play in a very fine theater with a marvelous actress who has helped make it such a strong cultural force for the Free People of Color."

"What about the prince?" Clancy demanded. "Is he gonna be here tonight when you open at the Majestic?"

"I'm afraid there is no—"

"Miss O'Malley is on her way to lunch," Robert said, and there was a hard edge to his voice. "She does not care to answer any more questions now."

"Who the hell are *you*?" Stevens cried.

"I'm Robert Courtland," he replied, "and if you value your job, I strongly suggest you desist. At once."

Stevens blanched. So did Clancy. Both men hastily departed, disappearing among the plants. Robert escorted me on outside where an open carriage waited in front of the hotel. It was of richly polished brown wood, with padded beige velvet upholstery. A driver in brown velvet livery perched up front, while two magnificent chestnuts stamped impatiently in harness, eager to prance. Robert gave instructions to the driver, assisted me up into the carriage and then took his place beside me.

"I suppose you know we'll both be in the evening editions," I said as we started down the street. "You will have given me a diamond ring once belonging to Empress Josephine and I will have promised to go meet your family in Natchez as soon as we close here."

"I have no family," he informed me, "and my name is never in the newspapers—unless I want it to be. Neither the *Picayune* nor the *Crescent* will mention our being together this afternoon."

"Oh?"

"Rest assured," he replied.

"Speaking of diamonds," I said, "after our week here in New Orleans, the season will be over, and I must give the diamond necklace back to you. You refused to take it back, I refused to keep it, we argued, and I finally agreed to wear it onstage during the run of the play, vowing to give it back just as soon as we closed."

"I seem to recall something like that."

"You'll take it back?"

"On the contrary, I intend to give you a bracelet and earrings to match as a token of my appreciation. As producer of the play, I get a hefty percentage of the box office. Because of you, the play has been tremendously successful. Consequently, you've made me an awful lot of money."

"But—"

"I don't intend to argue about it," he informed me.

I started to protest more, and then I smiled. Then I burst into laughter. Robert arched one brow, giving me an inquisitive look. I shook my head and, finally controlling my laughter, told him Laura's reaction when she first saw the necklace.

"Both of us were convinced you had dishonorable intentions," I explained, "and Laura suggested that I string you along—at least until I got a bracelet and earrings to match. She'll die when I tell her about this."

"I plan to give Miss Devon a gift, too."

"Diamonds?"

"Sapphire earrings to match her pendant."

"She'll be thrilled. You—you really are wealthy, aren't you?"

"Shockingly wealthy. Aren't you glad you strung me along?"

"I'm glad you've become my friend," I said. "It's nice to have an older man to go out with on occasion, someone I can talk to, someone I—I don't feel threatened by. I enjoy being with you very much, Robert."

We were riding past the elegant, exclusive shops now, their windows abloom with lavish displays, and I caught my breath as I saw Corinne's, a gorgeous apricot velvet gown and a wide-brimmed apricot chapeau with curling white ostrich plumes displayed in the front window. Dear Corinne. I really should pay her a visit, I thought. Would she remember the awed and nervous girl fresh from the swamps who first visited her salon, speaking in an atrocious squawk? Would she associate her with the notorious actress who, at this particular point in time, was one of the most famous women in the country? Traffic was heavy this afternoon in late May, and we were forced to slow down. I turned, gazing pensively as we passed the dress salon.

"You seem to know New Orleans quite well," Robert said. "Have you ever lived here?"

"I—I spent almost a year here," I said quietly.

"It wasn't a happy time?"

"It was—in some ways it was very happy. It was very sad, too. I left New Orleans a brokenhearted girl and—now I'm an entirely different person."

"Happier?"

"Much happier," I said firmly.

Robert didn't press, didn't ask me any more questions, and I was extremely grateful for that. Not quite two years had passed since I had left New Orleans on the steamboat bound for St. Louis, but it seemed like an eternity ago. Julian, Delia, Charles, the months I had spent at the Etienne mansion—all that might have happened in another lifetime, I thought, and I assured myself that I was completely over that painful first love. Still, I found myself tensing up as we neared Etienne's. We turned the corner now; and there it was. The last time I had seen it, it had been a charred and smoking ruin. Now in the early afternoon sunlight it stood as grand and impressive as ever with a new pink brick front, new plate glass windows, a new striped awning. I recognized a couple of the pieces displayed in the windows. They had once been in the east wing.

Though completely restored, the store seemed deserted, and, yes, the items displayed looked vaguely dusty. Business couldn't be very good, I thought, and I forced back the flood of memories. The fortune of the Etienne family was no concern of mine, I reminded myself. I was glad to see that the store was still in business, but it . . . it really didn't matter one way or another. I was in the city to perform for the paying customers, not to relive the past, and I had no intentions of contacting any of the family. They were naturally aware that I was in the city. After the barrage of advance publicity, everyone not closed up in a convent knew that I was in New Orleans and that our scandalous play was opening tonight at the Majestic Theater.

"The market is just ahead," Robert said. "Hungry?"

"Ravenous," I confessed. "I didn't have any breakfast, only a cup of coffee, and, I may as well confess it, I'm dying to try some pork rinds."

"Pork rinds?"

"I passed the stall a dozen times, but we never stopped— Jezebel told me that was 'po' folks food,' not fit for a fine lady like myself. They fry the pork rinds until they're crispy and golden and light as a feather, and they look delicious."

"Pork rinds you shall have," he told me.

"And one of those small bread loaves stuffed with oysters in butter sauce. I've had one of them before. They're really tasty."

"I'm sure," he said.

"And a cup of gumbo, of course."

"Of course," Robert agreed.

The market was every bit as colorful and intriguing as I remembered. Dozens of exotic smells filled the air, and some quite earthy, all blending together to make a heady perfume that hung over the area. It was a sultry afternoon, lazy rays of sunlight bathing the cobbles. Negro women with huge baskets moved lethargically through the labyrinth of stalls, sniffing at barrels of black eel and mounds of plump pink shrimp, examining racks of meat, arguing with the vendors over the price of oranges and vivid yellow lemons and juicy scarlet plums. Prostitutes idled about, eating slices of melon and eyeing the men, and respectable women strolled together, exchanging gossip, occasionally pausing to buy a bunch of dried herbs or a string of mauve onions. Dogs barked, scurrying about among the litter of wilted cabbage leaves and carrots. Robert held my elbow as we sauntered past cages of squawking chickens and carts of apples and a wonderland of vegetable stalls. He wore the patient expression of an adult indulging a favored child.

"You don't like the market?" I inquired.

"It's fascinating," he said dryly.

I smiled, leading him to the open-air café. We took a table beneath a big umbrella, and Robert sat me down and went to fetch our food from the stalls that encircled the area. The handsome, distinguished middle-aged man in his elegant attire looked completely out of place as he returned with pork rinds wrapped in grease-spotted paper. He brought oyster loaves as well, two cups of gumbo and glasses of iced lemonade. I ate with great relish. Robert tried one pork rind and made a face, poked at his oyster loaf with a fork, looked at his gumbo with a decided lack of enthusiasm.

"Poor dear," I said. "You're not enjoying yourself at all."

"On the contrary, I'm enjoying myself immensely."

"You'd rather be in a fancy restaurant with haughty waiters hovering about offering plates of hors d'oeuvres and pouring expensive wines into fine crystal glasses."

"Perhaps," he admitted, "but being with you is pleasure enough. Are you really going to eat the rest of those disgusting things?"

"They're delicious," I protested, reaching for another pork rind.

He shook his head, the faint half smile curling on his lips again. There were a number of women at the other tables, and I noticed several of them looking at Robert with interest, even longing. Middle-aged he might be, but he was in marvelous shape, his trim, superbly muscled body that of a much younger man. Sunlight burnished his dark auburn hair, gilding it with deep coppery red highlights, and his wise smoke-gray eyes were full of secrets, touched with sadness as well. No randy, hot-blooded youth, he had the strength, the authority, the maturity that many women found vastly appealing. He would always be in control of any situation, always in command. In the bedroom, too, I thought. I sensed incredible drive and energy behind that carefully maintained facade, great sensuality, too. I studied his strong hands, the palms wide, the fingers long and sinewy, those of his left hand curled tightly around his glass of lemonade. He would be very masterful in bed, I suspected, very demanding, but generous, too, giving as he took. I felt a blush tinting my cheeks as these thoughts materialized.

"Something wrong?" he inquired.

"Just—it's a little sunny."

Robert stood up and adjusted the umbrella so that I had more shade. As he sat back down, I sighed. Yes, I was attracted to him, I couldn't deny that. He was an extremely attractive man, his wealth and power adding an extra fillip of allure, but the feelings he aroused in me weren't primarily sexual. I felt secure with him, felt safe and warm and protected, and there was a closeness that had been there from the first, as though we really had known each other in some other lifetime. Even before we met, when I had been standing at the railing of the steamboat and he on the dock below and our eyes had met and held, there had been the feeling of our being bound together somehow. Mama Lou might have been able to explain it. I certainly couldn't.

"Have you decided what you are going to do this summer?" he asked.

"Not yet," I said. "After we finish our week here, the company will separate until September. Ollie is staying here in New Orleans with an old friend who used to be in the company, and Billy is going to vacation at the plantation of one of his belles—he's already met her family, they adore him, I fear he's finally hooked. Bartholomew and Theodore are going to visit an aunt in Cincinnati. I don't know what Laura and Michael are going to do, but whatever it is, they'll be doing it together."

"And Donovan?"

"Jason's going back to Atlanta. He plans to spend the entire summer working on his new play. He's almost finished writing it, the National is offering him tremendous terms, and he'd like to get the entire production mounted during our hiatus—sets built, costumes designed, all the details worked out. Dulcie and Jackson will be in Atlanta, too. It—they'll be incredibly busy and it'll be incredibly frantic and nerve wracking and—'' I hesitated, looking down at my empty glass.

"You don't want to go with him?"

"Jason and I—we're very close, and it isn't that I don't want to be with him, it's just—for the past two years there's been nothing but theater. The noise, the confusion, the tension. I love being in the theater and I love acting, but I—I need a little rest. I'd like to laze in the sunshine someplace quiet, read all the novels I wanted to read, wake up in the morning with no rehearsals and no responsibility, nothing whatsoever I had to do and no one I had to see."

"I quite understand."

"Do—do you think I'm being terribly selfish?"

"Everyone needs to replenish the wells now and then."

"That's it exactly," I said quietly. "I—the past months have been wonderful and I'm very grateful for all the success, but I— every night onstage I've poured myself out, given my all, and I feel exhausted. I feel emptied. I do need to replenish the wells. Jason doesn't understand that. He thinks I'm being very unreasonable."

I looked at him, and we were both silent for a few moments, then he got up and went to fetch more lemonade. I watched him moving among the tables, going over to the stall, calm, confident, a splendid male who was well past youth but still in his prime. How easy it was to talk to him. How I enjoyed being with him. I smiled as he returned with the drinks. It was even sultrier now, heat waves shimmering visibly in the air, but although I could feel tiny droplets of perspiration sliding down my spine, Robert looked cool and fresh. He handed me my glass of lemonade and sat down. He took a sip of his lemonade, gazed at the glass for a moment and then, as though reaching a decision, set it aside, looking at me with level gray eyes.

"You could come to Natchez," he said.

"Natchez?"

"I have a house there. Belle Mead. It's just outside town, surrounded by oaks and gardens, with a river walk. It's very quiet. You could laze in the sunshine all you liked. You could read all the novels you wanted to read. I have a full staff of servants who would take very good care of you."

"It—it sounds lovely," I said, taken aback by the invitation, "but I really don't think—"

Robert smiled. "I shall be away on business most of the summer, Dana, and I can assure you that during the time I was in residence, I wouldn't infringe on your solitude. You wouldn't even have to see me if you didn't want to. Everything would be quite proper. . . ." The smile flickered. "I could even bring in a respectable lady chaperone if it would make you feel easier."

"I'm sure that wouldn't be necessary," I told him.

"This isn't—I'm not making an immoral proposal, Dana."

"I realize that."

"If you would like a place to rest, relax and replenish your wells, Belle Mead is open to you. It's said to be one of the finest homes in the South. I wouldn't know about that, but I'm very proud of it. I only wish I could spend more time there."

He said no more, and we left the market a short while later. I appreciated his invitation and thought it very kind of him to make it, although I couldn't possibly accept it. It *would* be lovely to spend the summer at Belle Mead, to laze in the gardens and saunter along the river walk, but, under the circumstances, it was entirely out of the question. I stole a look at him as we rode slowly back toward the hotel. Robert Courtland had his own integrity. He knew I was involved with another man, and he would make no overt advances as long as I was committed to Jason, but . . . he was definitely in love with me. I suspected that Laura was right. Robert was merely biding his time, waiting for my tempestuous relationship with Jason to end. When he made his move, it would be major, but in the meantime he made do with our unusual friendship.

We drove by a gray stone wall ablaze with red and purple bougainvillea, an old gray stone church visible beyond the wall. A group of nuns made their solemn way through the wrought iron archway, arms folded, heads bowed. Further on there was an ancient convent, shaded by huge pecan trees, and then we were passing the shops again. New Orleans had its well-remembered aura of indolent old world charm, perfumed by the fragrance of a million blossoms. Robert seemed to be in a reflective mood, sitting close beside me, silent, smoke-gray eyes serious as he contemplated private matters.

"It was a lovely lunch," I told him. "Thank you very much."

Dismissing his grave thoughts, he gave me a warm smile. "I only hope you don't grow ill from those wretched pork rinds."

"They were wonderful. I could eat them every day."

"Every day?"

"Well, at least once a week."

"You're a remarkable creature," he said fondly. "You know, I really know very little about you. Only what I read in the papers. I suspect much of that is fanciful fabrication."

"All of it," I assured him.

"You obviously know New Orleans, but—we have never discussed your background. I know nothing about your childhood, your education, who your parents were, where you were brought up."

"It isn't—it isn't very interesting," I said hesitantly. "It isn't very pretty, either. I was raised poor, dirt-poor, and—"

Robert sensed my discomfort. He squeezed my arm.

"It's not important," he said firmly. "Where you come from doesn't matter. It's what you are that counts, and you're an intelligent, charming, very gifted young woman."

"You're terribly gallant," I told him.

"Just truthful. Did I say lovely, too? You're quite the loveliest woman I've ever known, but I'm sure many men have told you that."

"Never so sincerely. I—I don't really know anything about you, either. You mentioned earlier that—that you had no family. None at all?"

"My parents died when I was seven years old. I was put into an orphanage, broke out at fourteen to make my own way. Make it I did, with a lot of colorful misadventures along the way. I'm afraid I wasn't quite respectable when I was younger. It was only with maturity—and financial success—that I became the solid citizen you see now."

"What about women?" I inquired.

"I've always adored them."

"There've been many?"

"Many," he confessed.

"But none you cared to marry?"

"There was one . . ." His gray eyes turned dark, and I saw the sadness again. "There was one I should have married," he said, and his voice was flat, carefully controlled. "Through my own foolishness I—lost her. I was very young, but I should never have—"

We were nearing the hotel. Robert said nothing more until we had stopped in front of the elaborate portico. Fashionably dressed couples were strolling up and down the esplanade. The doorman held the door open as a plump woman in purple taffeta stepped out, a fluffy gray poodle in her arms. Lost in reverie, Robert made no effort to alight. After a moment he looked at me and shook his head.

"Sorry," he apologized.

"You must have loved her very much," I said.

"I did. I think I did. As I said, I was very young. There have been many other women in my life since then, but somehow they all fell short. None of them ever meant as much to me, until—"

He cut himself short. Until I met you, he had meant to say. I could see it in his eyes. He didn't say it. Instead, he alighted from the carriage and helped me down and led me to the door, waving the doorman aside. He was staying at the Fontaine, too, but he obviously didn't plan to come inside just now. He took both my hands in his, squeezing them tightly.

"I have some business to attend to at the bank," he told me. "I won't see you again until after the performance tonight. I know you're going to be brilliant."

"I—I'm a little nervous. I always am."

"They're going to love you," he promised. "I—uh—wonder if you would care to have a late supper with me after the show?"

"I'd love to, Robert, but—I'm not sure."

"I understand," he said. He released my hands.

"I'll let you know after the performance. Is—is that all right?"

"Fine. It's after three. You'd better get some rest. I've enjoyed this afternoon more than I could possibly say."

He took my hands and squeezed them again, then went back to the carriage. I passed the plant-filled lobby and went upstairs, not to my own suite but to Jason's. He had been extremely moody lately, immersed in the new play, testy and snappish, and if he had checked on me and found me gone, he would be testier still. Already nervous and not wanting an argument before the opening tonight, I decided to take the initiative and do some soothing before an explosion occurred. I needn't have bothered. His suite was empty. The sitting room was in deplorable condition, the large worktable he had requested strewn with papers and books and empty coffee cups, crumpled-up wads of paper littering the floor where he had missed the wastebasket. A bottle of ink had been spilled on the carpet—that was going to delight the management—and several cushions had been dumped off the sofa, as though hurled there in anger. Jason was going to have to leave the housekeeper a *very* big tip.

Walking over to the table, I saw amidst the mess one neat stack of pages, a heavy paperweight on top. The stack was rather high. I wondered if he had finally finished the last act. I had read the first two, and they were quite powerful. *Lady Caroline*, which he had fashioned especially for me, was based on one of the greatest scandals of the age, Lord Byron's affair with the gorgeous, seductive and very married Lady Caroline Lamb, a neurotic blonde who literally threw herself at the feet of the handsome, amoral poet and declared him "Mad, bad and dangerous to know." Jason had taken the existing facts and woven them into a rich, dramatic tapestry full of high color and heated emotions. When society discovered that Lord Byron was also having an affair with his own half sister, he hastily fled England, leaving Lady Caroline to shatter a champagne glass and slash her wrists, splattering blood all over her sumptuous satin gown.

Incest, adultery, great wealth, glamour, *Lady Caroline* had all the ingredients. With Michael as Lord Byron, it was certain to create a sensation and be every bit as controversial as *The Quadroon*, dealing as it did with the tempestuous private lives of celebrated figures of an age just past. Caroline Lamb was a marvelous role but one even more emotionally demanding than Janine. Before I immersed myself in it, I needed a long rest, and that was something Jason couldn't, wouldn't understand. As wonderful as our success had been, *The Quadroon* had drained me. I wasn't "artistic" or even particularly temperamental, merely a hard working actress, but after working so very hard for so long, my nerves needed a respite.

Back in my own suite, I set down my reticule and pulled off my long white gloves, thinking of the man whose life I shared. I had decided to have a bonbon and had had no intention of becoming deeply involved, but Jason had become much more than a bonbon. I still kept him at arm's length, still refused to let him know just how much I cared—this for my own protection—but care for him I did. Deeply. We might fight like two alley cats, we might disagree constantly, but he still made my heart sing. He was as endearing as he was exasperating, and in the bedroom he was a superbly masterful and satisfying lover. He was mercurial, volatile, a bully, but I was still lucky to have him. I was wise enough never to let *him* suspect I felt that way.

There was a knock at the door. I stood up. The door opened. Jason came in, his hair all atumble, his expression grim, his green-gray eyes full of silent accusation. He kicked the door shut behind him and stood there, looking at me, clearly spoiling for a fight. I felt my dander rise. He looked wonderfully appealing in his black broadcloth breeches and frock coat, his green and white striped satin vest and white silk neckcloth, but at the moment I was immune to that appeal. I longed for him to pull me into his arms, to hold me tight and tell me everything was going to be fine tonight, give me the reassurance I so badly needed, but I could see that wasn't going to happen. He continued to look at me with accusing eyes, and my dander rose even more.

"I know you didn't get out of bed on the wrong side this morning," I observed. "I recall the occasion distinctly. You woke me up, grumbling because you had to get back to your own suite before the maid appeared. Something is obviously bothering you."

"Where have you been?" he demanded.

"For the past two and a half hours I've been right here."

"I came down at three. I had something to *tell* you, something important. You weren't here. No one knew where you were. I thought maybe you'd gone to the theater early. I went there. No one had seen you. I thought maybe you'd gone to see Corey. I went to the little house she and Adam have near the Jewel. They hadn't seen you either. By that time I was *frantic*."

"I'm a grown woman, Jason. I'm perfectly capable of going out on my own without answering to anyone."

"Where were you?"

"Out," I said stubbornly.

"You don't intend to tell me?"

"It's none of your bloody business, and I don't like your attitude. You're not my keeper, Jason. I—we've both been under a lot of strain recently, and I'm rather tense about tonight. I'm really in no mood for one of your petulant tirades right now. If you don't have something pleasant to say, please get the hell out of here.''

''You—you're telling me to get *out*?'' He was appalled.

''If you don't have something pleasant to say, yes.''

''Just because you're a big star now, just because you've received a bunch of paltry offers from other managers, you think— you think—''

''Jason, my dear, I really *don't* want to fight just now.''

''I was worried about you! That's why I went looking for you. I happen to *love* you, you little slut, and—I didn't know *what* might have happened to you. This is a great big wicked city. You could have been *kidnapped* for all I knew!''

''Jesus,'' I said. ''You've written far too many melodramas.''

''*Lady Caroline* is *not* a melodrama!''

''I didn't say it was.''

''You hate it, don't you?''

''I didn't *men*tion *Lady Caroline*. You're spoiling for a fight, Jason, and I'm very likely to crown you with that teapot if you don't get out of here right this minute.''

''I finished it this afternoon,'' he said. ''That's what I wanted to tell you. I started to work as soon as I got back to my suite this morning, and I finished it at precisely two forty-seven.''

''Marvelous.''

''You needn't be sarcastic.''

''I wasn't.''

Jason strolled over to the tea table, picked up my cup, emptied it into a plant and poured himself a cup of tea, tiny spirals of steam swirling from the spout as he poured. He had calmed down considerably, but I was still fuming. How attractive he was. How infuriating. I really should throw the son of bitch out before I weakened.

''The National wants to see it at once. Did I tell you the kind of money they're talking? We'll leave for Atlanta as soon as we close here. Caroline is a very complex role, full of hidden depths and subtleties. I plan to coach you in the part this summer, while we're mounting the production, and when the rest of the company joins us in September, you'll be ready.''

''I told you before, Jason—I'm not going to Atlanta. Not until September, anyway. I'm taking the summer off.''

''You need the extra coaching, and I need you with me.''

''You've been working as hard as I have. It wouldn't hurt you to take the summer off, too. You've been pushing yourself, driving yourself. You're going to crack if—if you don't slow down."

Jason took another sip of tea. "We've got to go to Atlanta, Dana. We've got to be ready to open in—"

"Western civilization won't crumble if we open a couple of months later," I interrupted. "I can't go on at this pace, Jason. You can't, either. Both of us need a break. We've gone over this before. I told you—"

He set the cup down with a loud clatter. Tea sloshed over into the saucer.

"You're planning something, aren't you?"

"I'm planning to *rest*."

"You haven't signed for next season yet. Michael has signed. Laura has signed. Everyone's signed but you. You've been evasive ever since we drew up the contracts. It's that weasel Drummond, isn't it? He's talked you into going to New York, starring in—"

"No, Jason," I said patiently.

"Why won't you sign? You plan to drop me, don't you? I take you in and make you a star and—"

"*I* made me a star," I said hotly. "I worked my ass off. I gave my all. You wrote a wonderful play, yes, but how would it have gone with—with Carmelita playing Janine? I believe in credit where credit is due, but you did *not* create me. I created myself!"

"You ungrateful little—"

"Don't say it," I warned. "Just—don't—say it."

He didn't. He glared at me, eyes flashing emerald fires. I glared back at him. Several long moments passed. I finally sighed and walked over to the door, holding it open for him.

"We're both acting like children, Jason. We have to be at the theater at seven. There—there's no point in going on like this. Both of us are likely to say something we'll regret. I—I need to dress."

He moved past me, paused in the doorway, turned.

"I'll be down for you at six forty-five," he said. "We'll drive to the theater together."

I closed the door, utterly drained. How was I supposed to give a performance tonight, feeling like this? I probably wouldn't even remember my bloody lines. Tonight of all nights I was going to be abominable, a wreck, a joke, onstage. I went into the bedroom and dressed and brushed my hair, and when Jason appeared I gave him a cool nod and we went downstairs in silence. He was as cool as I was, his face expressionless, as stony as granite. He handed me into the waiting carriage without a word. I drew my skirts back to make room for him. They rustled crisply. We might have been total strangers as the carriage pulled away, heading toward the theater. New Orleans was never lovelier than at twilight, the sky a deep gray smeared with pink, the air tinted with a thickening mauve-blue haze, the lovely, gracious old buildings spread with velvety black shadows. The soft, splashing music of fountains could be heard from a hundred hidden courtyards, and, as always, the opulent perfume of flowers was heady and tantalizing. New Orleans was one of the most romantic cities in the world, but neither of us felt very romantic tonight.

"I brought the contract with me," Jason said icily. "It's in my breast pocket. I want you to sign it tonight."

"I'll sign it in September," I said.

"How can I be sure of that?"

"I suppose you'll have to trust me," I retorted.

"You'll sign it tonight or not at all," he informed me. "I can't start mounting an expensive production like this one with no leading lady under contract."

I made no comment. Jason thrust his jaw out.

"Did you hear what I said?" he asked sharply.

"I heard."

"And?"

"I don't intend to discuss it, Jason."

Jason said nothing more. He sat stiffly beside me. The haze thickened, growing darker, and lengthening shadows cloaked everything in black. We drove on, passing brightly lighted restaurants and cafés now, music spilling out into the street, the esplanades aswarm with merry couples eager to begin an evening of festivity. Fortunately the theater was now only a few blocks away. I didn't know how much more of this strained silence I could endure. We finally drove past the front of the theater and turned into the narrow passageway leading to the area in back. I sighed with relief when we stopped in front of the stage door, the single lamp hanging over it making a soft yellow pool over the rusty metal steps and landing.

"You're tense," Jason said, "nervous about your performance. I can understand why you don't want to discuss it now. We'll continue our talk after you've taken your curtain calls.''

"No," I said, "we won't."

I climbed out of the carriage without his assistance. He hurried out after me and caught up with me on the landing. He took my arm, glaring at me as the carriage drove on.

"I don't know why you're being so unreasonable, Dana."

"I'm not the one being unreasonable. Please let go of my arm."

"You know, sometimes you can be a total bitch."

"I know," I said.

I pulled my arm free. Jason looked exasperated now, worried, too.

"What you said earlier—you're right. We *are* acting like children. I'm sorry if—dammit, you drive me crazy! I'll take you out to dinner after the show. I'll buy you caviar and champagne and you can sign the contract and we can carry on like civilized adults."

"I'm sorry," I said. "I already have an engagement."

I opened the stage door and stepped inside and moved past stacks of flats and coils of rope toward the passageway leading to my dressing room. He soon caught up with me, seizing my arm again. I stopped, took hold of his hand and unloosened his fingers.

"What do you mean—you already have an engagement?"

"Robert is taking me out tonight."

"Robert?" He was puzzled for a moment, and then dark suspicion appeared in his eyes. "Courtland? You're going out with him? You—you were with him this afternoon, too, weren't you?"

"I was with him this afternoon."

"So that's how it goes," he said grimly. "All those supposedly innocent dinners in Atlanta, that party he took you to in Washington—I thought it was good public relations for our producer to be seen with our leading lady, and I gave you my blessing. I *trusted* you, and all the while—"

"Robert and I are merely friends, Jason."

"Sure," he said. "He's worth millions, and you—*that's* why you won't sign the contract. You think you're going to land yourself a millionaire, and you don't need—"

"Believe what you wish," I said. My voice was like ice.

I turned and moved resolutely down the passageway to the

door of my dressing room. Jason hurried after me. I started to open the door. He caught my shoulder and whirled me around.

"I haven't even *looked* at another woman since we've been together. I let you into my life. I let myself fall in love with you. Like the bloody fool I am, I thought—I forbid you to see him tonight! I forbid you to see him ever again!"

"It isn't your place to forbid me anything, Mr. Donovan."

"You can't *do* this to me!"

"I can do anything I bloody well please."

"Dana—"

"Go fuck yourself," I said sweetly. "You certainly aren't going to fuck *me* any longer."

I stepped into my dressing room and slammed the door, leaning against it. I was trembling inside, and I closed my eyes, telling myself I wasn't going to fall apart, I wasn't going to cry. I leaned there against the door for several minutes and, finally, full of steely resolve, stood up straight and stepped over to the dressing table. I had a performance to give tonight. Thank you, Jason Donovan, for making it well nigh impossible to give a decent one. Forty-five minutes later I was fully made-up and wearing my buttercup-yellow brushed cotton frock and, like a zombie, left my dressing room and took my place backstage. I could hear the audience settling down, growing quiet. Corey and the boys were already in position onstage. A few moments later the burly stagehand pulled the ropes and, with a creaking ring, the curtain slowly rose.

They were all out there, all those people who had judged and condemned me two years ago. How satisfied they would be when I dropped my lines, forgot my marks, made a total ass of myself. How they would titter and nudge each other and whisper behind their fans. My cue came. I moved onstage. I spoke the words I was supposed to speak and expressed the emotions I was supposed to express, but I did it by rote, purely by rote. It grew no better as the evening progressed, and in the final scene I was still completely removed, speaking my lines like an automaton. The curtain came down. Corey gave me a big hug and told me I had been brilliant, positively brilliant, and I gazed at her in wonderment. There were eleven curtain calls. I received a standing ovation and more bouquets of flowers than I could carry. It was a triumph.

Robert took me to New Orleans' grandest restaurant that evening, a splendid place with dark gold carpet and drapes and gleaming mahogany walls and exquisite etched-glass panels enclosing each private booth. He was charming and attentive, but I barely touched my thick turtle soup, my salad of crabmeat and artichoke hearts, my savory and steaming lobster thermidor. Sensing my mood, Robert said I looked tired, suggested I might like to skip dessert and go back to the hotel. I nodded thankfully. He gave my arm a squeeze as we left, so kind, so understanding, such a comfort. He curled his left arm lightly around my shoulders as we drove to the hotel, asking no questions, making no demands. At the door of my suite he told me good night, and I looked into his smoke-gray eyes and saw the veiled yearning in them and the concern, and I rested my hand lightly on his cheek for a moment, then went inside.

I'm not going to let this throw me, I promised myself the following morning. I'm not going to be hurt like . . . like last time. I can get along very well without Jason Donovan. I can get along magnificently, in fact. I'm not going to weep and I'm not going to pine. I finished my coffee and dressed and felt empty inside. I had slept little during the night. I had tossed and turned and watched the moonlight reflecting on the ceiling and yearned for the weight of his body beside me, the warmth of his skin, the sound of his breathing. I hadn't slept alone in months, and the bed seemed empty, seemed strange and alien without him. I hadn't cried. I was too stubborn for that. I had tried to hold on to the anger, but the anger soon evaporated and the hurt kept right on hurting.

He'll never know, I vowed, smoothing the skirt of my pale rose silk frock over the layers of white petticoat beneath. He'll never know how much he hurt me. He'll never know how much I cared. I sat down at the dressing table to brush my hair, and the eyes that looked back at me in the mirror stubbornly refused to reflect the pain inside. It's your own bloody fault, I told myself, brushing vigorously. You let yourself become attached to him. You let yourself care too much. You said you were merely taking a bonbon, but, admit it, you fell in love with the son of a bitch. Hair spilling to my shoulders in a glossy honey-blond cascade, I stood up, fetched parasol and reticule, and left the suite to go shopping with Laura and Michael.

It was after three when I returned. I was empty-handed, but only because Michael had taken charge of all our packages and promised to have mine sent up to my suite later on. I had been very bright, very merry, gossiping with Laura, teasing Michael, buying with abandon. We had lunched on crepes in a lovely little restaurant, and Michael had kept us entertained with tales of Texas. I was weary now as I opened the door, glad I no longer had to keep up a front. Hazy silver sunlight spilled through the sitting room windows, making pools on the floor and illuminating the gray velvet sofa. The woman who sat there rose slowly to her feet, and I gasped, startled, believing at first that she was an apparition, for, bathed in the light, that's what she resembled.

She was wearing a soft mauve velvet gown, and the fluffy cloud of silvery hair floated about her head like a dandelion cap. The gentle and beloved face was as delicate, as fey as I remembered, the complexion smooth and clear, like fine old ivory. Her light green eyes were shining. A hesitant smile trembled on her lips. My heart seemed to leap. Tears sprang to my eyes. Delia sighed and took a step forward.

"I do hope you don't mind my coming, dear," she said.

"I—" My voice seemed to catch in my throat.

"I'm afraid I told them a little story downstairs. They said you weren't in, and I told them I was your aunt and asked if I could wait in your suite. I was very convincing and the gentleman was most kind, escorting me up here himself."

"Oh, Delia—" I cried.

I ran to her then and we hugged and she patted my back and the tears fell and it was some time before I could pull myself together. I brushed the tears away and smiled and asked her to sit back down. I pulled a velvet cord hanging beside the drapes, and a few minutes later a maid appeared at the door. I asked her if she could have a lavish tea sent up. It arrived shortly thereafter: neatly quartered sandwiches of sliced tongue and cucumber, crusts trimmed away, tiny iced cakes and petit fours, steaming hot tea in a silver pot.

"My," Delia declared, eyeing the lavish display. "You do get wonderful service here, don't you?"

I nodded, composed now, pouring tea into the delicate porcelain cups. I handed one to her, and Delia smiled.

"I had to come, my dear," she said. "I couldn't leave New Orleans without seeing you."

"You—you're leaving?"

"I am going to Grande Villa again, to visit my friend Alicia

Duvall. You know how dreadfully uncomfortable New Orleans can be in this heat. I'll probably be away all summer. I'm leaving tomorrow morning. I always enjoy visiting Alicia. So many parties, so many balls . . ."

Delia sighed, fondly remembering previous visits, and I feared she was going to launch into one of her fuzzy monologues. She didn't. She set her cup down and looked into my eyes.

"I was in the audience last night, my dear. I went with friends. I was so proud of you. I wept real tears. That's our Dana up there, I told myself. You can't imagine how very happy I am for you, how pleased I am with your success."

"Thank you, Delia."

"I've read all about you in the papers, of course. Such outlandish stories, my dear. I took most of them with a grain of salt."

"As well you should have."

"Princes, suicides, fortunes in jewels. I knew that wasn't you, my dear. You're still the same sweet child—I can see that—but now you're successful and terribly famous."

"I've worked hard, Delia."

"I know you must have. I'm so proud of you. Would you believe that when I was a girl—back during the Bronze Age, this was—I dreamed of becoming an actress myself. It was out of the question, of course. Respectable girls didn't go onstage back then."

" 'Respectable' girls still don't," I said dryly.

"Do—do you enjoy the life, dear?"

"Yes—yes, I do. It's very demanding and frequently frustrating, but in the theater I—I'm somebody. I have respect. I have admiration. I belong. I'm part of a large, loving family, however quarrelsome, and no one looks down on me because my blood isn't blue, because I grew up in the swamps."

"I fear our people were very hard on you, child."

I thought of those haughty Creole aristocrats in the Quarter she referred to, and I thought of the snubs, the gossip. It all seemed so trivial and unimportant now.

"I wanted to be like them," I said quietly. "I wanted to be accepted. I soon realized that could never happen. Now I'm content merely to be myself. Being Dana O'Malley is—just fine."

"We—all of us were very upset when you left, child."

I looked away, remembering.

"I understood why you left," Delia continued in that soft, gentle voice. "I understood far more than you may have guessed, child, and I realized it was the—the best for all concerned. That didn't make it any easier. I missed you dreadfully. Poor Julian almost went out of his mind."

"I—I did it for him, Delia."

"I know. I think he eventually realized that, too. He didn't know about you and Charles. Charles never told him—I forbade him to. Julian believed you ran off because you wanted to spare him the ostracism that would have come if he had married you. He threw himself into his work, and—I suppose you've read about his success?"

"Julian has finally come into his own," I said. "I always believed he would."

"Success has been wonderful for him," Delia confided. "He's become an entirely different person, so confident, so self-assured. He loves the attention and the acclaim. He loves being recognized as an authority, loves giving lectures, signing copies of his book. You're right, child—he *has* come into his own, and he's happier than I've ever seen him."

"Was—was Julian in the audience last night?"

Delia shook her head. "He's in New York at the moment. One of the major publishing houses up there wants him to do another book, and they're negotiating. Once they agree on terms, he plans to vacation in Europe. He—he has a companion," she added hesitantly.

"Amelia Jameson," I said.

Delia looked surprised. "You know about her?"

"One hears these things," I replied. "I met her once. She is a very beautiful woman."

"She's very good for him, too," Delia admitted. "A man in Julian's circle can't afford to—to take the wrong wife, but he can take all the mistresses he pleases."

"I'm glad he has her," I said.

We both had more tea then and sampled the sandwiches and cakes, and I told her about life in the theater and all the friends I had made. Delia seemed to be fascinated. I answered all her questions and told her colorful anecdotes, all the while longing to ask her about Charles. I didn't. I couldn't. I had too much pride. Delia finished another petit four, glanced at the clock and said that she really mustn't keep me too long, I must have ever so many things to do.

"Nothing more important than talking to you," I said. "It—it truly is wonderful to see you, Delia. I thought of you so often. I wanted to write to you, but—"

"I understand, my dear."

"I happened to drive by Etienne's yesterday," I said, my voice extremely casual. "I was glad to see that it's been restored. It—it didn't look too busy."

"It's been closed," Delia told me. "As late as last week it looked as though we might even lose it."

"Lose Etienne's?" I was startled. "I thought—I understood Julian made quite—quite a lot of money with his book and was able to replenish the family coffers."

"He did, dear. Charles was able to restore Etienne's and get it back on its feet, and there was even some money left over. Things looked rosy indeed, and then there was that dreadful hailstorm—perhaps you read about it in the papers. Charles had purchased the crops of three plantations before they were picked. I'm hazy about the details—much too complicated—but it seems that by buying the cotton in advance, he wouldn't have to bid for it at auction and would make a much bigger profit."

"And the hailstorm destroyed the crops," I said.

Delia nodded, idly running her palm over the soft nap of her mauve velvet skirt. "We were almost wiped out. Julian has been traveling, and he doesn't know how dire the situation is. If things don't work out, we'll have to sell the house as well as the store, but Charles seems to have found the perfect solution."

"Oh?"

"Regina Belleau. Her father died last year. She's become an immensely wealthy heiress, and her mother would like nothing better than to see her marry into a family like the Etiennes. The Belleaus were never quite top drawer, you understand."

I remembered Regina Belleau quite distinctly. She was the haughty blonde I had encountered at Corinne's when I was being fitted for my first ball gown. She and her friend Bertha, the fat brunette, had come into the fitting room as I was changing behind the screen, had made vicious comments about me and Julian and had gone on to discuss their many sexual conquests. Regina was a tramp, but she belonged, and now she was very wealthy. The perfect solution indeed, I thought bitterly.

"Charles has been courting her for some time," Delia continued. "Regina *is* rather fast and, truth to tell, not to my taste, but she's lovely and vivacious and I've no doubt Charles will be able to keep her in line. He proposed to her last Tuesday. She accepted. They're to be married in September."

They deserve each other, I thought.

"I hope they'll be very happy," I said.

Delia sighed, her eyes doubtful. "Regina may surprise us all and make a good wife," she said. "At any rate the Etienne coffers will be full again. Full to overflowing," she added. "I suppose it's for the best."

I said nothing. Delia touched her soft cloud of silver hair and glanced at the clock. She rose then, soft mauve velvet rustling. I stood, too, feeling sad, feeling lost, feeling lonely.

"What about you, dear?" Delia asked. "Is there someone special in your life?"

"There—there is," I replied, "but things aren't—aren't going too well at the moment. I don't seem to have a great deal of luck with men."

Delia took my hand and squeezed it gently. "The course of love never did run smooth," she said. "I hope things work out for you, child. You've had enormous success. I hope you have happiness as well."

"Thank you, Delia."

"I really must go now, my dear. Jasper is waiting out front with the carriage. I—before I go, I want you to know you will always have a place in my heart."

Tears stung my eyes again. "And you in mine," I said.

We hugged each other once more, and I escorted Delia out to the carriage, waving as it drove away. My heart was heavy as I went up to my suite. I managed to get through the rest of the afternoon without breaking down, counting the minutes until it was time to leave for the theater. Jason didn't come down to fetch me. I rode to the theater with Ollie and Bart and Theodore, and I only caught brief glimpses of Jason backstage that evening. He was avoiding me. It was just as well. He continued to avoid me throughout the week, curt and cool when it was necessary for us to speak. I carried on, telling myself it didn't matter, telling myself I didn't need him, but each day seemed interminable, and each night was agony. I had promised myself I would never again suffer as I had suffered over Charles, had promised myself I would never again allow myself to care that much. I suffered. I cared. I had only myself to blame.

Robert Courtland was a great comfort. I saw him several times, and he was charming and attentive and, sensing my unhappiness, quietly supportive, letting me know without words that he understood, that he would be there for me should I need him. Laura and Corey and the rest of the cast were supportive as well. They couldn't help but be aware of the tension backstage, and, of course, they all knew the reasons for it. Corey took me to the small, charmingly furnished house she and Adam shared and cooked lunch for me and told me men were no damn good. Ollie clucked over me and patted my hand. Bartholomew brought Theodore to my dressing room to perform a new trick. I was blessed indeed to have such friends and I adored them all, but their kindness and concern only made things worse as I had to put on a brave front, pretend it didn't matter. When closing night finally arrived, I was relieved, eager to be done with it.

Laura arrived in my suite to accompany me to the theater. She looked radiant in deep sapphire-blue, raven locks tumbling to her shoulders in rich profusion. We left the hotel and climbed into the waiting carriage, and she gave a weary sigh as the carriage pulled away. I sat silently, gazing out the window at the thickening twilight. Laura adjusted her skirts, restless. I could see there was something she wanted to tell me.

"Have you and Michael decided what you're going to do during the summer?" I asked, giving her an opening.

"More or less," she replied. "I think I've lost my mind, love. I'm going to Texas. I'll probably be scalped, but Michael insists we go—he wouldn't take no for an answer. What's a girl to do?"

"How will you get there?"

"We take a steamboat upriver to Vicksburg, then travel by rail across to Shreveport—it's a small cotton port on the Red River, Michael tells me. At Shreveport we board a coach that'll take us on into Texas and to the ranch."

"Ranch?"

"His parents' ranch."

"I didn't know he *had* parents."

"Neither did I, love, but he does and he wants me to meet them. Apparently they own a huge spread of land with hundreds of cows and lots of rugged men working for them. The men round up the cows and brand them and stuff and carry six-shooters in case Comanches attack or the Mexican army gets too uppity. Actually, they're worth a *bundle*, love, and Michael's their only son and heir. He assures me they'll find me as adorable as he does."

"Somehow I can't see you on a ranch, Laura."

"Neither can I, love. Wide open spaces give me the jitters, but we won't be staying all summer—just long enough to get his parents' blessing and tie the knot. That's what they do in Texas, tie the knot. It sounds terribly final."

"You—you're getting *mar*ried?"

"I never thought it would happen," she confessed. "A girl like me, tied to one man, but when the man's Michael—"

"Laura, I—I'm so happy for you."

"I'm rather happy myself, love. Scared to death, too, of course, but—I really don't think I could do much better than Michael. I love him, Dana."

"I—I know you do. I've known it for some time."

"He had to do some serious arm twisting, but I finally decided— why not? I told him there was no way I would live on a ranch surrounded by bloodthirsty Comanches, and he quite agreed. We'll go right on acting. He's looking forward to playing Lord Byron, and of course, I have signed to play Augusta Leigh, Byron's half sister. I—I trust you'll still be playing Caroline, love."

"I—I don't know, Laura."

"You and Jason still haven't patched—"

"We haven't patched things up," I said dryly.

"I could *kick* him," she said. "He's always been bossy and unreasonable and stubborn as a mule, but—"

I stiffened and, realizing I didn't care to discuss it, Laura cut herself short. The carriage let us out in front of the stage door, and we went on into the theater. Laura looked bothered. I smiled and gave her a hug and told her again how happy I was for her.

"I—I feel guilty as hell, being so deliriously happy when you're so upset, but—"

"Seeing you happy makes me feel much better, darling. Michael is a very lucky man. You're lucky, too."

"Don't I know it," she said.

"I must get you something very special for a wedding present. Perhaps we can go shopping tomorrow morning. I—it's late, I suppose I'd better get to my dressing room. We—we'll talk after the show, darling."

The performance went very well indeed. Corey was magnificent, as usual, and Billy was brilliant, outdoing himself as the tormented Travis. Tall and ruggedly handsome, Michael was superlative in his one scene, giving his all as he brutally rejected me and knocked me to the floor. Painfully, I climbed to my feet and rubbed my cheek, tears flowing beautifully. I stepped over to the dressing table in my sumptuous white silk gown with its overlay of white tulle, narrow gold stripes glimmering. The diamonds sparkled at my throat. I began to repair damages and Corey entered and we said our final lines. The curtain came down. There was thunderous applause. There were cheers and loud bravos. We took our curtain calls. They seemed to go on forever, and when the curtain came down for the final time, I nodded to my fellow cast members and went wearily to my dressing room, carrying one of the many bouquets I had received.

Distracted, I stepped inside and closed the door, setting the white roses aside. I sensed a presence. I looked up. Jason stood, lean and handsome in evening attire. My heart skipped a beat. My wrists and knees felt suddenly weak. I stared at him, momentarily unable to speak.

"I've been waiting for you," he said.

His voice was quiet, not curt. His manner was polite, not icy. His gray-green eyes gazed at me without emotion, though, and I felt there was an invisible wall between us. How I longed to shatter it. How I longed to end this coldness between us. I couldn't. I had my pride, and I was every bit as stubborn as he. Love him I might, but I wouldn't allow him to bully me, and if after all this time he couldn't trust me, thought me disloyal, there could be no future for us.

"I'm very tired, Jason."

"I'm leaving for Atlanta tomorrow afternoon," he said. "I want you to come with me."

"I'm sorry."

"I have the contract here. I want you to sign it."

"I shan't sign it, Jason. Not now."

"I think we should discuss it."

"We've already discussed it." My voice was cool. "If you'll excuse me, I have an engagement tonight. I need to change."

"Courtland? You're going out with Courtland again?"

"Yes," I lied. Why did I lie?

"I see," he said.

I stepped over to the dressing table and removed the diamond necklace, and the gems shimmered and flashed as I put it down. Jason watched, his eyes hard and resentful now.

"You're keeping the necklace?"

"I'm keeping the necklace," I said. "He's giving me a bracelet and earrings to match."

"I see," he said again. "He can give you diamonds. I can't. I wanted to give you the world. I love you, but I'll get over it. Yes, by God, I'll get over it."

"Jason—"

"I wrote *Lady Caroline* for you, Dana, but you are not the only actress in the world. If—if you don't sign the contract now, if you don't come to Atlanta with me—"

He cut himself short. I gazed at him coolly.

"You're giving me an ultimatum?"

"I'm giving you an ultimatum," he retorted.

"Go to hell, Jason."

He looked at me for a moment and then stepped over to the door and opened it. He gripped the knob tightly, standing there in the doorway, his eyes holding mine. It's true, I thought, a heart that has been broken before can break again.

"I guess that's it, then," he said.

"I guess it is," I whispered.

"Good-bye, Dana."

He stepped outside and closed the door behind him. Oh yes, it was true. It was happening. My heart was breaking all over again.

Chapter Twenty-One

A CLEAR BLUE-WHITE SKY arched overhead like a translucent silk canopy, and dazzling silver sunlight streamed down in rich profusion as I strolled through the terraced gardens down toward the river walk. The air was fresh and invigorating, scented with the fragrance of hundreds of blooms, and a mild breeze caused light skeins of hair to blow against my cheek, caused my gold and cream striped skirt to billow gently. It was a glorious day, pleasantly warm but not as warm as it usually was in mid-August, Maudie assured me. Sometimes it was so hot a soul just felt like meltin' away, but this summer had been right cool for Natchez. I paused, brushing the hair from my cheek, admiring anew the beauty of the gardens. They had been laid out with great care and at great expense by a professional landscape architect from England, but while elaborate, the overall effect was one of charming simplicity, graceful walks leading through flower beds and under white wicker trellis arches, white marble steps leading from level to level.

Turning around, I looked back toward the house. Surrounded by cool green lawn shaded by the wide-spread boughs of lofty oaks, Belle Mead was incredibly beautiful with its pale tan brick walls, its tall white columns and graceful verandahs. It had clean, simple lines, with none of the fancy architectural furbelows that marred so many of the large houses. Gracious, elegant, it stood in the afternoon sunlight with quiet majesty, the loveliest house I had ever seen. The two and a half months I had spent here had been restful indeed, Robert's excellent staff of servants taking care of me as though I were a treasured daughter. Long, lazy, serene days followed one after another, no noise, no people, no pressure. Although Belle Mead had a large library, parcels of new books had arrived in the mail each week, mostly novels from England and France, forwarded by the bookstore in Atlanta where Robert had placed a standing order. How considerate he was. How thoughtful. I eagerly looked forward to seeing him again when he returned from his most recent business trip.

Moving on beneath one of the trellis arches festooned with fragrant yellow summer roses, I followed the walk past beds seemingly overgrown with multicolored blooms of varying heights, like Anne Hathaway's garden, I had learned from studying notes the Englishman had made. The flower beds were deliberately rather shaggy, and the shrubs were allowed to retain their natural shapes instead of being clipped into neat uniformity. A shoulder-high row of shrubs bordered the lowest level of gardens, a gateway leading to the river walk beyond. I opened the gate and strolled leisurely along the walk to the octagon-shaped white gazebo where I spent so much of my time. There were seats with plump pink cushions around each side, and lazing there one could look over honeysuckle-draped railings and see the grassy green slope of the levee and the mighty river beyond, a silvery brown this afternoon, ashimmer with sunlight. A large cotton barge and two fishing boats were passing by as I sank onto one of the cushioned seats and picked up the novel I had left there earlier in the day.

Bees buzzed quietly in the honeysuckle, and the light breeze caused leaves to rustle. It was cool and shady here in the gazebo, though idle rays of sunlight slanted across the railing and made flickering patterns on the floor. I could hear the muted rush of the river and the distant hoot of a horn. I dutifully turned the pages of the book, but the travails of Balzac's amorous and amoral comtesses held no interest for me this afternoon. I was tired of reading, and, although I was loath to admit it, I was tired of peace and quiet as well. Putting the book aside, I stood up and gazed at the river, thinking of the past weeks.

True to his word, Robert had spent very little time at Belle Mead this summer: three days in June, four days in July, a weekend early this month. During these brief visits, he had been utterly circumspect, treating me with courtesy, respect and unfailing kindness. A proper gentleman at all times, he was nevertheless unable to keep his feelings for me completely hidden. Several times as we lingered over the dinner table or sat on the verandah, watching the sunset, I had seen the adoration in his eyes. He had taken my hand several times and had squeezed my arm one evening as he told me good night at my bedroom door, but he had made no move that could even remotely be called forward.

I wondered why. I knew he was in love with me, knew he found me desirable and wanted to sleep with me, and I knew as well that he had a great deal of experience with women—potent sensuality clearly smoldered behind that proper facade. Why, then, did he continue to bide his time? He treated me like a demure young virgin, knowing full well I wasn't. When was he going to make that move both of us knew must be inevitable? I wondered and I wondered how I would react when he finally made it. That curious bond I felt was ever present, like a silent current of communication flowing between us, and I felt wonderfully secure in his presence. I found him sexually appealing, too—there was no question about that—but did I want an affair with him? The best way to get over a man is to get another man, Laura had said. I had taken her advice and I had indeed gotten over Charles Etienne, only to be hurt again just as badly. Robert would never hurt me, I sensed, and no, I wasn't a demure young virgin. I would probably sleep with him when he made that long-delayed move, but . . . was it what I wanted? A wide range of conflicting emotions assailed me when I thought about it.

But Robert had not made his move. A warm and genial host, he had taken me for several pleasant drives in the open carriage, showing me Natchez and its environs, the gracious homes, the gardens, the town itself with its shops and air of sunny indolence. There had also been a memorable meal in Natchez-Under-the-Hill, an infamous area crowded with brothels and taverns where brawls and stabbings were a common occurrence. Robert had been hesitant about taking me there, but, amidst the squalor, there was a dilapidated eating establishment that just happened to serve the best seafood in the South. He had kept his arm around my shoulders as we alighted from the carriage and went in. I was intrigued by the colorful surroundings and agreed that the seafood was indeed wonderful, even if it was served on chipped platters by a scowling waiter who looked like he would slit a throat without blinking. I longed to see some more of the area, but Robert hurried me out to the waiting carriage as soon as he had paid the bill. As he handed me into the carriage, his frock coat flapped open for an instant and I saw he had a pistol thrust into the waistband of his breeches. I had no doubt he knew how to use it—and with deadly accuracy. I enjoyed the outing immensely, and Robert was amused by my enthusiasm, saying he really shouldn't have taken me to the notorious district. I told him I wasn't quite the fragile flower he seemed to think I was. He chuckled and patted my hand, saying no more as we returned to the respectable part of town.

One evening in June we had gone to dine with Len Meredith and his wife Arlene in their modest but charming home. In his midthirties, Len was Robert's lawyer and business manager, with offices here in town. Tough, efficient, extremely cool-headed, he handled all of Robert's business and financial affairs, and I pitied anyone who tried to outsmart him. Formidable though he might be in business, he was quite engaging socially, witty, good-humored and exceedingly hospitable. Arlene, alas, was a sweet and timid young woman so intimidated by Robert's wealth and my fame that she could scarcely open her mouth. At Robert's request, Len called on me at Belle Mead once or twice a week to see how I was and ask if I needed anything. I enjoyed his calls a great deal, for he was as attractive as he was personable and clearly approved of me, claiming I had a very good influence on his employer.

Plucking one of the honeysuckle blossoms, I pulled the end off and put the blossom to my lips, tasting the sweet honey taste that enraptured the bees, and as I did so I saw a steamboat in the distance cruising slowly up the river like a miniature wedding cake. I wondered if it would dock at Natchez like the one I had been on two years ago. I remembered that morning so clearly, remembered seeing Robert standing there on the dock and the long, searching look we had exchanged and the curious force that seemed to draw us together and bind us. Had it been a premonition of things to come? Even though I had never laid eyes on Robert before, I had somehow sensed that he was going to play an important part in my life, and it had come to pass. Just how important a part was he going to play? As important a part as you allow him to play, a voice inside said, and I left the gazebo in a quandary.

I moved along the neat, well-kept river walk, the breeze lifting my skirt, toying with my hair, and then I turned back into the gardens and headed back up toward the house. Hollyhocks, iris, phlox, a dazzling variety of flowers grew all around in wild patchworks of color, but I was immune to the beauty now as I moved up another level and passed under one of the trellises. I saw his face, the slightly twisted nose, the dark, quirkily slanted eyebrows, the moody gray-green eyes and, try though I might to banish the image, it persisted as always. During these past weeks I had made a valiant effort not to think about him, had tried to forget the past and ignore the pain inside and, to a certain extent, I had succeeded. You must go on, I told myself. You must go on. You must forget him. I did forget, sometimes for an hour, sometimes for several hours at a time, but then it would catch me unawares, like now, and I would see that handsome face and feel the jabbing pain that was every bit as strong as it had been the night he told me good-bye and stepped out of my dressing room.

I loved him. I couldn't deny that. I loved the son of a bitch, son of a bitch though he was. He was volatile, temperamental, unreasonable, demanding, bossy, stubborn, impossible, but . . . he could be so vulnerable, he could be so warm and funny, he could be so loving. He was in Atlanta now, mounting *Lady Caroline*, and I felt another sharp jab of pain as I thought of the play opening with someone else in the lead. You don't need him, I told myself. You're better off without him. Forget him. It's over, and you've got to go on, just as you did before.

"My, you look very thoughtful this afternoon."

The voice startled me, and I looked up to see Len Meredith approaching me, tall and sturdy with sunlight burnishing his thick dark blond hair. Impeccably attired in gray breeches and frock coat, sky-blue waistcoat and white silk neckcloth, he had strong, clean-cut features and somber blue eyes that I knew could glow with warmth, as they did now. A smile curled on his wide lips. Many people found Len formidable, even intimidating, and there was no doubt he could be tough and unrelenting in business dealings, but I knew his other side and liked him very much.

"Len," I said. "I—didn't see you coming."

"Is that sadness I spy in your eyes?" he inquired.

"I was—was reading a novel. It had a very sad ending."

"How sensitive you women are. Arlene's the same way. She actually weeps over a sad book, weeps, sobs, wipes her eyes and then vows it's the most wonderful story she's ever read."

"How is Arlene?" I asked.

"She's fine. Looking forward to seeing you again."

We both knew that wasn't true, but Len was invariably polite. We moved up three flat white marble steps to another level. There was something very reassuring about his presence. I felt better already.

"Maudie told me you were out here. I just thought I'd stop by and see how you're doing."

"I'm doing fine, Len. Maudie and the others are taking marvelous care of me. I'm deplorably pampered, waited upon hand and foot. If you want to know the truth, I long to put on an apron and help Tilda with the chandeliers."

"She'd be horrified," Len assured me. "You don't enjoy being a lady of leisure?"

"It was lovely for the first couple of weeks but—one gets into the habit of working. I'm not the lady of leisure type, I fear. I'd rather be cleaning the windows than lolling on a sofa with a cool drink."

Len chuckled. "You're quite a remarkable young woman," he said. "I can see why Robert is so taken with you. By the way, I have a message. He's going to be back tomorrow. Just for one day and night, alas, but after the next trip, he'll be back for several weeks."

"Just for one day and night?"

I was terribly disappointed. Len heard it in my voice.

"You're extremely fond of him, aren't you?" he said.

"Extremely," I replied.

"I'm glad, Dana. He needs someone like you."

The great house cast cool blue-gray shadows over the back patio. We moved across it to the back verandah, shadier still. A lazy gray cat snoozed contentedly on the banister near one of the graceful white columns. Baskets of fern and ivy were suspended from the ceiling, their leaves moist from a recent watering. Wide French doors stood open, leading into the hallway. I could hear one of the servants humming inside as she leisurely did her chores. Robert had given all his "house Negroes" their freedom years ago, and they were all devoted to him, none more so than Maudie, who ran Belle Mead like a bossy but cheerful sergeant major.

"Robert has worked hard all his adult life," Len continued. "He's devoted his life to making a success, becoming someone of note, and he has succeeded beyond his wildest dreams. Now he has everything he's ever dreamed of having—wealth, power, position—and I fear he finds it's not enough.''

''He needs someone to share it with, you mean?''

Len nodded. His blue eyes were somber again. I could see that he was devoted to Robert, too, and fiercely loyal. Len, I knew, was a native of Natchez who had shocked and disappointed the local folk by going off to a Yankee university. After taking his degree from Harvard law school, he had had rough going when he returned to start a practice in his hometown. He had become ''Yankeefied,'' the locals felt, was too hard, too bright, too ambitious, but Robert had been impressed by the young man's zeal and determination and had turned some of his minor business transactions over to him. In less than a year Len was handling all Robert's business, working for him exclusively and making a very handsome living.

''He's in love with you, you know,'' Len told me.

''I—know,'' I said.

''There have been a lot of women in his life,'' he said, ''as I am sure you know, but—you're special. I have never seen him treat a woman like he treats you. Usually he—''

Len hesitated, afraid that he might have gone too far.

''Usually he puts them up in some fancy apartment and sleeps with them. Is that what you meant to say?''

''More or less. You—he respects you, Dana. He wants to do right by you. I think—'' Again he hesitated. ''I think he might even want to marry you. I'd like to see that.''

''You'd like to see your esteemed employer marry a notorious actress and be ostracized by all the local gentry?''

''I'd like to see him marry one of the finest young women I have ever met,'' he said, ''and as for the local gentry—they're not nearly as stiff-necked and snobbish as your New Orleans breed. Most of their ancestors were pioneers who sweated and toiled and lived in log cabins as they hacked away with axes, turning overgrown wilderness and mud flats into the Natchez you see today. They're consumed with curiosity about you and dying to meet you—can't wait for Robert to give a ball and introduce you. I have no doubts they will take you to their hearts immediately.''

I made no reply, and Len smoothed a palm over his thick blond hair, clearly still worried that he may have gone too far.

I gave him a reassuring smile and asked if he had time to come in for refreshments. Len shook his head, looking relieved.

"Afraid I can't, though I appreciate the invitation. I have mounds of papers to go through and a cutthroat cotton broker to best. Are you sure there's nothing you need?"

"Quite sure," I told him, smiling again. "I enjoyed seeing you, Len. Do give my best to Arlene."

Len promised he would do so and, nodding politely, went on around the verandah to the front of the house where his horse was waiting. I stepped through the French doors and moved down the wide corridor toward the front foyer. The interior of Belle Mead was as simple, as gracious as its exterior, large, sunny rooms opening one into another, each beautifully appointed with exquisite furniture. The front foyer was huge, done in yellow and white and gold, a glittering chandelier suspending from the high ceiling, a graceful white spiral staircase curving up to the second floor.

"Here you is!" Maudie exclaimed, bustling into the foyer. "An' dat Mister Len goin' off without takin' any refreshments! I done had Libby make up a pitcher of dat limeade he likes so well, an' I set out a plate of macaroons an' almon' cakes, too!"

"I'm sure they'll keep," I told her.

Maudie gave me an exasperated look. Not quite as tall as I, she was plump and rotund, her shiny brown face as round as a pumpkin. Invariably attired in black linen dress, crackling violet petticoat and violet bandanna turban, Maudie was a dynamo, full of energy and vitality. Bossy and imperious with the other servants, she was nevertheless warm and good-humored and had a deep and booming laugh which could be heard throughout the house several times a day.

"I'se gonna give him what-for next time I sees him," she told me. "Ain't no need-a him rushin' off like that, downright rude *I* call it. An' you, missy! You done look all tuckered out. Nap time, I think. I'se gonna draw the drapes in your room and you is gonna take a nice refreshin' nap. All dat gallivantin' around in th' gardens ain't good for a gal, an' all dat sunlight will sure nuff spoil your complexion."

"You're a tyrant, Maudie."

"I don't rightly know what dat means," she retorted, "but I'se *sure* it ain't flatterin'. Mister Robert done told me to take good care-a you, and dat's exactly what I means to do. You'se gonna have a glass of iced limeade and then you'se gonna have your nap, and I ain't takin' no lip about it."

I couldn't help but smile. "Tyrant you may be, but you do mean well."

"I mean for you to mind me, missy, dat's what I mean. Oh, I almost forgot about dese here letters." She pulled two crumpled envelopes out of her pocket, handing them to me. "Done arrived right after lunch, they did. Ain't neither of 'em from Mister Robert—I always recognize his writin'."

"Thank you, Maudie," I said, studying the envelopes.

"You go on an' read dem dere letters," she ordered, "an' then you get on up to your room. I'll have your limeade waitin' an' everything ready for your nap."

"Yes, ma'am."

"Lip," she grumbled, shuffling off. "Dat's all I get around here—lip! An' what's dis tie-runt I'se supposed to be? Tie-runt indeed! I knows my job an' I'se gonna do it and ain't no one gonna stop me—"

I carried the letters into the large library with its French windows looking out over the oak-shaded side lawn. Sunlight streaming in made bright pools on the polished hardwood floor with its rich Persian carpets and gleamed on the rows of leather-bound books filling the floor-to-ceiling shelves. Sitting down in one of the overstuffed chairs, I opened the first letter. It was from Corey and full of wry, loving comments about life with the ever-exasperating Adam and news about the forthcoming season at the Jewel. By popular demand she was going to reprise her Duchess of Malfi and, in addition to a new comedy, they were going to do Shakespeare's *Anthony and Cleopatra*. Adam was going to look divine in short tunic and breastplate, she confided, but she was worried about her final scene. They wanted her to use a real snake, just a tiny grass snake, harmless as could be, they claimed, but "Honey," she wrote, "there ain't no *way*!" She inquired about my health, sent her love and said she looked forward to hearing from me soon.

The second letter was from Laura, now Mrs. Michael Prichard, and it was a brief, hastily written missive informing me that she and Michael were back from Texas, in New Orleans now, and planning to come visit me in Natchez for a couple of days before going to Atlanta. She had *such* things to tell me, she confided, the ranch was incredible, Michael's parents were lovely, and she had learned how to shoot, had shot a rattlesnake and seen only one Indian. He hadn't tried to scalp her, had, instead, attempted to sell her a very smelly blanket. There were marvelous adventures to relate, and she couldn't wait to see me so that she could relate them at length. They would be arriving on the twentieth and trusted I would roll out the red carpet.

Setting the letter aside, I stood up, elated at the prospect of seeing her again. How I had missed her. I happened to look at the calendar and realized with some dismay that they would be arriving this coming Friday, only four days from now. I could barely contain my excitement as I left the library and moved up the curving staircase. Robert would be here tomorrow, Laura and Michael at the end of the week. The pervading lethargy of the past weeks melted away as I stepped into the dim, shadowy bedroom. I didn't take a nap. I pulled open the drapes and let the sunlight come pouring into the room and planned what I would wear for Robert tomorrow, how I would entertain Michael and Laura when they arrived on Friday.

It was well after ten when Robert reached Belle Mead the next morning. I was on the front verandah, watching the carriage come up the oak-lined drive and stop before the wide front steps. Nimble as a monkey, young Leroy leaped down from his perch to open the carriage door, and a dignified Herman came shuffling out to take care of the bags. Robert alighted, looking rather weary in a rumpled cream linen suit. He's been working much, much too hard, I thought. He said something to Herman and patted Leroy on the arm and then looked up and saw me standing there in my yellow silk frock. He smiled and the smile lit up his eyes and he looked like a much younger man then. I had the impression he wanted to bound up the steps and crush me to him. He didn't. He gave another instruction to Herman and then came up the steps with his usual quiet dignity and took my hand, telling me I looked quite lovely this morning.

"You look tired," I said.

"I am," he admitted. "I've been traveling in these clothes. I need to freshen up and change, and then we'll talk and have lunch."

"And you'll rest this afternoon," I told him.

Robert shook his head. His thick auburn hair was slightly tousled, giving him a curiously vulnerable look.

"I can't, Dana. I'm going to have to spend the entire afternoon with Len, going over business matters.'

"But—you're only here for the one day," I protested.

"I know. I'm sorry. We'll have a lovely dinner tonight and a nice visit afterwards. Don't be downcast. I'll make it up to you later, I promise." He curled his arm around my shoulders, leading me into the foyer. "It's wonderful to be back," he said, "if only for a brief time."

"It's wonderful to have you back."

He looked down at me with fond gray eyes. "Is it?"

"Of course it is."

"You've missed me?"

"Very much," I said.

It was true. The loneliness, the lethargy, the sense of isolation and emptiness that had pervaded my days had vanished the instant I saw him, and I felt alive and aglow and secure. Robert smiled again and then turned as Herman came in with the bags. Maudie bustled into the foyer, petticoat acrackle, and began to snap orders, telling Herman to carry dem bags straight up to Mister Robert's room, telling Robert he done looked done in an' he was havin' a hot bath immediately an' no argument about it, telling me to go on about my business, I could have him back soon as he was presentable again.

Robert brought me several small gifts, as he always did: three new novels, exquisitely shaped chocolates in a box covered with pale blue satin, a delicate and lovely yellow lace fan embroidered in white silk. I toyed with the fan as we lunched in the small, screened-in alcove on the side verandah. The crabmeat salad was delicious, the baked ham pink and tender, the flat round hush puppies crisp and golden and marvelously tasty, but I ate very little, feasting instead on his presence and the pleasure it gave me. Robert talked about his business dealings—cotton, lumber, real estate—and told me about the sawmill he had bought in Georgia and the timberland he had managed to acquire in Alabama, and then he paused and looked at me and smiled and said he must be boring me terribly. I shook my head and told him I was fascinated, as, indeed, I was, and he smiled again and poured himself some more iced tea.

"And what have you been doing?" he inquired.

"Reading, resting, taking walks. Last week young Leroy and I went fishing with bamboo poles. He caught five catfish and I got quite muddy and Maudie was outraged. She said it 'wudn't fittin' for a white gal like me to go traipsin' along the levee with a nigger boy.''

Robert chuckled, and I told him about Laura's letter and told him how much I looked forward to seeing her and Michael. Robert said he was sorry he wouldn't be here to see them himself and added that he would speak to Len and Maudie and see that arrangements were made to make their visit a pleasant and comfortable one. He finished his tea and we left the alcove, strolling around the verandah to the front steps. His carriage was waiting, Leroy standing by to perform his job as footman.

"It'll be late when I get back," Robert told me. "I'm sorry about this, Dana."

"I understand," I said.

"See you at dinner. We'll have a nice visit then."

The afternoon seemed interminable. I went down to the river walk and sat in the gazebo and listened to the humming buzz of the bees and finished the Balzac novel, and then I wandered around, restless, finally returning to the house around four. I answered Corey's letter and wrote to Ollie as well, and it wasn't quite five when I finished. I sealed the envelopes and set them aside and then sat gazing into space, thinking about Robert. I had indeed missed him, and seeing him again made me realize just how much he meant to me. No, I wasn't in love with him, but I was drawn to him, strongly drawn, and there had never been anyone whose company made me feel so . . . so warm, so secure, so safe. It was as though we belonged together, that curious force binding us. Was it possible we *had* known each other in another lifetime? I sighed, wondering how it would all end.

Robert returned shortly before seven. I had bathed and washed my hair and was in my bedroom when I heard the carriage coming up the drive. Dinner would be served at eight in the formal dining room. I brushed my hair until it shone with lustrous blond highlights, and then I put it up, arranging it in a French roll on the back of my head. I fastened a creamy white magnolia with tiny coral veins on one side, above my right temple and, sighing, stood up, the skirts of my white silk petticoat billowing softly. The gown I had selected was coral velvet, simple and elegant, with narrow off-the-shoulder sleeves, a low-cut bodice and snug waist. The full skirt spread out in sumptuous folds over the layers of my petticoat, making a soft, musical rustle as I stepped over to apply a dab of perfume behind my ears.

The sun had gone down and candles were glowing in the hallway as I left my room. As I moved slowly down the gracefully curving staircase I felt a curious premonition, a feeling that came over me all at once and was as real, as intangible as the air around me. Something was going to happen tonight, I knew, and I couldn't say how I knew it. The feeling persisted as I moved across the foyer and stepped into the spacious drawing room done in shades of white and pearl gray and soft blues, sumptuous Boulle furniture with its exquisite marquetry adding rich, gleaming browns and golds. Candles burned in the crystal wall sconces, and a gentle evening breeze caused the long blue brocade draperies to billow softly. Robert hadn't come down yet. I longed to pour myself a drink from one of the decanters on the Boulle side table. I didn't. I stepped over to one of the windows and gazed out at the hazy purple-gray sky and the shadows thickening on the lawn like folds of black velvet.

"Sorry I'm late," he said.

He stood in the doorway, looking resplendent in formal attire: shiny black pumps, black breeches and frock coat, elegant white satin waistcoat embroidered with white leaves, white silk neckcloth. His auburn hair was perfectly brushed and gleaming darkly. A quiet smile played on his lips, and his smoke-gray eyes gleamed with fond appreciation as he looked at me. What a splendid man he was, I thought. He was everything a woman could want, and I realized that I wanted him. I wanted him to step across the room and take me into his arms and caress me and kiss me until I was delirious, until I forgot everything but the rapture I knew he could summon from my senses. All those needs I had repressed for so many weeks seemed to surge to the surface, tormenting me, crying out for physical release.

"I just came down myself," I said demurely.

Robert moved across the room and took up one of the crystal decanters. He asked if I wanted a drink. I shook my head. He poured himself a brandy. How attractive he was, that mature face full of character and strength, those smoke-gray eyes full of wisdom, a little sad. He was a compassionate man, but there was a tough, ruthless quality as well. A man didn't attain Robert's power and position without it, and it made him all the more appealing. I didn't love him, no, I still loved Jason, but I felt strangely close to him and I sensed that he could, with time, make me forget all about the past. I sensed he could make me happy as well.

"I love this room," I said quietly. "Such beautiful Boulle."

Robert lifted a brow. "You know furniture?"

"I know a little about it. I certainly recognize the work of Boulle. The pieces you have here are the finest I have ever seen. You have so many beautiful things at Belle Mead, each perfect of its kind."

"I wanted only the best at Belle Mead. I wanted it to be a special place, full of beauty and harmony."

"It is certainly that," I told him.

Dinner was announced. Robert escorted me into the formal dining room with its elegant Chippendale sideboard, table and chairs, its walls hung in mulberry damask. Crystal and silver gleamed in the candle light, as did the Spode china with its exquisite gold, mulberry and indigo patterns. How perfect it all was, I thought as the turtle soup was served. I remembered the swamps and cornbread and greens with bacon grease served on the rickety wooden table in the kitchen. That was reality. I remembered Ma, her lined, weary face, and I had the feeling she was with me now in spirit, watching me, warning me. Why should she be warning me? The soup bowls were removed, the salad brought in. It was wonderful, but I ate very little of it. Yes, Ma was here with me. Why should I feel her presence so strongly tonight?

Robert was watching me. I couldn't just sit here, a prey to completely irrational feelings. I smiled. I asked him about the Spode china, and he told me it had been crafted by Josiah Spode himself at Stoke on Trent in the early 1780's. The damask on the walls here in the dining room had been hung especially to complement this particular set of china, he added. The breast of chicken cooked in orange sauce was served, along with the vegetables, and I ate enough to be polite and managed to keep the conversation going. Robert talked about the creation of Belle Mead and the expert help he had had in choosing the furnishings and appointments—he had known nothing about furniture and china and such, he admitted. It had taken a number of years to create the atmosphere he wanted. I told him he had the perfect place now.

"There is just one thing missing," he said.

"What's that?"

"I think you know, Dana," he told me.

He looked at me, and, yes, I knew. I lowered my eyes, toying with my wineglass. Our plates were removed and dessert brought in, a light chocolate pudding with sweet whipped cream. I didn't eat mine, but I did take a cup of coffee. Ma was here, I could feel her presence still, and the curious premonition I had felt on the stairs returned. I felt peculiar, felt I was in the grip of forces I could neither explain nor understand. When we had finished our coffee Robert suggested we go out on the verandah, and I readily agreed. Fresh air was just what I needed.

It did help. I felt better almost at once, and I wondered what could have come over me there in the dining room. The sky was a misty black now, shimmery with moonlight, and moonlight bathed the lawns, intensifying the shadows spread by the oak trees. We strolled slowly along the verandah for a while, both of us silent, and then we paused. Robert folded his arms across his chest and leaned against one of the slender white pillars, and I stood at the banister, looking out over the silvered, shadowy lawn. There was a mild evening breeze. The oak boughs creaked gently. Crickets made raspy music beneath the steps, and an owl hooted in the distance. It was all so serene, so lovely, like a dream that had to dissolve.

I could feel Robert watching me. I turned to face him.

"Feeling better now?" he asked.

I nodded. "Was it so obvious?"

"You merely seemed—a little distracted."

"I was thinking about the past," I said.

"I have the feeling it wasn't very pleasant."

"It wasn't—most of it wasn't. You don't know anything about me, Robert. You know Dana O'Malley, the successful actress. You—you don't know the girl who grew up in poverty, who had no education, who—"

"I know *you*," he said quietly, "and I know that the past is not important when two people—when two people feel kinship with each other."

"You—then you feel it, too?"

"I have from the first," he told me.

Robert stood up straight and, unfolding his arms, thrust his hands into his pockets. The owl hooted again, closer this time, and I heard a swooshing flutter of wings. Robert looked at me with solemn eyes.

"My meeting Jason Donovan in Atlanta was no accident, Dana," he said, and his voice was solemn, too. "It was very carefully planned. Donovan thought he was using me. Actually I was using him—to get to you."

"I—I don't understand."

A faint smile formed on his lips. "You wouldn't," he said. "I saw you once, Dana—you wouldn't remember. There's no reason why you should. It was here in Natchez. I had gone down to the docks on business, and a steamboat had just come in. I was going back to my carriage. I happened to look up. I saw you standing at the railing of the steamboat, looking down. Our eyes met, and I felt—" He paused, searching for the right words. "I felt I knew you. I felt I had known you for a long time."

I had never mentioned that morning to him before. I said nothing now. So it had not been just me. Robert had felt the same thing I felt, and he remembered that morning as vividly as I did.

"You reminded me of—of someone I once knew," he said, "but that wasn't enough to explain the feelings I had. I couldn't get you out of my mind. I'm not a reader of romantic novels and I don't believe in love at first sight, but something happened that day, something I couldn't explain. Try though I might, I couldn't forget you, couldn't get you out of my mind."

Wisps of cloud passed over the moon, and the silver rays streaming over the banister were replaced by shadows. I could barely see him now, but I felt the power of his presence, and for some reason it seemed even stronger in the semidarkness. His voice was deep and calm as he continued.

"Several months passed. One day I happened to be in Augusta, Georgia, and I saw your picture in the newspaper. It accompanied an article about the play that had just opened in the theater there. I recognized the picture immediately and when I went to the theater that evening and saw you perform, I felt that same—that same kinship, and I finally knew who you were."

"Augusta, Georgia," I said, casting back in memory. "We did *Lord Roderick's Revenge* there. I played Cora. You—you were in the audience."

"I had to meet you, but I didn't want to go backstage. I didn't want to be just another Stage Door Johnny chasing after a very popular young actress, so I began to investigate. I discovered that Donovan had written a play and wanted to have it performed at the National in Atlanta, discovered that he was leaving for Atlanta shortly thereafter.''

"You went there, too," I said.

"I went there, too. I spoke to the people at the National, told them that I was backing the play and would make up any losses on their part. They agreed to take it—and then I 'accidentally' encountered Donovan in the hotel bar and let him sell me on the idea of financing *The Quadroon*. He never knew I had already arranged things with the National.''

"I see."

"You all came to Atlanta. Rehearsals began. The production was mounted. I stayed in the background. I had learned that you and Donovan were very close, and I didn't want to try to take you from him—''

He hesitated, and as he did so the moonlight came pouring over the banister again and I saw his face. His expression was grave, his eyes dark and full of feelings I understood all too well. He stepped closer to me and placed his hands on my bare shoulders.

"I didn't want to play that stock figure, the Other Man, and I didn't want to alarm you or—or possibly alienate you. I realized that I was much older than you, and I realized that I hadn't Donovan's fire or looks or magnetism. I decided that my best chance was to win your trust, win your friendship—and do nothing to frighten you off.''

"You were biding your time," I said.

"Exactly. I was waiting for the right moment to tell you how I feel, and that moment has come.''

I waited, looking up at that grave, handsome face.

"I love you, Dana," he said.

"I—know. I've known for some time.''

"And?"

"I—I don't know what to say.''

"You—needn't say anything just yet.''

His hands were warm and heavy on my shoulders, and his fingers massaged my flesh and his eyes held mine there in the moonlight and sensations sprang alive inside me and I wanted more, much more. I wanted comfort and solace and tenderness.

I wanted strength to lean upon, and I wanted release. I trembled under his hands and he pulled me to him and the strength was there. He curled an arm around my waist and I looked into his eyes and the tenderness was there. Drawing me closer, he curled his other arm around the back of my shoulders. Sensations quickened within. I found comfort in his strength and solace in his nearness, and all that remained was release. My whole body craved it urgently now, and I clung to him as he parted his lips and tilted his head. He hesitated for an instant, and that instant seemed an eternity. When he finally kissed me, my senses reeled. It had been so long, so long. I had been so lonely. His mouth caressed mine, indescribably tender, firm, too, demanding the response I was so ready to give.

His arms tightened around me, holding me closer still, our bodies pressing together, flesh against flesh, bone against bone, separated only by thin layers of cloth, and his mouth continued that sweet plunder. I ran my palms over his back and up over his broad shoulders and finally wound my fingers into his hair and clasped the back of his head, drawing him to me. I felt his muscles tightening, felt the tension in his body, felt his own urgency mounting, and for several infinite moments both of us were bound by urgency and lost in the splendor, and then, abruptly, he pulled back, breathless.

"No," he gasped.

He released me. He stepped back. I thought I would fall. I thought my knees would give way. I caught my breath. Moments passed and control came and my heart stopped pounding and my breathing grew normal. Robert's chest heaved. His hands were curled into fists. Several more moments passed before he could speak, and then his voice was strained.

"Not this way," he said. "I don't want an affair with you, Dana,"

I didn't trust my own voice. I didn't speak.

"I've waited—all these months I've waited—and I want it to be right. I love you, Dana, and I want you—I've wanted you since I first saw you standing there at the railing of the steamboat—but I don't want another mistress. There've been—" He took a deep breath, hesitated, and when he continued his voice was controlled, calmer. "There have been many beautiful women and I have enjoyed them all, but you are different, Dana."

I waited, calm myself now. The oak boughs creaked gently. The crickets continued their raspy music. Moonlight shimmered, bathing us both in pale silver light. Robert smoothed his hair down, adjusted the hang of his frock coat, straightened his silk neckcloth. In complete control at last, he looked at me, and those moments of madness might never have occurred.

"I want to marry you," he said.

I nodded. I still didn't speak.

"I know I'm older, Dana. I know I'm not the dashing, exciting young hero women your age are said to desire, but I want to spend the rest of my life with you, and I think I could make you happy. We would live here at Belle Mead, and we would travel. I long to show you England, France, Italy, share with you the beauty and marvels to behold there. You would—if you married me, you would have all the luxuries life can offer."

He paused and moved closer to me. He wanted to take my hands. He didn't. He maintained tight, careful control.

"I know that you are fond of me," he continued, "and I feel there is a special empathy between us, a bond, if you will, a very strong bond. I realize you are not in love with me—you are still infatuated with Donovan, trying to forget him—but I think you might come to love me, Dana. I know that I would do everything in my power to make you the happiest woman on earth."

"I—Robert, I appreciate—"

"No," he said, "I don't want an answer now. I'm leaving in the morning, as you know, and I'll be gone for ten days. While I am away, I would like you to think about all I've said, and when I return—"

He hesitated. He did take my hands then. He held them lightly, for only a moment, and then he squeezed them and let them go and stepped back.

"I would like you to give me your answer when I return," he said.

"I will," I promised.

We went inside and Robert told me there were some papers he wanted to look over in his study, and we said good night in the foyer. He left very early the next morning, before I got up, and perhaps it was best, I thought. I needed to think about what had happened, and it might have been awkward seeing him before I reached my decision. It was a brilliant, sun-splashed day, and I wandered in the gardens and strolled along the river walk, reflecting, pondering, wondering what I should do. Robert loved me. There could be no question about that. He knew about my affair with Jason, knew I had what society would call a past, but he respected me nevertheless. He could have taken me to bed last night, and he had wanted to, but he wanted to do right by me. He wanted to make me his wife. I suspected that there were few men in this world as honorable as Robert Courtland.

Wednesday and Thursday were sunny, too, and Friday was glorious, the sun a silvery ball, the sky a shimmering blue. Len drove me to the docks to meet the boat, and I felt a great rush of joy as I saw Michael and Laura coming down the gangplank. I rushed to greet them. Michael grinned and nodded. Laura and I fell into each other's arms like schoolgirls, both of us talking at once. She looked elegant and sophisticated in white taffeta with mauve, purple and fuchsia stripes. Michael wore his familiar cowboy attire, the tan corduroy jacket a little the worse for wear. Laura showed me her rings, a thin, elegant gold band, a very large diamond of dazzling beauty. I took them over to Len and performed introductions and we got into the carriage and drove to Belle Mead, Laura chattering nonstop all the way.

It was wonderful to see them again, wonderful to have them with me. Laura was enchanted with Belle Mead and agreed with me that it was the most beautiful place she had ever seen. Maudie was enchanted with Michael, spoiling him outrageously during the three days of their visit. Laura told me all about her adventures in Texas and about the wedding and confided that Michael was often exasperating and still a bit bossy but added that she was keeping him in line and considered herself the luckiest woman alive. She was positively aglow with happiness, and Michael was happy, too. Although he teased her constantly and pretended a weary resignation to his fate, his eyes were full of adoration, and he couldn't keep them off her.

On Friday there was a tour of the house and gardens and a magnificent dinner and talk until after midnight. On Saturday morning Len drove us around the environs and into town, and although the shops in Natchez couldn't begin to compare with those in New Orleans, Laura went merrily berserk, buying with abandon. Michael and Len escaped to a tavern for drinks while she and I looked at dresses and tried on hats and bought a great many things we didn't need. In the afternoon Maudie supervised the packing of an enormous picnic hamper and we drove to a lovely wooded glade overlooking the river, Len apologizing that Arlene was unable to join us. After the superb lunch of fried chicken, potato salad, and chocolate cake, Michael and Len sat on stumps and talked about Indians and guns and such while Laura and I strolled idly down to the wildflower-strewn slope to watch the river winding its way along in the sunshine.

Sunday was a lovely, lazy day. We all slept late after another late night of talk. After lunch Michael went fishing with young Leroy, and Laura and I sat on the verandah, sipping iced lemonade and talking and looking out over the gardens. The multicolored patchwork of blossoms seemed to shimmer in the bright haze of afternoon sunlight. Michael and Leroy returned around five with a huge string of catfish and Maudie said she wudn't about to have Mamie clean an' cook all dem dere fish and Michael looked disappointed and said there was nothing he liked better than fresh catfish and, of course, we had them for dinner fried in a crisp golden batter and tasting divine. Michael retired early with a book of Restoration comedy he had found in the library, but Laura and I sat up late for the third night in a row.

At ten Monday morning, Len came by to drive Michael into town and show him his offices. The two men had taken to each other immediately. Laura and I had coffee on the verandah and then strolled down to the river walk, both of us subdued. They were leaving today, Len was driving us down to the dock right after lunch, and we didn't know how long it might be before we saw each other again. It was another beautiful morning, the sun not nearly so bright today, the sky a misty blue. The river was pewter-colored in the morning light, the gazebo with its pink-cushioned seats shady and inviting. Honeysuckle trembled in the warm breeze. Laura sighed, examined a book I had left on one of the seats and then moved over to look out at the vista of sky, slope and river.

"It really is beautiful here, love," she said. "It's like a little paradise, and it's worked wonders for you. I've never seen you so serene."

"This summer has—has been good for me. I was on the verge of a nervous collapse when I left New Orleans. The tension, the strain, the constant pressure—I needed a break."

"I know, love. I needed a break myself, not that Texas was all that *rest*ful."

"I'm so happy for you and Michael, darling."

"I can't believe I'm really married, and to an heir, no less. One day my vagabond actor husband will come into a great deal of wealth. In the meantime, we'll keep right on treading the boards. Acting's in his blood. Herding cattle leaves him cold. His parents are very sweet about it, very understanding. They just want him to be happy—and come visit a lot."

She smiled, and then there was a long silence. During all our cozy talks, there was one subject neither of us had mentioned. Laura had too much tact. I had too much pride. I swallowed my pride now, no longer able to endure not knowing.

"I—I suppose *Lady Caroline* is coming right along," I said.

Laura hesitated for a moment, then nodded. "Dulcie has kept us abreast of all developments through letters. The play won't be opening in September, but it should open shortly thereafter. Dulcie's already done most of the costumes. Michael will be very Byronic in a long sweeping black cape and white silk shirt with open collar, and she says the blue velvet riding habit I wear in the first act is stunning."

She was being evasive. I waited.

"Most of the sets have been constructed, too. Dulcie says they're spectacular. The National is sparing no expense. The ballroom will have real chandeliers and white damask walls with patterned gold panels, and there will be marble columns as well."

I was growing impatient. Laura saw that. She took a deep breath.

"He's found a leading lady, love," she told me.

"Oh?"

"Carmelita," she said.

"Carmelita!"

"Apparently she's done nothing but diet since she left the company. She's lost all that weight and looks terrific, Dulcie says, thinner than ever. Jason has been working on the part with her all summer and—seems to be quite satisfied with her."

My blood seemed to run cold. "I—can't believe it," I said.

"Neither could I," Laura confessed.

"She's all wrong for the part," I protested. "She's far too *old*, for one thing, and, fat or thin, she hasn't the sensitivity to convey the subtleties of the character. Her Caroline will be a cool, haughty aristocrat. The passion and the pathos will—''

I cut myself short. It didn't concern me, I reminded myself. It didn't concern me at all. The outrage and anger persisted nevertheless. He had written the part for me, tailored it for me, and I wasn't going to play it, I could accept that, but for him to have given the part to Carmelita Herring was like a personal affront.

"He had to do something," Laura said cautiously.

"I realize that."

"She's a competent actress, and she does have a following."

"That's quite true."

"I'm sorry, love. I—I didn't want to tell you."

"It's just as well," I said. "Actually, it's quite a break for Michael. He'll have to carry the play, and he'll undoubtedly score a tremendous personal triumph. I—I imagine we'd better be getting back to the house now, darling. Lunch will be served soon."

We left the gazebo and strolled along the river walk. I was calm, now, resigned. Sad, too. The sadness hung over me like a pall. Laura looked concerned.

"What are you going to do, love?" she asked as we moved through the gardens.

"I'm not sure," I said.

"You've had dozens of offers."

"Dozens," I agreed.

"Are you going to take one of them?"

"I may."

"What about Robert Courtland, love?"

I hadn't told her about the proposal. I saw no reason to do so now. Until I reached a decision, I felt it best to keep it to myself. As we moved up the flat marble steps to the next terrace, I saw that Len and Michael were back, waiting for us on the verandah.

"Robert's been wonderful," I said. "He's been very supportive and—as I told you, he's been a perfect gentleman. If—if anything develops, I'll let you know. Right now I just want you and Michael to have a safe and happy trip to Atlanta, and I want you to know how much I've enjoyed having you."

I hated to see them leave that afternoon. Len drove us down to the docks, and Laura and I were both rather teary. She hugged me tightly, and we promised to keep in close touch. Michael gave me a hug, too, said he was sure going to miss me and then escorted his wife up the gangplank. They stood at the railing and waved as the steamboat chugged and lurched and finally pulled away, and Len handed me into the carriage. I was silent as we rode back to Belle Mead, feeling lost, feeling orphaned and alone. For two years I had been part of a large, merry, unruly family, and now I no longer belonged. They were going on without me, and *Carmelita* had taken my place. That was the hardest blow of all.

The brilliant procession of sun-filled days ended. Blue skies turned gray, and mornings were misty and damp, although it never really rained. I had a decision to make, and I knew I must make it before Robert returned. I knew I hadn't really considered accepting his proposal before. Although I had never openly acknowledged it, in my heart of hearts I had believed that things would work out somehow, that I would join the others in Atlanta and open in *Lady Caroline*, but that foolish illusion was gone now. Jason didn't want me. He didn't need me. I bloody well didn't need him either, I told myself. Drummond would sign me up in a minute, as would at least a dozen other managers much more important and successful than Jason would ever be, but . . . I really didn't want that. I didn't want to be an international star, the toast of two continents. I didn't want fame and glory and adulation. I wanted to be part of that merry and rowdy and loving family in Atlanta.

It isn't going to happen, I told myself. You've got to face reality. You can leave Belle Mead and go to New York and sign up with Conrad Drummond or you can stay and marry Robert. I didn't love him. I acknowledged that frankly. I found him physically appealing and I was fond of him and felt very close to him and . . . and many successful marriages had been built on less, but would it be fair? I respected Robert too much to use him. He was a wonderful man. He was in love with me. He knew I didn't love him, but he wanted me nevertheless. He felt I would come to love him. Perhaps I would. With Robert there would be security and comfort and warmth, great luxury as well, and that snug, safe harbor was tempting indeed, yet . . . the reservations persisted. Day followed day, and I still couldn't reach a final decision. He would understand, I assured myself. Robert was nothing if not patient and understanding.

The day of his return dawned, damp and misty and gray, but

by ten the mist had evaporated and the sky had turned from slate to a pearly gray luminous with pale white sunlight. Robert was due to arrive at two-thirty in the afternoon, Len had advised me, and he should reach Belle Mead a little after three. I was unusually restless and nervous all during the morning, plagued by another irrational premonition I could neither explain nor shake. I had the feeling something was going to happen, something of monumental importance, and the very air seemed to reverberate with silent whispers, whispers felt, not heard, warning me to beware, beware, beware. It was totally absurd, I told myself, completely irrational, yet the feeling grew stronger, and, again, I felt Ma's presence nearby. She was here with me, I could feel her, and she was warning me, too, desperately trying to penetrate that invisible field separating us and warn me not to . . . not to do what?

You're nervous and upset, I told myself. You're imagining things. Belle Mead was peaceful and serene, and even the weather was clearing, sunlight growing stronger now, bathing the gardens in thin sliver-white light faintly touched with gold. There was no menace here, no threat. What could there possibly be to warn me about? What could I possibly need to beware of? I retired to my sitting room and busied myself writing letters, but those whispers still reverberated and Ma never left me, not for an instant. When Maudie came in to bring me a tray, I almost jumped out of my skin. She looked rather skittish herself, as though she, too, could sense something in the atmosphere.

"Lands-a-goshen, Missy! You done give me a turn, jumpin' like dat. You'se as white as a sheet!"

"You—you startled me," I said. My voice was strained.

"I—I know you done said you wudn't havin' any lunch, but you didn't have no breakfast, either, just dat coffee, an' I brung you dis omelet an' a glass of milk an' one of Mamie's applesauce pancakes, an' I wants you to eat it, missy."

"I really—"

"I ain't takin' no lip, missy. You jest eat dat food or you'll catch what for. Cain't have you lookin' all pale an' lis'less when Mister Robert gets in. Eat—you hear?"

I sighed and unfolded the white linen napkin and picked up the fork. Maudie waited until I cut off a piece of pancake with the edge of the fork, and then she shivered and scurried out of the room as though she couldn't get out quickly enough. The pancake was light and delicious, the omelet superb with mush-rooms and cheese and spices, but I ate only a few bites of each. The milk was icy cold. I drank it all, and I felt a little better then. It's your imagination, Dana, I assured myself. You're a grown woman now. You didn't even believe in ghosts when you were a little girl, living in the swamps, and it's preposterous to believe in them now.

I stepped over to the window and gazed down at the mighty oaks that spread soft mauve-gray shadows over the lawn. It was peaceful and lovely, without the faintest hint of anything omi-nous, yet as I returned to the writing table those whispers were louder than ever. Stubbornly I picked up pen and continued writing to Corey, sketching bright anecdotes about Laura and Michael's visit, but I had to strain to maintain that light touch, and often my pen stopped altogether as I raised my head and strained to decipher that felt-not-heard warning in the air. Frowning, I continued to write and discovered that I had run out of paper and would have to fetch some more if I was going to finish the letter. Ma was beside me as I stood up. Felt, not seen, she seemed to urge me on, to lead me out of the room and down the hall.

Robert had provided me with two boxes of the pale creamy tan paper. Where would I find more? In his study, I told myself. In his desk. *Yes, yes*, a silent voice agreed, and Ma led me down the graceful curving staircase and across the foyer and down the hall. I passed the drawing room and the library and finally reached the large, comfortable study with its brown and tan carpet, brown leather sofa and walls of polished golden oak hung with fine old English hunting prints. Pale yellow-white sunlight streamed in through the windows, making tiny sun-bursts on the bronze and orange globe standing in one corner and on the various brass pieces on the large golden oak desk.

Moving behind the desk, I opened the top right-hand drawer. No writing paper there, just folders and ledgers. The top middle drawer contained an account book and business papers, pens, ruler, a magnifying glass, and the top left-hand drawer con-tained bundles of what looked like business contracts. Every-thing was neat and tidy, as was to be expected from a man as orderly as Robert. I sighed, sat down in the leather-cushioned chair and pulled open the middle drawer on the right, and my own face looked up at me from a delicate oval miniature in a frame of gold filigree set with tiny diamonds and pearls. Startled, I lifted the miniature out of the drawer, wondering when he had had it done. I certainly hadn't sat for it. The artist had done a superb job, capturing my features perfectly. I might have been staring into a tiny mirror, only . . . I had never worn my hair in sausage ringlets, and . . . and I had never worn a white tulle dress sprigged with small daisies. The dress was old-fashioned, as least . . . at least twenty-five years out-of-date.

I knew then. I understood. Understanding came all at once and with shocking force. My pulses seemed to stop. I seemed to be encased in ice. With understanding came horror, and, though paralyzed, a trembling started inside and I closed my eyes and for several long minutes I seemed to swim in a dark, icy void. That curious bond between us . . . the feeling we had known each other in another lifetime . . . it was all clear now. The empathy, the affinity, the sense of security I felt when in his presence . . . blood and basic instincts had known, had responded, even if the rest of me was unaware. I felt a stirring around me, and I opened my eyes. The air was still. The atmosphere was clear. There was nothing there now. Ma was gone. She had done her job, and she was gone, and I looked at her face there in the miniature and understood everything.

I was no longer in the elegant study in Belle Mead. I was in that squalid room in the shack in the swamps, and Ma was there in her bed, all pale and waxen, her forehead moist, her graying honey-blond hair damp. She was dying, but her eyes filled with joyous recognition as she looked at me and saw not me but someone else. *If you had known—Oh, Robert, if you had known, you wouldn't have—I wanted to die then. I wanted to stop living, but I couldn't because—because I was carrying our little girl.* I heard her dear, fading voice whispering those words, and then I heard another voice, raspy and cracked and confused, and I saw Mama Lou's face in wildly flickering candlelight. *What he wants, it is unnatural, it is wrong and you must—you must not do this thing. It is wrong, against nature.*

My mother had loved Robert Courtland with all her heart. He was not of her class, not of her kind, did not belong to that exclusive circle of the New Orleans Creole aristocracy. She could have made a grand marriage, but she had loved him and had run away with him, and . . . he had loved her, too. *There was one,* he had told me that afternoon as we returned to the hotel after our lunch at the market. *There was one I should have married. Through my own foolishness I lost her. I was very young, but I should never have* . . . He had never forgotten her and he had seen me and I reminded him of her and he felt that curious bond, too. Robert had loved my mother, but he had left her, and he had never known that she was carrying a child.

I sat there at the desk, still stunned, immobile, all these thoughts parading through my mind in solemn procession, and I have no idea how much time might have passed when I finally heard his carriage pull up in front of the house. I ran my hand across my brow, trying to compose myself, but it was several minutes before I found the strength to stand. My knees felt weak, and I had a moment of panic as I heard his footsteps approaching the study. Standing behind the desk, I silently prayed for strength. He stepped through the doorway and paused just inside the room, smiling when he saw me.

"Here you are," he said.

The smile played on his lips. It was a beautiful smile, warm and loving, and his eyes were full of adoration he didn't even try to conceal. He was wearing pale tan breeches and frock coat and a brown and white striped satin waistcoat and a brown silk neckcloth, and his glossy auburn hair was neatly brushed, gleaming with rich highlights. How glorious he must have been all those years ago, I thought. He must have been a veritable Adonis.

"It's wonderful to see you," he said. "You have no idea how I've missed you."

I didn't say anything. I didn't trust myself to speak.

"I couldn't find you when I first got in. Maudie told me she thought you had come in here."

"I—I came to get some more writing paper," I told him.

My voice sounded stiff and seemed to be coming from someone else. Robert looked puzzled, and then he looked concerned.

"You—you're pale, Dana. Is something wrong?"

"I didn't find the paper," I said. "I found this."

I picked up the miniature and showed it to him, then placed it back on the desk.

"Clarisse," he said quietly.

"At first I thought you had had a miniature of me painted."

"You—you look remarkably like her," Robert said, and his

voice was hesitant. "That's what first drew me to you, I admit it, but I—I fell in love with *you*, Dana,"

"She was the one, wasn't she? The one you said you should have married."

Robert nodded. "It was a long time ago, I was very young, and I was very foolish."

"Tell me about her, Robert,"

"Dana, I see no point in—"

"Tell me about her."

"She—she came from a very distinguished family. I told you—I was an orphan. I had been on my own since I was fourteen years old. I made my living by my wits, by my charm. I wasn't bad, but—I wasn't respectable, either. I met Clarisse, and she believed in me. She believed I could *be* somebody, become a success. I—we ran off together. I loved her. I wanted to make her proud. I—after a few months I realized—"

He paused, looking very sad.

"After a few months I realized I could only make her unhappy. She was accustomed to luxury, to all the fine things in life, and we were living in a tiny flat and she was washing her own clothes and—I can't do this to her, I told myself. I had over three hundred dollars. One night while Clarisse was sleeping I left most of the money and a note and I crept out of the flat. The next morning I left town on the first train. I told myself I was doing it for her. I—perhaps I was merely frightened of commitment."

"And then what happened?"

"Two years later I went back to New Orleans. I had spent those two years working, working hard, and I had quite a bit of money. I had discovered that I had a knack for making shrewd deals, and I had made several by then. I no longer relied on my wits, on my charm. I planned to marry her. I planned—" He paused again, gazing into the past, his expression grave. "Her family wouldn't see me," he continued. "I learned that she had married someone else. I tried my best to forget her. I—never could. I devoted my life to making a fortune, and I succeeded. There were many women, but until I met you there was—no one like Clarisse."

There was a long silence. I moved over to one of the windows to gaze out at the lawn, trying to summon strength. Finally I turned and looked at him and saw his grave expression and his sad gray eyes, and I bit my lower lip. When I spoke, my voice trembled not at all.

"She married someone else because she had to," I told him.

He frowned, "How—how could you possibly—"

He cut himself short and looked at me, the furrow between his brows deepening, and realization came then. I saw the knowledge in his eyes, and I saw his cheeks turn ashen.

"She was pregnant," I said. "Her family refused to take her in. She got a room in a cheap waterfront hotel and—the money you left her eventually ran out. Clem O'Malley found her there. He was an overseer at one of the plantations she used to visit when she was a girl. He married her and took her back there, and I was born shortly thereafter. Clem O'Malley gave me his name, but he—he was not my father."

"My God," he whispered.

"He lost his job. We moved to the swamps. I was brought up there, living in a squalid shanty. Ma—Ma worked like a farmer's wife and her health seeped away little by little. She—never talked about the past. She never told me who my father was, but—" My voice threatened to break. I paused and took a deep breath. "She got the consumption, and—and as she was dying she looked at me and she thought I was you and—she said your name, just your first name. She loved you always."

These last words were a mere whisper. His face was completely drained of color now, and the pain in his eyes was terrible to behold. I wanted to go to him and comfort him. I wanted to hold him to me and tell him it was all right, but I couldn't. I couldn't move.

"I'm—sorry," he said. "You'll never know how sorry I am—about everything."

"It was—neither of us knew."

"Neither of us knew," he repeated.

He looked at me with that terrible pain in his eyes, and then he came over to me and put his arms around me and folded me to him. He held me close, held me tenderly, but only for a moment. "I'm sorry," he said again, and his voice was so faint I could barely hear the words. He released me and moved back, and then he turned and left the room.

He left the house a few minutes later. I was moving down the hall when I heard the carriage pulling away. Maudie met me in the foyer. She said Mister Robert done left an' he didn't say where he was goin'. She looked worried, and she was even more worried when dinnertime came and he hadn't returned. I let her bring a tray of food up to my sitting room, but I ate very little. Maudie fussed and fretted when she returned for the tray, said I looked poorly, said I wudn't to get all het up, there was bound to be a reason why Mister Robert hadn't come back. She was going to bring me a glass of warm milk and I was to get right to bed an' none of dat readin' till all hours.

I drank the milk. I went to bed. I didn't sleep. I watched misty silver moonbeams chase the shadows over the walls and ceiling and listened to the heavy oak boughs creaking gently in the night. It must have been after three when I finally drifted into a troubled sleep, and it seemed only a matter of minutes before I awoke to find Maudie bustling about with a breakfast tray. She pulled the curtains open and sunlight spilled into the room in brilliant rays. It was after ten o'clock, she told me, and no, Mister Robert hadn't come back yet. He was goin' to get what for when he *did*. Sure, he was a grown man, but it wudn't right, worryin' people half to death.

The day seemed interminable. Every hour seemed like ten. Robert didn't return. I wondered if I should pack my bags and leave quietly. Perhaps that would be the best thing for both of us. I could return to New Orleans and stay with Corey until I decided what I was going to do. No, that would be cowardly. He was my father. I couldn't run away. I would wait for him, and when he returned we would talk, we would work things out. I ate no lunch. I was sharp with Maudie when she kept fussing over me, and then I had to apologize and make things up with her. She had a feelin' in her bones, a bad feelin'. Dis wudn't like Mister Robert. I had a feeling, too, and I tried to ignore it as late afternoon sunshine made shadows lengthen across the lawn and I wandered under the oaks, my pink cotton skirt fluttering in the breeze.

I heard the hoofbeats on the drive. Relief flooded over me. I turned and saw the powerful black horse and the man in gray riding it, and the fading sunlight burnished his dark blond hair. Len. I was some distance from the house. He dismounted and gave the reins to Leroy and started toward me, his expression grim. I knew then. I stood there under the oaks as the shadows lengthened and I knew, even before he reached me, even before he spoke. He took my hands. He told me that Robert had come to his office yesterday afternoon and had insisted on making a new will. It was duly written and witnessed and signed, everything done with impeccable legal care.

"He provided for the servants, and he left me a small bequest, and he left everything else to you, Dana. Belle Mead. All his business interests. Everything. Millions."

I said nothing. I was unable to speak.

"He—he told me he needed to be alone for a while. He said he was going to take the boat out. He kept a small craft in a berth down on the river. He usually took at least two men with him as crew, but yesterday he went out alone. It was possible for one man to handle the boat."

"He—didn't come back," I whispered.

Len held my hands very tightly, so tightly I felt pain.

"They found the boat, Dana. It had cracked up on a sandbar, and there was a large hole in the bottom. They found Robert a short while later. He was—he had washed up onshore half a mile away."

"No," I whispered.

"It was an accident. Everyone believes it was an accident."

I shook my head. Len squeezed my hands even tighter.

"We must let them believe that," he said.

"You know."

Len nodded, and he finally released my hands.

"He told me. He said he wanted me to know. He—before he left the office he casually remarked that if anything should happen to him, he was depending on me to—take care of things for you. I should have sensed something was wrong. I should never have let him take the boat out."

"You mustn't blame yourself."

"He was not only my employer, Dana. He was also my best friend."

I nodded. Why couldn't I cry? Why wouldn't the tears fall? Why did I feel completely numb?

"There will be journalists, Dana," Len said. "You're a famous woman, and there is no way—"

"I understand."

"I'll do what I can."

He put his arm around my shoulders then, and we started back to the house, walking slowly beneath the oaks. The mauve-gray shadows were deepening to purple. Leaves rustled overhead. Maudie and Leroy and several other servants had gathered on the verandah, all of them anxious, all of them sensing something was wrong. Maudie was wringing her hands.

"What am I going to do, Len?" I asked. My voice was hollow.

"You're going to be strong," he said.

Oh yes, I thought, I'm going to be strong. I always am. I'm very good at it. I've had a great deal of experience. I'm going to be strong. That's all I can do.

Chapter Twenty-Two

MAUDIE HOVERED OVER THE BREAKFAST TABLE with her arms folded across her bosom and a stern expression on her face. I could feel my dander rising. She had been marvelous these past two weeks and I didn't know how I could have gotten through them without her, but there were times when I longed to drive a knife through her heart. Like now. Care and concern were one thing. Being a bossy, overbearing tyrant was another. Enough was enough. I had dutifully eaten two pieces of toast, one with jam, and I had drunk three cups of black coffee, but I would be damned if I was going to eat eggs, grits and fried ham as well. The mere thought of it was disgusting. I set my mouth in a resolute line, shoved the plate away from me and folded *my* arms across *my* bosom, looking at her with icy defiance.

"You'se as stubborn as a mule," she accused.

"I don't deny it."

"You still ain't strong an' you still looks puny. You needs dat food to gib you strength. How'se you gonna get better if you keeps on starvin' yourself? Dat ham is sugar-cured, an'—"

"You can take the ham, and the grits, *and* the eggs, and shove—"

"Don't you get lippy with me, missy! Don't you start talkin' ugly. You might be mistress here now an' you might be rich as dat guy Crow-shus, but Mister Robert done left *me* some money, too. I done went an' bought myself a new purple taff'ta petticoat an' some gold earbobs, an' Mister Len says I'se *still* a well-to-do woman. I'se free an' I'se rich, an' I don't hafta take no guff from *no* one."

"Then don't," I snapped.

"What's *dat* supposed to mean?"

494

"It means you can leave any time you choose."

"Leave! Ain't likely, missy!" Maudie placed her hands on her hips, her expression as defiant as my own. "My job's to take care-a dis house an' take care-a you, an' dat's what I 'tends to *do*. Now you eats dat dere food before I *really* gibs you what for."

"Damn you, Maudie."

"Don't you go damnin' me," she warned. "Eat dat food."

The eggs were fluffy and delicious, scrambled with herbs and cream. The ham was tender and tasty. I turned down the grits, but I had another piece of toast with guava jelly and another cup of coffee as well. Maudie was beaming when I finished. I still longed to stab her.

"Dere," she said. "Feels better, don't-ja?"

"Maybe." I was noncommittal.

"I knows you'se gettin' better 'cause you'se gettin' spunky. Rather see you dat way dan see you mopin' around all pale an' lis'less. You're gettin' de color back in your cheeks."

I sighed and stood up and started toward the door.

"Where's you goin?"

"I'm going for a walk."

"It done be rainin' for de past three days!" Maudie protested. "It's still damp out dere, all misty, too."

"I'm going for a walk," I said firmly.

"Not without your shawl, you ain't!"

I left the room and started down the side corridor to the French windows that opened onto the verandah. They were closed. I opened them and stepped outside. The air was indeed damp, but wonderfully clean and refreshing, and the gardens were wet and half-concealed by thin tendrils of mist that swirled lightly in the air. Overhead the sky was watery and gray, but a pale yellow ball was faintly visible. The sun might well come out after all, I thought. If I had to spend another day closed up in the house I would surely go out of my mind.

Maudie came charging down the corridor after me, her heavy tread seeming to shake the house. She burst out onto the verandah and gave a sigh of relief when she saw me standing beside one of the hanging plants. She was carrying a soft, lovely white shawl, and she wrapped it around my shoulders as tenderly as she might swaddle an infant. Bossy and overbearing she might be, but it was difficult to stay angry with her.

"Now you don't stay out dere too long! Dem steps're probably slippery, so watch 'em, an' don't you go gettin' your skirts wet on dem bushes. If you ain't back soon, I'se comin' out after you!"

Not *that* difficult, I thought.

"If anyone calls, Maudie, I—please tell them I'm out. I don't want to see any more journalists, and—"

"Ain't no one else likely to call dis mornin'. Dem 'ristocrats dat've been callin' don't never get outta bed 'fore noon, an' Mister Len ain't gonna be here till dis afternoon."

Wrapping the shawl around my arms like a stole, I started down the steps and crossed the patio, Maudie watching anxiously from the verandah. The tiles were wet, and I lifted the skirt of my deep pink frock a couple of inches, as well as the layers of white petticoat beneath. The thin tendrils of mist continued to swirl, lightly veiling the multicolored flower beds and creating an impression of blurry unreality that was both delicate and lovely. The blooms were damp, too, with dew, and tiny trickles of water dripped from the trellises. I sauntered slowly through the gardens down toward the river walk, and I tried not to think about my father and the funeral that had been so beautifully conducted and attended by over a dozen journalists and all the landed gentry for miles around.

Len had been right. I was a famous woman, and there was no way we could hold the journalists at bay. Sniffing blood, sniffing scandal, they had converged on Natchez in a rowdy pack, prepared to outdo themselves in sensational dispatches. I could imagine the headlines: Millionaire Dies Under Mysterious Circumstances, Leaves Entire Fortune to Actress-Mistress. I knew I had a decision to make. I didn't want my father's memory besmirched with sordid speculations. I knew journalists. I knew how to handle them. After a brief discussion with Len, I decided to give them a story far more interesting than any they could invent. I decided to give them the true story of Dana O'Malley and her parents and how my father and I had found each other after twenty years. With Len at my side, I invited them all to Belle Mead and served food and wine and told them the whole truth, omitting only my mother's maiden name to spare her folk embarrassment and implying that Robert and I had discovered our relationship before he backed *The Quadroon*.

I left holes, of course. I did not tell them about Clem's brutality, and I did not tell them about my time in New Orleans with the Etiennes. I simply said I left the swamps after my mother's death and eventually made my way into the theater, and they were so busy scribbling they didn't bother to ask any awkward questions. My father had planned to publicly acknowledge our kinship, I told them, and then the tragic accident had occurred. I was illegitimate, I concluded, but I had loved both my parents and was proud to be their child. The world could say what they liked about me, but I would always hold my head high. The journalists were intrigued. They were fascinated. They were, to a man, completely sympathetic, and the stories they filed created a sensation on front pages all over the South. I was the heroine of a star-crossed love story, and the journalists did everything but deify me.

The public response was overwhelming. They praised my honesty, my bravery, my indomitable spirit. How they loved the poor little girl who had left the swamp in rags, became a celebrated actress and was reunited with her long lost father, ultimately inheriting one of the greatest fortunes in the South. They clamored for more details, and more and more journalists appeared to interview me. Unlike the Creole aristocracy, who would surely have shunned me, the elite of Natchez and its environs were ready to accept me with open arms. Dowagers and their daughters came to call to express their sympathy and bring flowers, each and every one of them, it seemed, extremely close to my dear departed father. They issued invitations to parties and teas, and a number of them seemed to have perfectly marvelous sons who were quite eager to meet me. They were all eager to take me under their wings, and the fact that I was now the wealthiest woman in the South did not, I assured myself, have anything to do with it.

I moved down the three marble steps to the last terrace of gardens, surrounded by mist that swirled like thin, transparent white veils, now concealing, now revealing great patches of multicolored blooms. The mist was heavier down here, and I could barely see the tall line of shrubbery that hid the river walk. I moved on toward the gate, thinking about the surprise visit I had had three days ago. Conrad Drummond had been visiting in New Orleans and he had seen the stories and he had come to Natchez to beg me to return to New York with him. The stories were appearing in all of the northern papers, too, he informed me, and I could dictate my own terms. He would mount a fabulous production for me, any play I selected, and he would make me a legend in theatrical history. I thanked him politely. I took his address in New Orleans. I told him I would let him know.

The leaves of the shrubbery gleamed with moisture. The gate creaked as I opened it and left the gardens behind. I started up the river walk toward the gazebo, but the mist was so heavy here I couldn't see it. Clouds of mist drifted and danced, parting before me, and there was a strange silence broken only by the muted rush of the river. I had no desire to go to New York. I had no desire to become a theatrical legend. I longed to return to the theater, yes, but . . . I stubbornly closed my mind to that. I wasn't going to think about Atlanta. I wasn't going to think about Jason. I certainly didn't need him now. I was one of the richest women in the country, and I could do anything I wanted to do. Anything but what you really want to do, a voice inside said dryly, and I resolutely silenced it.

I walked through the drifting clouds of mist, and the gazebo was visible now, looming ahead like something out of a dream. The honeysuckle was damp, and the bees were gone. When I stepped inside, I saw that the pink cushions were slightly damp, too, but they would dry quickly enough in the sun, if the sun ever shined through. The rush of the river was clearer now, like distant music without melody, muted, monotonous, and as the mist lifted and swirled, I caught occasional glimpses. It looked like a shiny blue-gray ribbon undulating between the banks. Although the air was cool and moist, it was still too warm for the shawl. I removed it and draped it on the table, knowing I would incur Maudie's wrath, not caring in the least. The air seemed to gently caress my bare arms and shoulders. There in the gazebo, completely surrounded by the dancing, drifting clouds, I felt alone and adrift, and the sadness inside was almost more than I could bear.

You're rich, I told myself. You're rich, rich, rich. You can buy anything in the world. You have this lovely house and more money than you could possibly ever spend. Isn't that what most people long for? The wealth was precious little consolation. There were things I could do with it, yes, and I had already made arrangements with Len to dispose of some of it. Delia was going to receive a very large sum, enough to insure that she—and her family—would never again have to worry about losing the house or the business. Mathilde and Solange DuJardin were to receive a large sum, too, enough to enable them to leave that drab, pathetic house on Conti Street and live in comfort for the rest of their lives. I would never see them again, it was true, but they were blood kin and it seemed the right thing to do. It was what Ma would have wanted.

There were many other things I could do with the money as well. I could have the Jewel Theater completely refurbished and subsidize it and help Ollie and Bart and all my friends and . . . and there would still be a fortune left for Len to manage. I could do a great many things with the money, yes, but I couldn't buy the camaraderie and excitement and sense of fulfillment I had received as part of that merry, unruly family, and I couldn't buy . . . I couldn't buy . . . I closed my eyes, willing myself not to think about him, but I did. I remembered his warmth and his wit, his boyish enthusiasm and zest, his vulnerability and sweetness, his quick temper and his thorny pride, and I remembered his arms, his mouth, his lean, strong body and those words he always murmured so tenderly into my ear as he became a part of me. The old familiar feelings began to stir inside, the tender ache, the honied warmth that spread so slowly, so sweetly in my veins. Denying them as best I could, I left the gazebo and started back up the river walk.

I heard his footsteps. I stopped. The mist swirled, and the great river was nearby, and I knew it had all happened before, again and again, but in my dream. This was not a dream. It was real. I tried to tell myself it was real, but there was a shimmering quality of unreality and I still couldn't believe it was actually happening. He materialized out of the mist and he was wearing his most elegant attire and he stood there before me. Neither of us spoke. He took my hands and squeezed them and pulled me to him. I looked into those gray-green eyes and saw the love in them, and I knew he was the one. He wasn't perfect, he would never be that, but he was the one.

"It—it wasn't Charles," I whispered. "It was you—all along."

He let go of my hands and stepped back.

"Who the hell is Charles?" he asked.

"Someone—someone I once knew. I thought—in my dream, you see—"

"What are you talking about?"

How I loved that fascinating voice that was light, almost soft, but guttural and scratchy, too. How I had missed hearing it. I smiled. A flood of joy welled up inside, and it was all I could do to contain it. He was looking at me with one quirky eyebrow elevated, something very like a scowl forming on those wide lips.

"How did you get past Maudie?" I asked.

"The old dragon at the house? I told her I was a very close friend, and she said Miz Dana ain't seein' no one and I said is she in and she said maybe she is and maybe she ain't but you ain't seein' her, and I said look, lady, I've come all the way from Atlanta and if you don't tell me where she is I fully intend to wring your fat black neck."

"That sounds like something you'd say."

"She grinned then. She said I must be th' one Miz Dana done been pinin' for all dis time. She knowed dere was a man, she said, all along she knowed, an' she reckoned I must be th' one."

"That bitch," I said.

"*Have* you been pining for me?"

"Of course not," I retorted.

He jammed his hands into his pockets and scowled. A light breeze sprang up. The mist shifted, swirled, began to lift. I caught another glimpse of the river. Light golden spangles seemed to sparkle on its surface. The sun was coming out. The mist swallowed us up for a moment and then grew thinner, gradually dissolving. Jason looked miserable. How I longed to stroke that furrowed brow and run the ball of my thumb along that full, firm curve of his lower lip. How I loved him, but he had some crow to eat and some explaining to do before I let him know how much.

"Why did you come, Jason?" I asked. My voice was cool.

"I shouldn't have," he said. "I realize that, but—I thought maybe I could—well, help in some way, give you some kind of support. Laura and Ollie both said they were coming and I said no, you're staying here, I'm going. They both smiled and said that would be much, much better."

I said nothing. They'll pay, I vowed.

"You'll probably want to send me away, and I wouldn't blame you. I was very unfair to you, Dana. I was—I acted like a heel."

"You certainly did," I agreed.

"I—dammit, you're not making this very easy."

"I'm certainly not."

"Okay! I was very unfair. I acted like a heel. I've had the most miserable summer of my life. I love you, and I've lost you, and it's all my own bloody fault. So there!"

"It wasn't *all* your fault," I conceded.

"No?"

"I was—rather stubborn and intractable myself."

"That's for damn sure!"

I smiled again. The mist was dissolving rapidly now, white wisps floating furiously in the breeze, disappearing, and rays of sunlight broke through, shining rather weakly at first, growing brighter. He was no southern gentleman, true, but he'd never pretended to be. He was a rough-and-tumble artist, testy and temperamental and . . . quite wonderful. We would always fight, I knew, but he was the one and I loved him with all my heart, and I also knew I couldn't possibly live without him.

"We'd better go back to the house," I said.

"Anything you say."

He marched along sulkily beside me, his hands still thrust into his pockets, and when we reached the gate I stopped, waiting, and he scowled and gave an exasperated sigh and opened the gate, acting as though it were a great imposition. Poor darling. How miserable he was. The mist was completely gone from the gardens, but the air was still slightly hazy, and the flower beds were soft, multicolored blurs. As we started slowly toward the steps leading up to the next level, Jason sighed again, his bad temper dissolving. He looked at the flowers and then he looked at me, and when he finally spoke, his voice was quiet and full of compassion.

"I'm really sorry about your father, Dana."

"Thank you," I said.

"I can see why the two of you didn't want anyone to know, but—I wish you had told me. I thought—I assumed—"

"I know what you assumed."

He believed what he had read in the newspapers. He believed Robert and I had known of our relationship before, and . . . he would go right on believing that, I resolved. No one but Len would ever know the entire truth.

"It was very brave of you to give those interviews to the papers," Jason continued. "Everyone admires you for it. Everyone is behind you. I—I suppose you've made a great many plans for the future."

"A few," I said.

"You're rich now."

"Incredibly rich," I replied.

We moved up the steps. The air was clearer now. The sunlight streamed down brilliantly. The flowers were brighter. Jason stopped and turned to me, and his eyes were full of anguish.

"I wish you weren't!" he said violently. "I wish you were dirt-poor!"

"How can you say such a thing?" I demanded.

"If you were dirt-poor, I could marry you and I could offer you a job. I can't now. There's no way you would go back to the theater. Why should you? You're a bloody heiress. No doubt the fortune hunters are already lining up. You could marry anyone, a duke, a count—hell, you could even marry an impoverished prince if you wanted to."

"I don't want to," I said. "What kind of a job?"

"We've closed down the production of *Lady Caroline*. The National closed it down. They've already lost a bundle of money—sets, costumes—and they're afraid they'd lose even more if—" He paused, took a deep breath, made a full confession. "It's Carmelita. She's dreadful. She's too old and she's too affected and—well, she got into a row with one of the directors of the National and walked out. Now everyone's out of work."

"The slut never could act," I observed.

"I suppose you're going to gloat," he said.

"No," I replied, "I'm going to play Lady Caroline."

"You—" He was stunned. "You—you mean you would—"

"You bet your sweet ass," I said, "and if the directors of the National give us any trouble, I'll *buy* the place."

"Dana—"

"What's this about marrying me?" I asked.

"I—I—" He was even more stunned and, I saw, very uncomfortable. "I couldn't marry you *now*."

"Why not?" I demanded.

"You're—rich," he said. "People would think *I* was a fortune hunter."

"When have you ever given a damn what people think?"

Jason didn't reply. He set his mouth in a stubborn line and thrust his hands back into his pockets and strode on up the walk.

I trotted after him. We passed beds of brilliant flowers and passed under one of the trellises and moved up the steps onto the next level. Belle Mead was bathed with sunlight now, serene and elegant and incredibly beautiful. I saw that Maudie was waiting on the verandah. Oh Lord, I thought. I forgot the shawl. She's going to kill me. I wasn't going to worry about that now. I caught hold of Jason's arm and forced him to stop.

"Answer me," I said.

"Dana, I didn't come here to—I came here because—"

"I know why you came," I said.

"I didn't even intend to *tell* you about the play. I thought—I thought you might *need* someone, and—"

"I do," I said. "I do need someone."

"I won't have you thinking I—"

"Jason," I said patiently, "if you don't shut up and kiss me at once I swear I'll knock you flat. If you recall, I have a very powerful right."

He hesitated for only a moment and then he pulled me to him quite roughly and kissed me. It was perfunctory at first, a duty done, but I held on to him and he continued to kiss me and his lips grew very, very tender. He drew me closer and kissed me more, and when he let me go I was filled with beautiful sensations that shimmered and glowed inside. Jason curled his arm around my waist and we continued to stroll toward the house.

"About that marriage—" I began.

"We'll talk about it," he said tersely.

"We will," I said. "Believe me."

About the Author

JENNIFER WILDE lives in Texas in a three-story, octagon-shaped red brick house filled with books, paintings, antiques, and an old manual typewriter on which another bestseller is currently being written.

*Be sure to read Jennifer Wilde's bestselling
historical romance!*

ONCE
MORE,
MIRANDA

Growing up on the streets of London, fighting
for survival, Miranda James became an accomplished pickpocket and a remarkable beauty.

On a dare, bestselling pulp writer Cameron Gor-
don rescued Miranda from the gallows by in-
denturing her as his maid. Cam could not begin
to tame this feisty, bright street urchin. Instead,
he fell in love.

Each has a secret: *She* writes wildly successful novels under the pseudonym of "M.J." *He*
is the ringleader of an underground group of
Scottish rebels backing Bonnie Prince Char-
lie. ONCE MORE, MIRANDA is their tempestuous story!

*And Jennifer Wilde's
wonderful contemporary romance,*

THE SLIPPER

A sexy novel about three spectacular women,
and three glittering dreams . . .

NORA LEVIN: A saucy, wisecracking girl from
   Brooklyn, she went to college full of her
   dreams to write. After a stint in the fast-
   paced world of New York publishing, she
   got her wish. But a blockbuster novel
   could not take the place of love.

CAROL MARTIN: Cool and elegant, a blond
   beauty who wanted more than anything
   to be a movie star. Little did she know
   what it would take to see her name in
   lights.

JULIE HAMMOND: She was the most gifted
   of the three, transformed from a shy, self-
   effacing girl to a dynamic performer on
   the stage. She loved to act, but she loved
   her husband even more—and would give
   up everything for him.

ONCE MORE, MIRANDA SBN 30694-5 $3.95
THE SLIPPER SBN 35643-8 $4.95

Look for all of Jennifer Wilde's bestselling novels in a book store near you, or call toll-free
1-800-733-3000
to order with your American Express, MasterCard, or Visa. To expedite your order, please mention Interest Code "MRM 6." Postage charges are $1 for the first book, 50¢ for each additional book.

To order by mail, send check or money order (no cash or CODs please) to: Ballantine Mail Sales, 8-4, 201 E. 50th St., New York, NY 10022.

Prices and numbers subject to change without notice. All orders are subject to availability of books. Valid in U.S. only.